A Right to Bear Arms
Richard Savin

Matador®
9 Priory Business Park,
Wistow Road, Kibworth Beauchamp,
Leicestershire. LE8 0RX

For Mau

A NOTE ON TERMINOLOGY AND SPELLING

Readers may notice that I have used a mixture of American and English spelling throughout the book: those parts set in America use American spelling and those that take place in England have their English equivalents. I have applied the same rule to terminology and hence you will find that what is a 'pavement' in London becomes the 'sidewalk' in New York, and so on ...

I hope the reader finds that by doing this it helps to convey the atmosphere of the setting more vividly and improves the sense of being there.

REAL-LIFE CHARACTERS FEATURED IN THE STORY

The Americans

Franklin D Roosevelt: Franklin Delano Roosevelt, commonly known as FDR, was an American statesman and political leader who served as the 32nd President of the United States from 1933 until his death in 1945. He was the only president to serve an unprecedented four terms in office. Roosevelt was responsible for re-arming America and was a staunch supporter of Churchill in his struggle to convince congress to support Britain in its fight against Hitler and the Nazis.

Henry Stimson: Henry Lewis Stimson was an American statesman, lawyer, Republican Party politician and spokesman on foreign policy. He served Roosevelt loyally as Secretary of War, assisting in persuading Republicans that they should back a Democrat President in re-arming America.

Cordell Hull: Cordell Hull was an American politician from the U.S. state of Tennessee. He is known for being the longest-serving Secretary of State, holding the position for 11 years in the administration of President Roosevelt.

General George Marshall: George Catlett Marshall Jr. was an American statesman and soldier. He was Chief of Staff of the United States Army under presidents Franklin D. Roosevelt and Harry S. Truman. After the Second World War he served as Secretary of State and Secretary of Defense under Truman.

General George Patton: General George Smith Patton Jr. was a senior officer of the United States Army who commanded the U.S. Seventh Army in the Mediterranean and European theatres of the Second World War. He became famous for his aggressive tactics against the Germans in his march across France. He was equally famous for his strong language, which made him popular with his soldiers but was often condemned by fellow officers for being crude and coarse.

General 'Vinegar Joe' Stilwell: Joseph Warren Stilwell was a United States Army general who served in the China-Burma-India theatre during the Second World War. His caustic personality was reflected in the nickname 'Vinegar Joe', given him by those of his men who disliked his harsh discipline.

General Omar Bradley: General of the Army, Omar Nelson Bradley, nicknamed Brad, was a highly competent senior officer of the United States Army who saw distinguished service in North Africa and Western Europe during the Second World War, and later became General of the Army.

Colonel Karl Spaatz: Carl Andrew 'Tooey' Spaatz was promoted to the rank of Major General as World War II progressed. He became commander of Strategic Air Forces in Europe in 1944 where he successfully argued for the bombing of the enemy's oil production facilities as a priority over other targets.

Colonel James Doolittle: James Harold Doolittle was an American aviation pioneer and competition pilot. In 1925 he won the Schneider Trophy to take the world's air speed record. A reserve officer in the United States Army Air Corps, Doolittle was recalled to active duty during the Second World War where his most famous exploit was in leading a long-range reprisal attack on the Japanese mainland in retaliation for the attack on Pearl Harbour.

Admiral Ernest 'Joe' King: Ernest Joseph King was Commander in Chief, United States Fleet and Chief of Naval Operations during the Second World War. He was a self-professed Anglophobe, noted for his foul temper and his outspoken criticism of Churchill, whom he openly disliked.

Admiral Chester Nimitz: Chester William Nimitz Sr. was a fleet admiral of the United States Navy. He played a major role in the naval history of the Second World War as Commander in Chief, United States Pacific Fleet, including the famous battle of Midway in which his ships largely destroyed the Japanese carrier fleet.

Admiral Leahy: Fleet Admiral William Daniel Leahy was an American naval officer who served as the most senior United States military officer on active duty during the Second World War. He was a member of the Joint Chiefs of Staff.

General of the Army Air Corps 'Hap' Arnold: Henry Harley 'Hap' Arnold was an American general officer holding the grades of General of the Army and General of the Air Force; he was the only Air Force general to hold a five-star rank and the only officer to hold it in two services: the US Army and the US Air Force. He had fallen out with Roosevelt over policy in his early career and it was not until the onset of the Second World War that he came back into favour with the President.

General of the Army Air Corps Ira Eaker: General Ira Clarence Eaker was a general of the United States Army Air Forces. During the Second World War Eaker was second-in-command of the prospective Eighth Air Force and sent to England to form and organize its bomber command.

Bill Knudsen: William Signius Knudsen was a leading automotive industry executive who was for several years the president of General Motors. He was born in Copenhagen but became an American citizen and lived out his life in the USA. An expert in industrial management techniques, he was invited by Roosevelt to oversee and organize armaments production by private corporations that would supply his 'Arsenal of Democracy' programme. In 1942 he was given the rank of Lieutenant General, the highest induction rank ever given to a civilian.

The British

Lord Halifax: Edward Frederick Lindley Wood, 1st Earl of Halifax, KG, OM, GCSI, GCMG, GCIE, TD, PC, styled Lord Irwin from 1925 until 1934 and Viscount Halifax from 1934 until 1944, was one of the most senior British Conservative politicians of the 1930s. Whilst he distrusted Hitler, he was inclined towards appeasement when he served as Foreign Secretary in the government of Neville Chamberlain.

Neville Chamberlain: Arthur Neville Chamberlain, PC, FRS, was a British Conservative politician who served as Prime Minister of the United Kingdom from May 1937 to May 1940. He is best remembered for the disastrous Munich Agreement in which he was deceived by Hitler and in which he had vested much of his credibility. He resigned after the battle for Norway had been lost and Churchill took his place as Prime Minister.

Winston Churchill: Sir Winston Leonard Spencer-Churchill, KG, OM, CH, TD, PC, PCc, DL, FRS, RA, was a British politician and statesman who served as the Prime Minister of the United Kingdom from 1940 to 1945 and again from 1951 to 1955. Churchill had campaigned in Parliament for re-armament during the mid-1930s and warned against the rising threat of an emerging Nazi Germany. He lobbied the US Congress for support in the supply of arms to Britain. Hitler referred to him as a criminal and vowed to have him hung when Germany invaded Britain.

Clementine Churchill: Baroness and wife of Sir Winston Churchill.

Walter Thompson: A member of the Metropolitan Police Force and lifelong body guard to Winston Churchill, he reportedly saved Churchill's life on 20 occasions. There were numerous Nazi plots to assassinate Churchill.

Mary Shearburn: Junior Secretary to Winston Churchill. She married Walter Thompson and all three became very close over the years.

Hugh Dalton: Edward Hugh John Neale Dalton, Baron Dalton PC was a British Labour Party economist and politician who served as Chancellor of the Exchequer from 1945 to 1947. He was a member of Churchill's War Cabinet.

Anthony Eden: Robert Anthony Eden, 1st Earl of Avon, KG, MC, PC, was a British Conservative politician who served three periods as Foreign Secretary and then a relatively brief term as Prime Minister of the United Kingdom from 1955 to 1957. He married Sarah Churchill, the niece of Winston Churchill.

Ernest Bevin: Bevin was a British statesman and trade union leader as well as a Labour politician. He co-founded and served as General Secretary of the powerful Transport and General Workers' Union from 1922 to 1940. He was widely respected by all political parties for his honesty and strength of character.

General Alan Brooke: Promoted to Field Marshal in 1944, Alan Francis Brooke, 1st Viscount Alanbrooke, KG, GCB, OM, GCVO, DSO & Bar, was a senior officer of the British Army. He served in the Royal Artillery during the

First World War and distinguished himself in a number of engagements, including the Battle of the Somme and Vimy Ridge.

Air Chief Marshall Keith Park: Air Chief Marshal Sir Keith Rodney Park, GCB, KBE, MC & Bar, DFC, was a New Zealand soldier, First World War flying ace and Second World War Royal Air Force commander. Called by the Luftwaffe 'the Defender of London', Park's 11 Group were the key players in the Battle of Britain.

Sir Oswald Mosley: Sir Oswald Mosley, 6th Baronet, was a British politician who rose to fame in the 1920s as a Member of Parliament and in the 1930s became leader of the British Union of Fascists. Mosley was an admirer of both Mussolini and Hitler. His followers dressed in black paramilitary uniforms and paraded through the streets of London where they skirmished with Jewish and Communist protesters. Mosley was acquainted with Joseph Goebbels, the Nazi propaganda minister, and campaigned for a peace treaty with Nazi Germany. He was interned by the British government at the outbreak of the Second World War.

The Germans

Adolf Hitler: Adolf Hitler was a German politician and leader of the Nazi Party, Chancellor of Germany from 1933 to 1945, and Führer of Nazi Germany from 1934 to 1945. He was responsible for the re-arming of Germany during the interwar years when he ignored the Treaty of Versailles and expanded all three of Germany's armed services. His expansionist ambitions brought about the Second World War when his armies marched into Poland in September 1939.

Paul Schmidt: Paul-Otto Schmidt was an interpreter in the German Foreign Ministry from 1923 to 1945. During his career he served as the translator for Neville Chamberlain's negotiations with Adolf Hitler during negotiations for the Munich Agreement.

General Heinz Guderian: Heinz Wilhelm Guderian was a German general during the Second World War, noted for his success as a leader of Panzer units in Poland and France and for partial success in the Soviet Union. During the 1930s it was Guderian who had developed the concept of the armoured thrust, using fast-moving tank divisions supported by ground attack aircraft to swiftly punch holes in enemy lines, allowing the infantry to catch up afterwards to mop up. This became known as Blitzkrieg (lightning war). Guderian was widely respected by his fellow officers, who referred to him as 'Schneller Heinz' (speedy Heinz).

General Von Paulus: Friedrich Wilhelm Ernst Paulus was an officer in the German military from 1910 to 1945. He attained the rank of Generalfeldmarschall two hours before his defeat at Stalingrad in the Second World War. Hitler had bestowed the rank in an attempt to stop Von Paulus from surrendering to the Russians: no officer of that rank was permitted to surrender into captivity and Hitler expected him to shoot himself. In the event Von Paulus surrendered and survived the war, eventually returning to Germany.

Admiral Eric Raeder: Erich Raeder was a naval leader in Germany who played a major role in the naval history of the Second World War. He had planned to integrate the captured French navy assets into the Kreigsmarine. The plan was thwarted when the French scuttled their fleet at Toulon.

The Italians

Benito Mussolini: Benito Amilcare Andrea Mussolini was an Italian politician, journalist and leader of the National Fascist Party, ruling the country as Prime Minister from 1922 to 1943. Mussolini was an educated man, though often lampooned by the British press as a posturing buffoon. He had a university education and spoke three languages fluently. He had been a newspaper editor and was a published author. However, he was also a bully and often resorted to violence to achieve his ends. A one-time socialist, he fell out of love with the ideology and turned to National Socialism in its place. In April 1945 he was captured by partisans and executed by firing squad.

Carla Petacci: Clara Petacci, known as Claretta Petacci, was the mistress of Benito Mussolini. She was executed alongside him by the partisans.

Giuseppe Bastianini: Giuseppe Bastianini was an Italian politician and diplomat. Initially associated with the hard-line elements of the fascist movements, he later became a member of the dissident tendency. He was Ambassador to London during the run up to the Second World War

THE HISTORICAL BACKGROUND AGAINST WHICH THE STORY IS SET

I believe it is important that the reader should understand the context into which this story fits as a credible alternative to the true historical events that took place in the opening years of the Second World War. Accordingly, I have set out below a short narrative of the social and military facts of that time which I hope you the reader will find helpful.

It has become commonplace to think of America as always having been militarily strong and a leader among world powers, but this has not, in fact, been the case. This was especially not so during the interwar years from 1919 to 1939, when the nation had allowed its arms programmes to stagnate and its forces to be run down; so much so that by the middle of the decade its military capability reportedly stood only nineteenth in the order of world powers, ranking as weaker than Belgium and behind Portugal.

In 1933, in the midst of the Great Depression, American President Franklin D Roosevelt launched the New Deal and by 1939 the country was beginning to prosper. In a rising mood of optimism America hosted the World's Fair at Queens in New York; according to the slogans it was the age of new promise, of 'Building the World of Tomorrow'. This was a prosperous America and one that did not wish to contemplate war, preferring to believe that it could disengage from the rest of the world.

On the eve of the Second World War much of America was still committed to a policy of isolationism: Americans believed that they were insulated from danger by three thousand miles of salt water – the Atlantic Ocean. However, Roosevelt, his Joint Chiefs of Staff and his Secretary for War, Henry Stimson, had misgivings; they wanted America to re-arm but the mood in the country was split. Roosevelt saw the war clouds of Europe rolling across the Atlantic. He believed a conflict with Germany was inevitable and convinced Congress to increase spending on arms, creating what he called the 'Arsenal for Democracy'.

Notwithstanding this, as a German army of 1.5 million-strong invaded Poland with 2,750 tanks, America found itself with barely more than 350,000 men across its entire services. Its navy ranked behind Britain in the world order and its total armoured complement comprised 34 armoured cars and around 240 light tanks – many of which were obsolete. So depleted was America that in manoeuvres held during 1938 they had to use trucks with the word TANK written on the sides, and in some cases groups of infantry running along in block formation to represent a tank!

For Operation Barbarossa, the invasion of Russia, Hitler deployed over four million Axis military personnel and 600,000 vehicles of which it is estimated more than 4,000 were main battle tanks.

By contrast with the impoverished state of the American military, the arms held by the civilian population in the same era had steadily increased and by the outbreak of hostilities in Europe a census revealed that there were more than three million weapons in the hands of private households across the nation. Added to this was the unquantifiable number of arms that had grown over the years through unrecorded acquisition: guns passed down from father to son, guns that men had brought home with them from the Spanish-American War and from the demobilization after the First World War. Further, there was the arsenal held by the criminal underworld and the Mafia. So, although the official military forces may have been poorly armed, the nation as a whole was not and the notion that a man had a right to defend his home by force of arms was considered by many to be sacrosanct. To understand what this meant it is necessary to look back into history.

The question of who should have the right to possess and use firearms has exercised the conscience of the American People since the moment of that nation's birth. It was first manifested in the eighteenth century and vested in the belief that it was the duty of the citizenry to be armed and ready to repel tyranny. Later, in the early and middle years of the twentieth century, the idea that there was a right of self-defence played strongly alongside the sporting issues, the tradition of the wilderness and the right to hunt. Then, in the closing years of that century and with the dawn of the twenty-first, there came the birth of the argument that strict gun control should be exercised for the sake of good order in society; that people no longer needed to protect their homes by force of arms because society would undertake the role of protection for them, rendering the possession of arms unnecessary. This, it has been counter argued, would leave power exclusively in the hands of government who, if they abused that power in a tyranny against the people, could stand unopposed – and this, ultimately, is what the Founding Fathers had sought to prevent with the Second Amendment to the Constitution.

History also tells us that those who rule, either by consent or through force, hold in common the fear that an armed population will be difficult to govern and that it poses the constant threat that dissent will turn to armed revolt. The obvious response flowing from this is to restrict the access of arms by the population, but this in itself may prove counterproductive if the act of so doing itself causes dissent.

It has been forcefully argued by academics and historians that the real cause of the American Revolution was not the Boston Tea Party, nor the principle of 'no taxation without representation', but the avowed intent, and attempted implementation, by King George III's government to impose gun control on the colonists and seize, by force, the arms and powder of the citizenry.

The British had feared that an armed population would be uncontrollable and attempted to disarm it; and in so doing they sparked a revolution.

It was the memory of these acts which gave birth to the Second Amendment to the Constitution and granted the American People the 'right to bear arms'.

The Amendment was intended to protect the people from the tyranny of an unjust government as well as the threat from foreign invaders. In An Examination of the Leading Principles of the Federal Constitution, published on 10 October 1787, Noah Webster, better known for the dictionary he created, concluded that: *Before a standing army can rule, the people must be disarmed, as they are in almost every country in Europe. The supreme power in America cannot enforce unjust laws by the sword; because the whole body of the people are armed and constitute a force superior to any band of regular troops.*

For Webster it seemed clear; the people were armed and this guaranteed their freedom from oppression.

I have left the last words on this subject to an extract from an article by David B. Kopel, a member of the American Bar Association and commentator on the gun issues in America.

"Furious at the December 1773 Boston Tea Party, Parliament in 1774 passed the Coercive Acts. The particular provisions of the Coercive Acts were offensive to Americans, but it was the possibility that the British might deploy the army to enforce them that primed many colonists for armed resistance.

The Patriots of Lancaster County, Pennsylvania, resolved: "That in the event of Great Britain attempting to force unjust laws upon us by the strength of arms, our cause we leave to heaven and our rifles." A South Carolina newspaper essay, reprinted in Virginia, urged that any law that had to be enforced by the military was necessarily illegitimate.

The Royal Governor of Massachusetts, General Thomas Gage, had forbidden town meetings from taking place more than once a year. When he dispatched the Redcoats to break up an illegal town meeting in Salem, 3000 armed Americans appeared in response, and the British retreated. Gage's aide John Andrews explained that everyone in the area aged 16 years or older owned a gun and plenty of gunpowder.

Military rule would be difficult to impose on an armed populace. Gage had only 2,000 troops in Boston. There were thousands of armed men in Boston alone, and more in the surrounding area ... "

Finally, there is one further point I should like to make. In putting the words into the mouths of the then contemporary politicians and public figures, I have tried to get behind their thoughts as manifested in their speeches of the time, or in the published historical accounts of their lives and their biographies. However, none of the sentiments expressed are intended to represent fact. This is a work of fiction and none of the characters, other than those known to have been world players and household names, are meant to represent persons either living or dead. Any resemblance they may have to real persons is purely coincidental and unintended. In writing this I have tried to imagine how the players might have acted in the alternative history of the story – but it is only a story, an entertainment, not more than that.

Richard Savin
Southern France

'Those who hammer their guns into ploughshares
will plough for those who do not.'

Thomas Jefferson
Third President of the United States of America

CHAPTER 1

London, 4 June 1940

In a quiet fashionable Knightsbridge street, a short walk from Harrods and Sloane Square, a large Humber limousine drew up tight to the kerb, its blackness starkly silhouetted against the white of the elegant stone buildings. For a few moments the occupants lingered in conversation. Then the driver slid out from behind the wheel and, with a deferential stoop, opened the rear door. The passenger who emerged was a man in his late middle-age with thinning hair, a dark coat and a bow tie. He hauled himself out of the seat and on to the pavement. 'Wait for me here, Walter,' he quietly instructed the other passenger in the back of the limousine.

After a cursory nod to the driver he made his way up the steps to one of the large eighteenth-century town mansions. The front door, elegantly finished in a deep glossy midnight blue with ornate brass fittings, opened silently as he reached the final step and a man in something close to livery ushered him in. The driver lingered by the car, lit a cigarette and prepared to wait. The weather had been good for the end of May and the evening air was pleasantly warm. The broad secluded tree-lined street was quiet save for the occasional passing taxi. A little further up a group emerged from one of the houses. They laughed and chatted as they headed for an evening's entertainment somewhere in the West End. They seemed not to know there was a war on; either that or they just didn't care.

'Come in, Winston,' said a voice emerging from the end of the well-lit hall.

Inside the room three men stood close together, talking. The fourth, who had called to him, was just inside the door and conducted him through. He was tall and gaunt with a withered left arm. A pair of wire-framed spectacles perched awkwardly on his nose. He had a look of the aristocracy in the way he carried himself.

'Well, Edward,' Winston said, 'I've come at your request but you have not indicated what this is about.'

As they moved into the large room the group of three men who had been deep in conversation got up abruptly. Two moved away to the farthest corner while the third stepped forward to meet them.

Winston looked at him questioningly. 'Lord Chalfont – and how do we find you here, sir?'

'Like you, I was invited by Halifax here.' He gestured to the tall thin man standing next to Winston.

Halifax beckoned to a sturdy polished table. 'Come, let us sit down.'

Seated, the three men faced each other in silence; Halifax broke it. 'Winston,' he said with an air of solemnity, 'we've been adversaries these many years but we share the same politics.' He spoke the words like a man trying to justify what came next.

'We are now at a dreadful and critical juncture in this war, a war which we are losing and I believe – and Chalfont is supportive ...' – Chalfont nodded – '... that we must now make overtures for a negotiated settlement with Hitler.'

Winston grumped and was about to say something but Halifax cut him short. 'Hear me out.'

'Go on if you must, but you've already had the benefit of my views on this matter.' He pulled a cigar case from his pocket, selected a fat Havana and proceeded to light it.

'I have been contacted by Signor Bastianini, the Italian Ambassador, whom I believe to be an honourable man.' Halifax paused, hoping to judge the effect and Winston's reaction, but none came.

'Go on.'

'He has offered his services to mediate. He has informed me that were we to approach Signor Mussolini to intercede with Hitler he would receive the proposal favourably. By this avenue we perhaps may get a reasonable peace settlement and save the further dreadful loss of life that is inevitable if we continue on our present course.' Winston remained sitting in silence. He pulled hard on the cigar. Eyebrows raised, he looked from one man to the other.

Halifax continued. 'We should no doubt have to concede some territory as an incentive, perhaps the former German colonial holdings in East Africa, and I have no doubt Signor Mussolini has certain ambitions in the Mediterranean that might have to be accommodated, but overall we would save Europe from further pointless bloodshed.' He looked closely at Winston trying to detect a hint of sentiment to the proposal; there was none.

'I have spoken privately with Monsieur Reynaud, who has intimated that the French government is about to sign an armistice with Germany. If this is so, and I have no doubt but that this is so, then we in Britain will stand alone and isolated.' There was another pause.

Winston sat quiet for a moment. 'I find it difficult to believe,' he finally said, 'that either of you could be so naïve in this matter as to think the terms that could be achieved by such a compromise would be anything other than a demeaning of this nation's position in the eyes of the free world.' He waved the

2

Havana, causing the ash to drop on the table. 'This would mean subservience to a Nazi-dominated Europe.' It was worse than he had feared when he first got the invitation. He looked from one to the other through narrowing eyes.

'We should not give away our great history with all its glorious moments for such a mess of potage – and a mess it would be. It would be foolish to think that any agreement with Herr Hitler and his Nazis would be honoured for more than the time it took the ink to dry on the paper. Here is a tyrant whose whole being and philosophy is dedicated to mendacity, to duplicity. As for Signor Mussolini, I doubt he has the sway with Hitler that you suppose and, in any event, he would clearly be looking to take a sizeable bite from our unprotected backsides as Dane geld for his doubtful services. I cannot in all conscience contemplate an action in which we so betray the British nation and the people who entrusted us with their votes in such a low and cowardly manner.' His voice was serious and measured, full of what Halifax referred to as 'sonorous Churchilian stubbornness'.

'Operation Dynamo has been a success and we must now rebuild our forces so that we may resist this tyranny. If France wishes to throw in the towel then so be it, but we are able to fight on and we should fight on. After all, we shall obtain no worse terms if we are defeated than if we treat for peace on dishonourable terms now!'

Chalfont looked at Halifax but said nothing. He sat like the observer he so clearly was and waited for Halifax to respond. Halifax, despite his training as a diplomat, looked frustrated and irritated, but he kept a cool demeanour. In his view Winston was an adventurer with a checkered history of doubtful decisions and uncertain results. Now, here he was once more bent on sending good men to their deaths for a cause that could not, he believed, be won.

'This is rhetoric,' he said unsmilingly, 'and it does you no service that you are intent on the destruction of this entire nation. It speaks poorly of you that you are so unwilling to consider any other course than your own. I do not believe that I can continue to serve in a government that refuses to take the wider view of a negotiated peace.'

Winston held his silence. He thought for a moment, sensing the fragility of the position. A resignation at this time could be awkward. It could force a vote of confidence and then what? If it were lost there could be hell to pay with another pacifist cabinet and all the unthinkable consequences. He needed to buy time – lie if necessary, but keep them hopeful.

'Gentlemen, I have made my position clear. However, I am prepared to listen to what the rest of the War Cabinet may think of your proposal. I would not object if you indicated to Signor Bastianini that we are considering a negotiated settlement. In this way we may at least buy ourselves a little time and so prepare ourselves for whatever decision we come to. I shall leave you – we can discuss it further when we meet in the House tomorrow.'

'What do you think?' asked Chalfont as Winston was taken to the door.

'I think he is playing for time – the leopard will not change its spots.'

'I'll get the others back in. We shall have to act.'

Before Churchill had reached the front door he was approached by the man who had ushered him in. He bent his head forward courteously, 'If you wouldn't mind waiting a moment sir, I shall bring your coat and hat.' Winston thought it odd and not a little delinquent that a trained man of the house should have been so unprepared as to have to ask him to loiter in a hallway, but he let it go without comment. He remained preoccupied with the meeting he had just left.

Outside in the street two men in belted trench coats and wearing trilby hats approached the parked limousine. As they reached the car they moved apart. One went swiftly to where the driver stood smoking his cigarette. The man pulled something from his pocket and started talking to the driver in a quick low voice. In the same moment the second man opened the rear door to confront Walter Thompson, Churchill's bodyguard. Thompson was caught off guard and before he could reach for the gun he kept concealed in his coat pocket the second man blocked him with a tight grip. He too spoke quickly and in a hushed voice. Then suddenly both men broke off and, looking briefly around, left as rapidly as they had arrived.

Churchill emerged from the front door and stood for a moment at the top of the steps. Then he descended in a measured manner and walked to the car. The driver opened a door and he got in.

The car pulled away from the kerb and accelerated towards Westminster. At Victoria the driver turned right into Victoria Street and then took a left to join Vauxhall Bridge Road. Churchill looked surprised and tapped on the glass partition. 'Why are we going this way Stevens?'

'Small diversion, sir,' Stevens replied in a matter of fact tone, but when they crossed Vauxhall Bridge and turned right to join the Embankment heading south away from Nine Elms shunting yards, Churchill became suspicious. He looked at Thompson. 'All right, what's going on Walter?'

'Sir,' Thompson said awkwardly, 'there is a plot to get rid of you.'

'I know Walter; Viscount Halifax and some others; Chamberlain is one of them and I suspect Lord Chalfont. They're plotting to resign tomorrow in the House and call for a vote of no confidence.'

'It's more serious than that, sir.'

'What could be more serious than that? It's downright treachery.'

From Albert Bridge any passer-by who looked towards Albert Embankment could have seen the military roadblock. From the Humber, as it approached it looked like any of the check points that the authorities set up to control traffic in the vicinity of unexploded bombs or a burst main in the street.

A soldier stepped forward and raised his hand to stop the car.

CHAPTER 2

Washington, 6 June 1940

Franklin Delano Roosevelt – 32nd President of the United States of America and the man who was carried to victory on the promise that the sons of America would not be sent to die in another European war – sat at a table in the White House together with his Chiefs of Staff and pondered how he was now to keep that promise.

Sitting at that table with the same thoughts running through their collective minds were General George Marshall, Admiral Ernest King, Admiral Chester Nimitz, General of the Army Air Corps Hap Arnold and Henry L Stimson, Secretary for War.

Roosevelt had been up since dawn. He had been woken early by an aide with a transcript from his intelligence chief and the contents were disturbing. He surveyed the assembled company of military men.

'Gentlemen,' he said, 'I'll get right to the point. When I came to this high office I did so on the ticket that I would keep our boys out of foreign wars that were none of our damn business. I pledged not to send the sons of America to die for somebody else's cause! I pledged to keep this country isolated from the lunacy that has once again got European nations tearing at each other's throats.'

'Now I face a dilemma – we all face a dilemma, because those foreign wars are getting mighty close to our back yard and I don't know how close we can tolerate without putting up our fists and striking a blow. I got you here this morning because I need your thoughts.' He paused and picked up the report that each man had in front of him. 'You've all read the report?' There was a murmur of agreement.

'The British,' he continued, 'look like they are going to throw in the towel. This latest situation report from our Embassy in London says that Mr Churchill is out and Lord Halifax has taken over. Halifax is talking to Mussolini and Mussolini is talking to Hitler. It seems likely there will be a deal of some kind that takes the British out of the war.'

He paused again and leaned back a little in his chair. 'And then what? Where does Hitler go next? The German War Machine needs oil. So where does he go to get it. Turkey is neutral but that hasn't stopped him so far. They could drive right through to the Persian Gulf and it seems there wouldn't be a damned thing we could do to stop them. If he can secure his oil supply and he has rolled up all of Europe then he could start to look across the pond. He looked at Marshall, 'George, what do we think?'

Marshall grimaced. 'Mr President, I can't underestimate the seriousness of the impact this has on our position militarily. It's not so much that it weakens our position but it moves the threat of an attack on the US closer. As you know, I have always been particularly concerned about our Pacific coast security. It's been my belief the Japanese are looking in our direction with greedy eyes and I've long held the view that a confrontation somewhere in the Pacific region is inevitable. Now this latest report says to me that the problem is likely to get compounded and that we have to look at a threat from Germany in the North Atlantic.'

Roosevelt turned to Nimitz, his Commander in Chief for the Pacific Fleet. 'Chester, how strong are we in the Pacific?'

Nimitz had better news. 'Sir, we're in pretty good shape. We know Admiral Yamamoto has been building up the Japanese fleet and they are adding more carriers as we speak, but I still don't rate them as a match for our ships in that area. We outnumber them and we outgun them.'

Roosevelt leaned forward a little and settled his gaze on Admiral King. Ernest Joseph King was the Navy's hard man. Roosevelt knew him to be unsympathetic to the British; he was an openly professed Anglophobe and took every opportunity to display it. His fellow officers viewed him as confrontational and permanently in a bad humor (even his own family openly joked about his foul temper). But for all this he was an exemplary officer and Roosevelt knew that in a tight situation he was a good man to have in your corner. He took off his glasses and thoughtfully polished them.

'OK Joe,' – King preferred to be called Joe – 'tell us what you think.'

King looked sour and shook his head contemptuously. 'Well, I always said you could count on those Limeys to fold in a fight and now they've done it.'

Nimitz gave a wry smile, 'Hey, don't sugar the pill Joe, just tell it like it is.'

The others laughed but Roosevelt just looked over the top of his gold-rimmed spectacles. 'I need to know if we can protect our Eastern seaboard, Joe, should the Germans try to make an incursion into our waters, that's all.'

King shook his head slowly again and pursed his lips. 'It's gonna be tougher without the British Navy because between them and the French they've kept the goddam Krauts busy on the other side of the water. Now if they've both gone over to the other side that's a substantial shift in the balance. If the Krauts had sent the Limey fleet to the bottom of the ocean that would be one thing because there's a lot of cold, grey water between us and them so they would have to spread themselves out pretty thin. But that hasn't happened and if they combine their assets we would face potentially the biggest fleet in the world. Of course, you can't be sure that the British would not insist on being neutral in any settlement but I wouldn't want to put too many of my own greenbacks on that one.' He stopped for a moment as if weighing the odds then went on.

'But in the end I'm with Chester. I think the Japs are a bigger threat and we should deal with them first. Keep the Navy in the Pacific to knock out the Japs, that's my view. We're commissioning two new battleships – the North Carolina and the Washington – and four new cruisers are right behind them; and there are more on the slips. But Mr President, we need to build a lot more tonnage if we're going to head off an Atlantic threat – and we need to do it like we had fire up our ass.'

Roosevelt turned to Stimson who sat next to him. 'Henry, where are we in the procurement stakes?'

Henry L Stimson was Secretary for War. He was now 73 years old but still energetic with a strong and active mind. He had served in the same post during World War I under President Wilson. A lawyer and a lifelong Republican, he nevertheless served his Democrat president loyally and enthusiastically. Two years earlier he had outspokenly warned of the Japanese threat and urged Roosevelt to increase war preparations and allocations for the defence budget. He had not been without his critics but he got his way.

Since 1937 he had overseen the ramped up recruitment of men into the armed services. The Navy now had more than 350 warships in the combined fleets and more were being commissioned at the fastest rate in US history. The production of tanks was slowly being addressed but no significant design innovation had been undertaken by the Army since the Great War; reliance for procurement had been on British and French output. There had been an increase in the procurement of heavy artillery and aircraft were starting to be turned out in larger numbers. The American arsenal was growing but, Stimson thought, not fast enough.

In September of the previous year when the Nazis had invaded Poland, ripping up their pacts and agreements with the French and the British, he had urged Roosevelt to declare war on Germany and get on with what he saw as the inevitable conflict. Roosevelt was reluctant to do it while the balance of arms still favored the Germans. Besides, Roosevelt was trapped by the policy which had helped bring him his second term in office – that he would not involve America in foreign wars. Stimson sat at the table with a quiet confidence; he knew he had been right all along and this was vindication. He addressed his reply not to the President but to the whole group around the table. He sat with his elbow on the table prodding the air with a finger, punctuating each word.

'Gentlemen, preparations for a conflict on a major scale have been in hand for nearly two years. We are as well-equipped militarily now as at any time since 1918. In many ways we are better equipped. Innovation by our manufacturers can give us an edge over our potential adversaries – but we can't say how long this will take. The news of the potential loss of Britain both as an ally and a naval partner is not good. This is grave news not only because it makes numerical superiority harder to achieve, but equally concerning must be the boost it will give to German morale and therefore battle confidence.'

He paused for a moment and then added as an afterthought. 'I lament the loss of Churchill – and not just for strategic reasons. I liked the man. I shared many of his views and misgivings about the Nazis – and he had a good sense of humor; he'll be missed.'

At this Roosevelt nodded. He and Churchill had formed a bond in the early crisis. 'OK,' he went on, 'General Arnold, what's our strength in the air?'

Army Air Corps General Henry Arnold, known to his fellow officers and friends as Hap (short for happy) had been responsible for the shaping of the US air defences and its strike capability since 1937. But he was still not satisfied with the command structure, which he believed should be separated from the Army, a view which had earned him rancorous opposition at the highest levels in the military structure.

So caustic was the opposition to him that when, some years earlier, he had unofficially gone public with his views of an independent air corps, he narrowly escaped a court martial for insubordination. He had campaigned since long before then to create an independent air corps under its own command structure instead of using it as an adjunct of the Army. His view that the Army Air Force was a cumbersome and ineffective structure, poorly deployed as a military asset, had not been shared by Roosevelt, who found him a tiresome renegade who failed to tow the party line. This had made him so unpopular with the President that for eight months he had been banished from the White House. However, he had a patron in the shape of Henry Stimson. Stimson pushed his cause and persuaded Roosevelt that Hap was the best man to take control of the Air Corps and reshape it into an effective fighting arm. As a result of this patronage he had his seat at the table that day.

'I won't beat about the bush Mr President. You are aware of my views. I believe we have a better Air Force today than we have ever had – but like the Navy we're short. We need a lot more planes if we're going to cover all that water on both sides of this country. We need carrier-borne fighters and we need bombers. We need more and they need to be bigger, faster and better armed than the opposition. We have the production potential to achieve air superiority but we need to build and we need to do it fast. Our long-range bomber fleet is getting obsolete; it doesn't fly far enough or carry a big enough bomb load. I also happen to believe we have some of the best designers in the world. If we are going to protect America we need a much bigger budget allocation, at least double what we are spending now.'

Roosevelt nodded but said nothing. He turned to King again. 'I'm told the Germans have some pretty big guns in the Atlantic. Is that right Joe?'

'At 2,000 tons, Tirpitz is way and above the largest warship in that operational area. Scharnhorst isn't far behind. If they go on building stuff like this it's going to get very rough out there. But in the end it's as much about numbers – we need to be able to smother them.'

'What do you need and how much time do we have to close the gap?'

'Destroyers; lots of them – and carriers. I'm with Hap on that one; being able to deliver air power at sea is going to be vital.'

The conversation came back round to Marshall. 'George,' he said sombrely, 'it doesn't sound good but it's what we've got so we'd better get on with it.'

Roosevelt sat back and took off his glasses. There was a short silence and then he said, 'Gentlemen, I believe there is a war coming and I don't believe we can talk our way out of it; nor do I believe the Atlantic Ocean is big enough to keep us isolated from it. Let me make it very clear. I do not want to go down in history as the President who lost the United States. Regardless of who strikes the first blow, in whatever form it takes and no matter where it breaks out, we cannot allow ourselves to lose this war if it comes our way.' He stopped it there and then added his thanks, signifying that the meeting was at an end. As the room began to clear he put his hand on Stimson's arm.

'Hang on a bit, Henry, we have a few more things to discuss. You're going to have to convince some of those stubborn S.o.Bs over there in the Senate they need to dig a bit deeper into the military allocations budgets. We're behind the eight ball and we need to get out of the way.' Stimson nodded grimly.

CHAPTER 3

An End to Innocence

The road was long and straight for as far as his eye could see; running to a point of infinity where it disappeared over the horizon a good two miles off.

The sharp air felt clean and as he breathed it in he caught the scent of the long-fallen leaves now lying moldering in the nearby woods. Along both sides of the black macadam strip the forest on the margins had been cleared, given over to farmers.

It was early spring; the newly ploughed fields had been broken down by the winter frosts and now spread out in a furrowed carpet of rich black soil. On the far edge of the field, where the trees started again, standing like sentinels for the deeper woodland behind them, a solitary crow cawed from its perch high up in the crown of an oak, breaking the silent air, its raucous voice softened and muted by the distance.

He had already walked nearly a mile but he liked the sense of solitude and had turned down a lift. He had another three to walk before he got there, but then he was young and fit and walking was still a pleasure in is life. He stood for a while and looked around him, taking in the landscape, and the thought occurred to him that it was good to be alive and out there in the middle of it all under a vast, crystal-clear blue sky that arched from horizon to horizon, free and healthy. He moved on again, quickening his pace, getting into a marching rhythm.

In the distance his eye was drawn to a dark dot, a small moving object that he thought was coming towards him. He stopped and raised a hand to shade his eyes from the brightness of the low morning sun. There was definitely something there. Now he could see it moving. A gentle purring noise came to him through the still air, indicating it was motorized. As it got nearer the purring turned to a throb and, as that got louder, the crow in the oak abandoned its lonely vigil and, after giving up a last defiant caw, flapped away across the treetops like a scrap of black rag blown on the wind.

Now he could see it was a figure on a motorcycle that was heading towards him. As it came closer he saw it was weaving erratically, the rider struggling to control the machine. When it was not more than twenty to thirty yards away the rider gave up the struggle and lost control. The front wheel slipped out sideways

11

and the bike went down, careening along on its frame, grinding and gouging the macadam, dragging the rider with it until finally it slewed itself sideways and came to a halt, resting on the edge of a drainage ditch that flanked the road. He ran to where it lay.

The rider was still alive when he got to him but his leg looked to be broken; he sounded delirious and confused. 'They're coming,' he wheezed out between gasps for air. 'They're coming; they hit us by surprise, they got everyone, I don't think anyone survived.'

Carefully he pulled the rider free from the machine and as he did he saw the blood oozing out through a small hole in the back of his leather jacket.

CHAPTER 4

Rites of Passage

The idea that boys should take up the practice of arms in their educational years was not new. In 1864 during the Civil War a Union army officer, General Hazen, complained about the poor level of marksmanship and target training of his infantrymen. General William Tecumseh Sherman, a onetime friend of Hazen, took a similar view; he recommended to the Department for War that young men be trained early on in the practice of arms.

Ever since the patriotic war against the British it had been a requirement that the townspeople would form and maintain militias. Every household should keep a gun with enough powder and shot to be ready for an emergency; men should practice their marksmanship – but it was a very loose arrangement. Powder and shot fired at paper targets was powder and shot wasted; powder and shot were expensive so practice came with a paucity only ameliorated by those who hunted.

At the end of the Civil War in 1865, encouraged by Sherman, it was decreed that all boys over the age of 16 should be drilled in the use of arms and trained to become proficient at shooting.

However, fifty years on during the Great War, later known as the First World War, General J.J. Pershing, leader of the American Expeditionary Force in France, had cause for the same complaint – a great many of his men could not hit a target. Like Sherman before him, boys, he demanded, had to be trained in their marksmanship so that the nation would be ready in the event of another war. It had to become part of the national ethos for the sake of freedom.

For the Founding Fathers it had been simple: an honest man armed with a good rifle was a guarantee against tyranny, but it was no good arming honest men if they could not shoot straight.

Croton-on-Hudson, 1940

The village of Croton-on-Hudson sits on the banks of the Hudson River about seventy miles up the valley north of New York City. In the year of 1940 it had a population of around 5,000 souls, a hospital, two churches, and all the usual facilities and services normally associated with a community of that standing. It was also an important railroad depot, marking the point where the line heading north to Peekskill and on to Albany changes from the electric railroad to that of steam locomotion. Here the rolling stock coming down from the north gets a change of locomotive as similarly does that coming up from the great Manhattan terminus of Grand Central. Since the founding of the station and the marshaling yards in 1906 it had been a prosperous community, giving work to all manner of trades and skills related to the railway business. Away from the tracks the village was home to a prosperous middle-class community with neatly kept streets and some fine houses.

In common with most educational institutions of good standing in America, Croton High School had its own facility; there was a 25-yard shooting range in the basement and every week students were required to bring their rifles with them to the classroom for a lesson in marksmanship – and, if they had a mind to, some shooting practice in the gun club, which met in the evenings when school was out.

This was part of the curriculum, something to be done along with the three Rs or chemistry – it was in the culture. For some students it was a chore to be endured, like learning mathematical tables by rote or regurgitating passages from *Tom Sawyer*, but for most it held a certain level of appeal; for them it was more a sport, but without the grunt and sweat of football or the track. It was embedded deep within the psyche, in the folklore of their history; it had shades of the pioneering backwoodsmen about it – of Bowie, Crockett, the Alamo – of trails westward and winning the frontier. It was their heritage – part of becoming a man.

So strong was the value placed upon it that an enthusiasm for the sport was not considered to be out of the mainstream. For not only was it promoted as part of their education, a skill they were required to master, it was also a rite of passage for 16-year-old boys. It marked the recognition of approaching manhood and the preparation for that day when they may be called upon to serve the nation in arms. They couldn't vote and they couldn't get a drink in a bar; no matter that – they could be sent to war and they should be ready.

Spring 1930

It was the first day of the new semester at Croton High School; lessons had commenced at 9.00 a.m.

At around 9.20 that morning a boy, who by this time should already have been in his class, approached the main gate. He was a tallish boy, slim and not too broad in the shoulder with fair-to-brown hair and alert blue eyes. In his left hand he carried a school bag with pencils, notebook, geometry instruments and text books, all those things it would normally contain. It also contained another item, a small box marked 'Smith & Wesson .22 rimfire cartridges x 50 rounds'. On his right shoulder he had loosely slung a pump action rifle which swung on a webbing strap, keeping time with his steps as he walked.

He unslung the rifle, knocked nervously on the door of his classroom and entered. The class, who were taking a maths lesson, looked up as one and stared at the figure now entering the room. The teacher turned and fixed him with a questioning gaze. 'Thomas Jordan,' he said, 'what is this?'

Thomas Jordan said nothing for a moment.

The teacher looked at his watch, 'You're late. You can explain later – take your seat. I do not propose to recap, you will have to catch up however you can; for now put your gun in the corner with the others.'

At the end of the lesson each boy collected his own rifle from where it had been stacked and, shouldering the weapon, filed smartly out of the room.

That same afternoon the eleventh grade was to get its first introduction to the proficiency of arms and the art of marksmanship. In the school basement the students of Croton High gathered in the locker room at one end of the firing range. Their teacher looked at the boys in front of him; all eager-faced with anticipation.

'Okay,' he said, 'here's a question. It was reported that at the Battle of Shiloh in 1862 it took the weight of a man in lead shot to bring down one Confederate soldier.' He paused. 'Can anyone tell me why?'

One of the group put up a hand. He hoped it wasn't a trick question. He took a gamble. 'I guess the Union riflemen were just bad shots.'

The teacher turned on him, followed by the eyes of the entire class. 'You guess or you know?'

The boy shuffled uncomfortably. 'I guess.'

'What's your name?'

'Thomas Jordan, sir.'

'Well, Thomas Jordan, you guessed right.' There was a sigh of relief and a ripple of light laughter ran through the group.

'Yes, they were rotten shots. That great General Ulysses S. Grant once remarked, they couldn't hit a bull on the backside with a fiddle.'

The class again laughed and then they got down to the business of how to handle a gun safely – and, more importantly, how to hit what they were aiming at.

******

They had met at the High School when they were all in the eleventh grade; that time when they had taken their first lesson in the practice of arms. In the beginning it was just Tom Jordan and Mike Mescal who had become friends; a little later they were joined by Tony Gagliardi. And so – there they were, three

15

young men standing on the threshold of their lives, full of the expectations of a promising future, looking at the world in wonder and excited by its prospects.

When Tony Gagliardi had first arrived at Croton High he had not been naturally outgoing; he was a touch intense, a callow boy, serious for his years and eager to please. He was considered by his mentors to be a student of great promise. Anthony, as he was then known, would be a scholar. It was predicted he would go on to achieve great results – of that they were sure. From ninth to tenth grade they congratulated themselves on their astute prediction: Anthony was way out in front of his peers by a good country mile; there was the scent of an achievement award in the air, maybe a scholarship.

However, at the end of the winter break that year and the start of eleventh grade something in his character altered. His family had a vacation home in Miami, and while he was there to celebrate the Christmas holiday something strange had taken place; a change – one which was most distressing to his mentors.

******

'You know what?' Tom pulled up a chair and sat down at the table opposite his friend Mike Mescal. 'Something's changed,' he said. 'Did you notice Tony Gagliardi on the range? Something's different about him. I don't know what's happened, but he's different.'

Mike shrugged. He was a short, well-built boy with broad shoulders and a barrel chest, ideal for the football he liked to play. His voice and his expressions held traces of the Irishness gifted to him by his heritage. 'No idea – but you could be right. I don't really know him that well.'

'I think maybe he met a girl.'

'Are you serious, why?'

'Well because, first off, he's always been a teacher's pet, but since we got back from the Christmas holiday I notice he's dropped out of three classes.'

'Maybe he's sick.'

'Then there are his clothes. Here is a guy who has always looked like he slept in a garbage cart. Did you see the shoes and pants he had on today? That's expensive, classy stuff; not to mention he's changed his hairstyle. Actually he looks very cool.'

'You could be right,' Mike said; he lifted his wrist and looked at his watch. 'I gotta go, it's football practice.'

'So what do you think?'

Mike got up. 'I don't know,' he started for the exit. 'Why don't you ask him?' he shouted over his shoulder as he left.

'Okay,' Tom said to himself, 'I'll do that small thing.'

16

He finished the dregs of the cola he'd been drinking and made his way outside where he came across Tony Gagliardi waiting for a lift back to his home. As he walked up to him the first thing he noticed was that Gagliardi had grown over the holiday; he was definitely taller.

'Hi,' Tom said casually as he reached him. 'I saw you on the range today. That was pretty cool shooting.'

Gagliardi looked pleased by the remark. 'Thanks man, you know I think I'm really gonna to like the range – it has something about it that's kinda hip, neat. You know how I mean?'

This, Tom thought, was not Tony Gagliardi talking – this was some other person. He noticed his almost black hair had been molded into a quiff at the front and there was a smell of perfumed pomade; very slick – this was definitely not the same bookworm that had gone to Miami for Christmas.

'What happened to you?' Tom asked earnestly. 'You've changed.'

Tony Gagliardi thought about it for a moment – then he smiled and said casually, 'I grew up, that's all. It'll happen to you one day.'

His transport arrived. 'See you on the range again?'

'Sure,' Tom shouted after him, then said quietly to himself, 'Yup, it was a girl alright.'

******

In Miami that Christmas the Gagliardi family had gathered to celebrate. His Uncle Giorgi was there with his wife Gina, his grandfather and grandmother, Uncle Adolphus with Tia Doria, his Uncle Mario and another aunt, then the cousins. It had been two years since he had last seen his cousin Sophia. At first he didn't recognize her – she had changed; she had changed a lot. In place of the awkward, insecure 15-year-old with acne, he found himself confronted by a fully constructed and well developed goddess.

When they last met, Anthony, the teacher's pet, had been dismissive and not a little unflattering in his remarks to the shy teenager. Now she was going to have her revenge. She started by flaunting around him. He blushed and cringed. This was something he hadn't expected; he had no idea what to do about it. Then she shifted up a gear, taunting him about his schoolboy looks and uncool clothes. Finally she began to flirt – it was grotesque. His aunts all giggled about the performance and teased him about his awful embarrassment; his humiliation was complete. In the end he dreaded leaving his room, scared she was there – waiting to ambush him. Sophia worked on it; she had a lot of self-doubt to make up for; he would have to suffer a bit more. From breakfast to lunch, and worse at dinner, she cranked up the pressure and watched him squirm like worm on a hook. In desperation he consulted his Uncle Giorgi – the one person he trusted and admired more than anyone else in the family.

'What do I do?' he whined in desperation.

'Do?' Giorgi replied with a touch of incredulity in his voice and a broad grin on his face. 'To start with you stop acting like a *testa di cazzo* (Italian for dickhead). 'Play the same game. Take a look in a mirror sometime – you're a disgrace. Go and buy some new clothes before everyone shuts up for the holiday, and get Angelo the barber to do something with the hair. Shape up – you're 16 nearly 17 and going on 12, for Christ's sake!'

'Dio Mio!' Tia Doria exclaimed as he came back into the house. 'What happened, who is this?'

Giorgi let out a long, low, wolf whistle, 'Porca Madonna. Mario!' he shouted. 'Would you take a look at this?'

When Sophia saw the new Tony she smiled a delicious little smile. 'Mmm, come on,' she said, 'now you've grown up there's something I'm going show you.'

******

In spite of the disparity between the boys and the gulf of other interests that marked them out – Mike with football, Tom with baseball and Tony who now developed an appetite for the girls – they had formed a common bond around shooting. The high school Gun Club was extracurricular and optional and although the weekly shooting practice was mandatory and threw them together, it was the evenings shooting on the range that founded the friendship.

Throughout the last two summers of their final grade years they hung out together; they entered in the lists of the shooting competitions and they went hunting. They had become crack shots, always favorites to come home with the prizes and between them they accumulated more silver than anyone else in the school, though much of that was down to Tom. Dubbed 'the three musketeers' by their peer group, they enjoyed the limelight and the popularity that went with it. The camaraderie grew and they became like the brothers, which, in real life, they had all been denied.

'There's a competition.' Tony draped his arms around the shoulders of his two friends and grinned broadly at them. 'Wanna take a little wager on it?'

'I think I won't,' Mike said, shaking his head, 'Yer man here will walk away with it,' and he nudged Tom in the ribs. 'But I'll definitely shoot – just not for the money.'

'I'll miss the gun club,' Tony said with a touch of nostalgia in his voice.

This would be their last competition; the semester was drawing to a close and that would be an end to it; next year they would be at college. They would no longer be boys – they would become young men. These had been their salad days; they had basked in the sun and drunk the wine and now that would all too soon come to an end.

CHAPTER 5

The Anatomy of Conflict

College was a distant memory; they had graduated and each gone off to find their own place of work, but they'd stayed in touch and still went shooting together and then it was just like they had never moved on.

It was Saturday. In the town of Peekskill where he lived with his parents, Holly and Martha, Tom was putting together the things he needed for a hunt. He would join the others at Jennifer's Diner in Croton, not 15 minutes' drive south, just off Highway 9. Jennifer's was their regular meeting place; from there they could drive deep into the thickly wooded hills, leave the car and spend the day hunting.

In the living room his father looked set up for an argument.

It was one of those days, one of his hangdog days as Martha referred to them, when he'd got out of bed on the wrong side and nothing seemed to please him; days when his depression bore down on him with the full weight of the psychological baggage he had carried with him ever since he'd gone off to the Great War and seen all those terrible things. On those days nothing would lift him out of the abyss and he would sit for hours in numbed silence under the heavy shadow of his memories. In these times he could find fault with everything and in that fault he reserved a special dislike for guns and his son's enthusiasm for shooting.

'I don't know why you wanna go everywhere with that thing', he said grumpily.

'I can't hunt without a rifle, Dad,' Tom replied, trying to pass lightly over the remark, knowing how easily Holly could get all riled about it. His father shook his head slowly from side to side in ill-tempered resignation.

'Nothin' good ever came to anyone from guns,' he said in a voice loaded with irritation. 'Look at all those crazy people in Europe – and they say they're gonna be at it again; and what for? What damn good did it do them last time? All those years of slaughter – and for what? Now they're gonna start it all over again'.

'You said that once already, Dad'.

'Good, and I'll keep right on saying it; it's true – ain't it? Wasn't it enough for them last time. Give him a gun and sooner or later some damn fool will start shooting.'

'It isn't like that,' Tom replied, trying to back away from what he knew could end as a long rancorous row.

'Oh yes it is – that's exactly how it is!' Tom resisted the urge to respond and decided to let it rest there.

There was a silence between them as they mutually disengaged; they had said all there was to say and there was no point in saying more. It was always the same conversation, like a well-rehearsed play, they knew the plot. The dialogue sometimes changed as they spoke their lines but the ending was always the same sullen silence; neither wanted an encore. Tom moved towards the screen door. It was the start of the fall, but still warm, and there was the dry smell of dust in the air, hanging over from the hot summer just gone. A fly hummed in a corner of the living room. Occasionally it made a laconic sweep across the airless space; a pointless low buzzing transit from one corner to the other culminating in a random bouncing off glass panes before settling momentarily, after which it re-enacted the same futile exercise. Like Tom and Holly, it didn't seem to be able to grasp the futility of pointless repetition.

The Jordan house was quite large, colonial in style but it had seen better days. The white-painted weather board was faded and peeling in places. The front door, which led onto a porch, had seen happier times and the heavy wooden steps, which led down to the front lawn, were beginning to split. Tom kept the front grass tidy. Each Saturday from spring through to the fall he rose early, got out the old power mower and cut the grass on the front where it ran down to the street. Then he did the same at the back of the house where the garden stretched 200 feet to the back fence. There was a large planked back porch for sitting out in the evening. It had tall ornate arching supports under a roof of wood shingles. Here and there, when the rain was heavy, it dripped where the shingles had come loose – another job Tom would have to find time for. There were two old apple trees and a cherry his father had planted when they had first moved into the house – a quarter century before. They still fruited; the cherry did especially well. Each year it gave up its generous harvest of large plump black and purple fruit that marked the summer. Martha, his mother, made them into what she called 'pies to eat' and 'jams to keep'. The apples had not endured so well and were now showing their age: rot had set into the trunk of one of them. Tom needed to find the time to cut it down but there never seemed to be enough. His father didn't do much anymore. His physical health was right enough but mentally he had fallen into early decline and, although only just 50, there was already an old man inside his head.

'I'm going out now, Ma,' Tom called into the kitchen. 'I'll be back for supper'. His mother came fussing from her chores and hung around his neck.

'Give me a kiss then. You know I can't let you go without one.'

It was her ritual of survival, a talisman against disaster. As long as there was a goodbye kiss she knew he would return safe. If she ever missed one she fretted until he got back. Of course, it was silly; she knew that, but it had worked before. When her husband had gone to Europe for the Great War and she had kissed him for the last time as he boarded the transport, she knew that parting kiss had brought him home; it had saved him for their future life together. There he was, the living proof, sitting in an old broken-down chair, worn out by life and the Depression years, but still there and still alive. She knew she had saved him the day he embarked and she clung to that belief for nearly two years until he came home safe again. Since then she never let her loved ones go without that good luck kiss.

'Take care son,' she said quietly.

'We're only going hunting,' he protested with a chuckle.

'Sure,' she chided gently, 'but you take care none the less. I worry about accidents. You know how I am.'

'I'll take care, I always do.'

'I know, but you're going hunting aren't you. Accidents happen, just take double care. Are you going with Mike and Tony? I like Tony; he's a real nice young man.'

Tom pulled away gently, collected a big bore Remington rifle from where it rested against the jamb of the screen door and, with a wave, walked down the porch steps. Parked in the driveway, his father's old Chrysler was waiting. The car, like his father, had seen more promising times. Holly never drove it anymore and it had become Tom's by default.

Martha looked at the husk of her man sitting aimlessly in the old chair. They had seen out all these years together and now it seemed like they were near the end. Much of it had been hard, grinding effort on the borderline of poverty. They had used up the best of their life in the Depression years with not a lot to show for it.

'Holly, would you like some tea?'

He'd picked up the taste for tea in the war. He liked it well enough but it always reminded him of those bad years. It had a whiff of the trenches about it, but he drank it nevertheless even though it brought back the memories. All those years ago when he had enlisted ... then it seemed like the right thing to do. He was a farm boy, no real education but he'd been bright and quick to learn. So why not join the army, it made sense didn't it? In the army he found opportunities and he took them as they came along. He signed on to the training programs and worked his way up. His promotion had been rapid and he rose

22

through the ranks quickly from private to corporal, then platoon sergeant and finally sergeant first class.

Then along came the war and messed up everything; his life would be changed forever. The army life he'd once enjoyed now turned his work to a meaningless confrontation with slaughter; a purposeless acquaintance with injury, with degradation, with men sliding into mud-filled shell holes they would never get out of. The stink of death, of gangrenous wounds, blood stale dressings; the bloated decomposing corpses of dead mules left where they fell, some still propped up in the shafts of the shattered gun carriages they had been hauling. All abandoned because nobody had the time or the energy to cart them away to some isolated corner where they could rot in peace.

He had served in the American Expeditionary Force with General J.J. Pershing. Black Jack, they'd called him – those who didn't like his iron-hard discipline. Some thought him an over-ambitious career soldier who drove his men too hard just for his own glory; Black Jack and an army of men, mostly conscripted – the Doughboys, they'd called them. They disembarked in France with only light arms and for a while had to be propped up by French tanks and artillery, all because some fool bureaucrat stateside had forgotten to sign a piece of paper. That's how it had been in that war – bad organization, bad planning, bad leadership, pretty much bad everything.

At first, though, it hadn't seemed that bad. He had his buddies around him and he was in charge of a company of men under Captain Farrow, a man he had grown to like and respect. Farrow was a young man with a Harvard education and West Point training. He was a good officer, Holly had thought. He cared for his men. He made sure they got their mail from home and they never wanted for tobacco. In the evenings he would often sit with them and share a pipe. After the war, he said, he thought he would leave the army and train to be an architect. Like many in those forlorn days he had a girl at home waiting for him. As soon as he got back he wanted to marry and start a family.

In the beginning they shared their trenches with the Brits and the Aussies and it was there he got the taste for tea. They would sit around on the warmer days and drink it in tin mugs, occasionally during lulls, carelessly sitting out on the top of the trench walls where they could have been shot by sniper fire. On those days nobody seemed to care and the Boche could sometimes be seen doing the same. On the cold wet days they huddled together in the bottom of the trench or in one of the dugout shelters that pock-marked the trench walls – and here the tea was warming, comforting; just the act of accepting a mug from a comrade was like a social ritual and it brought them closer together.

The experience with the Australians had mostly been bearable because they were successful; their raids were intelligently planned and, although it was war, it had not seemed so terrible. Then there came Argonne Forest and all that changed.

Black Jack had at last got his heavy equipment and, along with his 22 full divisions, he joined with his allies to make his mark on the war. The Germans were weak in numbers at the start of the battle and the Americans, now at full strength, were confident and sure of success. It was 1918 and the war was in its waning months; it would soon be ending. The Americans had yet to gain the battle honours Pershing so craved to carry him home in triumph; he needed a victory, one that would crown his career, and time was running against him. The German Army was on the defensive and retreating on nearly every front. Now was his chance and he was determined to seize it. Backed up by French tanks to cover their flanks, Black Jack mounted a mass frontal attack with the expected outcome that many would die but that he would procure his victory. Many did die.

On a cold October morning they lined up in the trench and waited for the whistle that would send them over the top. Farrow went along the line of his men, handing out words of encouragement, reminding them that the best way to stay alive was to keep moving forward. He would be there with them. Then the shrill blast of the whistle pierced the silent cold air and they were up the ladders and onto the open field.

Farrow fell in front of his eyes, an instant casualty, shot through the head on the first charge. It was a sight so shocking and so ugly he would never forget it. They were barely ten yards from the trench where they had clambered up the wooden scaling ladder and gone over the top. Captain Farrow had a service revolver in one hand and was waving his men on with the other. Holly was close by him, the air humming with the sound of bullets like swarming bees – and then there was that distinctive thwack! Farrow crumpled on to his knees and toppled forward, his face buried in the black mud. The back of his head had come away and blood pumped and flowed like a thick glossy tide of deep red oil. His service revolver was still in his hand.

The battle lasted 46 days and Farrow didn't get to fire a single shot. In the end the Germans, although heavily reinforced, had to fall back and concede the ground on which nearly thirty thousand Doughboys gave away their lives. Whole regiments were lost in those terrible hours and days – friends he would never see again but would remember always as he lived out the life and the future they should have had but which they gave away, there in the forest.

Black Jack was heavily criticized and accused of being careless with the lives of the young men who did the dirty business of fighting. But, what the hell, he came home in triumph with his victory and in the end they decorated him anyway; and called him a hero, too.

Sometimes, alone in the evenings, while Martha busied herself in another part of the house and he dozed in his old chair, the ugly scenes would creep subtly into his soporific tranquility with the uninvited drumming of a machine gun. Or a shell would burst inside the depths of his brain, jerking him awake with a gasping intake of breath and a flash of light so bright it lit up the deepest corners of his subconscious mind. Then he would get up and turn on the radio, not because he wanted to listen to a particular program but just to hear the sounds of normal human voices; voices that were not panicking or shouting or screaming in the agony of their shattered bodies. The radio and Martha were what he now lived for; and, of course, Tom, their only son, but Tom could be a painful reminder. So like his father, he thought – bright, intelligent but this time with the advantage of a college education, and how they had struggled to provide for that education.

In the earlier years when he came home from the European war there had been some money saved but that was all lost in the crash of '29. Then the farm went, sold for a song because nobody wanted farms anymore. Now they lived off his meagre war pension. But Tom would be alright; he had a good job with Imperial Life Insurance in New York and he was making good money for a young man. He had prospects, Holly thought, and everything would be fine but for his fearful fascination with guns. He understood the hunting but not the gun club and the obsession with shooting off guns at paper targets; and worse, paper targets made in the image of men. It was unnatural; he should be out looking for a wife to make a home and he wasn't, and that caused some friction between them. It was only Martha who held the balance in those awkward moments with her gentle fussing over her boys.

'Holly,' Martha said quietly and coming up close, 'I've got you some tea, honey?' He nodded but said nothing. Then, after a short while, he sighed and mostly to himself said, 'Nothing good ever came of all that fighting; what a waste, what a waste.'

******

Tom liked to drive, even the old Chrysler which was beginning to feel its age; it was a symbol of the freedom his generation were beginning to enjoy. He planned some time to buy one of the new Fords or, better still if he had the money, a Hudson Coupe with a rumble seat, but for now he would put up with the old Chrysler and, as he drove, he looked out onto the world through the windshield and thought about making plans for his future. That future had started to look more promising since the Democrats had brought in what people were calling the Second New Deal. America was getting on the move again. The worst effects of the Depression had gone and there were jobs; people had

25

money. Middle America was on the way back and seemed unstoppable. Lots of homes now had new cars, radios and telephones. One day he would buy a house, he thought, one with a modern kitchen. There were new inventions coming along all the time; things were changing. He had seen a new kitchen in a magazine with all manner of gadgets and labor-saving devices. That was how he imagined his life – modern, bright and fun.

The neon sign on Jennifer's Diner peered in through the windshield of the old Chrysler and he put his thoughts on hold. He parked up next to Mike's smart new V8 Studebaker where it sat gleaming in the sun. Next to it, parked carelessly was a new Cord convertible, its long hood sprouting an exuberant display of chromed exhaust pipes. This was Tony; the car was a reflection of the man he had grown to become: exuberant, flamboyant and just a little bit flashy. What a change that Christmas in Miami had to answer for. He slammed the door on the Chrysler and locked it.

The day was fine though the air already had the touch of the impending fall about it and the leaves were on the turn. Up into the Adirondack forests the oaks and sugar maples were burning flame red, scattered in among the peaches and vivid yellows of birch and beech. Tom thought about the hills. There was game up there, maybe a buck if they were lucky.

Tony and Mike were sitting at a table drinking coffee and eating donuts when he arrived. They turned together.

'Hey, look who's finally got here,' Tony shouted as Tom came in through the door. 'You gonna get some breakfast?' he said, looking at his watch and tapping it with a finger indicating that Tom was late.

'Give the guy his breakfast,' Mike laughingly protested.

Tom came over and slapped him on the back. Mike had grown since high school but was still shorter than the other two; he had wild unruly flaming red hair, wiry as an engineer's brush that shouted out his Irish origins like a shamrock on St Patrick's Day.

Tom sat down and a pretty blond waitress came over to take his order. 'Hi,' he greeted the waitress. She smiled back, displaying a row of perfect white teeth.

'Coffee?' she asked. Tom nodded, 'and give me a bagel with that will you, miss?'

She poured the coffee steaming into his cup and smiled again, this time an intimate smile and he felt himself go a little hot around the neck. He was still not quite comfortable around women. The other two noticed it and pulled faces, then laughed.

Afterwards, up in the hills, Tony ribbed him about it. 'Are you going to ask her?'

Tom came back with a cautious drawn out, 'No-o-o-o.'

'Why not, you know she likes you?' Tom just shook his head.

'Come on now,' Mike joined in. 'A good-looking guy like yourself – she can't resist. It's sure she'd never say no. She'd make a fine wife.'

Tom smiled, but there was an edge to his voice when he said, 'I don't want a wife – OK?'

'But she's a really nice girl,' Mike persisted.

'I can do better than a waitress in a diner!' Tom snapped. There was a short silence. Mike pulled a sour face and everyone realized they should leave it there.

Early in the afternoon they picked up the trail of a white-tailed deer and tracked it till evening but never caught up with it. Mike, who had brought along a scatter gun, shot two cotton-tails and dropped them into a sack, although it was strictly still not yet the season. The day had taken them in a wide circle through the woods till eventually they got back to where they had started and to where the Chrysler waited in a clearing at the side of the track.

They threw the sack with the rabbits into the trunk and started back along the unmade trail towards the metaled road that would eventually join with the macadam of Highway 9 and then back to the diner and the other cars. They bumped along the uneven track in the fading evening light, the engine beating out a hollow burble through the exhaust and the gearbox whining. The Chrysler was old; it had been built in 1929 and was now showing its age, but it was still the best car for their needs. It was upright and boxy. It had wire-spoked wheels – no longer the fashion – with a flat windshield and large dumb irons sticking out in front of the radiator. It was yesterday's design, consigned to history by the latest automobiles with their flowing lines, lower chassis and headlights molded into one-piece fenders. But you could strap a stag to the old Chrysler's dumb irons and carry it home – and you couldn't do that with the latest models now coming out of Detroit.

Back at Jennifer's Diner they ordered beers and hotdogs. The blond waitress was still there and again she looked at Tom in that certain way, but this time Tony and Mike kept quiet. They considered the day and admitted they were really too early in the season for hunting buck, which strictly didn't start until the end of the month. There might have been a penalty if a ranger had come across them but they rarely saw one on the trails; mostly the rangers patrolled further north, the more popular hunting areas up by the Canadian border, looking for unlicensed tourists who came in from the cities to poach. The city dudes were looking for bigger game, trophies to be hung up on walls – stags, bears or coyote. A ranger wouldn't really be too fussed about a couple of cotton-tail rabbits in a bag. In the end, it had been a good day's trek.

They ordered more beers and the conversation shifted to Mike's wedding. Mike was getting married to Eileen. It had been on the calendar for two years since Mike was 25. You couldn't call it an arranged marriage but it was almost that. They had known each other since they were children and she was related, although only as a very distant cousin from the more remote reaches of the family. The New York Irish were very clannish, especially those who came over in the potato famine. They were proud people, proud of the struggles they had endured and survived; keeping clan ties was a tradition difficult to break.

His family had come from Cork and, although they were not farmers and not directly affected by the famine, grandfather Mescal could see no future in the old country and so, in 1846, the second year of the disaster, they took a ship from Dublin and after the hard and traumatic Atlantic voyage landed on Long Island a month later.

His grandfather had been a doctor; there was plenty of need for medical men and so the family prospered. By the second generation they were comfortable and Mike's father had started one of the first Irish community newspapers in the area, *The Irish American Echo*, but it had struggled. The overheads were high, especially the print bills. The making of the business and the family fortune occurred when his father set up his own press. He bought a rundown factory and installed second-hand machines and what he couldn't afford to buy he built himself. Then he expanded the business into the profitable area of general print and in a short time they were doing alright, getting out other peoples' broadsheets, printing calling cards; there were invitations too – weddings and funerals, births and anniversaries. In 1929, when Wall Street crashed, the Mescal family was in the fortunate position of holding nothing but its own stock and, better still, because they had always invested exclusively in their own business there was no bank hammering at their door, threatening eviction. Such prudent planning had left them in a strong position to sit out the Great Depression which had started a year following the Crash. Now the economy was mending and Mike was getting married; it would be a big event.

The wedding was set for the first Saturday in December because, as Mike explained, for the Irish it was considered lucky to marry in December.

CHAPTER 6

3 September 1939

Monday morning came round again and, as he always did, Tom walked to the station to catch the train to work. Imperial Life had offices in Manhattan. The train came into Grand Central and the Imperial building was a walk away on East 42nd Street.

The weather was turning; there was cloud blowing in from the east on a freshening breeze and a darkening sky promised rain. That morning at breakfast NBC radio had announced that the anticipated European war had now broken out. The British, together with their French allies, had declared war on Germany. He didn't properly understand why they were going to war but it had set Holly off again. The mood in the house was black as he left.

This Monday morning was otherwise like any other workday morning. The train stopped along the route gathering up commuters as it went; most were headed for New York City. The first stop down the line from Peekskill was Croton-on-Hudson. After that there was Ossining, where, if you were sitting on the right side of the car on the down track you could watch the scenic Hudson River flowing by. If, however, you were on the left side, you got a not so great view of Sing Sing prison, its bleak grey outline a depressing monument to the desperate souls it housed. Moving down the line there was Tarrytown and Irvington, followed by Dobbs Ferry and finally Yonkers, just up the track from Grand Central Terminus.

At each stop he watched with indifference as the passengers boarded. Sometimes he recognized the regulars, greeting them with a nod. It was the same old routine with the same old faces wearing the same old hats, mostly dark felt fedoras, and all reading the same old newspapers. Sometimes, as he sat wrapped in the tedium of the journey, he found himself wondering if this was how his life would be. If this was all there was or ever would be until, like his father, he sank into his retirement years and a slow decline?

Then something different happened, something that broke into his torpid reverie and shook him awake. At Dobbs Ferry a girl boarded his car. She was, he thought, the most stunningly beautiful girl he had ever seen. There were no seats so she stood, quite close by, hanging on one of the overhead straps. She had long dark hair in the Hollywood fashion of the moment with a small hat, like a beret, pinned to the back of her head. Occasionally she flicked her head in a sideways movement to shake away a few strands that had fallen across her eyes. As she did so the whole of her long hair swayed in a luxuriant rolling motion like a gentle ocean swell. Tom was transfixed. She stood there, tall and elegant, in a pencil-slim skirt covered by a short trench coat, tightly belted to emphasize her waist. Should he, he thought, offer to give up his seat. While he was thinking this thought and gazing at her something terrible happened: their eyes met; she had caught him looking at her. He looked away quickly but not quickly enough. It was a moment of acute embarrassment and he felt the heat rising from his collar up towards his face. Quick-witted, he pulled the morning newspaper from his satchel and buried his head in it, where he kept it for the remainder of the journey. She stayed on till Grand Central, the end of the line, but got down from the car before him and he quietly thanked God for saving him further embarrassment. He lingered on the concourse long enough for her to disappear.

Outside on the street he almost ran into her again. This time she was standing on the sidewalk just across from the Chrysler building, studying a city map. The first thought that struck him was she must be new to Manhattan, perhaps a tourist. Maybe he could offer to help her find her way. He hesitated and, in that momentary gap between the thought and the action, the large blue uniformed presence of a traffic cop stepped in to fill the void with a polite 'Can I help you miss?'

In turning to look at the officer she also found herself looking at a man who was looking intently at her, a man she had seen on the train.

Tom turned and walked resolutely in the direction of work. Jesus, he thought to himself, she must think I'm following her. Maybe she thinks I'm some kind of nut, a pervert even. Imperial Life was located in an impressive building about two blocks away from the Grand Central terminus. It was 78 floors and had been built for the corporation in 1923 when Imperial was on its way to becoming the largest provider of life insurance and mortgages in America. It took less than five minutes to walk there briskly. In that five minutes he rehearsed what he should have done and said maybe a hundred times.

At the main entrance a doorman touched his uniform cap. Every office building seemed to have one these days. Mostly they were ex-military and Tom wondered how it felt to spend the day opening doors and saluting people you didn't know or probably didn't even care about. But men were taking any job they could find since the Depression and there was still a hint of desperation in the air. The New Deal was working for some but there were still a lot of haunted men on the streets and a lot of hungry women and children in the poorer quarters of the city. It was better he told himself, but it wasn't fixed yet – not by a long stretch. Inside the high vaulted reception hall he punched the elevator call button and waited.

The elevator had been modernized; it was now automatic. It wasn't always so. It used to have an operator who greeted its passengers cheerfully and politely asked how their day was and which floor they wanted. But then one day back in the summer it had failed. It probably had a few more people on board than there should have been. Stanislav, the elderly Polish man who operated the elevator and who was known simply as Stan, was inclined to let his passengers take their own view on what was meant by maximum load. It was a Friday and everyone likes to get out on time for the weekend. There had been a sudden lurch and a loud crack like a whip being lashed, then it started downwards, in freefall. It fell rapidly through six floors before the automatic friction brakes kicked in and brought it to a halt. Nobody was hurt but there was a lot of hysteria and some screaming, and one woman fainted.

As the hubbub cooled down and people began to demand to know what was happening, Stan asked if anyone had a knife. A young man at the back produced a pearl-handled switch knife with a long blade and handed it over the heads of the other occupants, who were now beginning to get very hot and irritable. Someone shouted 'Pull the alarm cord', but Stan quietly pointed out that it was a very old lift and the alarm no longer worked. There were more irritable mutterings but Stan, ignoring all, inserted the knife blade between the doors and then with his fingers in the gap levered them apart. They were stalled midway between floors but Stan was still agile and, hauling himself up through the gap, alighted on the 23rd floor concourse. A young male passenger then pulled himself up through the gap and between them they helped haul the other occupants out. It was an undignified exit, especially for the ladies, and a lot of underwear went on display that should have remained secret. Ruffled but relieved, they thanked Stan; he was now the hero of the day.

The real estate manager had called in the elevator company to fix it and they recommended it be updated with the latest automatic control system. It was, he said, more reliable than a human operator and cheaper to run. So they fired Stanislav the Hero, and there it was – another jobless man in another welfare queue.

Tom's office was on the 11th floor, where he was now a junior underwriter in the Overseas Risks section. He pressed the button marked 11 and the conveyance rose silently to his destination. Marion, the receptionist looked up briefly and pushed a register at him. He picked up the pen from its stand on the reception counter, entered his name and time of arrival, then walked along the corridor to the open-plan office which was now the latest style in workplace design. Overseas Risks had its own dedicated space, which was hedged around with screens separating it from the main floor. Inside this glass corral his work colleagues were already at their desks; the incident with the girl had made him late.

That morning, talk in the office was all about the World's Fair. It had opened in the spring and was due to close in October, but only for the winter. The organizers had scheduled it to reopen for a new season in 1940 with the theme of 'Unity of Nations', but nobody had second-guessed the German invasion of Poland. True, Germany anyway had declined to open a pavilion at the Fair but had announced that it was on the grounds of cost. Now people questioned the truth of it, and the less charitable said they stayed away for other reasons. There was also the added complication that the British and the French had declared war on Germany – the international harmony the show had trumpeted was beginning to look a bit ragged.

Dan Johnson sat at a desk next to Tom and he'd been to the Fair.

'What do you think?' Tom said to him. 'When they close this fall will that be it do you think? Or will they open again for 1940?'

It was not a large office; the Overseas Risks business was a new venture for Imperial and was only provided as a service to major clients – those with large important portfolios in the mainstream risk spectrum like fire, marine and real estate. It included such diverse underwriting as automobile insurance for oil magnates and maharajas living in remote areas of the world, often with unpronounceable names. They insured private yachts and airplanes located in high-risk territories and they even supplied theft insurance for the private palace of the Grand Mufti of Arabia.

Because it was such an obscure part of the Imperial portfolio, there were only six of them working in it: Tom, Dan Johnson, Fred the junior clerk, a typist Miss McKinnon, Mavis who looked after the filing, and Dan Johnson's assistant, Margaret Higgins, an aloof blond girl who largely kept herself to herself and was likely to leave soon because she was due to get married at the end of the year.

Miss McKinnon also kept herself to herself. She did not consider she was part of the office. Her job was to type out the policy schedules and business letters for these important clients – confidential work which she did for the senior management and she only sat there among them. She did not consider she was with them – it was simply a space requirement.

So when Tom and Dan Johnson both looked at her and said, 'Adele, what do you think, will the Fair open again?' she simply sniffed. 'I don't have a crystal ball, I can't tell the future,' was all she said.

Dan shrugged off her indifference. 'I heard it cost the board more than sixty million dollars to build it and another hundred million from the sponsors. So I can't see them shutting just because those screwball Europeans are fighting again. It's nothing to do with us if they want to kill each other. Good to be shot of them!'

Tom nodded. 'I haven't seen it yet but I'd like to.'

Dan Johnson gave him a look of enthusiastic approval. 'You should. I took my wife and son. It's outstanding. I never saw anything like it. They say it's all about our future and I believe it. I saw a television there, amazing – Roosevelt broadcast a speech. And then afterwards I saw myself and my family on it. You just walk past a camera and the next thing you know there you are – on the screen. It's just fantastic and to think – they say every home will eventually have one. Now that is the future.'

In the corner of the office Fred, the junior clerk, got up and walked over to them. He was 18 and this was his first job. 'Mr Johnson,' he said with a hint of reticence, 'do you suppose, sir, there is any chance America could get caught up in this scrap the Germans and British are going to have – you know, like last time?'

Johnson smiled an assuring smile, 'I shouldn't think so, Fred.'

'It's just, well, my Dad took me to the Fair and I guess I've seen the future, like you say – but – well I kinda worry there might not be much of a future if I had to go and fight like my uncle did – and then get killed and all that.' They both laughed and Dan Johnson punched him a friendly nudge on the shoulder.

'Don't worry kid, it aint gonna happen. Roosevelt says so and I believe him. The worst I can see is a couple of foreign pavilions packing their traps and going home early. In my book the show will go on. I think the future's here to stay.'

'Was your uncle killed in the Great War?' Tom asked, almost as an afterthought.

'No, sir, but he came home in so many pieces he might just as well have been. He died last year.'

'Gee, I am sorry, that's tough kid, but you shouldn't worry. I'm pretty sure the future's here to stay.'

That evening, going home on the train, Tom found himself looking around for the girl. It was pointless, of course, because the chance of her getting the same train at the same time was pretty remote. The chance of her getting into the same car as him was even more remote. The train arrived in Peekskill. Tom got down and walked the short distance to his parents' house on Union Avenue. Over dinner he found himself thinking about the girl again. She really had been stunningly pretty.

'Are you going out tonight?' Martha asked him.

'I'm shooting over at Croton High. There's a two-two competition. I'm meeting Mike and Tony there.'

'Try not to let your father know,' she smiled gently. 'It'll only get him all heated up and it's bad for him.'

'Don't worry Ma, I'll keep it quiet.'

The .22 calibre competition had been organized by the high school club but was open to all shooters of any age just so long as they were members of affiliated clubs. They met in the school cafeteria; Mike, Tony and Tom. Having arrived early with time to kill there was nothing better to do than sit around drinking coffee and talking with other shooters, swapping stories about their guns, hunting trips and other competitions.

'That's new,' Tom said looking at the rifle Mike had just removed from its carrying case – German Mauser? I haven't seen that before.'

'Ah,' Mike said conspiratorially. 'Well now, let me tell you about this little beauty because it's got a bit of an interesting story behind it.' He leaned close to the others sitting around the table. 'You see this was a present to my Uncle Seamus. He got given it in Germany in '36. He'd been to see the Berlin Olympics. He saw Jesse Owens win four gold medals; he was greatly impressed.'

Tony shot a glance at Tom and grinned. 'Will you get on with it. I know about the Owens' medals; I saw it four years back on the Pathe. Tell us about the gun for Chrissakes, save the blarney.'

'Okay, he was invited over by the German American League and they gave him a really good time – but you know, they gave the Owens victory a pretty cool reception and when they were at a beer hall later an argument broke out. Some of the Germans were, shall we say, a little less than polite about Owens.'

He picked up the gun and handed it to Tom, 'Feel the balance, it's the business to be sure.'

Tony looked heavenward. 'Are you gonna tell us or are we expected to guess the rest?'

'Will you wait up!? There was this young guy – all fired up and he was very aggressive; a proper loud mouth. Well, the uncle tells me he started shouting out that this showed America as a degenerate nation. It seems he said something like in Nazi Germany the purity of the nation would not allow its national honor to be put in the hands of a Negro – no matter how fast he could run or how high he could jump. For a while, according to the uncle, things looked ugly and it seemed like a fight must come next. But the President of the League, he ruled the kid was out of order and had him sent out of the beer hall. The next day they put on a farewell lunch, and that's when the uncle found himself being presented with this very rifle in a smart embossed leather case – as an apology, he judged. Well, my uncle had no use for such a small calibre gun himself so he passed it to me – and there you have it.'

He took the rifle back from Tom and passed it around for inspection. 'But,' he said, 'the story doesn't finish there.'

'There's more?' Tony joked.

'Now,' he said resuming the tale, 'when the uncle gave it me, he did say something else, which I thought was very far sighted. He said, these German fellahs are a much organized bunch. They'll be marching all over Europe again – and not long now; you see if they don't. Just mark my words.'

He grinned at the satisfaction of telling the story. 'That was three years ago. He wasn't far wrong now, was he?'

In the contest Tom shot the top scores of the match and, as was often the case with Tom, he walked away with the competition in his hands: ten dollars and another certificate to hang on the wall. Shortly after it was over and they were packing their rifles, an army instructor who had come down from the National Shooting Range at Port Clinton to observe the contest walked over to where they were. He was a tall, gaunt-looking man with a chiselled chin and sergeant's stripes on his arms. He looked down at the three of them sitting around the table. He stood rigidly to attention and in a vaguely theatrical manner saluted them. 'Sergeant Henry Newman at your service,' he announced, continuing the air of drama. 'Fancy shooting,' he said. 'I like your style. Are you boys local?'

'These guys are,' Tom nodded in the direction of the other two. 'I'm Peekskill, just down for the day.'

'You boys ever think about bigger competition; something man-sized, maybe National Championships?'

Tony shrugged, 'Maybe.'

'We've got some fine facilities up at Camp Perry. You should come up there some time. It'd be a pleasure to show you around, maybe interest you in a little action on the range.'

'Are you with the National Rifle Training Program?' Tom asked.

'Sure am,' the sergeant replied. He took a card out of his tunic pocket and handed it to Tom.

'We train hundreds of young men in marksmanship every year. You could say Its Uncle Sam's investment in our nation's security. Of course, boys like you are pretty much on the mark but there's a lot who aren't and one day we may need a bigger army at short order.'

'What do you think about the news from Europe?' Mike asked.

The sergeant thought for a moment and then, carefully drawing out his words, said, 'Well, they say those Nazis are a tough bunch, but there's a lot of water to cross between here and them.'

'You don't think we'll get sucked in?' Tony questioned, 'Like last time?'

The sergeant shook his head slowly and pursed his lips. 'I don't think we need worry on that one, son. Government knows what happened last time. We'll just let the Europeans get on with it this time.' Then he added, 'I figure the French and the Brits between them ought to be able to handle it. We might have to sell them a few tanks and artillery pieces – but, hell, that's not getting involved; that's just good business.' With that he stood rigidly to attention again, saluted them and left.

'Well, what do you make of that?' Tony said, laughing as he got up from his chair; he stood rigidly to attention and, mimicking the sergeant, saluted stiffly and said, 'Right, men, I think you did real well so let's go over to the Coco Club, I could handle a drink!'

'Good to hear we're staying out of Europe,' Mike chipped in. Tom kept quiet but inside he had a nagging feeling that may not be right.

The Coco was on the corner of Main and Church Street. Outside it had a garishly lit palm tree adorned with three large coconuts. Inside, behind a long polished wood bar Jimmy Carroll, the barman, stood talking to a customer perched on a high bar stool. He turned his head and looked briefly at the three as they walked in and then resumed his conversation. The trio picked a table in one corner and sat down.

'What'll it be, boys?' the barman called from behind the counter. Tony went over to the bar. Throwing a glance at Tony, the barman broke off from his conversation with the customer on the stool and came over to him.

'Hi Tony, how ya keeping?'

'Good, Jimmy, yeah good.'

'What'll it be then?'

Tony turned to the other two, 'Bourbon?' he shouted. They nodded.

He put up three fingers, '… and make them large, Jimmy.'

He was about to pick up the drinks when his attention was diverted to the man seated on the high stool. He hesitated and leaving the glasses where Jimmy had set them down he moved along the bar until he was standing next to the stool. The man, who was sitting silently contemplating his drink, gave a short sideways glance at Tony and then continued staring into his drink. Tony put his hand on the man's shoulder; he looked up. Tom, who could see them from where he sat, judged the look to be sullen, slightly hostile. There was a short exchange of words, then the man stood up, put some money on the counter and abruptly left.

'What was that about?' Tom asked as Tony put the drinks on the table.

'A personal matter, nothing important.' He lifted his glass and, changing his tone to mock formality, joked in a parody of Sergeant Newman, 'To our champion shooter – a true son of America.'

'Here's to good friends,' Tom replied.

They sat for a while in near silence, then out of the blue Tom said, 'Do you believe in love at first sight?'

Mike and Tony looked at each other and then at Tom. Their look was apprehensive, as if to say 'Okay, go on, what comes next?' Mike said he thought it existed but that it wasn't in his experience commonplace. Love in his opinion was an evolutionary thing; it took time to mature. You meet someone and you spend time with them – maybe you see them on and off for months, even years, and sometimes you grow together.

Tony gazed up at the ceiling, then back at Mike. 'Come on, will ya! Believe me, there isn't anything else. If it doesn't smack you right here,' and slapped his palm on his face. 'The first time you clap eyes on her it aint never gonna last.' Then he pointed at Tom. 'OK, who is she?'

'It's the girl from the diner – the blond – isn't it?' Mike butted in. 'I knew it, I knew it. I could see the way you looked at her the first time we went in there. I told you these things take time and this proves it. Ha!'

Tony sat waiting but Tom said nothing. He took a deep breath and then said. 'It's not the waitress from the diner.'

There was another silence. 'I saw a girl this morning; on the train – she was the most outrageously beautiful girl I have ever seen.'

'Booff, there goes your theory,' Tony said, looking at Mike. 'So come on, are you going to tell us or do we sit here all night? We need another drink while the star struck among us have time to think. Same again, Jimmy!' he shouted across the room.

Tony walked over to the bar and collected three glasses. 'He met a girl!' he said, jerking his head in the direction of Tom. 'We're trying to find out who she is, but its slow in coming – the drink will help, but we may need more of this stuff before we get it all out of him.'

'A girl,' said Jimmy the barman in a voice loaded with disillusionment, 'that'll be trouble – eventually.'

Tony scooped up the glasses. 'Always is.'

'Right,' he said as he sat back down again, 'who's got the smokes.'

Mike pulled out a pack and threw it on the table. 'Luckies anyone?' Picking up the pack, Tom jerked it upwards with a deft flick of the wrist. A single cigarette popped up out of the pack. He captured the slim tobacco-filled paper tube between his lips and withdrew it. Then he took it out of his mouth and holding it vertically tapped one end on the table top to compress the tobacco more firmly.

'That's the trouble with Lucky Strike,' he said, as he casually examined the now firmer cigarette in his hand. He pinched off the spare paper from the now hollow end and lit up. 'They pack them too loose – makes them burn too hot.' He inhaled deeply, then blew a long trail of grey smoke into the air above their heads. There was another pause, while the other two got their cigarettes lit. Tony broke the silence. 'So are you gonna tell us?'

'I don't know, that's it – we didn't actually meet. She got on the train and we looked at each other; well, I looked at her,' Tom said wistfully. He went on to explain the encounter while the other two listened patiently.

At the end of the story it was Tony who came up with the suggestion. 'There's only one thing to do here, we need to go to Dobbs Ferry and look for her. A girl of such staggering beauty shouldn't be hard to find. The whole of Dobbs Ferry is bound to know her. Come on, we can take the Cord – we'll be there in no time.' Mike looked doubtfully at his watch. 'Yer man's mad, it's nearly ten, I've got a bed to go to and so have you if you're smart.'

Tony picked up the bar tab and they all wondered out into the night. Much of the town was already sleeping and, apart from some street lighting and the big flashing Pepsi sign over the general store, there was no sign of life.

'Don't forget the conies; they're still in the trunk from the hunt,' Tom reminded Mike. 'That's alright,' Mike replied, 'you have them, it's my gift, now go and find the girl.' He climbed into his Studebaker and slipped quietly away.

'Come on,' Tony said, 'we must be able to find a bar open in Dobbs Ferry – I seem to remember they have a hotel there. That'll do for a start.' They drove slowly down Main Street until they reached the intersection with the Albany Post Road.

'What was that with the guy in the bar?' Tom asked casually.

'Nothing really; he owes my old man, that's all.'

He turned onto the main highway, then let the car have its head. The deep-throated roar of the Cord's big chrome pipes broke the night air like a purposeful tenor in full voice. The air was still warm as they drove through it with the top down. If that girl was out there they would find her.

They started the search by going into the first bar they saw, ordering a drink and asking the barman a simple question. 'Who is the most beautiful girl in Dobbs Ferry?' The barman looked at them suspiciously, then said he didn't know. They moved on.

Not far away they found another saloon and put the same question. 'I know the answer to that,' said a man propping up the bar.

'Oh yeah?' Tony got excited – they had a lead.

'Sure, it's Dorothy Lamour – but she's only ever here when she's in a movie – otherwise the best we got is ugly Doris who runs the boarding house.' He collapsed into robust laughing as Tony told him they didn't appreciate a wise guy.

They tried another three bars, then finished up back at the Dobbs Ferry Hotel. 'You know what,' Tony said, his speech slurred and weaving slightly, 'I don't think this was such a good idea after all. I'm seeing four of everything. Even if we found her I don't think we'd know which one was the right one.'

They both fell about laughing. The barman in the Dobbs Ferry Hotel started putting the stools up on top of the bar. He wanted to close, he wanted them gone. 'We need to go home,' Tom said, 'I have to go to work in the morning.'

The next day he nursed a hangover all the way to Grand Central and didn't care much if the girl got on or not. He spent a subdued day in the office and drank lots of coffee, not that it seemed to help much. Finally, when it came time to go home and he signed himself out on the office register he was feeling much brighter and he started to think about the girl again. Once more he loitered on the platform, not boarding the train until the last minute in the hope that he might see her but, as before, it was a fruitless exercise. He probably had about as much chance of seeing her again as winning the City lottery. For all he knew she was a day tripper, a tourist, maybe even foreign. He knew it made no sense but he would go through the same hopeless exercise for the rest of the week, though without result.

On the journey home that evening he spent time thinking and rehearsing what it was he might say to her if, by some rare whim of fate, she did get on the train. It was during that process he realized that he hadn't a clue what to say. It was OK in the movies when someone like Gary Cooper accidently bumps into Mae West. They have a script. What if he just said 'hello' and she simply told him 'get lost!'? Maybe he could ask her opinion on the European war. He tried that in his mind: 'Hi, I know we've never met but what do you think about the Nazis and European domination?' No sooner had he thought it than he realized how stupid it sounded. In the end he gave up because he was getting nowhere.

He was staring at the front page of the paper held up by the man in the seat opposite. The headline read 'Phony War in Europe – will it all be over by Christmas?' That set him thinking on a different track and he forgot about the girl. The train arrived in Peekskill; it was Friday – tomorrow he would meet up with Mike and Tony at the diner and they would go hunting.

CHAPTER 7

7 June 1940

Viscount Halifax had been at the Cabinet Office all morning. He had been called there by Chamberlain, who now told him there was a flap on. Churchill had gone missing. He was due to address the House before lunch but nobody seemed to know where he was. His secretary could not be found either, nor Walter Thompson, his bodyguard.

'This is infamous,' he told Halifax, 'irresponsible. The nation is at a crossroads and now Winston is nowhere to be seen. There is a debate scheduled for the afternoon session, what am I to say?'

Halifax frowned and folded his arms. 'Neville, you know Winston and I have never been at one over the approach to Germany and this disastrous war. You know also, I believe, that it is my firm conviction we should negotiate terms while we still have our freedom, and that if we were to find ourselves at the table as a vanquished nation it would be very difficult, if not impossible, to obtain terms at all.'

Chamberlain looked tired; he already had the air of a beaten man cast across his face. Ever since the betrayal of Munich, when Hitler had torn up their agreement and he had been forced to go to war, there had been a grey pallor about him. Now he felt the tiredness deep inside and it drained him; he looked worn out. The surrender of the French Army and the desperate scramble to salvage what they could of the British Expeditionary Force from the beaches of Dunkirk had been a *tour de force*, but it had been Winston's *tour de force* and his alone. Chamberlain had been a bystander. Now Winston was missing and Chamberlain was being dragged, weary and unwilling, back into the front line, and the history of Munich was coming back to haunt him. The man who had been so confident less than a year before had left the room; he had gone, he no longer existed. In his place there was only this tired shell, bereft of self-assurance, deserted by courage, racked with doubt and anxiety.

'But Edward,' he virtually pleaded, 'can we trust Hitler in any negotiation? He has a long history of breaking his word.'

Halifax was not there to be swayed. 'I believe we have no choice in the matter', he insisted. 'But so long as we keep control of our armed forces we have some safeguard against a deceitful move on his part. If we go down fighting, as seems to be Winston's preference, we should come to the table with nothing in our hands but defeat.'

Halifax stood up. His hard poker face and strong flinty gaze drilled into Chamberlain, who gave up any further resistance. Halifax would have his way; he had dealt with devious men like Hitler before and had a reputation as a skilled negotiator. As Foreign Secretary he had always seen himself as a counterpoint to Churchill's gung-ho, barnstorming recklessness. He was first and foremost a diplomat; Churchill was the warrior. Worse, to Halifax's mind, he was a warrior with a history of flawed strategic decisions. Now, if he had his way, he would once again become the author of the nation's misery. His mind was made up and he had already committed himself to actions which would dispose of the man and his dangerous ambitions. Churchill had cast himself in the role of Caesar and now he would reap the legacy of Caesar. He looked over the rim of his wire-framed glasses straight into the face of Chamberlain.

'Whether Winston comes to the House or does not come to the House to make his statement this morning, I am set on a course to make a statement of my own. It will be contrary to what I know he has in his mind and which he will oppose with his usual passionate rhetoric. Nevertheless, I shall propose a negotiated settlement of this war – with immediate effect. If I am to succeed, I shall need you and other key members of the Cabinet to support me. Neville, is that clear? I do expect to rely upon you to bring the Cabinet with you. If you do not I shall resign and move for a vote of no confidence in this government. I judge that would bring it down and the chaos that will ensue would be on your shoulders. I need your pledge, Neville, your word that you will support me on the floor of the House.' He paused and waited for the answer.

Chamberlain nodded. He was not a man without honour but he no longer possessed the resolve of Halifax or Churchill. He had strived throughout his political life to seek harmony, often through compromise. He lacked the determination of Halifax even in better times. Now he had no fight left in him and he gave way without further argument. Secretly he hoped Winston would turn up and take the problem out of his hands. Where the devil was he and what was he playing at?

There was no sign of Churchill at the morning session of Parliament, nor was he present for the debate that afternoon. Rumours were flying about like bats in a midnight churchyard. You never knew where the next one was coming from.

The next day the *Daily Express* newspaper carried the banner headline:

WHERE IS CHURCHILL?
Prime Minister absent from key debate ousted as Halifax steps in

******

41

Union Avenue, Peekskill, NY

Holly sat dozing in his chair. Next to him a cup of tea stood cooling on a small table. It was hot outside. Across from him on a large sofa Martha was listening to the afternoon radio soap opera *Against the Storm*.

She had finished the chores around the house for the time being and this was her time of day. She would allow herself an hour each afternoon just to relax and do nothing other than listen to the radio or read a magazine. Later there would be the laundry, some shopping in Peekskill at the general store, and then the evening meal to prepare in time for when Tom got back from work. She had originally chosen this broadcast over others because its principal character, Professor Jason McKinley Allen, was portrayed as a pacifist anti-fascist and she thought it might strike a chord with her husband's own views. Holly listened to it on and off depending on his mood and how tired he was feeling. Now, after two years of following the program, Martha had become hooked on the story and the characters. They had become part of her social dialogue when she met with her few friends in the town.

Her life since the Great War had been 'fine' she would always say when asked and, although it had been a struggle in the Depression years, they had not suffered as badly as many. They had kept their house, which they had bought for cash from their share of the thin proceeds of the sale of his father's farm. They'd owned a car at a time when many others were walking or waiting for buses, and the veteran's pension, though small, had been just enough to keep them – and it was regular and reliable. Unlike many folk, Holly had no job to lose and they were spared the fear that went with that. Now Tom was working, with a good salary, he made their lives more comfortable. When she went for the groceries she no longer had to be so careful and she liked that; it was a small unspoken pleasure – simple but, like the radio soap, it was comforting. She was a giving woman with a gentle nature. She rarely complained and made the best of what she had. They'd had some good times together for a brief period before the war and they had Tom. She would have liked more children but they never came and now at nearly 50 it was too late. But she was content in a simple fashion and loved her two men with a comfortable, gentle love that came as they grew into the later years.

For now she listened to the newest episode of *Against the Storm*; later she planned to go shopping for a new dress she had seen at a fashion store on South Street – a pretty cotton floral print, bright and light, just perfect for what was left of the summer and she could wear it right on through the fall. It was a gift from Tom and she was excited. It was a long time since she had done anything other than make or mend her clothes. Now, for a change, she would have the pleasure of going into the store and browsing along the rails of dresses and coats, to feel the fabrics, not just look at the merchandise but to actually buy something.

It was the practice of NBC to break into the advertising intervals in the programs for short news broadcasts; this was signaled with three musical chimes. Occasionally, for something of national importance, they would break into the program itself without waiting for the sponsor's message. The precursor to these rare occasions was a fourth chime.

Martha got up and shook Holly by the arm. 'Honey,' she said, 'wake up, we just got four chimes!' They sat close by the radio as if they might miss something if they sat further away.

'Good afternoon, ladies and gentlemen,' said the disembodied voice.

'Is that Cronkite?' Holly whispered to Martha.

'Hush,' she put a finger up to her lips; 'listen – and no, Cronkite is CBS.'

The voice that came out of the radio was abrupt and stentorian; it had a note of urgency that made it feel like the roof was about to fall in; for some it would:

'We interrupt this program to bring you some important international news. It has today been announced by the British government that peace negotiations with Germany have been commenced and that a temporary lifting of hostilities has been agreed between the belligerents. President Roosevelt has cautiously welcomed the news of the ceasefire, saying if this brings peace to Europe it must be welcomed. However, he also warned that America must stand constantly vigilant in the face of the threat of further German aggression.

'In a strange turn of events, possibly connected to the negotiations, there is a rumour that Prime Minister Churchill has left the government and is missing; his whereabouts are unknown.

'This has been a special bulletin from NBC News. Now we return you to *Against the Storm*. Good afternoon.'

Tom arrived home around six. The journey from Grand Central to Peekskill took just under the hour. 'Have you heard the news?' his mother asked. 'Your father is very excited. I haven't seen him so bucked up since I don't when.'

That evening they sat on the back porch and talked. They talked at length about the European war, which Holly said he hoped was now done with and that folk over there could get on with proper lives instead of all this shooting and killing. 'Roosevelt is right,' he proclaimed, 'we need to stay in our own back yard but just keep an eye on the guy the other side of the fence. If he has some kind of quarrel with his kin we let him get on with it. We just make sure he doesn't come round to our place with his ruckus.'

Martha laughed, 'Can you imagine Alan and Irene in a ruckus?'

'Well,' said Tom, 'if they did, I doubt they'd make enough noise for us to hear it.'

At this they all laughed. Alan and Irene had been their neighbors for as long as they had been there. They were a very proper couple; God-fearing church goers was how Holly described them. She was like a church mouse, tiny and timid; he was a short man, stick thin, fussy in his dress, mild mannered and intensely polite. He wore stiff collars every day of the week even though he had long been retired from his job as a bank clerk. Holly thought him stuck back in another time by two or three decades when people were more formal and observed social niceties that were no longer with them in this new mechanical age. When they first came to the house on Union Avenue Irene had shown great neighborliness to them, especially to Martha whom she often invited round for coffee and cakes. So the idea of these two having strong words with each other was humorously absurd.

'Mike is getting married,' Tom said out of the blue.

'Oh, that'll be nice,' said his mother, 'when is the happy day?'

'They're planning for some time in December.'

'That's late in the year, isn't it? Everybody will be busy with Christmas.'

'It's an Irish tradition. Apparently some months are considered luckier than others. Mike says December is particularly good but May has to be avoided. Don't know why.'

'We married in May,' she said wistfully. 'I had the most beautiful gown. You know I still have it in the trunk upstairs? Maybe one day you'll bring a girl home and, who knows, she might like it for her wedding.'

'Yes, son,' Holly chipped in, 'when you gonna get a girl?'

'I just haven't met the right girl yet,' Tom protested.

'Your mother and me, we met at a dance. You should go to dances. Maybe you'd meet some nice girls.'

'Well, we go to Hops, you know. I'm going to one with Tony in Croton next week.'

'Yup, but you spend too much time with those damned guns of yours. Shooting is not attractive to women. You won't find too many girls that way.'

'Whatever became of that girl you were dating around the end of high school?' Martha asked. 'She was a nice girl – and very pretty.'

'Yeah,' Holly added, 'how come you let her loose?'

Tom laughed a little. 'Alice Rogers – now that's a thought. She was nice; that's a long way back – it was just school stuff. I think she's married now.'

Holly hauled himself out of his chair and stood up slowly straightening his back. 'Honey, I think it's time we were in our bed.'

'Sure,' she said, 'I'm coming.' She bent over Tom and kissed his forehead. 'Don't sit up too late son. Goodnight.'

'I won't,' he smiled up at her. 'Sleep well.'

The evening had gone well on the porch for a change. Holly had been on good form and Martha was pleased. He was so cantankerous a lot of the time and she could never be sure when he would sink into one of his difficult moods. If only he would get out more, drive the car a bit, take up a pastime or do something in the garden. He was different back then when they first met. He had plans for a career in the army. They went dancing a lot and then there was the new craze for the movies. He had been a deal of fun.

Holly had been one of three brothers. James, the oldest, had died back in '36 from a heart attack. They weren't close but when the news came he took it badly, more than Martha had reckoned with. Of the other two, Daniel, who was two years younger than Holly, had moved to the West coast after the farm had been sold. He met a girl out there, married and they had two daughters, but they rarely heard from them except for a note at Christmas. He put his farming days to good use, though, and became a salesman for an agricultural machinery company in Seattle. She had heard he was doing real well now and a few Christmases back he had sent a photograph of them all. The girls were so pretty with long blond hair in ringlets and their mother was a real catch too, educated and from a good family.

Nobody knew what happened to Ben. He simply disappeared. Maybe one day he would turn up but Holly hardly ever talked about him. He was the youngest of the boys. He hated the farm work and he was moody as a child. He would get easily bored and disappear off on his own for hours. One day Holly found him with a rope around his neck. He was standing on a hay bale and staring into the distance with the other end of the rope held aloft in his hand.

'What do you think it would feel like to be hung?' was all he said. Then he jumped off the bale. Taking off the noose, he threw the rope to the ground and walked away. It was years before Holly told Martha about it but he wouldn't discuss it after that. She wasn't sure how it had affected him, but she sensed it went deep.

Tom sat for a while thinking about his parents and how old his father seemed even though he was only 50. He contemplated what he might be like in another ten years but didn't really want to think too much about it. Maybe they were right; maybe he ought to make the effort and find the right girl. Grandchildren might help his father, give him something to fill his life and take away all that pain and guilt he had been carrying since those dreadful war years. He let his mind wander, thinking for a while about Alice from high school and what she might be doing now. He thought about the waitress at the diner; the other girls called her Dottie. She was pretty and attractive to him and he knew she was giving him the eye – but he just thought he should be looking for someone more ambitious than a waitress. Then, without warning, an image of the girl from Dobbs Ferry slipped into his mind. He had forgotten about her over the last six months. Now he found himself wondering where she was. She must be out there somewhere. He wondered where she lived, what her house looked like, who her parents were and what they did. Were they rich? Probably, because she dressed so elegantly and most of the folks in Dobbs Ferry were well to do. After a while he let the images and the fantasies go. He would probably never see her again anyway. His father was right; he ought to make an effort to find a girl and get settled. That, he knew, would make them happy, especially if there were grandchildren. It was, after all, at the heart of the American Dream, as the soap commercials liked to call it.

He sat for a while longer in the warm night air then hauled himself up out of the chair. 'Perhaps we should get a dog,' he found himself saying out loud. That would be a companion for his father. A nice medium-sized dog, nothing too big, maybe a Boston terrier or a retriever.

As he climbed the stairs to his room he forgot about the dog idea and again found himself thinking of the girl from Dobbs Ferry.

'Nope,' he said to himself quietly, 'that's not an answer.'

CHAPTER 8

9 June 1940

In London the day had not gone well. Halifax now found himself carrying the can – and when he opened it he saw it was full of worms. He sat in his office together with Ernest Bevin, Minister of Labour, and Hugh Dalton, leader of the Labour Party, and now both part of a coalition with the Conservatives. Spread out on a table in front of them were several newspapers. They were all staring at the copy of the *Daily Express*. 'SOLD OUT!' it shouted. Underneath it announced in no less strident terms, 'Britain to come under German rule in shameful deal for peace'. Hugh Dalton picked up a copy of *The Times*. 'Where's Churchill?' it cried. 'Your country needs you'. The *Daily Mirror* was even more vitriolic. 'Halifax the Traitor, dirty work in sell out to Nazi Germany'.

For two days prior to this uproar in the papers Churchill had been missing. Then came news that his wife, Clementine, had also disappeared. The press was beginning to smell a story and had started digging.

At the same time as the news hounds were off in search of a trail for Churchill, Halifax had met with the Italian Ambassador, Signor Bastianini, as a precursor to peace negotiations. Arrangements had been made for him to take a small delegation to Paris, which was now under German occupation. There they were to meet with the Italian leader, Mussolini, in the morning, then in the afternoon with Hitler. Halifax had hoped that the newspapers' preoccupation with the missing Winston would keep the talks off the front pages, but this had proved both naïve and forlorn.

The day before the talks were due to take place he had attended another meeting with Bastianini to lay down the parameters for the meeting and set an agenda. This had been encouraging and had been a lot easier than he had supposed. He was gambling on the Germans welcoming a truce and agreeing to stay put in the Pas de Calais.

Bastianini confirmed that he was instructed that this proposal was acceptable to Germany and that there were now no plans for the invasion of Britain, but that this position might change if other conditions for supporting a peace between them could not be agreed. In that event the Germans would consider it a rejection of the peace offer and an invasion might ensue. Halifax responded that the British armed forces were prepared for such an eventuality and, should it arise, would strenuously resist it. He added that he was confident they could repel an armed German assault on the British mainland. At this, the Italian smiled; it was clear from his expression that he dismissed the idea that the already beaten British army would be capable of holding out against the overwhelming might of the forces sitting just 23 miles away. In this Bastianini betrayed his lack of understanding of military matters. Halifax knew that an invasion across water involving beach landings would be strategically challenging, even for the Germans, and the outcome would by no means be certain. Hitler and his generals knew this, which is why they were prepared to talk.

But there would, he knew, be a price to pay for the peace. In his mind he had already ruled out any terms which left him or any succeeding British government running the country in the same way that Marshall Petin now administered southern France from Vichy or Quisling governed Norway. Bastianini noted the point, but added that he believed Hitler would be expecting a closer tie with the British, perhaps in the form of treaty arrangements.

There was an expectation that there would be demands for territory in exchange for halting the hostilities. Halifax knew he had to give something away and he wanted to keep that as small as possible.

Bastianini suggested that Mussolini would want some recompense for brokering a peace deal with the Axis alliance of which Italy was now a partner, together with Japan. Halifax had already had intelligence reports that the Italian demands would centre around the British possessions in North Africa, in particular Egypt and the Suez Canal, and so he'd had time to prepare for it. He told Bastianini this might be possible, although he had reservations about the Canal. He suggested that Hitler may also not want such a strategically important waterway to be exclusively in Italian hands. This was aimed at cooling the ambitions of Mussolini who Halifax judged would not want to go against Hitler. He needed to get the message back to the Italian dictator that there was a limit to any commission that might be gained through the intermediary offices he offered. After all, Halifax reasoned with himself, Mussolini was only a go-between at this point and he was determined to keep the price of his services as low as possible; even Egypt might be a territorial concession too far.

For the time being he would let Bastianini take back a message that was cooperative but non-committal. The act was one of fine balance. The Japanese were threatening in the Pacific and without the Americans coming in on their side the British supply routes to their eastern empire had to be through Suez. Japan had formed the Axis alliance with Germany and Italy and would certainly be pressing Hitler to close the route to British vessels, both merchant and naval.

Without Suez there was little chance of saving the Empire from the ravenous appetite of the rapid Japanese expansion in the region. The east and the west would be split and he could not rely on Hitler to keep any agreement if it suited his strategy to break it.

If he allowed the Italians to invest Suez, he was sure that sooner or later they would be forced by Hitler to allow German forces to take it over. The British fleet was still the supreme sea power but with Hitler in control of Suez the balance could be altered at his whim. At any time the Mediterranean fleet could be bottled up and the Pacific fleet split from its western counterpart. If that happened the Asian part of the British Empire would be lost.

Halifax judged that Bastianini was a diplomat, not a strategist. Therefore, his information was coming from others and by listening rather than proposing he hoped to tease out some intelligence on the real concessions that Hitler would accept in return for taking the British out of the war. When the Italian Ambassador stated that nothing less than a full return to the position of the German colonial possessions in Africa at the outset of the First World War would satisfy the Führer, Halifax was suspicious. It seemed inconsequential as the key demand and really told him nothing. Giving back to Germany her old colonies in East and West Africa would have little strategic impact on British security. So he conceded these could be on the table for discussion and waited to see what came next.

There was a pause while Bastianini went through a time-worn diplomatic ploy, which was to shuffle his papers in a matter-of-fact way that implied what came next was not a key issue. Germany, he explained, was concerned about the ambitions of Stalin and the threat of communist expansion into Europe. Hitler wanted a bilateral agreement that allowed a German naval base and limited ground forces in the north of Canada. This, he said, was to protect the Siberian flank in the event of Soviet aggression being launched through the Barents Sea. This would have to be a covert agreement so that the Soviets were not alerted and given time to pre-empt the physical logistics of its implementation. In this Halifax thought he saw an opportunity to counter the Italian suggestion that they should have Suez. If what Hitler was really after were strategic bases from which to fight a war against the Soviets and communism he could sign up to that, but only on terms that Britain kept Suez and Egypt. Mussolini would have to be satisfied with having ingratiated himself with Hitler; there would be no introductory commission for the Italians. Whatever crumbs of reward they got he had already decided would have to come from the Germans. The only difficulty he faced with such a treaty would be to get an agreement from the Canadians, but he was sure that in the interests of peace he would get their cooperation.

The meeting, which had been informal, ended with both parties agreeing that there was some mutuality in their individual requirements and that a meeting should now be arranged with Mussolini.

The meeting was fixed; it would be held in a private suite in the Georges V Hotel in Paris. The delegations were due to meet at 10.00 in the morning and Halifax's team was there on time. Halifax was anxious that this negotiation should have the widest possible parliamentary and public support. To achieve this, he had decided to invite both Hugh Dalton, who represented the Labour Party and Ernest Bevin for his trade union credentials. Halifax felt he could carry the Conservatives. Of the three, only Halifax had been wholly convinced that a deal could or should be signed up to.

The first indication that things might not be as planned was the late but triumphal arrival of Mussolini. Il Duce was in no hurry to accommodate the British. He had been ridiculed by the British press and especially the newsreels that had caricatured him as a puffed-up buffoon. Now he would exploit the moment to humiliate Halifax and his team.

On their arrival the British delegation had been herded into a cramped, airless side room with a window looking out onto the Avenue Georges V and from which they would have an opportunity to view the grand entrance of the Italian dictator. The front of the hotel was flanked by officers of Hitler's SS and inside the lobby some Gestapo men loitered obtrusively. When Halifax's press secretary, Charles Stevenson, tried to leave the room to find refreshments his way was blocked by a Gestapo man, who said abruptly, 'Go back and wait until you are called.' When he objected the man pushed him roughly back into the room and banged the door closed. There was the sound of a key in the lock. He looked at Halifax and said in shocked tones, 'Do you know, I think we are locked in, this is outrageous!' He took the handle of the door and tried it. It was locked. Next he rattled the door, at the same time knocking loudly on it. The door opened and the same man stood there barring the way.

'What is it you want?' he demanded.

'We need refreshments, and I need to know what is happening. On what authority are you confining this delegation in this room?'

The Gestapo man adopted an oily smile and changed his stance. 'I must apologise but I am responsible for your security and I can only guard you if you are in one place. There are still French resistance criminals out there and they would not hesitate to shoot you if they knew of your presence and purpose at such a meeting. We should not like anything to happen to our guests. I shall go and make enquiries Mein Herr. Perhaps the concierge can bring you something to drink.'

'Well, please do,' the secretary replied, trying to sound conciliatory.

He went through the huddle to where Halifax, Bevin and Dalton were looking out of the window.

'This is most unorthodox behaviour,' he said to Halifax, a note of worry in his voice, 'not at all acceptable. I have never experienced anything like it.' Halifax was beginning to share his worries, but simply asked the press secretary to go back and wait by the door in readiness for whatever may arrive at it.

Bevin was a huge figure of a man, tall, well-built and not easily intimidated. He was also a trade union man and not unused to being forced to cool his heels in halls and lobbies while those in power tried to gain a psychological advantage by leaving him waiting – in limbo. It cut no ice with him; he was made of tougher stuff. Halifax, however, was now concerned. He had dealt with difficult treaty negotiations before and knew the protocol. This did not feel right. This felt more like the prelude to a meeting with gangsters, not diplomats or responsible leaders of nations. For the first time since Churchill's disappearance he began to feel uneasy. It had all looked so good on paper. Now he wasn't quite so sure that reason and argument would prevail.

After about half an hour the door opened again. This time it was an Italian.

'Secret service,' the press secretary thought, 'not a waiter', and there was no sign of refreshments. The man who stood confronting Stevenson was quite short, thick set with a thuggish look about him. He seemed more like a Hollywood caricature of the archetypal Chicago gangster as he peered in through the doorway at the uncomfortable looking delegation. His mouth formed a malevolent grin as he commanded in a voice that was almost contralto, 'Sorry, but you must wait here in this room until Il Duce arrives; it is for your security.' Then he added sharply as an afterthought, 'and you must stay quiet!'

Il Duce finally arrived more than an hour late. He arrived in a style so flamboyant it could be described as theatrical. First, there were four motorcycle outriders in Wehrmacht field grey uniforms. They pulled up to the front of the hotel and flanked the entrance, standing off a short distance. Next, a black Mercedes drew up and disgorged an honour guard in the black and grey ceremonial dress uniform of the SS. Finally, a large Horch cabriolet, with fixed Italian and German pennants attached to the fenders, drew up level with the front doors of the hotel. 'He's here,' said Halifax quietly to the others.

Mussolini was dressed in a uniform of the Fascist Party with a Shako style military hat. The door of the car was opened by one of the SS guards and Mussolini stepped out followed by two other men in military uniform. He stood for a moment, hands on hips, legs slightly apart, and looked around him as if he were waiting for some ovation from adoring bystanders. However, this was Paris and not Rome and there were no admirers, just sullen Parisians who were in any event too far removed from the spectacle by the cordon of security men and guards. With a flourish of his arms he walked in through the main entrance of the hotel.

Dalton looked at Halifax and then at Bevin. 'Extraordinary behaviour,' he said almost inaudibly, 'like something out of a cheap operetta!' The door to the room opened. 'Il Duce is ready to meet with you, gentlemen. Please come this way.'

There was no real substance to the meeting. It was, Halifax judged, a softening-up exercise. The purpose was to sound out the British delegation and test their resolve on certain key issues. Mussolini was only the messenger boy. Hitler would make the real decisions based on what Mussolini reported back to him. The extraordinary episode of their confinement in the room off the lobby had been calculated to humiliate the British and in this they had partially succeeded. Uncertainty over what kind of behaviour might come next gave rise to a sense of insecurity which touched even the veteran diplomat, Halifax. Only Bevin was unmoved by it.

He had experienced these tactics before, in his career as a trade union negotiator and at the hands of those holding trump cards. He instinctively knew what came next. He had been there before and was not intimidated by it. In fact, he was heartened by it, he told Halifax after the meeting was over. 'If you have to get up to these daft pranks it usually means one thing: you've got very little in your hand. You need to scare your opposition a bit, unsettle them because you're going to be doing quite a lot of bluffing.' They waited for the next piece of theatre; they did not have to wait long.

The room in which they met was large with a high ceiling and generous windows which flooded it with summer light. There was a long oval table in polished mahogany with chairs drawn up on either side. The two sides sat facing each other. Mussolini sat in a carver chair with padded arms which was wider, deeper and slightly higher than the rest of the furniture. He sat like a king on a throne, slightly elevated to reinforce his superiority. It was as though he were giving an audience rather than engaging in a dialogue of equals. It breached all the normal codes of diplomatic protocol. He was flanked by two Italian military men dressed in the uniform of generals, Giovanni Messe and Annibale Bergonzoli. Again, Bevin was not impressed; he thought they were there to give substance to an insubstantial forum.

The generals also sat in well upholstered carvers with padded arms, but they were slightly lower than Mussolini's throne. Just behind Mussolini there stood a strategically placed interpreter, although in fact Mussolini spoke passably good English. He was, Halifax knew, an educated man and not simply the clownish caricature lampooned by the British press. This strutting about, arms stiffly folded, head slightly back with the chin jutting out was merely a performance for the adoring crowd. In common with Hitler, he saved the impassioned ranting and the posturing for public consumption. In private there was another, altogether more measured Mussolini. He had once been an academic, having studied Social Sciences at the University of Lausanne and was in fact highly literate, speaking both English and German as well has his native Italian. He played music and had published essays on a wide variety of political subjects as well as a novel; he had been a newspaper editor and a teacher.

In his earlier life he had been an enthusiastic trade union activist and a promoter of socialism. He had been a crowd agitator, giving street corner speeches urging and assisting in the growing spread of communism in Europe. He had been jailed three times for his activities in encouraging strikes and in the battles for workers' rights. Then, in 1914 he fell out of love with socialism. The socialist policy was anti-war and pacifist. A younger Mussolini had for some time been moving towards a more nationalistic view. He had read Plato's *Republic*, which he later professed had greatly influenced his ideas on the importance of national identity as had the works of Nietzsche whose philosophy of the strong had convinced him that liberalism and socialism were both decadent and marked the decline of a nation.

In 1914 he went to war. Curiously, and in common with Hitler, he had served in the trenches and been promoted to corporal. In 1917 he had been injured by a grenade that exploded in his trench, leaving him with more than 40 shards of shrapnel in his body which would stay there for the rest of his life.

When he returned from the war Mussolini had abandoned all notions of socialism. He no longer believed in the equality of all people but instead had converted to nationalism. He was convinced of the need to find a strong leader to rebuild the Italian nation and it would have to be done using Nietzsche's philosophy of elitism.

Ironically, as Halifax knew only too well, the dictator who sat opposite him in the elevated chair had been given his start in political life by secret payments from the British government. In late 1917 the British Secret Service had begun making payments of £100 a week to Mussolini for publishing propaganda articles against the anti-war movement that still existed at that time in Italy. Italy was fighting on the Allied side in the Great War and the British needed to keep her there. The payments had been authorized by his predecessor at the Foreign Office, Sir Samuel Hoare!

In 1919, with his British funds, Mussolini sowed the first seeds of his National Fascist Party. Here, then, was an intellectual, a man of learning, a man who should have been reasonable and rational to deal with, but he was not. There was a darker side to his nature. There were threads of extremism, obsession and paranoia running through his character, giving rise to a megalomania and self-delusion.

Halifax believed that sitting there in front of him was a greatly competent, charismatic and gifted politician who was wholly convinced of his mission to create a stronger, more prosperous Italy. Yet he also knew Mussolini had abused those gifts to ruthlessly eradicate all opposition in his country, using the means most readily at his disposal: force, intimidation and murder. In his view he was about to enter into negotiations with a gangster and, what was worse, a gangster whom his government had been an instrument in creating! He knew that any pact or treaty would be temporary and that the Axis would rip it up when it suited. His only hope therefore was to buy time, to win a breathing space in which Britain could build up its armed forces and try to persuade America to come in on her side.

Mussolini looked over the table at the British delegation. It crossed his mind that he had once fought on the same side with the British in a different war. But things change, and he had changed. He believed this war had been started too soon. Hitler had miscalculated with Chamberlain after Munich. He had judged him too weak and the British too unprepared for a war. He should have waited longer before testing their resolve by marching into Poland. Italy, he knew, was not yet able to fight a long campaign in a modern mechanized war. She was militarily depleted and weak. He needed time to arm. The army was too small and poorly equipped. More than anything else he needed tanks, heavy tanks. The Air Force, too, he knew would be no match for the British RAF and even the mighty German Kreigsmarine could not be sure of defeating the Royal Navy. He was reliant upon the alliance with Germany to keep what land he had managed to secure in Albania and North Africa. Now he needed further conquests, but he wanted them without fighting and with this negotiation he thought he might get them.

Mussolini had long been persuaded that the critical mass of Italy was insufficient to create a powerful modern industrialized nation. Like Hitler, he craved more land and a larger population – at least sixty million citizens would be the target he needed to achieve. He had already issued a directive to Italian women to be more productive and bear more children for the greater good of the nation. In his mind he conjured up the dream that Italy could one day regain the former glories of antiquity, a new Roman Empire. He knew that if he had any hope of achieving his ambition of creating a new Roman Empire covering the historical territory conquered by his ancestors, the Axis would have to defeat the British or make peace. It nagged at his mind that Hitler had ambitions to expand eastwards and, as with Poland, he might misjudge it and strike too soon, before he or the Germans were really ready.

The Russians were not well equipped and their armies were poorly trained and poorly led. The officer corps had been all but annihilated during the purges only two years before when Stalin's paranoia over plots to assassinate or remove him had precipitated the arrest and execution of over half the senior ranks; the cream of the officer corps had been extinguished at a stroke. This might tempt Hitler to move sooner rather than later. The Red Army was in no condition to match the Wehrmacht in the field, but the Soviet manpower resources were huge and it would be a tight match of technology against massive numbers; the outcome would be uncertain. He was uneasy. If Hitler decided to invade Russia and there was no peace treaty with the British, they would find themselves fighting on two fronts, which would be unsustainable at that time. They needed to buy some time and to do so required two things: a deal with the British, and continued American neutrality. They could always tear up any agreement with the British at a later date when they were ready. In the meantime it was folly to pull the lion's tail while they still had their head in its mouth.

Both sides needed peace for the same reason; they needed to buy time. But as they sat and faced each other across the table neither party knew this of the other.

Mussolini now dropped the theatrical performance and donned the clothes of a rational negotiator. 'Benvenuto signori, welcome gentlemen. Would you prefer to conduct our business in English?'

Halifax nodded agreement. 'Thank you, that would be most useful.'

'Good, then we shall, and if my limited skill in English is not enough I have Signor Agnelli here who shall interpret for us all.' He folded his arms, resting them on his chest and leaned back. 'So where do you wish we should start?'

Halifax, ever the cautious diplomat, merely stated that His Majesty's government did not wish to pursue a state of conflict with the Italians and the Germans and was prepared to cease hostilities on certain terms. He continued by saying that clearly Great Britain wanted peace in Europe but that there were conditions. Britain was prepared to enter into an immediate ceasefire provided all parties agreed to halt hostilities both in Europe and North Africa. There had to be guarantees that all sides would refrain from further annexation or illegal expansion into neighbouring countries by means of an internationally binding treaty.

Mussolini was silent for a moment. He nodded sagely then said, 'I believe this does not create a problem; however ...' Here come the unreasonable demands, thought Halifax and steeled himself for the response.

Mussolini continued. 'We too do not wish to prolong this conflict but we find ourselves in a difficult position. If we cease to engage you on all fronts then there has to be compensation. After all, we do not believe that ultimately your country could withstand an invasion from across the English Channel. Of course, we realize it would be costly in lives because it is not easy to make an invasion from the sea. But in the end you would almost certainly lose and it is better to find a compromise than send all those letters to the grieving mothers of our soldiers. We also believe that the real threat to Europe comes not from the reorganization of frontiers,' and here he smiled at the term, seeming gratified to have framed it, 'but from further east, from the spread of the communist ideology and the tyranny of the Soviet Union. Stalin would be happy to see Britain in his grasp.'

Bevin looked at Halifax, the old trade union man in him emerging bluntly. 'When's he going to get on with it?' He turned to Mussolini, 'Get to the point man and stop blathering. What is it you want?'

Mussolini stiffened perceptibly. In any other place he would have this man taken out and shot, but here he did not have that option. He remained measured and diplomatic while mentally he noted down Bevin as a man he would personally have executed once the British were defeated.

'We shall want in return certain territories of the British Empire, as part of the guarantee that you remain neutral.' Here it comes, thought Halifax.

'And they are to be?' He posed the question slowly.

'Egypt and the British occupied areas and colonies of Sudan, Kenya and Somalia will be ceded to Italy and your government will recognize the Italian colony of Ethiopia as legitimately part of the Italian Empire. The German colonies in East and West Africa that were confiscated in the Great War will return to Germany. All existing frontiers as they now stand are to be recognized as legal and you will use your persuasion with the Americans to accept this.'

Halifax held up a hand to interrupt him. 'Signor Mussolini,' he said in his best diplomatic tone, 'I am sure you must understand that I cannot speak for the Americans in these matters and it would be improper for me to suggest I could.'

Mussolini nodded and brushed it aside with a small movement of his hand, then continued: 'The territories of Singapore and Malaya will be ceded jointly to the Axis powers with the naval base of Singapore being handed over to Japan. Finally the Suez Canal is to become jointly administered by Germany, Italy and Great Britain.' He paused before adding, 'These are Herr Hitler's terms, gentlemen, for not invading your country.'

There was a silence while it all sank in. 'I think,' said Halifax, 'we need a break in the meeting to discuss your proposals.'

The delegation stood up and the Italians responded politely by doing the same. The British were shown to an annexed room where they could consider their position in private. Mussolini was pleased with the morning so far. They lit up cigarettes while Mussolini joked with his generals that he didn't believe the British had it in them for more fighting.

In the annex they discussed the proposals. 'These are nothing less than surrender terms,' said Bevin angrily. 'We can't sign up to them, or anything like them – we're miles apart.' Dalton agreed and added that the loss of Singapore would mean the loss of the British Empire. Suez, he thought, might be practical but only with a watertight agreement and a major British military presence to guarantee that agreement. Egypt could be sacrificed so long as there was a broad neutral zone on the eastern bank of Suez and that the British remained in possession of the Palestine. He suggested there would be a need to reinforce the troops holding that area, troops that Britain did not actually have. The British Expeditionary Force, which had been lifted off the beaches at Dunkirk less than two weeks before, was an exhausted, dispirited and depleted force. It had lost 70,000 men during the French campaign: dead, wounded, captured or just simply missing. They had escaped with light arms only. Tanks, trucks, heavy field artillery, half-tracks, tons of ammunition and stores, in fact everything that was needed to wage a war had been abandoned there, on the beaches at Dunkirk and the roads leading to them. Britain had an effective army of less than half a million operational men. Dalton had secretly thought Churchill reckless to demand that they carried on fighting, even though he publicly supported him in the War Cabinet. He now began to see that it might be better to go down fighting with at least a chance of victory. The Navy and the RAF were both intact and the Navy, in particular, was still a formidable force. What was being demanded looked like it might be the thin edge of a very forceful wedge. It would certainly reduce the potency of the Navy.

Halifax had been silent since they entered the annex. He wanted to hear the others' views. Now he made his own known to them.

'Well,' he said, 'we are in a cleft stick. We are in no condition to repulse a German invasion of our shores. We have neither the men nor the equipment to defend ourselves were the Germans to gain a foothold. We need time to rebuild our military strength and that time comes with a price to pay. If we refuse to pay the price demanded they will come at us, and if they succeed they will take by force what at the moment they are asking for conditionally – and we should not be able to stop them. We must therefore be prepared to give something, or at least appear to be giving something, while at the same time creating delays in the final implementation of any legally binding treaties so that we can back out of them honourably when we are in a position so to do. Are we in agreement?' Bevin and Dalton nodded. 'Then let me put some flesh on it.'

'The African territories are expendable,' he put it bluntly. 'I agree that we could jointly run the Canal with the Germans. I doubt they would let Mussolini have a hand in it but that would be simpler for us. There have been suggestions in the past that it should become an international zone and since American shipping makes use of it, that in itself would partly guarantee that Hitler stuck to the agreement. He could not afford to create a situation which drew the Americans into the war, and were he to do so, it would be greatly to our advantage. Subject to the small print, I believe we could agree to the principle of that proposal. You are right, Hugh, when you say we need to improve our military strength in the Palestine if we are to safeguard our rights there. But there is another way of looking at this. We could counter-propose that the Canal becomes an international zone and this would bring the Americans in to keep Hitler in line.'

'It is totally out of the question that we hand over anything to the Japanese. They are already threatening our borders in the north of Malaya with the Siam alliance, and I fear for Burma in the same way.'

'For this reason I believe we should vigorously oppose any concessions in the Pacific and Far East. By the same token, any loss of control over the Canal, even in a joint agreement, would be to commit suicide. The Royal Navy must have free access and full rights of access at all times. No arrangement in which we are subordinate to Germany or Italy in these matters would be acceptable.'

Bevin was looking puzzled. 'Isn't there something missing here? When you met with Bastianini there was talk of them wanting a base in Canada. We seem to have lost that, so what's that about?' Halifax agreed. 'To me it indicates that they might feel it was a demand too far and probably not significant enough to be worth jeopardizing the talks. I think it betrays something they are hiding.'

'Go on,' said Dalton.

'Well, my instinct tells me they are unsure of themselves and don't want to overload the demands for fear we reject the talks and walk away. If that is so then it follows they are far from sure that they can defeat us on our home soil, and if that is correct they are more anxious than we have supposed to avoid further conflict. So, I think we should try batting a little harder and see where that takes us. I suggest we say a flat 'no' to the Far East demands and propose an international agreement on the administration of Suez which includes the Americans. This will require further talks that would need to include the Roosevelt administration and that will take time. In the interim we agree to a temporary ceasefire. They can have the colonies but we want a demilitarized zone along the French Channel coast – I would suggest 50 kilometers with our own observers being allowed to monitor on the ground. In that way we would get some warning if they started to build up an invasion force.'

Halifax waited for a response. Dalton and Bevin nodded.

'Right, then I think we are ready to go back in.'

It was clear from his expression that Mussolini was not pleased as he listened to the British counter-terms. However, he was only the messenger and he had been given the message to take back to Hitler. Now they would have to wait for the afternoon meeting, which was scheduled for three o'clock at the Élysée Palace. Mussolini left the meeting; it had taken less than an hour. On his way to Hitler he congratulated himself that at least he had got what he wanted. It was a step on the road to his policy of *spazio vitalie*, more living space, a concept held in common with Hitler's *lebensraum*, and the building of his imperial ambitions. In this respect he welcomed the British offer over Suez. Italy needed time to consolidate.

Negotiations with America would give him that time and perhaps the added advantage that the Italian Navy would have the opportunity to break out of its prison in the Mediterranean. The Italian Navy was already large, ranking fourth in the world, and they were building more ships, but many of them were old and outdated. They lacked the technology of the Royal Navy whose ships were also better armoured. If they were to move freely in the Mediterranean they would either have to defeat the Royal Navy, which Mussolini knew would be difficult if not impossible, or they must get the British out of the war. If Franco had not refused to join the Axis they could have included Gibraltar in their demands, opening the way to the Atlantic. But following extensive persuasion by the British Ambassador in Madrid, both General Franco and his Portuguese neighbour, the dictator Salazar, had declined to get involved in the European war, leaving the British comfortably perched on the Rock and able to harass Italian shipping trying to supply its North African colonies or making passage to the Atlantic. Here, then, was another reason for keeping the British on side. A cease in hostilities would open the Gibraltar Straits.

Hitler, he thought, would be angered by the British response. It concerned him that he would do something precipitate and squander the opportunity to settle the western front, thus depriving them of the freedom to concentrate where they wished: Germany in the East, Italy in North Africa and Mediterranean Europe. The British, he knew, would not be bullied but he judged they could be cajoled. Mussolini distrusted the German dictator and thought him often irrational in his decision making. His experience was that Hitler was prone to fits of depression and emotional outbursts. He had once confided to his mistress, Clara Petacci, that he found Hitler prone to weak and emotional decisions and referred to him as a 'teary eyed sentimentalist'. What he now wanted to avoid was further military engagement until Italy was ready.

When he arrived at the Élysée Palace Hitler's response was not what he had expected. He found the German Führer in a euphoric mood. He was laughing and slapping his thighs like a Bavarian dancer. He greeted Mussolini enthusiastically without bothering to salute but instead shaking him by the hand vigorously. 'Good news,' he said, 'great news, yes wonderful, wonderful.' He looked at Mussolini with satisfaction on his face. 'Two of our ships have sunk the British aircraft carrier *Glorious* and two of its escorting destroyers. *Gneisenau* and *Scharnhorst* – two of my best battlecruisers. So, the Royal Navy is not invincible. Perhaps this will help Lord Halifax in his decisions?' Then he changed the tempo and in a more serious tone said, 'Come, I have arranged food and we can discuss the British while we eat. This news has improved my appetite.'

Over lunch Mussolini imparted the British response. Hitler listened intently but said little. That he did not fly into a rage at what Mussolini thought of as

British arrogance in the face of overwhelming odds and certain defeat surprised and encouraged him. He diplomatically suggested that the most important outcome was to get a temporary truce which would park the British on the sidelines until they were ready to deal with them. This, he suggested, could best be achieved by scaling back the demands so that they were seen to be conciliatory. This would give the British a sense of having bargained successfully and they would not go back to their people with empty hands and repeat the shame of Chamberlain. Hitler nodded, listened, and continued to say little in reply. When he did enter the conversation it was only to make mild comments; he gave nothing away.

Secretly Hitler regarded the Italian with suspicion. He believed Il Duce had already made some bad strategic decisions which had stretched his country's resources to their limits. His regime had a bad track record on security. The French Deuxième Bureau had compromised Italian radio codes and there was little doubt they would have passed this on to the British. Italian security was leaky, it was full of holes. He was not about to pass on his thoughts to this garrulous Italian who could not be trusted to keep his mouth shut. There was a mutual contempt between the two dictators, though at the time neither showed it. The conversation finished with coffee and Mussolini left. He was not invited to be present at the final meeting with the British. His job as the go-between was done and he would have to await the outcome.

Between lunch and meeting with the British, Hitler found a well-padded *chaise longue* where he put his feet up and, comforted by the news of his ships, settled down for a nap.

A little before three, Paul Schmidt, his interpreter, woke him to announce the arrival of the British team. The Führer's valet brought a freshly pressed Nazi uniform jacket. Hitler straightened his tie and smoothed down his hair. 'Now,' he said to Schmidt, 'I shall tell the British what they don't want to hear: the price they must pay for survival.'

In the conference room they all shook hands then sat down at a long table. Hitler was joined by a colonel of military intelligence, but he was not introduced. On the other side the Halifax delegation sat eagerly waiting to hear their proposals to the British counter-terms. Hitler looked at Schmidt, said something in German, then handed him a sheet of paper to read from.

'These are the terms the Führer is prepared to offer you, gentlemen.' Then he read from the list in front of him. The unknown colonel sat and made notes.

'One: a Suez conference to agree the joint administration of the Canal comprising Germany, America and Britain.' Halifax looked satisfied with that – so far so good.

'Two: Egypt can remain in British control but is to be demilitarized; there will be a division of the Afrika Korps stationed at Cairo to ensure no breaches occur.'

'Acceptable,' Halifax responded.

'Three: Britain returns to Germany all the African colonies appropriated under the Treaty of Versailles.'

Halifax looked at the other two for approval; all three nodded 'yes'.

'Four: British Somalia and the Sudan are to be formally handed over to Italy.'

'Agreed.' Halifax was beginning to think things were going their way and inwardly congratulated himself.

'Five: Singapore and Malaya to be handed over to the Japanese in return for a ceasefire and a halt to further expansion.'

Halifax had expected this last demand but had always said he would resist it. It would mean an end to British naval supremacy in the Far East and probably the eventual loss of India and Burma. Now when he tried to raise an objection Hitler simply said, 'Nein!' He signalled to Schmidt to continue. Halifax was horrified at the off-hand undiplomatic response but when he tried to raise it Hitler simply shouted 'nein' even more emphatically. Schmidt ignored the interruption and ploughed on.

'Six: A German naval base in Canada – to be kept secret to avoid alerting the Russians.'

'I don't understand the point,' Halifax had started to say, but Schmidt simply held up a hand to silence him.

'Please allow me to finish and we can talk about it afterwards.'

'Seven: Germany to be consulted over Royal Navy movements in the Channel and the Atlantic.'

'Eight: Italy to be consulted over Royal Navy movements in the Mediterranean.'

'Nine: The same to apply to Japan for the Pacific.'

'Ten: RAF flights to be limited to UK and coastal movements.'

Bevin and Dalton were shaking their heads in resigned disbelief. None of this had come up in the pre-discussion with Mussolini.

'Eleven: The scaling down of the Royal Air Force and the British Army to be stripped of its heavy weaponry.'

'Twelve: German observers to be put in place at strategically important naval bases and some key military establishments.'

'Thirteen: The establishment of a permanent German Legation in London.'

'Fourteen: The port of Hull to be leased to the Third Reich for a period of 99 years.'

The list came to an end with one final demand: point fifteen – one which Halifax and the others thought both odd and inconsequential. Sir Oswald

Mosley was to be appointed to head up a policing organization which would sit somewhere between the Legation and the British government. It would have powers of arrest in exceptional circumstances where there was a conflict between the Legation and the British civil authorities. It was, Schmidt assured them, a measure for the security of both sides and would be relied upon to act impartially at the request of both sides. 'It is a measure which will help to ensure civil harmony between all sides,' he said with a flourish.

'Now,' he continued, 'on the German side we are offering the following concessions.'

'One: Germany will suspend all plans to invade Britain.'

'Hardly a concession,' Bevin whispered leaning over to Dalton. 'They've already done it under the terms on offer.' Schmidt paused and looked disapprovingly at the whispering Bevin. He looked at the Führer who was smiling with satisfaction at the humiliation of the other side. He signalled Schmidt to go on.

'Two: Germany will create a 50 kilometer demilitarized strip from Antwerp down to Biarritz on the Spanish border.'

'Well, that's something,' Halifax muttered under his breath.

'Three: Germany will enter into a treaty safeguarding the countries of the British Empire.'

Schmidt stopped; the British waited for point four but there wasn't a point four and Schmidt sat down. Hitler grinned and said something to Schmidt. Schmidt looked along the row of expectant faces lined up opposite him.

'The Führer thanks you for attending this meeting and hopes this will promote a long-lasting peace between our two countries.'

Hitler stood up and left. Then Schmidt and the colonel got up and prepared to leave. 'Thank you, gentlemen – goodbye.'

There was silence around the table and then Bevin said, 'Is that it? What happened to the negotiation?'

In truth there hadn't been a negotiation at all; they had attended like naughty children and been told what their punishment was to be, and that really was it – take it or we invade.

They left in a sombre mood; Halifax knew he had been outmanoeuvred. He instructed his secretary to make arrangements for the civil servants to meet with the other side and draw up the treaty document.

'This isn't a treaty,' Bevin complained sourly, 'it's just surrender terms.'

CHAPTER 9

10 June 1940

Saturday had come round again and they had planned to visit the World's Fair in New York. The day was hot and clear with a peerless blue sky and just the hint of a breeze coming off the Hudson. It was shaping up for a perfect day at the show. Tom took a leisurely drive down from Peekskill in the Chrysler. He would pick up Mike from his parents' home. The Mescals lived on the fashionable side of the town where the streets were broad and tree-lined. They owned one of the largest houses in Croton, Cutlers Hall.

The Hall had been built in the 1881 by a wealthy merchant, Thomas Cutler, who had got rich supplying the Union army with a coarse serge cloth for uniforms during and after the Civil War. The mansion, and it was a mansion in every sense, was built of mellow red brick; it had fine carved stone coins and lintels with a porch supported by massive sandstone columns. The sash windows were tall and gracious in the Colonial style. An expansive gravelled drive wound its way through venerable maples and ornamental shrubs up to the entrance of the house where it culminated in a sweeping semi-circle, which had originally been laid out for horse-drawn carriages but now served the comings and goings of their mechanical successors.

He drove in through imposing ornamental iron gates which stood sentinel at the front of the property and scrunched to a halt on the gravel, just short of the steps leading up to the front door.

Mike was one of five children and the only boy. Michael Mescal senior had wanted more sons who he planned would carry on the family business but Mike's siblings were all girls, and so all of his father's expectations fell about his shoulders like a heavy mantle.

Of the girls Ellie, the oldest, was married and long gone from the house. Next there were the twins, Shelagh and Rosheen, who were both now enrolled at a private school in Croton. Finally there was Ruby, who had come as a late surprise and was by far the youngest at 11 years old. Mr Mescal senior's valet came to the door in response to the jangle of the old-style mechanical bells. Behind him and looking shyly out was Ruby. Having seen Tom, she ran down the long hallway shouting for Mike and announcing Tom's arrival. Eleanor Mescal, Mike's mother, emerged from the large maple wood-panelled salon where they entertained guests and greeted Tom informally. She was a short but elegant woman in her fifties, but carried her years lightly. Her carefully permed greying hair was still tinged with the red that she had given Mike, though it was now more auburn. Her fine-boned features gave her face a slight air of mischief and he wondered how she could ever have made herself look cross for the sake of disciplining the children.

'She makes a dreadful noise that girl,' Mrs Mescal smiled apologetically. 'It's a grand day for your visit to the Fair. I do hope you'll enjoy it.'

'Thank you, Mrs Mescal, I'm sure we shall. Have you been to see it?'

'Indeed, we did. Mr Mescal took me and the twins to the opening and, you know, we saw President Roosevelt. He gave a fine speech about peace and hoped the European nations could find a way to live in harmony with each other.' Then she laughed and added, 'Not that there's much chance of that. It's a mercy we're well away from it and where it can't touch us. Mr Roosevelt is right. We should not get involved this time.' Then she added ruefully, 'I wouldn't like to think of you or Michael being sent over there to get yourselves killed; that I would not.'

Mike appeared in the hallway, followed by Ruby who danced around her big brother and looked shyly at Tom. They said their goodbyes and left.

From Cutlers Hall they drove the short distance to Croton railroad station where they abandoned the car and boarded a train. Tony had been in New York for a couple of days on some kind of business errand for his father, though he wouldn't say what. When they got to Grand Central he was waiting there on the concourse under the big clock. From Grand Central they took the subway out to Queens, where the Fair had been built.

The Fair was monumental, laid out over 1,216 acres of reclaimed land. Passing through the gates was like entering a city, but a city of the future. The pavilions were not what the word conveys – not temporary structures of canvas or wood. They rose like gigantic monuments, hundreds of feet into the air – a vision of some strange and exotic empire fashioned in concrete, glass, aluminum, plastic and brightly polished steel. It was a city traversed by wide avenues lined with tall trees, connecting gardens that folded around each building. Large plazas punctuated by fountains graced the spaces between each building, pumping millions of gallons of glittering water along little canals, connecting in their turn to a host of lakes and water features. Within its zones this city held not only the idea of the wealth and power of the nation – Ford, General Motors, the Chrysler Corporation, the manufacturers and the household names of America – but also the representatives of more than half the nations of the developed world. It represented the hope and potential of a modern future.

But hidden away behind this optimism there were doubts and anxiety. The slogans for the Fair, when it first opened in April 1939, were 'Dawn of a New Day' and 'World of Tomorrow'.

But in 1940, as the new day dawned, the future that arrived with the second year of the show was a little less bright. It had been dulled by the events in Europe. Germany, which had declined an invitation to host a pavilion at the great show, had instead invaded Poland. The future was beginning to go rusty. The air of hope was tinged with a chill more like winter than the spring of great promise. The organizers quickly changed the slogan to 'For Peace and Freedom' – something more inward looking, something that reflected America's growing determination to remain isolated from European events.

They entered the Fair through Concordia Gate and were immediately confronted by a vast open panorama. In front of them was the main avenue. 'Wow, man, this is the future,' Tom said as they walked through the gates. 'And you know what, I like it. We're only just inside the gates and I like what I see. The future looks good to me.'

Tony snorted a short, derisive, phony little chuckle. 'Hey, hold up their buddy, what about the European war? Is that part of your good-looking future?'

'Well, now that's interesting. Your folks are Italian, where do you figure to be in all this?' Tony put his arm around Tom's shoulder.

'Oh, I'm American – through and through. My family may have been Italian but they're sure as hell no part of those crazies.'

'Does that go for your old man?'

'Especially my old man. You know he was just a kid when our grandfather decided to make the move. They were a pretty well-heeled family. We had standing in the community.'

'So why'd they leave?'

'Vendetta. We're from the south; there was some kinda vendetta going on – I don't know what, they never talk about it. It was enough to make them decide to make the move. I think someone got killed – I don't really know.'

'So they never go back there?'

'Hell, no – and what for? Like I said we're Americans; Italian Americans maybe but Americans right through to the soft center. Cut me open and I've got the Stars and Stripes running all the way through. My old man – I guess he thinks Mussolini is probably good for Italy but that's about it. Maybe the Fascists can bring some stability to the country. I don't know. He never really discusses it.'

As they reached the end of the first broad avenue they came in sight of the Fair's signature buildings, the Trylon and the Perisphere. The three stopped and let the images sink in. The structure ahead of them was a combination of a three-sided obelisk rising 610 feet to its point, connected to a huge sphere of around 200 feet in diameter. The combined buildings were joined by an elevated walkway. The structures dominated the skyline. The only buildings in the fairground painted white, they stood out from the rest, shimmering in the bright sunlight, dappled by the reflections of rippling water in the surrounding lake. It was an impressive sight and looked more like a Hollywood set than anything real.

'Holy cow!' Tony shouted and threw his arms out wide as if to encompass the sight that stood before him. 'That is one truly amazing piece of construction! Can you believe this whole site was just a dump for garbage four years ago. I heard the government spent a hundred million bucks getting this place cleaned up and knocked into shape.'

They stood for a while looking up at it. 'I've seen pictures of it before,' said Mike 'but I never realized it was so big.'

On one side of the Trylon there was an entrance through which a continuous stream of visitors passed. Once inside, they were confronted by yet another wonder of the modern age: an escalator. It was, the makers claimed, the longest escalator in the world. As they followed the queue and stepped onto the moving stairway, Tom looked up to the destination high above him. It was, he thought, like a stairway to the stars. If America could do this kind of thing, he told himself, she could do anything; she was unchallengeable. At the top of the stairway they stepped into the giant sphere. A walkway spread itself all the way round the walls in a great equatorial circle suspended above the void. Below, in a huge auditorium, a vision of a city of the future had been laid out as a giant model, complete with elevated roads, skyscrapers and moving traffic. Onto the model a series of photographic slides was projected, bringing about almost magical changes to the structures and perspectives.

The Fair was divided into zones but not all of them were worth spending time on, Tom thought. The foreign pavilions represented the outside world but they held little interest for any of them. In common with many Americans, what was happening inside America had all their attention and there was little thought left over for the rest of the world, except perhaps the European war and how to stay out of it.

From the Trylon they made their way through more wide avenues and gardens till they got to the transport zone. Here they spent most of the morning. The Ford building took a lot of their time. It was the largest single pavilion at the show, covering around seven acres of ground. It was packed with exhibits demonstrating the manufacturing processes of modern mass production. There was a static display of Ford cars starting in 1905 right up to the latest Mercurys and the luxurious V12 Lincoln Zephyr limousine. There were cutaway models with moving pistons and valves, demonstrating how the modern internal combustion engine worked. Winding its way up to the roof a spiral vehicle ramp took visitors, driven in Ford cars, right to the top of the building, demonstrating how ramps could be used in modern road construction to get cars up onto elevated freeways, which were increasingly being seen as the way to take the growing motor traffic through city centers. On top of the roof of the building a half mile of road had been laid out in a grand ellipse. As they rode round it, lounging in the back of a Lincoln sedan, they were treated to the best panoramic view anywhere in the fairground. Below them the scene stretched away into the distance across the avenues dotted with thousands of visitors, the lakes and the pavilions, their flags swirling in the light midday breeze, right into the far distance where Manhattan skyscrapers jutted up, piercing the clear blue horizon. This they agreed was America at its most impressive.

It was after two when they wandered into the food zone where they stopped at a kiosk and bought hot dogs and sodas.
'Time out for a rest,' Mike suggested, 'let's find a bench and sit down.'
Tony stretched out his legs full length in front of him and arched his back against the bench. 'How much more of this do we wanna do? My feet are flatter than a New York cop's.'
Mike fell in with that sentiment. They'd seen most of what they came to see and what was left they didn't think would be that interesting. It was while they were sitting contemplating what, if anything, they might explore next that they heard a familiar sound. There was a solid crack from a rifle shot. Tom stood up and looked in the direction of the sound. There was another crack and another, followed by seven more.
Tom turned his head on one side. 'Listen, there's another one. It's gotta be a range. Well, dammit there must be a range somewhere in here. I didn't know they had a range here?' Tony held up a finger calling for silence. 'It must be over in the Amusement Zone. Shall we take a look, gentlemen?'
'Why not?' the other two agreed. Tony got up and looked around. 'This way I figure.' He started off in the direction of the sounds, the others following up.
The construction of an Amusement Zone had not been well received by the organizing committee who deemed it unfitting for such a great and important event, but pressure from business to have it included won the day. It was popular with the visitors; they came there and spent money. It was a little light relief from the sombre worthies and the well intentioned. As they entered the zone the first thing they encountered was Billy Rose's Aquacade, a water show. The grand art deco building hosting this show was like everything else in the park – gigantic, exuberant, a bold statement of the latest architecture. The auditorium could hold 11,000.
'Holy Mary, will you look at this place,' Mike said, waving his arm generally in the direction of the exhibit.

The Aquacade was rated the most popular venue of the entire show. It featured lots of girls in swimsuits, water dancing and synchronized swimming – though the less charitable claimed it was no more than an opportunity for grown men to come and gawp at girls with not too many clothes on. Some of the exhibits, which included girlie shows, ran close to what was legal and from time to time they got raided by the New York Vice Squad. But in the main it was tame enough to take the kids and get an ice cream.

They found the shooting attraction stuck away at the back of the site overlooking Meadow Lake. It was a 100-yard range with targets mounted in butts on the lake shore. The large expanse of water beyond was more than two miles long and an ideal backdrop for spent rounds to fall harmlessly into it.

The range was fenced and obscured with advertising hoardings. A substantial canvas tent stretched across the width of it; a wooden kiosk with illustrations from the Wild West was set at the entrance. Outside, a huckster was calling to the passing visitors to come in and try their luck. He was dressed in the style of a Confederate soldier from the Civil War. His quasi-military uniform with brass buttons and a polished silver belt buckle was more in keeping with a vaudeville gallery than a serious shooting range. Nevertheless, as they approached they knew instinctively they had to go in. This was not to be missed.

'Okay boys,' the huckster shouted, 'you look like you could handle a gun, how about it? Try your luck? We're handing out mighty fine prizes today. Why you could win a hundred dollars. Put a down payment on one of Mr Ford's nice new shiny automobiles with that. Whadya say boys. Will'ya take a chance?'

He turned his attention to another group and started the same spiel again, this time adding, 'A quarter for the gun, a dime a round, big cash prizes for the highest scores. Try your luck.'

They paid their quarters at the kiosk and filed in through a narrow entrance. Inside, the ground was covered with duck boards. The back of the tent was open to the range, which stretched out to the lake at the far end. Low bunds of earth had been raised along its length to curb any stray rounds and to stop the careless from wondering onto the range and stopping a round. At the end, 100 yards distant, another bund, this one lateral, formed the butts. There were ten target lanes spread across the range, each one with wire and pulleys to wind the targets in and out to and from the butts. The firing line was a series of trestle tables stood end to end. To one side a small office had been curtained off and next to that was a long wooden gun rack.

As they filed in they were greeted by a youth also attired in Confederate grey. He directed them to choose from the gun rack. The choice was small, mostly old lever action Winchesters, together with a couple of bolt action Brownings left over from the Great War.

Another man, also dressed in Civil War garb, ushered them forward to the firing line. 'Okie Dokie', he said grinning, 'you gentlemen familiar with the fine art of handling firearms, would you say?' They nodded.

'Here's the drill then. A dollar gets you a string of ten rounds. The range is one hundred yards but we'll be shooting at fifty; any two bulls gets you a handsome ten Simoleons. Three gets you thirty. After that it raises at ten bucks a bull all the way to a lip-smacking, tongue-tingling one hundred smackeroons. You fire from the standing position, one minute for the string. Are we ready?'

Tom looked at the man. 'Just one thing. I'd like to buy an extra round.'

'He'd like to buy an extra round', the man repeated, looking from Tony to Mike. 'Anyone else like extra rounds? No? Tell me son, why would you want an extra round when the rules are ten rounds and you win ten bucks a shell if you're real good or real lucky?'

Tom looked at the old Winchester and then at the man. 'I'd just like to get the feel of the gun before I go for real. You know, feel it against my shoulder – see how hard it pulls up when I shoot. I haven't used a gun like this before. I won't shoot at the target – just out onto the lake.'

The man shrugged and heaved a sigh of resignation. 'Okay, son, if it settles your nerves you can get the extra shot. But not at the target – understood?'

Tom loaded the Winchester and fired out to the edge of the lake. The round struck the earth to one side of the targets. There was a puff of dust where the bullet bit into the dirt bund. Tom stood looking at the lingering dust for a moment then turned to the man.

'OK?' asked the man.

'Ready as I'll ever be.' Tom stepped up to the line.

At the far end of the line a man, watched by his wife and son, finished a string and wound in his target. He looked disappointed. They wandered over to where the boys were shaping up to shoot, joining a small gaggle of spectators who had drifted in through the unattended door.

'Shooters only inside, folks', said the man in the uniform and herded them back out of the kiosk. 'I'm a shooter,' said the man who had just finished his string. 'You sure are mister; you and the family can stay.'

Mike shot first. It wasn't his best performance; everything went into the outer ring except one that just got into the inner. He shrugged, 'Now you wouldn't want to be shooting at barn doors with this yoke,' he said looking with derision at the rifle he held, 'because I don't think you'd hit it.'

Tony was better, although his first shot was so wide it missed the target altogether. 'The sights are all over the place', he said to Tom, and laughed. The second shot was better and by the last he finally placed a bull. He put down the gun. 'Right, now let's watch the master.'

Tom fired off his string methodically and without expression. When they reeled in the target there was nothing left of the bull; it was shot to pieces. The rest of the target was virgin.

'I think that's a hundred bucks,' Tony said pulling a grimace at the man in the Civil War uniform who stood there with a look of disbelief on his face. 'Wait here,' he said, and went behind a curtain at the back of the kiosk.

The woman who had been spectating turned to her husband. 'Well, I never did see anything like that. I don't think Annie Oakley could've done better.' Her husband nodded agreement. 'Fancy shooting, young man.'

'The extra shell?' Tony asked.

'Ranging the sights on that small white rock out there.' Tom pointed to the edge of the lake where a discarded white stone sat. 'They were all over the place. I just compensated and hoped for the best.'

'Remind me never to play golf with you.'

The man returned. 'Well,' he said, 'you're a real dandy shot – and that aint no lie. So how would you like to go up against one of my professional boys? We got some real keen shots staying with us to do some exhibition shooting. Whadya say to your hundred dollar winnings against a thousand; best of three rounds winner takes all?'

For a moment nobody spoke. Then Mike shook his head. 'It seems to me a man could buy an awful lot of things with a hundred dollars.'

'True,' said Tom, 'but I came in with nothing so what if I go out with nothing.'   He looked at Tony. 'OK, wise guy, what do you think?' Tony arched his shoulders in a deep shrug. 'It's your call. Mike's right, you can buy a hell of a lot with a hundred – but you can buy even more with a grand.'

'I'll do it.'

The man who next stepped out from behind the curtain looked familiar. He walked forward and shook hands with all three in turn. 'Didn't we meet somewhere before?' Tom asked.

'Henry Newman, sergeant of the army, attached to the marksman training program at Fort Perry. We sure have met before; I saw you shoot at Croton High School a while back – in a .22 match. Do you still wanna go up against me?'

'I guess.'

'OK, but I'm gonna be shooting with my own gun. It's the army's latest carbine, the M1 – you OK with that?'

'It's all the same to me,' said Tom, 'I'll stay with the Winchester.'

'All right, Mr Tubbs sir, some targets please.' The man in the Civil War uniform wheeled out two targets and ranged them at 100 yards. He pulled a silver quarter from his pants pocket. 'OK, we'll toss this quarter for who shoots first?' Tom nodded.

'You can call it,' Newman offered.

Tom nodded again and called heads. It came down tails.

'Right off,' said Tubbs. Three rounds and if there aint no winner you shoot one for one until one or other drops a shot. Understood? Good! Mr Newman sir, please step up to the mark.'

Newman pulled the carbine tight into his shoulder and squinted down the sights. Standing there in that pose, shoulders hunched, head forward leaning into the weapon, he cut a strong figure. For the first time Tom noticed that what had first seemed a gaunt individual was in fact a trim, well-muscled professional soldier. At six feet two he was taller than Tom by two inches. The carbine was a semi-automatic and Newman got off his three rounds in quick succession. When the target was wound in there wcrc three holes neatly grouped in the bull.

'Nice shooting,' Tom commented.

'Why, thank you son – and good luck to yourself.'

The woman and her husband both clapped and she gave out a little squeak of admiration. Tubbs scowled at the woman. 'We have to have quiet in here please; this is serious business with high rollin' stakes – we don't want no distractions.' The woman looked embarrassed and gave a little nod.

As Tom took up his position on the firing line, Mike gave him a reassuring pat on the shoulder. 'Just for luck.'

'Good luck,' squeaked the woman. Tubbs looked irritated. 'Keep the noise down folks if you want to stay and watch. Don't want any claims of distraction here.'

Tom tucked the Winchester tight into his shoulder, breathed out gently and, as the breath expired, squeezed the trigger. The crack of the shot was louder than the M1. He pulled down the lever and ejected the empty cartridge which bounced on the duck boards with a metallic clatter. He lifted the rifle to his shoulder and prepared to fire again. Tom got off the three rounds smoothly and methodically without any sense of hurry or tension. The targets were slowly wound back to where they all stood, rigid with anticipation. Newman's shots had each clipped the bull but were more inside than out so they counted. Tom's target displayed three overlapping holes where each shot had been so close to the center that they clipped each other. There was a sigh of relief from Mike and Tony let out a low whistle.

'Well,' said Tubbs, 'this is some fine and fancy shooting – I congratulate both contestants. But we must find a winner.'

Tony suggested that since Tom's shots were grouped closer to the center of the bull than Newman's surely he should be pronounced the winner – and walk away with the grand. Mike jumped in and agreed. The fake Confederate soldier Tubbs shook his head. 'In the bulls eye was the rule boys, in the bull's eye – and that's where all the shots fell. They have to shoot another round. Sergeant Newman, sir,' and he waved a hand to beckon Newman to the line.

'One shell apiece.'

Newman's clip magazine held five rounds so he didn't need to reload. New targets were wound out on the pulley wires, wobbling like uncertain butterflies hanging on a stem in a breeze.

Newman resumed the firing stance. There was a crack and the shot was gone. He stepped back abruptly and stood to attention as if complying with the shooters manual on protocol.

Tubbs took up a pair of field glasses and focused on the target. 'That's a bull,' he announced offering the glasses around. 'Anyone wanna take a look?' Mike took them and peered down the range. 'Confirmed.'

Tom cocked the Winchester and took his shot. At first it looked like he'd missed the target altogether and Tubbs let out a whoop, announcing in a loud voice, 'I think we may have a winner!' Tony and Mike both looked stunned – how could he miss a target that size at that range? And this was no ordinary shooter, this was Tom Jordan.

However, as the target came wobbling back up the wires it became clear that they had not got a winner. The man in the grey fake uniform muttered 'Ah shit!' It was another bull, but this time it was so geometrically central that it was difficult to detect through the glasses. Tony and Mike gathered around Tom congratulating him and showing clearly their relief. The man and his wife joined in patting him on the shoulder.

Another shot and two more bulls later the guns needed reloading. Sergeant Newman pushed the five-shot clip into the breach of his M1. Tubbs took a handful of shells and passed them to Tom who loaded the Winchester.

Two shots later it was all over. Newman's round was barely in the bull but Tom's was a long way shy. It had punched the inner ring well below the bull. The boys were devastated. Mike just stood there shaking his head slowly from side to side, all the time saying it was unbelievable. Tony, arms outstretched palms open, looked around at everyone. 'What happened?' he kept repeating. 'Tom, what happened?'

'The best shot won, that's what happened,' said Tubbs, tugging on the belt of his fake Confederate pants. 'Well shot, Sergeant Newman!' he shouted, congratulating him and pumping his hand up and down. 'Sorry boys, this young man shot well but not well enough. Bad luck.'

All the while Tom had remained silent. He looked at Newman and the other man. He was holding the Winchester against his cheek. 'Nope', he said calmly, 'you didn't win.'

Tubbs, the fake Confederate, couldn't believe it. 'What! Are you crazy? He got the bull – you missed.'

'Yeah,' said Tom calmly, 'but you cheated and that's a disqualification.'

Newman looked angry but stayed cool. 'Don't be a sore loser, son. It does you no credit.'

'That last shell was short weighted on powder; I could feel it in the recoil. And the breech isn't as hot as it should be. Maybe you're not in on it, I don't know, but that shell was rigged to miss.' He turned his attention to Tubbs. 'So, I'll thank you to give me the thousand bucks I just won.'

Tubbs went red in the face. 'Don't gimme that shit. You lost, now get your ass outa here before I kick it outa here.'

Now Newman joined in. He stepped forward and began to prod Tom in the chest with his knuckle, snarling that he was no cheat and how he wasn't in cahoots with the fake Confederate and even if he was there was nothing Tom could do about it except apologize if he wanted to get out of the kiosk with all his teeth in the right place. Mike stood there horrified. Newman was big and fit and Mike was a good half a foot shorter and no longer very athletic. He shouted at Newman to get his hands off Tom, who by now had been grasped by the lapels of his jacket and was being demanded for an apology on pain of getting his head punched. Newman let go of Tom and advanced on Mike.

'OK, wise guy, and what you gonna do to make me stop? I think you all need a lesson,' and he shoved Mike hard in the chest so that he stumbled backwards till he fell against the wall of the kiosk. Newman now stood there waiting for Mike to get up saying, 'I don't hit a man when he's down but you got some punishment coming, so get up on your feet, mister.'

Mike gasped for breath. Newman was looking ugly. He was very strong and the push had almost been a punch. It had taken the wind out of him. Newman moved in for the execution and as he did so Tom tried to get between them. Newman let out an angry laugh. 'Don't rush into it, son, your turn to get a whopping is next.'

Now the man who had been watching intervened. 'Look here, sir', he said sternly but politely, 'there's no call for a rough house. This young man may have a point and it should be properly considered.'

Newman turned his attention on the man coldly. 'Shut the fuck up and butt out of what's not your business – unless, that is, you want me to rip your head off and give it to your wife to take home in a bag.' The man backed off indignantly.

Tubbs stood there watching with a look of belligerent satisfaction wreathing his face. He was preparing to throw his two cents worth into the fracas but stopped short when Tony stepped forward. He was shorter than Newman and no match for the big man. In a stand-up fight he'd get pulverized. But he felt he had to do something.

'Hold up there, guys,' he said. He walked right up to Newman. 'Sergeant Newman, let me apologize for everyone. This whole thing has been a big misunderstanding.' He held out his hand to Newman, who paused for a minute. 'Let's shake on it and all go our road. Whadya say. Shall we shake?'

Newman put out his hand. 'I've got no quarrel with you mister and I'll gladly take the apology for these two from your mouth. You seem like a gentleman. But you gotta understand these two can't leave without a little chastisement. They gotta feel a little pain. It's cleansing. Don't worry, I won't hurt them too much – but they have to learn a lesson.' He smiled an ugly brutal smile as he contemplated the work in hand.

What happened next was not expected. It surprised everyone present; especially it surprised Newman. The handshake he had been offered suddenly morphed into something quite different. First he felt his wrist and forearm gripped and for a moment the thought ran through his head that this was some kind of foreign handshake, the sort of thing he had seen ancient warriors do in the movies. Next his arm was being raised above his head. Then, with a move like a ballet dancer Tony ducked under Newman's armpit, taking the bemused sergeant's arm with him and twisting it behind his back in a painful lock. In the same move he hooked Newman's feet from under him and the big man crashed to the floor with an angry yell. It had all happened so fast it left Newman wondering what the hell had gone on. A torrent of foul language came out of his mouth but this only caused Tony to pull the arm up tighter, increasing the pain. Newman got the message and stopped yelling. He knelt down beside Newman, folding the man's arm tighter behind his back until he could whisper in his ear. There was a moment of calm when nobody said anything. Tony slowly let go. Tubbs, the fake grey Confederate who had all the while stood paralyzed, suddenly let out a sort of whinnying noise like a startled pony, and bolted for the exit. Tony stood away from Newman and simply said to the others, 'I think we should leave quietly now before that chiseller comes back with the cops and makes some lying allegations.'

Outside, they made their way to the exit and left the fairground. All the while they had been silent about the ruckus; now Mike broke it. 'Thanks,' he said gratefully, 'I think we all owe you,' then added admiringly, 'I didn't know you could do that kind of stuff. What did you say to him? He went kinda placid for a hooligan.'

Tony grinned, 'I told him my old man was a Mafia boss and if he ever bothered you again I'd finger him and the mob would take care of it.'

'You didn't.'

'Yup.'

'That's outrageous – is he?'

'Is he what?'

'A Mafia boss?'

'Are you kidding me – get outa here!' They all laughed.

74

'It worked though,' Mike observed a little later as they walked to the subway. 'I didn't know you could do the old ju-jitsu thing, though. Where the devil did you learn that?'

'In high school.'

'Is that for real?' Tom cut in. 'I didn't think you did anything in high school – 'cept maybe fool around with girls.'

'Oh yeah, who told you that?'

'Well, it's true isn't it?'

Tony grinned a long, thoughtful grin and nodded his head slowly. 'Maybe,' he said, 'maybe.'

******

Tom found the dog in an unexpected place. He hadn't been thinking about it. It just happened out of the blue. As they climbed the steps into Grand Central, they had the idea they should go to the lower level and maybe buy something to eat from the food vendors. 'There's a Chinaman who does a mean chow mien,' he promised.

They descended to the lower hall where the food of the vendors filled the air, competing with the smell of cigar smoke, cigarettes and pipe tobacco. As they walked along the line of stalls and barrows with their little fires and rising columns of steam, the vendors called out their wares. Hustlers hawked at customers, nagging them to buy something from this stall or that, offering deals of extra portions. An old Chinaman had grabbed Tom and was insistently pushing is wares. 'You get two bowl of special fried rice – only pay one.'

From further along the line Mike called to the others, 'Will you just look at these little fellahs – aren't they just so sharp?'

Tom and Tony arrived to find him crouched down with his hand in a large wicker basket, stroking a very small puppy. Next to him was a roughly dressed man with threadbare pants and a newsboy cap. He wore an old, poorly fitting jacket that had once been fashionable tweed but was now stained and frayed. Out of the generous patch pockets the heads of two more small dogs emerged.

The basket was a tumbling mass of small white and tan puppies, squeaking and yapping and biting each other's tails with needle sharp teeth. Mike scooped one out of the basket and held it up. 'How could you possibly not take this away with you?'

Tom looked at the dog. The dog looked back at Tom. It cocked its head to one side as if it was weighing him up, the small black nose like a little leather patch twitching as it took the scent of the air. Tom smiled. The dog let out a high-pitched yap. Tom laughed and put out a hand to stroke its head. The dog sniffed the hand suspiciously and then licked it. It had an alert, intelligent look about it.

75

Having decided the hand was not good to eat but also not dangerous either the dog allowed its head to be stroked. Finally it completed the act by wagging its short docked tail vigorously.

And so, on a day when he had not thought about it and without prior intent, Tom bought a dog. It was, he thought, probably some kind of cross breed but it looked much like a wire haired terrier with a very sharp muzzle, mutton chop whiskers and bright button eyes. It had an irresistible look about it.

'What would you want with a dog?' was his father's only comment when they entered the house together that evening.

'How was the Fair?' his mother called from the kitchen.

'Good,' he shouted back, 'a real eye opener. I'll tell you about it over supper.'

He set the dog down. 'Actually, Dad, it's not for me – it's for you.'

Holly was silent for a moment. 'What would I do with a dog?' he stated querulously. 'These things need a lot of looking after!' He waved the back of his hand towards it. 'Where would I find the time for that sort of thing?'

'Well, you don't have much else to do in your day and I figured you could walk him now and then. The exercise would be good for you.'

At that moment his mother walked in but before she could say anything Holly turned to her from where he sat in his chair. 'Martha, look what the damn fool boy has brought home – and he says it's for me. I don't need a dog, what would I do with it?'

Martha looked at the dog, which sat there on the rug, wagging its stumpy tail. It looked at her and yapped. 'Well,' she said, 'oh my, aren't you the cute little fellow.' The dog jumped up at her then scampered around the room for a bit. Then in the excitement it let go a small stream of yellow water.

'Well, that's just dandy,' said Holly, looking grumpy. 'It's pissed on the rug.' Tom scooped up the puppy and took it out onto the back porch.

Martha shot him a look of exasperation. 'Now you've upset the boy. How could you be so clumsy Holly, he was only thinking of you?'

'I know, I know,' he grumbled, 'but maybe for once people could stop treating me like I was ready for the old folks home. If I wanted a dog I would have gone right out and bought one myself.'

'My, but you can be a sour patch, Holly Jordan,' she said, shaking her head and went back into the kitchen, 'such a cute little critter too.'

Over supper Tom told them about the Fair, leaving out the confrontation with Newman. 'You two should go,' he told his mother after they had eaten and she had cleared away the dishes. 'I could get you some tickets.'

'Well, that would be nice, but I don't think your father would like it. He's got no interest in anything anymore.'

'I'm sorry, Ma. I know he can make life tough.'

She thought for a moment, then added with a thinly disguised sadness in her voice, 'He wasn't always like this, you know. Time was when he was so full of life, full of ideas, energy – we used to go to dances, picnics; we'd go swimming in the lakes. He was a good man and I loved him. Then that durned war came along and everything got different. What came back was what you see in there,' and she nodded towards the room where Holly sat in his old chair.

'Now he does nothing but think and the thinking's no good to him at all.' She let out a little sigh then put her arms around Tom. 'At least we had you. I don't think it would have been bearable but for having you.' She let go and stood back, smoothing the apron she was wearing and Tom saw a tear forming in her eye. He carefully put his arms around her and gave her a squeeze.

'I know, you don't have to say. I understand.'

He looked at her and thought how fragile she seemed and yet how strong she was; a strength that had been tempered by the constant struggle over all those years of Holly and the war and then the Depression.

'I'm sorry about the dog. I should have asked first. I didn't think he might take it badly but I should have guessed. It's just that the other evening on the back porch he seemed to be on much better form and I got to thinking about what I might do to help; stupid really.'

'Oh don't fuss about it. I can look after the little critter; where is he anyway?'

'On the porch, I put a noose on him and tied him to the rail.'

'Well, that's no place for the little fellah, I've got an old box out back I'll bring into the kitchen. That'll do with a piece of scrap blanket for the moment. Tomorrow we can make proper arrangements.'

'I'm for bed, Ma, it's been a long day and we covered a lot of ground.'

'You get along; I'll look after our new guest.'

'Good night, Dad,' he called, but there was no reply.

Up in the quiet of his own room he thought about the events of the day. He realized how much he owed to Tony for saving what had been more than an awkward situation. What if Newman had given him a beating? That he could take but for him to have come home for his mother to see him all bloodied and bruised would have hurt him more deeply. Her pain would have been heartbreaking and he couldn't bear to think on it. He resolved to find a way to thank his friend.

CHAPTER 10

Washington, DC

The mood In the White House was sombre. Roosevelt was less than optimistic as the shape of the Paris agreement emerged.

The news, which had broken overnight, landed on his breakfast table with an unwelcome thump the following morning. The report was starvation thin: just the bones of the deal with nearly no flesh on it and no one was sure where it might be leading, but it was enough to set alarms ringing in the presidential aide's offices.

'This isn't an agreement, it's a goddamned diktat,' he growled at Marguerite who'd brought it to him. He had a line put through to the Department for War.

'Henry, we could be heading for a crisis. Round up the Chiefs and get on over here. We need to talk this through.'

He looked at his watch: 10 a.m. George Marshall had arrived with Stimson; they were taken straight to the Oval Office. Roosevelt was already sitting behind his desk when Marshall and Henry Stimson entered the room.

'Pull up some chairs, George,' he said to Marshall. 'Henry, you come and sit round here on one side of me. You know Bill Knudson here, don't you?' He inclined his head towards a tall grey-haired man in his sixties already sitting on the other side of him. Knudson, a Dane who had emigrated to America as a young man, had a distinguished record in manufacturing and was now head of General Motors. Roosevelt had brought him in to kick some order into the armaments procurement program, which was struggling to meet its targets, largely because of poor management interfaces with the industrial community.

'We've met from time to time.' Henry leaned across and shook hands with the Dane, then sat down. Ten minutes later the other Chiefs showed up.

He had called the meeting, Roosevelt said, as a matter of national emergency.

They pulled their chairs up close to his desk and now they sat in a tight little huddle. In the middle was George Marshall. He was flanked by the egregious Joe King; next to him 'Hap' Arnold. With Arnold was another new Air Force general, Ira Eaker; formerly a fighter pilot, he was now charged with creating a bomber force.

Roosevelt looked grim-faced as he confronted the assembled men. 'I was informed by our Embassy this morning that the British have tossed in the towel.' He let the words out slowly, deliberately, loading them with the gravity he now felt weighing on his mind.

'They've done a deal with the Germans; I don't think I have to tell you how serious this could prove.' He paused and looked around at the small group. 'I don't exaggerate when I say that our worst fears have been realized. Unless we do something to head off this situation now, we face perhaps the gravest threat to our independence in the history of America.'

He picked up a few sheets of typescript stapled at one corner, holding it up for a second. 'You've all seen this. It's sketchy and we don't have the full picture. There hasn't been time to get out a full report. There's more intelligence coming in as we speak. The fact is this thing is moving so fast it's caught us napping.'

He dumped it down on the desk in front of him. 'Now I don't blame the British for trying to save their asses because we might do the same in their shoes, but they have gone a long way beyond just a peace deal. This is a pact dressed up to look like something it is not. It is my view that the British have effectively joined the Axis.'

He took off his glasses and surveyed the assembled faces, serious-looking men in military uniform. 'What the fuck,' he said silently to himself, 'is the good of all this gold braid if we let ourselves get caught on the hop like this?' He turned to King. 'OK Joe, just how bad is it for you?'

'It's pretty damn serious if I read this right. The Germans now have access to all British naval bases and harbors. That will give them virtual command of the North Atlantic.'

'They don't have the British fleet though.'

'No, sir, I don't believe they do, but that doesn't mean they won't some time further down the line. Shit – right now we're outgunned and outmanoeuvred. If they were to join hands with the Wops and the Limeys we'd be in pretty poor shape for a showdown. Right now, if they decide to come into home waters we'd have a tough fight on our hands trying to stop them.'

'What do we need to redress the balance?'

'A miracle, Mr President – a goddam miracle.'

'Joe, we do the impossible in this office; we leave miracles to the Almighty. Where are we deficient?'

King sounded grim; his voice was hard and measured. 'Nearly everywhere you look – men, ships, support equipment, everything right down to a liberty boat. The procurement program is up to speed based on what we knew; we're twice the Navy we were ten years ago – but hell, we didn't see this coming. We're going to need a whole lot more assets to take on this new situation.'

'Priorities?'

'Carriers. I can't rob Chester's Pacific fleet. I need new ones – and planes to fly off them.'

'George,' he said, turning to General Marshall, 'I need a full assessment of how we're fixed, here,' he tapped his finger on the table top, 'on my desk, by 0800 tomorrow – Army, Navy and the Air Corps.' There was a lull while he considered the position. In the back of his mind the thought was emerging that this could develop into the worst nightmare of his administration. 'I don't expect them to be stupid enough to try to invade us – but we need to be ready for anything and right now, gentlemen, it's my view we're ready for nothing.'

Marshall nodded solemnly. 'I'll have my team get on it right away. We do have one area where the priorities can be downgraded in support of the Atlantic demands: Hawaii. In my judgement Admiral Stark can get by on the assets in place. Right now, we're giving the Philippines priority because of the Jap threat but that can easily be changed. Men and materiel can be diverted to start beefing up the Atlantic commitment. What we were supplying to the British can go into the pot but it's mostly small arms, tanks and munitions; it doesn't amount to a lot. The ships are mostly mothballed stuff but they'll help fill the gap, though I can't say they'd bring us up to the required strength to take on the Germans, particularly if they get support from the Italians and, even worse, the British fleet. That just leaves the support we're sending to China.' Marshall waited for a response. He knew the Chinese would probably fold if the US left them to it.

Roosevelt shook his head. 'I don't want to withdraw support from General Chiang. We can't say what the effect might be and at this hour we need to keep the Generalissimo on side. They're not very effective but they're keeping the Japs occupied – and besides, what we're shipping to them is not going to help much in the Atlantic if that becomes a new theater in its own right.' Marshall nodded assent. 'Agreed.'

Roosevelt leaned back in his chair; he folded his arms purposefully. 'I want to know the real position with recruitment,' he said after a second or two's deliberation. 'How many men do we have; and not just bodies? How many are properly trained – battle ready?'

He turned to the Air Corps, but instead of addressing his remarks to Hap Arnold he spoke directly to Eaker. It was an indication that Arnold was not yet rehabilitated in Roosevelt's eyes after they had clashed over the creation of the new Air Corps. Eaker was junior to Arnold and Roosevelt was making his point. 'General Eaker,' he said soberly, 'what shape are we in with this new Air Corps you've created?' He assumed a slightly dismissive air as he said it, using the opportunity to snub Arnold.

Ira Clarence Eaker was a two-star general, outranked by everyone else in the room. Just six weeks before he had celebrated his 44th birthday. A square-jawed solidly built Texan who spoke with a slow drawl and who smoked a pipe; a family man with a dry sense of humor who was popular with the men under his command.

Arnold wanted him on board to restructure the Air Corps but when he called on his services, Eaker held the relatively lowly rank of colonel. Arnold needed a man with more clout and pressed Congress for his promotion to brigadier general, a rank that was in line with the job he was to take on. But the commission required presidential support and Roosevelt was in no humor to oblige. In the final analysis, though, the presence of looming war clouds weighed heavier on Roosevelt's mind than his chagrin with Arnold – and the balance was tilted: Eaker got his promotion.

Eaker responded with deference. Unlike the others he did not feel he was part of the White House inner circle. 'Mr President, sir, my role is principally to create a long-range bomber force and in aiding that task I judge that the Air Corps is performing well.'

Roosevelt softened; maybe he was going to hear some more positive news after the litany of gloom from the other generals.

Eaker became more confident in what he was about to deliver. 'The new Boeing B17 Flying Fortress is being procured in significant numbers. Trials have so far shown that this is a formidable weapons platform, strongly built to take considerable enemy fire damage and still keep flying. It has a comprehensive defence armament with eight gun positions packing thirteen .50 calibre machine guns. That's enough firepower to make it a real prickly character for enemy pursuit aircraft. It has a bomb payload of forty-eight hundred pounds, an altitude ceiling of twenty-eight thousand feet, can attain air speeds of over two-hundred-and-fifty miles per hour and an operational range of two thousand miles. I believe that at this moment it outclasses anything our adversaries have in their armory. As of now we have on order 512 B17s with just under 200 delivered. Our present state of readiness is high, both in trained crew and the craft available to fly. This would allow us to get our full complement airborne today if so required.' He paused for a moment but Roosevelt said nothing. He continued to look at Eaker as if anticipating more.

'The role we are developing for these aircraft is one of long-range strategic bombing. In this respect I can report that we have the capability to support the Navy in engaging enemy ships in almost all parts of any potential North Atlantic theater. I have the utmost confidence in our preparedness to successfully engage an enemy provided that enemy does not come at us with overwhelming force. Should we find ourselves confronted by the full potential of German naval forces, and if we need to take on other commitments such as coastal protection, then we shall need to increase our procurement four-fold which, on current production levels, would take us through to 1945.'

Roosevelt leaned forward on his desk, lifted by the optimism of Eaker's response.

'Gentlemen, as most of you will know, I have long held the view that the spread of both the war in Europe and the war in Asia is inevitable – and that it will, one day, reach the shores of our nation. That day has been brought closer by the events that have taken place with the British. There is a war coming our way and we should not delude ourselves into thinking otherwise. Furthermore, I am not convinced that time is on our side. Consequently, what's painted here might lead some people to think that it all makes a depressing picture – but let me say this. No man ever got anything done by letting himself get depressed. We're going to have to put on the pressure to manage this crisis, but manage it we shall. I have faith in you and I have faith in the American people.'

He turned to Stimson. 'Henry, you'd better get over to Capitol Hill; we're going to need some friends in the Senate to get the necessary appropriations through – and we need to do it without sending the nation into a panic.' He looked around briefly at the others then continued.

'Now I'm sure all present realize that getting the appropriations through Congress is only one part of the problem. We can pay the piper; now we need to make sure the piper can play the tune.' He leant to one side and looked at the Dane, who had all this time been sitting expressionless while Roosevelt had been talking.

'I've appointed Bill Knudson here to take on the role of chairman for the Office of Production Management; he has also agreed to join the Defence Advisory Commission. Most of you here will already know Bill as the top man at General Motors. His job is to create an interface between industry and the Defence Department, to get you the tools you need to do your jobs. I have confidence that his team will be able to harness the great manufacturing power of America and put it to good use in the cause of freedom. I expect everyone to pull in the same direction. Get your people briefed and get everyone talking to each other. I don't want to see rivalry or competition for resources. I want to see cooperation and smart use of men and materials. Be in no doubt there is a war coming. We need to be ready for it.'

Again he paused, then satisfied that everything that needed to be said had been said called time on the meeting. 'Gentlemen, for the moment that is all.'

He half turned to his secretary who was sitting back a little behind his right shoulder. 'Marguerite, get hold of the networks. I need to let the nation in on this before the press get hold of it and cause wholesale panic. We need to get the message out: a re-armed America is a strong America.'

*****

Croton-on-Hudson, NY State

Dottie had finished her shift at the diner and was getting ready to hand over. The two boys in the kitchen waved and whistled as she took off her cap and shook out her hair. A cascade of blond fell to her shoulders. Now she quickly rolled it up into a pleat and pushed in a comb to hold it in place. The lunch shift finished at three and outside the June afternoon was hot. Jennifer, who owned the diner with her husband Dan, was standing in the sun taking time for a cigarette and talking to another waitress, Dolores.

Dottie walked over to where they were chatting. 'Hi,' she said holding up her small apron. 'Here, can you take that back in for me. I forgot to take it off – those boys in the kitchen made me forget – really, they're embarrassing.'

'Oh, they're only joshing, honey,' Dolores giggled.

'I know, but it's silly, they're like kids the way they carry on.'

Jennifer blew out a stream of smoke and smiled. 'It's because they know you're sweet on that boy who comes in here with those other two. You know, the ones who go hunting. How is that, has he asked for a date yet?'

Dottie shook her head, looking thoughtful. 'No, and I don't think he ever will.'

'You know why,' Dolores confided, 'he thinks you're just a stupid waitress without a brain; a dumb blond.'

'I know; I've heard them.'

'Once I overheard him saying he could do better than a waitress in a diner.'

Jennifer shrugged and looked scornful. 'Huh, that's cute coming from a guy who drives around in a beat up old jalopy. You should put him straight. Tell him you're working your way through college. The dumb klutz needs educating. I'll do it the next time he comes in if you'd like, hun.' She folded her arms and looked resolutely at Dottie.

'Hey, no, leave it. I'd be so embarrassed. Just leave it. I don't want a boy just because he thinks I come from a good family. I want to be liked for who I am. And if who I am isn't good enough, then I don't want him anyway. I've got to go. Bye and see you tomorrow.'

'Bye Dottie,' they both chorused.

'She's forgotten and walked off with that apron,' Jennifer noted, taking a long draw on her cigarette.

'Love sick,' Dolores said, lighting up her own cigarette.

'Love sick,' agreed Jennifer, and they both fell to laughing.

Jennifer dropped the cigarette butt and ground it into the gravel with her heel. They stood for a moment watching as the diminutive figure of Dottie gradually shrunk into the horizon. Dolores shook her head slowly. 'I can't think what she sees in the guy. Me, personally, I'd go for the shorter one, the one that drives that gorgeous Cord convertible. I'd go for a ride in that anytime.' Then she waved her hand dismissively. 'What the hell, I gotta go get ready', she said and walked towards the diner. Clip-clopping on her high heels, her dark hair in pleats as was the latest fashion and her blue and white polka-dot dress swinging rhythmically from her hips, she disappeared in through the front door. A moment later Jennifer heard the familiar sound of wolf whistles coming out of the kitchen and some muffled laughter. I have to talk to those two goofs in the kitchen, she told herself.

Dottie could have taken the bus but it was only two stops. The afternoon was warm with a gentle breeze; just right, she decided, for a walk home. Sometimes she liked to be on her own, to think and enjoy the quiet. She thought quite a lot about Tom Jordan and wondered if she would ever get to know him. She liked his blue eyes and his gentle manner. He never seemed brash like the other two boys he came in with. He was somehow more thoughtful, intellectual, and she imagined he could be kind. This, she concluded, was what she found attractive about him. Of course, he was also tall and slim and not a little good looking, and she smiled at the thought of what it might feel like to have his arms around her.

The walk home was not far; it took her around twenty minutes from the diner on the Albany Post Road to her front gate. The house was set back from the street with a broad well-kept lawn surrounded by a neat white picket fence. It was a modern house built for her father seven years before when they moved to Croton.

James Brent was a doctor – a popular man in the town and well regarded for his skills as a surgeon. He had a particular claim to fame in that he had once assisted in an operation on Teddy Roosevelt following a hunting accident while serving his internship at the Walter Reed Hospital in DC. Teddy had a reputation as a bear hunter, although he had a great respect for the beasts. It was rumored that Teddy had accidentally shot himself while out with a hunting party. It had happened in the last year of his presidency and strenuous efforts were made to hush it up. Around the hospital all reference to it was forbidden and so, secretly, it was referred to as the bear's revenge; a lot of jokes grew up around it.

At dinner that evening the conversation turned to college and how Dottie was progressing. There was an issue with her mother; she could not understand why her daughter felt the need to work to pay her college fees.

'Dottie, dear,' she said in a slightly frustrated tone, 'I do wish you would give up on this idea of working to pay your college fees. Your father is well able to afford it and would be relieved to do so. You can't possibly give it your best if you are worn out with this menial job you've taken on. Besides, it's undignified.'

Dottie shrugged and politely dismissed it. 'Mom, it's what I want to do,'

'But why? I can't see the point of it.'

''The point of it, Mom, is that I want to be independent. I want to make my own decisions. Dad, you can understand that, can't you?'

Her father pondered his response. He was caught between two loyalties. 'Well, young lady,' he said after a moment. 'Your mother has a point. I can well afford those fees and I guess it does look a bit strange to our friends and our neighbors to see you packing yourself off to that diner at all hours,' and here he threw a quick conciliatory glance to his wife, 'but I guess, Eleanor, we can put up with that if that's what she really want's, don't you think?'

Her mother let go a little sigh of resignation. 'If you say so, Jim – but I must confess I don't quite understand it. I had hoped that by now you might have found a nice young man and be walking out. Don't leave yourself on the shelf too long; a single life would not be very suitable you know.'

Dottie winced. 'Mom, I'm all of twenty years. I'm really not an old maid yet.'

'Oh, I don't think there's any chance of that, my dear,' her father said. 'Our girl is too pretty by half to get left on the shelf. She'll get snapped up by some handsome young buck before not very long – of that I'm sure.'

'Maybe, but you don't find many eligible young men frequenting diners – and that's a fact. What about at college,' her mother persisted, 'there must be a lot of nice young men there?'

'Mom,' said Dottie, putting her fork down with a forceful clatter on her plate, 'I go to college to study,' and she shook her head in exasperation. 'It's an institution for learning not a marriage bureau.' Her mother assumed an expression of reluctant resignation. 'Very well, very well,' and she huffed a little sigh as if to say I don't understand you at all.

'Why don't we leave it there?' her husband suggested diplomatically and changed the subject. 'I hear the President is going to make a broadcast this evening. I think we should listen to what he has to say. It could be important. I think the economy is mending, you know.'

'Do you think the war in Europe will affect us?' Dottie asked, 'There's a lot of talk in college right now.'

'I think it could very well improve the economic outlook. We are a stable nation with a good manufacturing base and right now the rest of the world needs our goods – even more so since the British and the Germans are concentrating on destroying each other's production capabilities.'

After dinner Dottie helped her mother clear away the dishes and tidy up, then went to her room to read. James Brent retired to the living room where he dropped into an easy chair to smoke a pipe and listen to the broadcast. Close to the fireplace a large walnut cabinet housed the radio set. After a few puffs on the pipe he got up and turned the switch to the 'on' position. For a while nothing happened; then there was a low humming noise as the tubes warmed up. He turned the tuning dial, searching for the wavelength of NBC. There was a low whine punctuated by some crackling and then finally the sound of dance music came out of the set. He sat back down in the large stuffed armchair, drew on the pipe and waited for the announcement of the President's broadcast. Roosevelt used what he termed his 'fireside chats' to keep the nation in touch with events and to reassure his public that the various concerns and issues were being tended to and were under control. The European situation was tricky because what they called the Great War was still painfully fresh in the public memory; this had given rise to a widespread resistance to anything that even hinted at a possible American involvement in another European adventure. But he also knew that America had to prepare; he held to his deep conviction that a war was coming and they had to be ready.

The music faded and a voice announced the President of the United States, Franklin D. Roosevelt. There was a pause and then the voice of the President:

'Good evening friends,' he began.

'It is my sombre task this evening to let you know of the most recent events that have taken place in Europe and the European war, events that will have a profound and far-reaching effect on all of our lives.

'You will know that for the past months we have supported the British in their valiant struggle to hold back the Nazi war machine, which is slowly devouring that continent and driving it into the depths of an abyss so dark and so evil that it defies description. With the consent of Congress your government has provided arms and munitions together with vital food supplies to keep our allies, the British, from sinking into that abyss. But it has been ultimately down to their heroism and fortitude that the Nazi beast has been kept at bay.

'Now I am sad to have to report to you that the British have given up that struggle. They are no longer a bastion against the evils of Hitler and his dark legions of death and torture. The British have been forced to a peace treaty with the Axis. Just over a week ago Prime Minister Winston Churchill was reported by our embassy in London has having gone missing and we must now fear for his safety. There is a new regime in London, headed by their former Foreign Secretary, Lord Halifax. We do not know how this new leader will steer his country. We do not know to what extent he is independent of the Nazi forces with whom he has now decided to sit down and parley. We do not know if this peace deal he has negotiated makes Britain an ally of the Germans or simply a non-combatant; and we do not know if this makes them a member of the Axis or a sovereign neutral nation.

'What we do know is that the German Navy now has access to British ports and naval bases around that island and there is a strong likelihood that they will at some time in the future have access to British navy ships. If this should happen it would make the Germans together with the Italian Navy the greatest naval force in the world. They would have overwhelming superiority and they would control all of the waters of the Atlantic Ocean.

'So let us sit down together, you and I, to consider our own pressing problems that now confront us.

'There are many among us who in the past closed their eyes to events abroad – because they believed in utter good faith what some of their fellow Americans told them – that what was taking place in Europe was none of our business; that no matter what happened over there, the United States could always pursue its peaceful and unique course in the world.

'There are many among us who closed their eyes, from lack of interest or lack of knowledge. 'There are some among us who were persuaded by minority groups that we could maintain our physical safety by retiring within our continental boundaries. And, finally, there are a few among us who have deliberately and consciously closed their eyes because they were determined to be opposed to their government, its foreign policy and every other policy.

'To those who have closed their eyes for any of these many reasons, to those who would not admit the possibility of the approaching storm – to all of these, the latest events will mean the shattering of many illusions. They must now put aside the illusion that we are remote and isolated and, therefore, secure against the dangers from which no other land is free.'

Roosevelt then went into the detail of procurements that his administration had already made, running through lists of materials, costs and outcomes, improvements that had been made. It was a long list of boats and guns and planes. The Army, he said confidently, now had 250,000 men who were combat ready – but then he added they needed more.

The broadcast was paving the way to the military readiness he knew he had to achieve; he had to convince his audience this was necessary. To do it he had to make the threat real; not just the war in Europe – that was too far removed. He needed to bring it closer to home, to bring the fear of an enemy on the doorstep. The broadcast had been on for nearly an hour and the message continued to be the same: build up the nation's armory and be prepared to make a stand. The ostrich had to get its head out of the sand. Now he was coming to his final flourish.

'I am certain that out of the hearts of every man, woman and child in this land, in every waking minute, a supplication goes up to Almighty God; that all of us beg that suffering and starving, that death and destruction, may end – and that peace may return to the world. In common affection for all mankind, your prayers join with mine – that God will heal the wounds and the hearts of humanity.'

The voice ceased and there was a moment of quiet, then the announcer: 'You have just listened to the voice of the President, Franklin D. Roosevelt, in *A Fireside Chat.*'

James Brent sat expressionless for a few moments, contemplating what he had just heard, letting the layers of information sink into his consciousness. Carefully he absorbed the impact of the broadcast and what it might mean. He got up slowly from the armchair, stooped at the cabinet and turned off the radio. Then he went into the kitchen.

In the kitchen Eleanor was putting away the last of the dishes. He came up behind her, put his arms around her waist and kissed the top of her head. 'Is Dottie in her room?'

'She is; she went up straightway after we finished the dishes.' She turned and saw that his faced looked strained and serious.

'Its war,' he said in a flat voice without waiting for the question. 'There's going to be another war. Thank God we don't have a son.' He pulled his wife closer to him and tightened his arms around her. 'I saw it last time. We thought it would never happen again but Roosevelt says its coming and I believe him. It was hell on earth last time and it was supposed to be the war to end all wars. Now here we are again heading for the same lunacy.' She stood with her head buried in his shoulder.

'Will you be called to go?'

'I don't think so – I'm too old. I'll be required to stay here and try to patch up the boys who make it home in less than one piece.'

CHAPTER 11

A Girl with a Book

Earlier that month, standing on Albert Bridge, a casual passer-by noted that an army road block had stopped a large black limousine down on the Embankment. Two men emerged from the car and stood surrounded by armed soldiers. The muted sound of muffled voices rose up through the still night air, inaudible but with a sense of urgency. After a short discussion the two men climbed into the back of an army truck that was parked close to the barrier. A few minutes later two large shadowy bundles were carried over to the car; the barriers were dismantled and put into the back of the truck. The engine wound into life, there was a crunch of gears engaging. It lurched forward and, to the sound of a whining axle, drove off in the direction of Wandsworth.

For a while the seemingly abandoned limousine stood silent at the kerb, quiet and lifeless. The air was still and warm and the only sound was the muted slushing of the river as the tide ran out. A man emerged from the driver's door of the limousine and walked round to the back. He opened the lid of the trunk and retrieved a jerry can. Quickly, he splashed the contents over the car and into the interior. As the passer-by reached the Chelsea side of the bridge there was a sound like somebody beating a carpet – a whoompf – followed by a flash of light. As the passer-by leaned over the parapet of the bridge it was clear that the limousine had exploded and was now a blazing inferno. What the passer-by could not see was the figure of a man in a chauffeur's uniform walking rapidly away from the incinerating vehicle. Later, all that remained of the incident were some scars on the tarmac where it had melted and then later reset.

******

It was Friday and there was a weekend coming up. They had planned to spend it up on the edge of Lake Champlain. There was a shallow trout stream Mike had discovered three falls back that ran into the lake. There could be good fly fishing in the stream or they could line fish on the lake if the trout weren't biting. They had rented the same small cabin by the lake shore for the last two years and there was a little clinker-built dinghy with a single cylinder engine that was just fine for slopping around offshore. But as Tom caught the train to his office that morning the shine seemed to have been knocked off the day.

He had heard the President's broadcast. His father had become morose and depressed by the news – once more he had withdrawn into himself. Martha set about worrying; if it was going to be war then Tom would be called and most likely end up in a front line somewhere. Later, after the broadcast he had found her in the kitchen worrying quietly to herself, secretly so that Tom might not notice her anxiety. It had taken him some time to assure her with the logic that this was only 'maybe' and that war had not actually been declared and probably never would be. The Navy would keep the shores of the country safe and any fighting would be done at sea. Since he was not a sailor it was highly unlikely that he would be called upon to see any action.

The train was crowded as usual. Men and women with their heads buried in their newspapers and all the bannered headlines were about the broadcast. 'FDR SAYS IT'S WAR' was splashed large across *The Westchester Post*. *The New York Times* was more reserved: 'AMERICA WILL STAND FAST FOR FREEDOM' it announced. *The Peekskill Gazette*, which Tom took on the train every workday morning, reported 'ROOSEVELT PROMISES A STRONG AMERICA', and then in smaller print underneath, 'Congress to provide unprecedented appropriations for war readiness'.

The car had a different feel that morning. On any other weekday the commuter train would be packed with silent faces busy with their newspapers, occasionally whispering to a known companion; barely a sound to smother the rustling of newsprint pages and the low-pitched whistle of exhaled cigarette smoke. But this morning was different. There was a hum of conversation as complete strangers, who would not normally even catch the eye of another passenger, struck up worried conversations about the real meaning of Roosevelt's words. Was it really conceivable there was a chance this European war would land right on their doorsteps? A complete stranger sitting opposite Tom leaned forward and said, 'Looks like 1917 all over again.' He leant back into his seat. 'There's going to be a war and the American people are too goddam stupid to realize it.'

Tom felt angered by the remark, though he thought it was probably true – at least for half the country. 'I don't think they're stupid,' he said, scowling at the man. 'They just don't want to believe it. People like my dad. He fought in the last one. It destroyed him. He's just tired, that's all. He doesn't want to see it again.'

The stranger looked embarrassed. 'Sorry, young man,' he said quickly, 'no offense meant.'

Tom shook his head and said there was none taken and personally he didn't think it was actually that bad; then he looked out of the window to avoid further conversation. He just didn't feel like talking. They were at Croton and more commuters boarded; the car was filling up, some of the passengers having to stand holding on to the leather straps that danced in rows along the ceiling. The train slowed for the next station, Dobbs Ferry.

As it slid slowly to a halt Tom could see a loose string of expectant passengers gazing up at the windows, all hoping to see an empty seat. It stopped with a final jerk and there, framed perfectly in the window, was that girl again, standing on the quay waiting for the train to stop. Her dark hair hung around her cupid face like an oval frame with another hat pinned in place, tilted to the back of her head. She wore a tightly belted camel-hair coat, pulled in at the waist to show off her perfect form. As she climbed aboard Tom was dumbstruck. Over the past months she had slipped from his memory. He had long dismissed the idea of ever seeing her again and now here she was. His mind went gluey as he tried to think of some way to meet her. He couldn't bungle the opportunity a second time – but how? His brain had temporarily ceased to function. His pulse went up and for a moment he felt the blood rise to his head.

He almost couldn't believe his luck when she stopped next to his seat, reaching up and taking a strap. Her delicate fingers with bright red polished nails hung elegantly in the loop of the old leather strap, which she had hitched round her wrist. The train started again with a little jerk, causing all the standing passengers to stagger slightly as they readjusted their balance. Tom noticed she was wearing very high heels and wondered how she could hold her poise with the train in motion as it rocked and clattered across the points and track changes. Without thinking, he stood up. 'Please,' he said, 'have my seat. It's still a long way to Grand Central.' She smiled and sat down. As she did so the sweet delicate scent of her perfume wafted across his face. Tom had never really given any thought before to a woman's perfume. Now he was entering into a new world of experience, the exotic world of girls. It was a world he had never contemplated till then. His mother was the only woman with whom he had any close contact and she smelled mostly of carbolic soap and fresh linen – or sometimes the homey smell of cooking. The new aroma excited him.

The man sitting opposite who had remarked on the similarity to 1917 caught Tom's eye. He raised his eyebrows and shot him a quick knowing grin as if to say 'Good move.'

She looked up from her newly donated seat. She was still smiling. 'How did you know I was going to Grand Central?' She was talking to him – my god, she was talking to him! He could relax; not too much though, mustn't blow it. Don't say something stupid, he told himself.

'I've seen you on the train a couple of times before. You always got off there.'

'Full marks,' she said, 'for observation that is.' She pulled a book out of her handbag and opened it. It was a signal that the conversation was at an end. 'You will excuse me won't you?'

'Of course.' His heart rate shot up till he thought she must be able to hear it pounding. The man opposite caught Tom's eye again. This time with a small shrug and a turned down mouth that said, 'Nice try, too bad about the result.' The rest of the journey was passed in silence and only once did she look up from her book, but it was only to glance out of the window.

At Grand Central he stood aside to let her get up. She smiled but said nothing and got down from the car, disappearing quickly into the tide of commuters heading for the exits. He got down from the train himself and stood for a moment to light up a cigarette and console his disappointment. He had the perfect chance to shine, to say something clever, to get her interested, and he had screwed up. The odds of ever having that moment again were worse than remote. It had been a one-shot opportunity and it had gone south. He was about to move on when he heard a voice behind him. 'You're a lucky son of a bitch.'

He turned to see the man from the opposite seat, the man who thought it was 1917 all over.

'How so?'

'She's taken a shine to you and that's no kidding.'

Tom shrugged, 'Oh yeah, how do you make that then? She cut me dead after the first few words.'

The man shook his head slowly from side to side. 'Funny things women. They speak a different language, you know. Here – she left you an invitation.'

He handed Tom the book she had been reading. 'It was on the seat for you to find, 'cept you missed it. There's one of those business cards inside.' He looked up at the great clock in the high vaulted station ceiling. 'If that's not an invitation, I don't know what is. Go to it buddy, it's sitting on a plate – and it's a real tasty cracker.'

Tom stood for a moment longer in the milling crowd that was coming and going all over the concourse. People with things to do and places to go, with hopes, fears, anxiety, elation; people who had worries about money or health. How many, he wondered as he looked at the anonymous crowd, would be carrying around burdens of great sadness or crushing concern, and here he was in the midst of all these unknown emotions with an overwhelming sense of exuberance. Life once again felt great. Thoughts of a war were far away on distant horizons. They were not his concern. As he walked towards the exit his mind was buzzing with thoughts of her and the sweet smell of that perfume she was wearing. He opened the book and there was the card; printed in gold and black it was headlined 'Kolinsky Gallery'. Underneath it read 'Modern

American and Fine Art', then at the bottom – 'Caroline Grace Taylor, Senior Consultant'.

When he arrived at the office unexpectedly it occurred to him that he couldn't remember the walk from the station, such was his preoccupation. In the lift going up he began to plan their first date. He would, he thought, go over to her office around midday, deliver her back the book and invite her to lunch with him. When he went to sign in he was still clutching the book she had left on the train seat. He had a wide grin on his face that was a dead giveaway. Marion looked at him, 'my, but we look sunny this morning – in love are we?'

Tom just winked an eye and went to his office. Only Adele was there, sitting at her desk, preoccupied with her work. She was always first in every morning and last to leave at the end of the day. 'She only has a cat to go home to,' Dan Johnson joked.

Tom sat at his desk for a moment and contemplated the card. The address was East and 14th Street – he could walk that in less than ten minutes. He began to work out how he would handle the suggestion of lunch. He imagined and re-imagined the meeting. Should he be relaxed and laid back, like he'd seen in the movies? Maybe it was best to be formal, polite, perhaps even slightly reserved? He couldn't make up his mind. In the end he decided to deal with it on the hoof; after all, she had been the one to leave the invitation behind in the form of the book and the card. She was, he argued to himself, hardly going to just take the book, say thanks and turn her back on him.

He put the book to one side and turned to the task of reading the morning mail in his 'in' tray. On top was a memo from the chief underwriter. He picked it up and read that there was to be an emergency meeting at midday to consider the potential impact of the FDR speech on risks and premiums. There would be a talk by the Head of the Actuarial Department and all underwriters were ordered to be present. His heart sank and a mild sense of panic gripped him. For a moment he actually thought of ducking out of the meeting; he could leave the office on the pretext of some errand and then apologize for getting back late. It was a lame idea and he quickly abandoned it. Dan Johnson and Fred the junior both arrived at the same time. Tom waved the memo at Dan.

'I heard the chat last night,' Dan said. 'I'm not convinced we should get involved. I don't actually think it will come to anything for us; we're too remote from it.'

Tom looked dubious. 'I'm not so sure, but I hope you're right.'

Fred, who had been standing in earshot, looked anxiously at them both. 'Do you really think so, Mr Johnson?'

'This is just politicking in my view.' He shrugged and sat down, picking up his copy of the memo. 'But I guess we have to go listen to what our masters have to say on the subject.'

Fred looked relieved, 'Gee, I do hope so.'

They didn't get out of the meeting till nearly three o'clock and any idea of meeting Caroline Grace Taylor was out of the window. As Tom left the office he was psychologically on his knees. What had been a great start to the day had disintegrated and had, once again, crumbled to a handful of nothing. He boarded the train to Peekskill in a state of resignation. It was a lousy way to start the weekend.

He had looked around hopefully at Grand Central but there was no sign of her. At Dobbs Ferry he half thought about getting off the train and staking out the station in the vain hope that he might see her, but in the event he had no enthusiasm and let the moment pass.

CHAPTER 12

Champlain

The morning sky was dark and threatening. It felt close and there was a smell of rain on the air. The prospect was not great for the weekend; a storm was brewing. Tom packed the Chrysler, stowing fishing rods, reels, line, keep net and bait can into a large canvas kitbag which he laid across the dumb irons on the front of the car then lashed down and around the bumper bar with a piece of rope and an old leather strap. The kitbag bore a faded name, number and army rank just visible in chalky white against the khaki canvas. Holly had brought it back from the war and thrown it in the trash. It was the only reminder of that war he had come home with, a war that had so ruined his life. He had wanted to destroy it but Martha had saved it, not for sentimental reasons but for its utility. It was a good piece of canvas and you didn't throw away things like that, it might come in useful one day. It had lain in the attic for 20 years, waiting for its day of usefulness until Tom came across it and that day finally arrived.

Next he loaded the Remington into the trunk. It was not yet the hunting season but there were bears in those parts. The black bears weren't too much of a problem, except they would raid the garbage cans and throw stuff everywhere, but grizzlies were another story and you just didn't want to meet one without a gun about you, especially if there were cubs around. They could get very bad tempered. Although there were almost no grizzlies as far east as Champlain the animals had a huge territorial range; he had once had a difficult encounter with a stray and it had made him cautious.

He wrapped a change of clothes in a blanket and a piece of fine muslin which he could put over his head and cover with his slouch hat to keep the black fly and the mosquitoes off his face while fishing. Finally he threw a few useful things into a small grip: hunting knife, can opener, canteen set, toothbrush, comb, soap and a large box of Vesta matches. He dropped the grip into the trunk and closed the lid. He was ready to go.

Martha came out to kiss him and wave him off, but before she let him go she pressed a parcel in into his hands. It was neatly tied up in brown paper with a double bow on the string. 'Here,' she said with a caring look and a sweet smile.

'It's a fresh pillow. You'll sleep all the better for having something soft and cool to rest your head on.'

Tom shook his head slowly from side to side, smiling as he did so but he didn't resist her because he knew it would only make her unhappy. There were straw sacks up at the cabin and they were good enough for young men living rough. The others would laugh but it didn't matter. He laid it carefully on the rear seat and went back into the house to say goodbye to Holly.

'I'm off, Dad,' he called, but there was no reply. His father was still in a black mood and dwelling back in the past of the Argonne Forest. The puppy got up from where it had been lying in the old orange crate lined with the piece of blanket Martha had found. He came to the door and looked out at the preparations for departure. Seeing Tom, he wagged his tail and let out a little yap. Tom bent down and ruffled its head. 'We need to give this mutt a name.'

The plan was he would drive down to Croton, pick up Tony and Mike and then head back north up Route 9 through the Hudson Valley to Lake Champlain. It would take the best part of the day to cover the distance but the fishing was good: walleye, brown trout and, sweetest of all, yellow perch – real good to eat. Tom had arranged to take two days off so they wouldn't come back till Tuesday – two whole days of fishing.

As the Chrysler rumbled out onto Route 9 and turned its blunt nose south, the first spots of rain started to fall. A little further and the wind got up, pushing the rain across the highway in busy gushing rivulets. There was a long rumble of distant thunder but no lightning. The heart of the storm, he judged, was passing away to the west of him. The rain stepped up its pace and began drumming on the metal roof. Along the margins of the road the drainage ditches began to fill with fast-moving water, swirling round the fallen debris of snapped off tree branches left there from the winter gales. It sloshed and danced over pieces of junk casually dumped by those who just wanted to be rid of it. The big maple trees lining the road swayed menacingly under the buffeting of the wind, which attacked them in violent squalls, testing and tugging their limbs, ripping the leaves and snapping small twigs. They were heavy with their summer crowns and vulnerable to the storm. They creaked and groaned under the weight of their water-soaked foliage. Some of them had been there since the War of Independence. They were old and hollow and occasionally one would succumb and come crashing down across the highway, blocking the traffic; and once, he read, one hit a truck, crushing the cab and killing the driver.

By the time he reached the village of Montrose the highway was awash. The rain lashed the windshield with sheets of water that defied the wiper blades and inside the glass began to mist over. He wiped it with the back of his hand but that only made the vision worse. For a while he pressed on but in the end there was nothing for it but to pull over and wait till the worst had passed. Just outside

Montrose he found a truck stop and parked up to sit it out. He pulled the window down a little, trying to get rid of the condensation that was now fogging every piece of glass in the vehicle. As he did so a faint smell of coffee came to him on the wet air. It smelled inviting and he decided he might as well go get some. He opened the door and made a dash for it, hopping and splashing his way the short distance across the rutted muddy parking lot to the warmth of the gas station diner.

Inside the air was dry and warm. He took off his hat and slapped it against his side to dislodge the water droplets that clung to it. Then he sat with coffee and a donut, watching the relentless rain slash at the plate glass in wind-driven gusts. His thoughts turned to the girl and he wondered what she might be doing right then. Was she thinking of him? She must have given him some thought, otherwise why leave the book on the train – and with the card inside? Then another less positive thought occurred. Maybe it wasn't that way at all. Maybe she had genuinely forgotten the book and the card inside was just a bookmark. That was possible, wasn't it? As he chewed that over in his mind it developed more substance than the other proposition, which was now looking pretty shaky. After all, if she really wanted to take up with him she would have continued with the conversation he had kicked off, but she didn't – she had retreated into her book. Now he questioned if he was reading into that book a message that simply wasn't there. By the time he finished his coffee he had concluded the book was a blind alley; it would lead nowhere.

The waitress came over and asked if he would like more coffee. He was about to refuse but then he had an idea. He nodded and she poured the refill; he asked for another donut. When she returned with his order he said, 'Do you mind if I ask you a question?' She looked like she'd heard this line before.

'Forget it, kid,' she said sardonically, 'I'm already taken – I married some jerk – that's the reason I work in this joint.'

Tom held up a hand in protest. 'Hold up, don't get ahead of me. I need an opinion on something – I thought you might be able to help.'

She raised her eyebrows. 'Well, I'm not Einstein but go ahead. Who knows, I might have the answer to the universe.' She looked at him patronizingly but he decided to ask anyway.

'I met this girl – but I'm not sure what to make of it. I just thought you might be able – you being a female and all that.'

'Well, you got the sex right – so go on, what's the pitch?'

The waitress listened to the story of the book on the train. There was a pause. She looked at him a little sideways. 'Well, you're a pretty good-looking guy – I'd leave a book on a train for you.'

'Yes, but did she?'

'I dunno. Why don't you just go ask her? After all, you've got the address. You've got nothing to lose, honey. The worst you can hear is thanks for returning the book. At least that will put you out of your misery.' She moved away to serve another customer, leaving him to think on what she'd said. It hadn't really helped but she was probably right.

The rain eased and then, as abruptly as it had started, it stopped. As he walked back to the car the only sound was the splat of the rainwater dripping from the trees. For a moment the air was quiet again. The kit bag tied to the front was sodden but it would dry out as he drove, and anyway it was only filled with the fishing gear.

The highway was almost empty as he continued towards Croton with nothing but the throb of the engine and the splashing of the tires on the wet road. The storm had driven most of the traffic to take shelter and now only slowly they were venturing back again.

Mike and Tony were walking in the drive as Tom pulled up to the house. 'Tony, good to see you man! Hi Mike. Are we set up to go?'

Ruby, who had been playing on the front lawn rushed over to greet him. 'Hi Tom, are you staying a while?'

'Fraid not Ruby, we're going up country to fish for the weekend.' Ruby looked disappointed. 'Oh gee, you should stop over some time. You never do. Tony stayed the night, you know'. She turned and ran across the lawn to the house.

'She's got a crush on you,' Mike said laughing. 'The storm was bad. Did you catch it?'

'Yup, ran smack dab into it. I pulled over at Montrose to let it pass. Hope we don't have it for the weekend.'

'The Da says it'll be fine but we'll see. Have you a poncho with you?'

'I have.'

'Then it's sure to be fine.' They loaded their tackle into the kitbag, which was now dry again, then put what they could into the trunk, piling what wouldn't go in onto the back seat. As they turned out of the drive onto the street and headed for the main highway the skies cleared and the sun broke through.

Mike lounged across the back seat and lit up a smoke. 'Anyone want?' he asked and tossed a pack of Camels into the front. The pack had been carelessly ripped open and the cigarettes flew all over the front floor.

The drive to Champlain took around five hours and it was mid-afternoon by the time they reached the cabin. Tony looked at his watch. 'We'd best go to Crows Crossing for supplies if we want an early start tomorrow. We need eggs, we need coffee, sugar, beans – anything else?'

'Bread,' said Mike, 'and we should get some bourbon.'

'And bacon,' Tom added. 'You can't have breakfast without bacon.'

Crows Crossing was close to the shoreline, a village of around two thousand inhabitants. It had a general store, a gas station with a diner, and a small jetty with a boat repair shop where you could buy bait and fishing tackle.

It was around seven in the evening by the time they had loaded the Chrysler with supplies. Mike suggested they go to the diner and eat. Inside, a cheerful looking man in cook's whites was leaning on the counter top, talking to a sheriff's officer. The place was empty but for a couple sitting at one end and a lone man staring into a cup of coffee. The cook broke off the conversation with the officer. 'What'll it be boys? We got burgers, we got ham, we got eggs and I can do ya fries.'

'I'm a burger,' said Tony. 'Me too,' Mike chipped in. Tom thought for a minute. 'Make mine ham with fries – and two eggs sunny side up.'

'And let's have three beers,' Tony added, 'what've you got?'

'We got Bud, we got Miller, or we got Molson from across the border. Take ya pick.'

'Make it three Bud,' Tony called from the table.

The officer turned on his bar stool. 'You boys new here?'

Tom nodded, 'Up from New York State for a weekend of fishing.'

'You couldn't have picked a better spot; they bite real good around here. Where are you staying?'

'We're in a cabin along the foreshore, just by Shelstone Farm.'

'OK, that's a good spot, I know Jim Shelstone. Do you rent his little lugger with the donkey engine?'

'Sure do.'

The officer got up and pulled on his hat. 'Well, nice to meet you boys. Have a good stay and – oh, in case you should need anything I'm Al, Al Cardy. You'll find me down at the Sheriff's Office just along the way there.'

As he got to the door he paused and came back to the table. He fished out a photo and put it down in front of them. 'I don't suppose you came across this guy over where you are? Tall man, big in the chest.' They shook their heads. 'What's he done?' Tom asked.

'Oh, he's done nothing. He's a missing person; Will Tennant is our local park ranger. There was a report of strangers out in the backwoods. I expect you know this is all State Park around these parts.'

'Sure do,' Tom replied.

'A local man called in to say he'd seen three men who looked like they might be hunting out of season. Will went out to take a look but he didn't come back. He could have taken a fall or something. Would be much obliged if you'd let us know if you see anything while you're out there.'

The food arrived and was put down on the table. It was freshly made and looked good.

Back at the cabin they set up for the night, laying out blankets on the bunks and putting the stores in a vermin-proof cupboard. By ten o'clock it was dusk. The light was just right to start some night fishing. They gathered up their rods and made their way to Shelstone jetty where the little clinker-built lugger was tied up. The engine kicked into life and Mike cast off. Slowly they made their way out towards the middle of the lake. It was flat calm with no wind; perfect for catching walleye. The waters of the lake lay on a north/south line starting quite narrow at the southern end and getting wider as it progressed up to touch the Canadian border just south of Montreal. About a mile out they stopped to let it drift. Lines were cast, reeled in and cast again. After half an hour they had caught nothing and decided to move closer inshore. Mike cranked the starting handle and the engine puttered into life. The new spot was much closer to the shoreline and as they fished they caught the sound of another boat coming from the north. Then they caught site of a red navigation light away in the distance.

Tony lifted his head. 'That's moving fast. Kinda risky running a sports boat at those speeds in this light.'

Mike laughed. 'What light is that then? It's dark where I'm sitting.' Suddenly there was the sound of a reel racing.

'Got one on the line,' Tony shouted, 'and it's a good size, I'd say!' He started to play the fish, slowly reeling it in. Then Tom's reel started to sing. Within seconds Mike also had one on. 'They're biting,' he shouted, 'and this one's got some fight in it!'

For the next twenty minutes there was a frenzy of singing reels, splashing and writhing water, flashing silver and shiny brown scales brought to life under the reflected moonlight. Then, as quickly as it had started, it all went quiet again. The fish stopped biting; the shoal had either gone deeper or moved on. There were seven good-sized fish in the bottom of the boat. Tom thought they must have thrown back at least as many again, if not more, just on account of they were too small. For a while they waited, sitting silently under the moon to see if the walleye would bite again, but they didn't. In the distance they heard the other boat again; a big powerful launch with the unmistakable throb of twin engines. Then they saw the navigation light, but it was green this time.

Tony looked at his watch, the dial just visible in the pale moonlight. It was gone midnight. 'That's an odd time to be getting out on the water. What d'ya think he's up to?'

Tom looked out across the water to where the light was fast disappearing. 'If it was ten years ago I'd say he was a bootlegger down from Canada. Now – he's probably night fishing like us.'

'Ha, we'll he won't catch much at that speed,' Mike said laughingly. 'And by the look of it we probably won't either. Shall I start the old engine now?'

They'd had the best of the night, Tom concluded, as they chugged back to the landing. After securing the lines they tramped the short distance to the cabin and lit the iron stove to make coffee. 'Why don't we just open up the Bourbon?' Mike suggested. 'A snort before bed and we'll all sleep the sounder.'

As he dozed off Tom thought he caught the sound of that motor boat again – but it could have been his imagination. That night he dreamed of the girl. She was in the boat talking to him, but he had to leave her there because his father was on the shore calling for help. Now he was on the shore with his father and she had fallen overboard and was yelling for help. Now he was in the water but it was his mother who was clinging on to him, pulling him down. His legs were caught in a rope that was floating just beneath him in the crystal clear water and he could see a great shoal of walleye deep down at the bottom of the lake. Then Tony was there coming to the rescue in a fast launch, but it morphed into the Chrysler and began to sink. He struggled to dive down to the Chrysler, which was sinking deeper through the water, getting smaller and smaller, but his legs were entangled and the rope wouldn't let him go down – it kept pulling him up.

He woke sweating, his legs tangled in the blanket. It was four o'clock and the first blush of dawn light washed the cabin window. He pulled the blanket over his head and went back to sleep.

Mike was out early. He had gone looking for wood to get the stove going and when he got back he was hugging a large bundle of kindling. Tony was sitting on the wood-decked porch at the front of the cabin sorting out the tackle from the previous night. Meanwhile Tom was out back gutting the catch. 'We have to give some of these away!' he shouted to anyone who was in earshot. 'It's more than we can eat.'

Mike dumped his bundle onto the floor of the front porch. 'I saw that boat again this morning; you know, the one from last night. It's tucked up neat as you like in a small cove just up the foreshore. You can see it from the top of a ridge out the back there but I reckon you wouldn't see it from the lake. It's literally around the corner from us. It's an ugly looking thing too; at least half is engines and it must be all of sixty foot, very fast I'd say; bit of a monster. I wonder we didn't hear it come back, it's that close.'

Tom came in, wiping his hands on a cloth. 'I think I did – in the early hours. Any sign of the crew?'

'I heard some voices but I couldn't see anyone. I think they were ashore.'

'We should take a look after breakfast,' Tony suggested. 'It's always good to know who your neighbors are.'

There was a small garden behind the cabin with a rough picket fence and a gate letting on to a clearing, beyond which the ground rose directly into dense woodland. 'Why don't you bring your Remington,' Tony suggested, 'the scope might give us a better view.'

The ridge was no more than a few hundred yards from the cabin. The ground was loose and thick with the detritus from a hundred seasons of fallen leaves and branches. Above them in the thick maple canopy birds were calling and somewhere close by came the coarse croaking sound of a cock pheasant.

They broke through onto the ridge. Here, the wood thinned and, there, suddenly they could see it – not fifty yards below the motor boat was tied off fore and aft to a couple of small trees on the shore. Tom took the scope off the Remington and put it up to his eye. As he did so, a man appeared on deck. He was followed by another, who then turned to take something from a third man who was down inside the boat's cabin.

'What do you think that is?' He passed the scope to Tony. 'No idea.' He handed the scope to Mike. 'I think it's a tripod – the kind you put a camera on.'

Tom took back the scope and looked again. 'They're getting off with it, whatever that is. And they've got a box – could be a camera – and there's some kind of pole. What do you think?'

Tony took the scope and adjusted the focus to get a better look. A third man came out from below deck. Tony took his eye away from the scope and rubbed it, then put it back to his eye again. 'Holy shit, what's he doing here?'

He had a puzzled look on his face as he turned to Tom. 'Take a look at this will ya, and tell me I'm not wrong.'

'What is it?'

'It's that asshole Newman, the one you had the ruckus with at the shooting gallery.'

Tom peered through the scope. 'Jesus, what the hell's he doing here?'

He passed the scope to Mike. He looked for just a moment then said quickly, 'They're coming this way; we might want to move back a bit.'

In the cabin they thought about what they had seen and tried to make some sense of it, but no sense came of it. Crows Crossing was a long way from Lake Eyrie and Newman's camp so why was he out there, and what was he up to? The other two men with Newman, who were they? And what was the equipment they took off the boat? They weren't fishing that was sure; the boat wasn't right and they had no gear. Maybe they were trying to make something out of nothing. After all, they were on holiday so why not Newman? In the end Tom gave up on it. Whatever they were doing, it was not their business. All they needed to do was to avoid Newman for the next two days and then forget about him. In the absence of answers they decided to go fishing; it was, Tom pointed out, what they had come for.

It was around mid-afternoon when they got back. They were tying up the boat to the jetty when Mike said, 'Do you think those three are the ones that deputy talked about yesterday – and shouldn't we maybe tell someone, perhaps call in on the Sheriff's Office?' He looked at the other two and waited for a response.

102

'I thought we agreed to leave it and just stay out of their way,' said Tony. Tom turned the idea over in his head for a moment. 'True, we did say that but Mike has a point and if they are connected to the missing ranger then we ought to tell someone.'

Tony didn't much like the idea of getting involved; it just wasn't in his nature and he said so, but in the end he went along with the others. 'Why don't we just drop by with some of those fresh walleye? That way we could slip it into the conversation without making it look like we were trying to put these guys in trouble.'

Tom pulled the Chrysler up to the curb across the road from the Sheriff's Office and was preparing to get out when he saw a man emerge from the office doorway; it was Newman. A minute or two later and he would have run slap into him. Tony was half way out of the car when Tom grabbed him by the shoulder and pulled him back into the seat. 'Newman,' he said pointing across the road.

'What the hell's he doing here?'

Mike crouched close to the window, peering out to get a better look. Newman stood for a moment while he lit up a cigarette, loitering on the threshold. From under the brim of his hat he looked furtively right and left, up and down and across the street. It was as if he was expecting to see somebody. Then a black Plymouth pulled up to the curb; Newman got in.

Tom started the engine on the Chrysler and as the Plymouth moved off with Newman inside he pulled away from the curb and made a U-turn.

'What are you doing?' Mike called from the back.

'Following him, I want to see where he goes.'

'Is that a good move?' Tony asked.

'Nothing's ever a good move but it might tell us a bit more about what is going on.'

'Do we need to know that?'

'No idea, depends where he goes. I figure something's going down round here and if we know what it is we might be able to avoid a whole mess of trouble.'

The driver of the Plymouth began to speed up as it headed out of Crows Crossing. At the edge of town it turned onto a road that headed north towards Essex. The distance between the cars widened as the Chrysler struggled to keep up with the newer car.

'Old straight six against the latest V8, not a contest really,' Tony remarked as the Plymouth got into its stride.

He wasn't really taking the chase or Tom seriously. What would they do if they did catch up with them? One confrontation with Newman was enough, he thought. He didn't relish going up against him a second time. But Tom was determined, and he wasn't going to stop him whatever he said, so he decided to

103

say nothing. In the end fate took a hand as so often it does in these things. Up ahead was a railroad crossing. The lights were flashing red and a bell was clanging. At first the brake lights on the Plymouth blinked then the driver changed his mind and it bucked across the tracks, kicking up dust and stones as it went.

As they got closer they saw the approaching locomotive hauling a long line of freight cars and belching grey black smoke. At the last minute Tom knew he wouldn't make it and hit the brakes hard, causing the suspension to hop. The Chrysler's tires tramped, skipped and skidded on the unmade surface, finally coming to a halt side on to the track. They watched as the train rumbled by in a long panorama of freight wagons. When at last the Caboose had passed they could again see the road ahead; it was deserted.

'We might as well turn back,' Tony suggested. 'There's no point in going any further.'

On the way back to Crows Crossing Tom was all for making the call on Al Cardy. Maybe they could find out what was going on. Tony was not so convinced it was a good idea. What had they got, he argued, nothing but a bunch of circumstances, no real facts. So what did it boil down to? Three men with a powerful boat cached away in a hidden cove who drove around the lake flat out in the dark. Crazy but not criminal – at least not until they hit someone. Newman was probably just a nasty coincidence. His appearance coming out of the Sheriff's Office could mean anything – maybe he went in for directions or some other local information. As for chasing after the Plymouth, that, said Tony, was just about the craziest thing in the whole stupid affair. What had Tom been thinking about?

'No idea,' Tom said angrily, 'it was just an impulse. If I thought anything it was it might give us some clue about what these guys are up to.' There was a pause and then he added, 'They have to be here for a reason.'

'Vacation?' Tony suggested.

Tom shook his head. 'I don't buy that. They're not on vacation, they look too serious – no, they're up to something.'

'He's got a point,' Mike added, laughing. 'After all, who goes on vacation with a theodolite, for Christ's sake?'

Tom looked over his shoulder and the car went off course. He swerved sharply to bring it back, narrowly missing the drainage ditch that ran along the margin. 'A what?' he shouted.

'A theodolite,' Mike repeated, 'and watch the road will ya!'

'What's that – a theodolite?'

'It's a thing surveyors use to measure the height of land. You see them on construction sites. I knew that tripod was familiar and then I remembered this morning where I'd seen one before. They were using them when they built my old man's new factory.'

'That does it,' said Tom emphatically. 'Let's go visit Deputy Cardy. He must know something, and if he doesn't we need to tell him what we've seen and what we know.'

Tony looked unconvinced. 'And what is it that we know exactly?'

'Come on!' Tom spat the words out angrily. 'These guys are suspicious as hell. For all we know they could be connected to the disappearance of that ranger – what was his name?'

'Will Tennant,' Mike reminded him.

'OK, I say we do it; we go talk with Deputy Cardy.' Then he reconsidered. 'No, let's not all go in like a mob; it'll look fishy. I'll go alone – you guys stay here. Does that sound right?'

Tony looked up at the cloth headlining in the Chrysler's roof. 'Sure thing – you can give him the walleye in the trunk; that's one more thing that probably smells a bit fishy by now.'

'Dammit, I'd forgotten those. Do you think they'll still be fresh? They've been in there since this morning and that sun's hot.'

They pulled up outside the Sheriff's Office for the second time that day. Tom opened the trunk. The walleye were still OK. Just inside the office a secretary was seated at a desk tapping on her typewriter. She looked up from a bundle of papers and over the rim of her glasses. She looked, Tom thought, like his mother. There was a hominess about her face and she had kind eyes.

She smiled. 'Good day. How can I help you?'

'I came to see the deputy, Officer Cardy,' Tom replied. 'I brought him some fresh fish. I had a really good catch last night and it's too much for one person; seems a shame to let it go to waste.' He opened up the old newspaper wrapper and displayed the catch.

'Oh, I'm sorry, I'm afraid the deputy stepped out of the office a short while ago and I don't know when he might be back.'

She looked at the fish glistening in the open paper; their eyes were still fresh and the gills looked good. 'My, but they're handsome,' she said smiling. 'Let me take them and I'll give them to him later. There's a cooler cabinet out back – I can put them there. Is there anything I can help you with?'

Tom hesitated for a minute, calculating if he dare put up a question about Newman. It might flush a few birds out of the trees; on the other hand, he could be exposing them all to who knew what. He was beginning to think that maybe Cardy had a connection with Newman and if that was right and Newman was up to something then Cardy could be in it with him. He decided to take the chance.

'Well, ma'am,' he said, trying to be as naïve as possible in the hope of disarming her, 'I guess you might be able to at that.'

Here we go, he said to himself; in head first. He tried to sound casual.

'I was looking for someone I know; I think he's vacationing hereabouts but I don't know where.'

'What's his name? It's possible we might know of him.'

'Henry Newman, ma'am; he's an army man, tall, kind of rugged looking – likes the backwoods and getting out on the water.'

She showed no reaction but shook her head a little. 'No,' she said after a short consideration, 'I can't say I know anyone of that name or that description. Sorry I can't help. I'll ask Deputy Cardy when he comes back again. Who shall I say called by?'

That caught him wrong-footed. He had not intended to hand out his identity, but he hadn't really thought about it. 'Oh, I don't know him personally. We just met briefly the other day at the diner. He said if I wanted anything to let him know but I'm out of here later today, back to New York, so not to worry.'

'New York,' she raised her eyebrows, 'now that's a big city – which part are you from?'

The conversation was going in the wrong direction. It was time to bail out before he dug himself in too deep. Maybe the question was a bad idea.

He looked at his watch. 'I have to get on the road, ma'am. Please do excuse me. It's a long way to New York – thanks for your help. Hope Deputy Cardy enjoys the fish.' He stepped out into the street and walked quickly back to the car without turning his head to see if he was being watched. He was, and the others told him so.

'Shit,' he said as he got in. 'Shit, you were right. I shouldn't have gone in there.'

As they were about to drive away Tony let out a low whistle. He put a hand on Tom's shoulder. 'Look at that,' he almost whispered the words. The black Plymouth they had followed now pulled up outside the Sheriff's Office. The driver got out and walked into the office. It was Deputy Sheriff Cardy.

'I think we need to get outa here,' Tony said, 'and let's make it quick.'

As Al Cardy stepped into the office his secretary got up. 'I think we may have a problem, Al,' she said, looking out of the office window at where the Chrysler still stood parked up to the curb.

'Dammit,' Tom kept saying as they headed back to the cabin, until Tony butted in. 'Dammit won't fix it buddy; we need a plan.' He turned to look over the seat back, 'Any ideas Mike?'

Mike raised his red eyebrows and put on a wry smile. 'Well, let's look at what we've got here because we may be making a storm out of a few puffs of wind.'

Tony looked quizzical, 'Okay.'

'One, we don't know that Newman is doing anything sinister. Being here could be a coincidence.'

'What's he doing in the Sheriff's Office?'

'That's a good question, but if you stand away from it for a minute and stop looking for trouble what do you have. An army man with two sidekicks doing a land survey. Who would he work with locally – the Sheriff's Office?'

'OK,' said Tom over his shoulder, 'but why did the secretary lie about him being there?'

'Could be she genuinely didn't know or maybe it's a covert project. Do you want to go back and ask the question?'

Tony smacked his hand on his forehead, then threw his arms up in the air. 'Are you out of your head. Why don't we just can it?' Then he added, 'You know what, when you think on it Mike is probably right. My vote says we carry on like nothing's happened. Let's do some fishing.'

Later that day Al Cardy came by to thank Tom for the fish. 'I figured it must have been you boys,' he said. 'It looks like the fishing has been real good.' He stayed for a while and drank coffee with them, then he took his leave. No mention was made of Newman or the missing ranger.

In the night Tom again woke to the rumble of engines and the sound of a boat on the water. It droned away into the distance.

Next morning when they went to look the boat had gone. They climbed down the ridge to where it had been tied up to the trees and stood where Newman and the others had stood, not because they expected to find anything but because subconsciously just standing up close to where it had been in a way seemed to exorcise the ghosts of the unknown. It turned the shades of yesterday's events into something tangible; it brought an air of ordinariness about them.

The ground had been trodden down and there were signs that well-shod feet had passed and repassed along the shoreline and up into the wooded ridges. One track was particularly well beaten. Tom pointed to the bent over saplings and snapped twigs. 'They must have used this a lot from the way it's beaten down.'

The track led up through the trees, slowly climbing over one ridge and then another, each one taking them a little higher. Finally they came on a clearing. There was evidence of a fire. Tony bent down and picked up a discarded cigarette pack. 'Look at this,' he said holding it out to the other two. 'You don't buy these in the US.'

It was a rectangular stiff cardboard pack with a card tray that slid open to reveal the cigarettes. It bore the image of a ship ploughing through a heavy sea at speed. Above it was the brand name "CORVETTE Cigarette Deluxe". On the back printed in black were the words FOR EXPORT ONLY.

Mike looked at it. 'I've not seen that before.'

'Canadian,' Tony observed, tossing it back on the ground. I went up there once when I was a kid. My old man had some business up there. I remember seeing these; they're a popular brand – like Camels here.'

On one edge of the clearing Tom stood and looked out through the trees. He could see the lake below and in the far distance he could just make out a road, probably Highway 9 going north.

'Come and look at this,' he called to the others. 'That's some view. You can see the far side of the lake; that must be Burlington out there in the distance.'

'So what do you think they were doing up here? They sure as hell weren't sightseeing.'

Tony kicked at the cigarette pack. He held up a finger, paused for a moment and then said, 'Well, maybe that's exactly what they were doing.' He picked up the empty pack again. 'See this,' he held it in his palm, displaying the front of the pack to each of them in turn. 'You know what this is?'

'Sure,' said Mike, 'you'd have to be blind not to – it's a cigarette pack; well, an empty cigarette pack.'

'Well, you're not quite right there, my shamrock green buddy. This a duty free empty cigarette pack – and you know what that means?'

'Go on'.

'It means it's bonded stores; loaded duty free under customs seal in Canada and brought down here on that boat. And I'll bet they never paid US duty on it either.'

'You mean they were smuggling Canadian cigarettes into the US?' Tom looked at him disbelievingly. 'Come on, there's no market for Canadian smokes here.'

'True, but this would only be part of the bonded stores. What else would you bring across the border duty free from Canada?'

'Well?'

'Ah,' said Mike, 'liquor!'

'Not just liquor. Scotch whisky and French brandy: premium liquor. Buy them duty free there and you sell them here at a market discount and still make an obscene profit. There's a high protection tariff this side of the border on that stuff. It's simple if you look at it that way. Newman is a modern bootlegger.'

Tom thought on it. 'What about Cardy, the deputy? How does he fit into it?'

'That's simple. He's in it for the greenbacks. Five years ago half the cops in the country were being paid to look the other way – payoffs, that's how it worked. Even some senators were in on the game. I think the stuff was being landed here and he was paid to cover for them.'

Mike nodded agreement. 'But that doesn't explain the tripod and theodolite.'

'Well how do we know if it was a theodolite. We didn't see what was in the box; we just saw the tripod and you assumed that's what it was.'

'What else could it be?'

'I think it was a big pair of those ships night glasses, or a telescope. Mount it on a tripod up here and you would see right into the landings at Burlington –

exactly where customs and police launches could be waiting to intercept stuff coming down from north of the border. Someone sitting up here with a powerful set of glasses could scan the whole area for patrol boats and radio their position directly to that big fast boat they had. That's what I think we're looking at here. And when we turned up at the Sheriff's Office they shoved off quick.'

Tony flicked the packet into the ashes of the extinguished fire. As it fell the card tray slipped out and floated down behind it. Something caught his eye and he bent down again and retrieved it. It had something scribbled on it in pencil as if it had been made as a makeshift note.

'What's that?' Mike asked. 'There's something written on it.'

Tony turned it towards them. The writing was difficult to read. 'It says,' Tony squinted at it. 'Got, erm, got something – and some numbers.' He handed it to Mike, 'See if you can make anything from it.'

Tom leaned over Mike's shoulder. 'There's two Ts in that – it says Gottlieb, then 9 87 225; what's that – some kind of phone number?' Mike shook his head. 'Not one I've heard of.' Tony shrugged. 'Means nothing to me.' He took the card from Mike, turned it around a couple of times then lobbed it into the ashes.

There was nothing more to be said. They made their way back down to the cabin in the warm morning sun; all thoughts now on lunch because it was getting towards that hour. 'Just one more thing,' Tom said as they were nearing the cabin. 'What about the missing ranger, Tennant?' Tony shrugged, 'I have no idea.'

Monday was turning out to be an altogether better day. The anxieties of running into Newman had gone with the departure of the boat. Tony's version of the events made sense and there were yellow perch biting. Perhaps they would catch the big one. They spent the rest of the day sitting offshore in the little wooden lugger with a bucket full of cold beers. It was funny, Tom remarked, how much better the beer tasted just slopping around in that little boat on a gentle swell with the smell of the old wooden timbers mixed with the exotic aroma of the fuel oil from the engine.

By evening they had caught four perch and a stray brown trout, but the big one had evaded them. Back at the cabin, they lit a fire out front of the cabin and cooked the fish on sticks in the ashes. They came out a bit charred but they were good. They ate them off the sticks, pulling the burnt skin away. Underneath they were deliciously smoky and together with a few shots of bourbon put a perfect cap on the day.

That night Tom slept without dreaming – or at least if he did he couldn't remember it in the morning. His first thoughts when he woke were about the girl. He would go and see her tomorrow and ask her to have lunch. Perhaps, he thought as he lay there, she might even spend the day with him on Thursday – it would be July fourth.

Next morning they set out early to drive back down to Croton. For the first hour Tom kept looking in the rear view mirror, each time half expecting to see the black Plymouth – but it was never there.

On the road the talk was mostly about Mike's upcoming wedding and how Tom was going to handle his first meeting with the lovely Caroline. Tony, who had lots of experience in these matters, offered one simple piece of advice. Play it cool, don't look too enthusiastic and, above all, don't rush at her. Just casually go into her office and in a disinterested sort of way let her know you're only there to return her lost property. Try to make her laugh if you can – women, he proclaimed, like a man with a sense of humor. But, he added, there's a fine line between funny and cheesy so just don't crack some god awful corny joke because then she's going to think you're some kind of Oaky fresh off the last train from Hicksville.

That was all very well for him, Tom had said, because Tony was quick on his feet. He'd dated a lot of girls and he always knew what to say and when to say it. He always had just the right response up his sleeve. But they were talking Tom Jordan, a man with zilch experience and not very good with words at the best of times. He could trip over his own name on a really bad day.

Then, during a lull, the conversation turned to the events around Newman and Deputy Sheriff Al Cardy. 'What do you suppose that was about?' Tom asked. 'What was in behind that business with the boat charging around in the dark?'

'My money's on smuggling. It's duty free for me,' Mike called out from the back seat.

Tony agreed, with an affirmative nod. 'I'm with Mike on that one. I think it's the most likely explanation. My old man gets approaches all the time from guys in that racket wanting to supply the club. He always tells them to get lost, but there's a lot of it going on.'

They arrived back in Croton around five in the afternoon and, having taken his leave of the other two, Tom turned the Chrysler north again and headed for home.

As soon as she heard the car on the gravel at the front of the house Martha came out of the kitchen. She was standing there on the porch as he got out of the car. She came down the steps and before he could start unpacking she folded her arms around him and hugged him tight. 'How was the trip?' she asked, so happy to see him back again that the answer really didn't matter.

'Well, you know,' he laughed, 'fishing is a lot of waiting about and little bits of action – but it was good. I've got a pair of big perch caught just last night. We could have them for supper.'

'Oh, and I've baked a pie especially for you coming home – will they keep a day?' Tom said he thought they would if they were kept in the cooler. One day, he said to himself, he would buy a refrigerator for the house, with a freezer tray, and then they could have iced drinks in the summer and ice cream whenever the fancy took them.

He took the canvas bag off the front of the car and unpacked the trunk. Lastly he got the Remington out of the trunk and took it back up to his room where he propped it against the wall just behind the door.

Downstairs Martha busied herself in the kitchen with preparations for the evening meal. For a while Tom sat in his room. He cast his mind back over the bizarre events of the last few days and wondered if he should tell his mother about it. But what was the point, he reasoned. To make sense of it he would also have to tell her of the encounter with Newman at the Fair and that, he knew, would worry her. She had no idea what had happened either there or later up on the lake and that, he decided, was for the best.

As he came into the kitchen he noticed that the puppy had gone from the old crate. 'Where's the dog, Ma?' he asked curiously.

'Oh, my goodness, I forgot to tell you.' She moved around him and quietly closed the kitchen door. Then she said in a hushed whisper, 'The most wonderful thing has happened. Your father has taken to the mutt. You go into the front parlour and you'll see it for yourself.'

Tom smiled in quiet disbelief. 'How did it happen?'

'I don't know. I just walked in yesterday morning and there he was talking to it just like it was a kid; just like he used to talk with you when you were a kid. Just go take a look.'

Tom walked into the front room. His father was sitting in his old chair with the puppy curled up on the floor beside him. The puppy jumped up at the sound of Tom coming in and his father put out a hand to pat it on the head.

'Hi Dad,' Tom said cheerfully, 'I see you got on okay with the mutt.'

His father picked up the puppy and sat it on his lap. 'He aint a mutt. He's a wire-haired fox terrier as it happens.'

Tom tried to sound interested. 'Is that so; how did you find out?'

The question seemed to worry his father for a moment; Tom thought he might have put his foot in it. His father looked thoughtful and far away as if trying to remember something; a frown settled on his forehead. Then he looked up at Tom and in a slightly sad voice said, 'We had one once – in the trenches. We used him to run messages. He had a little canister strapped round his neck and we would put messages in it. He would go back and forth between the lines and our command post. Back and forth and back and forth. You see, a dog could go places where no company runner could get through.'

He looked at the dog in silence for a moment and then added, 'Then one day he went out and never came back again. We found him a week later between the lines – dead; shot, probably by a sniper. We buried him there and put up a little wooden cross with his name on it. Wheels is what he was called; plucky little fellah. Just like this one,' and he fondled the puppy's muzzle.

Tom was taken aback. He had not heard his father speak so tenderly about anything or anyone before and now this memory had stirred something in him. 'Why Wheels?'

His father smiled. 'After those toy dogs that kids push around – you know, a dog on wheels. You remember – you had one when you were a kid. Yup,' he said, brightening up visibly, 'so that's what I'm calling this little fellah – he ain't no mutt, son.' He stroked the dog affectionately.

'Sounds like a good name, Dad.' Inside he felt a warm glow – he had never seen his father so engaged.

CHAPTER 13

The Shack

The phone rang – a long jangling ring, followed by another and another, demanding attention. General of the Army Air Corps, Hap Arnold, was still in his pajamas.

'Hello'.

The voice at the other end was tense. 'Hap?'

'Yup.'

'It's Ira. One of my boys has spotted something and you should know about it.'

'Is it important?'

'Damn right it is.'

'Where are you?'

'At the Shack.'

'I'll be right over.'

In the 20 minutes it took for the drive across Washington, Arnold sat in the back of the car, staring out of the window and contemplating what it might be that Ira had thought important enough to get him out of bed on his day off. And what was he doing at the Shack when he operated out of Fort Myer across the river? There was an intelligence unit at the Shack and that, he supposed, must be the reason. As they came down the National Mall, lined with cherry trees and classical architecture, he wondered what in God's name they had been thinking when they allowed the Shack to be built. Teddy Roosevelt, he concluded, was not a man of taste when it came to matters of architecture.

The Shack, as it was derisively known by many in Washington, had been built at the time of the Great War to house US army workers, and was more properly known by the title of the Munitions Building. As the car turned into the parking lot the full impact of what George Patton had described as 'one hell of an ugly bitch' presented itself full in the face. It was a squat, unlovely, two-storey concrete rectangle sitting alongside buildings of much greater architectural merit. Like the hunchback swinging in the bell tower of Notre Dame, it was grotesquely out of place. Built at the same time and joined to it like an ugly twin was the Main Navy Building. Together they took up an entire block between 19th and 20th Streets fronting Constitution Avenue. Over the years it had been

113

condemned by DC residents as inappropriate for the National Mall, which had originally been conceived as an avenue of great public buildings.

'They ought to pull this thing down,' he said to his driver as he got out of the car. But he knew they wouldn't. The pressure on administrative space in the capital was so great that nobody could afford to let it go. Early the year before, Henry Stimson and George Marshall found themselves moving their offices there after they had been booted out of the State War Navy Building by the pressure on space from the incoming Department of State. The State War Navy Building was, by comparison, an eloquent expression of late nineteenth-century design in the French manner. It had been a pleasure to work in its well-proportioned, high ceilinged rooms; now they were dumped down here in the Shack.

Ira Eaker sat at a borrowed desk. He filled a pipe with tobacco and lit it. Behind him on the wall was a large map of the world marked with zones of conflict. It had pins with national flags stuck into it showing the disposition of the belligerents. On the desk was a photo of a dog. Next to the photo sat a plain white plaque with a message engraved on it in black. It read THINK SMALL: IT'S THE LITTLE THINGS THAT KILL YOU – YOU JUST DON'T SEE THEM COMING. Eaker didn't know whose desk it was but he liked the message on the plaque. He thought he might put that up in his own office.

'The British are up to something and we're not sure what.' He pushed a large grainy blow-up of a black-and-white reconnaissance photo across the desk at his boss. 'That came in this morning from one of our flyers. Lately we've been getting reports of a lot of activity around Nova Scotia and up towards the Barents Sea. There's been an unusual amount of shipping movements. Mostly transports. We had a Navy flyer on border patrol off the Maine coast, so we sent him up north to take a look.'

'What am I looking at?'

Eaker got up, holding the pipe by its bowl and tapped the map with the stem. 'Here, around Prince Edward Island and here up in Hudson Bay. They're constructing what looks like a harbor with landing stages.' General Arnold said nothing while he studied the picture.

'They've been landing a lot of stuff up there – and the Hudson Bay site is wilderness. Look at these here.' He put a finger down on a blurred row of small dark rectangles. 'We think these might be prefab barrack huts – that means a lot of personnel. Why would you want to put that many men out there in the wilderness, unless of course it's a transit camp? In which case where are they in transit to?'

'Do we know the status of the equipment?'

114

'It's hard to say from this altitude. Intelligence thinks it's most likely military stuff – artillery, trucks, tanks, but they can't be sure. And there may be airplanes; we think these might be hangers but again we can't be sure.'

Arnold tapped a finger on the photo. 'Don't like it. It's got an odd smell to it, Ira. Damned odd.'

'They could be trying to clear out Britain and set up something in Canada.'

'They'd need German cooperation. They'd never get across the water without it, not in these numbers.'

'How close can our boys get to the landing stages?'

'It's difficult. The Canadians have put a major security cordon around the whole area. Most of the north east of the country is under travel restrictions.'

There was a knock on the door and a corporal came in. 'Pardon the interruption, sir, but Major Gregson thinks you should see this.' He saluted and stood to attention. Eaker read the note and handed it to Arnold. There was a silence, then Eaker said, 'Ask the Major to step in here, please Corporal.' A few minutes later there was another knock at the door. Gregson entered and saluted, then shook hands with Arnold.

'OK, what do we know?' Arnold asked, getting straight to the point.

'Not a lot. A Pan Am pilot reported seeing what he thinks was a full bomber wing inbound towards Halifax. And get this – we just got notified by the FAA that Canada closed its airspace all the way from the Baffin Bay right down to Montreal.'

Arnold ran a hand across his mouth, rubbing the stubble on his chin. 'Who else has this at the moment?'

'No one,' Gregson replied. 'None of this is more than an hour old.'

'OK, then you'd better get this up to Admiral King's office and to George Marshall. I'll get a meeting with them later,' he looked at his watch. 'I've got to go, Ira – stay on the case and keep me up to speed. We need to get to the bottom of this one; it's got a bad feel to it.'

They met over lunch – Marshall, Arnold, and King. Together they formed the Joint Chiefs of Staff responsible only to the President. Henry Stimson joined them. He had more disturbing news.

'We think Churchill is dead.' There was a momentary pause. 'I've just come from the White House. FDR got a report this morning from our embassy in London. They tell us his official limousine was found burned out in a street somewhere along the edge of the Thames. There were two charred bodies in it, too badly burned to identify but they think its Churchill and his bodyguard. The British are keeping it under wraps at the moment. They're not even telling their own people about it. Officially he is still just missing.'

'Murdered?' George Marshall looked round the table.

'Assassinated – it's political', Stimson observed casually.

'Same thing in the end result, Henry'.

'Poor bastard,' King grunted. 'I never liked him personally but he was useful. They got any clues about who?'

'We've got one of our people inside the British Special Branch. He says there's a rumor that Hitler got a hitman into the country. They think it was set up by some Fascist grouping run by that guy from the aristocracy, Sir Oswald Mosley. It's just rumor, nobody knows for sure. The theory goes that with Churchill out of the way, Halifax would be clear to go; he could do a deal with the Nazis, which is what we know he did.'

Marshall gave an understanding nod. 'Adds up in my book. I'd probably do the same in Hitler's shoes.'

The lunch arrived served by an orderly in uniform. They sat in silence for a moment until the food was laid out and the orderly had withdrawn, then Marshall broke it. The first course was soup. Marshall scooped up a spoonful, blew on it and swallowed. He looked around the table. 'OK, we know why we're here – so what's going on up North; what are the British up to?'

'Ira is talking with the Signals Intelligence boys,' Arnold responded. 'You're aware they have a group in this building?' The others acknowledged with a nod. The Signals Intelligence Group had an analysis team that was listening in on world traffic. They had already successfully broken the Japanese code 'Purple', giving the War Department an invaluable ability to intercept and understand messages being transmitted between Tokyo and its Embassy in Washington. Now they were concentrating a team on the British communications in the North Atlantic.

Joe King stared into the soup bowl in front of him, then put his spoon down. 'You all know how I feel about the Brits.' A ripple of laughter went round the table. 'They're tricky. It's possible what we may be looking at here is an attempt to get set up in Canada – get as much hardware out of reach of the Germans.'

'How practical would it be for us to send some ships up there to intercept and find out first hand what's going on, Joe?' Marshall asked.

'Possible, but we run the risk of German U-boats. There could be confrontation.'

'And if there was, how would we be?'

King looked serious. 'George, if we get into a shooting war in the North Atlantic right now it would not be good. You could be sure the Italian Navy would weigh in and, who knows, maybe the Brits too. I'd have to strip the Pacific fleet and move it through the Canal. That would take time and in the same moment leave us exposed to the Japs – and you don't even have to guess what those bastards would do. I say we stand back and watch what develops.'

'We need to avoid a confrontation,' Stimson quickly interjected. 'We're nothing like ready to get into a fight yet.' The others agreed; America would need another year to bring its armed forces up to fighting strength; and that went right across the board.

'Hap,' Marshall turned to Arnold. 'Could we get an overflight; get some aerial reconnaissance boys to fly low over those ships and snap a few close ups?'

'It's do-able but we'd have to do it closer to Canada than Europe. We need to keep out of the way of German air cover. The Luftwaffe is pretty free now the RAF is grounded.'

'Do we have any evidence they're covering the British movements?'

'There's no evidence. We can try?'

Stimson agreed. 'It's probably diplomatically risky,' he cautioned, 'but, short of any other solution, it's the one we have to run with. We need to know what's going on up there in the North. It's too close to home to be comfortable.'

Marshall thought for a moment. 'Henry, I suppose there's no reason we couldn't just ask the British outright what they're up to? The worst they can do is tell us to go to hell – and if they do, we'll know they're up to something.'

'No reason at all but keep in mind it will alert them to the fact that we are suspicious. How do you feel about that, Joe? It's your patch they'll be treading on if it comes to a showdown.'

'Henry, I don't think we have too many options – do you?'

'Anybody else got a view – Hap?'

'Henry, I guess my only thought on this is if we call them and then draw a blank card, the stakes go up for a flyover. They'll be watching for us.'

Marshall signaled agreement. 'How long would it take us to get one in the air and back?'

'Maybe later today; we've got plenty of daylight up there at this time of year. Tomorrow, first light at the latest I guess.'

'Let's do it then. At least, Henry, you'll have an ace in the hole with whatever it is we've learned.' Marshall looked at the other two for approval. They nodded and then Arnold added, 'You know, Henry, we could do with better reconnaissance planes and more of them. All we've got right now is a handful of modified P38s. The British are way in front of us on that one. We need to catch up – and fast.'

They finished the lunch with routine procurement business, then left. Tomorrow would be Independence Day. Each one of them would have a full agenda of public duties to perform. As he was driven home that afternoon Arnold wondered where it was all heading. He was saddened by the news of Churchill. Personally he liked this tenacious Englishman whom he had met on two occasions. He had shown determination and a deep sense of patriotism in his struggle to save the British from Nazi domination. Joe King was wrong

117

about the British, he mused, or at least about Churchill, but that was Joe – aggressive, opinionated, and a downright hard man. Roosevelt once said, 'Joe is so abrasive he probably shaves with a blowtorch in the morning.' But he was a good sailor and a strong commander and this was what you needed in a war – and Hap, like the others, was more than ever coming round to the idea that there *was* going to be a war for America. Not today, not tomorrow – but soon.

New York City
The traffic in Manhattan was lighter than usual, but then it was the day before the Fourth of July and a lot of the offices would be emptying out early so that people could get home and ready for the holiday.

Tom walked briskly along East 42nd Street, clutching the book from the train – her book, his ticket to an introduction. He lifted the book to his face and breathed deeply. It still carried the barely detectable aroma of her perfume. He'd read the book up on the lake and thought it a strange kind of novel for a girl to read. Richard Wright's *Native Son* was a best seller that year and he'd heard about the book before he read it. It was a controversial story of a poverty-stricken black criminal laced with sexual violence, rape, murder, and a graphic catalogue of misery. He had somehow imagined that she would have read a romantic novel, perhaps a period piece set in the Deep South or a classical English nineteenth-century author. This was a story without the redemption of a happy ending; of brutality without morality, unrepentant even at its finish. He had been brought up with a strong investment in the American Dream and this didn't correlate. The book had shocked him, but what had shocked him even more was that she should be reading it; it was not the character he had constructed in his fantasy of what she would be. But when he put it to the others they had just laughed and Tony remarked that he was most likely getting involved with a very sophisticated woman so he'd best keep his provincial opinions covered up if he didn't want her to dump him after the first date.

He reached Eighth Avenue and turned onto 14th Street. The gallery was just along from Scribner's Bank. Scribner had been a casualty of the '29 crash and remained empty for years. It was a fine Art Nouveau building, fronted by lofty columns in high relief. Now clear plate glass had replaced the frosted windows that hid the tellers at their cages inside and gave privacy to its customers. In the place of the counter and the cashiers there was now a display of fashion garments for ladies of wealth and taste. Mannequins adorned in the latest from the fashion houses of Paris and Milan graced the floors and were lit so they could be seen from the street. He set off down 14th Street, looking at the store fronts for their numbers. Scribner had been 539; he would find her at 627 according to the card in the book: Kolinsky's Gallery of Modern American Art.

When he found the building it was not what he had been expecting. The idea of an art gallery in his mind was of a small boutique business, a charmingly decorated shop front with bright lights illuminating paintings and objects carefully set out for its audience to browse. 627 was in the same style as Scribner's Bank. It was a large imposing stone building with solid grey portals and a pair of highly polished strong teak doors. These were open to reveal more doors this time in glass. They were set back inside a marble flag-stoned lobby and beyond this he could see a person seated at a large desk facing the doors; another was standing by the desk. He had one hand on a corner, imparting an air of proprietorship.

Tom hesitated for a moment and then crossed the threshold. The cool marble floor threw back the light from an ornate crystal chandelier hung high up in the distant ceiling, illuminating everything around it. It was like walking on very thin ice over fine milky water. As he approached the desk the two men stiffened. They looked at him like the hounds of hell guarding the entrance to the underworld. They were immaculately dressed in pale grey suits with stark white shirts and small bow ties. But when he finally stood there in front of them he realized they were less the hounds of Hades, but more lap dogs. The white shirts were not, in fact, white at all – one was lilac and the other pale pink. And instead of snarling like guard dogs, they simultaneously broke into broad welcoming smiles.

'How can I help, sir?' said the seated man.

Tom pulled the card from the book and presented it. 'I've come to see this lady. Is she here today?' The man looked at it then up at Tom. 'Ah,' he said, with what Tom thought was an air of impertinence, 'the vision of loveliness.' He turned to his colleague. 'Patrick, could you let Miss Caroline know that she has a gentleman waiting to see her.'

He turned back to Tom. 'If you would be so kind as to take a seat over there, my colleague will see if she is available.' He pointed towards a small eighteenth-century *escritoire* with a seat next to it; 'Over there, sir.'

Tom walked over to the corner and sat down. The space felt very large, like a railway terminus. The sound of steps going up a marble staircase echoed back across the hallway at him. He put the book on the little antique desk and looked around him. The walls were hung with huge modern paintings and he found himself wondering what kind of people lived in houses big enough to hang such stuff. After a while he looked at his watch; he had been waiting 11 minutes but it seemed a lot longer. He began to feel uncomfortable. He was out of his depth in this place and he knew it. The man at the desk looked over at him and shrugged a little gesture of helpless resignation. Tom wondered if maybe the gesture signified that the man at the desk had seen this all before and knew exactly what might be coming – or possibly not coming – next. After another

119

few minutes he decided it might be best if he abandoned the quest. He got up and was walking towards the desk when the chill silence of the room was broken by the sound of shoe heels rapidly clattering down the marble stairs. Then she was there at the desk. The man said something to her and pointed at Tom. He stopped in mid-stride. Damn! Now what to do? He didn't know whether to turn back or go forward to meet her. His composure crumbled like dry ashes. He stood there as she advanced towards him with a purposeful little stride. She seemed shorter than he remembered. Then as she came up to him he realized it was not her at all; it was someone completely different, someone he had never seen before. He stood there with his mouth open and was about to say something silly when she stopped him.

'Caroline is awfully sorry but she is busy right now. Can I help with your enquiry?'

He tried to say something but he couldn't quite form the words. Then he got out 'Well,' followed by 'Er, I'm not sure – that is.' He held up the book. She smiled, 'Is this for her?'

He looked at her stupidly, then blurted out, 'It's hers – she left it on the train. I found it. Well, I didn't, but someone else did and he said I ought to let her have it.' As the words fell out of his mouth he realized they didn't sound right and wished he'd just handed over the book and left. She let out a little laugh and gave him an old fashioned look. 'Well, that's one way of saying it, I guess.'

He started to feel himself getting flushed and tried to get himself out of the corner he had just backed into. 'Sorry,' he said, 'I put it badly.'

'Don't be,' she replied, taking the book from his hand. She smiled again. 'I thought it was naïvely charming actually. Shall I take it to her?' Tom felt relieved and let it go. All he wanted to do was get out of the place. 'Thanks, please do.'

'And who shall I say left if for her?'

'Oh, Tom Jordan, but she won't know me.'

'Any number to call if she wants to say thanks?' He shook his head. 'Not really.'

'Are you close by? Maybe you could come back again?'

'It wasn't that important. I just thought she might like to have the book back – that's all. It wasn't really out of my way. I work at the Imperial Life Building on East 42nd. I'm a junior underwriter there, overseas risks – it's kinda specialist. Tell her not to worry about it.'

'Are you sure?'

He had regained his composure and now he felt a sense of relief. The tension of the moment had dissolved. 'Yes, I think I am.'

He was about to move away from her and then he stopped. 'By the way, what sort of place is this? It wasn't what I was expecting from her card. I had more in mind a small store of some kind.'

Again she smiled. 'We procure art for specialist clients. Wealthy people and institutions. We're not really a public art gallery in the true sense of the word. It's mostly modern American but we do get asked to hunt down some of the classical stuff. There's a lot being brought over from Europe looking for shelter from the war over there. The richer refugees bring things with them – very valuable things and they want to dispose of them, they need cash you see, particularly the Jews; they have some very nice things. It's a tragedy really but that's our business.'

'Thanks again,' he said, and left.

On the way back to the office he turned over in his mind what had happened. Curiously he did not feel any real disappointment, just a lightening of his mood, as if a weight had been lifted off his chest. He concluded that the whole adventure was a crazy notion and best put behind him. If the encounter with the girl who had come down to see him was anything to go by then a meeting with the 'vision of loveliness', as the man on the desk had called her, could have been worse than a rerun of the Wall Street Crash. He concluded he had been saved.

In the office he looked at his watch. It was still only 12.30. He was surprised how little time he'd actually spent on the whole episode. He phoned Tony. 'You got time for a quick lunch?'

'What about the girl?'

'It was a no show – I'll tell you about it over a salt beef sandwich. How about we meet up at Katz's Deli?'

Katz's was a short cab ride away. Inside they queued at the counter to order. The place had been popular since the Great War; it was always crowded but the service was good and you got a lot for the money.

'I'll pay,' Tony said, offering a dollar bill to the assistant behind the counter. They took their sandwiches to a table and sat down.

'So what went wrong?' Tony looked him straight in the eye. 'Don't tell me you blew it.'

'No, I didn't blow it; she just declined to come down from her office to see me. She sent a messenger. That's all – just that.'

Tony bit into his sandwich and, after he'd munched the contents of his mouth down to a manageable size, said through the slurry, 'Did you leave her a card, your phone number – anything?'

Tom, with his mouth full, just looked at his friend. He gave a little shake of his head. Tony looked exasperated. 'Nothing!' It was a statement, rhetorical and agitated. He slapped his forehead with the palm of his hand. There was an audible thwack. 'Nothing', he repeated quietly. Tom swallowed the mouthful.

'What did you expect me to do?'

'Well, you could have left the door open. Why didn't you send a message back with her friend, for Christ sake? Suggested you meet another time. Tell her you read the book and found it interesting and you'd like to meet the sort of girl who takes literature seriously.' Tom laughed a short forced laugh. 'Are you kidding – the book was garbage.'

'So tell her it was garbage. Who knows, it might get you into a conversation with her. Better still it might even get you into a bed with her.'

Tom waved the remark aside. 'She's not that kind of girl.'

'Well, in that case my friend you've got your moolah on the wrong pony.'

There was a long quiet interlude as they both finished their food. Tony swept up the last of a few fragments and tossed them into the back of his mouth. Tom looked at his watch. 'I have to get back. Thanks for the sandwich.'

'It's cool. Are you doing anything for the holiday?'

'It'll be the same as usual, I guess – home with the folks. You?'

'I'm putting a picnic together and inviting a couple of girls. There's a great little stretch of beach just off Croton Point – join us if you're free.'

'Do I know the girls?'

'You do; they work at Jennifer's Diner.'

'Not the blond?'

'Yes, the blond – and her friend, the dark haired one. Anyway, what have you got against the blond?'

'Nothing, I just don't see myself hooked up with a waitress in a diner. It's not how I see my future.'

'Well, if you change your mind come along. You might have fun.'

They got up and headed for the door where they would part company, Tom for his office and Tony on yet another errand for his father.

'About the picnic,' Tom called out as a parting shot. 'I'll take a rain check on that one if it's OK.'

'Why not, but if you change your mind you know where to find us.' His friend flagged down a cab and he was gone.

When he got back to the office there was a message. Marion, the girl on reception, called him as he went towards his office. 'You had a visitor but she couldn't wait.'

Tom stopped and turned back to the desk. He could feel his heart start to speed up. 'Who was she? Did she say what she wanted?'

Marion looked impassively at him. 'Didn't say.' Then, reaching in under the desk, pulled out a book and handed it to him. 'She left this though. Said you had her number and to give her a call.'

Tom stood looking at the cover: *A Native Son* by Richard Wright. 'What's it like – is it any good?'

He smiled a big open grin of a smile – the sort of smile that says I feel like a kid at Christmas. 'Yeah,' he said, 'it's probably the best book I've ever read.'

For a while he sat at his desk and just stared at the book. After a few minutes he opened it. There between the pages was what he had hoped to find – the card with her number on it. He felt a flutter of anticipation inside him. He would call her, right now, and he would propose to meet after work for a drink, maybe discuss the book. Then he would accompany her on the train and before they got to Dobbs Ferry he would invite her to join him for the holiday – go out on a picnic or come back into New York to watch the pageant and later the fireworks. Yes, he had a plan. Tony would be impressed.

As he reached for the phone Fred intervened with a pile of papers. 'It's the new guide on territories,' he said, dumping them down on the desk. 'Places you won't be able to quote on. There's a lot of them.'

Tom nodded. 'There sure are, the free world is getting smaller by the minute.'

Fred hovered around Tom's desk for a moment, looking like he wanted to say something. 'You know how you and Mr Johnson said the other day that you didn't think America would get involved in the European war.'

'Sure.'

'Do you still think that?'

Tom hesitated. Was there any point in hiding what he now thought was inevitable, that they would get sucked into the whole lousy mess and it could be the Great War all over again – probably worse this time because the weapons were bigger, more accurate and much, much, more deadly? He decided to lie. 'Don't worry. I think it'll be OK. There's a big ocean between us and that war.'

Fred looked unconvinced. 'I saw a newsreel the other day. It had planes in there, big bombers they claim could cross the Atlantic.'

It was a conversation Tom did not want to get involved in. He just wanted some time to make the phone call. 'Fred,' he said, 'think about it this way. Even if the Germans or the Japs could fly all the way over here, how are they going to get back home again? It's a six thousand mile round trip just coast to coast without coming inland to bomb anything. It isn't possible, so stop worrying about it.'

'Okay, if you say so,' he said reluctantly, though he still looked worried, but he said he guessed Tom must be right then ambled back to his desk in the corner.

Dan Johnson came over and, pulling up a chair, sat down beside him. This new territorial guide was going to make things a tad difficult, he told Tom. He thought they should discuss how it could be applied. It was simple enough in the well-defined combat zones but there were some areas that were marginal and there needed to be a clear strategy. For example, he pointed out, there was no war in neutral Turkey, or in Arabia, but they had been marked up as high risk because the Germans had shown no respect for neutrality and they were already sitting in Romania – right on the Turkish border – and that could be a direct route through to the Arabian oil fields.

By the time they had combed through every risk in the guide it was late. Fred had left and the outer offices were empty. Only the diligent Miss McKinnon still sat at her desk, her fingers busy clattering on the keys of the typewriter. At Zanzibar, Dan Johnson finally stopped, realizing, as he said, that they had talked for longer than he had anticipated and he must go because his wife needed him to run some errands and do some late shopping for the holiday celebration.

At last Dan Johnson had gone. Tom picked up the phone to dial the number. There was nothing, just the faint empty hum of the electric current running through the instrument – the girl on the switchboard had gone home.

Disappointment hung about him like a heavy wet overcoat. It had been a rollercoaster of a day. Up and down; elation then crash. As he stepped outside the air crackled with the early summer heat. Bright sunlight hit the pavement with an eye-watering glare. Light bounced off the windshields of the passing automobiles, throwing dazzling shafts in his face. He reached into his pocket for sunglasses and as he put them on became aware that she was standing there looking at him. She had a wide-brimmed hat that sheltered her face and a tightly tailored blouse, nipped in at the waist by a broad shiny black belt. She smiled.

'I'm sorry I missed you.' She made a little gesture with the bag she was clutching. 'Actually, I missed you twice, which is quite awful.'

He stood there dumb for a minute then, realizing he was still holding the book, held it out to her. 'You left this behind on the train. I found your card in it. I thought I ought to return it to you – that's all.'

'That was very sweet of you. I'd finished it so I left it there in case someone else might like to read it. I always use a business card as a book mark.'

Ah, he thought, so there was a rational explanation after all. The man on the train had got it completely wrong. It wasn't an invitation, just a random action with those inevitable unpredictable consequences that flow from them. Still, there she was and here he was and they were talking, so that was something. After all, hadn't he been trying to engineer a meeting ever since he first saw her? He'd ask her if she'd like to go somewhere for a drink, perhaps a cocktail, but before he could get it out she beat him to it.

'You can keep the book,' she said, 'if you'd like to.' Tom looked at it still half held out towards her. 'Thanks – er – that would be nice.'

'It doesn't seem much for all the trouble you went to. Why don't you let me buy you a drink, just to say thanks. How about it?'

'That would be nice,' he said, 'but you've already given me the book.' For a moment he couldn't believe what he was saying. It was like being in a dream, a really bad dream when you do things and say things and you can see them happening but you can't stop them.

'No, I insist – the book was rubbish anyway. Come on, we can take a cab. I know a shishi little bar not far from here.' She stepped off the sidewalk and waved down a cab – and in doing so she saved the day.

'Sorry, I forgot to ask your name,' she said, laughing as she got into the back of the cab.

'Tom, Tom Jordan.'

She settled herself into the seat with a little wriggle, then straightened out her dress. He couldn't help noticing the curve of her body under the folds of the light material.

'Hello Tom,' she said, smiling again and offering a hand which he shook politely. 'Is that short for Thomas? I like Thomas, it's a strong name. I think I shall call you Tommy. Do you mind if I call you Tommy? I'm Caroline,' she went on rapidly, hardly drawing a breath, 'but I prefer Carey. You can call me Carey if you like. My friends all call me Carey.'

'Okay – Carey it is.'

In the cab she talked non-stop about her job and how she held an executive position on account of her father, who was the industrialist Warren H. Taylor and a major patron of the Kolinsky gallery. The words tumbled out of her like a sweet cornucopia. Tom sat fascinated, transfixed by the movement of her delicate mouth and the dark eyes that swept across him as she devoured him with the intensity of her glances.

'Where are we going?'

'You'll see when we get there. Some of my friends discovered it last year and we often go there.'

The cab made its way to Lexington Avenue and there it stopped outside a small restaurant. Over the door a sign advertised Tarwids Russian Bear Restaurant and Cocktail Bar. The window was filled with a large bear lounging in a reclining chair, sipping from a champagne glass complete with a cherry on a stick. Carey pulled him from the cab and linked her arm around his. Standing beside him, he noticed for the first time how tall she was. At five eight in high heels she almost met him eye to eye. Inside they found a table and sat down. 'Now,' she said with an air of authority. 'What will you have, and before you say anything I'm buying – I insist. It was so considerate of you to bring me back the book.'

Tom looked blankly at the list of drinks, most of which he didn't recognize. 'You choose,' he said. 'Surprise me.'

'Do you like whisky?' He indicated he did. 'Then you should have a Manhattan. Now tell me who you are and what you do.'

'I live in Peekskill, with my folks, which is up the line from you. That's where I'd seen you before. We've sometimes shared the same railcar. You get on at Dobbs Ferry. We spoke once – very briefly, but I don't suppose you would remember.'

'No,' she said, 'I don't think I do.'

Their cocktails arrived. They touched their glasses together. Carey smiled at him over the rim of something colorful with bubbles in it. 'Here's to us, Tommy Jordan – we should get to know each other better.'

A little flock of birds took flight somewhere inside him.

'Can you play tennis?' she asked. He shook his head. 'Don't know – never tried it.'

'Do you play golf?'

'Fraid not.'

'Can you ride?'

'Probably – it doesn't look too difficult.'

'Okay – what can you do'?

'I shoot, in competitions. I hunt in the fall and winter, I like fishing, I can sail a boat and … ' She held up a hand to stop him. 'Oh how fascinating – an outdoors man – I like that.' Then she added as an afterthought, 'Why don't you take me sailing some time?'

'That's a thought,' he said draining his glass. 'Now that is a thought!'

'Here, let me get you another drink. Then you can tell me more about yourself.'

They were on their third when Carey had what she called a good idea. 'Come on,' she told him, 'I'm hungry.' They should, she insisted, go to a restaurant and she knew just the one. It was in another part of the city and they would need a cab.

Outside, the sun had dropped behind the tall buildings but the air was still warm and balmy. They walked a block, then two, but didn't manage to get a cab. Everything seemed to be full or had the flag down going for a pickup or going off shift. Tom hailed and whistled for a third block until finally Carey spotted one emptying out it passengers just a few yards back behind them. As they walked towards it, the driver waved at them indicating he was no longer for hire.

'Oh no you don't, buddy,' she said, and stepping off into the street stood arms outstretched, blocking his getaway. The driver got angry and sounded the horn, then leaning out of the window looked at her appealingly.

'Come on, lady, gimme a break will ya? I got a home to go to and I've been in this crate all day.'

126

'Double charge if you take us – no make that triple. How about it? I can stand here all night if you like.' The driver relented. 'Okay, lady, you win. Where to?'

'Do you know the El Morocco?'

'Of course, what cab doesn't?'

'Good – take us there.'

'That was disgraceful,' Tom told her, laughing as they sat in the back. 'You hijacked the poor guy. You know you can get arrested for that kind of thing.'

'Are you crazy – did you want to walk? It's half way across town.'

When they arrived at the restaurant there was a queue waiting for a table but Carey simply walked round it and, finding the maître d', arranged to have them seated.

'I'm sorry, but I can't afford to eat here,' Tom said looking uncomfortable. 'And anyway, how did you manage that?'

'My father has his own table here,' she said, smiling sweetly, 'and you're not paying, he is. How many times do I have to tell you – it's my invitation.'

'Won't he mind?' Tom asked, almost innocently.

'He won't know and he wouldn't care even if he did.'

The maître d' arrived and gave a little deferential bow, a white napkin draped across one arm.

'Let's have some champagne,' Carey decided. 'Do we have any of the Krug '28 left, Herbert?'

'You do Miss Taylor.'

'A bottle of the '28 then.'

She sat there for a moment, elbows on the table, her hands cupped under her chin and with a slightly impish look curling around her mouth. 'This is nice,' she said, leaning intimately towards him. 'We should do this again.' She let out a little contented sigh, then put out a hand and brushed it against his. 'Now then, tell me more things about you; where you go hunting – and sailing – I want to hear all about you, everything you do, what you think; everything.'

It was late when they finally got to Grand Central. As they boarded the train the large hands on the main concourse clock slumped silently on to midnight.

They sat together on the train, side by side. The car was empty except for the two of them and as it rumbled through the dark she linked her arm round his and put her head on his shoulder. 'Do you mind?' she said, half lifting her head for a moment.

'No, that's fine,' he whispered, and gave her arm a gentle caress. With a trace of a smile on her lips she closed her eyes and dozed. Tom sat there contented, enveloped in the headiness of the moment and the perfume of her hair, hardly daring to move for fear he should disturb her.

When she got down from the train at Dobbs Ferry it was with the promise to spend tomorrow together. He leaned out of the window to wave goodbye and, just as the train gave its first intimation of movement, she kissed her hand, held it up towards his face and with the smallest puff sent it gently fluttering towards him.

He watched her standing there on the platform until she fell from his sight, then sat down and with a little shudder of elation squeezed his hands together. He felt like a child at Christmas. Tony was not going to believe this. After all, he could barely believe it himself.

CHAPTER 14

Carey

'Churchill is dead. I can't believe it.'

'Is it important?' she asked naïvely.

'Yes, I think so; I think it means we'll go to war with Germany – probably Japan as well.'

He put down the newspaper and rolled over onto one elbow. With his hand he gently brushed aside her hair then dropped the lightest kiss onto her forehead. She looked up at him with sleepy eyes and he wondered how in the world he had got here – into her bed. Then she put up a hand and brushed the back of it against his cheek. She smiled a little girly smile. 'Hey, hog face – you need a shave.'

'I don't have a razor with me – remember; this wasn't exactly planned.'

'There's one of my father's in his room. I'll go get it later but not yet. Cuddle me Tommy.' She rolled over pulling the sheet up under her chin and pushed her back against him.

He moved closer to her, putting one arm under her neck and the other round her waist. He gently folded her into the curve of his own body. She felt warm and smooth to his touch. Her skin was, he thought, the softest thing he had ever touched, like fine silky velvet. He gave her a little squeeze and kissed the back of her neck. She gave a little wriggle, sighed lightly and pushed his hand down onto her thigh. For a second time they came together, folding their bodies around each other, kissing and touching until that moment came when they simply lay in each other's arms and let the passion subside into a warm comfortable, half-world half-dream state of being. Wrapped around in a perfect layer of euphoria, they dozed for a while, him on his back, her with her head on his shoulder and one arm draped across his chest. Eventually Tom gently drew his shoulder away and let her face nestle into the pillow. He quietly got out of bed and left her to sleep. In the bathroom he splashed water onto his body. Then he came back into the bedroom and stood at one of the large windows looking out onto the gardens. He opened the window an inch or two till he could feel the breeze on his naked body. Standing there in her room he still couldn't believe everything that had happened in just 48 hours since they met outside his office. And here he was, without a stitch on, gazing out onto what was building up to be another fine day and a hot one.

Yesterday he had driven down to Dobbs Ferry in the Chrysler. Martins, the family chauffeur, had driven them down to Manhattan in a huge Packard Victoria and they had sat in the back like two giggling kids excited about their Independence Day out. Martins took them to Times Square and dropped them there with instructions to collect them that evening. Carey had planned the day. They had seen the parades and the marching bands in the morning and then had lunch at the Stork Club, where it turned out her father had yet another private table. Afterwards they had gone for a quiet stroll in Central Park and there she had kissed him and told him she had fallen for him. Later, in the afternoon, after she had pulled him by the arm around Saks, they had tea at Macy's. As it got dark they watched the fireworks until at last it came time for dinner and they ended up at Tarwids, gazing at the bear with the cocktail glass in his paw and laughing romantically at how far they had come since that meeting in front of the Imperial Life building. This, they agreed, would forever be their place. They would always remember it as the start of their love and they vowed there and then always to come back to celebrate their anniversary.

'If we ever break up,' she said, 'I want you to promise never to return here again. I don't think I could bear the thought of you being here with someone else; this is our place.'

Tom leaned across and kissed her then, slowly shaking his head, said, 'I can't believe how lovely you are or how lucky I am.' Then he added, 'Do you know what those two on the front desk at Kolinsky's call you?'

'I hate to think, it'll be something bitchy if I know those two – go on, tell me.'

'The vision of loveliness.'

She laughed, then taking his hand tenderly in hers said, 'You know something – I don't think I have ever been happier than I am now, here with you in this funny little restaurant with that stupid bear watching us. This is oh so perfect – let's never let it go away.'

'Why would I?' Tom said. 'I'll tell you a secret – I fell in love with you the first time I saw you, that day on the train. I knew then I had to find you.'

'So,' she teased him, 'what took you so long?'

Then he told her how he and Tony had decided to go looking for her one night in Dobbs Ferry with the crazy notion that if they simply visited all the bars and asked who is the most beautiful girl in town, somebody would be bound to know her.

She laughed some more and after the waiter had taken their order and left them alone again she said she had a little guilty secret of her own and she wanted to tell him, but he must first promise not to hate her for it. 'I've got a confession to make. The book, the one you returned to me, the one I left on the train …' Here she paused.

'Go on.'

'I didn't just dump it. I left it there because I hoped you would pick it up and bring it back to me – just like you did.'

'That's not a guilty secret, that's romantic.'

'No wait, that's not the guilty bit.' Tom looked cautiously at her, wondering what was coming next. He couldn't imagine anything making him hate her.

'When you didn't turn up that day, or the next, I got sore at you. I felt angry that you hadn't come running immediately you got off the train. Then when you did turn up, days later, I did something really dumb. I wasn't really busy that morning; I just had this silly idea I'd teach you a lesson – and I nearly lost you. How stupid can a girl be? I was lucky. Kate, the girl I sent to give you the brush off, remembered what you'd said about Imperial Life. We spent an eternity tracking you down.'

'You needn't have worried. I was going to come looking for you. I wasn't going to give up that easily.'

In the soft light of the little restaurant, after all the other diners had gone and the tables had been cleared, they sat there holding hands across the table and waited for Martins and the Packard to take them home. Sitting in the plush comfort of the back seat, they linked arms and watched the lights of New York slowly give way to the deep black velvet of the countryside – the night full of stars massed like fairy lights hung on some invisible web. For Tom it was the start of a new era and nothing would ever be the same again, although not in the way he was now thinking. Just now his thoughts were filled with that intimate little restaurant with the silly bear in the window. She was right, he could never go back there again; not without her – he knew it would break his heart.

******

'Don't you have just the most perfect butt?' a voice said from behind him. He turned to see her sitting up in bed, propped against the pillow. 'Throw me that pack of cigarettes, will you. We should get up – I'll tell Patience to make us some breakfast. What would you like? We have everything.'

Over breakfast he asked her about her father. 'He's a complete shit and he doesn't really live with us any longer – thank God. He's the Taylor in the Taylor Engineering and Steel Corporation. He's massively wealthy, the richest man in America, they say.' She looked up from a plate of scrambled eggs, 'Did I tell you that yesterday?'

131

'You told me who he was and that he got you the position with Kolinsky, but that was it. Oh, and you told me about your younger sister who lives here and your mother. Where are they, by the way?'

Carey made little circles in the air with her fork to indicate it didn't matter, then added, 'They're away for the holiday, visiting my aunt in California – they're gone for a week. So we have the place to ourselves.' She gave her shoulder a little wiggle as if to say won't that be fun. Every time she made a little gesture like that Tom was captured and then recaptured, a prisoner to his pleasure of just looking at her. She was not only beautiful, but he now saw her as alluringly sexual and every time she made one of those little movements he just wanted to scoop her up in his arms and consume her.

'And your father?'

'He won't show his face around here. He'll be away somewhere on his yacht with one of his floozies. He didn't exactly walk out on us, but as good as; let's just call it creeping infidelity.'

'Why doesn't your mother divorce him?'

'Stupid though it may seem, she still loves him – in an odd sort of way – and he provides all this.' She waved the fork in a great circle around the room.

There was silence as she paused briefly to bite a neat little arc out of a piece of toast. After a moment of thought, and accompanied by the crisp sound of her perfect white teeth crunching on it, added, 'Besides, have you any idea what that would be like for a lone woman going up against that kind of man with all that power and wealth? His ego couldn't tolerate it. He'd crush her. She wouldn't get to first base before she was wiped out financially; much better this way.' She finished the toast and dabbed at her mouth with her napkin.

She pushed back her chair and stood up, then called to Patience, the downstairs maid, to clear away the table. 'Come on,' she said, 'I want to have a bath – you can come in with me – and you need to shave.' She got up and pulled him along by one arm.

'You know,' she said, 'I want to be an artist. I'm learning to paint – I have a private tutor.'

The bathroom was cavernous, like a ballroom. It was bigger than anything Tom had ever seen before, even in the movies. Inside, the upstairs maid was standing by the huge sunken tub, except it wasn't a tub, more a small swimming pool.

'Thank you, Constance,' she said, dismissing her. 'I had her run it earlier because it takes so damn long to fill but it will still be warm enough.' She slipped out of her silk robe, revealing the perfect curves of her body and the delicate arch of her neck. Tom marvelled at her lack of self-consciousness as she stood there stripped. She half turned, holding her cupped hands over her breasts in an act of mock coyness, then with a little grin dropped into the warm water with a splash and sat down.

'I have the day planned,' she announced. 'It's Friday, we should go to the city and see a show on Broadway. Martins has the day off but we can drive – but not in that antique flivver of yours. My father has some exotic foreign thing in the auto shed, we'll take that. We can get down there in time for a late lunch.'

Tom laughed, and splashed her. 'Slow down a minute. I don't have a change of clothes with me. I have nothing fresh to wear. I need to go home first and get a few things.'

'No, no,' she protested. 'You can choose something from my father's wardrobe. He left all kinds of stuff behind.'

'Is he my size?'

She looked down at him through the water then put her hand over her mouth and giggled, 'Probably not.' She shuffled up closer till her legs rested on top of his then she pulled herself onto him and wrapped her legs around his waist. For the third time they sank into the arms of the deliciously mischievous cupid until they were completely filled with each other. Lying back, they let the water roll across their bodies. It really was turning out to be a most perfect day.

In her father's dressing room Tom tried on a pair of casual pants. She laughed. He put on a jacket. It hung around him like a shroud. She shook her head. Tom stood holding up the pants by the waistband. He looked in the mirror and then at Carey. 'I don't think this is going to work. Yeah, I think he is definitely bigger than me.'

Again she laughed, 'Well, definitely round the waistband.' She came up close and, reaching up on tiptoes, kissed his ear and whispered, 'But not everywhere.' He put his arms around her and the oversize pants fell down round his ankles. 'Pull 'em up, bub,' she joked. 'You've had all you're getting for one morning.'

'I have to go home and get things.'

'No, no', she countered, 'we'll go into the village. There's a men's shop. We'll buy what you need. I don't want to lose you for half the day.'

He took her face in his hands and gave it a little squeeze. 'It's Friday, I've taken the whole day off work, we can have the weekend together. Besides, I have to let my folks know my plans. It's only fair – they have their own lives and, besides, my mother is a worrier. If she doesn't hear from me she'll think the worst has happened – that's how she is.'

'Oh, not a momma's boy, are we?'

'No, but my dad got shot to hell in the last war and she doesn't really trust fate any more – that's all.'

'I thought he was still alive.'

'He is, but only from the neck down. What's in his head is anybody's guess. I wouldn't want to go through the hell he went through. He relives it nearly every day now.'

Carey hung her arms round his neck for a moment. 'Couldn't you just phone them?'

'I told you yesterday, we don't have a phone at the house. My father is phono phobic.'

'What's that?'

He laughed, 'Someone who has a fear of phones.'

She looked at him sternly. 'Are you kidding me?'

'Uh-huh, look it up in a dictionary if you don't believe me. I have to go and see them; I won't be long. Besides, I've already taken the day off work and we've got the whole weekend coming up.'

He went back into her bedroom. His clothes lay draped over a chair where he had discarded them last night. Carey followed him in with a large bottle of cologne water, which she dabbed on his shoulders and then splashed on to his chest. 'Here,' she said, rubbing her hands across him and massaging it into his body, 'this will make you feel really fresh and you'll smell oh so good.' Then, without warning, she stopped. 'No,' she said, 'this is not a good idea. This is my father's and you'll end up smelling like him and I wouldn't like that. I wouldn't like that at all. Quickly, go and wash it off.' It took Tom by surprise but he didn't argue. If it upset her then he would do as she asked.

When he was dressed she walked with him to where the Chrysler was parked at the back of the house. Martins had washed it and valeted the inside. He couldn't remember when it had last looked so clean.

'Don't be long, I'll miss you.'

'I'll hurry back,' he said, lingering for one last long soft kiss. 'I am going to hate being away from you.'

The Chrysler slowly crunched its way along the drive, turned into the street and then it was out of sight. Carey stood for a moment with her arms wrapped around herself, then she slowly walked back to the house. She went up the steps through the monumental front door of the outer lobby then through the pair of plate glass doors, opaque with engraved decorations, into the main hallway. She stood for a brief moment and contemplated their hideous enormity. Her father had commissioned the doors especially for the house. They had been created by the French designer, René Lalique, and manufactured in Paris. On them had been engraved images of modern industrial scenes with half-naked men toiling over crucibles of molten steel. As a child she had never liked the doors; they left her with dark thoughts and a sense of insecurity. There was something crude and rough about these images of working men with their iron-bound muscles and coarse features. Although she had not known it until her mother told her years after the event, there had been a serious falling out between her father and the architect, Frank Lloyd Wright, who thought that Lalique belonged to the earlier Art Nouveau movement and his work was not acceptable to be incorporated into the design. Wright relented only when he was allowed to dictate the theme of the engraved glass work.

Inside, the main hallway was palatial. The floors were marble flags with coloured stone inlays set in a geometrical pattern. On each side of the space two stairways swept in a curve up to the ceiling where they met on a concrete balcony with wrought iron balustrades. She found Constance polishing the hand rail on one of the stairways. She was talking with Vera, the housekeeper. They both stopped and looked down at the small figure standing in the large lonely space. 'Is there anything you'd like me to do for you Miss Caroline?' the housekeeper called out.

'No,' she said in a small abstract voice, and carried on into the depths of the house.

******

Tom reached home around three and found Martha busy as usual fussing over things in the kitchen. He could see her through the window as he came up the front steps. She looked pleased, he thought, and seemed to be singing. As he opened the front door she called out, 'Is that you Holly? How was the walk?' He stuck his head round the kitchen door, 'Hi, Ma.'

She dropped the large skillet she was holding onto the top of the stove and came over to him excitedly. She threw her arms around him and gave him the mandatory long hug. Then she stepped back and, still holding his arms, stood and looked at him admiringly. 'Good to see you, son. I was getting a tad worried when you didn't come home last night but I figured you'd be OK. I thought it was your father coming back in.'

'Dad has gone out. What's going on?'

'Oh, it's the dog. He's taken a real shine to that little critter. This is the third time in two days he's been out walking him. I don't know why but he's taken to it and that's a fact. You know he calls it Wheels?' Tom cocked his head a little to one side. There was a faint barking, then the sound of claws clicking on the steps.

'I think that's them now.' They both walked into the front hall to see the door open. The terrier was first through it and ran to Tom, jumping up at him and yapping excitedly. Tom went down on his haunches and it jumped into his arms. He stood up to see his father – a broad smile wreathed his face. He did not often see his father smile and it gave him a warm feeling to see it now. He hoped it would last, but secretly he held the fear that it was only temporary. He knew

135

how fragile his father was and knew that almost anything could destroy the moment. A wrong word or an old memory could wipe it all away and the blackness would return. But for now it was good – for now the mutt seemed to have saved him.

'How was the walk, Dad?'

'It was fine son, just fine. He got out there and chased a dog ten times his size. He's a spunky little guy; gonna be a real terror that one; aren't ya, Wheels.' He bent down towards the puppy and slapped his hands on his thighs, encouraging it to jump up. Wheels jumped in the air and, scooping him up in mid-jump, he cradled him in his arms and headed for the living room.

'How about some tea, honey?' he called over his shoulder. 'Come and sit with me a bit, son, and tell me how you are. Your mother was worried when you didn't come home last night – did she tell you?'

Martha motioned with her head towards the living room. 'Go and join him. Would you like some coffee?' Tom said he would and followed his father through to where he had installed himself in his comfortable chair and was playing with the puppy.

'So where did you stay last night?' His father asked. Martha came into the room with a tray and set it down on a small table.

Tom wasn't sure how he was going to handle this. He could say he had stayed with Tony but he hated to lie. On the other hand he was not quite ready to tell them he had spent the night with a girl and was planning to do the same for the next two nights. It wasn't so much that they would be shocked or disapprove as much as he was acutely embarrassed. They were his parents, a generation apart, their codes were different; it was a quandary. So he figured the best route out was to be as vague as possible – maybe modify the truth a little.

'I went for a drink with a friend I met through work,' he said, 'and we did the day in New York, watched the parades, saw the fireworks, had something to eat, and all went out for a few drinks. It got kinda late so they let me bunk down at their place.' He paused to see how that went down.

'That sounds like a fine day out,' Martha said, handing Holly his tea. 'Put the dog down, Holly, or you'll upset the cup.'

They sat for a while and talked about the parades. Holly said they'd had a quiet day but it was nice and they'd had lunch on the back porch, shaded from the sun. It was small talk and Tom was pleased to see his father so changed from his normal sullen mood, but at the back of his mind was Carey and he couldn't wait to get back to her. He felt a strange panicky sensation as if she might dissolve or change her mind, or just not be there when he got back. It was only a couple of hours and he was missing her irrationally. He just needed to be near her, to smell her perfume and touch her hair. And he hadn't yet told them he would be out all weekend. How the hell was he going to cover over that one without one daddy of a lie? In the end it was Martha who brought it to a head. She had gone back into the kitchen where she was rolling out pastry. 'I'm making a pie for dinner,' she called out. 'Are you in for dinner, Tom?'

He got up and went into the kitchen, looking over her shoulder. 'Looks like it'll be a great pie, Ma, but I'm not in tonight. I'll be going back to meet up with the others for a barbeque. It's down at Dobbs Ferry so I'll probably stay overnight.'

'Well, that'll be nice,' she said lovingly, 'it's good you have friends you can get together with? Will Tony and Mike be there?'

Tom hesitated and then said he didn't think so, they both had other things planned. 'I'll just go upstairs and throw a few things in a grip.'

Fifteen minutes later he came down and she kissed him her talisman kiss. He hugged her and said his goodbyes. 'It's really good about Dad and the dog,' he whispered, 'hope he hangs on in there.' Martha squeezed him tightly in one last hug, then let him go.

He went in to the front parlour where his father was sitting. 'I'm off, Dad, I'm away for the weekend.'

Holly smiled, 'I heard you tell your mother.' Then he beckoned him closer and, speaking softly so that Martha shouldn't hear, said, 'You can tell me her name later,' and he reached forward and gave Tom a friendly nudge on the shoulder. Then he put out a hand and both men shook on the secret.

'It's Carey, Dad, but don't say anything to Ma. It's early days yet and I don't know where it's going.'

'You can count on me son – good luck.'

As he walked to the front door the puppy followed, his stubby docked tail sticking up like an aerial as he pegged along in Tom's wake, his little claws clicking on the polished oak floor. Tom opened the door. The puppy sat down and looked up at him, expecting to go on another expedition into the new world beyond the front steps. Tom stood and looked down at the little animal. The puppy looked back at him, his sharp eyes like two black buttons sewn on to a toy. He marvelled at how this small creature seemed to be bringing such a profound change into his father's world. He didn't understand why, but a new man had appeared. The old Holly, the one Tom had known all his life, the one who had dwelt deep inside the morose darkness of a troubled soul, damaged by things Tom could never properly understand, was changing. He seemed to be coming out into the light. It was as if something deep inside had flipped a switch. Martha came to the door for a final hug and a kiss. When she finally let him go he bent down again to the dog and ran his hand across its little muzzle, tweaking the small leather patch of a nose.

'Sorry, Wheels, not this time. You look after Holly – you're doing a good job.'

Wheels yapped, Martha picked him up and, standing on the top step with the puppy cradled in her arms, waved Tom off.

The Chrysler seemed slow and clumsy after the ride in the Packard. He felt every bump on the route but every turn of the wheel and every jarring pothole took him closer to Carey and he was impatient to be there, just to be with her.

When he arrived the best of the afternoon had gone. Carey came running out of the house. She looked as if she had been crying. In one hand she held a large handkerchief. It wasn't what he'd been expecting. Since they'd first met she'd always been so self-assured, so much in control, so unshakably confident; now she was blubbing like a frightened little girl. He felt confused.

'Where have you been?' She cried, throwing her arms around his neck. She began kissing him desperately, violently. She clung to him and started to sob. 'I thought you were never coming back. I thought something awful had happened to you. What took you so long?'

He held her there, close to him, stroking her hair, telling her in a soft voice that everything was OK until the sobbing gradually tailed off into a whimper and then ceased. 'It's okay, honey,' he found himself whispering, though in fact he wasn't sure if it was or what had set her off.

She relaxed her arms and just stood there for a moment sniffling. Then she pulled back as if nothing had happened and linked her arm around his. She dabbed at her cheeks with the handkerchief she had been carrying. 'Now look what you've done,' she smiled her little girl smile. 'You've made me cry and now my nose is all red and my eyes have gone puffy. Let's go inside. I'll tell Patience to make us some tea. Then we can talk and I shall feel better – but first I need to go and fix my face. I look awful.'

He squeezed her gently then let his hand slip down until it rested on her perfectly formed bottom. 'You look fantastic just as you are.'

'No,' she said, 'I'll see you in the drawing room.'

He laughed, 'Which one is that?'

'The big one on the front that looks over the lawns, silly.'

Tom entered through a pair of high teak doors decorated with intricate rare wood marquetry. The room was very large; it had ceiling to floor windows with metal glazing bars in the latest Art Deco style and it struck him that the house had been designed as a single entity, right the way down to the furnishings. It was a monster of a building. It trumpeted power and money; it was redolent of the aggressive dynamism that had built the Taylor empire.

Outside, the whitewashed concrete facades with curved corners and a low domed roof, snaked around by the sinuous curves of a fluid balcony, did less to soften it than give it an air of menace. It squatted among the lawns and ornamental trees like a large pale concrete toad. It felt more like a bunker than a house. Tom remembered that as he had entered the property he had driven through a large iron gateway with the name of the house arching over the top: BRUNESSEMER – a combination of Brunel and Bessemer, two great names associated with the metal on which Warren Taylor had founded his fortune.

He sat on a modern Mackintosh chair and Patience brought in tea and cakes. She set the tray down on a small onyx table with chromed metal legs, and left him to wait. The china was fine Limoges; bright colours and geometric patterns.

'This house is too big for three people to live in,' Tom said casually after Carey had finally joined him.

'There are four of us,' she replied in a matter-of-fact voice. 'I have a brother, Wendell, but he doesn't come home often. He spends most of his time with his friends in Philadelphia.'

'What does he do – in Philadelphia, that is?'

'Oh, I don't know,' she said, sounding bored. 'Do we have to talk about him?'

Tom felt flustered; he had upset her and he pulled back rapidly. 'No, of course not. I didn't mean to pry.'

'Of course, we have the hired help too,' she went on. 'Patience and Constance have rooms upstairs and Martins lodges in the annex with Mrs Martins – she's the cook – and then there's our housekeeper, Vera, she lives in. So you see that's quite a lot of people, and then we need rooms for the guests when they stop over. We used to have a butler but Mother didn't like having a man in the house – not after my father and all that.' Her voice had gone flat and the tone was irritated. There was a hint of something that seemed to say, 'Okay, if you want me to justify my home, I can.'

Then, without warning, she smiled again and her face softened. It was a smile full of warmth; it was as if something had darkened her world momentarily, like when a cloud passes across the sun fleetingly, blotting out its light and bringing a sudden chill to the air. Then, as quickly as it came it is gone and the world seems bright again.

'Of course,' she added with a mischievous grin, 'we don't need a guest room for you – you can share mine.'

She got up and, standing behind his chair, draped her arms around his neck and pushed his head deep into her soft breasts. 'Although, if you stay here when Mother is home we'll need to put you in one of the guest rooms. Mother is a bit of a prude.' She ruffled his hair.

'After our tea we can go to bed,' she said, kissing and nibbling his ear, 'and then this evening we'll take one of the cars and drive down to Broadway. Let's go and dance at the Roxy. Fred Waring is playing there – I think Fred Waring is brilliant – don't you, darling? Or, if you would prefer, we could go to the theatre. There's a brand new musical, *Pal Joey*; it's got Gene Kelly taking the lead. Don't you just love his dancing? I think he's better than Astaire – don't you think so?'

139

In the garage they found Martins who had custody of all the auto keys. 'We'll take the convertible, Martins,' she said. 'You can bring it round to the front.'

The car was breathtaking. Martins got out and handed the keys to Tom. 'I think, sir,' he said in a clipped English accent, 'that you will enjoy driving this motor, if I may say so.' Here he used the English word 'motor' referring to the car. Before coming to America he had been in service with the Earl of Suffolk and the gloss of the aristocracy had stuck to him – especially in his very precise speech – it was why Warren Taylor had chosen to employ him. There was an air of impeccability that surrounded him.

Tom took the keys but just stood there looking at this thing in front of him. It was streamlined and elegantly sleek. The lines were simple but seductive. The fenders flowed over the wheels like a wave passing over a shoal of sand. All the lamps, the door handles, the hood clips were discreetly faired into the bodywork so that nothing seemed clumsy or out of place. He had never seen a more beautiful automobile. Compared with this, Tony's much admired Cord looked like a hippopotamus standing alongside a gazelle.

'What is it, Martins?' Carey said, looking at it as if she had not really noticed it before.

'It's French, Miss Caroline; it's a Bugatti – a Bugatti Type 57sc. I understand it to be one of the finest touring motors in the world.'

Martins was right; the drive was like a dream. The ride was flawlessly smooth but Tom always felt in control. It went through the bends like it was on rails and the acceleration was an instant response that built rapidly and inexorably. When the speedo needle flicked over the 110 mark she slipped her hand down inside his pants and stroked his bare thigh. The grin of pleasure on her face was as broad as a Cheshire cat. 'God,' she shouted through the roar of the exhausts and the rush of the slipstream, 'I never knew a car could be so erotic!'

They went to the Roxy and danced to Fred Waring's Syncho Sympho band until they dropped. 'You know,' she said later, 'you were pretty good back there on the dance floor – for a backwoodsman, that is.' After they could dance no more they went on to the Stork Club for supper. When they drew up outside the restaurant the car pulled such a crowd the doorman had to hold it back just to let them step out of it. Afterwards Tom laughed and said he would bet they were trying to guess who the celebrities were driving in it.

Later, as they drove back up to Dobbs Ferry, he took it easy so she could doze comfortably on his shoulder. The day had been hot and the night air was still deliciously warm. 'Tomorrow,' she said sleepily, 'I'm going to teach you how to play tennis.'

******

140

He woke lying flat on his back with the sheets of the bed wound round his legs. Carey was still sleeping, her head settled softly on his chest and her arm thrown over his shoulder, her dark tousled hair covering her face. He moved slightly, trying not to wake her but she lifted her head and murmured a comfortable little sigh. She cuddled up closer to him, then moving her head down his body kissed his belly. Taking her in both his hands he lifted her bodily up the bed until her face was up against his and their lips met in a long soft embrace. Then he wrapped her body in his arms and gently rolled over until he was looking down on her.

'Now, what's this about tennis?' he said.

'Later, it's too early and I want you. You should make love to me before we do anything else this morning.' He looked longingly at her and the only thing he could think of was how good it was just to be there holding her. He pulled her close to him feeling the soft warmth of her body.

They drove to the tennis club in the Bugatti. I could get used to this, Tom thought to himself as he sat back in the pale tan leather seat and let his hand slide over the ivory and chrome spoked steering wheel.

As they drove into the club grounds two couples who had been standing talking to each other stopped and looked at the car. Then one of their number recognized Carey and waved. They came over and greeted her. The two men were attired in tennis slacks and wore their shirts with the neck open. One had a gaudy silk cravat knotted around his throat. Tom was immediately conscious that the grey flannels he was wearing might not be quite the thing in this place. The women were both in the new fashionable shorts with a skirt overlay that showed a lot of leg but modestly hid everything above mid-thigh.

'Darling,' one of the women said in an exaggerated voice, 'so nice to see you again. We haven't seen you for ages. Where have you been hiding?' She looked over at Tom who was just getting out of the car. 'Hmm, that's nice – where did you find it – and what's happened to Douglas?'

'Hello, Cynthia'. Carey leant forward and kissed the woman in the continental manner, touching her cheek but kissing the air to one side. She did it twice in what was then the Parisian fashion. 'Douglas is the ex,' she responded to the question. 'We don't talk about him anymore.'

The other woman joined them and embraced in the same formal manner. She had a bright blue Alice band across her forehead, holding back a main of blond hair. Both women had that look that spoke of careful grooming in expensive salons. 'Hello Carey, are you well?' There was more formality than inquiry about the question of her health.

'No Douglas, I see.'

'No, darling, done and dumped,' Carey replied sharply, 'and before you ask, Nigel went the same way too.'

'My, but we're racy – and who is this divine vision?' said Cynthia, casting an eye over towards Tom who had now become engaged in conversation with the two men.

'His name is Tommy,' she replied curtly, 'and Margaret,' she looked fiercely at the women with the blue band, 'just stow it. This is something special and I don't want you spoiling it. Okay!'

'Darling,' Cynthia replied in breathless hushed tones, 'Do I hear wedding bells at last?'

'Just can it,' Carey hissed. 'Come and meet him and try to behave like ladies – if you know how to – and if you don't, then button up.' She led the two women over to where the men had gathered around the Bugatti and were talking cars. They had the hood up and were poking around the engine compartment.

'David, Jerry, how nice to see you again,' she said, with a hint of forced enthusiasm. She had known the two couples for years and had been at school with the girls. But they were too closely associated with her past and there were things they might say that she didn't want said, especially in front of Tom.

Jerry, sporting the paisley cravat, had married Cynthia five years earlier and the wedding had been a biggish society affair. His family were bankers but they had been hit hard by the stock market crash and there was more facade than substance to them.

David and Margaret were similar but a rung lower down the social ladder. David owned and operated a car showroom and his father had been the owner of a small gas station and garage. Margaret was more pretentious; her father was an accountant who had married into a relatively wealthy family, but they too had been hit hard by the crash and they were no longer quite top drawer.

They all kissed again and this time Tom had to join in the charade. David dropped down the hood and secured it. 'Beautiful car, Carey; didn't know Warren had such exotic tastes. Coachwork by Van Vooren, I believe – very stylish.'

'Well, you know my father, David; a man with impeccable tastes.' She assumed a contemptuous expression.

'What do you do Tom?' Jerry asked.

'I'm with Imperial Life in their New York office.'

'Is it interesting work?' David said in tones that were meant to sound dismissive. It was David's style and Carey had seen it before. He was an insecure person and liked to put others down, to diminish them and make them look inferior. He liked to build his ego at the expense of others and she was not going to let it happen to Tom.

She quickly butted in before Tom had a chance to answer. 'We have some tennis to play, will you excuse us?' She linked her arm in his and walked away

142

with him calling out over her shoulder, 'Nice to see you; we must meet up again when there is more time.'

'I hate them,' she said, looking at Tom, 'they're so pretentious.'

Carey did not teach Tom to play tennis that afternoon. Instead she introduced him to the club coach, then sat and watched him practice. Seeing him like that, she realized how lithe and agile he was. His body moved with a natural harmony; he was quick to learn and from his poise she guessed he would be a good partner to have in a match. Afterwards the coach pronounced that he was a natural and said he couldn't believe Tom hadn't played the game before. Tom said he had watched it but, like shooting, it was all about having an eye for a moving target, and hitting a ball was no different from shooting a running buck. All he needed was practice.

That evening Vera made them a supper of cold cuts and afterwards, as the sun went down, they sat out on the lawn with glasses of champagne and watched the sky, looking for shooting stars.

'What would you like to do tomorrow?' Carey asked as they lay there on the still warm grass, her on her back and him with his head in her lap, and then followed quickly with, 'I know, why don't we go into the country,' before he could answer. 'I could get Vera to pack us a picnic,' she went on.

'You know what I would like to do in the evening,' Tom said slowly, still gazing up at the stars.

'Tell me.'

'I would like to go back to the Russian restaurant and have a quiet intimate supper; just you, me and that bear.'

'Then that's what we'll do.' She sat up and smoothed his cheek with the back of her hand. 'Have you ever hunted bears?'

He shook his head. 'Some people do but I can't see the point; they're not good to eat and mostly they stay out of your way. They're quite shy really, although you don't want to be around them when there are cubs. Mothers with cubs can get aggressive – and you need to stay clear of big males if they are marking out their territory.'

He was silent for a moment, then admitted, 'I shot one once – a big male grizzly, but then he had me cornered and he was really bad tempered. I didn't have a choice. I felt a bit sad about it afterwards.'

'Never mind,' she said, stroking his forehead. 'Our bear won't get bad tempered – as long as he has a cocktail.'

They both laughed, then Tom sat up and kissed her; a long, slow, warm, kiss.

CHAPTER 15

Hudson Bay, 8 July 1940

Tom arrived in the office early. He'd met Carey at Dobbs Ferry, hanging out of the window waving frantically until she saw him. On the train they had sat side by side and talked about their plans to meet as often as they could each week and have lunch together; and they would have the weekends too.

'With Mother around you'll have to stay in the guest wing,' Carey warned him with a little laugh. 'She's very priggish but we won't let that spoil things. I can come to your room secretly at night – we'll be like secret lovers. It'll be so exciting,' and she linked her arm with his and gave it a squeeze.

At the terminus they parted with a kiss and went their separate ways.

******

Two hundred miles south, at the Shack in Washington DC, General Marshall had called a meeting. A group of military personnel and advisors had been ordered to attend the meeting which was being held to provide a briefing document for the President. They were to meet in the conference suite; there they gathered around a large oval table. Marshall sat center stage, flanked by Joe King and Hap Arnold, the three of them comprising the Joint Chiefs of Staff. Either side of them were Ira Eaker, Henry Stimson, the only civilian in the room, and there was a major of the Intelligence Corps. Sitting on the opposing side of the curve were Generals Patton and Stilwell – 'Vinegar Joe' as he was known to his men. Next to them sat Fleet Admirals Leahy and Stark. Finally there were two Army Air Corps officers: Colonel James Doolittle and Colonel Carl Spaatz. Both the flyers were heavily outranked by the rest of the room.

Marshall cleared his throat. He looked serious. 'Gentlemen, thank you for making yourselves available at such short notice. I know some of you were on furlough and have had to break it to be here and I apologize to you and your families if it has interrupted a special time or disrupted a vacation. However, I have brought you together here today because you represent some of the best expertise at my disposal.' He looked along the line of expectant faces for a moment.

'I won't beat about the bush. We face a serious problem. As you all know, in the last 48 hours some intelligence has come into our hands that is a cause for grave concern.' He turned to the officer from the Signals Intelligence Group. 'Major Gregson – you're on.'

Gregson stood up, then picking up a sheaf photos pushed them across the table to Stilwell who was directly opposite. 'General, if you would be so good as to distribute these right and left of you. There are two photos, please retain one of each.'

Stilwell split the pile, passing some in each direction and holding back two for him. They were grainy shots in monochrome: one was of the deck of a vessel, which was clearly a supply ship; the other appeared to show some landing stages, sheds and cranes.

Gregson continued, 'Last week we got a report from one of our agents operating in northern Canada. According to that report there is an unusually high volume of shipping in an area from Halifax in the south up to and into Hudson Bay. The agent was not able to get close enough on the ground to investigate. He reports that the whole area had been closed to public traffic. However, he was able to get this photo before he had to quit the area. The photo was taken from the cover of the wooded hills just south of the Hudson Bay foreshore.' He held up the picture of the landing stages.

'We have analyzed these structures within the image and conclude that the pontoons you see in the middle ground of the picture are a prefabricated harbor, which is being assembled on the southernmost landfall of the bay. You will also see what appears to be a road leading away to the edge of the picture. Comparing it with maps we have of the area, we believe this to be a newly constructed road. Now this road looks likely to be heading for an intersection with a good quality logging road lying just south of that area. That logging road in turn continues south all the way through to Highway 1, the Trans Canadian.'

He paused to drink some water, then went on. He held up the photo and pointed to the crane-like structures. 'We think this is heavy lifting gear. From the mass and the shape of these objects we believe we are looking at wharf cranes. The lines you see radiating from them back to those dark patches are almost certainly rails. We think the darker patches are concrete hard-standing for whatever those cranes are lifting.'

Patton interrupted. He raised his hand perfunctorily. 'Major, a question. Do we have any idea of the lift capacity of those cranes? Could they lift a tank – say, a main battle tank for example?'

'It's hard to say, but again the mass indicates a substantial lifting ability, maybe as much as 100 tons.'

'So, they'd lift a tank?'

'I think that is a safe assumption, General.'

'Thank you, Major. Do continue.'

Gregson put the photo down on the table and picked up the second one. 'Item two.' Again he held up the photo. 'Item two is a photo of a supply ship shot by one of our reconnaissance planes that overflew the area two days ago. The vessel is an RFA ship. We have identified it as HMS *Regent*, a supply and repair vessel of the British Navy, but it now appears to be carrying cargo.'

'Look at these dark patches,' he pointed to the deck of the ship. 'What you are looking at there are cargo covers. This ship is carrying deck cargo, which suggests that below decks she's stuffed to the gunwales. We cannot be sure at this time why a repair and supply vessel, which would normally carry parts and fuel for fleet maintenance at sea, is carrying this kind of load. It was not part of a large convoy but instead a link in what appears to be a shuttle operation, which we believe is now operating between the port of Portsmouth on the south coast of Britain and the areas around Hudson Bay and Prince Edward Island. We know it is a British vessel and it is flying British colors. However, we are picking up radio traffic from the ships involved in this operation and, surprisingly, much of that traffic is in German. It is, of course, in code and we aren't yet able to decipher what is being sent.'

He put down the photo and paused again, giving time for the information to sink in.

'Item three. Four days ago Canada closed its airspace to all commercial overflights from Quebec up to the Hudson Bay. That air space remains closed as I speak.

'Finally we have item four. You will be aware that we have broken the Japanese code named Purple. This allows us to monitor all Japanese radio transmissions in and out of their Embassy here in Washington. Yesterday we intercepted a signal from Tokyo into that Embassy. It was an instruction to dispatch a high-ranking member of their military attaché's office to Ottawa for a meeting with his opposite number in the German Embassy. The subject of the visit was identified as a top secret operation code named Gottlieb. We have not previously picked up any reference to this so we must assume it relates to a new initiative between the Germans and the Japanese.'

He paused for a moment, then concluded, 'That gentlemen, is the picture as we have it at this time.' He sat down. There was a murmur of conversation in the room as those around the table exchanged brief views with their colleagues.

Marshall leant forward with both hands resting on the table in front of him. A hush fell over the room. 'Thank you, Major.'

For a moment his gaze swept the men sitting around the table then, addressing them all, said, 'Individually, each or any of these items would arouse our interest because they are happening close to our borders and it is our business to take note of anything that may affect our interests. However, put them together and they take on a new character that is not simply interesting; it starts to look menacing. So, what do we know and what should we do? Canada is sovereign territory and the British are now declared neutrals. They are entitled to go about their own business in their own backyards. Until now both have been allies of the US and if no longer as close as they were, nevertheless would normally be viewed as friendly neighbors – or at least as non-hostile to US interests.' Again, he stopped for a moment to let what he had said penetrate his audience.

'But the situation here no longer allows us to view the activity up there as normal. We can't be sure but it looks like the British, probably in concert with the Germans, are establishing some kind of base. We have no way of knowing for the present what their intentions are but clearly it has a purpose and I think we can safely assume it has a connection with Gottlieb – whatever that is. We need to monitor this activity closely. We need to know what this is. Is it a transit camp of some kind and, if so, why up there? Is it a supply dump – if so, what is it going to supply? What's going on up there?'

For a moment there was silence in the room, then Patton interrupted it by addressing Hap Arnold. 'Can your fly boys get more photo reconnaissance?'

Arnold threw the question over to the airmen, looking at Doolittle and Spaatz. 'Carl, can we?'

Spaatz shrugged. 'We can do high-level overflights but with closed airspace we'd need to be very high – unless you want to upset the Canadians. I'm not sure they would tell us much more than we already have.' Henry Stimson indicated he didn't like the prospect of a diplomatic incident.

Stilwell looked down the table at Spaatz. 'What about a low-level buzz in an unmarked plane? Is that possible?' Spaatz looked at Doolittle. 'How about that, Jimmy?'

Doolittle raised his eyebrows and rubbed his nose, then smiled. 'It'll be a challenge but we can try. I can't say how they'll respond if they get on to us. I might just give that one a go myself.'

James Doolittle already had a reputation in the Corps for being someone who would take on risky assignments. Before he came into the military he had been a barnstormer in a flying circus and was well respected as a man for a dangerous mission. 'The best way in would be off the deck of a carrier. I could come down from the north and get in a low pass. We'd need to trick the plane up a bit to make it hard to identify and I don't think we'd get more than one pass – two would be tops.'

Admiral King nodded his agreement. 'Bill,' he looked across the table at Leahy, 'who's best placed for this one?'

Leahy turned to Stark. 'We've got a light carrier we could use, the USS *Long Island*. She's down in Virginia right now but she could be got up north in maybe three days.'

Stark nodded his agreement. 'I think that's do-able.'

Marshall looked around his audience again. 'We can't say what's going on up there right now but we need to start guessing. We need to ask ourselves what it is we would be doing in their shoes.' He looked across at Patton. 'George, what would you do?'

'Well, I sure as hell wouldn't pile up stuff like that unless I had plans to use it, so you have to look around and ask where that stuff is going.'

'Too damn right. Those Limey quitters won't be going to all this trouble without a plan,' Stilwell said in his usual acerbic tone. 'The weather up there is shit for half the year and barely tolerable for the rest, so why choose that spot – unless it's right on the doorstep of where you're gonna use it?'

Patton cut in again. 'Of course, it might just be they're dumping there because they figure it's hard for us to see what's going on from this distance and they wanna keep this thing under wraps. And if that is the case and that's why they're up there then we better start worrying because you don't do that kinda thing unless you're planning to get the jump on someone.'

Marshall folded his arms and leant forward again; he looked up and down the table. 'How about Alaska – the oil fields; could that be the target?'

Patton thought for a moment. 'It would make sense. It's the one thing they're most short on – oil. Stilwell agreed. Logistically he thought it made sense.

'OK,' Marshall said in a slow deliberate tone, 'Henry, do you want to add in your two cents?'

Henry Stimson, who had all this time been listening and saying nothing, now took off his glasses and slowly polished them. It was as if he were giving his audience time to build up their expectation. 'Gentlemen, I want to add another small piece in this jigsaw we have in front of us. Following the uncovering of these events I requested the State Department to call in the Ambassadors of Britain, Germany and Canada. We asked them for an explanation.' He paused.

'And?' Patton questioned.

'Well, it's kind of interesting. The British say it forms part of an agreement in their peace deal with the Germans. They have agreed to provide bases in Britain and their colonies to supply German naval requirements. They claim they have placed the Canadian base as far away from the American border as they practically can in order not to alarm the US government.'

Stilwell let out a derisive grunt. 'Sounds like a goddam lie to me. Are we going to believe them?'

'General,' Stimson continued, 'the protocol of diplomacy proscribes outright lying but allows evasion.' He paused again, then continued, 'The German Ambassador attended in person, which tells me they think it's important to keep us happy. He confirmed what the British had said but added that their concern was to prevent an incursion into Canada by the Soviets. Notwithstanding that, for the moment, Russia and Germany have signed a non-aggression pact. It appears the Nazis see communism as the next major struggle. They tell us the Soviets will eventually mount an all-out attack on capitalism. They think America and Eastern Europe will become the prime targets in any such encounter.'

Stilwell again grunted. 'Of course, we know the Krauts are bigger damn liars than the Limeys'.

'I won't take issue with that for the moment, General; however, we can't discount what they say – but let's move on. The Canadians tell us they have acquiesced in the establishment of a number of facilities by the British as a condition precedent to a full independence treaty they are currently negotiating. This makes sense to me and I am inclined to believe what the Canadians are saying.'

Stilwell turned to Patton with a look that questioned the logic of Stimson's last statement. 'If you'll excuse the forthright question, Mr Secretary, are you saying we believe the Germans are looking to shield us from some speculated attack by the Soviets?'

Stimson raised his index finger to interrupt Patton. 'No, General,' he said in a measured tone, 'that's not what I have said. I'll put it a little more plainly. I believe the Canadians probably are trading that Hudson Bay base with the British as part of an independence deal. I don't think they necessarily know what the British and Germans are planning to do with it, though. Of course, when it comes to the British it's a little different. I think it's highly likely they are being duped by the Germans and most probably don't have any real idea of what is going on. I am sure they believe the official line the Germans are feeding to us. When it comes to the Germans, do I believe this is a maneuver to protect capitalism?' And here Stimson smiled sardonically, 'It could be true. But I would counsel you to approach it with caution.'

He held up both hands in feigned protest. 'I am only the Secretary for War; you gentlemen are the soldiers. You must decide and advise.'

'Did we ask about Gottlieb?' Patton queried.

Stimson shook his head. 'No, to do so might get them thinking we had broken Purple and we wouldn't want that.'

Stark now joined the fray. 'It seems to me that the Germans and the British Navy are coming together and that is going to make life real edgy up in the North Atlantic. We are going to need a lot more ships if it comes to a showdown.'

King motioned with his hand to where Stimson sat. 'Henry is getting that seen to. We are about to go to the House with the biggest appropriations bill in US history. I just hope they are smart enough up there to see the sense of it.'

'We're going to build a lot more of everything,' Marshall added, 'and the President is again upping the recruitment initiative, so there will be a lot more men across the services.' He surveyed the room and then looked right and left at his colleagues, nodding as he did so and indicating that he was winding up the meeting.

'Gentlemen, thank you for your attendance here today. I don't have to tell you that today's briefing is of the highest level of secrecy. You will need to go away and think on the situation and you will be kept updated on any developments. If we could crack the German code as we have with Purple we could find out just who is lying and about what. Until then we need to be ready for anything. That is all, gentlemen.'

Marshall stood up; the assembled company came to its feet and saluted.

CHAPTER 16

1 August 1940

In the back garden Wheels was barking loudly, running round in circles chasing his tail and anything else that caught his attention. He was no longer a puppy; he had grown quite a bit in the last six weeks or so. Holly had now become devoted to the little dog and went everywhere with him. Martha marveled at the change in the man she had loved and nursed through all of the past twenty years and then some. Since the mutt arrived Holly had changed so much and so quickly it must be, she thought, a miracle. Every night she prayed that his deliverance would survive another day. Every morning she woke to the same anxiety that he would relapse into the old morose Holly and during the day she would keep asking him if everything was alright, at which he would smile and say, 'Everything is just fine, honey.'

Tom woke to the sound of the dog and turned over lazily in his bed. It was Saturday and there was no going to the office, but there was work to do nevertheless. In the garden the cherries had all been picked a month before and now the apples were ripening and would need to be gathered. The grass had to be mowed. There were logs to be split for the winter. He lay there a while longer listening to the dog until it was interrupted by another sound. An engine burst into life. Then he heard the sound of the mower. The dog got even more excited and barked louder. For a few moments he lay there listening to the noise and wondering what was going on. Now fully awake, he sat up. He was the only person in the household to use the mower, but there it was with the little engine sputtering away and the blades ringing as they engaged with the chain that drove them, spinning frantically through the grass, snipping it short and spitting it into the catcher box behind. He went to the window and opened it to look out and see who was using the machine. The warm green smell of freshly cut summer grass filled his senses. Down on the lawn below he was greeted by a sight he had never thought to see. Holly was hanging on to the handle bars and striding behind the machine with Wheels bouncing along behind him, barking and snapping at the green stream of grass that flowed up from the blades in a magical arc then fell to be caught neatly in the open mouth of the catcher.

Downstairs Martha was watching. 'It's another first,' she said as she kissed her son good morning.

'I can't believe it Ma – he's changed so much.' They both went to the back porch and stood there for a moment watching, then Martha called out that he should stop and come in for breakfast.

'Do you have plans for the day?' she asked Tom.

'I was going to cut the grass but it seems these days we have a new gardener. Then I was figuring on going to play tennis at this new club I've joined in Dobbs Ferry.'

'Well now,' Holly butted in, 'you can find something else to do, I'm sure, but right now me and Wheels just found out how much fun you can have with that thing.' He leant down and patted the dog, which had just parked itself by his chair. Wheels looked up expectantly and Holly picked up a piece of bacon from his plate, handing it down to him.

Martha tutted but smiled. 'Don't let him have yours,' she scolded Holly, 'he can have his afterwards.'

Holly looked down at the dog, raising his eyebrows and shaking his head in mock disapproval. 'You hear that, Wheels. Ma says you have to wait. So you go sit in your box now.' He pointed to the box and to Tom's surprise it went obediently over to the old wooden crate, stepped in, curled round a couple of times and then, having found a comfortable space, lay down with its chin on its paws.

'I'm impressed,' Tom said.

'Training and discipline,' Holly replied, looking a little bit cocky. 'And I tell you he learns real quick.'

'You know Dad, we should get him a proper dog basket. That old crate doesn't look too comfortable.'

'Maybe you're right.'

After breakfast Holly and Wheels resumed their game in the garden. 'I'm off,' Tom said. As she kissed him Martha said softly, 'When are you going to bring her home to meet us?' She took a step back and looked lovingly at him.

'How did you know?'

'Oh, just little things; you've been out a lot, and you look happier – and that's not just because your father has improved. A woman notices these things; especially a mother.' Tom shuffled uncomfortably.

'I will, Ma, when the time is right – when I'm more sure.'

Martha hugged him again. 'So aren't you at least going to tell me her name?' Tom looked sheepish. He felt a little guilty at not having told his mother and what with her having guessed all along.

'It's Carey, Ma, and she's wonderful – I can't tell you how wonderful.'

'So bring her home and show her off. Has she met your friends?'

'No, nobody; not Tony, not Mike – nobody.'

'Why not?'

He shrugged. 'I don't really know. I suppose I'm scared we might not make it together and it would be so hard to bear if she'd met everyone and become part of my life. I guess I'm frightened of losing her.' He gave a little shrug, closing the conversation.

Martha let out her breath in a long sigh and tilted her head to one side. Shaking her head very gently, she looked deep into his eyes seeing the uncertainty that hid there. 'Well,' she said after a moment, 'I guess we'll have to wait until you're ready. But don't keep us waiting too long.' She folded her arms giving him a long sideways look and thought how beautiful he looked standing there. 'You know what I think – she's a lucky girl to find a boy like you. You're kind and thoughtful, the way your father was when I first met him – and is becoming again.'

Then she suddenly became quite animated as she remembered some news she had forgotten to give him. 'Did I tell you he's going to take me to a dance? I haven't danced in more than twenty years. Can you imagine that? It's almost like we were young again.'

'I'm so happy for you both, Ma. You deserved to be dealt a better hand than you got.'

Out back the sound of the motor mower spluttered to a halt and a moment later Holly came into the kitchen with Wheels running at his heels. 'Boy I don't know when I had such fun. I'd forgotten how useful a machine can be.'

'You'll be wanting to drive the car next,' Tom joked. 'Then what'll I do?'

Holly looked slightly awkward. 'Well, now you come to mention it, I probably will. It's the darndest thing but I never thought about how we would get to this dance we're going to next week. It's too far to walk. I guess I'll just have to get back behind the wheel again and learn how to use it.'

At this they all laughed because the idea of Holly ever driving again had never really entered their thoughts before. Now he was recovering his old self and everything seemed to be happening so fast, it slowly sank into Tom that he would have to make other arrangements – to find a car of his own. He had some money saved but he'd always thought of it as a security, something to fall back on if times ever got bad again. It was true the Depression years were waning; more men had jobs and America was working again, but those bad years of his childhood still colored his attitude towards the way he planned his life. Like a lot of Americans, deep down inside he took nothing on trust. Everything, he knew, could change on a dime; a fortune could disappear overnight and what felt solid and reliable one day could crumble on the next and be blown away on the wind.

******

He met Carey at the country club and for the first time they played tennis together. He was, as the coach had said, a natural and he had to restrain himself from winning the game too quickly. After two wins in quick succession he let her beat him but she knew he'd deliberately lost and gently chastised him.

'You know,' she said as they left the court, 'we should challenge Jerry and Cynthia to a doubles match. They're so smug because they always win everything, but you know what? I think we'd beat them.' And she swung on his arm adding, 'Well, you would beat them, I'd just be along for the ride.'

In the clubhouse they had lunch and talked about what they would do with the weekend. Tom was apprehensive. He would be staying as a house guest at Brunessemer and it had the feel of an official invitation about it. He would be meeting her mother and sister for the first time. It was unknown territory and he wasn't sure how to respond.

On Friday he had left the office during the lunch break and gone to a menswear store on Fifth Avenue. There he had taken advice from the sales assistant who had guided him through what he might be expected to wear in the morning and how to dress for the evening. He'd bought tennis whites for the court, then two shirts, a pair of cavalry twill pants, a silk paisley patterned cravat in reds and yellows as well as a light jacket and a pair of Italian shoes in soft brown leather. The sales assistant was a dapper looking man in his middle age. Attired in an impeccable dark suit, he had an air of quiet patronizing authority about him. Painstakingly he led Tom away from what he considered poor choices, looking disdainfully every time he picked up something he considered 'not quite right for sir'. When it came to the evening wear he said in his opinion it was unlikely he would be expected to dress formally for dinner. It was, he assured Tom, no longer the custom. The world, he stated with great authority, had moved properly into the twentieth century and the latest fashion was casual. It was, he counselled, still *de rigueur* for banquets and official occasions or grand gatherings like a ball; however, for country weekends it was no longer in vogue. But at the last minute Tom had packed a tuxedo just in case – though he wasn't at all sure if it was the right thing to wear for the evening.

He arrived at the house feeling uncertain of himself. This was to be the first time of meeting her family. What would they think of him? What if they didn't like him or were openly hostile? Christ, he thought, this could be a disaster. On the drive down from Peekskill he imagined and reimagined a procession of nightmares that could bring his fragile world down around him in ashes. He harrowed the fertile ground of self-doubt over and over until finally he realized there was no point. Like a man condemned to the certainty of a walk from death row to the electric chair, his fate was now in the hands of others. He was who he was, he decided, and they would have to take him as he was, though tucked away in the back of his mind there still lurked the nagging doubt that he might somehow get caught out, wrong footed, made to look foolish like some dumb Okie. Then what would she think of him?

As he came into the driveway he felt self-conscious and exposed. Not for the first time he realized the old Chrysler marked him out for what he was. It was a giveaway – it shouted 'Look at me I'm poor!' The car scrunched noisily to a halt on the gravel. OK, he told himself, this is it.

Then Carey came down the steps and interrupted his paranoia. She flung her arms around his neck and hugged him tightly, almost like a child. And when she told him that her mother and sister had gone shopping in the village he immediately felt better. Patience took his bag and disappeared into the house. Tom started for the steps but Carey just stood there looking at him admiringly.

'Come on,' she shouted, 'let's go to the club. I want to see how you play. You can put the jalopy round the back – I'm not going out in that. We can take Wendell's car, that French thing. It's almost as beautiful as you.' She laughed loudly. 'Here,' she said throwing him the keys, 'I got these from Martins before he drove Mother to the village.'

It was late afternoon when they arrived back at the house. The big Packard was parked at the front door and Martins was handing bags and boxes to Patience and Vera, the housekeeper. The foreboding came right back at Tom like a boomerang and hit him hard in the chest. As they parked Martins walked over. 'Would you like me to take it back for you sir?' Martins held out his hand for the keys.

They walked up the steps. Inside the house Carey called out, 'Mother, we're back!'

Mrs Taylor appeared in the hallway. 'I wish you wouldn't shout like that, Carey.' She had almost sighed the words as if in resignation. 'It's so jarring.'

Standing there, she was exactly what Tom had been expecting. She was statuesquely tall. In his mind Tom had built up a picture of somebody imposing with the same startling looks he imagined she had passed on to her daughter – and here she was, in the flesh. He found himself confronted by a very self-assured woman. She was dressed in a remarkable floral silk print shirt and sheer black trousers with wide bell bottoms. A tight white shiny patent leather belt nipped her waist into an absurdly small circle. She wore her hair tight around her face, rinsed blue and with little kiss curls stuck tightly to her high cheek bones just in front of the ears. It had been crimped and permed in yesterday's style but it added a sense of purpose to an already powerful image. She walked across the hallway towards them.

'You must be Tom.' She held a long cigarette holder in one hand, which she waved in an exaggerated gesture. 'How nice to meet you. Carey has told me absolutely nothing about you but, never mind that, you can tell us all about yourself over dinner. I understand she calls you Tommy. Is it all right if we call you Tommy, or is that too familiar?'

Then, without waiting for his reply, she called out for Vera. 'Tell Mrs Martins we're five for dinner and find out what she is proposing.' Then, addressing Tom, said, 'I really don't have time for these domestic arrangements. Carey, show your young man to his room, there's a good girl. Cocktails on the terrace at seven fifteen and dinner is at eight.' Before Tom could gather himself she had turned and headed for another room.

Carey shrugged. 'I know what you're thinking – just don't say it.'

'I wasn't thinking anything – I didn't have time to think.'

'Precisely, nobody gets a word in with Mother. It's a performance; she's like it with everyone the first time. Our doctor says it's a nervous reaction. She's neurotic; terrified of new people.'

The first encounter had gone off OK. Tom felt better – more in control; perhaps the weekend wasn't going to be so bad after all.

At 7.30 he came onto the terrace wearing the twill pants, the light jacket and the cravat loosely tied at his throat. He instantly realized he was over-dressed. Carey and her mother were wearing blue jeans with shirts tied at the waist – it was the young look for 1940. Then, as if to make things worse, her sister appeared through the doorway. She was accompanied by a man; Tom guessed him to be in his mid-forties though his exaggerated Pancho Villa moustache made it hard to be sure. Maybe he was younger. He, too, was dressed very casual in a bright print shirt hanging loosely on his body and canvas trousers tied at the waist with a Mexican sash. Tom began to feel like an overdressed clown in a funeral procession.

'Nigel's an artist,' Carey whispered to Tom.

'This is my younger daughter, Alicia,' Mrs Taylor said in a voice that sounded like she was announcing a train arrival. 'Aly, come and meet Tom – or should I call you Tommy? Which do you think sounds better?'

'No, Mother,' Carey said coldly, 'you can call him Tom. Tommy is reserved for me!' She moved closer and took his arm as if to say this is my property – keep off. She looked at him for confirmation of the statement. There was a difficult silence. Tom shuffled uncomfortably. He couldn't think of what to say so he just gave her a peck on the cheek. It seemed to have filled the moment better than any words and Carey gave him a little squeeze.

Aly came over and kissed Tom lightly on the cheek. She was 17 and still had the slightly pudgy look of the high school about her. She was shorter than Carey and more filled out; more rounded and curvy with mid-length brown hair that was loose and bouncy. A red band across the forehead held it off her face. She was not plain, Tom thought; in fact she was quite pretty but she lacked the

156

stunning looks of her older sister. Like the others, Aly was also casually dressed; her simple blouse and skirt a careless understatement.

There was another silence. This time Nigel came to the rescue. He held out his hand and shook Tom's. It was a handshake of surprising vigor. 'Hello, I'm Nigel.' His grip was unexpectedly strong. He was not as tall as Tom and looked quite slender, but the look was deceptive. Underneath the loose shirt was a man with wiry muscles and no fat to spare. He had the look of an artist but not the feel of an artist. As if to compound the anomaly, he stepped lightly over to Mrs Taylor and with a little bow took hold of her hand and kissed the back of it.

'Irena, darling,' he said, raising his voice half an octave. 'How are we on this fine summer evening? So nice of you to invite me to your exquisite rock pile.' Then, turning to Tom with a wry look, he went on with, 'Actually, dear boy, it's the ugliest house I have ever had the displeasure of passing my eyes over. Such a brutal attack on the senses.'

Irena clipped the back of his hand with a mock slap. 'Behave, or I shall send you home,' she joked and, looking at Tom, said, 'such a ghastly person, you know – I can't think why I invite him.'

She picked up a small bell and gave it a shake. 'Now,' she said commandingly, 'let's have cocktails.' Patience came out onto the terrace with a tray of glasses.

At dinner they sat in an impossibly large room spread out around a black lacquered Japanese dining table on the most uncomfortable chairs Tom had ever encountered. He had slipped off the jacket and left it on the terrace. He felt less conspicuous, less out of place; he was beginning to assert himself.

Then Irena asked the question he had come to dread. 'So where do you live Tom, are you local? I don't think I know of any Jordans in the area. What do you do for a living? Carey has told us absolutely nothing about you.'

He sidestepped the first question. 'I work in New York, Mrs Taylor.'

'That's where we met,' Carey interjected.

'You needn't be so formal, Tom,' she said, throwing a glance at Carey that said please note I am calling him by the approved name. 'Call me Irena, please do.'

'Are you connected to the arts – the Kolinsky perhaps?' Nigel asked.

Tom shook his head. 'No, not the arts; I work for Imperial Life, I'm an underwriter there. I deal with overseas risks.'

'Overseas risks,' Nigel said trying to sound enthusiastic. 'That sounds exciting.'

'Not really,' Tom replied, 'though it has become more interesting recently with the war in Europe; we insure quite a lot in that area. But now the fighting's spreading and the risks need greater analysis.' He shrugged because he couldn't think of more to say and ended with, 'That's what I do.'

'Do you see this war as spreading then?'

'Yes, Irena, I do.'

'Tom is convinced America will get involved,' Carey added with an air of authority and in support of her man.

Nigel looked skeptical. 'Really? I understood our country to be wedded to a policy of isolation. No more sending our boys to die on foreign fields and all that.'

'Surely,' Irena commented, putting down her fork. 'Surely we wouldn't let ourselves get sucked into Europe again?'

'Our teachers think it will happen,' Aly said. 'They say if we don't stand up to Hitler and his European bullies he'll come knocking on America's door next.'

Irena looked irritated by this. 'I'm not sure I like them filling your head with such silly notions. Not at the fees I pay for your education.'

'Which school do you attend?' Tom asked, trying to turn the conversation away from the subject of war, which seemed to be irritating Irena. Besides, he was thinking, what would they know about it? They lived impossibly privileged lives; they were isolated from the real world.

'I'm at the Masters School in Croton-on-Hudson. Do you know it?'

'Not really'.

'I'm not surprised; it's a private school for girls. Carey went there – she hated it.'

'And will you go on to college?'

'Not really, I'll probably just get married – though I might like to be a vet someday. I like animals – especially horses. I have a pure bred Appaloosa; she's beautiful.'

Nigel pulled them back to the war again. 'What makes you think they would try to attack America?'

'Churchill's dead and Tommy thinks that will bring us into the war, don't you darling?' It was the first time he had heard her refer to him as 'darling' in public and he could have kissed her for it right there in front of everyone. It was a statement that said she claimed him and wanted everyone to know it. It made him feel good.

Nigel assumed a quizzical look. 'Who is this Churchill? Do I know him?'

Carey laughed but it was a phony, forced, slightly taunting laugh and she rolled eyes towards the ceiling. 'Nigel, don't you read newspapers?'

'He's the British leader,' Tom chipped in, 'or he was till they murdered him about a month ago. It's reckoned he was assassinated by a Nazi hit squad sent over from Germany – and it looks like the British Fascists might have had a hand in it too.'

'So what's that got to do with us?' Nigel looked openly dismissive, holding up his hands in mock horror. 'Do we care if they kill each other? After all they've been doing it for centuries – what's new?'

Irena clapped, 'Well said, Nigel. So come on Tom, why should we care? They are after all – what is it, three thousand miles away across an ocean.'

Tom looked round the table and wondered where to begin. Did these people want a history lesson on the complex relationships between America and the warring states of Europe? They were clearly invested heavily into the belief of the safety of isolation. There was, after all, no evidence of danger in the world they inhabited. They had only been marginally affected by the Depression years and that had washed right up to their highly polished front doors. If they had barely noticed that, other than as a passing inconvenience, why should they believe or concern themselves with something that was playing itself out on the other side of the ocean, remote from their world? Where do you start when you're speaking in a language the audience doesn't understand? He would have to put it in simple terms.

'There were Brits who wanted to do a peace deal with Hitler and Churchill was against it.'

'Who's Hitler?' Irena asked. Aly looked up at the ceiling, horrified by her mother's seemingly naïve question. 'Mother,' she said with an air of contempt, 'even, I know that!'

'Hitler is the Nazi leader in Germany. He's a dictator. Anyway, with Churchill out of the way there was nothing stopping the others from broking a deal with Germany, and that's what they did.'

'So, does that matter?' Irena butted in again.

'Well, it does because the British Navy was keeping the Germans busy in the North Atlantic and now they aren't. And I know from the work I do at Imperial Life some people consider the risk of German expansion into areas like South America and the Middle East has suddenly become much more real. Premiums are going up – barriers are coming down – blocking off whole areas where the risk of invasion is becoming real.' He waited to let that sink in.

Aly looked concerned. 'Do you think they would try to come into America?' she asked with a hint of nervousness in her voice.

'Oh, don't be foolish Aly,' Irena said dismissively.

'It's possible,' Tom said, 'but at the moment it's more likely they'll go for a foothold in Brazil or Argentina.'

Nigel raised his eyebrows a little. 'It's an opinion,' he said airily, 'not one I share personally but I believe there are some who do.'

The table went quiet. Irena pushed her chair back. 'This is all too depressing. Excuse me, won't you. I shall go out to the terrace for a little air.'

159

After dinner they sat round the table talking for a while, then Carey announced she was going to bed. She came and stood behind Tom's chair and after running her hand through his hair put her head down and kissed his cheek.

'Don't make me wait too long,' she whispered. Tom waited a bit then excused himself, but as he was leaving Irena re-appeared from the terrace. She stood in the doorway for a moment then beckoned Tom.

'Do come out onto the terrace and talk to me for a while,' she said, and then taking his hand led him out into the warm night air. They sat down in the wicker chairs and looked across at each other. Tom wasn't sure where this was going but he didn't want to stay out there any longer than he had to. Upstairs Carey was waiting, and anyway he wasn't good at making small talk.

Irena smiled, 'You know it's very good to have guests in the house. This place is so large it really feels empty unless we have guests. The hired help don't count; they're invisible, a bit like the furniture really; you only notice it when you use it. I don't know why my husband wanted such a huge edifice – that's what it is, you know – it's an edifice, a monument to his overinflated ego.'

Tom's mind was going numb; he had nothing to say. What could he say? He'd heard of Warren Taylor – who hadn't, he was one of America's top industrialists. There was hardly a day when he was not mentioned in one newspaper or another. In America he was probably more famous than Hitler. But that didn't help. How was he to talk about a man he knew she detested? Throw mud as well? That was likely to be fraught with all kinds of traps. Throw shit at Hitler, that was fine, but throw it at her husband and she could well take it as a personal insult. So he said nothing. There was another little silence.

'Did you know he was once a senator?'

Tom said he didn't. He wanted to go to Carey and his mind was searching for an excuse to escape.

'He even saw himself as a presidential hopeful – him, huh – the arrogance of the man.' She spat the words into the air like venom coming out of an angry rattlesnake. 'He hates Roosevelt, you know – he hates all Democrats. He thinks the Wall Street Crash was a good thing. Can you believe that! He says that it got rid of the phoney and the inefficient and brought the country back to its senses. He claims it's put the little man back where he belongs, working for a handful of pennies. Oh yes, he loved it – all that cheap labor queueing up outside his plants, doffing their caps and begging for work.'

She stopped and sighed. 'I should never have married him – worst mistake of my life.'

Again silence reigned. Irena sat for a moment, staring thoughtfully at nothing in particular. Tom shifted in the wicker chair. 'I think I'll probably go to bed now if you'll excuse me,' he said with as much polite tact as he could muster.

160

'Yes, of course. I'm sorry I didn't mean to keep you. It's nice to have someone new to talk to. Nigel's sweet but doesn't have much to say except small talk and art. And Carey – well we don't have a lot to say. Aly's my real prop in the family.'

He stood up but she remained sitting in her chair. She held up her hand. He guessed from what he'd seen of Nigel's performance earlier he was expected to kiss it but at the last minute he changed his mind. It seemed an alien thing to do, so he just shook it instead.

Irena smiled. 'Tom,' she let the word fall softly from her lips. 'Please be careful with Carey. She is a delicate flower and easily bruised. She had a difficult time as a child and she carries it with her. I know she seems highly confident, but don't be fooled – she's fragile. She can be unpredictable and I wouldn't want to see anybody hurt.'

Again he was caught off balance. Again he couldn't think of anything that seemed to be the right thing to say. 'Of course,' he said awkwardly, then as an afterthought, 'I love her. I would never hurt her.'

'I know,' said Irena, 'but I wasn't thinking about her – I was thinking about you.'

When he got to his room he knew she had been there. The sheets were rumpled and warm. She had been there waiting for him. The bed smelled of her perfume. He climbed into the bed and buried his face in the pillow where she had lain, breathing in the sweet scent of her. For a while he lay there on his back, staring at the ceiling and hoping she would return – but she didn't. As he drifted into sleep he quietly cursed her mother for holding him on the terrace when she had been there all the while, waiting for him.

Tom woke early and lay in bed for a while wondering if she would come to his room. After a while he got up, bathed, and then decided to go down to breakfast. He walked the long open corridor that led from the guest wing to the main staircase. The corridor, like the rest of the house, was white, bright and stark in the minimalist style. He hovered on the landing where the long flight of stairs intersected the two wings and listened. He wandered if he should chance going further along to where Carey had her room. Voices drifted up from the terrace, female voices. He waited a little longer then went down the stairs in search of the voices, hoping he would find her there.

In the dining room he found Patience setting up for breakfast on a long polished mahogany buffet bar. There were hot eggs and bacon under a covered salver, cold ham and turkey on open trays and slices of Monterey Jack. There was French bread, Danish pastries, a stack of pancakes, waffles and muffins; there were jams and maple syrup. At one end a silver urn of hot coffee steamed. Next to that there was a silver creamer, matching sugar bowl, small pieces of butter in a cut crystal dish surrounded by a sea of crushed ice, and two large plain glass jugs containing freshly squeezed orange juice. Finally there was a monstrous pierced and fretted silver basket piled high with shiny apples, deep yellow California peaches and a pineapple from Hawaii.

He watched Patience carefully folding white linen napkins and laying them on the bar where the plates and cutlery had been arranged in a neat formation. He stood silent for a while and then when she became aware of him he asked if Miss Caroline had come down yet.

'No sir,' Patience said formally. 'I ain't seen her yet this morning but she could be out on the terrace. Miss Alicia is already out there.'

'Thanks,' he said.

The terrace was bathed with the early morning sunlight and through the doorway he could see Aly talking with her mother. He turned around and headed back up the staircase and along the corridor to Carey's room. He tapped lightly on the door. There was only silence. Maybe she had gone to his room again. He looked along the corridor. There was no sign of anyone so he quickly walked back across the open landing and into the guest wing. He opened the door to his bedroom, hoping to find her hiding under the blankets or in the bathroom, but the room was empty. He thought for a minute, then decided to go back to her room once more. Maybe she had been asleep and not heard him. As he reached the landing he heard the voices coming up from the terrace, then there was a laugh – it was unmistakably Carey. He mentally kicked himself; she must have been there all along.

As he came onto the terrace three heads turned to look at him. Irena broke off and came over. 'Good morning, I hope you slept well.'

Tom nodded, 'Thanks, I did,' but all the time he was looking at Carey who, having given him a glance, then ignored him; she carried on the conversation with her sister. He couldn't understand why, but she had looked at him coldly. He walked the half dozen paces to where she stood but she had turned away as he came towards her and by now had her back to him.

'Hi,' he said, trying to sound casual, but it came out slightly croaky and nervous. Carey turned her head briefly. 'Hello,' she said coldly, then carried on talking to Aly.

It was Irena who came to his aid. Nigel had just joined her. 'Darling Nigel,' she said, 'hold on to this and wait here for a moment, will you. Somebody needs my help.' She passed him a glass of orange juice she had been sipping then went to join the girls.

'Aly,' she said, taking her by the arm, 'Nigel and I want to talk to you about something. Carey darling, why don't you take Tom for a walk around the gardens before we all have breakfast.' As she marched Aly away she looked back stonily at Carey – a look that said I know what you are doing and just stop it.

162

They stood staring at each other, Tom not knowing what to say or what had gone wrong – but something was wrong. After several cavernous seconds that seemed like hours she jerked her head in the direction of the garden. They went down the steps onto the lawn in silence and crossed it to where it gave way to a large arboretum. When they reached the trees Tom stopped. 'Honey, what's the matter?'

'I waited for you – I waited and waited and you never came.' She looked angry. 'Instead you preferred her company. You hung around talking to her. I wanted you and I couldn't bear it. Why did you do that to me?' Tears welled up in her eyes. Tom was flustered; he had no idea what to do or what to say, but seeing her start to cry he put his arms around her and pulled her close to him. At first she resisted, then she let herself be folded into the embrace and finally she pressed her head onto his chest.

'I couldn't get away,' he whispered. 'I tried but she just kept on talking and when I did you were gone. I waited too; I lay there hoping you would come back. I knew you'd been to my room – your perfume was everywhere; God, how I missed you.'

At first she said nothing, then she slowly pulled away from his arms. She stepped back a pace. He let his hands slip down to her waist, not wanting to let her go completely. She drew in a slow deep breath, clasped her arms tightly around her own shoulders, arching them up till her head nestled in the hollow they formed and her ears were almost engulfed. She gripped herself and, locked in that embrace, gave a tiny shudder as if trying to exorcise some unwanted feeling. 'I'm sorry. I don't know why I do this. I think it's because I'm frightened. I get scared you'll walk away and I'll lose you.'

He pulled her to him again. 'Don't be scared – you'll never lose me; I'll always be here.'

She leant back a little to free her arms, then with her delicate fingers started to tidy the collar of his shirt. Then she adjusted the buttons and smoothed down the material. She sniffed and patted him on the chest.

'Nigel wants me to spend some time with him this afternoon. You know he's my art tutor don't you.'

'I guessed from what you'd said before.'

'He wants me to do something on landscapes. I hate landscapes. I prefer abstract. I like Picasso – do you know Picasso?'

'I've seen something but I don't know much about him or his work.'

'He's disturbing – not him but what he paints. Have you seen Guernica?' Tom indicated he hadn't. 'It's about a town in Spain. The Germans bombed it in the civil war there. It's so haunted.' She hugged her shoulders again and once more gave a little shiver.

Then she brightened. 'I know, let's go to MoMA; they've got a Picasso exhibition that's on right now. I can show you his work and tell you all about him. Let's do that – it would be exciting. I'll get Martins to drive us there.'

'What about Nigel and the landscape tutorial?' She laughed and all trace of the melancholy had gone. 'Oh, fuck Nigel and his landscapes – I'd rather spend the afternoon with you and Picasso.' He'd never heard her talk like that before. It was slightly shocking but he didn't care, he had her back – she was his normal Carey again.

Martins drove them to New York and the day was perfect.

CHAPTER 17

The Shadows of War, 31 August 1940

Dr Brent dropped into an easy chair by the radio and turned the small white Bakelite knob to the 'on' position. When the tubes had warmed enough for the sound to come through he tuned the dial to where he knew he would find the CBS channel. It was his habit to listen to the news broadcast around the mid-point of the day. It was one o'clock in the afternoon; he had closed the morning surgery at noon, and then sat with his wife over lunch. Now he had fifteen minutes to relax before preparing his bag to make house calls. At five he would be back in the surgery again for the late afternoon appointments.

As the needle on the dial settled at the CBS channel, anchorman Paul White was reporting on the morning's press briefing at the White House. White reported that Roosevelt had been steady and measured as he addressed the assembled journalists and radio reporters but that his tone had been sombre.

'The President' ... the deep rich voice of White said ... 'talked about what he called the gathering gloom of troubles coming over the horizon from Europe.'

The bulletin cut to a live recording of Roosevelt's address.

'This morning I have an announcement of some gravity.' Roosevelt weighed his words carefully, enunciating and punctuating in a way that was quintessentially Roosevelt. There was a cadence to his speech which was unmistakably his and, like other great orators, it lent him gravitas.

'I don't need to tell you,' he went on 'that the war in Europe is escalating and expanding in the scope of its conduct. It is my belief that the Germans, and in particular their leader, Herr Hitler, will seek to extend their hegemony over their weaker neighbors and that in the coming months they will be looking to expand their theatre of operations into new territories.' He paused, giving his words time to impact on his audience, then added solemnly, 'Possibly our territories – those places where America has special interests.' Another pause.

'We cannot be sure where they will cast their eyes next but we must be vigilant. There is a real and grave danger that America may be caught up in these events, however unwillingly. If that is to be the case – and we most sincerely hope that it will not be the case – then the nation must ready itself to defend its sovereignty and the freedom of the American people.

'You will all be aware that in recent months I have strengthened our armed forces with unparalleled appropriations of millions of dollars spent on ships, airplanes, tanks and artillery of all classes. I have sought to harness the formidable might of American industry to fulfill those requirements so that in the event of any threat whatsoever, from whomsoever and from wheresoever, we shall be prepared to meet the challenge and come through victorious. But to have this great and expanding armory is not of itself enough. Now we must recruit and train the men whose task it will be to use these tools, should it be forced upon us, in the defence of this nation.'

Again he stopped, leaving a little dramatic gap, a gap to give more import to what came next.

'You will know that last month I asked Congress to pass a bill requiring all American male citizens to register for military service. Many will consider that this will be a great inconvenience and they may be right to think so. But I have not done this lightly, nor have I done this without thought and regard as to how this may affect the lives of many American families. There are always times in a nation's history where great sacrifices may be called for. I hope most sincerely that in this case the sacrifice will not be great but merely an inconvenience that must be borne for the readiness of the nation. We must be ready and we must be capable.

'It has always been my belief and my policy that whilst we must hope for the best, we must also prepare for the worst. In order to prepare for the worst I have this day signed into law the Selective Training and Service Act. This new law will require all men aged 18 to 45 to register for military service. However, registration alone will not for the moment require these men to go immediately into military service. The Act proposes a lottery.'

Again he put the speech on hold, giving just enough time for what he had said to fully register with his listeners.

'To oversee these measures we have authorized the setting up of District Draft Boards. The District Draft Boards will be the point of registration and all those eligible should seek out their nearest Board Office and complete their registration. May I say that I most honestly believe this is not just a legal requirement but a call to duty which all our young men will feel proud to answer. There can be no higher honor than to serve in a cause that lies at the heart of the freedom of your nation.

'Finally, let me conclude by assuring you that your government will do everything that is necessary to protect the safety of this great nation of ours and will not rest until we are fully prepared for all and any eventuality. Thank you.'

The bulletin returned to Paul White where he finished with news from Wall Street and a round-up of stocks. Then the anchorman signed off.

'That was the news at the top of the hour, I'm Paul White – have a good afternoon.'

Dr Brent sat for a while, contemplating Roosevelt's words, wondering where it would all end. Now they were going to be calling up the young men and that could only mean one thing. It was what he had feared after he'd listened to the *Fireside Chat* broadcast. His government was starting to slide down the slippery slope towards a war.

He pulled himself up out of the chair, switched off the radio and went through to the front hallway. 'They're going to start drafting men,' he called out to his wife. 'I've just heard it on the radio. It's the first peace time conscription in this country's history. Mind you, I'm not surprised – I guessed all along it would come to this. Now it's happened. They're doing it by lottery; they'll draw names out of a hat. If your name comes up you have to go.'

'You said this would happen – you were right. Did they say when they'll start registration?'

'No, but I imagine the call up papers will start dropping into mail boxes pretty soon. It's bound to be with immediate effect.'

'Oh dear,' was all she said. She was perplexed by it all – like a lot of people she couldn't fully grasp what was happening.

'I'd better be getting along,' he said. 'I've got three house calls before I can get back into the surgery. Is Dottie working at her diner place today?'

'Yes, she is,' his wife replied without enthusiasm. 'I don't know where she finds the energy to do that and her college work. I wish she'd give it up. She'll wear herself out.'

He headed for the front door. 'She's young; the young can do these things. Have you seen a pack of cigarettes, I left them on the table here?'

'You left them in the parlor, I'll get them.'

'There,' she said, pushing the pack into the pocket of his shirt. 'What time do you expect to be back – in case anyone calls?'

'Around 3.30.' He gave her a peck on the cheek. 'I'm calling in on Mike and Eleanor; little Ruby has gone down with something. Did you know their boy was getting married?'

'No.'

'Well, he is – later this year. Let's hope he doesn't get drafted.'

******

For Tom and Carey meeting on the train had become their habit; it was now almost a routine. He had bought a new suit and she told him how good he looked in it. Carey talked a lot about the news of the draft. It worried her. She knew Tom was pretty good at looking out for himself but what if there was a war; a real shooting war? What if he was sent to fight? He could get hurt, wounded – even worse, he could get himself killed. Wasn't there any way he could avoid it? She asked. Wasn't his job important enough to get him exempted? Tom didn't think it was and anyway he figured he had a patriotic duty to join in the defence of his country. Then she said she had a plan. Her father was influential and well connected; although he was a lifelong Republican he knew people in high places, people who were close to the President, people who could arrange for him not to be drafted. At this, Tom put a finger on her lips and pressed it gently there. He didn't want to be ghosted out of the system. He would, he said quietly, feel uncomfortable if others had to do their duty while he hid behind her father's high-placed connections. There was nothing for it – if he was called he would have to go.

At Grand Central they kissed their usual kiss and went their own ways.

Tom had come to a decision. If she cared so much for him that she would seek the help of her father – a man she hated – to keep him safe then it was time he showed her around. She ought to meet his friends and his family. He would start with Tony and Mike.

It was evening when he went to the District Draft Registration office in Peekskill. Outside the building he was surprised to see a queue had formed. It simply hadn't occurred to him just how many eligible men there were living in the Peekskill district. Men across the age range stood patiently in an orderly queue while they waited their turn to identify themselves. Here and there along the line little groups formed like knots in a rope as men talked to each other and speculated about what the future might hold. They bunched together, occasionally shuffling forward to keep up with the turgid flow as it crept towards the recruiting office door.

A man passing by stopped close to where Tom stood in the line. 'It ain't gonna be no picnic,' he called out to nobody in particular, 'you'll see.' There was an embarrassed silence as the queue continued to shuffle forward. He must have been in the last war Tom thought – he was of that age.

Shortly after the man had moved on there was a noise up at the head of the queue. At first it was just a tempo, a sort of muffled beat. Then it got louder and he could hear chanting. There was a murmur of voices up ahead which started to turn into shouting. Then he saw it, a group of men with a banner were taking up position in the street, partially blocking it, causing the traffic to honk and swerve around them. The group was about fifty strong and had rallied by the banner. Angry drivers shouted abuse at them, but they ignored it. The slogan on the banner read 'America First Committee'. At its head a man with a tin megaphone was shouting something and each time he did the group around him repeated it. At first Tom couldn't make out what they were shouting, but as they took up a closer position and the queue moved forward he heard it.

'No war – no draft! No war – no draft!'

Somewhere a man in the queue shouted, 'Get the fuck out of here you cowardly bastards!' Then other voices added to the abuse. Tom sensed it was getting nasty as the individual voices merged into a clutter of expletives. A man somewhere near the front stepped out of the line and grabbed the megaphone and threw it down the road. The line and the protestors broke ranks at the same moment and there was a scuffle with men squaring up to each other, chests out, pushing and shoving at their opponents. The pushing and shoving quickly degenerated and fists started to fly. In moments it had turned into a full-scale fight. Tom had run forward without thinking and now found himself in the thick of it, hitting out and being hit. The man who had grabbed the megaphone went down under a sea of protestors but there were far more men in the line than the protest group and the tide quickly went the other way. Two men had grasped the banner and were ripping it to pieces as the defeated America First Committee demonstrators turned and ran. A police officer had appeared from nowhere and was shouting at the men to get back in line. 'OK, calm down boys, calm down, it's all over.'

Two officials emerged cautiously out of the registration office. One of them laughed. 'Well done lads,' he crowed, 'that's the way we deal with Uncle Sam's enemies.'

As Tom was inspecting his sorely bruised knuckles and rubbing his cheek where he had been struck a blow in the ruckus, he saw the man who had started it all slowly get back up off the ground. Tom walked over to him and offered an arm to steady him. As he helped him over to a street bench he realized he knew the man; he was a park ranger who patrolled the Adirondacks north of Croton in the Westchester district. He put a hand on the ranger's shoulder to steady him. 'Dave, Dave Hanson,' it's me Tom Jordan. Are you OK?'

Hanson nodded slowly. 'Yeah.' Then the light of consciousness switched on and he recognized Tom. 'Of course,' he said, 'Tommy Jordan – sorry, I didn't know you there for a minute. Hell, I didn't know anyone come to that. That was a real haymaker put me down.'

'So what are you doing up here in Peekskill? You're from Croton, aren't you?'

Hanson rubbed his neck and winced as he touched a tender spot. 'My folks live up here and this is where my address shows. I only work out of Croton – that's where the office is located.'

'Oh, right.'

'Hell, I'm gonna be sore tomorrow. Still, it was good to get a shot off at those cowardly bastards. Thanks for pitching in. If there's anything I can do for you anytime – maybe when you're up in the woods – just holler. I owe you one.'

'Don't think about it buddy, I'd do the same for most guys I know.'

169

Then a thought occurred to him. 'Tell you what, there is one thing you can maybe do. I was up on Champlain with the guys I hunt with a couple of weeks back – we got in some real good fishing.'

'Sounds nice.'

'Yeah, it was, they were biting alright. But while we were up there we heard a local rangcr had gone missing and I wandered if you would have any way of finding out if he came out of it OK – if you had any contacts, that is.'

'Sure, that's easy if you know his name. How do I get back to you?'

'Good point – you know Jennifer's Diner in Croton?'

'Yup, of course.'

'Well, you could leave a message with one of the waitresses. I'm in there from timc to time – and, oh, his name is William Tennant.'

Tom helped Hanson to his feet and walked him to the head of the line. 'Anybody mind if the hero of the day does a little queue jumping?' A cheer rippled along the line and a few men shouted 'good man.'

That evening over supper he told his parents that he had registered but kept back the story of the street fight. Instead he excused his torn shirt and bruised face on a fall. He was surprised Holly took the news of his registration so well; there was no acid or morose commentary but Tom could hear a note of sadness in his voice when he said, 'Well, I just hope we're not going down that road again.'

'He has changed a lot,' he told his mother later.

'Yes,' she replied, 'he's holding out well – I just pray every night that we're not sliding back into the same mess as last time. I don't want you coming back all torn into shreds as well. I don't think I could bear that a second time.'

For a fleeting moment he thought about Carey and the idea of her father's help. It would save all Martha's anxiety – but he knew he could never take it. How would he live with himself afterwards if good men had died while he stayed home – out of harm's way? It wasn't a road he could let himself travel. It wasn't the road he wanted to travel.

Friday morning, as he boarded the train for work, Tom was carrying a grip, a copy of *The Westchester Post* and a yellowish-black bruise high up on the right cheek bone. In the grip he had a change of clothes enough for two days. He was going to spend a second weekend at Brunessemer but this time there was no uncertainty; he knew what to expect and he was comfortable with it. He just wasn't sure yet how he would explain the bruise on his face.

For the first time that week they did not meet on the train. Instead Carey had gone with her sister, who wanted to buy a whole new wardrobe. On the Sunday Aly would be returning to Masters School in Croton where she would be boarded for the fall semester.

Martins was at the station to meet him with the Packard. Holly had finally repossessed the old Chrysler and now Tom would have to find some wheels of his own. He didn't mind though – it was wonderful to see his father recover so much of himself in such a short time. He still hadn't got used to the idea of living alongside someone who, for as long as he could remember, had been little more than a passenger passing through life and who now, without any prior indication, had turned into a fellow traveler.

Exercising impeccable etiquette, Martins politely ignored the bruise on Tom's face; Irena did not. She threw up her hands in a theatrical gesture of horror and immediately demanded an explanation. He saw no point in avoiding it so told her the truth and, to his surprise, she responded as if he had become some kind of hero. It was not what he had expected and as she led him through to the drawing room she fussed around him and insisted he tell her all about the encounter. Patience brought in tea and together they talked about the ruckus, then the prospect of war and then a whole raft of small inconsequential matters. As he sat there in command of the conversation, the ogres of the household etiquette, the dress code, the formalities of how to greet and what to say all shrank to become nothing more threatening than tiny shadows. For all their money they were really no different from him.

After a while the conversation turned to the girls who had gone to New York for the day and would be home soon. They had taken the train and now Martins had gone with the Packard to wait for them at the station. 'I do hope they're not going to hold us up,' she said, glancing down at her wrist where a delicately crafted Swiss watch hung languidly on a diamond bracelet. Tom looked at it briefly and the thought crossed his mind that it probably cost more than the car he was about to buy.

'You know,' she went on, 'Carey has no sense of time – she just takes off as she fancies with never a thought for those who have to hang around waiting for her.' Tom thought that sounded familiar.

'Now Tom,' she continued, 'I want to ask you a very great favor.' He mentally winced at what might be coming next – with Irena you could never tell.

'Aly has to go back to school at Croton on Sunday afternoon. Martins has the day off and I shall be too busy. I wonder if you would mind very much taking Aly up to Croton on your way home and just depositing her at the school.' She smiled an ingratiating little smile, leaning across to touch his arm. 'I would be so grateful.'

Tom smiled back. 'The problem is,' he said, trying to sound apologetic, 'I don't have a car with me. Martins collected me from the station if you remember – I'll be going home by train.'

'Oh, silly boy – that's not a problem. We're awash with cars. You can use mine.' Then she paused. 'No, no you can't; I shall need it with Martins off. I know, simple, why don't you take that absurd French thing my equally absurd husband bought for our dissolute son. Complete lunacy really – Wendell can't drive and has no inclination to learn.' She stopped abruptly then added, 'You will do it, won't you?' Tom reluctantly agreed. He didn't want to spend any more time away from Carey than he had to and driving her sister up to Croton had not been on his agenda.

Just after seven the girls arrived home. They came noisily in through the front door, full of chatter about what they had bought. Carey dropped her bags on the hall floor and started pulling things out of them, oblivious of Tom who had come out of the drawing room when he heard the commotion of their arrival and now stood watching as she pulled out stuff and held it up. She was like a child with a new play box, a play box full of pretty, frivolous things.

After taking out several items she noticed Tom. She dropped the dress she was holding and put her arms around his neck. 'Sweetheart,' she squeaked excitedly, 'come look at what I've bought.' She pulled on his arm until they stood among the bags and boxes that were now spilled and tumbled around the floor. Although she kissed him, she didn't seem to notice the dark brooding lump just under his right eye.

'God, we've pounded Fifth Avenue. I think I must have worn out my shoes on the sidewalk.' It was as if her mind was somewhere else. Aly had quietly called Constance to take her purchases to her room and came over to look at the mess Carey was creating.

'Hello Tom,' she said, leaning up and giving him a peck on each cheek, 'nice to see you again.' She stepped back and looked at his face. 'Ouch, that's a bit of a shiner – what did you do, run into a wall?'

'Something like that,' he replied, trying to dismiss it.

'Carey,' she called to her sister, 'have you seen this?' She put up a hand and brushed his face with the tips of her fingers. Carey dropped what she was holding.

'Tommy, what have you done?' she said almost breathlessly, letting the words out in a little gasp. She looked closely for a moment. 'How did you do it, honey? Does it hurt?' He shook his head 'No, it's fine – I'll tell you all about it later.'

It was just before they went down to dinner that Carey came to his room. She took off all her clothes and then slipped in between the sheets. 'Come on,' she said, 'I'm taking no chances on you getting cornered by Mother again after dinner. This time I want a little something before the main course.'

'Jeeze,' he said, getting into the bed with a huge grin on his face. 'You're so naughty.'

Cuddled up under the sheet he ran his hands across her body, feeling every curve and dimple until eventually they couldn't hold off any longer. As they slipped together and their desires took over she gave a little squeak of satisfaction and gently bit his shoulder; the moment consumed them both in the lust of a raging hot fire.

Then there they were, calm again. Tom laid on his back and she on her belly propped up on her elbows, her chin resting gently in her cupped hands. She leant slightly sideways and taking one hand away from her chin lightly brushed his bruised cheek with her fingers. 'Does it hurt?'

'It did, but not anymore.'

'How did it happen?'

'Well,' he said, hesitating, 'I was hoping it would go down yesterday and I wouldn't have to tell you but your mother saw it and I told her so what the heck, it's out' – and he went on to recount the story. When he finished she looked at him questioningly.

'So why didn't you want to tell me?'

'I guess I thought you might think it was just some common low-rent roughhousing. I can't imagine Nigel or your friends at the tennis club getting into a brawl.' She laughed at the idea of Nigel fighting, and as for the others, 'They don't have it in them. I'm proud of you for standing up for a friend,' she said softly, stroking the wound. 'I think there's a little bit of the hero in you, Tommy Jordan.' Then she laughed her little girly laugh that he'd heard the first time he'd slept with her; putting her arm across him, she snuggled her face into the warm space between his neck and his shoulder.

After a minute she lifted her head and stared into his face. 'You're such a strong man, but I think you will be careless with your life. You make me feel safe but nothing is forever. I'm frightened they'll draft you and send you to fight. And you'll go and you'll put yourself in harm's way because that's the kind of man you are. You're a hero and they always kill the heroes first. I hate that beastly war.' She spread herself across him and lay there listening to his heart beat for a moment.

'Tomorrow,' she whispered, 'let's go to the city and just walk around Central Park. The leaves are starting to turn and it will soon be the fall. I'd like some time together, just us. I always think of the fall as a slightly sad time of the year – the summer is dying and soon it'll be gone – and who knows what else with it.'

She lifted herself off him and sat up. 'And after the park we could go to Tarwids and say hello to the bear. Maybe we'll even buy him a drink.'

'That,' said Tom, 'is the best idea yet.' He kissed his finger tip and touched it on the end of her nose. 'Don't be frightened, I won't get killed. If I have to go I'll be careful, and I'll come back and be there to look out for you – always.'

Late Saturday afternoon they drove out of the grounds at Brunessemer in the Bugatti and made their way down to Manhattan. The Park was lovely. The leaves were turning and here and there they fell, swinging and twirling as they performed their whimsical descent – a slow, spiral dance. It would soon be September and although the days were still warm there was a nostalgic feel of something passing away in the air. People were lighting their fires in the evening and from time to time there was the smell of wood smoke on the breeze. As they walked he thought about the Adirondacks, about hunting and about the others. He hadn't seen Tony or Mike since July 4th and the fishing trip – and he still hadn't taken her to meet anyone.

They got to Tarwids as the light was shortening into evening. The bear was there, grinning as always, a glass in one paw, laid back and taking its ease. They found their favorite table in the corner and a waiter came over to hand them a menu and light a candle. Carey ordered their drinks: champagne for her, Manhattan for him. Then she smiled and held his hand across the table.

It was too perfect to last, he thought. She was right – this war was going to change everything.

CHAPTER 18

The Bodies in Rochester Row, 1 September 1940

It was two days short of a year since the war had been declared. It had lasted until the retreat to Dunkirk and its evacuation, barely nine months. Then a grateful nation thanked Halifax and Chamberlain for their statesmen-like diplomacy, for saving the nation from more blood and the inevitable defeat at which the weary population believed they had been staring. They had bought peace, but it had been at a price and now the grateful began to wonder if the price had actually been right, if the statesmen had not sold out too cheaply. They had peace but it was not the peace they had expected. As the full extent of the terms emerged, so the misgivings grew. True, there was no more blitz and ordinary people could sleep soundly in their houses. The ghostly wail of the siren in the night no longer terrified children as they ran in panic for the nearest shelter. The boom of the ack-ack batteries had been silenced, the drone of the bombers overhead was only a memory. There was no blackout; the children trudging to school no longer had gas masks slung across their shoulders; there was plenty of milk and most foods were back in the shops again.

But it was a strange peace that had been purchased. Slowly the reality of what had been done sank in, like a creeping osmosis insidiously oozing into the consciousness of those who must now live with it. The ordinary man in the street, the reasonable thinking man – and some less reasonable too – was beginning to regret what had been served up to him; it had a bitter aftertaste – it was giving him indigestion. People in their houses everywhere were waking up to this new reality and it now dawned on them that perhaps there was more to life than a full belly and a good night's sleep. The talk in the pubs began to question if this was life or just passive existence. What about sovereignty, self-determination, respect for your neighbour, trust in authority? These things were beginning to erode, carved away, sliced like salami and replaced with new rules enforced by new men in new uniforms.

Mosley's Blackshirts were on the streets again, strutting about, bullying those who didn't show respect for the new diktats. But there was a difference: where the old Blackshirts had carried sticks, now they were carrying guns. The civilian police remained unarmed.

175

At Portsmouth and Dover there were German ships in the harbours. Wehrmacht officers were shopping in Oxford Street. Increasingly SS uniforms had been turning up in Whitehall and further west, at Lancaster Gate, where the Reich had installed its Legation.

Under the terms of the peace treaty the Germans had insisted they should have a presence in London and be free to move around Britain. There were observers based at the Legation building whose task it was to make sure that the British did not re-arm beyond the narrow limits that had been imposed in the treaty. The Army had been capped at the 300,000 men who had been repatriated from the beaches of Dunkirk; the Air Force had been virtually dismantled. There were a handful of Spitfires and Hurricanes left over from the combat but no more were to be manufactured. Bomber Command had been disbanded, save for a few lumbering Blenheims that were permitted to be used for coastal patrol. The senior ranks had been thinned, pared down to a few lower-ranking personnel, and there was a German civilian, the Shadow Controller of Unilateral Movements – unofficially referred to as the SCUM – whose function was to observe all air movements. It was said that every airfield now had its German Scum – watching silently and reporting daily to the Legation in Lancaster Gate. Of the big names, Dowding, Harris, Park and a handful of others had been retired from the service and returned to civilian life. Only the Royal Navy had been left untouched. There was dissent in the ranks when the full extent of the reductions in the other services was made known; mutterings of mutiny and accusations of treachery were rife. There had been desertions; senior men had left their posts, simply disappeared and gone to ground – nobody knew where. There was open talk of resistance. Everywhere there was talk that the country was as good as occupied.

The traffic in Park Lane was ugly. A turgid, tangled file of taxis, buses, trucks and cars competed with horse-drawn delivery vans for road space. Barrow boys pushed their carts in between the hooting cacophony; everything struggled against the inertia of the choked up jam. In among this a black Horch limousine slowly made its way towards the roundabout at the intersection with Piccadilly. Mounted on each of the front wings two pennants advertised its authority: one carried the Swastika and the other the insignia of the German Legation. It inched its way round Wellington Gate and then, peeling off left into Constitution Hill, broke loose from the river of metal and headed for the Mall. The Mall was quiet and clear of traffic. Just a handful of curious tourists stood looking at Buckingham Palace.

As the car picked up speed, the two men occupying the back seat stared out at the autumn sky. One of them, Sir Oswald Mosley, displayed a self-satisfied composure. At the outbreak of war he had been interned together with Lady Mosley. Their fascist views and quasi-military organization had had the odour of the Nazis about it. Churchill had been quick to act but the Mosleys had a friend in Hitler and when it came time to sign the peace treaty the Führer had made it a condition that Mosley should be freed and his Blackshirts given a role in the new governance of Britain.

The car moved along the Mall; Mosley turned to look out of the small rear window at the diminishing view of the Palace. 'I do wonder what we shall do with them,' he said to the other occupant, jerking his head in the direction of the great building. 'Does the monarchy have a role in the future, would you think, Herr Major?'

Major Linz grinned. 'Why not?' he said, running a gloved hand over the smooth leather arm rest that separated him from Mosley. He didn't much care for this arrogant Englishman but if he could be useful to the Führer then he would be civil with him. Those were his orders. 'We don't want to destroy the history and traditions of this country of yours,' he said, then added, 'We might perhaps replace the King with his older brother.' But he had said it with an effusion that hid the antipathy he actually felt. His father had fought in the first war and he had no love of the Tommies. The German nation had been betrayed, humiliated, insulted; now it was a time for revenge.

'You know,' he continued, 'it was once great and anyway it has always been very much admired by the Führer. He has often said how he marvels at the way in which the British have managed to control such a large empire with such a small number of men to police it. It is a lesson we are keen to learn.' Mosley looked gratified. Quietly, in delusory moments he saw himself as the head of the nation.

Linz again ran his hand over the leather armrest. 'This is a beautifully made car, do you not think? This is what German industry can do.' He looked around the interior admiringly. 'It is the Führer's favourite; he likes this make much better than the Mercedes.' He paused and tapped the armrest.

'Hitler is a man of taste, you know. He will keep the best of the history and the institutions of the Reich. We are developing a great culture; cleansing our nation of decadence, of the sub-human values and Zionist trash that has been allowed to infest the fatherland. We were once a pure nation and shall be so again. The Führer will see to it – and he will see to it that Britain is great again.'

Mosley was flattered by the thought that Hitler could hold Britain, his country, in such high esteem. 'Heil Hitler!' he shouted, and gave the Nazi salute.

The Horch emerged from the Mall, drove round Trafalgar Square, then proceeded up Whitehall. About a third of the way along the car slowed and then swung left into Great Scotland Yard, pulling up outside the old police headquarters. It had long since ceased to be a police station but the office of the Commissioner was still located in the front of the building. The driver jumped out and opened the door for Linz; he left Mosley to fend for himself. A police constable on duty outside the main entrance saluted. It had now become a requirement for all men in uniform to salute anyone they knew to be a Nazi official. Inside, a sergeant was waiting for them – he too saluted. They were led down a brightly lit corridor with dark wood-block flooring. Linz's boots hammered out the urgency of their progress. They stopped at a heavy wooden door with a name plate on it: Commissioner David Peters. The sergeant knocked, then turned the handle and opened the door. Linz and Mosley strode in. Peters looked up and grudgingly offered the semblance of a salute. He waved a hand to indicate that they were invited to sit then, closing the file he had been studying, sat up to his full height and looked at the two men.

'You know why we are here,' Mosley said. It was a statement not a question.

The Commissioner nodded, 'I do.'

'Are they here?' Linz asked perfunctorily.

'No, they are over at Rochester Row in the morgue.'

'In that case, Commissioner, we should like to see them.'

'I'm not sure it will help you.'

Linz looked irritated. 'I shall be the judge of that, Commissioner.'

Peters lifted the phone on his desk and, after a short pause, spoke into it. 'If anyone wants me I'll be over at Rochester Row.' He stood up. At six feet two inches he was taller than both the German and Mosley. 'All right,' he said in a matter of fact way, 'follow me.' They stamped their way back along the corridor to where the sergeant sat at his desk in the entrance hall. He stood to attention and saluted.

'Ask my driver to bring the car around please.' Peters had no intention of sharing a car with the other two. He turned to Mosley. 'You go on ahead and I'll meet up with you there. You know the way I take it?'

'Of course.'

'Good, then wait for me there.'

******

A mortician in a white coat wheeled out two trolleys, each one draped over with a rubber sheet. The sheets clung to the corpses beneath like damp brick red shrouds outlining the features that in life would have made them recognizable. But as the covers were drawn back it was clear those features had been erased. The bodies were badly charred and only their stature gave any indication of who they might have been in life. One was broader in the shoulder and the hips, but other than that there was little to tell them apart.

Mosley strutted slowly round the trolleys with his hands clasped behind his back, his head poked forward like some large wading bird paddling through a swamp. He said nothing as he made his inspection of the deceased. Peters

178

indulged the charade in silence for a moment then turned to the mortician. 'What do we know?'

The mortician pursed his lips and screwed up his mouth into an expression indicating there was not much he could say. 'Both male, of course; badly burned – more charred actually. The heat was intense; it was caused by a highly volatile fluid, almost certainly petrol. The bodies are too badly damaged to be precise but we calculate they were both around six feet tall. This chap,' he tapped the leg of the corpse with the larger structured bones, 'would have been quite a muscular individual, fairly imposing in life I'd say.'

There was a silence. Linz looked at Mosley, then at Peters. 'Did not they have something about them that could survive the fire?' he said. His English was almost perfect but the syntax and the accent betrayed his origins. Peters nodded at the mortician, indicating his consent to reveal more.

'Nothing survives in a fire like that.'

'Commissioner, as you know my office believes these two men may have been German. We should like to carry out our own forensic investigation of the bodies.'

'I regret, Major Linz, that will not be possible for the moment – at least not until we have concluded our own enquiries.' Linz didn't like the answer but for the moment took it without responding.

As they drove back he said nothing but his expression was dark and brooding. Silently, in his mind he accused Peters of insubordination, of holding back information that he should have divulged to the Legation weeks ago. Under the Treaty Peters was effectively of inferior standing to the German in matters relating to the security of the Reich. This Linz considered an offence against his office and rank and he had already determined that he would report it to Berlin as soon as he was back at Lancaster Gate. For a person of a defeated nation, which is how Linz saw Britain, this English policeman showed no deference to the victors or accorded them the respect they were due. For his part Peters felt a sense of moral superiority over the German whom he considered loutish and aggressive.

They did not sit when they reached the office but instead stood around the Commissioner's desk. It was Mosley who spoke first. 'Neither of those bodies is Churchill!'

'We cannot be sure of that,' Peters replied with a look of barely disguised derision.

'How do you know this thing?' Linz butted in angrily.

'They are both too big. Churchill is a small man,' Mosley said importantly, 'no more than five seven or eight, and a quite slight build.'

Linz looked coldly at Peters. 'And you have known this fact for many weeks. Why did you not let my office know?'

Peters hardened his attitude. He looked resolutely at Mosley. 'Bodies change substantially when they are subjected to that kind of heat. We still have not properly identified the bodies. One of them is quite possibly Churchill and the other his bodyguard. I need to investigate who these men were, what they were doing and how they came to their end. Besides, I considered it was purely a police matter and not your concern.'

'When it comes to Herr Churchill everything is my concern, Commissioner. Hitler has declared it so. Hitler has declared him an enemy of the Reich. He is a criminal.'

Underneath Peters felt a burning desire to fell Linz, to arrest him there on the spot and throw him in a cell, but he knew it would be pointless; the German would be sprung in less than an hour and he would replace him in the cell. He was powerless; the British government was powerless. They had let the spider in and it was spinning its web across the whole of London and eventually it would extend up and down and across the nation to every town, village and hamlet. So Peters stayed outwardly calm. 'No, Major, that is not correct. Under British law Mr Churchill is a politician and at the moment he is missing. Our concern is to find him – only that.'

Linz looked angry. 'We shall see how Berlin feels about that.'

Peters knew he was on dangerous ground. He had known for some time that the bodies at Rochester Row were almost certainly German. Under the Treaty obligations he should have shared this information with the Legation, but he had needed time – time to find out who these dead men were, how they got into Churchill's car, why they were incinerated and, even more importantly, time to find Churchill – and help him if he could. Peters was increasingly certain that the two men had been sent to murder Churchill. He guessed Churchill had somehow been warned and helped. Churchill had been with Walter Thompson. Thompson would have been carrying a revolver but neither of these men had been shot; their necks had been broken. Thompson would not have been able to take on two men of their strength even if Churchill had been able to help, which was doubtful. Also, he had lied to Linz back at the morgue. Not everything had been incinerated. One of the bodies had a ring on its finger.

Linz looked intently at Peters and when he next spoke there was an air of menace in his voice. 'You must make immediate arrangements to hand over the bodies of these men to the Legation. There should be no delay. Is that understood?'

Peters held his ground. 'I can't let you do that, Major. The bodies are part of a criminal investigation and they must remain where they are.'

Linz's tone became more threatening. 'I believe, Herr Commissioner, that you have overstepped your authority in this matter. That is a most serious miscalculation for you. I am ordering you that you hand over the bodies of these men to the Legation. I shall make arrangements.'

'Major,' Peters said in a calm, flat tone, 'I believe these two men may have been implicated in the disappearance of Mr Churchill. Indeed, one of the bodies may well be that of Mr Churchill, so until I have concluded my investigation they will remain in my custody.' Peters pressed a buzzer on his desk and almost immediately a sergeant came into the office. 'Sergeant, take these gentlemen to the front desk and sign them out please.'

He turned to Mosley, who had all this time remained stony-faced but silent. 'Sir Oswald, I am sure you will understand my position. You could, of course, take it up with the Home Office if that is what the Major wishes.' He offered his hand but neither man took it. Instead both men gave the Nazi salute. The sergeant who had been standing with the door open now led the way back along the corridor.

When they had gone Peters sat in silence, thinking through what had happened. After a few minutes he pulled open a drawer in his desk and fished out a brown paper evidence bag. He shook it and a metal ring fell out. It bounced and clattered on the desk, then came to rest. He picked it up and turned it thoughtfully between his thumb and forefinger. There was an inscription running round the inner side: Gott Mit Uns – God is with us, the motto carried on the belt buckle of every German soldier in the previous war. The ring was clearly German and the owner had probably fought in the Great War.

******

Halifax sat at the great table in the Cabinet room, his back to the fireplace which lay cold and unlit. The summer had been hot and even now in mid-autumn there was a warm touch to the air. Things had not gone well since the meeting with Hitler. The terms of the Treaty were harsher than he had bargained. The civil servants in the Foreign Office who had drafted the document constantly complained that their German counterparts were obdurate and unbending. The process had not been a true negotiation but a thinly veiled dictation of German demands. Word by word and line by line, ground had been lost. Promises and safeguards had been watered down as the document grew into nothing more than German hegemony. Their independence was illusory – they were in no better state than Quisling in Norway or Petin in Vichy; Halifax had set out to save the nation but, like Chamberlain at Munich, he had been foolishly deceived. He had sold his nation for sixpence and that had bought him nothing. He was just another puppet and the bitter realization now broke his will to resist.

Chamberlain came into the room with Anthony Eden, who had now taken over as Foreign Secretary. Eden was a close friend of Churchill; he had been his protégé, had married his niece. Now Churchill was no longer with them. He had been a political rock but now he was missing, probably dead; Eden was feeling insecure.

Chamberlain looked pale and ill; he had never really recovered from the disappointment of Munich and colleagues had begged him to rest. Now the disgrace of the Paris Treaty looked like finishing him off and, of course, there was the business of Churchill. Minutes later, Hugh Dalton came in with Sir Stafford Cripps, British Ambassador to Moscow. Dalton, like Chamberlain, was suffering the shame of public denigration. He had been humiliated and traduced by the press for his part in the Paris meeting with Hitler.

There was a sound outside the room and the door opened. Ernest Bevin entered. He didn't bother to knock; he no longer felt there was any moral authority in the room he was entering. He had been the only man at Paris to stand up to Hitler. Behind the scenes he had tried to put some backbone into the delegation but in that he had also failed. His only consolation was that his stance had been reported in the foreign press. The Germans had branded him obstructive and obstinate; this had gone down well with the British and now he enjoyed something of a heroic reputation.

Another member entered the room. This one was strongly built with a rugged face and a look of determination. He was alone among the assembled company to have an air of confidence about him. 'Beaverbrook,' Halifax greeted him, 'so glad you were able to attend, dear chap.'

Lord Beaverbrook was the last to join the meeting. Canadian by birth, he alone had no real misgivings about the Treaty. He had long admired the energy of the Germans in their recovery from the Treaty of Versailles in 1918, and had helped Halifax and Eden in their secret negotiations with Canada to get the agreement for the Anglo-German bases now being established in Hudson Bay and Prince Edward Island.

Halifax invited the men to take their places around the table. There was a short period of quiet while each of them laid out their papers on the blotters in front of them. The tops were unscrewed from fountain pens and neatly set down beside the papers in readiness to take notes. Halifax cleared his throat. He looked around at his colleagues, then opened the meeting. 'Thank you all for attending. As you know things have not gone as we had expected. They have not gone well. I am ashamed to admit it but I believe we have been bested by the other team.'

Dalton looked sourly across the table, 'Duped more like it.' There were nods and murmurs around the table.

Halifax sensed a simmering resentment amongst Dalton, Bevin and Cripps. These Labourites had been difficult to deal with at the meeting with Hitler, and ever since. They made no effort to hide their dislike of appeasement and their contempt for Chamberlain in particular. If Churchill had still been leader they would have been solidly with him even though he was a Conservative. Halifax now moved to head them off.

'I deeply regret it,' he said boldly, 'and I take full responsibility for it but we had little room to negotiate.' He looked reprovingly at Dalton. 'You were there, you know quite well how it was, but I believe we got the best deal we could under the circumstances.' He looked around for approval and then, judging his position was sound, added, 'However, if it is the consensus here that I should go because of this Treaty I will offer the house my resignation in the morning.' He looked directly at Beaverbrook. 'Max, it would seem we may have been wrong. Now we have to take steps to put things right.'

Beaverbrook shook his head and looked round the table at the others. He had been a long-time appeaser and a supporter of Chamberlain at Munich but he was also a skilled negotiator. Now, like Bevin, he knew they had been outmanoeuvred in Paris, but for Halifax to resign would be to admit it to the nation. There were already signs of public unrest. There was no indication that anyone felt such a move would help.

'Resignation?'

Bevin looked stony-faced across the table. He and Hugh Dalton had gone to Paris as the anchors of the delegation. They were supposed to have put the brakes on the German demands but they had totally underestimated Hitler. They had failed, and now they sat at the table wearing the same cloak of guilt as Halifax.

'Resignation doesn't help,' Bevin said grumpily. 'It would only make us look weak – and God knows we're weak enough without parading it before the people. The Germans would laugh all the way to Berlin! We are all responsible – we must all find the way out.'

Having got the resignation issue out of the way, the group then floundered around the subject of how they might get a better deal. There seemed no room left for manoeuvre either in the wording of the Treaty or in the real position on the ground. The Germans were here and they would not be easily shifted. The army was weak. Under the Treaty all the heavy weapons, artillery and tanks had been put in secure storage and each depot had a German inspector on site to ensure its isolation. There were protocols restricting military movement outside barracks. The army was no longer in control of its own command structure. There were Germans everywhere – 'There's one in every bloody cupboard you open,' Bevin had observed angrily. The fact was that they had gained peace but in the process they had slammed the door on any hope of resistance. There was a lull. Nobody seemed to have any ideas.

'Is there any news on Winston?' Chamberlain asked, changing the subject.

'That's another mess,' Halifax replied. He'd had a report from the Home Office about an hour before the meeting had convened and the news was no more conclusive than it had been a month ago.

'Is he dead,' Bevin asked pointedly, 'or isn't he?'

Halifax held his hands up. 'We have no idea. But there have been developments. We know the men in his car were not him and Walter Thompson. They were two Germans; one, they think, from the SS. Scotland Yard are certain they were German agents sent here with orders either to abduct Winston or to murder him. We know they didn't succeed. And there's another thing. Winston's wife, Clementine; she has also disappeared.'

'Gone with him?' Bevin asked bluntly. 'Done a bunk together have they?'

Eden butted in angrily. 'Winston would not do a bunk, as you so crudely put it.'

Halifax held up a hand to signal he wanted no feuding. 'We simply don't know, although we do know she didn't disappear till two days after Winston. The fear is she may have been abducted, but we just don't know.'

Eden looked straight at Bevin and said calmly, 'If I know anything of Winston I'd say he's probably gone underground to organize some kind of resistance. He's not a man to run away to save his own skin.'

'Resistance?' Bevin said, raising his voice. 'What resistance – farmers with pitchforks and a few 12-bore shotguns? There's nothing else out there to resist with. The Germans put paid to that with this bloody treaty.'

Halifax looked across at Stafford Cripps. 'What about our Soviet friends? Is there any ground to be explored there?'

Like a lot of his contemporaries, Cripps had dallied with Marxism while a student at university. Although he had moved away from the extremes of the doctrine and was seen as mainstream in the Labour party, he had maintained close ties with the Russians and with their Ambassador in London. 'I'm not sure where they stand at the moment,' he admitted. 'The Molotov–Ribbentrop Pact is still holding up but my contacts tell me that they don't think it will last. They're nervous about the build-up of the Canadian bases, especially Hudson Bay – they think it's all aimed at them. They think Hitler plans to choke off the Barents Sea and then launch an attack.'

Bevin folded his arms with a mixture frustration and derision, 'Well, isn't that sodding wonderful? If they fall out it'll be bloody awkward. We'll be stuffed back into the firing line again, and this time we won't even be fighting for our own freedom!'

'Stafford,' Halifax said, 'we should see if we can open a dialogue with the Soviets. It might help to balance our present position.'

Cripps looked doubtful. 'I'll see what I can do, Prime Minister.'

'Good, let's move on. We still have a country to run.'

******

The sergeant on desk duty saluted. 'Will you want a driver sir? There's a car handy in the pool if you'd like it.'

'No, that's OK sergeant. It's a nice afternoon, I think I'll walk home.'

The walk to Peters' house took him along Whitehall. As he passed the Cenotaph he caught the sound of German. Two men, probably off-duty soldiers he thought, were taking photographs of the memorial. It struck him as a strange anomaly. They were photographing a monument that commemorated a German defeat in the First World War. Now barely more than two decades later, here they were as victors. As he turned right into King Charles Street he heard more German being spoken. This time it was two young couples ambling along arm in arm enjoying the autumn afternoon sunshine. London had become a popular destination since the peace. He crossed Horse Guards Road and went into St James's Park, heading diagonally across the south side along one of the paths that would lead him into Bird Cage Walk. From there it was a short step to Queen Anne's Gate where he had his London flat. The flat was part of a large and elegant late Georgian mansion block built in soft red brick. As he let himself in through the heavy wooden front door, he again heard the sound of Germans in the street.

He climbed the wide staircase to the first floor. On the right side of the broad landing he opened the front door to his flat and stepped inside. The hall he entered was large with a high ceiling and oak wood panelling. At the end of the hall was a generous kitchen with a large multi-paned window which flooded the room with light. In it he could hear his wife Muriel clattering about.

'I'm home,' he called out, as he hung up his jacket on a coat stand. He walked half way along the hall and then turned left into their bedroom. He changed out of his uniform and hung it in the wardrobe. Then, feeling more comfortable, he went along to the kitchen. Muriel gave him a peck on the cheek. 'How was your day dear?'

'Bloody,' he said in a matter of fact way, 'perfectly bloody. How was yours?'

'Oh, fine. I went shopping with Thelma, over in Knightsbridge. We went to Peter Jones and then we had lunch at Fortnums. Everywhere's full of Germans though; they seem to have money to burn. Go into the sitting room and I'll bring you some tea. Then you can tell me about your bloody awful day.'

He slumped down into a stuffed armchair and looked at the flower-printed covers. They reminded him of the country with their big, bright, gaudy flowers spread across the fabric in extravagant splashes of colour.

They had a house in Surrey, close to the town of Guildford. It had a large garden and before the war he had commuted to London on the Southern Electric Line. Then the war started and this made things difficult. The trains did not

185

always run and there were air raids. The service offered him the flat so that he could be on hand during the week if needed. To begin with Muriel stayed out in the country; it was thought safer what with the risk of air raids, and he went home at weekends. But increasingly he found himself caught up in work at the weekends, too, and Surrey was out of the question. Originally it was the war making demands on manpower. Then, after the Paris Treaty, it had been setting up the interface with the Germans and their damned Legation. Now it was the bureaucracy that was taking the time. He seemed to spend more of his day filling in forms than doing the job he had signed up for. Eventually Muriel moved up to London and, although she missed the clean country air and the open spaces, she found compensation in the shops, the restaurants and the theatres. If only the Germans would go home, life could be very good, she thought.

'How would you like to go to the house for the weekend?' he called to her. She came in with a tray of tea and set it down on a small occasional table.

'That would be nice. Can you get away then?'

'Yes, I think so – I need the break. I thought we might go over to Wisley and walk round the gardens. I might go to the club and play a round of golf. I feel the need to get away from all these bloody Germans.'

'Are you having trouble with the Legation again?'

'I am.'

'Anything special?'

'Yes, it's the Churchill case. We still have no idea where he is, if he's alive or what it's about. All we've got are two dead Germans found in Churchill's burned-out Humber. I think Special Branch know more than they are letting on. And then this morning I get a visit from a Major Linz, demanding the bodies be handed over to the Legation. You can't carry out an investigation if people keep pinching the evidence.'

'Can't you refuse to release them?'

'I tried but it was met with threats of retaliation. I don't want to get shipped off to Berlin.'

'Surely, they couldn't – could they?'

Peters leant forward and picked up his cup. He sipped the hot tea and thought about the meeting with Linz. 'Anything seems possible these days. The government is too weak to resist.' He paused for a second and then added. 'Do you know that bloody German had the temerity to walk into my office this morning wearing a side arm? He had an automatic pistol in a holster in full view. Not only that but he came accompanied by that odious little man Mosley – and he was armed too!'

'Good grief!'

'And here's a salutary tale. Linz and Mosley had the latest German automatic pistols – P38s. Do you know what I have in my desk drawer back at the office? An old Webley and Scott 45 revolver. It was made in 1912 and you couldn't hit a barn door at 50 feet. That's what makes anything possible; that's the difference between us and them.'

On a table in the corner the phone started ringing. He got up slowly and walked across to it. He looked over at Muriel. 'The office no doubt.' His voice displayed no enthusiasm for the prospect; there would only be a problem at the other end of the line. They only called him when there was a problem. He lifted the receiver. 'Whitehall 1304.' A voice at the other end sounded agitated.

'Good afternoon, sir. I'm the desk sergeant at Rochester Row Police Station. Sorry to disturb you, sir. It's that Major Linz again, the one who came over earlier to look at the bodies. He's turned up mob-handed and he's demanding the release of the two scorched stiffs.'

'Does he have any paperwork with him – any authority?'

'I don't know, but I'll tell you what, they've got a lot of guns with them. I don't really want to argue with this lot if I can avoid it, sir.'

Peters thought for a moment. There was no point in a showdown but it rankled nonetheless. There was nothing he could do about it and the last thing he wanted was an incident. Linz, he knew, would throw his weight around. It was too late to get hold of anyone in the Home Office so it would have to be his decision. 'All right, put the Major on. I'll talk to him.'

There was a short delay and then, 'Commissioner, how can I help you?' Linz sounded tense and Peters sensed he was in a nasty mood.

'Well, you could start by telling me what you are doing at Rochester Row police station with a group of armed men.'

'I have come for the bodies of the two German citizens which you are holding illegally.'

'I see. Forgive me, but I am surprised that you should be doing this.'

'You should not be surprised, Commissioner. I told you I would come for them.'

'And do you have any written authority to do this, Major?'

The response was slow and threatening. Linz stabbed out the words. 'I do not need any written authority. I represent the Legation and that is enough authority for me. Be careful, Commissioner, you have already obstructed the Reich once today; it would be unwise to do it again.'

That did it for Peters. He was not going to have his authority usurped any further. If he allowed the Germans to get away with this it would set a dangerous precedent and who knew where that might end. His mind churned, searching for a way to stop Linz taking the bodies. The nearest armed response unit was at Snow Hill. If he could get enough men down to Rochester Row in time he could probably force the Germans to a stand-off. It would take them a good half-hour to draw weapons from the armoury and get across to Westminster. It was unlikely that Linz would give them that much time. The only other option was at Horse Guards, but he wasn't sure they would move for him. He knew a colonel at the barracks; it was a risky strategy but it was worth a try.

'Major,' he tried to sound measured, 'unlike you I'm afraid I don't have the same authority to make decisions. I shall need an authorization from the Home Office to release the bodies. I can get this now but it will require a little time. I shall have to ask you to be patient and wait while I make the arrangements?'

There was silence at the other end. He could hear Linz breathing and then the sound of muffled voices speaking in German. Linz had his hand over the mouthpiece; Peters could not hear what was being said. He waited. 'All right Commissioner, I will wait for you, but I shall give you only a half hour. After that I shall order my men to take the bodies – by force if necessary. Is that clear?'

'Thank you, Major. That should be enough time. Let me speak again with the sergeant and I will instruct him.'

The sergeant was back on the line. 'Sir?'

'Where are they at the moment?'

'Here in the main entrance.'

'Keep them there if you can, I'm sending for help. Do you have any armed officers in the building?'

'One or two.'

'Alert them.'

'I already have sir.'

'Good man, just sit tight for the moment. I'm on my way over to you.'

Half an hour was better than he had hoped for. Now the idea occurred to him that he might try to get both Snow Hill and the Horse Guards into the action. He picked up the phone again and dialled a new number.

'Guardroom,' said a voice at the other end of the line.

'Oh, good evening. This is Commissioner Peters speaking. Can you put me through to Colonel Anderson please.' There was a wait, then the sound of a line connecting.

'Colonel Anderson's office.'

'Can I speak to the Colonel? It's Police Commissioner David Peters here.'

'Sorry sir, he's away from the office for the moment. Can I give him a message, or you could call back later?'

It took Peters no more than 15 minutes in a taxi to get over to Rochester Row. As the cab turned the final corner he could see clearly a group of men standing in front of the steps of the station building. They were in civilian clothing, but

188

they were armed. Two of them were dressed in black shirts – Mosley's men, he thought contemptuously. There were two cars and a van parked close by; each one bore the Swastika pennant, their drivers gathered around the van smoking. He walked up the steps, brushing aside one man who tried to bar his entry. He could see Linz inside standing in the main reception hallway. He was decked out in full military uniform. He bore the air of a man who was feeling supremely confident.

'Sir,' the desk sergeant saluted.

Peters returned it and then turned to Linz. He now had to stall for time. It would be another quarter hour before the men from Snow Hill could get there. He had no idea if Anderson would show or if he had even got his message. He thought it unlikely that help would be coming from that quarter.

'Well,' Linz said abruptly, 'do you have your authority?'

'Not yet.' Linz looked at his watch.

'Don't test my patience, Commissioner. You have ten minutes – no more. What do you have to do?' Desperately he groped around for a plan. If he could get Linz out of the main lobby and into an office he could isolate him from the thugs outside and interrupt the chain of command. Without him, they would be less able to resist help whenever that arrived. It would also make it easier for him to stall the German.

'I need to call my superiors at the Home Office. I cannot do anything without proper authority. Sergeant, have we got an office we can use? I am sure this matter will shortly be resolved.' He hoped Linz's sense of orderliness would prevail. It did; Peters gestured to the sergeant to lead the way.

'In here, sir – you can use the Super's office.'

'Be seated, please.'

Linz sat down stiffly, his back straight, his gloved hands clasped in his lap.

'Sergeant, can you rustle up some tea? Would you care for tea, Major?' Linz dismissed it with a wave of one hand.

'Commissioner, you are nearly out of time. Unless you do something I shall not wait longer.'

Peters picked up the phone then put it down. 'Of course, the switchboard is closed.'

'Then you have run out of time.'

'No, no, the sergeant here can get me a line.' Peters hurriedly scribbled on a piece of paper and handed it to the sergeant. 'Go back to the front desk and look out for this.'

Linz stood up abruptly. He held out his hand. 'Let me see that!'

The sergeant looked at Peters, uncertain about what he should do and waiting for some kind of order, but before he got a response Linz grabbed the paper out of his hand. He unfolded it and read the words EXPECT COMPANY. He turned angrily on Peters, screwed up the note and threw it onto the desk.

'What is the meaning of this? What are you up to Commissioner?'

'This simply means I am hoping for someone to arrive from the Home Office. I am sure they will be here shortly.'

'Enough of this, I shall order my men to remove the bodies and you will not stop me. Is that understood?' He left the room with Peters and the sergeant right behind him.

'Bugger. Now the game's well and truly up.'

As they reached the main lobby Peters tried again to buy time but Linz shrugged him off. He removed his pistol from its holster and stood threateningly in front of Peters. 'You will not interfere with this further. Go back to your office and wait. I will come with my men and you will release the bodies to them.'

A small group of station officers had now assembled by the main reception desk. Others were standing in a doorway. There were no more than a handful on duty at that time of the day and most of them were elsewhere in the building. They looked uncertain about what to do. Linz pulled open the door to the main entrance. He stood on the steps and signalled to the men loitering around the vehicles parked in the street. One of them opened the back door of the van and pulled out two canvas stretchers. The group carried them across to where Linz stood, then walked up the steps. Inside, Linz gave them his orders in German. The police officers around the desk just stared helplessly as the stretchers disappeared down the corridor, the orderly stamp of boots charting their progress.

A short while later the echo of returning boots was heard again. Linz looked triumphant – he had what he had come for. Now, ignoring Peters, he marched out through the main door and down the steps. As the second stretcher disappeared the desk sergeant walked the few paces to where Peters stood. He looked disappointed. 'Sir, a message came in while you were in the morgue. Snow Hill won't be coming. It seems some daft fanny upstairs overruled your orders. Sorry.'

Peters looked sourly in the direction of the doors. Through the glass he saw the last of Linz's armed men walking down the steps. 'Well, we tried,' he replied. 'Let's get this place back in order shall we. I shall have to make a report.'

He stood there staring at the main entrance door for a moment longer, wondering what the consequences of the confrontation with Linz might be. He would probably be carpeted but he felt justified in his actions. The Germans would carry out their forensics and conclude that Churchill was probably still alive, although he was already certain they had concluded this from the morning visit when Mosley had said as much. The two burned bodies were probably sent to assassinate Churchill, or kidnap him for a show trial in Berlin. So they would try again to find him.

His thoughts were interrupted by a noise outside on the steps. A man in khaki battledress pushed the door open. His uniform bore the insignia and rank of a colonel of the Household Cavalry. He strode across to Peters smiling broadly. 'David, sorry to be a bit late.' He shook Peters warmly by the hand. 'I was across the road with the Tank boys when your SOS came through. There wasn't time to get my lot together so I borrowed some of theirs. What's this all about?'

There was more noise and then another man came in. It was Linz; he was escorted by two of Anderson's men and he was ragingly angry. 'How dare you interfere with a member of the Legation!' Linz's face was pale and pinched with pent-up anger. 'You will pay a high price for this.' He turned on Anderson. 'You, too, Colonel will find yourself facing a court martial. Berlin will not allow you to get away with this. You would be advised to withdraw your soldiers and leave. It is an offence under the Treaty to try to detain me or my men.'

Anderson looked thoughtful. 'You are not detained, Major. You and your men are free to go.'

'And the bodies?'

Anderson looked at Peters. There was the hint of a question in his eyes; he knew the situation was not good and he didn't want to make it worse if he could help it.

Three of Linz's men then came into the room followed closely by more of Anderson's men. At the back of the hall, taking up positions behind the bulk of the substantial oak reception desk, several police officers now appeared with handguns. Everybody now seemed to be armed.

Peters knew there was every chance this thing could end up bloody. It would only take one ill-considered move, one twitchy trigger finger, one hothead to suddenly lose his nerve and the whole place could explode. He saw that Linz now had his hand resting on the butt of his gun. Christ, he thought, he's going to draw the bloody thing and start a gun fight. Linz hesitated, probably realizing he was now outnumbered and outgunned. He stood there motionless for a moment, his hand still on the butt of the pistol. Every man in the room stiffened, waiting, watching, and ready to act, but nothing happened – it was a stalemate. 'Very well,' Linz said slowly. 'I shall leave, Colonel, but don't think you have won, Commissioner. We shall be back.'

Peters said nothing for fear of setting Linz off again, but inside he was jubilant – the Nazi lout had been defeated. But as one of Linz's men reached out and pulled the door open, another player stepped in, unexpected and unannounced.

The newcomer was a slight, youngish looking man in his mid-twenties with a fresh complexion and startlingly blue eyes framed by a pair of cheap steel-rimmed glasses. He wore a charcoal-grey suit and a black bowler hat. He was not armed and not in military dress, but he strode in confidently. He seemed unconcerned by the guns and the nervous men holding onto them. The appearance was so unexpected that for a moment nobody moved and through that small gap in time the fresh-faced man deftly stepped, placing himself between Linz and Peters.

He half turned his back to Peters and held out a hand to Linz. Linz removed his hand from where it had been hovering over the butt of his sidearm and accepted the offer to shake. He looked warily at the newcomer.

'Grainger, Home Office,' he said quietly and politely. 'We had a call from your office, Major Linz – I take it you are Major Linz?'

'Of course.'

'Good.' He turned his head to Peters. 'I believe we have a little problem here and I've been sent round to see if I can't sort it out. He waved a piece of paper at them; it bore the Home Office crest. 'Commissioner, would you mind awfully, sir, if we used an office to talk in private? I think it best.'

Neither Linz nor Peters replied; they just stood there, a look of surprise on their faces. 'Excellent. First class – oh, and gentlemen can we clear this lobby, please. Colonel, I don't want to see any guns around here when I come back. All I want to see is policemen in this lobby. Major, please arrange to have your men wait outside in the street.' The three trooped off to the Super's office out of which Linz had just recently stormed.

Inside the office Grainger immediately sat down in the Super's chair and, by that simple expedient, made it clear who was in charge. He laid out the paper he had been carrying, planted both elbows on the desk and leant forward. There was half a grimace and half a smile smeared across his face.

'Gentlemen, I am here with instructions both from the Home Office – Commissioner Peters – and from the German Legation to His Majesty's Government – Major Linz. You', and here he glanced at them both, 'will take your instructions from me. This is my authority.' He picked up the paper and then let it drop back onto the desk.

'So, let us look at the problem. There are two corpses. You, Major, say you want them because you say they are German citizens.' Linz opened his mouth to respond but Grainger held up a hand, 'Let me finish, please. Commissioner, you say you want them because they are evidence.'

'That is correct.'

'Well, one thing is clear, you can't both have them.' He raised his eyebrows over the rim of his glasses like a school teacher addressing two naughty children. 'Commissioner, the minister is most unhappy about what has happened here and he is especially concerned about the confrontation that has occurred. However, he wants a resolution to this matter that will be acceptable to the Legation. The bodies are to be released into the custody of Major Linz.'

Linz smelled victory. 'Thank you, Herr Grainger.'

Grainger put on a sterner look. 'There are conditions. There are conditions because there are complications. It is the view of both parties, the Legation and my Minister, that this incident is best forgotten. Neither side wishes to engage in a diplomatic row. Therefore, you will be required to withdraw your complaint, Major.'

Linz stiffened. 'Herr Grainger, the Reich has been insulted and I will not just walk away and forget this matter. I was held against my will by your police and that is a clear breach of protocol within our Treaty. I have already made my complaint through my office.'

'Nevertheless it must be withdrawn.'

Linz looked grim again. Inside he boiled; how insolent these people were, how arrogant for a defeated nation. Had they no shame?

Grainger ignored the signs of ire and carried on, now reading from the paper in front of him. 'Commissioner Peters, sir, the Minister wants you to know there will need to be an internal inquiry. It is only fair to warn you that you may be disciplined.'

Peters nodded but said nothing. Linz looked interested. 'Will this inquiry mean a punishment?'

'That is not for me to say.'

Linz looked satisfied. 'Very well, I shall withdraw my complaint.'

Grainger stood up, indicating the meeting was at an end. He plucked the paper off the desk. 'Now we need to get these bodies out of here.'

'They are already in our vehicle.'

'Yes, Major, but there is a process to be observed. You will have to return them to this building and then the correct paperwork has to be completed. After that you can take them back to your vehicle.' With that he walked briskly up the corridor to the main lobby, which was now empty of all but the sergeant and three constables.

'Sergeant, take these men and round up another one please. We need a stretcher party.'

'Is this absolutely necessary, Herr Grainger?'

'I regret so – we have to observe the rules. Is that not so, Sergeant?'

The sergeant grinned. 'That's how we've managed to run an empire for all these years, sir,' he said smugly, then walked off to find another constable for the party.

The bodies came back in, were formally identified, documented, signed for and taken back out of the building to the waiting van. Linz shook hands with the man from the Home Office, who had now put the papers in his brief case and was once again wearing his bowler hat. Linz looked churlishly at Peters and gave a perfunctory grunt for his goodbye. Then he clicked his heels like a Hollywood stereotype, raised his right arm vigorously in a Nazi salute and shouted a brisk 'Heil Hitler!'

Linz left; he had his bodies – now he was determined Peters should pay a price for the slight. As he went down the front steps he passed Anderson coming up. Anderson saluted but the German ignored him.

'Pleasant character,' he joked as he joined Peters and Grainger. 'I imagine that's not the last we'll hear from him and his bloody Legation on the matter, though.'

Peters looked dejected. 'I almost wished he'd tried it on. It would have been a pleasure to see him shot. Thanks for the support, Harry. Oh, this is Harry Anderson by the way, an old friend of mine. Hope it doesn't get you into hot water, Harry.'

Anderson touched his cap. 'Shouldn't worry too much on my score – happy to oblige. He turned to Grainger. 'Bit difficult for David here I imagine. Can't see the Kraut taking it lying down – even if he did get his bloody corpses.'

Grainger looked apologetic. 'Yes, a bit awkward old chap, but Linz did walk into a government building waving a firearm, and that is a clear breach of the Treaty as well – one for which he could be legally detained,' he paused, smiled and then added, 'under the Treaty, that is.'

Later that evening, during dinner, the phone rang in the flat. Muriel answered it. 'It's the Home Office.' The conversation was brief and when he sat down he was subdued.

'I've been suspended. It's temporary, of course – the Home Secretary thinks it's best – just for a few weeks. He wants to cover his back over today's business. He thinks we need to show the Legation we're taking the incident seriously.'

'Will there be a disciplinary hearing?'

'Probably – just for show.'

'I don't understand why the government doesn't support you more.'

'It can't. The truth is we have no power, no real power – we bartered it away for a bag of beans – only there isn't going to be any giant beanstalk, there isn't going to be any Jack the Giant killer and there's no damned golden goose either.'

They finished the meal in silence. Muriel made coffee and sat next to him on the settee, holding his hand. 'Well, at least you will get some time off. Let's go home tomorrow – I don't like it here at the moment.'

He patted her hand. 'What about the shops and the restaurants, won't you miss them? I thought you liked being in London.'

'There are shops in Guildford – and restaurants too. We should go out to a restaurant as soon as we get back to the house. An evening out – just the two of us, like we used to do before this wretched war came along,' and she gave him a little hug. He had, she thought, been such a handsome young man when they first met and at 54 he still was. He had looked after himself and he still looked good in his dress uniform. She was proud to stand alongside him at public functions. But, even so, the war had aged him – but then it had aged everyone.

On Saturday morning they went in a taxi to Waterloo station and from there took the 8.55 Portsmouth Harbour train as far as Guildford. In normal times they would have been driven down to the house by a police driver, but these times were not normal. His superiors had suggested it might not look good if he was seen to be still benefiting from 'company perks'. The Germans saw everything and they would see this. It didn't worry him but it angered him. The reality was unpalatable; call it what they would, this was an occupation. The future that lay before him no longer looked appetizing; he saw the scrap heap looming on the horizon.

As the train slipped out of London they watched the city slowly merge into the suburbs. With the first stop, Surbiton, they were finally into Surrey. The streets were lined with large London plane trees, planted more than a century before. Their massive gnarled trunks, mottled grey and white as they peeled off the summer growth and shed the bark like wafer thin shingles. They still had leaves, though they were turning yellow and falling.

Peters stared abstractly out of the window at the passengers standing on the platform getting on and off the train. Just for a moment he idly wondered how their lives must have changed, but it was only a passing thought and he quickly went back to thinking about his own position. In his mind it was beginning to look darker than he had first thought and pangs of doubt started to invade his mind. Now the decision to oppose Linz was looking like a bad one. Linz had got his way in the end so it had all been for nothing. Worse, he realized he may have traded his career for a very uncertain future. How different things may now be because of that one decision.

The train jerked and started slowly to pull away and, as it did so, a man in a brown raincoat pushed his way through the people who lined the platform. For a moment he hesitated. Then he ran alongside the moving train, grasped a brass handle, opened a door and jumped into a carriage. It was about three compartments up from where he was sitting and when Peters heard the door slam a thought flashed through his mind. How important was it to catch that particular train? The man had taken a risk in jumping aboard like that – had it been worth it? What if, say, his sleeve had caught around the handle and he had been dragged along the platform, possibly killed. Like him, the man may have ended up worse off for making a split-second decision that turned out to be a bad decision – even though it might have seemed like the right idea at the time. It made him realize that people did that kind of thing all the time and that harrowing over the consequences was a waste of time. It would change nothing; he had to live with it and take control of what flowed from it. The train gathered pace and he began to feel more positive about the future. He would fight any attempt to scapegoat him by the Service or the Home Office. This was not Berlin; it was London and for the moment justice could still be relied upon. He would fight.

Woking was the last stop before their destination. It was a depressingly ugly town built only a hundred years before to provide a watering halt for the steam locos before the line had been electrified. Then, the early steamers coming out of London were heading for Southampton, but they could only get as far as Woking before they had to top up their water tanks. The water towers were still there, gaunt ugly frameworks with heavy black steel tanks sitting on top, the hoses dangling from gantries like grotesque elephant trunks. There were still steam locos using the line but not so many now. Behind them, looking back, he could just see the green dome of a mosque. The Shah Jehan mosque had been built for the railway workers, Afghans who had laboured to construct the line in the previous century. It seemed curiously out of place, this item of oriental exotica in a dull Surrey town.

As the train began to move, the man who had jumped aboard so precariously at Surbiton suddenly decided to leave and at the very last moment jumped out onto the platform. Peters just caught a glimpse of him as he brusquely made his way towards the exit, then he was gone from sight. He laughed to himself; maybe the man just liked to take risks – to tempt fate. He had come across people like that in his career. Often they were criminals, although his friend Harry Anderson was similarly driven, which was why he joined a Guards regiment; he liked the challenge, he liked to measure himself against risky endeavours. The thought drifted out of his mind as the train passed by the village of Pyrford in the distance. He just caught a glimpse of the golf club through the thinning autumn foliage of the tall poplar trees. He would be able to get in a game or two now he was on temporary leave.

Guildford looked pretty in the morning sunshine. The sun lit up the pavement giving the flagstones a warm ochre hue. Muriel immediately felt she had come home. She was a local girl; she had been born in this busy little market town. There were more cars now but they still had the cattle market every Saturday and people came from all over the county when they held the annual agricultural show.

'I think we should go and find some elevensies.'

Muriel laughed, 'Elevensies? Don't be silly, darling, it's not even ten o'clock.'

'Then we shall have a late breakfast – I'm starving. Come on. We should be able to get something at the George.'

They left the station and walked at a good pace up North Street heading for the Upper High Street. Half way up she paused briefly and looked behind her towards Stag Hill. She could just see the partly built structure of the new cathedral rising up out of the mound. She had never really liked the design with its modern neo-gothic interpretation in reddish buff brick; somehow it seemed wrong for a place to worship the almighty creator. It was four years since work had started but the war had called a halt to the construction. Now the visitor was confronted by the stump of the knave caged around by rusting scaffolds and nobody was sure if it would ever be finished. However, as she stood for that brief moment and gazed at its forlorn outline, she felt a little warm emotion, a feeling of coming home, a sense of comfortable security. It was an ugly building but it was familiar and she liked that. Reaching the top of North Street, they turned left and started up the steep cobbled ascent of the High Street until finally they reached the George Hotel near the top.

Peters pulled open the big glass-panelled door and the smell of warm baking and coffee filled his nose. He took a big breath of the inviting aromas. 'Come on, old thing,' he said affectionately, 'we're in luck.' Contented, they sat for a while looking out of the window at the activity in the busy High Street. It all seemed nicely parochial and quietly he thought it would be good to spend some time away from the dirty air, the noise and the soot-stained buildings of London.

They walked back down towards the station and found a taxi to take them home. It was a short drive out of Guildford to the house in the nearby village of Merrow. The village had a pub on one corner and a flint-built Norman church on the other. Between them a lane passed close to their walls, then wound its way up to the chalky heights of the Surrey Hills. A short way up the lane Peters tapped on the window that separated them from the driver.

'Just here cabby, the next drive on the right.' The cab turned in through a rustic gate and drove the short distance to the front of the house.

It was not a large building but it was secluded and set back from the road; they had liked it the moment they saw it nearly twenty-six years before. Its half-timbered front was Elizabethan and so was the imposing front door. Its solid oak planks were studded with black iron bolt heads and it hung on heavy ornamental strap hinges. It had a sturdy air about it, the air of a fortress. Beyond the façade, however, the house was quite modern. Sometime in the early 1900s it had been reshaped into a more convenient dwelling and, once beyond the original entrance hall, it opened out into comfortable spaces with higher ceilings and large metal-framed windows.

The cab driver carried their suitcases into the hallway and then, having received a generous tip, doffed his cap in the old-fashioned manner and got back into his cab. But before he pulled away he hesitated and, leaning out of the window, called to Peters. There was a short conversation and then the taxi left. 'What was that about,' Muriel asked?

'I don't know. The cabby said somebody at the station had asked him about this address. Asked him if he knew where it was. He wondered if we were expecting a visitor. Apparently he sounded like an American.'

'We're not are we – expecting anyone?'

'Not that I know of. Especially not American – I don't know any Americans.'

'Well Tudor Cottage is a fairly common name.'

'Yes, but Trodds Lane isn't and the cabby was quite definite that he was looking for Trodds Lane in Merrow.'

'How very odd. You don't suppose it has anything to do with this ghastly Legation affair – do you?'

'I shouldn't think so – unless it's one of the Home Office Johnnies come to give me a ticking off. But the cabby said he thought he was American. Curious though.'

'So did he say what he looked like – this man?'

He looked thoughtful for a moment then, dismissing it, he shrugged. 'He didn't say. I suppose we'll find out when he turns up – if he turns up.'

******

Sunday morning announced another fine autumn day.

'Let's go to Wisley and walk round the gardens,' he said. 'It's such a nice day and the exercise will do us some good. I'll get the Riley up and running. We can have a spot of lunch in the restaurant there. The trees should look splendid by now – the leaves'll be turning colour on the maples and the liquidambars should be glorious.'

Arriving at the gardens, they parked the Riley and made their way to the ticket booth. The Royal Horticultural Society had opened the gardens at Wisley to the public in 1909 and it had immediately been popular with visitors. Sundays always attracted a good crowd especially when the weather was favourable. As they joined the queue, Peters stiffened. Muriel felt it and looked at him quizzically.

'What is it, darling?'

'Bloody Germans', he said, nodding in the direction of the entrance where three young men in the uniform of the Kreigsmarine loitered around the visitor gate, smoking and laughing. 'They're everywhere – we might just as well be occupied.'

'Come on', she said, linking her arm through his. 'Ignore them; let's not let it spoil such a lovely day.'

They climbed the path up to the top of Battleston Hill and admired the view over the open Surrey countryside, then worked their way along the tracks to admire the new rhododendron plantings. They had started to develop this part of the gardens three years before and already it had acquired a touch of maturity. Most of the shrubs were long past flowering but here and there late varieties, stimulated by the still warm weather, delighted them with sudden displays of brilliant reds, blues and whites.

It was as they were coming down the hill, heading for the restaurant, that Peters first caught a glimpse of something odd. They were almost at the bottom when he got the sense they were being followed. He glanced over his shoulder and was just in time to see what he thought was a familiar figure. It looked very much like the man who had jumped on the train at the last minute in Surbiton – the same man who'd made a last minute bailout at Woking. As they went into the restaurant he saw the man pass. He was wearing the same raincoat but his face was hidden by his hat and he couldn't be sure. As they were seated he looked out of the window but the man had gone. Peters dismissed it as a coincidence and then he remembered the conversation of the previous day with the cabby.

The food in the restaurant was not memorable, but it wasn't about the food; it was about being there, together, in old familiar surroundings, in the warmth of each other's company. They were out of London and back on their own ground and it felt good, even though the Linz affair lurked in the back of his mind. He thought about Merrow and Tudor Cottage and began to realize that this would probably be his life from now on. He thought, with luck, the Home Office would kick him upstairs with a gong and a pension. At worst, he might not get the gong – but so what, he had never thought much of medals. They had, he realized, been happier at Tudor Cottage than in the London flat. They had lived there since they were married in 1914. The early years had been exciting and full of promise. As a young detective sergeant in the Surrey Constabulary he had been spared the horror of the trenches and instead had spent his war following the trails and rumours of spies, undercover agents and subversives. The Irish question and the Sinn Feiners had been a major part of his life then and he had worked closely with the Special Branch and MI5. He had enjoyed his life and his career and the only one regret he really had was that they had never managed to have any children. Muriel, he thought, would have made a wonderful mother, but they had not been blessed and as the years passed and they turned to middle age they had come to terms with the idea that they would die childless. That did make him sad to think back on and he tried to put it away from his mind, though from time to time it crept slyly into his subconscious and there ambushed him with a brief moment of nostalgia and remorse.

Out in the foyer of the restaurant he left her and made his way to the washroom. He pushed open the door and there was the man from Surbiton station. He was medium height, strongly built and he still wore the raincoat. Peters looked around the cubicles – they were alone. The man from Surbiton station reached into the inside of his jacket. My God, he thought, he's got a gun, I'm done for. For a split second he thought of Muriel waiting outside and how she would survive his death. Then the policeman in him took over and, stepping forward to close on his assailant, he grasped his wrist before it came fully out of the jacket.

'Special Branch,' the man from Surbiton station spat out the words in a hushed but urgent voice. He pulled his wrist away from Peters' grasp and revealed a warrant card. 'I have to be quick because I'm sure I've been tailed.'

'I saw you jumping on at Surbiton. Was that what it was about?'

'Yes. Now just listen, don't say anything. The bodies they took from Rochester Row – neither of them was Churchill – they were two hit men sent by Berlin.'

'I guessed as much. Where is Churchill – is he still alive?'

'I don't know and it's better if you don't. Just listen; I can't stay in here too long.'

Before he could say more the door opened. Both men froze but it was only an elderly man with a walking stick who looked almost apologetically at them as if he felt he had intruded. They ignored him as he shut himself in a cubicle.

'The Legation now knows for certain that neither of those bodies was Churchill and they'll be out there looking for him – to finish the job. We know they have a new man coming over from Canada; we think he's a contract killer – an American. Trouble is we don't know who he is or what he looks like, and he may already be here.'

'How do you know?'

'We have an informant planted inside the Legation, but he doesn't have anything more than that.'

There was the sound of a toilet being flushed. There was the snap of a lock and the elderly man came out of the cubicle. He washed his hands slowly and methodically dried them. Then he left giving a little polite nod to each of them.

'Do you have a gun?'

Peters shook his head, 'No, I left my service revolver back in my office. Why, do I need one?'

'We think they may come after you, They probably think you know something.'

'Are you my bodyguard then?'

'No – I've been sent to warn you. You're on your own, I'm afraid. Officially I'm not supposed to be here but you've got friends in Special Branch; they sent me.'

Peters felt the blood draining from his brain; a cold sensation gripped his chest. All thoughts of a comfortable retirement in Merrow dissolved; a sense of near panic invaded his whole being. He looked intently at the other man.

'Tell me, did you ask a cabby at the station about my house – where it was?'

'No, why?'

'Someone did.'

The man from Special Branch looked grim. 'They're already here. You need to   leave. Is there anywhere else you can go to lie low?'

'Only the London flat, but they'll be watching that.'

'Find a hotel, go to ground. Get a gun because I think you'll need one. Is there anyone you can stay with – a relative – brother or sister? What about your wife, has she got anyone?'

'We're both only children, our parents are dead. We're all that's left. Isn't there anything you can do?'

'No, I have to go. I'm sorry, I can't help you. You leave first; I'll wait for a moment.'

When he came out of the washroom Muriel was not there. The first thing to go through his mind was that she'd been abducted. A frisson of fear ran through his body like an electric shock. He began to imagine the worst. Frantically he walked the short distance to the exit, stepped through it and looked outside. He scanned the crowd of visitors but she was not there. He turned back into the lobby, sweating with anxiety. Then he saw her coming out of the restaurant with a waiter and relief flowed over him like a warm wave.

'Oh, there you are. You were so long in there I was worried something might have happened. This waiter had kindly offered to go in and look for you. Are you all right?'

'Yes, I'm fine,' he said quickly. 'We have to leave – now,' and taking her by the arm almost pulled her through the exit and into the crowd. Muriel looked perplexed.

'David what's going on? What's the matter?'

'I'll tell you in the car, come on.' He felt less exposed walking among the crowd and the bright sunlight made things seem more normal, but he knew that was just an illusion. Things were going very wrong.

******

The man from Surbiton station was the first to hear. He grabbed his raincoat and a trilby hat and made his way to the underground garage where he requisitioned an inconspicuous black Ford. As he crossed the Thames at Putney it began to rain. Why does it always seem to rain on Monday, he idly thought? The traffic going up Putney Hill was messy and slow. A bus was grinding its way laboriously up the steep street, held up by a brewery dray pulled by two dripping Shire horses. After a frustrating ten minutes he emerged onto Tibbet's Corner. It still had a gibbet in the middle of the traffic island where they had hung the last highwayman sometime in the previous century. The traffic thinned as he went down through Roehampton and when he finally joined the Kingston bypass he was managing a good 60 miles an hour. He passed west of the town of Kingston and joined the Portsmouth Road, heading south towards Guildford.

Nearly an hour later he turned into the driveway at Tudor Cottage. A constable immediately stepped in front of the car to bar the way. He held up his warrant card and, leaving the constable standing by the car, walked briskly to the house and through the Tudor oak door. A number of uniformed officers were moving carefully around the living room, examining the scene for evidence. In the middle of the room the officer in charge of the investigation was scratching down notes in a small book.

Still holding his card he introduced himself. 'Detective Sergeant Loughlin, Special Branch. Nasty business.'

'Superintendent Arbuckle, Guildford police. Yes, it's nasty all right. They seem to have been knocked about a bit before they were killed. It looks like they were tortured. Can't say for how long; afterwards they were shot. That's what alerted us – somebody heard shots and reported it. Here, I'll show you.'

They went into the dining room where the two bodies lay draped with sheets. Loughlin pulled back the covers and looked briefly. 'Poor buggers,' he said under his breath. 'You know who they were, of course?'

'Oh yes, they were quite well thought of around these parts. I've been ordered to report direct to the PM's office.' Arbuckle hesitated, 'I've been told not to make too much of a fuss out of this one. Was it political, do you think?'

'It's possible – or maybe just a revenge killing. He worked with the Branch on the Irish problem back in the fourteen-eighteen war. He was a clever and dedicated policeman. Who knows how many enemies you make in a career like his?'

'Frankly, and between us, I doubt we'll ever get to the bottom of what went on here.'

'I wouldn't try too hard. They'll probably sweep it all under the carpet anyway. It doesn't send out the right message to the public when you let your top policeman and his missus get knocked off. They'll give him a posthumous knighthood and put it all to bed. There aren't any relatives to grieve, you know.

No children, no brothers or sisters, parents are long dead. Strange really; they were the last of their line – slate wiped clean you could say. I must go. Good luck.'

Loughlin got into his car and drove back down to Guildford. At the top of the High Street he passed the George where two days before Peters and his wife had sat planning his retirement, but instead of turning right for London he carried on down to the bottom, crossed the Woodbridge that took him over the river Wey and headed south on the road to Portsmouth.

The late edition of the *Daily Express* bannered the headline TOP POLICEMAN AND WIFE KILLED AT HOME IN VIOLENT BURGLARY.

CHAPTER 19

Portsmouth, 3 September 1940

In Portsmouth, Loughlin's car stopped in a street close to the Bridge Tavern. Inside he sat watching in the rear mirror for anything suspicious; there was nothing. Satisfied he had not been followed he got out and made his way towards the pub. He pulled open the door of the saloon bar; the place was packed. He paused and looked around then elbowed his way through the press of sweating bodies, making his way to the public bar; it was full of sailors, mostly Royal Navy men with just a few Canadians – there were no Kreigsmarine. Antipathy had grown between the German sailors and the British; now everyone stayed in their own place. Segregation was the rule – unwritten, but the rule. Down the road a bit and close to the old Gun Wharf the Germans had set up their own *bierkellers* where they kept themselves to themselves; interlopers were discouraged.

In the public bar the air hung thick with the blue-grey smoke of tobacco. Men stood packed against each other, drinking and talking as frothing pints of mild ale and bitter were handed over the tops of heads to those who couldn't reach the bar counter. Slowly, he squeezed his way through the room until he got to a door leading into a corridor. The crush stopped at the mouth of the corridor and once into it he walked freely to the end and turned left. He looked around, checking that there was no one in sight, then went in through a door marked 'Gentlemen'. It was empty. He stepped up onto the tiled plinth in front of the long, rank-smelling urinal trough and stood looking down at the brown stained porcelain. Burnt-out cigarette butts sat in the residue of piss that puddled in the bottom of the gulley; soggy and deconstructing, the shreds of tobacco fanning out and floating freely in the shallow, fetid yellow pool. He waited to see if anyone had followed him, breathing in the acrid stench of the fag-tainted ammonia. Nobody came.

He moved quickly into a cubicle, shut the door and stood up on the edge of the toilet bowl. It was as it had been described to him when he was briefed; he knew exactly what he was going to find. Behind the toilet a large window with frosted glass opened onto the pub yard. Very carefully he turned the handle and pulled. It was stuck; countless coats of paint carelessly applied to cover the ruin of centuries now held it fast. He tugged on it until, with a noisy crack, it opened.

Cautiously he looked out into the yard. It was stacked with barrels and beer crates but there was nobody around. He was about to climb out through the window when the sound of someone coming into the toilet made him stop. He stood still, balanced on the edge of the toilet rim and listened. There were voices, two or more and the sound of splashing as the intruders relieved themselves. One of them told a joke and the others laughed. Then it was quiet again; they had left. Loughlin pulled himself up to the ledge and, putting one leg through the opening, he ducked under the lintel and let himself drop gently to the ground. He pulled the window shut until it jammed fast on the paint; crossing the yard, let himself out through the back gate.

Quickly he walked to the end of the road, crossed over and headed for the Gosport Ferry. The old chain ferry had run the cross-harbour service connecting the Gosport peninsular with the city of Portsmouth for nearly a hundred years. He heard the hooting siren that told him it was about to dock; as he turned the corner he could see the smoke rising from the steamer's stack as it moored stern-to on the jetty. A line was thrown around a capstan and then, with the front ramp lowered, the passengers poured off, spilling out into the street leading to the harbour station. As he crossed the road to the ticket office he looked around to see if he'd been followed, but there were so many people milling about the wharf it was impossible to tell.

The woman in front of him in the ticket queue was arguing about the price to take on a child and push chair. Again he scanned the crowd and the pavement on the far side of the road. If he missed this crossing he would be left standing around for a quarter hour waiting for the next one, exposed, in the open. At last the woman moved away. 'Give me a return,' he said through the hatch, dropping a shilling into the tray in front of the window. He was going to make it.

Once on board he went into the saloon where he installed himself on a bench and sat looking out of the window. The ferry quickly filled; there was a rumble from the machinery and a blast on the whistle – then it lurched as the winding gear took up the slack on the chain. It took less than ten minutes to cover the distance across the Sound to the Gosport pontoon. He waited till he was about half way across then he left the saloon and went out on deck. He moved along the side till he found a spot that was out of view of the saloon but from where he could see the door. He waited; nobody had followed him out.

Minutes later the ferry neared its destination. The passengers started to press forward, eager to get off and onward to wherever they were bound. As they shoved and jostled to disembark he allowed himself to be towed along by the flow until he was opposite a flight of steps that went below decks to the engine room. The door was open and he could feel the heat coming up from the furnace and boiler tanks. He stepped sideways as he came to the door and then, silently, he descended the metal steps. At the bottom there was another open door leading to the engine room. Inside two stokers were leaning on their shovels, taking a break from the back-breaking task of shovelling coal from a large steel bunker into the hungry mouth of the fire box. Unseen by the stokers, he slipped into a gap between the bunker and the bulkhead; it was suffocatingly hot. After a short while he heard the scrape of shovels and the clatter of coals being thrown into the fire, then the rumble of machinery and they were under way again. He stayed hidden until the ferry was almost back at Portsmouth and then, as quietly as he had come, he surreptitiously stepped through the hatchway and climbed the stairs. On deck once more he waited, scanning the wharf and the pontoon, looking for anyone suspicious. The coast was clear.

As satisfied as he could be that he was not being tailed he set out in the direction of Queens Street. About half way along it he turned left, heading towards the naval dockyard. He arrived at the main gate where he presented his warrant card and was waved through. A corporal in the Military Police saluted stiffly and then escorted him to a small brick-built guard house. Inside, a man in naval uniform was sitting at a table; he wore the insignia of commander. As Loughlin entered he stood up and, smiling, put out a hand to greet him. 'Jimmy Banks – Commander. Good to see you made it OK.'

'Fred Loughlin – Sergeant, Special Branch.' They shook hands warmly.

'Yes, we were expecting you,' Banks said casually, 'You weren't spotted by Jerry, I take it?'

'Are they here on the base?'

Banks looked sourly out of the window. 'Over there in one of the basins and the Semaphore Tower. They're around but mostly they stay out of our way.'

'I'm pretty sure no one followed me ...'

'Good show.'

'... but I've left a car just round the corner from the old Bridge Tavern. I'll need somebody to pick it up and take it back to London. It'll raise suspicions if it's left there too long.'

'We can arrange that. I'll find a man about your build and just to be sure can I suggest you let him have your hat and coat. We'll kit you out with something else.'

'Good idea.'

'Right then. Let's go and see the top brass. You're going to need briefing.'

Outside, the sky had clouded, grey and miserable. The fragile warmth of the September sun quickly turned to a chill and it started to drizzle with rain; a damp, uncomfortable wind-driven spray spattered his face. Loughlin pulled down the brim of his trilby, bent his head to the elements and followed Banks along a wide cobbled roadway. Underfoot the flint cobbles glistened black with a thin sheen of oily water, which made them feel slippery and unsure. A fivetonner with a canvas back trundled past. Inside it a group of sailors sat in two rows, gazing disinterestedly out of the open rear at the grey spray thrown up by the wheels. It started to rain harder. Then a staff car behind them hooted. As it pulled alongside them the driver wound down the window. 'Would you like a lift, sir?' They got in, hats dripping, and sat perched on the back seat.

'Turning nasty,' the driver said. 'Whereabouts do you need to go, sir?'

'The Commissioner's House.'

'Very good, sir.'

Admiral Sir William James had been His Majesty's Naval Base commander at Portsmouth for just over a year. He'd come to the office at the outset of the war with high ambitions and an appetite to fight the German Kreigsmarine, which he believed to be an inferior force to the Royal Navy, but he had not had the chance to prove his mettle or that of his ships. After the Paris Treaty he found himself faced with the indignity of sharing Portsmouth Sound and the Solent with his very enemy and it chafed him. He had close connections with government and this had helped his career, but now he felt that the government had betrayed him – him, his men, the whole country. Churchill, he knew, would have fought on, and he had been for it. In a straight fight he knew he could take on the best of the Kreigsmarine and beat them. Now he sat in port kicking his heels, his ships locked up in harbour while the Germans anchored off the Isle of Wight watched his every move. Since June there had been two giant battlecruisers, the *Scharnhorst* and the *Gneisenau*, moored in Number 4 basin, and there was a German observer presence in the Semaphore Tower monitoring shipping movements. He had been highly thought of in Admiralty House and widely tipped to become First Sea Lord, but that hope had faded with the Treaty and now, as he sat in his office contemplating his future, it all looked very bleak.

Loughlin and Banks jumped out of the staff car and ran for the entrance of an elegant eighteenth-century building known as the Commissioner's House. It had been built as a residence for the Port Commissioner but was now used to house the Commander - in - Chief of the Portsmouth fleet. Inside, a naval rating stood quickly to attention and saluted. They made their way up a grand staircase to the first-floor landing where a young lieutenant was sitting at a desk. He jumped up at the sight of the approaching senior officer and saluted. 'To see the Admiral,' Banks said, returning the salute.

'I'll leave you here,' he said to Loughlin. 'This lieutenant will take you in. Good luck, old chap.' The lieutenant led Loughlin the short distance to a large polished wooden door and knocked. He waited for a reply, then opened it and ushered Loughlin in. 'Sergeant Loughlin, Admiral.'

'Come in, Sergeant,' Admiral James said warmly. 'Do sit down.'

Loughlin drew back a chair away from the desk and sat. There was a knock and another visitor came in. The new man was dressed in a well-tailored pin-striped business suit with a dark blue polka-dot tie and a matching handkerchief tucked into the breast pocket. Loughlin calculated he was in his mid-fifties. He had a good head of hair that had gone grey in places and the face was firm, although around the eyes were the tell-tale lines of advancing years. The new man had an urbane, almost languid, look about him, but there was also an air of confidence that spoke of authority. Loughlin stood up in deference to the newcomer.

'Sit down, do sit down.' Loughlin sat again. The new man pulled another chair away from the desk and sat a bit off from him and at an angle so that all three now faced each other. James motioned to the other man. 'Let me introduce you. This is Sir Charles Armitage. Sir Charles is from MI5.'

Armitage looked at Loughlin for a moment as if assessing the man. 'You're a single man they tell me. Have you never thought to marry?'

'I did, sir, but it didn't work out. My career got in the way and she married another.'

'Anybody else in mind? Anyone close or special?'

'Not at the moment.'

'Good. You know we need a single unattached man for this task?'

'I had been told, sir.'

James opened a brown folder that sat on the desk in front of him. It was a thick folder, bulging with papers and tied together with green tape. He pulled out a few sheets and studied them. 'I see here that you have a very commendable service record.'

'Thank you, sir.'

'It says you are an expert in unarmed combat – and a qualified marksman.'

'Yes, I like to compete in ju-jitsu.'

'You've won medals.'

'Yes.'

'You also speak German.'

'I do.'

'Fluently?'

'With a Berlin accent, they tell me.'

The Admiral closed the folder and looked over to Armitage. 'Over to you then, Charlie.'

Armitage thought for a moment, choosing his words carefully. 'I have a highly sensitive assignment – a difficult and potentially dangerous assignment. Whoever does it may be putting themselves at risk. It involves going abroad for some time, possibly quite a long time. It is a top secret mission, so sensitive no word of it can be allowed to get out – not the slightest hint. It is so sensitive that even our own government does not know of it.'

He stopped, studying Loughlin's face to see the reaction. There was none, Loughlin just looked blankly back at him, waiting for whatever came next. Armitage leaned back in his chair. Slowly he said, 'I've been looking for a man to carry it out and I think you might be my man.'

'Will I be required to transfer from the Branch, sir?'

'I've already had you seconded – you're in my service now. I don't need to remind you that you are already bound under the Official Secrets Act. No, of course not – but, just in case, you need to know that this is Most Secret and to breath a word of it would be treason.' Loughlin nodded. He knew when he had been sent out from the office that morning there was some top op going on. That was why he had covered his trail so well.

'Where will I go to be briefed, sir?'

'Nowhere. I'm briefing you here – now. Bill, would you like to lay it out for our young sergeant.'

Admiral James drummed his fingers on the desk top. He looked serious. 'The Soviet-German Peace Pact, you will have heard of that.' Loughlin nodded.

'You will also be aware, I am sure, that there are tensions. Our intelligence has for some time been convinced it's fraying round the edges. You'll also know we're cooperating with the Germans on an operation to establish a supply base in the north of Canada. Our German partners tell us this is being set up to counter a possible Soviet aggression. We, however, do not believe this. We think the Germans are laying the ground for a multi-pronged attack on the Russians. Canada, we think, will be used as a base to close off the Barents Sea. If they can deny that exit to the Russians, all they have to do is stop up the Baltic and they're hemmed in, blockaded. With the Japanese controlling the Pacific coast they would be surrounded.

'Point number two. The Prime Minister has been toying with the idea that the Russians might be persuaded to help rid us of the Germans. Nobody believes in the Paris Treaty any more. It's a flimsy veil over what was has turned out to be an invasion through the back door. If the Germans do invade Russia, then the Soviets could become our ally – or they could just become a replacement for the Germans. Our worry is swapping a German tyranny for a Russian tyranny. We don't think this government is anywhere near tough enough to make a strong deal with the Soviet bear.'

So far, this was nothing Loughlin didn't already know. This stuff was not top secret; it had been common gossip around the office for months, ever since the Canadian operation had commenced. He wondered what might be coming next.

'A bit over three months ago, just before the first meeting of the Paris Treaty negotiators, we got a tip-off that two of Hitler's Nazi thugs were on their way to

London with orders to kidnap or kill Churchill; we weren't sure which. Before we could intercept them two Polish agents working for MI6 got to them and killed them.'

'The bodies held at Rochester Row.'

'Exactly.'

'So what happened to Churchill?'

'I'll come to that. A week ago a man – possibly an American though we're not sure – came into Britain. Two days ago we think he murdered Police Commissioner Peters and his wife. Peters and his wife both showed signs of having been tortured – you saw the bodies – but they weren't the target. It was Churchill they were after and we're pretty sure the killer thought Peters knew where Churchill was.'

'I knew about the American. It was our contact in the Legation who tipped us off. My chief sent me to warn Peters. What I don't understand is why the Home Office didn't do more to protect him.'

'The government is weak,' Armitage said, taking over the conversation. 'It's under the thumb of the Germans; they can't be trusted. They have to go before they do any more damage. They've sold out the Army and there's virtually no Air Force left any more. Only the Navy has the power to take over.'

'A coup!' Loughlin gasped. He had expected a surprise but he hadn't seen that one coming. 'Does that give you a problem of conscience?' James asked him.

'No.'

'Good, because what we have planned isn't going to be easy. It's going to need good patriotic men to see it through and it'll need a strong leader once we've got back the reins. We can't move yet; the Navy could secure the country in the short term but it wouldn't be able to hold it for long. But if we are right and the Germans tear up the Berlin–Moscow pact that would change the game. We need to be ready. With the Germans committed in Russia, we'd just about be able to pull it off. We could easily neutralize whatever bit of their fleet they leave here and they have virtually no Wehrmacht in the country. The Army think they could take them on.'

He stopped and waited, studying Loughlin to gauge a reaction. It was important they had the right man, a committed man, for the task they had for him. Loughlin betrayed nothing by his facial expression.

'Then we come to the afterwards. It is not the intention that His Majesty's Navy should hold on to power once we have secured the nation; it has to be returned to democratic government, but it has to be a government that can be trusted to hold on to the country, not give it away like this lot. Britain will need a strong leader, a man of integrity, someone the country will stand behind. In short, we need Churchill.'

'He's here?'

'He is. When we got wind of the plot, the Army lifted him and brought him here. That was in June and he's been here ever since – right under the noses of the Kreigsmarine.'

'So he's not dead. I was sure he wasn't. Peters hung onto the bodies because he didn't want the Legation to find out it wasn't Churchill, of course. So the American …'

'… was here to get Churchill; that's what we think.' Armitage finished the question for him. 'Now we have to get Mr Churchill out of the country to a safe haven.'

'Where's the American now?'

'We don't know. We think the Germans got him out to Canada on one of the supply ships.'

Armitage leaned closer to Loughlin. 'Churchill is to go to America; you're going with him. He'll need protection, even in America – especially in America because we don't know how the Americans will take his arrival there.'

'They don't know he's going?'

'Nobody knows he's going except me, the Admiral here and, of course, Mr Churchill – and now you. You've made all the necessary arrangements for a long stay away, I take it?'

'The office has taken care of it. They haven't told me much – just I would be out on this assignment for some time.'

Armitage stood up. 'Good. We can't have you wandering around out there; not now you have all this information. Come on, let's take you to your new quarters.'

Admiral James didn't bother to stand. He looked firmly at Loughlin. 'Good luck,' he said curtly. 'Don't blow it, there's a lot riding on this.'

'Understood, sir.'

'Off you go then.'

They went past the lieutenant still seated at his desk, down the stairs, then past a number of rooms until they reached a dark narrow hallway which led to the kitchens; there they found Commander Banks waiting. They stood in the kitchen for a moment. Armitage pointed to some clothes lying on one of the kitchen tables. 'You'll need a change. Can't have you wondering around in civvies. Could give the game away. Here, get into these.' Loughlin picked up the bundle; it was the uniform of a second lieutenant in the Fleet Auxiliary. Quickly, he stripped down and changed into his new clothes. Armitage handed him a canvas duffle bag. 'Here,' he said, pushing it towards him. 'Everything you'll need is in there including your orders. Once you've read them get rid of the paper; burn it. Good luck. Ever been to America?' Loughlin shook his head, indicating he hadn't. 'You'll like it. Everything's in colour, not black and brown like here.'

The *Regent* was on a berth in an outer basin, its grey silhouette almost merging with the miserable sky that hung over it. There was a dock crane working alongside loading cargo. Banks left him as they reached the dock. A forward gang plank was down and he made his way towards it. With the kit bag slung over his shoulder, he climbed the slippery wooden structure and entered through an opening in the hull to a covered walkway. As he stepped onto the deck he was met by a Chief Petty Officer. 'Follow me, sir,' he said curtly, and led the way aft. A man came walking towards them. 'Atkins,' the CPO said curtly, 'take this officer to his quarters – he's in A17 – and then go topside and join the loading crew, and look smart about. We shove off at seventeen hundred. That's less than three hours.'

'Aye aye, Chief.' Atkins nodded his head in the direction he had just come from, beckoning Loughlin to follow. 'This way, sir.'

The cabin was cramped. Through a small porthole he could just see out across the rain-pocked water to the outer mole. He took off his wet coat and put it on a hook where it hung damp and limp like some veiled spectre. There was a small bunk, no more than a pipe cot, and another one over the top, though that was stripped and he deduced he was the only occupant. There was a small table fixed to one of the bulkheads and a chair. Next to the cots were two fixed lockers.

He opened the neck of the duffle bag and pulled out the contents onto the lower bunk. It didn't contain a lot: some civilian clothing, a wash bag with razor and toothbrush, a tablet of soap. Deeper into the bag he found a pack of 20 cigarettes and a lighter, then right at the bottom an oilcloth packet tied with a string and sealed with an admiralty wax. He could feel there was something hard inside. He broke the seal and unrolled the packet. The hard object was a small 32-calibre automatic pistol: Belgian, made by FN. There was a box of ammunition and a spare clip. The last item in the packet was a manila envelope; on it was written NOT TO BE OPENED UNTIL AT SEA. He sat down at the desk and looked at the envelope. In the corridor outside he could hear the sound of men passing and repassing as they prepared the ship for departure. He supposed he would be summoned at some point but, for the moment, there was nothing to do but wait, so he lay down on the bunk and lit one of the cigarettes. It had been a long day and now it was good just to stretch out and unwind. After a bit, he stubbed out the cigarette and dozed.

He was awoken by the sound of the ships engines; the motion in the cabin told him they were at sea. He looked at his watch; it was seven o'clock – they must have been under way for a couple of hours. He went back to the desk and picked up the manila envelope. Pushing his finger in under the flap he tore it open. There was one folded quarto sheet of closely typed paper inside. Slowly he read his instructions. Churchill and a small entourage were on board. Walter

Thompson, his bodyguard was with him. Loughlin was to join forces with Thompson and keep Churchill safe while they established themselves in America, but he was not to make himself known to Churchill. His only contact was to be with Thompson. There was one further instruction. He was to make contact in America with an MI6 agent code-named Amber Rose; there was a contact phone number and a password – that was all. The instruction was clear on one thing: MI5 was convinced the Germans would make an assassination attempt in America once they knew of Churchill's whereabouts. Using the lighter, he set fire to the paper in an ash tray and watched it burn. He sat and stared idly as the paper flared up, then disintegrated into a wafer of black ash; small sparks glimmered around the edges and then, with a small wisp of smoke, it was dead. He prodded the incinerated remains into a fine powder.

There was a knock on the cabin door. Opening it, he was confronted by a rating; the rating saluted. Loughlin almost forgot to return it – a fundamental give away he thought; he must remember to return salutes and to salute senior officers.

'Excuse me, sir, but the captain would like to see you on the bridge. Can you follow me?' Loughlin attempted to leave but the sailor barred his way. 'Don't forget your cap, sir. Wouldn't do to get put on report the first day aboard.'

'Thanks; only just woke up – still a bit dozy.'

As they made their way along the open deck he could see more ships stretched out around them. They appeared to be in a convoy. The light had almost gone but the sky had cleared and there was a strong breeze blowing. The sailor clattered up the iron steps in front of him, then opened the door to the bridge; he saluted the officers inside. 'Second Lieutenant Loughlin, sir,' he announced, then stood back to let Loughlin through. The door banged shut behind him. From the vantage of the bridge he could now see the extent of the convoy. It was huge and stretched right to the horizon.

He tried to stand to attention and remembered to salute. The captain smiled as Loughlin steadied himself with one hand on the compass binnacle. He knew this was no sailor in front of him. 'Stand easy, Loughlin,' he said cheerfully, 'you'll soon get your sea legs.' He pointed out to the convoy ahead. 'Just wanted you to see this; there's as many again behind us. We need to have a chat – we'll go to my quarters. Take over, Number One.'

'My name's Davidson by the way,' he said as they walked along the companionway that led to his cabin. 'Don't worry, I know who you are, but be careful, I'm the only one who does. I suggest you keep to your cabin as much as you can. We shan't have you with us for long.'

Inside his cabin Davidson got out a decanter and two glasses. 'Here, have a glass of this – it's a good single malt.' He poured two generous measures, then sat down. 'How much do you know?'

'Only my assignment orders – otherwise nothing.'

'So you know what this ship is?'

'Well, from the uniforms I'd guess it's some kind of Royal Fleet Auxiliary.'

'That's right. The *Regent* is a repair ship and right now we're in a convoy bound for Hudson Bay. When we're two days out we'll get a call from one of the escort destroyers, the *Tenacious*, to say she's got damage to her steering gear. We'll detach from the convoy and hang around for a bit, then make our way to where she'll be slopping around. This will give the rest of the convoy time to get over the horizon. When we rendezvous with the destroyer we'll transfer our guests to her – and that will include you. From there it'll take *Tenacious* two days to get into the safety of American waters. Once you're inside, the Germans arc unlikely to follow. I don't think even that lunatic Hitler wants to upset the Americans; they're already touchy about the Canadian bases on their doorstep. Anyway, we're banking on the Kreigsmarine not spotting what's going on until it's too late, if they ever realize it at all.'

'How much does your crew know?'

'Nothing. Only my four officers know the real mission and even they don't know the identity of our guests. We didn't dare run the risk of this thing leaking out. If the Germans were to find out all hell would break loose.'

'And what's our port in America?'

'No idea. Once we've transferred you're on your own.'

Davidson got up, abruptly finishing the conversation. 'Right, shall we go to the mess? I expect you're starving.'

******

It was barely first light when he detected a change in the engine noise. The *Regent* was slowing and changing course. It was beginning. A short while later there was a knock on the cabin door and he was again summoned to the bridge. 'There she is,' Davidson said casually.   'That small light on the horizon – that's our man.' He held out his binoculars to Loughlin. 'You can just make her out on the horizon.'

It was twenty minutes later when Davidson spotted something else; there was a second light – it shouldn't be there. 'They've got a visitor, Number One. Take a look'. He pointed to the horizon and just right of the destroyer's running lights. 'About ten degrees to starboard. Can you see it?'

'You're right, sir.'

'Damn, what's that doing there?'

'Could be Jerry coming to assist.'

'Well, we don't damn well need that.'

As they closed, they could see the second vessel more clearly. It sat low in the water and rolled precariously in the grey Atlantic swell. The weather was worsening, a wind was getting up and was forecast to go to six or seven. If it got any worse it would make the transfer risky even for an experienced seaman. A bosun's chair was difficult enough in good weather, but in a storm it could be suicidal, especially for Churchill who was no longer a young man.

'It's Jerry all right. Looks like a U-boat. So what the hell's he doing there?'

'It's a type seven,' somebody said.

As the distance closed the U-boat moved its position so that it sat between the two vessels. 'Get some men on the guns, Number One, but make sure they keep their heads down; we don't want to raise any suspicion or panic Jerry. Best be ready though, just in case. Then let's get him on the radio – see if we can find out what's going on.'

On the main deck a group of men made their way forward to where a battery of four 4-inch AA guns were mounted in the bow. They moved quickly, crouching low, trying to stay out of sight of the U-boat. Hidden behind the armour-plated firing shields, they methodically set up the loading racks, ready to go into action if the order came.

In the radio room Davidson put out a call to the U-boat. There was a short, quiet delay then the receiver crackled into life. The U-boat captain came on the air. Davidson exchanged greetings then said, 'We are the repair vessel Regent. We are here to assist Tenacious. She has damaged her steering gear. What is your mission? Over.'

There was a long silence, longer than Davidson liked. Then the U-boat came back, 'Regent, we are patrolling this area. We picked up the call for assistance and came to see if we would be able to help. Is there anything we can do? Over.'

'U-boat, thank you, but we are fully equipped to handle the task. Over.'

'Regent, good, then we shall leave it in your hands. Good chances. Over.'

'U-boat, thanks and good sailing. Over and out.'

In another corner of the cramped radio room a sonar operator lifted off his headset. 'They're moving, sir.' Davidson let out a long, slow, pent-up breath. 'Thank the Pope for that.'

As he started back to the bridge, though, the idea struck him that something wasn't quite right. Had that been too easy? The U-boat had left without really questioning the destroyer's mechanical failure, which was something he hadn't expected. After all, the Germans had been monitoring British naval movements ever since *Ark Royal* had bolted for Australia with a small flotilla, following the Paris Treaty. He went back to the radio room and stuck his head round the door. 'Keep your ears open for that sub. Let me know if we pick it up again.'

The sun was up, but the light was watery and diffused by a heavy belt of cloud that socked in the sky. Around them the empty waste of the Atlantic stretched from horizon to horizon, a grey sheet of troubled water. The swell was cresting with white caps of salty spume drawn out in lines of spray. The wind was getting stronger. The transfer was not going to be comfortable or easy. Both ships were holding their position, their bows head up to the swollen water. Davidson had brought *Regent* as close to the destroyer as he judged safe. He looked out at the heaving deck of *Tenacious*; the crew had deployed a stairway but the base was constantly smashing into the rising waves, sending huge gouts of sea water surging across the lower steps. It would be difficult to get even a young fit man onto the stairs without having him immediately washed into the sea. With Churchill it would be impossible. There was no way for it – they would have to rig a bosun's chair. They got a Boxer rocket line across the destroyer. It took more than an hour to get the rig set up, and as the two ships see-sawed in the water, the chair swung violently from side to side, sometimes dipping so low it almost touched the ocean.

For the first time since he had boarded *Regent* Loughlin saw his charges: four figures huddled together on the bridge, looking anxiously at the contraption that was to convey them to the safe haven of *Tenacious* – two men and two women. He recognized Churchill and assumed the other man was Thompson; one of the women he thought must be Churchill's wife, Clementine, but he had no idea about the fourth member of the party. She was younger than the others, probably in her late twenties.

Davidson smiled wryly at Loughlin. 'Right, I need you to go over first. Make sure it works. If this bloody thing fails, you're the most expendable member of the group. Ever been in one before?'

'No – it looks precarious.'

'It is. Funny things, bosun's chairs. They're okay as long as you keep the two ships head-on to the sea, but if you let them get beam on then it can get a bit exciting.'

Loughlin settled himself into the canvas sling. It was, he thought, like sitting in a small hammock. They strapped a safety harness to him and secured it tightly to the ropes; then, with a jerk, they had launched him off the deck and there he was swaying in the wind with the water churning angrily beneath him. The progress was slow to start with but once the sailors working the ropes had found their rhythm it all began to run smoothly. The ride became more violent as he reached the midway point and he began to think he would be thrown clear into the ocean, but the harness held him firm, and although the chair yawed and swayed in great arcs he stayed in the seat. It took about ten minutes to reach the deck of *Tenacious*. Two anxious-looking sailors released him from the harness; he was thankful to be standing on a deck again. The chair started on its way back. Loughlin stood and watched it go. Now it was empty it moved more quickly and the canvas chair, without any weight to stabilize it, flapped wildly in the wind like a huge manic bat.

He stood for a while, then made his way forward until he reached the stairs that led up to the bridge. As he was about to mount the first rung, a crewman appeared at the top and started on his way down. As he came closer Loughlin thought for a moment that something was odd about his appearance, but before he could put a finger on it the man had gone. He climbed the stairs and, as he opened the door leading to the bridge, he saw it again on the first sailor standing just inside – he was wearing sub-mariner's boots. When the first officer turned to face him, he was dressed in a Kreigsmarine uniform. Loughlin was momentarily confused but, by the time he had gathered his thoughts, the sailor just inside the door had drawn a pistol and had it pointed at him.

The officer looked at him for a moment observing the shock on Loughlin's face. 'Don't be surprised, Lieutenant. I came aboard before your ship arrived and, I have to say, when the sea was a lot calmer, so I was spared the indignity of your style of arrival.'

'You came off the submarine?'

'Of course. We have known of the plans to move Herr Churchill for some time. We just didn't know when.' Loughlin's thoughts were now racing. Churchill would be the next one across, if he hadn't arrived already, and he'd fall right into their hands. He looked around him and realized that there were too many of them to do anything.

'Captain,' he said, addressing the German in front of him, 'if that's what you are. This is a gross breach of protocol. You have no right to board one of His Majesty's ships. This amounts to an act of piracy. What have you done with the crew?'

The German sneered. 'We have every right. We have the only right there is – it comes with having the power, you see. Your leaders signed away your country's rights at Paris? Have you forgotten so soon? Take him below. He can be introduced to the crew.' He felt the gun prod him in the back. The German behind him took hold of his collar and pulled him round to face the door. Loughlin resisted and the seam on his jacket shoulder parted. A second crewman grabbed the other shoulder and they slammed him hard against a bulkhead, splitting his forehead where it made contact with a locker handle. The pain shot through him, making him feel faint. He sagged at the knees. For a moment everything in his vision went a pale shade of green and he thought he was going to pass out. Slowly he recovered.

The captain grabbed him by his necktie and jerked him towards him. He shouted angrily at Loughlin, pulling him right up to his face. 'If you resist, you'll be shot! Don't act stupidly. It isn't necessary; you can't hope to achieve something.' There was a moment of tense silence. The captain let go of the tie and, with a slight jerk of his head, signalled his removal. Loughlin shook himself free.

'All right, I'm going,' he snapped, and moved towards the door. He was blocked by another submariner, this one with a submachine gun.

'You will go with him. Walk slowly in the direction he tells you and behave properly, or he has orders to shoot you. Is that all clear, Lieutenant?'

Loughlin grunted.

'Good – so don't do anything foolish.'

The door was opened and Loughlin again felt the barrel of a gun in his back. He went cautiously down the steel steps, still feeling unsteady, but his mind was now calmer and he started to examine his position. As they went in through a hatch, he just caught a glimpse of the chair arriving. It must be Churchill. His heart sank at the thought of what might happen once they had everyone aboard. As his guard stepped through the hatch the ship lurched, hit by a heavier wave. It flung the man violently against the wall of the companionway they had just entered and, for a moment, he went off balance. There was just time in that moment for Loughlin to see the other man's face. He was not as young as the others; his hair was greying and he moved uncertainly. He might not be too difficult to overpower, especially if they were caught by another wave like the last one.

He decided to move more slowly; he stumbled a little pretending to be weak from the blow to the head, forcing the submariner to stay close and keep prodding him with the muzzle of his weapon. At the end of the companionway they encountered another flight of stairs. This, he thought, might be his chance. He moved slowly down the steep steps, hoping for another big wave, but as they descended into the depths of the destroyer the effect of the wave motion became less. They went through another hatch and then stopped. In front of them was the entrance to an ammunition lift. The guard shoved him to one side and pushed a button with the muzzle of his weapon. There was a loud humming noise and clanking of chains followed by a dull thump, announcing that the lift had arrived. The German slid the door open. Inside it was dully lit by a small bulkhead light. He felt the prod in the back again and stepped in. The walls were flanked by shell racks; there was little room to move. He stood facing the back wall, all the time searching furtively for an opportunity, a chance to catch the man off guard. The doors shut and the lift started its slow descent.

They reached the bottom and still he had found nothing; time was ebbing away. He knew that once he was locked away in the bowels of the ship there would be nothing he could do. Between the lift and his final destination it could not be far, so it had to be then or not at all. The doors opened and Loughlin turned to get his first good look at the German – he was definitely a much older man. He motioned towards the exit with the gun. Loughlin got to the threshold; this, he thought, was his last opportunity.

He faked a stumble, clinging on to the edge of the lift as if he were about to pass out. The German kicked at him angrily and, as he did so, Loughlin caught him neatly by the boot and up-ended him. He heard the crack as the man's ankle snapped under the weight of his twisting body. The German was vaulted backwards by the force of the move, then his head banged loudly against the back of the lift. The machine gun flew out of his grasp and spun round his neck on its strap. The German was down flat on his back, his head wedged up against the ammo racking at an awkward angle. He lay still except for one leg, which was twitching. Loughlin dragged him out of the lift and propped him up against the wall. He felt for a pulse but found none; his neck had broken in the fall. He was dead. It was the first time he had ever used his skills in real combat – they had worked. For a moment he looked at the corpse. The open eyes stared emptily at him and the mouth was locked wide open, frozen in a last gasp, an uneven row of teeth still wet with saliva. A small trickle of blood was beginning to dribble from one corner of the open mouth. In that moment the thought flashed through his mind that somewhere someone was going to get the desperate news that would probably devastate their lives. Just for a second he felt a pang of guilt that he had killed a man, but it passed as quickly as it came.

Frantically he searched the tunic pockets of the dead sailor. He found a key in one of them but he had no idea where he was in the ship or where the crew were being held. The *Tenacious* would normally have a complement of around five hundred but he knew it was running on a skeleton crew; even so, there couldn't have been fewer than around forty to fifty men. Where would you keep that number? It would have to be one of the store rooms; most of the hatches and doors were without locks that required keys. He worked his way along the ship, moving towards the bow where the larger store areas were located. He found nine of them in the forward boatswain's store, cramped up together in the narrow isles between the ceiling to floor shelving. As he pushed open the door he heard the combined intake of anxious breath. As they scrambled out of the store he saw they were all officers, among them was the captain.

'Well done, Lieutenant. How did you manage it?'

'I'm not a lieutenant – don't let the uniform fool you. I'm MI5 and somehow I have to neutralize that lot on the bridge. How did they get aboard? What happened?'

'They surfaced about half an hour before our rendezvous. They said they'd picked up our call and offered to send an engineer over to look at the problem. We couldn't refuse without arousing suspicion. Three of them came on; they were armed and they jumped us before we could do anything. Then more of them came over.'

'How many are there?'

'Ten, I think. I don't know if they've brought any more on board.'

'Well, they're one less now.'

'What's happening? How did you get here?'

'There's no time, I'll explain later. We have to take back the ship. Where are the rest of your men?'

'They're locked in the kitchens. Follow me, I'll show you.'

In the kitchens they found the remainder of the crew, another thirty-two men. They had armed themselves with chef's knives and butcher's cleavers and were fired up for fight. At the sight of their captain they pressed forward, all asking questions at the same time and making more noise than sense. The captain held up one hand and put the other over his mouth, signifying they needed to be quiet.

Loughlin thought for a moment. 'This is going to be tricky. There were no more than five on the bridge so the rest must be working the bosun's chair. I counted four of them on the ropes when I came aboard. There's one lying dead by the ammo lift, so that means probably one more is roaming around somewhere. We have to find him and neutralize him before we can go for the bridge. When we take it, we have to do it quickly – we have to take them out before they get a chance to radio that U-boat. Are there any small arms we can get to?'

'There's an arms locker but the key is on the bridge.'

'Could we break it open?'

'Shouldn't think so, not without making a terrible racket. They'd be sure to hear.'

'OK, then we have to go with what we've got. I need you captain, your radio officer and the three fittest ratings you've got. The rest stay here – out of sight – and I need someone to help me get that body out of the way; we can stick him in a store room for now. Right, let's go, and stay behind me – I don't want any of you between me and a target if comes to shooting.'

As they got to the body they heard the whirring of an electric motor. The door of the ammo lift closed with a dull metallic clunk. Then there was the whine of the lift ascending. They stood frozen for a moment. The whine started again; the lift was coming back down.

'Get that bloody body out of here. Now. Quick!' The two ratings grabbed the corpse, one under each arm, and hoisted it off the floor. They ran down the corridor with it and barely made it out of sight when the lift arrived at the bottom. Loughlin went to the nearest bulkhead light and smashed it with the butt of the machine gun. The immediate area of the corridor was plunged into gloom. He moved back into the shadow and pressed himself flat against the bulkhead and waited, his heart pounding. There was a thump from the lift as it halted at the bottom. For a moment nothing happened and he thought that perhaps it was a false alarm and that the lift had come down empty. He waited – then the door slid open. A shaft of dull yellow light split the darkness of the corridor and he heard a voice curse grumpily in German. A figure stepped cautiously out of the lift. A short, portly man in a heavy woollen navy coat stood uncertainly in the gloom, peering into the dark corridor. From inside the lift an arm appeared and pushed the man in the small of the back. He tottered forward. As he emerged the Kreigsmarine escort also stopped for a moment, trying to accustom his eyes to the sudden change of light to dark. As he turned towards his captive Loughlin stuck the barrel of the machine gun into the German's back.

'Keep still and put your hands in the air,' Loughlin said in perfect German. The German turned swiftly round, swinging a blow at Loughlin which caught him on the side of his arm, knocking and sending the gun flying. The move had been so quick and so unexpected, it had caught him totally off his guard. The German came at him, both arms wide open, ready to hit him again. Loughlin made it to his feet and, as the German swung his fist, he caught it, turned under his arm and flipped the German on his back. Then he grabbed his neck and, finding the carotid artery, dug his finger into it as hard as he could. The German, who had been winded by the fall, tried to get up but it was too late and with Loughlin still holding on to his throat he slowly passed out.

'That was a most energetic defence, young man. I congratulate you.' Loughlin jumped up. In the heat of things he had forgotten the other man. Even in the gloom of the partly lit corridor he could see it was Churchill. He picked up the machine gun, then went through the pockets of the German. He was not armed. He handed the gun to Churchill.

'Do you know how to use this, sir?'

'I do.'

'Watch him. He's an ugly character.'

Churchill smiled. 'Well, Lieutenant, if you think he's ugly you should see some of the lady members in the House of Commons.'

'I'll get some help.'

He came back moments later with the two ratings and the captain. The German had not moved. 'Is he dead?' Loughlin put a hand on his throat. 'No, there's still a pulse but he's not going to be walking anywhere. Shove him in the room with the dead one. Bind his hands and feet – use his belt and see what else you can find – and watch him. If he comes round he may be difficult to handle. He's as strong as an ox.'

He turned to the third rating. 'Take Mr Churchill back to the kitchen and look after him there. There's still eight more to deal with. Captain, is there another way up to the bridge other than that stairway? I want to avoid those men at the chair ropes.'

'Through my cabin – it's the back way in.'

'Good, lead the way. Everyone else follow but hold back a bit till we get inside. Once they're disarmed I'll need two of you to guard them while we neutralize the others. Okay, let's see if we can finish the job.'

On board the *Regent* Davidson was watching anxiously as Clementine Churchill made the transit. She had proved remarkably calm and not at all flustered by the experience, remarking that if her husband could endure this for his country then she could certainly manage it too. As he watched her dangling over the cold ocean with the sling bouncing and waltzing like a child's yo-yo that had lost control, he got a message from the sonar operator. They had detected the U-boat again. It was stooging around just on the margin of the range of their signal. It was below periscope depth, so it must be waiting for a radio transmission.

Davidson knew he had to warn the others but didn't want to use the radio; it would certainly alert the U boat. His best option was the signal lamp. 'Get a signaller on the Aldis lamp and send the message: Our visitor is back.' The signalman went out onto the deck, uncovered the lamp and sent his message. He waited for a return and was surprised when he didn't get a reply. He waited; there was nothing. He sent the same signal again but there was still no reply.

On the bridge of the *Tenacious* the Germans were occupied with the signal transmission when Loughlin and the captain burst in behind them. There was no resistance; nobody had time to reach for a weapon; it was all surprisingly easy. The other two officers joined them. 'Search them for weapons. We don't want a random gun fight in these close quarters.' The search yielded two Luger pistols and another submachine gun.

Loughlin handed the pistols over to each of the junior officers, first pulling back the breeches to arm them ready to fire. He herded the four captives into a corner. In fluent German he ordered them to sit on the floor in a circle facing inward. Then he told them the others had orders to shoot them without warning if they moved from that position. He handed the machine gun to the captain. Now they were both armed.

'We need to split up if we're going to surprise them. If I go down the outside stairs to the deck, is there a way you can get the other side of them.'

'Yes.'

'Good, how long will it take you?'

'Minutes.'

'Is there anywhere you can keep out of their sight but still watch them.'

'The hatch I come out of is close enough. What have you in mind?'

'The best chance we have is when they try to get the next person out of the chair. At that point I'll approach them and shout something in German. That should take their attention away from you. By the time they realize there's something wrong you need to be up on the other side of them. We'll need to be quick because they might try to use whoever is in the chair as a shield. Does that all sound sensible?'

'It does.'

'Okay, good luck. I'll give you five minutes to get into position, then I'll make my way down the other stairs.'

On deck the chair was almost onto the ship when Loughlin stepped into their view. He started to walk towards them when one shouted at him. 'Johan, where have you been? We have another one to go below – and where the hell is Karl?'

Karl, he thought, must be the one who was dead. 'He's guarding the prisoners,' Loughlin called back, and as he did so he saw the captain advancing towards them on the other side.

At this moment Clementine's feet touched the deck. She was wet and her hair hung about her face like string, sticking to her cheeks. Her face was pinched with the cold and as she came out of the harness she slumped forward into the arms of the sailor nearest too her. It was just what had worried Loughlin most – she was now in a position to be used as a shield.

Loughlin and the captain now closed rapidly on the four men. As they got to within feet of them the Kreigsmarine men realized something was wrong, but it was too late. Loughlin barked at them in German to stand aside. He walked straight up to the man holding Clementine and with the palm of his hand hit him sharply under the chin. The man fell like a stone. The remaining three stood there in shock while Loughlin told them they were now prisoners.

'Right, Captain,' he said, 'we need to get her into something warm and quickly.'

Clementine was dazed by what had happened but kept her feet. 'What's going on?' she kept saying, 'and where is Winston? Is he all right? Will somebody please tell me what's happened?'

'Take her down to Mr Churchill and get the crew back to their stations. We need to get this ship out of here. I'll take this lot back to the bridge, then we can bang them all up somewhere secure. And get a signalman; we need to let *Regent* know what's going on.'

When the first signal reached Davidson he had already deduced that there was something wrong on board *Tenacious*, but he had not guessed anything close to the real situation. Now he had to come up with something. That U-boat was sitting out there and was probably expecting to take off Churchill; he didn't think they would bother with the others. Once on board, anything could happen. They might shoot him and dump his body overboard, but he thought that

223

unlikely – if they were going to do it they would have done it as soon as he came aboard *Tenacious*. He thought it more likely they would take him to Kiel or one of the other northern ports, and then on to Berlin. Hitler would find some way to publicly humiliate him, and afterwards probably execute him.

They had to find a way to neutralize the U-boat without it alerting anyone else in the area. They were away from the convoy but if the U-boat commander was waiting for them then there would be others, probably surface ships. The signal went back to *Tenacious*: Come across – urgent discuss plan of action.

Aboard *Regent* Loughlin quickly explained what had happened. As they talked the crew worked to get Thompson and the young woman across in the chair. 'Who's the girl with Thompson?' Loughlin asked. 'Churchill's junior secretary, Mary Shearburn - soon to become Mrs Mary Thompson.'

Loughlin looked out across the water to the horizon. The U-boat was out there somewhere and sooner or later it would return, expecting to transfer Churchill and take him who knew where. He had to find a way to stop them.

'The way I see it, there's only one way to knock out the U-boat and that's by boarding it.'

'How would we do that?'

'Not we – me, and I'd take one other with me. If you're right about them taking Churchill off then they'll have to surface and come close alongside. In this weather it's going to be difficult; they'll need to get some lines attached and raft up tight alongside.'

'What if they just send out an inflatable and pick him up that way?'

'Then I'll have to find a way to get on board and cross with them. I could take one seaman from *Tenacious*, dress him like Churchill – they won't know him, leastways not the ordinary mariners. No one will get a good look at him until we're inside the hull and by then it'll be too late. All we need to do is knock out the radio before they can transmit. After that it's just a roundup. Type V11s only have a crew of forty and ten of them are on *Tenacious*. The rest will be spread all along the hull. They won't know what's happening till it's too late. Anyway, that's the plan.'

Davidson looked concerned. 'It's one hell of a risk.'

'Well, if we fail then I can only suggest *Tenacious* legs it out of here as fast as she can. She's got more than twice the surface speed of that U-boat. Then it'll be every man for himself.'

'What about you?'

Loughlin shrugged. 'It's what I signed up for.'

'Do you have family? Are you married?' There was silence for a moment; Davidson guessed he'd touched a nerve and wished he hadn't asked the question. It was insensitive really, asking a man about those dear to him when he was about to stick his neck on the line – probably get killed.

'No,' he replied slowly, 'just my mother. There was a girl once but she found a better prospect – I think he was something in the City, rich. Can't blame her really. Look at what I've come to.'

'You'd better get back to *Tenacious*; at least we've got everyone where they should be. The best thing I can do is shove off and get *Regent* back to the convoy. That way the U-boat will think things have gone to their plan.' He stood up and put a hand on Loughlin's shoulder. 'Good luck, old boy. Send me a one-word Morse if you succeed. That way if I don't hear anything I can at least say a prayer for you.'

'Any word in particular?'

'Yes, try Moggerhanger. It's my wife's cat, scruffy old thing but she loves it.'

'Moggerhanger it is then.'

'Oh, and don't forget your kit.' He handed Loughlin the bag he had first brought on board. 'You'll need this stuff if you do get to America.'

Davidson watched him go, slung in the chair clutching the bag and swinging wildly. He stood there until it reached the other side. 'Poor sod,' he said to himself, 'I wouldn't want to be in his shoes.' He went up to the bridge again. 'Get ready to wrap it up Number One. As soon as the tackle's in let's get under way. Get a signal off to the convoy commander that we've left *Tenacious* and we're rejoining the group. Let's pretend it's all been routine.'

CHAPTER 20

Arrest

Tom turned the key, then pressed the starter button. The Bugatti sprang into life. It was another peerless day with a cobalt sky, quartz crystal air and clear right out to the horizon. It had been a glorious summer and, although it was now dying, the fall still held the promise of more fine days to come with the painted beauty of the turning leaves gilded by long, gentle rays of a lowering sun; and there would be days with Carey.

He waited out front on the wide gravel sweep of the drive at Brunessemer, the engine quietly ticking over with a barely perceptible sigh as it sucked in air and gas through the carburetors at the front, burned it and sent it quietly throbbing out through the exhaust. He liked cars – but he loved this one.

It would, he thought, be a great day for a drive out – go up to the Adirondacks and maybe take a picnic – but today he had promised Irena he'd take Aly up to her school at Croton. She came trotting lightly down the steps, crisply dressed in a white cotton blouse with a mid-length plaid skirt and shiny, black court shoes. All she carried was a small purse on a long strap swinging from her shoulder.

'Is that all you're taking?' Tom asked with a slight note of incredulity.

She laughed. 'Hell no, Martins took a whole car trunk full over there last week. Today you're carrying just me.' She slid into the seat next to him and pulled a straw boater firmly onto her head. She didn't want the wind to make a mess of her hair. Irena came out to say her goodbyes to her daughter. She leaned into the car and kissed her. 'Study hard and no wild parties – you hear me.'

Aly waved away the remark simply commenting, 'As if.' Irena stood back, 'Drive carefully Tom. She's precious cargo, you know.' Tom nodded, selected a gear and the car moved smoothly forward, out of the drive and into the street.

As they got onto the main highway he became conscious that Aly was looking at him. She had half turned in the seat and now sat watching him. It made him feel uncomfortable; it distracted him, so that at first as they rounded a bend he didn't notice there was a truck coming down the centre of the road – right at them. At the last moment Tom swerved to miss it; it was close. As he jerked the car back into control again she fell towards him and put out a hand to steady herself. It landed on his leg and for an unnerving moment she left it there.

'Sorry,' he said, 'I didn't see that coming.'

Aly laughed. 'That's okay, it was exciting.'

'I don't think your mother would have thought so, especially if I'd managed to get us both wiped out.'

She laughed again and then did something that really unsettled him. She deliberately reached out and put her hand onto his right thigh. He wasn't sure what he should do, how to respond. Maybe she had done it without thinking. Then she moved her fingers – just a little but it was a perceptible caress. She made little circular movements with her index finger. He could feel the heat of her palm where it pressed against the cloth of his pants. For a moment he was lost for a response, searching for a way out of the situation. She squeezed his thigh looking at him intensely, watching for his reaction. 'Uh oh', he thought, 'this won't do.'

Then she started to move her hand further round his thigh. She was undeniably pretty but this wasn't what he wanted. In the end he found his exit. He reached down, clasped her hand and lifted it gently but firmly away from him and let it drop into her lap. He smiled and shook his head slowly. She smiled back, let out a little sigh of resignation and, pulling the boater forward so that the brim almost covered her eyes, settled herself deeper into the leather seat. 'You know,' she said without looking at him, 'you need to be careful with Carey.'

'How so?' he replied, but without enthusiasm for the conversation.

'She isn't always what she seems. Carey is for Carey – that's all.'

The rest of the short journey passed in silence. As they drove in through the college gates a group of girls loitering near the entrance recognized her and, in a flurry of swishing skirts and raffish laughs, came over to greet her. One stood back and admired the Bugatti. 'Now that's to die for.'

'Isn't he,' said a friend close to her, 'and the car looks pretty good too.'

They all laughed and Tom felt the color rising in his face. Aly got out and flipped the door shut. Leaning deep into the car she gave him a little kiss on the cheek. Another girl in the group let out a whoop. 'Where *did* you find that?' she taunted jokingly.

'Don't get overheated – sister's boyfriend,' Aly shouted back. She looked at Tom for a moment longer, then said, 'You're a nice guy, Tommy Jordan – much too good for that sister of mine.' As she walked into the gaggle of girls she turned one last time. 'Thanks for the lift,' she called back at him. 'Hope I'll see you at Christmas.'

He started the engine and waved as he slowly maneuvered the car towards the entrance. A raucous cheer went up from the group and a dozen hands waved in the air – then he was out of the gates and away.

'He's gorgeous,' said one of the girls. 'How did you keep your hands off him sitting that close for so long?'

'With difficulty,' Aly replied, 'with difficulty.' Inside she smiled to herself as she thought about the journey and wondered if Carey really understood what she had in Tom.

******

In Croton the streets were almost deserted; they had the air of Sunday quiet about them. As he drove slowly down Grand Street the last of the congregation was spilling out onto the grass in front of the old stone church. They stood around in little knots – some couples, some family groups – chatting briefly before taking their parting and drifting slowly along the sidewalk towards their homes and a lazy Sunday lunch. Briefly he imagined himself with Carey coming out of that church, part of a congregation, comfortably content, happy to have her on his arm, saying hello to his neighbors. Then a darker feeling crept in and spoiled the image. He knew this scene of small town tranquility was a mirage; there was a more dangerous world out there, hidden just over the horizon, lying in wait to ambush this contentment and claw its fabric into shreds of insecurity and fear.

He thought of Carey and what Aly had said. He didn't know what she had meant by it but she had touched on a nerve. He thought again about Carey coming out of that church with him and knew it was an illusion – she wouldn't fit in, she would want to be off to New York or just out somewhere, flying around crazily with the wind in her hair and having fun; flitting like a beautifully painted moth, dancing from one candle to the next. He shook away all the thoughts save for Carey. He had planned to drive round and see Mike while he was in Croton but now he changed his mind; he decided to get back to Brunessemer and Carey without bothering. He hated being away from her.

When he got back to the house she wasn't there. She had, Irena told him, gone to New York with Nigel. 'Oh, and those other two – Jerry and Cynthia,' she added. They had gone to some exhibition of modern art and would most likely be back late. 'You just can't tell with Carey,' she said, shrugging her shoulders. 'Why don't we have a little lunch? Come along, I'll make some cocktails – you like a Manhattan don't you?'

It was around seven when Carey came back. He heard a car door slam and voices, then the sound of a car moving off. After a short while a key was turned in the front door. He got up and walked quickly into the hall. For a moment she just stood and looked at him as if he were a stranger. She gave him a frosty stare. 'So you're back then,' she said with a trace of petulance in her voice, 'so nice to see you again.'

This wasn't at all what he had expected. Now what was wrong? That old sense of panic rose up in his chest; his face felt numb and he fought for something to say. He had no idea what had gotten into her. 'Did you have a good day? Was the exhibition okay?' His voice sounded clumsy; the words came out of his mouth and fell flat onto the great tiled expanse of the cavernous hall – like a ball of pizza dough dropped off the balcony. 'I'm tired,' she said irritably, and headed towards the stairway.

He stood there helpless, without a plan and totally confused. 'What's wrong?' he called abruptly after her, but she ignored him and ran up the stairs. At first he thought he should follow but then thought what the hell good would that do? He stood for a while looking at the empty staircase then, letting out a noisy breath of resignation, retreated to the drawing room and Irena. Irena raised her eyebrows and shrugged. 'She'll come round in a moment, you'll see – let me make you another Manhattan.' Tom waved away the offer and slumped into one of armchairs. 'Don't let her see you like that. Go out onto the veranda – she'll be down in a moment, if only to see what effect it's had on you. That's the way Carey is. Go on outside. I'll send her out to you and she'll be ready to make up with you. Go on, you'll see.'

He waited for her and it seemed an age before she appeared, but it was exactly as Irena had said. She walked over to him all shy and schoolgirlish, looping her arm round his and laying her head on his shoulder. 'I'm sorry – I panicked,' was all she said. He put his arms around her and caressed her, gently resting his chin on her soft warm hair. She smelled sweet and perfumed the way she did the first time he had kissed her. They stood in a silent embrace while he rocked her gently in his arms, not wanting to speak in case he said the wrong thing and broke the newly woven spell that now surrounded them.

Eventually she said, 'Why did you take so long to come back. Did Aly try to get you to stay with her? She does that, you know. I think she does it just to spite me.'

'Why would she want to spite you?' he asked guardedly.

She didn't respond immediately, instead she just looked into his eyes with a long, sad gaze. Then she stood back and pulled her arms around her shoulders as if she were cold. 'I'll tell you. I've been trying to find the courage to tell you ever since we met but the right moment never seemed to come along. I'm going to tell you now – but you must promise you won't hate me if I tell you because I don't think I could live if I told you and you hated me and left me. I think I would die. Will you promise?' He stood looking at her, nodding his head, saying nothing, unsure what was coming next.

'I promise,' he said quietly.

She walked in a little circle, all the while biting her lip, wondering how to put her most dreadful secret. Then she took him by the hand and led him to one of the loungers. There they sat down together and, still holding his hand, she started her confession.

229

'When I was much younger – when I was at school …' she faltered, and looked down at her shoes. He wondered what might be coming next. She still kept her eyes downcast and he thought he heard a quiet whimper. There was more silence and he put his arm around her shoulder to comfort her, but she shrugged it off and when finally she turned her face to him there was no trace of sadness – that was gone, replaced by a grim look of anger. 'My father took advantage of me.' She blurted out the words with a vehemence he had not seen in her before. 'He forced his lust on me. I wasn't even in my teens, dammit – I was just a girl. He raped me and afterwards he made me feel guilt and shame and a horrible, horrible loathing of myself, saying it was my fault and that I had deliberately tempted him.' She spat out the words in single staccato syllables, punctuating each one by hitting into her lap with clenched fists until she broke into deep anguished sobbing.

He tried to console her but she recoiled from his touch and he backed away realizing he had to give her space.

The crying stopped and she pulled out a handkerchief and dabbed at her eyes. The anger and the emotion had gone. It was like the passing of a storm. It was quiet again. 'He kept on doing it for years,' she said calmly. 'Then, when I was older, just before my sixteenth birthday I exposed him. Over dinner one evening I just came out and said it. We were all there – Mother, Aly, Wendell, me and him. I told them he had been using me and I wanted it to stop – it had to stop.' She looked at him again – this time it was her little girl look, the look that said, I'm sorry but I feel a bit lost and scared.

Tom had no idea what to say. He wasn't equipped for this kind of revelation. He was at one and the same time shocked, horrified and embarrassed. Why, he wondered, could he never find the right things to say? He was tongue tied, like always. Carey came to the rescue. 'You don't hate me do you? Please say you don't hate me.' He pulled her close and kissed her.

'I love you, honey. How could I ever hate you? You're everything to me – you've become my world.'

She looked at him, reassured, and in that moment it occurred to him that for once he had found the right words – not very good words, not very clever or eloquent words, but at least they seemed to be the right words for the situation. And there was something else. Behind the anguish and the tears a clue had emerged, an explanation. Now some of the fog around Carey's often irrational behaviour started to clear away; it began to give voice to her insecurities, but he was still confused; he couldn't see how Aly came into all of this. Now he thought he would venture a little further into the dangerous territory of a question.

'Now I understand why your father is no longer at the house. But why would Aly want to spite you over this?' He waited for the response, mentally flinching

230

as he did so. Carey's face darkened and he thought he'd said the wrong thing, but it passed.

'She was always his favorite. She blamed me for driving him out of the house. Mother wouldn't let him stay. He protested, of course, but not much, and then he left. I think it was a convenient excuse for him – he'd been having a string of affairs for years. Mother always turned a blind eye to it but this was too much even for her; so he went. Now it's out I'd like to forget it if we can, Tommy. Would that be all right?'

He said it would and they left it there.

Monday morning dawned; there was a chill in the air. He had slept alone in the guest wing because she'd said she needed to be alone. But she had kissed him gently before she went to her room and they had clung together in a long gentle embrace till she had slowly pulled away and he felt content that everything was alright.

Outside, the leaves were beginning to fall. They lay wet and glistening with dew, spreading a yellow carpet across the length of the gravel drive, softening the noise of the cars and the footsteps running over it. He looked through the window. The gardener, who came each day to look after the lawns and the borders, was out there sweeping them up and piling them into a barrow. Downstairs Carey was already eating breakfast; hardly eating really, she just nibbled at the edge of a piece of toast delicately smeared with a touch of melted butter. She got up and kissed him. 'Did you sleep okay?' she asked. Tom smiled back at her, 'Like a log – how about you?'

'Not really. I had a really bad dream and I felt frightened. I dreamed I was out there up in the forest. I was alone but there was something out there with me. I could hear it but everything was so dark. Then I found a house – silly really, because you don't just find houses in the woods, do you?' He leant across the table and squeezed her hand.

'Dreams are strange, aren't they?'

'The door was open and I went in, but it was empty. Then I was in a room and I tried to switch on the light, but it didn't work. It came on for a split second then the bulb just blew. Then I tried to get out but the room had lots of doors and every time I opened one it led into another room – exactly the same room as I was standing in. It was horrible. Then I woke up all hot and trembling. I wanted to come to you and snuggle up close to you – I felt so frightened.'

'You should have, why didn't you?'

'I didn't want to wake you.'

'I wouldn't have minded.'

She smiled gently at him and put out her hand, laying it on top of his. 'Oh Tommy, you're so beautiful to me and sometimes I know I'm awful to you. Can you forgive me?'

231

Tom just nodded and smiled. She was such a bundle of enigmas but he knew he could forgive her anything. He looked at his watch then downed his coffee. 'We have to go,' he said, 'or we'll miss the train.' Martins drove them to the station where they boarded the train for New York. At Grand Central they parted once again. 'See you for lunch,' she said as her parting shot.

'Sure – 12.30?'

'Okay.'

He had been in the office for around an hour when he realized that one member was missing. 'Hey Dan, where's Fred?'

Dan looked up from the worksheet spread out on his desk. 'Didn't you hear? He's been drafted. Turns out he's one of the first out of the goldfish bowl. Did you know that's how they do it? There's a great big glass bowl with all the eligible drafts in it and someone shoves his hand in it, stirs it up and picks out a ticket; it's a lottery. Apparently, that's how they did it in the last war and this one's no different.'

There was a look of mild surprise and a touch of disbelief as he listened to Dan Johnson's explanation. 'Well, that's rough,' he said quietly. 'How unlucky can you get. Poor young Fred; and him just a kid. Doesn't seem right really.'

'I'd save your tears – they made a real fuss over him, being one of the first and all. I heard they gave him a pretty good send off and a whole lot of dollars too.'

Tom found himself thinking about how Carey would have taken it had it been him. 'Still, it won't be much fun for a kid at boot camp.'

'I'd better go home tonight,' Tom told her over lunch. 'I need to see my folks and, besides, I have to get a car sorted out. Dad has really taken over the old Chrysler.'

'That's okay,' she said, 'but you can use Wendell's car if you want. He's never going to use it and no one else even likes it, except you – and maybe Martins, that is.'

He shook his head and laughed a little. 'It's a nice idea but I need to get my own wheels. Anyway, I wouldn't feel right driving around in it all the time. Don't get me wrong, I love her, she's beautiful but she's not really right for everyday use. I'd stick out like a sore thumb going some places. It'd be like hitching a thoroughbred to a plough. It'd be out of place. It just wouldn't look right.'

'Boys,' she said, leaning across and messing up his hair, 'you're such strange creatures – but take it when you need it.' In the end she persuaded him to take the Bugatti just to get him home and until he managed to buy something.

He arrived home around six. There was a smell of baking coming from the kitchen. As usual Martha saw him arrive through the window and went out onto the front step. 'My, that's a lovely automobile,' she said, looking at the car, though on second thoughts,' she added, 'not so practical; doesn't have a lot of stowage by the looks of it. Still, mighty pretty – and the girls will love it.' She laughed. Tom climbed the steps and she hugged him. 'Good to see you, Ma. How's Dad?'

'He's fine. He's out on the back porch – with the dog.'

Tom went through to the back of the house and found Holly sitting reading the paper with Wheels snoozing on the floor next to him. At the sound of his shoe on the boards, the dog lifted his head and barked. Its stubby tail started to wag and he jumped up putting his front paws into Tom's outstretched hands.

'Hi Dad, how's things?'

'Oh, pretty good, pretty good.'

'I notice the Chrysler isn't out front. Is it still running OK or have you trashed it?'

They both laughed. 'No it's down at the garage; just a few small things that needed attending to. I left it there this morning – they were gonna bring it back for me this afternoon. He pulled out a silver pocket watch, flipped open the cover and looked at it. 'Should've been here by now.' He snapped the cover shut again.

Martha called from the kitchen and they both went in to eat. About midway into the meal, when Tom was telling them about Fred's draft, they were interrupted by someone at the front door. 'Now, who's that at this time?'

'Probably that young man from the garage coming to bring the car back; they said they would.' Tom went to move. 'I'll get it,' Holly said, standing up from his chair. Wheels jumped up and trotted out to the hall where he stood guard looking at the silhouette of a figure standing outside.

From the kitchen where they had been sitting eating they heard the door open and the sound of muffled voices. The talking carried on for some time until Martha finally got up and went out to see what was going on. The front door was wide open and she could see two men standing there. As she got closer she saw that one was in police uniform. The other, she supposed, must be a detective. 'What is it Holly?' she asked as she reached her husband. Behind her Tom could now hear more talking and when he heard Martha say in a loud voice, 'Oh my, how dreadful,' he decided to investigate.

As he got to the front door the first thing he heard was Holly saying, 'Well, he came by here to collect the car and take it to the garage. It needed a couple of things fixing.'

'What's happened?' Tom asked pointedly, looking at the man in the suit.

'Detective Hobbs,' the man replied, pulling a badge out of his pocket and holding it up for Tom to see. 'This here's Sergeant Browkovski. As I was telling this gentleman, here …,' he nodded towards Holly – 'That's my dad,' Tom butted in. '…Well, son,' the detective continued, 'I regret to tell you there's been a shooting and your dad's car has been involved.'

'How so?'

Holly turned to Tom. 'Seems the young man from the garage was driving the car back up here and when he stopped on a red in Main Street some hoodlum just stepped out and shot him.' Martha stood there in shock. All she could say was, 'Oh my lord, oh my lord!'

Tom looked puzzled. 'Why would someone do that? Did he have any background, with the mob or anyone like that?'

'Nope, not a trace of anything at all. He was just a regular ordinary guy like you; about your age too. No criminal record, nothing.'

He turned to Holly, 'I'd be obliged to you, sir, if you would come by the station sometime soon. We just need a short statement about when the victim picked up the car, just some background. Nothing special, just routine.'

'Sure thing, happy to help.'

'Fraid you won't be seeing the car for a while – least not for a few days. It's evidence; forensics will need to go over it. Got a couple of neat holes in it where the slugs went in. It'll need fixing again, I guess.'

The shooting dominated the conversation over the rest of the meal and, although Holly gave Tom the usual lecture about men with guns and how no good always came of it, in the end he never once became agitated or morose about it. That, Tom noticed with satisfaction, was a different Holly.

That night as he lay in bed, waiting for sleep to fall on him, he got to thinking about the boy who got shot. Not a boy really but a man just like him, and a thought began to invade his mind. What if it was a mistaken identity? What if those three shots had been meant for him? He was, after all, of a similar age and look to Tom and for years Tom had been the only driver of the old Chrysler. Most people around those parts knew that. But why? He had no enemies – not that he knew about. No, it was far-fetched. He put the idea out of his mind and drifted off.

He'd taken the next day off work to find and buy a car. He thought he might go down to Croton, maybe see if Tony or Mike were around. He stopped at the first phone booth he came across and called Tony's number but there was no reply. He hung up and tried Mike. Mrs Mescal answered. Where had he been, she wanted to know. Mike had wondered if there'd been an accident or some such thing because he hadn't heard from him since they'd been fishing. Tom laughed and started to tell her about Carey, then remembered to ask if Mike was actually there. He wasn't but he would be back later. 'Okay,' Tom told her,' I've got to go out and arrange to buy a car. My dad's taken over the old Chrysler so I need something, otherwise I'm walking. Could you let him know I'll be driving down to Croton later so maybe you could ask him if he wants to

234

meet up? I'll be at the diner around four. If you could tell him that I'd be real grateful, Mrs M.'

Inside the diner Dottie stood behind the counter polishing glasses. Jennifer was over at the window looking out into the car park. The lunchtime had been busy and they had been packed but the afternoon was slow; there were no customers and it gave them a chance to clear up and relax a little. As she stood there, idly drawing on a cigarette and slowly blowing out a long lazy trail of smoke, she saw the Bugatti pull onto the parking lot.

'Hey, will you get a load of this,' she called over to Dottie. 'This guy must be loaded.'

Dottie came over and stood beside her. 'Isn't that just the fanciest car you ever saw?'

The car door opened and Tom got out. Jennifer blew a long, low wolf whistle. 'Do you see what I see?' She nudged Dottie with her elbow. 'Now what d'ya think's going on there? Last time I saw him he didn't look like he had more than two nickels to his name.'

Dottie shrugged, and in a disinterested voice said, 'I have no idea.'

'Well, make a play for him honey, don't let him get away – he could be the catch of the season.'

Dottie waved the idea away. 'I already did but he isn't interested.'

'Well, try again girly, and this time try harder. There aren't too many around like that and, besides, he doesn't look half bad either. Go after him!'

Tom pushed open the door, nodded to the girls and sat down. Dottie came over and smiled, 'Hi, how are we today? What'll it be?'

Tom smiled back, 'I'll take a coffee please, miss. I don't suppose anyone has left a message for me, have they? The name's Tom Jordan. I was hoping one of the rangers might have left a message for me.'

'I'll ask,' she said.

After a short while she came back with his coffee. She held out a small piece of paper. 'You're in luck. This was left with one of the girls the other evening. It was one of the rangers. He asked if you could call him on this number.'

'Thanks – er – Dorothy; that is your name, isn't it?'

She felt her heart beat go up. This was the first time he had really taken any notice of her. 'Yes, but my friends call me Dottie.'

'Well thanks, Dottie, I'm grateful. I'm Tom by the way.' Now a cloud of butterflies took off somewhere around her middle and flew about all over the place. She tried hard not to blush.

At first he had thought he might phone the number later but there was no sign of Mike and he had time on his hands. There was a phone hung on the wall outside. Tom dialled up the number.

'Dave Hanson – it's me, Tom Jordan. I got your message. Did you find out anything?'

'Well, I did.' There was a pause.

'Are you still there?'

'Yeh, I'm here. Tom, did you get involved in some kind of trouble up there?'

'No. Why do you ask?'

'Well, my enquiry sure caused a stir. You must have ruffled somebody's feathers because shortly after I called them I got a visit from the FBI asking if I knew where you were. I told them I didn't know, but they weren't happy.'

'I don't know what that could be about.'

'Well, I don't either, but they sure seem anxious to find you.'

'Did they leave any contact number or a message, anything like that?'

'Nope – nothing.'

'Strange.'

'Yeh, I thought so too.'

'Okay, well thanks for letting me know. I'm not sure what I can do about it though.'

'No – and good luck anyway.'

'But what about Tennant? Did you get anything?'

'Yeh, that's strange too. He did go missing and they found him alright, 'cept he was dead. Didn't you say they were looking for him a couple of months back?'

'That's right.'

'Well, that don't make sense. According to the records William Tennant died more than a year before.'

'That's really weird.'

'Listen, Tom I gotta go. I don't know what you might'a got into here but I'd prefer not to get caught up in it with you. Hope you understand, but I've got a wife and two kids to consider. Good luck – you just take care now.'

The line went dead.

Back in the diner Tom ordered more coffee. Something was wrong and he didn't know what, but whatever it was it was beginning to look serious. He hoped Mike would turn up; it would be good to have someone to share it with.

As he sat drinking his coffee and thinking about the conversation with Dave Hanson a black Plymouth car drove onto the parking lot at the front of the diner and two men got out. At first he only caught it out of the corner of his eye and didn't pay much attention – cars came on and off the lot all the time. The two men started to walk towards the diner. They had covered about half the distance when, for no good reason, Tom looked again out of the window. This time his focus settled on one of the men in particular and he immediately recognized him; it was the deputy from Crows Crossing – Al Cardy.

Tom sat frozen with disbelief for no more than a second, then jumped up and walked quickly to the washroom. He locked himself in. His mind was buzzing. What the hell was Cardy doing there? He was miles out of his county. He looked at the window but it was too small for him to get through. There was no way out so he waited. He must have stood there in silence for around a quarter hour when he heard what he thought was Cardy talking to the other man. He reckoned they must be outside, probably just under the window because he heard them quite clearly. They stood around for a bit, then the one he thought was Cardy said, 'aint gonna catch no fish here, let's go.'

The sound of the voices trailed away and after a bit he thought he heard car doors being slammed. He waited a while longer then, with his heart rate up, he carefully turned the latch and inched open the door. They had gone. He walked back to his seat and slid in. Dottie came over. 'Hi, you're back – where did you go? I didn't see you go – and, by the way, you didn't pay.' She laughed a little. 'We don't want too many customers like you. What'll you have?' 'Oh, the usual coffee,' he said, beginning to relax.

'Make that two, please, missy,' said a voice from behind. A large, strongly built man eased his way onto the bench seat next to Tom, pushing him into the corner. He put his hand into the inside pocket of his jacket and pulled out a badge in a leather holder. He held it up to Tom's face, almost touching his nose with it. 'FBI son. Agent Parkes. I think you and I have a little business to attend.'

Cardy came back in through the door. He had a gratified smirk on his face. 'I didn't think you'd fall for that old trick. Come on, you didn't think we was really gone now, did ya?'

'I'm afraid you need to come with us, son,' Parkes said soberly. 'We have a few questions for you to answer and this place is a bit too public.' Tom stared at the two men; he couldn't believe this was happening. 'I don't understand what this is about.'

'You will, son, you will.'

'Are you arresting me? If so, for what?'

Parkes pulled on the cloak of a reasonable man. 'No, no, not arresting you – just exercising my duty as a public servant to Uncle Sam and requesting you to accompany me to another place which is more private and where we can have a civilized discussion about things we think you might know.'

'And if I refuse?'

'Well, then, I might have to arrest you.' Dottie arrived with the coffee. Parkes put a dollar bill down on the table. 'Hold the coffee; it'll be cold before we're back.'

They left the diner with Cardy in front and Parkes behind. As they reached the Plymouth Mike's car drove onto the lot and stopped a few yards away. He saw Tom, got out, and walked towards them. As he closed on them he could see something was not quite right. Tom stood awkwardly between the two men, who looked like they were escorting him. He recognized Cardy and stopped. He wasn't sure what to do. Tom moved as if to step out from between the two men but Parkes shot out a hand and grasped him by the arm. It was a firm, powerful grip and he knew he wasn't going to shake it off.,

'Hi Tom,' Mike called to him, still not sure if he should get any closer. 'Everything OK with you?' Tom shook his head. Mike looked from Cardy to Parkes.

'What's going on here mister?' he said directly to Parkes.

Parkes pulled out his badge again and held it up. 'FBI, sir. We are taking this man in for questioning. Do you know him, sir?' Mike nodded, all the time keeping an eye on Cardy. 'Uh ha, he's a neighbor.'

Now Cardy pulled a badge from his jacket. 'I'm Deputy Cardy, sir. This man is assisting us in our enquiries. Unless you have any business here then I must ask you to leave.' Mike said nothing and for a moment there was a silence as the men stood looking at each other.

Outside the diner a small group had gathered to see what was going on. Cardy opened the rear door of the Plymouth. Parkes, still gripping his right arm, pushed Tom into the car. 'Duck down, son. Don't want you bruising your head. Don't want to be accused of ruffing you up, now.' As Tom bent to get into the car his left hand let something drop. It settled there on the ground just next to the rear wheel; neither Cardy nor Parkes noticed it. Parkes got into the back seat and sat next to Tom, who was now looking shell-shocked and confused. The engine in the Plymouth roared into life. Cardy swung the car off the parking lot and accelerated hard. A shower of gravel flew out from under the rear wheels as he pushed its nose up the highway in the direction of Peekskill.

For a moment Mike stood there watching the car disappear. His first thought was that Cardy had not recognized him. He walked to where he had seen the object fall from Tom's hand, bent down and picked it up. It was a car key attached to a fob; on the fob was engraved an address with the words 'if found please return to ...'

Dottie and another waitress had been standing in the small group that had gathered to watch the spectacle. She walked over to where Mike stood examining the key. 'What was that about?' Mike shook his head. 'I don't know. Which car was he in?'

She pointed to the Bugatti. 'Is he in trouble?'

'I think he must be. Is there a phone here?' Dottie pointed to the booth on the side of the diner wall. 'You're his friend aren't you? I've seen you in here with

238

him, you and that other boy with the sport coupé. Could you let me know what happens? I'd like to know – that's all.'

'Sure,' Mike replied, not really listening to her. His mind was elsewhere trying to put together what had just happened and all sorts of alarm bells were ringing. What the hell was Cardy doing there?

The telephone rang in Tony's apartment. The tinny sound of Mike's voice came through the earpiece. 'You'd better get over here quick.'

Mike was on his second coffee when he saw the Cord fly onto the parking lot.

'Okay, tell me about it. I'll have a beer, miss, please.'

They talked through the events then stepped outside to look at the car. Tony ran a hand over the curve of a front fender. 'That's one hell of a jalopy, these things cost a fortune.' He looked quizzically at Mike and grinned. 'Maybe he stole it – maybe that's what this thing is about.'

'Do you think so?'

'Nah. Not our Tom's style. Anyway, why would Cardy be here for an auto theft? He's way off his patch – and the FBI. This has to be something serious. You're sure he didn't recognize you?'

'Didn't seem to. What d'ya suppose Tom wanted us to do with this?'

Tony shrugged and walked around the car. 'Return it to the owner, I guess. You know he's been acting strange lately. I haven't seen him since – oh – July fourth.'

'Me neither, but he called our house this morning looking for me – told my mother he was here to buy a car. Do you suppose this is it?'

'Get outa here. He'd need to hold up a bank to buy this – maybe two banks. Maybe he got in with a bad crowd. Maybe this is some kind of payoff.'

'I don't think that's right. He told my mother he'd been seeing a girl.'

'That sounds more like it. She must be loaded if she's got this *voiture*.'

'What's a *voiture*?' Tony threw up his hands in mock horror. 'A *voiture* is French for a car, you ignoramus; and this is a French car. Don't you know nothing?'

They stood for a moment contemplating the car. 'I guess we should return this thing, then,' Tony said. 'What's the address?'

Mike turned over the fob. 'Dobbs Ferry. That rings a bell.'

'The beauty on the train!' They both said almost in unison.

'I'll drive,' Tony said, holding his hand out for the key. 'You can follow and drive us back. Maybe the girl can throw some light on what's been going on.'

******

In Washington a White House aide stuck his head round the door of the Oval Office. 'FDR's not available,' said the secretary, busy setting out some papers for a meeting.

'Okay, but this is important. The coast guard has intercepted a British destroyer inside our waters – they're asking for asylum. The intelligence guys over at the Shack are getting all frothy about it. They think they may have the German naval code aboard. The JCs are waiting for a report right now.'

She stopped paper shuffling. 'Is it priority?'

'I'd say so.'

General George Marshall looked round the table at the others: Admirals Leahy and King, and Hap Arnold.

'How the hell did this one get so close to the eastern seaboard without anyone noticing, for fuck's sake? What if it had been a German, for crying out loud – or two or three – or the whole of Admiral Raeder's Atlantic fleet? Hap?'

General Hap Arnold held out two open hands and gently lifted them up and down as if he was weighing some invisible package. 'George, we don't have the planes to patrol the pond. I told the President this at the last meeting. You know the story. We need more surveillance aircraft. It's as simple as that.'

'Do we know what they were up to – what they're doing here?'

Marshall looked round the table then fixed on Admiral King. 'Joe, what's your assessment?'

King pulled a sour face. 'Limeys, Krauts, there's not much to choose – I don't trust either of them. This could be some kind of intelligence mission. We need to get them ashore and go over that ship with bloodhounds. My guess is they're up to something. I don't like it. It's got an odd feel about it.' He prodded a finger at the single sheet of the intelligence report they had all been studying. 'It says here they sent out a signal just as the boys in the coast guard nailed them – just one word – Moggerhanger. What in the name of all that's holy does that mean?'

One floor up from the joint chiefs, the intelligence team were scrabbling for answers; then a telephone rang. Someone picked it up. He lifted one hand above his head signaling he wanted silence. There was a pause. All he said was, 'Uh, huh,' then replaced the receiver back onto the cradle. He got up from his chair and stood for a moment, looking round the room. Then came the outburst. 'Holy shit, holy Alamo!' he shouted. 'You won't guess who's on that Can out there. It's that goddam Limey leader – Churchill. Someone get downstairs and tell them.'

Down below the news was greeted with a mixture of relief and disbelief. Nobody had seen this one coming and at first, as the news was dropped on them, the two generals and two admirals looked at each other, speechless. Joe King was the first to speak. 'Well, that son of a bitch – I was sure he was a goner.' Hap Arnold smiled; he had always liked Churchill and he was pleased the man had survived. 'This could be the best bit of news we've had for some time. I'll bet he has a whole mess of things to tell.'

There were three phones on the desk. Marshall picked up the one with a direct line to the White House.

As their limousine sped down Constitution Avenue the four military men speculated on what this might mean. Churchill had been missing for months; everybody had been sure he was dead. Now here he was asking for asylum. That could be good and that could be bad. If the Germans got wind of it there would be demands to hand him over. Things were tense with the Nazis as it was. Canada had made things difficult and right now they could do with keeping a lid on the relationship. On the flip side he would be coming with inside information. The British Ambassador had been tight-lipped ever since the Paris Treaty; now here was someone who had the inside track. That could be of inestimable value.

Then again, there was the question of security. All four were convinced the Germans would try to get to Churchill, either to abduct him or assassinate him. The intelligence team upstairs at the Shack had already warned them that might be an issue. The word was they should keep the whole thing secret for as long as possible. Everybody was agreed – he should not stay in Washington. Word would get around no matter how quiet they kept it; it was a gossipy town and Churchill was the kind of story it fed on. The moment it got out that he was there and a guest in the White House, it would go through the city like fire. He had to be kept out of view, underground, somewhere he would not be recognized. Of that they were all convinced.

The Washington Hotel is the best address in DC. Its location next door to the White House had turned it into the venue of choice for the great, the good and the famous. Not just anyone could stay there. It had become more like a club than a hotel – it was a legend of discretion. Churchill arrived at the Washington late that afternoon. He came in through the back entrance, pushed along in a wheelchair, covered up to his chin with a blanket, a slouch hat pulled down across his face. Not even the FBI knew he was there. Thompson and Loughlin came in through the main lobby of the hotel and were sent directly to a suite of rooms on one of the less gracious floors, rooms that would not attract attention. The two women arrived shortly afterwards, discreetly dressed and inconspicuous: Clementine wearing a hat with a veil, Mary posing as a ladies travelling companion. They passed unnoticed to the lift and went directly to one of the rooms.

'I don't much care for this skulking about. It makes me feel like a criminal.' Churchill stood at one of the full-length windows looking out onto Pennsylvania Avenue. It wasn't much of a view; just the broad street with cars and people

241

going briskly about their business, and the corner of the Willard Hotel which jutted out into his field of vision, cutting a severe perpendicular architectural statement.

'Come away from the window, Winston,' Clementine warned him. 'Do you want the world to see you?' Then added, 'Yes, you probably do.'

'From here I'm more obscure than the Liberal Party,' he joked. Then his mood changed and he thought about everything he'd left behind. What a mess poor Halifax had made of things. Such a good man but so naïve, just another Chamberlain as it turned out. What fools they had been to trust Hitler, to bargain away their country for a worthless treaty and some hollowed out promises. They should have stood their ground and fought. Now he was here, probably the last bastion of freedom. He hated running away, which was how he saw it, but there had been no other option. He could do more good in Washington than slammed up in a grey building in Berlin or, even worse, dead at the hands of some Nazi thugs. How useless that would have been.

Less than an hour after they had first entered the hotel a car arrived. Once again Churchill was covered up with a blanket and wheeled away in the chair. This time only Thompson accompanied him. Loughlin had another errand: he needed to make contact with Amber Rose. As the car headed for the White House, less than a block away, he casually made his way down to the front lobby. There he looked at the bank of phone booths but decided it was too dangerous to call from the hotel. Hotel phone operators were notorious for feeding the rumor mill and tipping off the press. He couldn't take the risk; he would have to go out and look for a pay phone somewhere on the street. After a short walk along Pennsylvania Avenue he found one, dropped a coin into the slot and dialed the number. It rang for a while but no one answered. He let it continue for a bit longer, then hung up. She must be out he thought. What to do? There was no option but to kill time. The others wouldn't be back much before late afternoon and until he heard how the Americans had taken to Churchill dumping himself in their midst he would have to cool his heels.

For a short while he stood looking at the traffic flowing like a river of steel along the broad avenue. It struck him that these American cars were much bigger than the cars he was used to in London; they growled along like bad-tempered bears, their exhausts grumbling. And the streets, the streets were wider and straighter than he was used to. The horizons were further away and the sky seemed bigger and somehow more open. In London the buildings were close and the streets winding and narrow; you wore them like an overcoat. Here, he felt dwarfed and at the same time exposed as if he was standing out on some great open prairie. He fished a paper map out of his pocket that he'd picked up from the hotel reception and pinpointed his position. He would walk a few blocks, try to get a feel for the location, but it was all more of the same. Finally he decided to abandon the exercise and go back to the hotel. It was lunchtime and he might as well get something to eat. Arriving at the Washington, he took the elevator to the suite and looked in to see if the others had returned, but there was only Clementine and Mary Shearburn. They both shook their heads when he asked if there was any news. He thought Clementine looked drawn and tired; the strain of what she had endured over the past weeks was showing. After politely enquiring if there was anything he could do or get for them and having received an equally polite response that they were well provisioned, he made his way back down to the main lobby, then walked the short distance to the restaurant.

As he reached the entrance to the restaurant a bell boy in hotel livery pulled open the big glass-paned door and held it back. Loughlin, not seeing at first that the door was being held open for another, started to walk through it and narrowly escaped a collision with an exiting diner. He stepped back and apologized. The man he had nearly knocked off his feet was elderly and carried a walking cane. He nodded curtly to Loughlin. As he left he paused for a moment and handed the bell boy a folded dollar bill. The recipient nodded and touched his forehead in an obsequious gesture, wishing the diner to have a good day. The man walked off in the direction of the lobby and, as he did so, a sense of something familiar struck Loughlin. Did he know that man? The man reminded him of someone, though he couldn't readily think who. He was sure they had met before; he had a good memory for putting names to faces. It wasn't one he could recall, but there was something about him that struck a chord in his subconscious.

The waiter showed him to a table and took his order. He sat thinking about the day and what lay ahead, but in the back of his mind the elderly man still nagged at him, lurking there on the shadowy edge of his memory. As the waiter arrived with a plate, Loughlin stood up. There was nothing for it but he would go to the lobby and see if the man was there. 'I'll be back in a moment,' he told the waiter, who looked thoroughly put out by the idea that the food should wait.

Loughlin pulled open the glass door and walked as quickly as seemed polite along the short distance of the corridor to the lobby. The mellow tones of a jazz band drifted in from somewhere. The lobby was almost deserted; most people, he guessed, must be out at lunch. He went over to the desk and asked the girl on reception if she had seen a man fitting the description of the elderly diner. The receptionist regretted she was unable to help; she had only just that moment come on to the desk and the others were all at lunch. 'Why don't you ask Harold, over there?' She pointed to where the concierge was standing at his station, reading a newspaper. 'He sees most of what goes on round here.'

Loughlin thanked her and walked across to the concierge. 'How can we help, sir?' he said stiffly.

'I'm looking for a man who left the restaurant a few minutes back – an elderly man, short, well dressed in an old-fashioned style. He was carrying a walking cane. I just wondered if you might have seen him – maybe even know him?' The concierge adjusted his glasses, delicately taking the right-hand lens frame between his forefinger and thumb. He lifted the frame off the bridge of his nose, looked over the top at Loughlin and then repositioned them, settling them back down again on the bridge. There was a pause; the concierge lifted his eyebrows a little and lightly furrowed his brow but said nothing. Loughlin was slightly puzzled for a moment, then said, 'Of course,' and, pulling out a dollar bill, pressed it into the hand of the concierge.

'I do recall seeing the gentleman in question. He crossed the hall and left through the main entrance.'

'Do you know him?'

'I regret not, but I can tell you he is not a guest – and he is a stranger to the Washington.'

'What makes you think that?'

'Simply that when he came in earlier he had to ask for directions to the washrooms and a regular guest would have known that.'

Loughlin went back to the restaurant and sat at his table. There was no sign of his lunch. He had drawn a blank card. Maybe he was mistaken; maybe the man just reminded him of someone else. It would come to him eventually, he thought. The waiter came over to his table. 'I trust we are now fully ready to be served, sir,' he said disdainfully. Loughlin agreed that he was and assured the waiter there would be no further unscheduled perambulations.

******

When they had arrived at the White House Thompson was asked to hand over the revolver he was carrying. It would be returned when they left, he was assured by a very young secretary. Thompson watched critically as she walked away, holding the heavy gun in a tiny hand. He didn't like the idea of being disarmed by a woman – and this one hardly a girl, barely out of college, he thought.

An aide dressed in a sharp suit took them to a side room close to the President's office and asked them to wait. Having provided them with refreshments, he left them in the comfortable surroundings with the promise that the President would see Mr Churchill shortly, but half an hour later they were still parked there with no idea of what was happening.

'This is a fine thing, Walter,' Churchill said gloomily. 'Sitting here not knowing if we are welcome or not – treated with suspicion no less.'

A dark mood had come over him; he felt the black depression that haunted him in moments of self-doubt. It crept like a shadow across his mind and made him feel cold and nauseous. It sapped his will when it was most needed. It drained the energy from his body and froze his mind. What had seemed like a great endeavor when they started out was now beginning to stall, turning into a potential disaster.

Now he questioned the wisdom of what he had become involved in, but what else could he have done? The threats had not been illusory, and he had been left with no option when the army had scooped him up on Albert Embankment and spirited him away to Portsmouth. On that rough ride down to the sanctuary of the Navy it had seemed to make good sense. Now it was fast taking on the shape of a criminal conspiracy which would have no legitimacy if the Navy coup failed. He was in Washington and safe for the moment – not as the leader of a government in exile but as a fugitive, a man on the run in a stolen warship, a man on the dodge.

Thompson said nothing but his face acknowledged the remark. He too had been raking over their position and it looked precarious. They had turned up uninvited, on the run from the Germans who were now in de facto control of Britain. He and the others all had guilty knowledge – they knew there was a coup being planned by the top brass in the Admiralty and that could make them an accessory if it failed. Churchill wanted to get the country back but he had no clear plans on how to do it. It would have been easier if there had been an invasion by Germany; then at least the country would be under foreign occupation and there would be a clear cause to fight for. But the Germans were there in a lawful capacity, under the terms of a treaty, and no matter how distasteful that was it had the force of international law behind it.

Then there was the incident with the U-boat. By now the Germans would know that *Tenacious* had escaped and their U-boat had gone missing. A German submariner had been killed in the retaking of *Tenacious* and another one so seriously injured it was quite likely he too would die. They had sent the U-boat to the bottom, opened up the seacocks and scuttled her. They were not at war so it was piracy; that was a hanging offence. Worse, when Loughlin took the U-boat, he captured the entire crew who were now locked up on the destroyer. They would have to be handed over to the American authorities. They, the Americans, would be bound to hand them over to the Germans – after all, they were not at war with Germany, they had no cause to keep them. When they did hand them over the cat would be out of the bag; Jerry would be demanding they also hand over Loughlin, Churchill and everyone else aboard *Tenacious*.

That would set alarm bells ringing in London, and there would be an investigation. That could well compromise the plans for the coup being plotted in Portsmouth. It was all a bloody mess and he could see no way out. It was only a matter of time before the press got hold of the story. He had seen the disaster unfolding right from the beginning but he had been Churchill's bodyguard for a long time and he felt a loyalty that made it hard to walk away. The only concession he had asked was that they take Mary with them. If he was to be stranded in America, then at least it would be bearable with her by his side. He was thinking about her and how brave she had been when the aide in the sharp suit bounced cheerily through the door.

'The President will see you now, Mr Churchill, if you would kindly follow me. Not you sir,' he said to Thompson, smiling, 'please wait here'.

Roosevelt and Churchill sat side by side at the presidential desk in the Oval Office. When the two men had met earlier that morning Churchill had been greeted warmly by the President. Now, in seating Churchill next to him, Roosevelt was sending out the message that he supported the British leader and expected others around him to do the same. He knew there was some antipathy towards the British generally, with Joe King and Joe Stilwell downright hostile. Churchill's position was precarious, finely balanced between the strong bond of support he had enjoyed from his old friend in the past and the disinterest of a nation who had no wish to get mired in the intrigues and ambitions of Europe's politics. He knew that for many of Washington's elite politicos he was at best a spent force, a leader without a country to lead, booted out of office, politically irrelevant – a man in limbo, without a future. To others he was a dinosaur from the old world of colonial ambitions, an embarrassing anachronism that should be abandoned to its fate, dumped in a dark corner and left to die.

Churchill was not a man to flinch in the face of an attack, but he knew his position was weak and it was going to be a difficult fight to convince Congress to give him support. He thought he could probably rely on the Senate, which was dominated by Republicans, but the Democrats might be another story: there was a tenacious lobby of isolationists in the party and they held the House. He set his mind to expect a rough ride. They would be difficult, he was sure, but he could take it. His black mood had passed. He was the old Churchill again and ready to do battle; he had a cause. With that thought uppermost he sat with his eyes fixed on the door waiting for the military chiefs to enter.

When they did, it was not as he had expected. There was a knock and a secretary appeared. She held the door open. The four chiefs filed in. It was George Marshall who set the mood. He came forward, smiling, and put out a hand to Churchill, which the other took and shook warmly. Roosevelt remained seated; Churchill followed his lead.

'Gentlemen, be seated,' Roosevelt said. They sat down in four large carver chairs that had been lined up in front of the desk.

'I've had an opportunity to have a long chat with Prime Minister Churchill and we have discussed the delicate matter of his being here in a clandestine fashion, so to speak. He has told me some extraordinary things about what is going on in Britain right now and I know you will be interested, as indeed I am, to hear his account of things. What we have to say in this room is most secret, as you will all understand. What he can tell you I believe to be vital to our country's security.'

Churchill smiled. It was the moment for the power of oration. Here was the opportunity to convince if only he could find the right words; he would have to choose them carefully. 'Gentlemen,' he said, still smiling. 'Let me say right at the outset that I am most grateful to you and to my good friend the President for granting me the opportunity to meet with you all today. It is an honor to be here in the company of great men at this dark and terrible moment in history.'

Admiral King folded his arms firmly, his face draped in skepticism. He fixed Churchill with a hard, stony stare that said 'this better be good'.

'Our two countries have been friends and allies for over a hundred years and there has always been a special bond between us. Less than a quarter of a century has passed since the dreadful Hun raised his ugly head and went rampaging across Europe. The life blood was being drained from us; our nation was in the direst peril. In that time the formidable industrial might of America came to our aid and, standing steadfastly alongside us, put an end to the threat. Now, once again, the ravenous specter of German hegemony has risen from out of its lair and is casting its grim shadow across all of Europe. Near history has shown us it will not be appeased by this tidbit or that. It is devouring nations in ravenous gulps, swallowing them whole with hardly a pause for breath. My country is not yet lost but it is in mortal peril and already encircled in the poisonous embrace of Nazi intrigue. In the spirit of that bond, which saw us fight together against a universal foe in the Great War, I come before you in the bold hope that I can convince you to extend the hand of friendship and help us once more.'

Churchill paused to judge his audience. The gap was just long enough for King to interrupt. 'Sir, these are fine words but we need facts, not gilded rhetoric – I can get that from the Senate any time I care to walk up Capitol Hill.'

Seeing where the opposition would come from, he changed his stance. Flattery and soft words would cut no ice with King, who would speak his mind even if it didn't accord with Roosevelt. He hardened his face and, addressing King directly, said, 'The Germans are disembarking a large force in the north of Canada. At the moment that force is facing towards Stalin's Soviet Union, but let us not delude ourselves that it could not as easily be turned around to face the other way. The Molotov–Ribbentrop Pact is just another piece of paper which Hitler, as soon has he is ready, will tear up and throw away – with no more regard than he would for an old newspaper. Now that Britain is out of the war he is no longer restrained in the West. For now his ambition is looking towards the East, but I believe that once he has subdued Russia, which is very likely to be quick – the flat plains of the Steppes were made for tank warfare and he will roll them up like an old Turkey carpet – then he will look west again. He has already crossed the Atlantic and is sitting on your doorstep. His ships, together with those of his Fascist friend Mussolini, are a formidable force. The French fleet is now in their hands and slowly they are tightening their hold on the British Navy. Together, all those ships will create the greatest naval battle fleet since the Spanish Armada.'

He stopped, hoping to give dramatic emphasis to his words, then continued, 'If that should happen, the seas and oceans of all the world would be theirs. This nation, which is the last hope of the free world, would itself be in great peril. It must not be allowed to happen. It must at all costs be prevented.'

Again he paused and surveyed his audience, looking for a sign that they were with him, but no sign came. Instead there was silence. Again King broke it. 'Well, sir,' he said, with a note of thinly disguised sarcasm, 'and how do you propose that the United States should go about preventing this? We are a neutral nation, in case you had missed that point. Besides, a united Europe may not be such a bad thing even if it is under Hitler. Maybe that'd put a stop to the endless bloodletting and chaos that your people have been up to this last thousand years or so. Who knows, it may not be such a bad idea at all when you think on it. Not bad at all.'

Churchill took it on the chin – but it hurt. These were supposed to be his allies. He had anticipated problems with King but outright hostility was not what he'd expected. The level of hostility took him by surprise. The mood in the room was going sour. He knew that this was the one chance left to him if he was ever to have any hope of getting Britain out of the German grip. He had to make them understand the danger they all faced, that they were in this thing together.

'Well, sir, I understand your dilemma, but I am bound to say that if you sit back and let this thing happen there will be untold consequences, not just for us in Britain – not just for Europe – not even just for you now sitting comfortably behind your walls and fences. There will be consequences for the whole world. I cannot impress upon you more forcefully the dark future which is being laid out before us if nothing is done to stop this megalomaniac from achieving his ambitions.'

Joe King looked patronizingly at his opponent. He sat tight-lipped for a moment, letting the silence do as much damage as it could before responding, trying to unsettle the man. Churchill waited to see what would come next. King looked directly at Roosevelt. 'Mr President, I speak for the Navy when I say we cannot afford to get embroiled in this European squabble. We don't yet have the resources to take on the Germans at sea with enough degree of certainty.'

Roosevelt frowned. He knew King of old; he knew he would always put forward the worst case – which was good in some ways because understating is always better than overstating – but he had his suspicions that the Admiral might be letting his personal dislike of Churchill get in the way of sound judgement. 'Joe, are you saying we wouldn't win? You've had a lot of new ships since we last had this conversation.'

'I think it is still too close to call, Mr President.'

Roosevelt turned to Hap Arnold, his least liked general. 'Okay, General, what's your view?'

'Mr President, I don't fully share the Admiral's view. The conduct of war is changing. The airplane now has a much wider role to play. In my view a combined deployment of strategic bombers, together with our current level of naval assets, could defeat the Germans at sea – even if they did join with the Italian fleet.'

King was about to take issue with Arnold, but Roosevelt saw it coming and headed them off. This was not what he had brought them together for, and things were getting side-tracked. He held up a hand to stop them, took off his glasses and rubbed both eyes; then, having slowly replaced them in a deliberate gesture that commanded their attention, passed the conversation back to Churchill.

'I am delighted to hear that General Arnold is able to provide such a positive view of an outcome in the event of a German naval encounter. Here, I may be able to add a little more to that optimism.' He drew a long breath and looked around the assembled company. He was about to share something important; something he hoped would convince them to support his cause.

'You are all aware of the Paris Treaty and the shameless terms under which the German Kreigsmarine has been given access to British naval bases, particularly the important harbor of Portsmouth and the sheltered haven of the Solent waters. Their presence there has become ever more intrusive and their control over British shipping movements, both of the Royal Navy and our Merchant Marine, has become ever more unacceptable. They seek, through devious methods, to monitor our movements. They raise the most fatuous objections, claiming that we are often in breach of this Treaty when they know full well that is not the case. Worse than this, however, there has been unwarranted pressure put upon His Majesty's elected government to allow German interference in social, commercial and political life on a broad spectrum throughout the length and breadth of our island. This interference is an intolerable breach of the Paris Treaty – a document, I might say, which is in and of itself an aberration of all that is acceptable to a free nation in any event.

'Nevertheless, the pressure to allow this interference is so great that men of less resolve than should otherwise be the case are caving in to it, giving up when they should be standing up. Lamentably, there are those in the British political class who have acquiesced in this, with the mistaken and deluded view that Nazi control of British politics would give them great power and prizes which they have been unable to gain through the democracy of the ballot box. These puppets are giving away their country for their own base self-interest. Against this backdrop of infamy, certain high-placed officers in the Admiralty, together with their counterparts serving on His Majesty's ships, have decided to take matters into their own hands. Rightly, in my view, they have concluded that those politicians who have so carelessly and spinelessly given away our nation – and who, even now, run hither and thither doing the bidding of the Nazi criminals – should be replaced, and that better men should take hold of the reins.

'In the coming days the Royal Navy will move to wrest control from the present government in Britain so that the country may be returned to the control of those who have Britain's interests closest to their hearts and not that of our evil occupiers – and let there be no uncertainty in your minds, my country is occupied. When they have accomplished this task I shall be called upon as the properly elected leader of the British Parliament to return to those shores and preside over new elections so that the country may once again enjoy the confidence of a free and impartial government to carry out their will. It is with this mission that I have come to your country to seek assistance in our cause. I do not come as some refugee, running and hiding, looking for sanctuary. I am here as the legally elected prime minister of a sovereign nation that hopes to enlist the help of an old and trusted ally.'

He barely paused, but inclined his look towards King so that the latter would know the words were addressed to him.

'Of course, should we manage to accomplish our mission, then the fear of a superior German naval presence in the Atlantic, bolstered by Mussolini's Italian fleet, would dissolve like so much mist in the morning sunlight. The British fleet would see to it that Signor Mussolini would stay bottled up in the Mediterranean Sea. Our garrisons and our bases in Suez and Gibraltar would keep him firmly penned in.

'Whilst I have no doubt that our Navy is more than a match for the Kreigsmarine, the same, regrettably cannot be said to be true of our Army or our Air Force. They have been decimated, broken up, given away and betrayed wholesale under the terms of this wretched and forlorn treaty. In this we shall need your help. If we are to succeed, and keep the free world out of the clutches of Hitler and his Nazi thugs, this can only be done if we have the strength of American guarantees behind us. The threat that the US would come to our aid if Germany tried again to mount an invasion of Britain would, I believe, give them pause for very serious thought. I believe most sincerely that the future prosperity, the well-being and the security of both our nations will best be served by marching forward together. And, therefore, in the cause of the greater good, I urgently ask you to give your support to us and our mission.'

Churchill sat back and waited to see how his words had been received. He didn't have to wait long. Roosevelt was quick to respond. 'Winston, that was more of a speech than a dialogue,' he said, laughing. The others joined in the laughing – even Joe King cracked an uncharacteristic smile. In that moment Churchill knew he had their support.

'George,' Roosevelt addressed Marshall, 'this is going to raise some security issues. We can't have news of this leaking out. It'll have to be carefully controlled. If the Germans get wind of it we are going to have our hands full. This has to stay with the military for the moment. I don't want Hoover or any of the FBI in on it yet.'

Marshall nodded. 'We'll have to give some thought to getting Mr. Churchill out of Washington for the time being. This town's as leaky as an old bucket.'

'We're on top of that one. Winston, we're going to put you at the home of an old friend of mine, Warren Taylor. He has a fine house in Upstate New York, tucked away discreetly along the Hudson. You'll be as safe there as anywhere. The Germans may still want you dead so we can't take any chances.'

George Marshall laughed, 'I thought Taylor was a Republican.'

'I have friends beyond politics, George – you should know that.'

As they drove back to the hotel Churchill smiled quietly to himself. He had pulled it off; he had done it. A warm glow welled up inside him; the black mood was gone and his mind started to plan the next moves. Everything now hung on Admiral James and the Navy. Their success would be pivotal. The idea of being back on the floor of the House excited him. Images and ideas flooded across his brain. Now he would get the nation back to strength, build up the armed forces with the aid of America, take on Hitler and bring honor back to Britain. It was, he thought, good to be alive and good to be doing things again.

CHAPTER 21

Incarceration

The black Plymouth made its way north. Tom watched the road slip by and searched his mind for answers. He was confused; what the hell was Cardy doing here? Then he remembered the events of the evening before. The Chrysler had been shot up and the driver killed. Was there a connection?

A few miles along the Albany Post Road the Plymouth turned off and joined Interstate Highway 9 heading for Crugers. It was familiar territory; at least for the moment he knew where they were. As the car slowed at the junction it occurred to Tom he might jump out and make a run for it. Parkes seemed to sense his thoughts – maybe it was the way he looked or some small movement of his body that gave it away.

Parkes half turned his head to Tom and, with a deadpan look that showed no emotion, slowly shook his head; the tone of his voice was flat but it carried a hint of menace. 'Don't think about it, son. I've seen men kill themselves just by jumping out at ten miles an hour. You could break a leg, maybe even break your neck. Even if you didn't you'd be a fugitive and then I'd have to gun you down. So you'd get yourself killed either way. Just sit back and enjoy the ride.'

'It'd be easier if you'd tell me what it's about.'

'Time'll come.'

Crugers passed away to their left. Cardy was now whistling some tune or other – so out of tune Tom couldn't recognize it. His thoughts began to settle down, but he still had a knot in his stomach and his chest was tight with stress and adrenalin. In his mind new ideas were forming, dark sinister ideas. If they wanted to question him, why take him so far away? Why not just use the Sheriff's Office in Croton? He began to think the worst. Maybe they were just going to murder him and dump his body somewhere, but that had no logic to it – why would they want him dead? He put it out of his head. Rationally he thought they could be going to Peekskill; they were heading in that direction; that's where the shooting took place; that would make sense. But then he came back to Cardy. Why would he be here? He wasn't connected with the shooting; that didn't make sense either. Nothing was making sense.

'Where are you taking me? Where are we going?'

'Not long now – you'll see,' was all Parkes would say. Cardy ignored him and kept up his tuneless whistling.

As they passed through Montrose Tom spotted the truck stop where he'd laid over when the storm hit just before they'd gone fishing. For the first time since the events of that day it made him think of Carey, and a new sense of panic welled up inside him. He felt the desperate urge to get away, to free himself and get back to her. It intensified his sense of powerlessness. He felt like he was bound, a helpless fly cocooned in sticky spider silk. He thought of wrestling Parkes for the handgun he could see just under the agent's jacket. He would shoot his way out if he had to; kill them both. He began to feel a deep hate for Cardy as he sat behind the wheel blowing his flat tuneless whistle.

At Buchanan the Plymouth took a left and went to the center of the town. It slowed as they came to the police station, a newly built red-brick building, and came to a halt at the curb. Tom felt a sense of relief. This was something different; it bore the hallmarks of officialdom and normality. The fears of the unknown were retreating. They could hardly bump him off quietly here; there would be too many witnesses. Now maybe he would get some explanations.

Parkes got out and stepped quickly round to the sidewalk. He pulled open the nearside door. 'Okay, out,' he ordered curtly. As Tom stepped out and stood up Parkes took hold of his wrist. There was a clicking sound and he looked down to see he was now cuffed to the agent. Parkes grinned, 'Just in case you decide to do something stupid. Don't want to have to fill out a report that says why I had to shoot you – it's an awful lot of paper.'

They marched up a short paved path that led up to the doors of the police station. Through the glass Tom could see the desk sergeant. He began to feel more confident. The man behind the desk looked friendly, just an ordinary cop; maybe now he could get some answers. 'Agent Parkes, FBI'. Parkes dumped his badge on the desk.

'I was warned you were coming. This here the prisoner?'

'It is.'

'Okeydokey, young man, empty your pockets, please, and take off that wrist watch.' Tom took out the contents: a pocket book containing his driver's license together with a few dollars and some loose change, a folded clasp knife and a picture of Carey. The desk sergeant picked up the photo and whistled. 'Nice looking girl. Shame you probably won't be seeing her again.' Tom felt the ground wobble under his feet.

'Why do you say that? I've done nothing – why am I here?'

The sergeant raised his eyebrows and looked at Parkes. 'They all say that. Is there a charge sheet?'

'Not yet, he's been picked up for interrogation. We're taking him over to Hoover Avenue. Do you have the keys? They should have been left with you.'

The sergeant picked up what looked like a bunch of house keys and shook them, making a jangling noise, then dropped them into Parkes' outstretched hand. He pushed a sheet of paper over to Tom and offered him a pen. 'Okay, Thomas Jordan, sign this; it's a receipt for your belongings. You'll get them back when they let you go; if they ever do, that is. Have you told him he could go to the chair for this?'

Parkes looked coldly at him. 'Nope'.

They got back into the car. Parkes took off his end of the cuff and clipped it round the door pull. 'There, that'll do just nicely.'

The house on Hoover Avenue was unremarkable, as was Hoover Avenue; a quiet suburban street a short walk from the Hudson River. The only feature that stood it apart was a high fence either side shielding it from its neighbors. Otherwise it was just another ordinary family home in Anywheresville. It had five bedrooms on the first floor and a deep basement beneath the ground floor.

'What's this?' Tom said suspiciously as Cardy drew the Plymouth up onto the drive.

'It's a safe house,' Parkes replied in a matter-of-fact tone. 'It's where we hide people if we think they're in danger. You've heard of witness protection, haven't you?' Tom nodded.

'It's gonna be home for the time being.'

'What do you mean – and what did that desk sergeant mean about the chair?'

'Forget it, he was joshing – he's a man with a bad sense of humor. You'll be fine. We just need to ask you a few questions to clear up a mystery. It's routine – don't worry. We'll soon have you out of here and on your way back home.'

Cardy got out and walked round to the back of the car, looked around to see if there was anybody about, then signaled it was all clear to Parkes. 'Right, Tom, I'm going to take these bracelets off and when I do I want you to walk casually up to the front door and ring the bell. I'll be one step behind you. Don't get any funny ideas about going on the run – because I *will* shoot you. Okay, off you go.'

Tom reached the door; he pressed the bell. There was a sound of footsteps, then of the door being unlocked. It was pulled open. A tall, rugged-looking man was framed in the opening: it was Newman.

******

The drive to Dobbs Ferry took less than half an hour. On the way back he told Mike the Bugatti made the Cord feel like a plodding donkey. It took a few attempts to find Brunessemer and when they eventually drove up to the front they weren't quite sure what they had come to. Martins was the first to see them. He came up to Tony smiling, then as he realized it was a stranger at the wheel his look turned to one of suspicion. 'I don't understand,' he said in his stiff English accent. 'Where is Mr Jordan?'

Mike had got out of the Studebaker and was about to start on an explanation when the front door opened and Carey came tripping down the steps, the heels of her shoes clicking on the stone. 'Tommy!' she shouted, then like Martins saw the mistake. She walked stiffly up to the car. 'What's this about? Where's Tommy?' There was a moment of shocked silence.

'I'm Mike, this is Tony. We're friends of Tom.'

Carey turned pale. 'What's happened? Has there been an accident? Please say there hasn't. Please say he's alright.'

'No accident,' Tony added quickly. 'He's been arrested.'

Carey stood with her mouth open and lost for words. 'Arrested?' she finally said. 'Why arrested – for what?'

'We don't know,' Mike butted in. 'He was picked up by the FBI and a sheriff's deputy, but they didn't say why. They just dragged him off. Can we come in and maybe explain.'

Carey had composed herself. 'Martins,' she said, 'take the car. You two had better come in. We need to talk to my mother. She's good at solving problems.'

'Is that it?' Irena said after they had recounted what little they knew.

'That's everything,' Mike replied. He felt almost apologetic. He should, he told himself later, have challenged the FBI agent about Cardy. It had to be connected to Lake Champlain and Crows Crossing. He should have asked for an explanation, but he didn't want to get too close in case Cardy recognized him.

'We should have some tea', Irena said after a few minutes. 'It helps my brain function.' She rang the small bell on the table and instructed Prudence to arrange it.

They drank the tea in near silence at the end of which Irena seemed to come to a decision. 'There's only one thing for it. I'll have to speak to your father. He knows people; he's well connected. If anyone can do anything it will be him.'

The dark shadow on Carey's face told the story. 'Must we, Mother? Don't we know anyone else who could help?'

Irena put her hand on Carey's and patted it gently to soothe what she knew would be the distressing emotion welling up in her daughter. 'If I thought there was another way I would take it, but I don't think there is. Think of poor Tom locked up who knows where.'

It was dusk when Mike and Tony left. On the way back they raked over what little they knew and concluded that somehow Cardy and Newman must be in there somewhere – but in what?

******

255

In Hoover Avenue they took Tom down to the basement.

'Can I get something to eat?' he asked Parkes. 'I haven't eaten since breakfast, I'm starving, and I need a drink. Can I get some water?'

'I'll see to it but I'm gonna have to lock you in here for a while.'

They had descended a short, steep flight of steps to a cramped hallway. There was a door in front of them and when it was opened it let onto a single large room, dimly lit with a very small rectangular window, almost too small even for a cat to get through. It cast a faint shaft of the afternoon light diagonally across the room. There was a light switch on the wall close to the door and when he switched it on it lit a single dull bulb hanging from a wire in the ceiling.

'I'm gonna have to leave you for a spell – you be good now.'

Parkes shut the door and he heard the key turn in the lock. He was alone. His first thought was of escape. He wasn't sure how, but he started by exploring his prison.

In one corner there was a metal-framed bed and, close by, what looked like a set of electrical jump leads for starting a car with a dead battery. In the far corner there was an old bicycle and piles of old newspapers. The place smelled sour. It was at the same time damp and dusty; it felt like it hadn't been used in a while. In the middle of the room there was an old brown-wood table and four chairs tucked underneath it, one on each side. At the far end there was a closet with batwing doors; he looked inside and found what passed for a wash room – except it had no running water, just a bucket and a chair with a hole cut in the seat.

Having checked out each corner of the room, he sat on the edge of the bed. For a while he sat motionless, deep in thought, trying to find some logic in the situation he now faced, but there were more questions than answers. His mind strayed round to Carey and then the remark made by the desk sergeant that he would never see her again. The thought freaked him; by now she would be worried sick. He thought about Mike and hoped he had spotted the car keys and had made the connection with the address on the fob. After what he judged must have been an hour he realized Parkes was not coming back with food. That made him angry; he was starving and his throat burned from the dryness. He knew he was in a really bad hole and he had no idea how he was going to get out.

It must have been near to midnight when he heard the sound of somebody coming down the staircase. He heard voices, then the grate of a key in the door. He thought at last he would get something to eat, but there was no food. Instead of Parkes it was Newman and Cardy, who had come down the steep staircase from the ground floor. They shut the door behind them, locked it, then came over to the bed where Tom was still sitting.

'Stand up,' Newman said abruptly. Tom pulled himself up off the bed and as he did Newman hit him with a short jab in the stomach. A searing pain shot through his body and he fell back onto the bed. 'That,' said Newman maliciously, 'was what you had coming for your slack mouth and lying remarks last time we met.' He grabbed Tom by the lapel on his jacket and hauled him upright. He hit him again, this time lower down in the abdomen, then threw him back onto the mattress. He turned and walked over to the table where Cardy had already sat down.

'And that,' he said over his shoulder, 'is for that lying Mafia pig, who pitched me over with some low and sneaky move. Just what I'd expect from an oily wop.'

Tom lay on the mattress groaning and close to vomiting. 'When you're feeling up to it,' Cardy said, 'please come over here and sit down. We need to talk about things; but don't feel rushed, we've got plenty of time. Yes, sir, we got all the time in the world.'

Tom struggled to find his feet. The pain in his gut still throbbing, he got off the bed and, bent forward to ease the nausea, he made it the short distance across the room and grabbed hold of the back of a chair. He stood there for a moment finding it hard to breath. 'Sit down,' Newman said curtly.

Tom slumped onto the chair but barely kept his balance. He leant forward to rest on the table but the chair tipped sideways and the legs came out from under it. He fell to the floor, hitting his chin on the table edge as he went down.

There was a knock at the door. 'It's Parkes; open up.' Cardy got up and unlocked the door while Newman started to pull Tom upright and tried to sit him in the chair, but he was out. The hit on the table had knocked him unconscious and in the end Newman had to dump him on the mattress. Parkes looked over at the body near lifeless on the bed, then from Newman to Cardy. He had a paper sack in one hand and a bottle of Coke in the other. 'Here,' he said, dumping them on the table. 'He needs to eat something. What's been going on? Have you been roughing him up?'

Parkes walked over to where Tom lay still unconscious and barely breathing. 'He fell off the chair,' Cardy called after him, 'hit his head on the table. I think it's put him out, that's all. He'll come round sooner or later.'

Parkes looked angry. He walked back to the table but didn't take a seat. 'See here and listen up good. I don't want to see this boy knocked about. A dead prisoner is no good to me – he's not going to tell us anything like this. I need his story – is that clear?'

Newman looked coldly back at Parkes, then stood up. 'Agent,' he said in a low deliberate tone, 'I'll remind you I'm here on military intelligence business. I work under orders from the commander-in-chief, the President of these United States and I'll decide how we go about the interrogation of this prisoner.' He shot a glance at Cardy and gestured towards the door with a quick jerk of his head. 'And, for the book, he fell off the chair and hit his chin on the table.' As he went Newman snatched up the bottle of Coke from the table and, using his teeth, lifted the lid off it. He downed the contents in one, belched loudly, banged the empty bottle down on the table and walked out.

Parkes went back over to Tom and put a hand on his chest; he could feel the heartbeat. At least he was still alive. He looked at the chin, turning his head carefully to reveal a livid bruise that was coloring up. Maybe Newman was telling the truth. Tom groaned and his eyes flickered open. He stared up at Parkes and tried to say something but the words stuck in the dryness of his throat and all that came out was a crackling sound. 'Lie still. I'll go get you some water.'

Eventually Parkes came back with a large enameled jug and a tin mug. He found Tom lying propped up against the bed head. Parkes picked up a chair and dropped it down beside the bed, putting the jug and mug on it. He poured out some water and offered it to Tom. 'I'm going to get you some bedding. Don't try to move around. See if you can drink some water. There's a couple of dogs in that bag if you think you can eat, but watch how you swallow – small bites or you'll choke.' He grabbed the bag from the table and dumped it next to the water. 'All I need is for you to choke to death,' he said under his breath as he left the room.

Tom sipped at the water. He cast his eyes around the miserable panorama of the room but didn't really take anything in. After a bit he dipped his hand into the paper sack and fished out a hot dog. He took a bite but the bread was too dry. He opened it up and took out the frankfurter. Slowly he nibbled at the sausage; at least the pain and the nausea in his gut had subsided. Parkes came back with a pillow and a blanket. 'Here,' he said, 'try to get some sleep. I'll make sure you're not interrupted. You should feel better by the morning.'

As he left Parkes flipped off the light switch and the room went instantly black. In the darkness Tom pulled the blanket over him and tried again to make sense of the day. Things were connected; there were threads but he couldn't join them into anything coherent. It had to have something to do with the boat on Champlain – of that he was certain – and the killing in the Chrysler, but what? And why had Cardy lied about the dead ranger, William Tennant? Why did he need to do that? He struggled with his thoughts for a while until eventually sleep overcame him.

He slept fitfully, the pain around his chin and neck kept lifting him in and out of confused dreams. From time to time he heard voices on the floor above; at one point they were raised and it sounded like an argument was taking place. In the end exhaustion defeated the pain and he blacked out into a deeper sleep.

He woke to see a bright shaft of sunlight streaming through the small window, cutting a line across the room. The night's sleep had worked; he felt a lot better though his ribs were still sore and the area where he'd struck his chin was tender to the touch. He sat up and reached for the water in the tin mug. It was cold and refreshing but what he really wanted was coffee. Carefully he dropped his legs over the edge of the bed and was surprised to find the movement did not increase any of his pains. Standing up, he carefully picked his way to the door where he knew the light switch was located. He found the switch and flicked it on and, as he did so, he saw a spark flash from inside the cover plate; it was old and loose. He made a mental note not to touch it with a wet hand. Then by the light of the single bulb he went to the closet and relieved himself. There was no wash basin. He fetched the jug Parkes had brought down to him. It had about a quart of water in it. He took it back into the closet and, standing over the bucket, poured some into one cupped hand and rinsed his face. Then he poured more sparingly over the other and rubbed them both together, the excess water splashing into the bucket and onto the chair seat where it missed the hole.

He had no notion of what time it was but there was daylight and he felt hungry so he figured it must be around six or seven in the morning. He looked into the paper sack. There was still one of the hotdogs and a crust from the one he had attacked last night. He put a hand into the sack and a cockroach scuttled out; blackish brown and shiny. It caught him by surprise and made him jump. He looked at the dog and thought about discarding it but he was too hungry. He tipped up the bag to make sure there were no more visitors and then set about his breakfast. He wondered when they would come down again and if there was going to be another assault. He looked around to see if he could find something to use as a weapon, but there was nothing. He knew he was no match for Newman if it came down to bare hands. He sat and waited but nobody came. Time seemed to be dragging but without a watch he had no idea of the hour – he thought it might be around midday, but that was only because he was hungry again. It dawned on him that life was punctuated by a series of small events with references to time. Take that away and the world becomes empty. Without his watch he was becoming disorientated.

It was early afternoon. He could see from the light coming through the narrow window that the sun was dropping. He was beginning to feel pains from the hunger and there wasn't much water left. He went over to the door and tested the handle – it was firmly locked. He banged on it with his fists but it made nearly no noise. When he kicked it he concluded it must have a metal core – it was too solid to be wood.

The light faded and still he was alone. He sipped carefully at the remaining water, allowing himself just enough to fill his mouth. He washed it around his teeth and let it settle on his tongue, savoring the relief it brought before swallowing it. He went over to the small window and examined it. It was less a window than an observation slit – the kind you might find in a fortified bunker. He could see from the way it was set that the basement had very thick concrete walls – they must be eighteen inches thick, he guessed. He walked around the room for a bit, counting the paces he made. As he sat down on the bed again the thought came to him that he was entombed and that they could easily leave him there to starve.

The light finally went and the night settled in. The house was quiet; he hadn't actually heard any noise since yesterday. In the end he dropped down on the bed and went to sleep, hungry and parched. He wondered how much longer he could survive this. The hunger pains weren't too bad; his stomach was beginning to get used to being empty, but the dryness in his throat was getting worse. He could feel his tongue swelling. He'd drunk the last few sips of water from the tin jug. Now the absolute desperation of his position fell on him as he came to terms with the facts; this could be the end of his life – this could be where it all finished.

******

It was two days since the incident and still there was no news of Tom or his whereabouts. Irena told Carey that her father would see what he could do but the message that came back was not to hope for too much. She had informed him of everything Mike and Tony had related and his only comment was 'There must be more to it than that.' He did not, she had emphasized to Carey, like to interfere with the process of the law but he would try to find out why Tom had been arrested and where he was. That was the most she could hope for.

On the third day of Tom's disappearance Tony came down to Dobbs Ferry, collected Carey and drove with her to the diner where Mike was waiting for them. On the way up she told him how she and Tom had met and how she now missed him so terribly she hadn't slept. 'Don't worry,' Tony assured her. He was certain he and Mike could find a way through this. She smiled at the reassurance and thanked him. 'You've both been so kind; Tommy is lucky to have such good friends.'

At the diner they sat and drank coffee and tried to come up with something new but there seemed to be no rational reason for his abduction. From behind the counter Dottie watched them and caught snatches of the conversation. She looked at the dark-haired girl and thought how beautiful she was and, at the same time, that this was her rival and she had no chance against her in a contest for Tom's affection.

She had watched the drama played out three days before as it unfolded in front of her. When the two men had first come in they seemed like ordinary

260

customers but then they started acting oddly, moving along the lines of banquettes, staring at each customer and then moving on. That was when she had first noticed Tom was no longer there. But there had been something else she remembered – another man. It was nothing definite but he was there hanging around in the background and at one point the other two had spoken briefly with him. With that in her mind she went over to where Tony and the others sat.

'Sorry to butt in,' she said hesitantly, 'I don't mean to interrupt but I couldn't help hearing what you were saying. I saw what happened the other day – I saw it all.' Tony shot a glance at Mike. 'You're not interrupting,' he assured her. 'Any new information would be good. Why don't you sit down and tell us what happened.'

'Yes,' Carey said enthusiastically, 'please do sit down.'

'I can't, I'm working but I could meet you after work. If you can wait half an hour I'll be free.'

They hung on until she finished her shift. Dottie sat down and recounted the events that led up to Tom's arrest, but it didn't throw up anything new or anything they could use as a lead. 'Is that all?' Mike asked at the end of it.

'Pretty much,' Dottie said, sensing their disappointment. 'There was one other thing though – and it may not be connected – but a park ranger came in a couple of days before that and said he wanted your friend to call him; he left a number. I think he called him from the booth outside.'

The news immediately picked up Tony's interest. 'Do you know what it was about?'

'No, your friend didn't say, but it was shortly after that the three men turned up.'

'Wait a minute,' Mike butted in. 'You said three men – I only saw the FBI agent and Cardy; that makes two.'

'No, there was another one with them,' Dottie assured him. 'I didn't see where he went after your friend was arrested because everyone was watching that happen – but he stopped and spoke with them. It wasn't like a passing stranger making a casual comment; it was more intimate than that.'

'What did he look like, this other man?'

'I didn't notice a lot. He was much shorter than the other two – and older, he had grey hair – and I think he walked with a cane. That's all I can remember really.'

'Let's go back to the ranger,' Tony suggested. 'Do you know him? Has he been in here before?'

'Yes, but I don't know his name. He seemed to know all three of you, though, and described you – I'm sorry I don't know your name – as being a friend of

Tom – it is Tom isn't it? He actually talked about all three of you as being hunters.'

'I'm Tony incidentally, and that's Mike and this is Carey, Tom's girl.'

'That has to be Dave Hanson,' Mike said, looking at Tony. 'That's got to be our first serious lead.'

'How do we find him?' Carey asked anxiously.

'That's easy. The rangers have an office right here in Croton. I suggest we pay him a visit.'

Mike looked at his watch. 'Tony, I have to get back, I've got an appointment to get measured – for a suit – remember, I'm getting married in just over a month.'

'It's okay, I can do it,' Tony assured him.

'I'd like to come too,' Carey said, 'if that's all right – then I could catch the train home or I'll get Martins to pick me up.'

On the way to the ranger station Carey asked him, 'Tell me about you; I want to know all about Tom's friends. He should have introduced us weeks ago but he never somehow got round to it.'

'There's not a lot to tell. I work for my father doing this and that.'

'What does he do – your father?'

'Oh, this and that.' They both laughed and she realized it was the first time she had laughed since she'd had the news of Tom three days ago.

'He and my Uncle Giorgio have clubs: Miami, New York, Atlantic City and Chicago. My dad's in Miami – he prefers it there.'

They found Dave Hanson in the front office at the public desk just before he was about to go on a patrol. He was not happy to see them. 'I never saw a man so jumpy,' Tony told Mike later, 'he really didn't want to see us.' It was a tense meeting. At first Hanson didn't want to talk about it at all but Tony wouldn't let up; he raised his voice so that others in the office could hear. 'This is a friend of mine we're talking about here,' he said loudly, 'and I'm not about to leave until I find out just what the hell is going on.'

'Okay, okay,' Hanson said, and led them into his office where they sat down to listen.

'About a week or so back Tom asked me if I could make some enquiries about a ranger up north.'

'Crows Crossing?'

'How'd you know?'

'I was there.' That seemed to unsettle Hanson but he went on in a lowered voice, 'It turned out the ranger was dead; he'd been dead a year or more.' Tony let out a low, slow whistle. Hanson put his head closer. 'Then, within an hour of making that call I had a visit from the FBI. They had questions, lots of questions about Tom. They wouldn't tell me what it was about and they told me to keep my mouth shut about their visit; said if I said anything I could be arrested on grounds of national security. They said Tom was in serious trouble and under suspicion of being involved in espionage and betraying America to its enemies.'

'You can't be serious.' Tony could not believe what he was listening to. 'How did they find Tom, did you tell them?'

'No, of course not. I left a message at the diner and he phoned me.'

'They must have put a wiretap on your phone. That's how they got to him. From what I can see they turned up just after he phoned you.'

'That's all I can tell you – I don't know anything else. I'd like you to leave now – I don't want any trouble – I don't want to get involved.'

Back in the car Tony said he ought to go and see Tom's parents, let them know what happened before they heard rumors. 'They must already be wondering where he is. Do you think you could come along too? I think it might help them to see you.' Carey hesitated for a moment, then agreed that perhaps she should and it would be a good way for them to meet her.

They arrived in Peekskill and went straight to Tom's home. Carey got out of the car and stood looking at the house for a moment. 'I somehow didn't expect it to look like this,' she said.

'What were you expecting?'

'I don't know, bigger I suppose – more modern.' Tony laughed, 'Not everyone lives in a mansion like you. Come on.'

At the front door they were greeted by Martha. 'Tony,' she said excitedly, 'how nice to see you – it's been so long, not since before July fourth, isn't it? Come in do. Holly we've got visitors.' Martha took them into the front room. 'And who is this?' she said knowingly, 'Aren't you going to introduce me?'

Before he could answer Holly came into the room with Wheels close behind him. He put out a hand to Tony. Wheels, seeing a new face with a new smell, decided to investigate. He jumped up at Carey, who let out a shriek and shrunk back. 'Take it away, take it away!' she screamed hysterically and hid behind Tony. Holly grabbed Wheels by the collar and picked him up. 'Don't worry, honey,' he said reassuringly, 'he's harmless – he just wants to be friendly, that's all.' Carey was trembling. 'What's the matter, dear, don't you like dogs?' Carey didn't reply but just stood close to Tony, shivering. Holly took Wheels out and shut him in the kitchen where he could be heard whining for some time.

'Why don't you sit down and I'll make us some tea,' Martha said, trying to calm the atmosphere, but Tony sensing that Carey was not at all at home in the house declined for them both. 'We weren't planning to stop. We'd come to tell you about Tom.'

'What about Tom?' Holly sounded worried. 'He hasn't been home for two nights but he often goes off to stay with his girl these days.' Tony was about to say, 'Well, this is his girl,' but Carey guessed and kicked him. He turned and she looked at him with eyes that said 'No – not now!'

'He's been arrested,' Tony said abruptly.

There was a silence, then they all sat down and Tony recounted the story. When they left nearly an hour later Martha was crying. Holly thanked them and saw them away. Then he sat down in his chair for a moment to think. After a minute or two he went to find Martha. She was in the kitchen, sobbing. Wheels sat on the floor next to her, looking up, not understanding what was wrong but knowing something wasn't quite right. Holly put his arms around her and rested a hand on her head, stroking back her hair. 'Come on,' he said softly, 'you're making your nose go all red. Let's make that tea, then we can sit down and work out what to do. There'll be a simple answer in there somewhere.' Martha sniffed and softly pulled away. Then she kissed her man and set about making the tea. 'I know you're right,' she said, 'but it's just such a shock.'

******

'What do you think?' Carey asked him as they left and started to drive south again.

'About what? Holly and Martha?'

'No, Hanson and his story.'

'I don't know for now – it's coming clearer. I now know the players but I still don't know what the game is.'

They were passing Buchanan when Carey suddenly said, 'I didn't like that house, you know. It wasn't what I was expecting. I felt uncomfortable there. I thought his parents were nice enough but again not at all what I had expected.'

'So?'

'Oh nothing; it's just all been most upsetting. I wish it hadn't happened.' She sighed, then kept quiet for the rest of the journey.

'I could take you all the way home if you like,' he offered when they arrived at Croton, 'it's not that much further for me.' She smiled sweetly but said no, she wanted time on her own to think and the train would be good for that. 'Besides Martins will be waiting and I don't think it would be fair to leave him hanging about for nothing.'

Just before she boarded the train Carey gave him a hug and a small kiss on the cheek. 'I don't know how to thank you,' she said. 'You've been a true friend to Tommy.'

He watched the train go, then went back to the diner. When he got there Dottie had gone home so he sat over a coffee and thought about what had happened. What Hanson had said worried him. He'd been at Crows Crossing so he too could be in the firing line. He finished his coffee and left, then drove into the center of Croton and found a public phone booth.

'Ciao Uncle Giorgi, comme va? Good – and Tia – she's well; buono. Listen, Uncle, I need to ask you a favor.'

******

'We're on the move, Clemmy,' Churchill announced when he got back to the Washington. 'It was a great success. They're won over, though I thought that blighter King was going to be a problem. He's an ill-tempered cuss but I brought him round. He could see the sense of it in the end. Now we just have to wait it out until Admiral James and his boys get control back at home.' He rubbed his hands together with satisfaction and smiled broadly at his wife. 'We're going to the country. You'll like it. We'll be able to rest for a while and recover our strength.'

Clementine laughed a little at the suggestion of taking it easy. 'Come now, Winston, when did you ever rest? You won't rest, you'll be plotting and planning and lobbying. You can't rest, it's not a word you understand.'

He patted her hand – short, rapid, excited little pats. 'It'll be good nonetheless – you'll see.' But she wasn't assured; she had lived with Churchill too long to know there would be ups and downs. He was fine with the big picture but not so good when it came to the detail.

'And what shall we do for money?' she said, slightly exasperated. 'I had to leave nearly everything behind when we left in such a hurry – and I don't really wish to sell my jewellery, not if it can be avoided. Do we have anything, Winston, or are we to be beggars at the President's table?' At this Churchill laughed out loud. 'My dear girl, don't worry. The strong room on *Tenacious* is stuffed full with money, not to mention quite a lot of gold. That splendid fellow Charlie Armitage and his team saw to that. I knew Armitage at Sandhurst, you know; bit of a dullard at the time but he turned out all right. I've told FDR and he has agreed to get it ashore and put it at my disposal. Don't worry – we shall not starve.'

Loughlin excused himself and left the others packing their bags. Again he took the stairs – there was a good overview of the lobby from the final landing and he quickly scanned the floor for anything suspicious. In Philadelphia Avenue he found the same phone and dialed the number. It rang twice and someone picked it up. It was a man's voice; he thought he detected a note of hesitance in it.

'Hello.'

'I'm looking for Amber, Amber Rose, is she there.'

'Who's calling?'

'Fred from Ealing.'

'What's it about?'

'The dog is unwell.'

There was silence at the other end. He had gone through all the passwords he'd been given; now he waited.

'Okay,' said the voice at the other end. 'Go back to the hotel; sit in the lobby – Amber Rose will find you.'

In the lobby of the Washington Loughlin sat in an easy chair where he could watch the door. People came and went but nobody approached him. After an hour had passed he decided something must have gone wrong. Perhaps, he thought, he should try phoning again. He got up and, as he did so, a smartly dressed woman in her twenties came out of the lift and walked straight to him.

'Mr Loughlin'?

'Amber Rose?'

The woman shrugged. 'No, I've come to tell you the others have gone on. When you're ready ask for me at the reception. I'm Jane Harper – I've got your transport arrangements.' She turned and walked away.

He sat down again. Another forty minutes passed, then another person approached him. This time it was a man. He came in through the main entrance, looked briefly around until his eyes lighted on Loughlin. The man in his early forties was unremarkable but for a freshly inflicted wound under his left eye which had barely healed. The scar it had left was quite red and small flakes of dried blood still clung to it.

He stopped close by the chair Loughlin sat in but didn't look at him. Instead he seemed to be looking towards the staircase. 'If you'd care to take a walk along the avenue,' he said out of the corner of his mouth, 'I'll come and join you.'

Loughlin got up and walked to the entrance. Out on the street he started walking slowly in the direction of the White House, then turned right. He walked along the west side of the hotel, then took the next street on the right. As he rounded the corner the man with the fresh scar emerged through the doors of the hotel back entrance. After a few paces he caught up with Loughlin but instead of walking alongside him he kept two paces behind and a bit off his left shoulder.

'Fred from Ealing?' It was just about audible above the noise in the street.

'I was expecting a woman.'

'Sorry to disappoint you.'

'I was told to contact you if I needed anything.'

'And do you – need anything'?

'Not at the moment but I will do. As soon as we're settled I'll need a car.'

'That's easy. Where are the others? Are they in the hotel?'

'No, they've already gone.'

'Where to?'

Loughlin shrugged. 'Don't know at the moment. I'm to catch up with them later. Somewhere north I think. I'll be in touch when I've joined them.'

'I'll wait for your call then.'

He walked on for about half a block but the voice behind him remained silent. When he turned to look he found there was no one; Amber Rose had gone.

******

Churchill's party had left the Washington the way they came: him in a wheelchair through the back door, with Clementine and Mary Shearburn going out of the main entrance where they got into a waiting taxi that had been sent to collect them. Churchill and Walter Thompson got into another car as they came out of the rear entrance. The cars left Washington heading north on State Highway 295 – it was going to be a long drive.

Just after South Laurel, and before they got into the Baltimore suburbs, both cars pulled off the road and disappeared into a tree-lined driveway. The drive led to a large colonial mansion where the cars stopped. 'Is this it?' Thompson asked the driver as he opened the door and got out. The house was one of the most elegant he had seen since he arrived. The driver shook his head. 'Just a change of horses.'

Shortly afterwards the long nose of the Taylors' Packard limousine emerged with Martins at the wheel. It turned back onto the highway and continued its journey north. Now they were all together. In the back the Churchill party relaxed and watched as they passed one small town after another. Behind them, following at a short distance but always in sight, was another car with four armed military officers in it. Each had been chosen for his discretion but none of them knew who they were guarding – only that if there was an attempt to abduct or interfere with the passengers of the car in front they were not to challenge, just shoot to kill.

When he arrived and got his first look at Brunessemer Churchill was moved to remark that it bore a strong resemblance to something Hitler might have built. Clementine told him to remember he was a guest. 'Well it's not exactly Chartwell,' he said under his breath.

Irena came out to greet the party. She stood at the top of the steps, looking down on them. She had heard a lot about Churchill and had often thought it might be interesting to meet him. Now he was here – her house guest. As they climbed the steps she was surprised to see how small he looked; he was quite a short man. His reputation was clearly larger than the physical man and it reminded her of once having met some stars of the silver screen on a gala occasion hosted by her husband and then being surprised at how small and ordinary they were. Like the stars, her only previous encounter with Churchill had been on the Pathe Newsreels projected onto a big screen; when somebody is spread across a forty-foot screen of course they would look big.

As the Churchills reached the top of the steps Irena greeted them and apologized that her husband was unable to be present, but that he was away on business. He would, she assured them, pay a visit and meet them personally when he returned.

'Oh Winston, this is lovely,' Clementine said when she saw the rooms they were to be staying in. 'Everything is so modern and spacious – you know we really must clear out some of the clutter at Chartwell.'

'I like clutter,' was all he said and went to inspect the bathroom. 'Jolly good plumbing though,' he called out, 'and two baths – that's extravagant.'

Mary Shearburn and Walter Thompson were put into separate rooms across the corridor with Thompson directly opposite so could be close to his charges. Churchill told Thompson that he thought it unlikely he would be in any danger here, tucked away in a small backwater town a long way from Washington. Thompson agreed, but kept his revolver with him at all times and kept it loaded. He knew he couldn't afford to be complacent – they would be out there somewhere, hunting for them, looking for an opportunity.

Loughlin arrived that evening, just in time for dinner. He was given a room next to Walter Thompson – now Churchill was flanked by bodyguards.

Before they went in he took Churchill to one side. 'Bad news I'm afraid, sir. The balloon's gone up; the Germans are on to us. Berlin sent a diplomatic note this morning to the State Department and is demanding they hand over the captain and crew of *Tenacious* – on charges of piracy and abduction.'

'They're releasing the crew of the U-boat tomorrow,' Loughlin informed him as they talked over the situation. 'They're handing them over to the German Embassy tomorrow morning.' 'Not good,' Churchill replied gloomily. 'They were bound to get on to it sooner or later but I had hoped it would be later. We must try to anticipate what they will do next.'

'The Americans think they'll get a demand from London for the return of *Tenacious* some time tomorrow. That'll be harder to resist. Have we got everything off her we need to?'

'I hope so. We need the gold and the money if we have to set up here for long. It's essential that they hold off doing anything until Admiral James makes his move. It won't be good for those poor beggars aboard if they have to go back before the takeover.'

Over dinner that night Irena asked if he thought Germany was a threat they should be worried about. 'Well, madam,' he replied, 'they're already on your doorstep and if you open your door and find a rabid dog sitting there then I think you would be right to worry.'

'Do you really think they would attack the United States? We are a neutral country.'

'In my experience Herr Hitler is no respecter of other people's property, as he has shown time and again in Europe.'

After dinner Churchill and Loughlin sat out on the terrace and talked about the implications of the events. If the Americans caved in then things could get sticky. They could find themselves carted off to Germany and put in front of a firing squad. 'I am surprised the Germans found out so quickly about us,' Churchill mused over his brandy. He looked dolefully into the glass. 'I much prefer whisky you know.'

'I think there might be a leak in US security. According to the sources I met in Washington, *Tenacious* was well hidden away. Someone must have said something.'

'Have you any ideas where this leak is?'

'No – I need to think about it.'

The night air was now becoming chill and Clementine came down with his warm navy duffle coat, insisting that he wear it. A moment or two later Irena came out on to the terrace. She gave a little shiver. 'It's far too cold,' she announced. 'Come along, Mrs Churchill, let's go inside – leave them to their brandy and cigars. Would you care for a nightcap? Do you mind if I call you Clementine? I do so dislike formality with my house guests.'

'Of course, and I'll call you Irena if that is all right.'

'Please do. You know the trouble living with powerful men is they're such crashing bores most of the time. It comes of being single-minded, driven.'

CHAPTER 22

England, November 1940

Admiral James left the navy base at Portsmouth in his staff car. To the guard on the gate who came rigidly to attention and saluted it all looked very routine. The sky was heavy with cloud and the mercury was almost down to freezing. There was the threat of an early snow fall. As the car trundled over the bridge at Tipner and onto the mainland he could see the lights of the fleet anchored out in the roads of the Solent. A signal had come in that morning a little after zero three hundred hours: *Tenacious* had been picked up by a US navy coastal patrol boat just off New England. Churchill was safe in Washington. It was the news he had been waiting for. It was time to set things in motion.

Using a driver he knew he could trust, James had left early and long before it was light. He needed to be in London when the balloon went up, alongside Charlie Armitage and those politicians he knew he could trust. Bevin and Dalton had been taken into their confidence and were now co-conspirators in the plot to seize power. It had been a risk to involve civilians but they needed experienced politicians who knew the Westminster machine and how it worked. They had to avoid a vacuum in government at almost any cost, or there would be chaos. It had taken months of planning and nobody underestimated the risk; if things went wrong it would be treason. Time after time James had pulled back from approaching some of his most senior officers for fear that it could become mess room gossip. But he had finally achieved it with a small contingent of key commanders who were now in place waiting for the order to head off the Kreigsmarine and keep it hemmed into the Solent. Out on the cold, grey sea his ships waited for the order to take up positions and blockade both ends of the narrow strip of water. It would be checkmate before the Germans realized the game had even started.

After two hours on the road they reached Hook, the Surrey village that marked the outer edge of London's new middle-class suburbs in the south. On his left he could dimly make out the Ace of Spades public house. It was still in darkness but it was intermittently illuminated by a flashing orange beacon that marked the large roundabout carrying the A24 interchange. To the left, out there in the darkness, was Kingston where his friend Harry Hawker had set up his aircraft factory back in 1920. Throughout the Depression of the early 1930s Hawker's company had prospered to become Britain's most successful aircraft company. Then came the Paris Treaty, the terms of which demanded a halt in the manufacture of war materials and the factory had stopped aircraft production. Now it was reduced to making tractor parts and agricultural machinery. Back in the previous summer, following the signing of the Treaty, James and Armitage had met Hawker in the Kingston Hotel and, over lunch in the privacy of the Oak Room lounge, had first mooted the coup that was now being put into motion. Hawker had agreed not to scrap the tooling for his most successful fighter, the Hurricane, and had secretly held back a stockpile of parts and airframes now hidden away in a warehouse at Brooklands flying club nearby in Weybridge. Once the coup had started there was an area of the factory that could immediately be put into production.

Over in the other direction the road ran towards Chessington where there was still a battery of anti-aircraft guns which had yet to be dismantled. They were unmanned other than by a solitary warden left to guard them. James knew these guns would be vital if he had to plug the main A3 route from Portsmouth into London. His own plan was to run trucks along that road, ferrying armed sailors up from Portsmouth. But the Germans might also try to mobilize their forces now sitting on the Isle of Wight; if they succeeded in breaking out he had some chance of stopping them at the Ace of Spades, which was well within the range of the battery.   Armitage had put together a small commando group to be led by an MI5 officer; their job would be to take out the warden and arm the battery. To do this they had secretly moved an ammunition truck down from the Woolwich arsenal where, curiously, a stock of shells had been overlooked when the disarmament programme had been invoked by the Treaty. They had been stored in the Royal Laboratory and had been scheduled for testing but had been forgotten when Woolwich closed down – another casualty of the Treaty. Now they sat in a truck hidden in a Nissen hut up a narrow track at the back of the Chessington Zoological Gardens, with nothing but wolves and monkeys for company.

The flashing beacon marked the start of the Kingston bypass, which would take him to Putney, 15 miles away. There he could join the Embankment alongside the Thames and drive straight to the Mall and his office in Admiralty House. From there he was a walk away from Downing Street and five minutes' drive to Westminster. At Admiralty House he planned a rendezvous with chief of the Army, General Sir Alan Brooke, and Air Vice Marshal Keith Park. Brooke was a close friend of Churchill and James knew he was utterly trustworthy and committed. Park was an unknown quantity but he was popular with the men he commanded and had personally flown with them, in the thick of it, supporting the retreat to Dunkirk. Hawker knew him and had vouched for his loyalty, and that was good enough for James. These were the men he would have to rely on.

As the car crossed over the Thames at Putney Bridge he heard the muffled sound of Big Ben coming through the damp, grey air; it struck six. A pale yellow fog came smoking up from the river, clinging to the bridge and draping it in a dripping coat of liquid soot. The road was almost deserted save for a single policeman who had just taken up point duty on the Chelsea side of the bridge. Here and there a few of the river workers were making their way to their labours – lightermen and porters mostly, but some clerks and the tallymen, those who kept account of what was loaded and unloaded. A solitary double-decker bus was groaning along the Embankment, the lights inside splashing out onto the pavement as it passed. It was nearly empty – the rush would not start for another hour.

Shortly before 6.30 the staff car arrived in front of Admiralty House, where it was saluted by a sentry dressed in the ceremonial uniform of the Horse Guards. James got out and, once standing, returned the salute. Then, with his cap under his arm, he strode into the building. A young lieutenant snapped to attention; James handed him his coat then made his way up the sweeping ornamental staircase to a room on the first floor. The others were already there: Armitage, Brooke and Park, together with Bevin and Dalton.

******

At Brunessemer Loughlin had set up his Morse transmitter and was waiting. Earlier he had put out his call sign and received back an answer. The British end now knew he was in place and ready. All he had to do was wait for the message that would tell him the coup had started. Once it was under way he would contact Amber Rose, who would pass on the position to his handler in Washington. It would be vital for the coup that it was immediately acknowledged as legitimate by the Americans, who would notify the German Embassy with a clear statement that any action by Berlin to intervene would be met by strong condemnation. James had wanted a stronger statement. He had hoped the Americans might be persuaded to threaten military retaliation in the event of German aggression, but that was a step too far. In private Churchill had cajoled his old friend Roosevelt to take a tough stance in the diplomatic note, but he had brushed it aside, chuckling at Churchill's audacity and telling him he would do a lot for his friend but that did not include pitching America into a foreign war.

******

As James made his way to London, a convoy of eight heavy articulated trucks was rumbling its laborious way down the Great North Road. It had left the German naval dockyard at Hull under cover of dark in the late evening of the previous day. Around midnight, it had passed through Peterborough and was now close to St Neots where it pulled off the road onto the large muddy truck park of a transport café. The drivers were all British because, by a small oversight in the Treaty, the Germans had allowed a restriction to be put on the movement of heavy goods by German drivers around the UK; the British had argued that the use of foreign drivers breached a Transport and General Workers Union agreement and this would result in disruptive strikes. The unions had insisted on it and so it found its way into the document. But although the drivers were British, the cargo was not.

In ones and twos the men and their mates climbed down from the truck cabs and made their way towards the lights of the café. One of them split away from the group. 'I'm going round the back for a piss,' he told his mate. 'There'll be a queue a mile long for the bogs in there.'

Walking round behind the café building, he disappeared into the dark. Looking around him to ensure that he was now alone and the others had all gone into the café, he changed direction and hurriedly made his way towards the road. On the edge of the park he found what he was looking for – a red GPO telephone box. He let several coins drop into the slot then dialled a number. A voice at the other end simply said 'hello', then there was silence. He pressed the button marked with a large A and heard the coins clatter into the box below; he was connected.

'It's Alpha Six. They're here.'

'How many?'

'Eight.'

Back in the café a man behind the counter wearing a greasy blue-and-white striped apron asked what he wanted. 'Eggs, bacon, sausage, beans and mushrooms – and a cuppa char,' he said enthusiastically, adding, 'and a fried slice.' He turned to his mate, 'I'm absolutely bloody starving.'

'That was a bloody long piss. What kept you,' the other man said, but it was a comment rather than a question.

'Got lost in the dark, didn't I.'

'Well, don't make a habit of it – you're driving the next shift and old Fritz over there will give you shit if you get this little lot lost.' He pointed to a table in the corner where a man in a German army field coat sat talking to another man in a black leather coat. They had arrived separately in a car shortly before the convoy. Now as they talked they leaned close to each other to avoid being overheard.

'What's he about then?'

'That's Major Linz. He's going to guide us round London and onto the Portsmouth Road – so as we don't get lost, like.'

There was a lull in the conversation while the man in the greasy apron dumped a plate and a mug on the counter top. 'Full English with fried slice and a cuppa – who wants it comes and gets it,' he shouted, 'and bring one and a tanner with ya.'

Alpha Six got to his feet, went to the counter and paid over one shilling and six pence then, returning with the plate and a steaming mug of tea, sat down and started to eat. 'Who's the geezer with him in the black leather then?' He motioned with his head to where Linz and the other man sat.

'Haven't a clue.'

An hour later the convoy pulled back onto the road to continue its journey south. In the lead truck Alpha Six took his turn at the wheel. Squashed in next to him on the kerb side of the cab Linz sat, staring ahead and saying nothing. He looked at the man behind the wheel and thought he looked familiar, but then concluded that all these English look alike: pale, weedy and undernourished.

******

In Admiralty House James confronted the small gathering. There was apprehension in his voice as he addressed them.

'We all know why we're here,' he said solemnly. 'This government is weak and ineffective and has to be replaced. It's let the country down and betrayed it – but let's be clear why it has to be replaced. The Germans are slowly infiltrating all our institutions. Ever since Paris they've been chipping away at promise after promise; they've altered a phrase here a word there, argued meanings, all to gain greater control over the country. They've rendered the army almost useless under the re-armaments clause in this damnable treaty. The RAF no longer exists, it's been dismantled – our own politicians have done the job the Luftwaffe couldn't manage. If this continues for a further six months we shall be nothing more than another vassal state in Hitler's Reich, like Vichy. And, as with Vichy, you'll have noticed he has not disbanded the Navy. The bulk of the French fleet is sitting in Toulon, twiddling its thumbs, just as we have been sitting idly in Portsmouth – that is, until recently when the Canadian convoys started. I believe that using the Royal Navy to assist in this operation is just the thin edge of the wedge. Intelligence reports are telling us that Hitler has a plan for both these fleets to eventually come under the single command of Admiral Raeder. It's not only the Atlantic and the Med he'll control; he'll have the Indian Ocean and half the Pacific.

'To achieve their aim they'll have to persuade Halifax and Chamberlain to hand over our Navy to the German High Command. Yes, Halifax is weak but he's no traitor. I don't believe he could be duped into doing something that crass. So that would leave Hitler with only one other viable option – a forcible removal of this government and its replacement with another, more to his liking – an acquiescent group with a leader who would do his bidding. There are no shortage of contenders sitting out there – Aitken, for example. I think he could convince himself that it would be for the greater good if he led the country. So, since the Germans plan to replace our government, it's best we do it for them – before they do it for us.'

There was a knock and the door to the room opened. Every head turned to look; a woman in a WREN's uniform came in and saluted. She handed a note to James. 'Important sir – just come in.' She saluted again and left. James opened the note, paused for a moment and then said, 'There's a convoy of heavy trucks just north of London and they're heading for Portsmouth. They're carrying eight battle tanks: Panzer Mark IVs – two of them are F class – fitted with flame throwers. One of our agents is in the convoy.'

Everyone in the room stood in silence. Dalton looked worried. 'So what the hell does this mean Admiral. Are they on to us?'

'I don't think so. We've known there was a movement pending for some time. We just didn't know when – or why for that matter. Our intelligence on this has been around for some time so I don't think it's connected – just a coincidence in my view.' He looked at Brooke, 'What do you think Alan?'

'It could be connected with what you've just been outlining. They could be getting those tanks into position ready for a takeover of the government. The easy way would be to declare martial law and use that as an excuse to put their own military on the streets. We've got nothing that could go up against a Panzer IV.'

'Would eight tanks be enough, General?' Bevin asked sceptically.

Brooke was forthright; he didn't mince his words. 'Definitely. They could easily subdue any resistance on the ground in the area around the dockyard. All they'd need is some infantry in support. There's no shortage of Kreigsmarine men stationed in Ryde and Cowes. They could bring them in on E-boats – there're plenty of them over there – but that's not the whole picture. We haven't a clue what else they might've been shipping into Hull. They could have no end of kit in there by now – and thanks to your crazy treaty we can't do a damn thing about it. It's German sovereign territory for the next hundred years.'

He turned to Parks. 'What do you think, Parky? Are they flying stuff in there too?' The Air Marshal shrugged his shoulders. 'Bound to be. Wouldn't you? There's enough room for a long strip, the docks spread out for miles. You'd easily get transports in and out.'

James held up a hand to halt the speculation. 'I think that does it. We have to move. So let's get down to the plan'. He pointed to the chairs laid out around a table.

'We don't have a lot of time to do this thing; we've set zero hour for Friday next, at midday. The Germans like a two-hour lunch; with a bit of luck we'll have it done and dusted while they're still getting stuck into their sausage and sauerkraut. That's in three days. It doesn't give us much time and there's a lot to be done. Charlie, we need to slow down those tanks – anything you can do?'

'I'm already ahead of you on that one.'

'Good, so *modus operandi*: tomorrow Park goes down to Kingston to link up with Hawker's team. They've started an assembly line. It's tucked away out of sight of inspectors and they haven't seen anyone from the Legation in weeks. There are some men from the Royal Surrey Regiment already there – not very well armed I'm afraid – Bren guns and a couple of rocket launchers, but hopefully you won't need them. There's small battery of Bofors guns on the roof of the Elite cinema building that might come in handy. Like Chessington, they've only got a caretaker. Over the next week it'll be up to you to get as many planes ferried out of there as Harry can turn out. Move them at night to the Brooklands strip; it's no distance and you're unlikely to come up against any Jerry flights. Once we've got control of Downing Street we'll stop all inspections anyway and the factory will go over to flat-out production. You're going to have to keep the Germans out of the sky. What else have you got Parky?'

'There's the best part of Eleven Fighter Wing mothballed over at Northolt and a couple of brand new Mosquitoes sitting on the ground at Croydon. The Germans were planning to take them over to Canada. Our best intelligence is that they're all operational but nothing is armed except the Mosquitoes. Northolt is pretty heavily invested with Wehrmacht, but mostly pen-pushers; it's down to the Army here to secure it.' He nodded in the direction of General Brooke.

'I've got a company of unemployed commandos I've borrowed from Lovett's 4th Brigade. Brooke said, grinning. 'They're armed with gate passes and they'll go in wearing civilian clothing. Once inside they'll meet up with one of Charlie's men who will take them to an arms cache we've set up in the canteen. The first thing they'll do is knock out the radio room in the control tower. After that, it's back to Parky again to get some of his flyers in and make everything operational.'

'It'll be tight,' Park admitted. 'We'll only have a short time to get crew mobilized – couldn't risk advanced mustering.'

James turned to the politicians, who had all this time been nodding with approval and occasionally smiling at the prospects of getting the country back. 'We'll swamp the area around the Legation with men from Chelsea Barracks and keep them boxed inside. We'll do what we can to intercept or jam radio traffic. What they don't know at the moment is that we've cracked the code they use to talk to Berlin. It's how we know so much about their plans.

'The tank regiment in Queen Anne's Gate and the Horse Guards will protect Parliament and Number 10. All you have to do is announce the new measures to restrict the Treaty. You've got enough breaches to cite and, besides, it hasn't yet been formally ratified by the House. The Americans will deliver their note to Berlin as soon as you make a statement to Parliament. We don't know what the German response will be but they'll need to get direct orders from Hitler and we know he is away from Berlin that weekend and will be on a train heading for Berchtesgaden. No one will make a move without his order so we shall have some time before they respond. We need to avoid an immediate fight on the ground if we can. We shall be at our weakest in the first 48 hours. If we can secure our positions so that they're difficult to assault then we can probably bog them down in negotiations. But make no mistake, in the end we shall have to stand and fight – this is too big a prize for either side to walk away. Any questions?' He looked round the table; nobody said anything.

'Good. Let's get down to the detailed planning. Mr Dalton, you and Mr Bevin here will need to get a meeting at Number 10. This has to be set up for eleven thirty in the morning. Once you're in position telephone me here. Your call sign will be 'sorry wrong number'. Don't wait for a response – just hang up. Then arrange for the constable on the door to let us in. Once inside, we'll replace the security Bobbies with our own men. They'll keep any unwanted visitors out. Brooke and I will then come up to meet you in the Cabinet room where we'll hold Halifax and Chamberlain till they make resignation statements in writing.'

'What if they won't?' Bevin said tersely.

'You will have to persuade them it's for the good of the country – then you'll need to get their statements to the House and there make your own statement confirming that Churchill is alive and still the legally elected Prime Minister. We can say he is in America, holding bilateral cooperation talks with the US government and you are acting as caretakers until his return. We've arranged for Churchill to make an address to the British people in a radio broadcast at six o'clock that evening. Reinstate Anthony Eden as Foreign Secretary and get him back to Number 10 where we can brief him. He can start talks with the Legation who, by then, will be wondering what hit them.

'Charlie, tell us what MI5 and Special Branch are doing to get key men in position in the ministries.'

'The problem is there are known German sympathizers in the Home Office and the Foreign and Commonwealth Office. We can't afford subversion or non-cooperation at the outset. We think we've identified most of the potential trouble makers, largely in London, and I have men marking them. The ministries will have to get the new policy stance out to the counties. We'll need every official down to the last policeman on the beat to know and understand their position and their duty to the new government.'

James took the floor again. 'Thanks Charlie,' he said, then added solemnly, 'bloody shame they murdered David Peters. He would have been a good man to manage the police forces. I'd like to get my hands on the swine that did it.' He turned again to the politicians. 'We need a general transport strike – will the Unions cooperate?'

'They will,' said Bevin, with certainty.

'Good, we need a picket on the Hull docks; no drivers in or out, and let's get all the dockworkers out. We don't want anything moving out of there. We want to keep the Germans locked inside for as long as possible.'

******

Just south east of Roxton the main A1 route passes over the river Great Ouse. The convoy had been on the road for barely an hour when it stopped again – this time there was a police road block. Ahead was the small village of Tempsford. A constable halted the convoy; he was standing in the middle of the road with one arm held up in the air.

'What is this?' Linz scowled.

Alpha Six stood on the brakes and wrestled the truck slowly to a halt. Linz immediately jumped down and started shouting at the constable to get out of the way. A sergeant then appeared, together with an inspector. Linz was outnumbered. 'What is happening?' he said testily. 'Why you are stopping us?'

The inspector saluted Linz, trying to placate him with a show of deference. 'The bridge ahead of you is blocked, sir. There has been an accident. You will have to wait, I'm afraid, or else go back and around Roxton - you can pick up the A421 then come back through Great Barford.'

'How long will it take to clear?'

'It's hard to say, sir. We're waiting for an ambulance and the fire brigade. It could take a few hours before we can let you across. Your best bet would be to turn around and go back, sir.' Linz looked around him at the open countryside, trying to work out a solution. There was no obvious way round the problem. He couldn't turn the convoy; there wasn't any room. Besides the ground looked too soft; he didn't dare chance bogging them down. He was becoming frustrated and angry.

'That is not practical,' he retorted angrily. 'I can't turn these trucks around here. We don't have the room; it is impossible. You must move the wrecks out of our way. We have to pass.'

The sergeant looked scathingly at Linz, then set off to inspect the position of the trucks. 'I'll just take a look, sir,' he said to his inspector. Casually he wondered along to the first truck, stopped by the driver's cab and looked up at Alpha Six. 'Could you hop down a moment, mate?' Alpha Six climbed down from the cab. The morning air caught his breath and made it condense into a fine misty vapour. 'Bit parky down here.'

'It must be nice and warm in that cab,' the policeman laughed, 'sitting on top of that big diesel engine.' Both men moved to the front of the truck and leant against the front grill of the radiator. It was comfortingly warm. The sergeant hesitated for a moment. He looked around him, then satisfied there was nobody else in earshot said, 'Are you Al?'

'Fa,' Alpha Six replied, finishing the word for him.

'Good, I've got a message.' He leant close and whispered. Alpha Six climbed back up into the cab and slammed the door. He settled into the warm seat and rubbed his hands. 'Bloody bitter out there,' he said. The sergeant wondered back to where Linz was still protesting at the hold up.

'Well, sir', the constable chipped in, looking at his inspector, 'there is the layby just up the road from here. There might be enough room to get them turned there. Of course, it'll be tight but it's probably do-able.'

'Thank you constable.' The inspector turned to Linz 'How about that, sir – does that help?'

Linz came back to the lead truck and issued instructions on the plan to Alpha Six. 'I'll go and tell the rest of the drivers,' Alpha Six volunteered. 'We don't want them all following us down the road like sheep – it'll create an even bigger traffic jam.' He set off back to the next vehicle. There he gave some instructions to the driver and asked him to pass them down the line to the others.

Back in his own cab he fired up the big diesel engine. There was a crunch as he engaged the first of its six gears and the truck slowly started to move forward. He was into fourth by the time he rounded the first bend and picked up speed. The rest of the convoy had slipped out of sight. About a quarter of a mile away he could see the layby; it wasn't very deep. This could be fun, he thought.

Linz got down from the cab again. There was no sign of the police or their car. In the distance, across the flat fields, they could just make out a village: Tempsford. Linz had been a tank commander before he was attached to the Legation. He had attended General Guderian's tank school in 1935 and witnessed the birth of the Panzers. He was equally familiar with tank transporters and knew the space he had to turn this one around was going to make it tight. He took a few paces off the road and tested the ground beyond the layby. It was hard but there had been a frost and he knew that could be misleading; the underlying ground beneath the frost-hardened crust could be soft. He went further away from the road and hacked at the surface with the heel of his boot. A few stones scattered up behind him; chalk and flint bound together with clay. He would have preferred gravel and sands but he thought the clay looked dry and cold enough not to slip.

Standing in front of the truck he signalled Alpha Six to start making the first part of the turn. Alpha Six hauled on the steering wheel and got the wheels as far to the right as they would go, then slowly let out the clutch. He took the giant truck as far across the road as he could without going onto the unmade ground. It sat there across both lanes in a huge arc blocking the whole of the road. 'Halt, halt!' Linz shouted above the din of the engine. 'Okay, so now you go to the other side with the steering and come back, but don't let the semi-trailer go onto the field so far, otherwise it will sink. I will tell you when.'

The truck started to move back but there wasn't enough room to induce the trailer to change its position and they ended up back where they started. Linz thought about it. 'Okay, we try to go a little further into the field this time – but slowly, we don't want it to sink.'

'Oh yes we do,' Alpha Six thought to himself. 'That's exactly what we want.'

There was a clunk as reverse gear was engaged. Leaning out of the window, he could see Linz waving him back towards the hard frozen ground of the field. He let out the clutch slowly until he could feel the drive take up. In the rear view mirror he saw the final axle wheels of the semi-trailer cross the layby and go onto the field. He stopped and waited to see what happened, but the ground held firm. Damn, he cursed under his breath – he had hoped the near total weight of 40 tons of tank and trailer would cause the whole thing to sink. Linz was still waving and shouting for him to move back further. Not until the whole of the trailer was standing on the field did Linz order him to halt. 'Right,' he shouted, holding his arm out like a Nazi salute, 'now go forward – but slow.'

Alpha Six looked in the mirror again. At last the ground was beginning to give under the weight but he was too far into the field and that was no good. He needed the truck to get stuck when the front of it was far enough into the road to block both carriageways and make it impassable.

'Go forward,' Linz was shouting. There was nothing for it, he had to move. He had reached the optimum point in the turn with the tractor part of the vehicle blocking the road and the trailer still on the soft ground when a desperate idea came into his head. He depressed the clutch, engaged sixth gear, then let the clutch up abruptly. The giant truck lurched, then the engine died. Under the bulkhead just by the steering wheel there was a valve in the diesel supply line; it went directly to the pump that supplied each cylinder with its injection of fuel. He turned the tap of the valve to 'off', then he pulled the starter. The engine turned slowly, then started to fire, but it was intermittent and it struggled to keep going. The huge engine gasped and faltered; he was starving it and shortly it would die. After a final cough, it gave up and stalled. Now he wanted to make sure it couldn't be restarted. He spun the starter again, emptying the fuel pump of the last dregs of diesel and filling it with air. It had taken less than a minute to kill it but the job was done. He knew it couldn't be started without the pump being bled; that would need a mechanic and would take time. If the day warmed there was every chance the back end of the trailer would sink and there would be nothing for it but to unload the tank and get a recovery truck to haul everything out.

By the time Linz had got to the cab Alpha Six had turned the fuel back to 'on' and was getting down from behind the wheel. 'What is it?' Linz grumbled abruptly. 'Why have you stopped?'

'I don't know. I'll have a look.' He opened a hatch under the cab, pulled out a heavy tool box and carried it round to the front of the truck. Lifting the engine cover, he looked in, then selected a heavy wrench. Linz was standing by looking over his shoulder. 'Can you see what it is?'

'No.' He needed to get rid of the nosey German if he was going to finish off the job but Linz stood there obstinately, watching and asking questions. Then he said something helpful. 'Is there anything I can do?' Alpha Six couldn't believe his lucky break. He pulled his head out from the engine compartment and pointed up to the cab. 'If you could go up top and pull the starter when I shout, that would be good.' Linz brightened at the prospect of doing something that might move the problem to a solution. 'Of course,' he said.

Free from the intrusion, he located the fuel line to the pump and, using the wrench, hit it until it snapped. 'Okay,' he shouted up to Linz, 'hit the starter.' The engine turned freely but refused to fire; a thick slick of diesel spurted from the fuel line, sprayed round the engine compartment and dribbled down onto the ground beneath where it started to form a large black pool. 'Stop! Shut it off!' he yelled up to the cab where Linz was still enthusiastically winding the motor round.

Linz got down. 'What is it? Have you found it? Can it be fixed?'

'Yes, I've found it, but no I can't fix it.' He bent down and pointed at the pool of black diesel on the ground. 'The main line to the fuel pump is broken. It's going to need a new one.'

Linz looked irritated. 'Well, we can't leave it here.'

'I could always go back to the convoy and uncouple a tractor from one of the trailers and bring it back here. That way we could at least get this one back on the road again; tow it to the nearest garage.'

Linz thought for a moment. 'That is a good idea but I will go. You stay here and guard this one.' He had started to move away from the stricken truck when he stopped and turned to look back. 'Have we met before?' he asked quizzically. 'You seem familiar.'

'No, I don't think so. I'd remember if we had. I'm often in the docks at Hull – I work on the transport there. Maybe that's where you've seen me. I don't know you, though.'

As Linz disappeared around the bend Alpha Six smiled and started to walk in the other direction. After a while he saw the police car parked at the side of the road. 'We've been waiting for you. What kept you?'

'Oh, not a lot really. I just needed to buy a bit of time for the other lads. There'll be one grumpy Boche when friend Linz reaches the convoy, though. I told the lads to leg it as soon as we'd gone out of site. They've all buggered off to find a café in Roxton. Linz'll have to move the fucking truck on his own – unless, of course, you fancy giving him a push.'

The sergeant laughed. 'Leave it out, I've done my bit for the war – I was at Dunkirk you know. I spent two days pushing trucks over the cliffs to stop Jerry getting his hands on them. Okay, Constable McGee, drive on, and when we get to the station give them a call over at Roxton. Ask them to sort out a lift for those lads. We don't want them going back to help Herr Shittenfürher.'

Back at the Admiralty the WREN again knocked on the door and handed James a note. He unfolded it and read it. He smiled at Armitage. 'Well done, Charlie – I'm impressed.'

'Good news is it then?'

'Yes. Apparently there's a major traffic jam on the A1. Some fool's got a truck stuck across both the north and south bound carriageways. The tailback goes for miles – it's chaos.'

******

At Brunessemer it was quiet and things had taken on a holiday mood. Irena took Clementine to New York where they lunched and shopped, saw the sights and then in the afternoon, following tea in one of the many fashionable salons, were driven back home by Martins in the vast comfortable back seats of the Packard. Clementine was beginning to enjoy the relaxation and the female company after the anxiety and privations of their escape aboard the *Tenacious*. She was, she confided in Irena, finding the whole experience very agreeable, especially the female conversation. It was, she stated quite emphatically, totally pointless to even try to talk to Winston about a new dress or some piece of jewellery. He simply did not understand that shoes and purses had to match or that one needed more than just one hat. Irena, for her part, was delighted to have a house guest with such a famous profile, even if it was resting on the reputation of her husband. The only frustration was that she could not make more of her; everyone around them was obsessed with the fear that there would be an assassination attempt on Churchill. So she found herself limited to family when it came to entertaining and with Thanksgiving coming up she thought it would be a very dull affair with nothing more than her two daughters, the Churchills and their bodyguards for the celebration. Then there was Carey fretting away in the background over Tom.

'Poor girl,' she told Clementine as they sat in the dining room after lunch, 'it's been the most dreadful affair.'

'Is there nothing anyone can do?'

'Warren has been trying to get to the bottom of it but it seems there's some kind of spy mystery surrounding it and nobody's saying anything. It's just awful. She's never been the easiest of girls, you know. She's very highly strung. I worry about what may happen if it ends in tragedy for her young man.'

'Could it, do you think?'

Irena made a little frustrated gesture, raising her eyes to the ceiling and shrugging her shoulders. 'I really don't know, but the one bright spot is his friend – a nice young man, from an Italian family, I think. He's been a great assistance, running around and making enquiries. It's been something of a comfort to her. I guess it helps to have someone she can talk to who is close to Tom.'

'You know,' Clementine said, trying to sound positive, 'in the heat of the fray things often seem worse than they are. I'm sure things will turn out for the best. Is she very much in love with her young man?' Irena sighed in resignation. 'I should like to say yes, but with Carey who knows?'

'Ah,' Clementine said knowingly. 'I imagine this will test it then?'

'Carey is for Carey. You can never be sure what is going on in that head of hers. It comes from being such an appallingly beautiful woman; she expects adoration, she commands it. She can be very hurtful if she's not the center of attention; too much beauty is a curse, you know.' Clementine nodded knowingly. 'I imagine there have been others then.' Irena threw up her hands, 'Oh many, my dear, and every one played out like a Greek tragedy.' She laughed an exasperated, unenthusiastic laugh, 'I'll ask Patience to bring us some tea – would you like tea?'

'I would love tea; that would be perfect.'

'Come on, we can have it in the drawing room.'

'We had hoped this young man, Tom, was at last going to be the right one; she seemed so settled when he was around and fretted when he wasn't. We were so hopeful – and now this comes along. It really is too tiresome.'

It was good to gossip again, Clementine thought. For months she had had no one other than Mary Shearburn to talk to: first when they were spirited away to Portsmouth and kept out of sight on the *Regent* and then for the desperate dash on *Tenacious*. Thrown together they had relied on each other's company to break the boredom but they were companions of convenience and had very little in common intellectually, and even less socially. Since they had arrived Mary had been working constantly on Winston's speech and they had hardly seen her except occasionally at dinner. She had elected to take most of her meals in her room and whatever time she had off duty she spent with Walter. They could often be seen walking arm in arm around the garden or just sitting wrapped up on the terrace enjoying a sunny November afternoon. They seemed very content, Irena said, like two characters out of a Hollywood romance.

As much as Clementine was enjoying her stay, Winston, by contrast, was restless. He was becoming more moody by the day; he wanted to see some action. He had prepared his speech to the nation and now he wanted to deliver it. He paced about the garden and growled a lot at Loughlin.

'Can't they get a move on over there in London?' he said one evening as Loughlin accompanied him around the lawns. 'Have we had no news at all? We're sat out here, fiddling around, not knowing what's going on, who's doing what. Oh, our American cousins are being very sympathetic all right but we need to see some action and I get the feeling we're a bit of an embarrassment. They just want us to stay quiet and not make a fuss. I feel like a bloody eunuch in a Turkey whore house – I've been neutered, Fred – I've had my balls cut off.'

******

It was Friday; it had been nearly a week since Tom had been taken and still no news. Tony called to say he was passing by that morning and would be happy to meet up with Carey and talk over the position if she would like that? Carey said she would like it very much and was grateful to him for his constant consideration but, she told him, 'You can't come here. We've got these strange, creepy English guests that we're not supposed to talk about. There's a prohibition on visitors. I even have to go over to Nigel's studio for my art class; he's not allowed near the house. Can you imagine that? Poor Nigel, he's so sensitive; he's devastated.'

Tony suggested she could walk to the end of the drive and he would pick her up there; that way nobody would see him. Carey didn't like that idea; it was too much like creeping away for some sort of secret assignation and people might get the wrong idea. Besides, she said, exaggerating, 'the gardens and the driveway were crawling with FBI men and security guards.'

'Do you have another suggestion?'

'I'll meet you in Croton,' she said.

Martins drove her to the diner but she didn't want to stay there. She said it reminded her too much of Tom and if she couldn't have him she didn't want to be reminded of him. Tony suggested they go to the cocktail bar in Croton but she didn't much like that either, so he suggested the hotel for lunch. In the end she said, 'Let's go to New York. I need to stick my head round the door at the gallery where I work. I haven't been there since Tom went missing; old Kolinsky will think I'm dead.'

When she suggested El Morocco for lunch, Tony said no. He knew she had taken Tom there when they'd first met and he didn't like the idea – it was like walking in dead men's shoes. All he'd wanted to do was have a talk with her and try to assure her that he was pulling out all the stops in his search to find Tom, and now she had turned it into a junket around New York.

'I have a better idea,' he said, trying not to sound like he was lecturing her. 'We can go to a deli and get a sandwich and I'll tell you what I've heard on the grapevine – that is, if you want to hear it.' She stood there silently and nodded her head vigorously like a naughty child who had just been scolded for talking out of turn.

'I hate driving around New York,' he said, 'I'm going to dump the car at my apartment and we can walk from there.' The apartment had originally been acquired by his father when he'd opened his first club in New York, but the family had moved to Miami for the opening of the second club and preferred it there. Like Tom with the Chrysler, he had inherited it because his father simply never used it. If he wanted anything done in New York he got Tony to do it for him. That was how Tony earned his keep.

Over lunch he told her the news didn't sound good. He'd tried several friends who had connections in both the police and the FBI. Nobody had heard anything about the arrest. Worst of all, one of his contacts thought it might have something to do with US military security and there was a story circulating of someone being killed, but it was only a rumor.

'Do you think Tommy's dead?' she asked, looking at him blankly. Her face had gone pale and he thought she might cry.

'I don't know but I don't think so.'

'Why not?'

'Because I couldn't bear to think he was.' His voice was edgy and she could feel the tension in it. She began to cry. This was the last thing he wanted. He felt bad as it was without her dissolving into tears on him. 'Come on,' he said, trying to show sympathy, 'let's get out of here – it's not far to the park. We can walk a bit and get some fresh air. It'll help settle you down.'

They walked along the east side in silence; neither could find anything to say to the other. After a while Carey looped her arm through his. The action took him by surprise, but he didn't pull away. 'Do you mind if I do this? It just makes me feel better? Tommy and I used to come here and walk sometimes.'

'It's OK', he said patting her arm gently, 'it's OK.'

They walked on still saying nothing. A cold wind was beginning to get up and the sky was darkening. 'I think we may be due for some rain,' he said, breaking the long hiatus. 'We should think about getting you back to your place.'

She shook her head solemnly and stood there for a moment, and he thought how like a lost child she looked. 'I don't want to go back there – not just yet anyway.' She tugged on his arm. 'Come on, let's walk a bit more, it's helping me to think.'

After another long silence they came to the Pond near to the south east corner of the park. Here she stopped and stood for a moment, aimlessly looking into the greyish brown, murky water. 'This is a very sad little lake,' she eventually said. 'They should do something to cheer it up.' She let out a short abrupt little sigh – almost a snort. 'Tommy used to say it looked like someone had drowned in it.' She took his arm again but showed no sign of wanting to move on. She just continued looking down into the water. 'I think Tommy is dead,' she said in a laconic voice that trailed away into a whisper. 'I think he's dead.'

Tony wasn't sure what to do and ended up saying, 'Why don't we find a place to go that's under cover? This wind is beginning to bite.'

'Sorry,' she said, 'I'm getting morbid. We could walk over to Broadway and find a newsreel theatre; see if they're showing the latest Mickey Mouse – that would cheer us up. Come on.' They sat in the dark of the theatre, munched popcorn and laughed at the latest Disney cartoons. The newsreel was full of the World's Fair and America on the Move.

'Have you been?' he whispered to her.

'No.'

'You should go. I went with Tom and Mike. It's amazing.'

'Would you take me?'

'Well,' he said awkwardly, 'I guess Tom would like to do that once we get him free.'

Carey didn't respond and then there was a news clip from Germany. It was a rally in some monumental stadium built in gleaming white stone, but before the newsman had said where it was she stood up abruptly. 'Let's go. I don't want to watch this.'

He followed her out into the fading light of the late afternoon. Here and there lamps were going on; the theaters began to glow with the gaudy brashness of rows of colored fairy lights. They walked as far as Fifth Avenue, then Tony hailed a cab. 'It's too cold for my hot Latin blood,' he joked. She laughed as they bundled into the warmth of the cab.

'Where to?' the cabby asked. They looked at each other blankly; neither of them had given much thought to where they were actually going when Tony had decided to take a cab. The driver waited.

'Let's find a drink,' she blurted out. 'I could murder a Margarita.'

'Okay, I know just the place. Do you know Tiro a Segno?' he shouted to the cab driver. 'It's south of the village on MacDougal Street.' The cabby laughed, 'What good Italian doesn't know that?' Tony turned to Carey, who had snuggled herself up into the corner of the back seat. 'You'll like it,' he said, smiling. 'They serve the best Italian food in New York – no make that all of America; but don't tell my mamma I said so.' Carey laughed. 'Is it a restaurant? I don't know it.'

'Yes, but it's a club – very exclusive – you have to be Italian to be a member. My Uncle Giorgio is one but they know me and they'll let us in. We can have a drink then maybe stay for dinner if you'd like.' 'Yes,' she said looking happier. The melancholy of the Pond episode had disappeared and she was feeling like the old Carey again.

As they entered the club it was clear from the greeting that everyone knew Tony. There were handshakes and back slapping all the way to the bar. People kept shouting 'Hey Tony, che bella,' and each time he stopped to explain that the beautiful girl was just a friend he was met with a look that said 'Oh yeah.' In the end he gave up and simply nodded knowingly. 'Sorry,' he said, 'if I had thought about it I would have suggested going somewhere people didn't know me.'

'It doesn't matter,' she said graciously, 'I don't mind – it's quite flattering actually.'

They sat in two large comfortable buttoned leather chairs and sipped their drinks. 'Will you be shooting this evening Mr Tony?' a waiter came over to ask. 'No,' Tony replied, then looking at Carey explained, 'there's a shooting gallery in the basement. I come here sometimes to get in a little practice.'

'Of course,' she said, 'you and Tommy used to hunt together – and your friend Mike. He's getting married soon, isn't he? Will you go to the wedding?'

'Of course.'

'Hmm,' she said wistfully, 'would you take me with you?'

Tony looked embarrassed. 'Well, I hope by then we'll have got Tom back again. He will want to take you – that's for sure.'

'Yes', she said under her breath, 'I had forgotten that.'

It was late when they got back to the apartment. After one in the morning. Tony asked the concierge if he would bring the car up to the front.

'Are we going up?' she said, looking at him coyly. 'Maybe we could have a nightcap?' The concierge arrived out front with the Cord.

'No, I'm driving you home.'

'It's late – and it's dark.'

'I like night driving.'

'You won't be able to drive me up to the house.'

'I'll drop you at the station. You can get your chauffeur man to pick you up from there.'

She looked at him pleadingly with an impish curl of her lips. 'Please. I don't think I could support being alone with my mother and her weird guests.'

'Okay,' he said reluctantly, 'but you sleep on the couch in the lounge and it's not very comfortable.'

'Doesn't matter – that will do; I won't be a nuisance, I promise.' He apologized to the concierge, gave him a tip and asked him to put the car back down in the underground garage.

At around three in the morning he woke with a start and found her standing there, naked. He sat up abruptly but she just stayed there motionless. The shock of seeing her had made him speechless. 'Oh no,' he eventually said, 'no, this is not good.'

'Please,' she said pathetically, 'don't turn me away.' He gave in and she slid under the covers. Her body felt quite cold as he folded his arms around her. She twisted round so that her back pressed against his chest and his chin rested gently on her pale shoulder.

In the morning he woke to the greatest conflict of his life. There was no one like her that he had ever met. She had consumed him and now he had to tell his closest friend how he had betrayed him, if he ever was to see him again – if he was still alive.

'We can't do this again,' he told her earnestly. 'We have to stop it now before we do so much damage we regret it for all our lives. We must stop.' She sobbed and hung on to his shoulder. 'I can't, I can't, not now I've found the only person I've ever really wanted. I have to hold on to you or I'll die.' He looked down at her tear-stained face and knew she was right. There could be no going back, no second thoughts, no walking away. It was their nemesis. If they tried to escape, it would pursue them without relenting. They knew then they would have to live with it.

CHAPTER 23

Coup d'état

In London the minute hand on the clock at the Palace of Westminster dropped silently on to the twelve mark covering the hour hand and setting in motion the chimes. Then the sonorous clang of Big Ben vibrated out across the waters of the Thames. As it struck twelve James and Armitage walked the short distance to Downing Street and rang the bell. They were let in by an armed police officer. Behind James and Armitage a third man entered the building; he was armed with a submachine gun. 'Don't worry,' James assured the policeman, 'he's here to help you protect us – it'll be all right.'

Hugh Dalton met them in the hallway and took them up to the Prime Minister's private office.

Inside Halifax had dismissed his PPS and now waited with Chamberlain and Bevin. 'What is this about, Admiral James?' Halifax asked impatiently, having invited them all to sit down.

In the street outside a number of armed soldiers had taken up defensive positions; the road was blocked at each end with light armoured cars and barbed wire barriers had been put in place. Behind the barriers two men with Bren machine guns stood at the ready.

James looked steadfastly at the gaunt figure of the man who had only a few months ago given away his country. Going through his mind now was the realization that the next few words he spoke could be the most dangerous he had ever spoken: he was about to commit treason. Between then and the success of their mission, in that short interval, he would be a criminal in the eyes of those who held the reins of power – and he would only be absolved when that power had been wrested from them.

'Lord Halifax, Mr Chamberlain, I have come for your resignations.' He said formally and sombrely.

Chamberlain looked stunned. Halifax, showing his long years of diplomatic experience looked calmly back at the two men in front of him. He knew Sir Charles Armitage personally and now he bypassed James, ignoring him in his remarks. 'What is this about, Charlie?' he said warily. 'What exactly is being proposed here?'

'We need your resignation, old man – and Neville's here.'

'You make it sound like a military coup.'

'Afraid so.'

'This is treason.'

'Not if you sign the resignations. We have them here, all typed and ready for the ink.' James opened his brief case and pulled out two typed sheets; he put them on the table in front of the two politicians. Dalton and Bevin looked on in silence.

'And who will take over? Who is to replace us? Not the armed forces I hope.'

'Bevin and Dalton will stand in for you until we can get Churchill back.'

Halifax now adopted the look of a disapproving schoolmaster glaring at Bevin and Dalton. 'Is this true, Ernest?'

'It is.'

'It's treason.'

'No, it's democracy. Just sign and I'll put it to the House. Now we know Churchill is safe they'll support us. Your time is up whichever way we do this thing.'

'And if we refuse to sign, Admiral – what then?' His tone was belligerent; his look one of barely disguised ire.

'Please don't do that, my lord. Think of it as your patriotic duty. Try to think of it as doing it for your country and the people you are pledged to serve.'

Halifax said nothing in reply but instead turned the document with one finger, twisting it through 180 degrees so that he could read it. Chamberlain all the while had sat there pale-faced; his hand trembled as he weakly picked up his copy of the text and examined it. 'This is not constitutional,' he muttered, 'not right at all. I really cannot sign a resignation that is forced upon me in this way. We need time to think about this document; it is too simplistic – it gives you de facto approval – there need to be safeguards. What is to happen post signature for example?'

James was getting frustrated. He had not expected this prevarication and time was now running against them. Dalton and Bevin had to be in the House and a vote taken to reject the Paris Treaty, and it had to happen before Churchill made his American broadcast. 'Gentlemen,' he said gravely, 'if you do not sign then I will declare martial law and arrest you for treason. Is that how you wish history to remember you?'

'It's outrageous.' Halifax spat out the words in an uncharacteristic display of emotion. He was a diplomat; he was used to dealing with dictators and tyrants, but to be threatened by his own side in this fashion was an affront to all his normal expectations of proper conduct. He wrestled with the reality of his position and the distaste he felt at being forced – almost at gunpoint – to acquiesce in what to his narrow view of political etiquette went beyond the pale.

Eventually the reality of his position broke through the dense prejudice of his diplomatic breeding. He agreed to sign, saying that in doing so he was acting under duress and not of his own free will, notwithstanding anything stated to the contrary in the document. As Halifax signed, Chamberlain caved in and followed him. Armed with the resignations, Dalton and Bevin headed for the Palace of Westminster and the emergency debate. The first brick was in the wall – now they had to build on it.

Chamberlain looked forlorn but relieved. He was tired; he should have got out of politics and handed over to Winston when he had the chance. The Treaty and what followed had worn him out and he knew it. He sat there stoically in his chair, his thin neck poking up through his starched collar, slightly bent forward with his beak-like nose and thinning hair – he looked, James thought, like an old, tired bird barely clinging to its perch.

'What now?' Halifax asked, having recovered his urbane manner.

'How about tea.' Charlie Armitage smiled indulgently. 'That's always good in a crisis.'

******

Brunessemer, Croton-on-Hudson

It was seven in the morning and barely light. Loughlin had been up and dressed since six. He set up the Morse transmitter, put on the headset and tapped out his one-word call sign: 'Jabberwocky'. He waited; there was silence. He tried again and then the reply came: 'Alice has stepped through the looking glass'. He acknowledged, then shut down. Without putting things away, he left his room and crossed the corridor to Churchill's suite where he tapped lightly on the door and waited. After a short while it opened and Churchill stood there in his dressing gown.

'The balloon's gone up, sir.'

A broad grin spread across Churchill's face; he rubbed his hands together vigorously in satisfaction at the news. 'Has it, by Jove, then we must get on. History is in the making and it won't do to be late.'

Back in his room Loughlin put in a call to Amber Rose. 'It's under way in London; your end should start the process. We'll make the broadcast later this morning from New York – it's scheduled for a six pm broadcast in London.'

'Do you still need the car?'

'Yes, can you arrange it? Something low profile, everything here is too noticeable.'

'Of course, where are you?'

'Up in the Hudson Valley. I can't say where; it would breach security.'

'Naturally. So where do I deliver it?'

'Croton-on-Hudson. Do you know it?'

'I can find it.'

'Good. There's a diner on the outskirts, it fronts onto State 9 – Jennifer's Diner; you can leave the keys with one of the waitresses. I can collect it from there.'

Next he knocked on Thompson's door. They would all have to go to New York with Churchill – Thompson to guard, Mary with the speech and he would manage the liaison with Washington. Only Clementine would stay behind, a state of affairs with which, she confided to Irena, she was perfectly content. She had found a very good book in the household library and would welcome some time alone. She came out with Winston to see them all off. Martins drove the party in the Packard and, as the big limousine made its way down the drive leaving a wispy trail of pale exhaust vapour in the bright crisp morning air, she felt a weight had been lifted.

For more than a week Winston had stalked the house and the grounds – impatient, grumpy and brooding. Now, with action on the agenda, she knew he would be fully absorbed and out from under her feet. He had been in a very good mood over breakfast and didn't even complain about the marmalade, which he was convinced the Americans could not make nor did they understand it – far too thin and sugary he had announced on their first morning at Brunessemer. Later she apologized to Irena who simply threw up her hands and laughed; 'Men are such children,' she had said, 'they get moody when they're bored. They're only really happy when they have games to play. They never grow up, you know.'

For a while she stood there enjoying the solitude. She looked around her at the big trees lining the drive, statuesque sculptures now that their leaves had fallen. Like the house, where they stood as sentinels, guarding the way to its entrance, there was a comforting solidity about them. Unlike Winston she had become used to the building, to its style and space – she quite liked it.

Irena came down the steps wrapped in a brightly colored Kimono. 'It's going to be a lovely day,' she said. 'Now your Winston is away and all his gunmen gone with him, I thought I would invite two friends over after lunch and we can make up a four for bridge. That's if you'd like to?' Clementine looked happy at that and went off to spend the rest of the morning with her book.

At three o'clock sharp the two bridge partners arrived. Amelia Jackson was quite young, Clementine thought, probably no more than 30. She was suavely turned out in a pencil-slim skirt, bolero jacket with pitched up shoulders, a small coquettish hat and a mink stole. The other guest, Monica Dandridge, was older, a little on the dowdy side but her jewellery spoke of wealth and taste. However, the fox furs she sported were quite out of fashion with the younger generation. Draped about her shoulders with snappy jaws clamped together, they made her

292

look dumpier than she really was. Irena had not intended that they should know how famous Clementine was and simply introduced her as her friend Clementine from England. At first Amelia thought she had met Clementine before. 'I'm sure we have,' she kept saying, 'but I'm darned if I can remember where. Give me a minute or two and I'll remember.'

It was when they were half way through the second game that Amelia suddenly dropped her cards on the table and blurted out, delighted. 'Now I know who you are – you're Mrs Churchill. I saw you on a Pathe newsreel at the movies just a couple of days ago. How absolutely thrilling to meet you. My husband will never believe me when I tell him I've met the wife of the great Winston Churchill; he admires his leadership so much. Daniel is a senator, you know.'

Clementine said politely that she didn't but was flattered by the compliment. Irena, on the other hand, was less charmed. 'No Amelia,' she said, fixing the other woman firmly with an almost imperial gaze. 'You can't do that. No, you mustn't.'

'Why ever not?'

'Because I say you mustn't. And if that isn't enough we have all been sworn to secrecy. There are people out there who would like to see poor Mr Churchill dead; assassins – nasty vulgar foreign assassins. I cannot have you blurting it out at your next dinner party or the country club and putting lives at risk. So there is an end to it. Now pick up your cards and bid.'

Mrs Dandridge put out a hand and touched Clementine on the arm. 'My dear,' she said sympathetically, 'you are quite the heroine you know. The story of your escape from England is all over the papers. What an ordeal.'

******

James Brent picked up the *Westchester Post* and read the syndicated headline: 'BRITS TEAR UP PARIS PACT – British government in state of turmoil as new leaders bid to take over. Full story on page 23'. He sat down in his favorite armchair and flicked through the pages until he found the lead story. 'Churchill is in Washington,' he called through to his wife, who was in the dining room with their daughter. 'Did you hear that?'

She came into the room, followed by Dottie, and stood looking at him. 'Jim, Dottie has a question and we think you might be able to help – but we aren't sure.'

'He made a speech to the British nation this morning,' he continued, ignoring the question, 'through NBC – and now he's in Washington looking for help. It says here there has been a takeover by British politicians backed by the military. Listen to this – today the Parliament of Great Britain announced that Prime

Minister Halifax and Cabinet Minister Chamberlain have been deposed in a Latin American-style coup. The new strong man Ernest Bevin, who has the backing of the military, has formally advised the German Legation in London that they are no longer prepared to ratify the Paris Treaty, which the Parliament almost unanimously rejected in an emergency session earlier today at just after two o'clock in the afternoon, Greenwich Mean Time.'

The two women looked at each other. 'Jim,' his wife repeated, 'did you hear what I said? Your daughter needs your advice on something. Never mind the British; they're a long way off.'

Dr Brent stopped and put down the newspaper. He pulled himself up straight in the chair and looked across at the two women who had now maneuvred themselves onto a settee opposite him and were sitting on the edge leaning forward slightly, waiting to get his attention. 'I'm sorry,' he said indulgently – what did you want to know?

'A friend of mine,' Dottie said, with some hesitation in her voice, 'has been arrested by the FBI – well, not exactly a friend, but he's someone I know and rather like – but nobody seems to know what's happened to him. He seems to have disappeared. I haven't an idea about how to start looking for him. I thought you might know.'

He sat silently for a moment, pursed his lips and breathed out slowly, letting the air out through his nostrils. Then he said, 'I've heard about this from one of my patients, Mike Mescal. He got it from his boy, Mike Junior. Do you know him?'

'I didn't but I do now – at least I've met him – but I didn't know who he was. Is that his wedding next month?'

'It is.'

'Is there anything we can do, Dad – some way of finding out at least what happened? You have some influential patients don't you? Somebody must know something. This is America, it's supposed to be the world's greatest democracy. Surely someone can't just disappear – can they?'

Her father looked perplexed. Although he'd heard the story he'd thought little about it. It had been no more than a local story, local chatter, something of passing interest. Now it somehow involved his daughter. 'I'll ask around,' was all he said. 'I'll see what we can find out.' Then as an afterthought he added, 'Is this young man important to you in any close sort of way?'

'Not especially so, I don't really know him too well – he comes into the diner occasionally with his friends.'

'Okay, I'll see what I can find out. How's that?'

'Oh thanks Dad that would be so good.'

'One thing, though, Dottie. It isn't always such a good idea to get too involved with people who get arrested by the FBI. Be careful – try to keep your distance, huh?'

'Well,' he said to his wife in a low voice after Dottie had left the room, 'is she carrying a torch for this young man?'

'I would think so. Is there anything you can do?'

'I don't know. I'll ask around, but I don't much like the sound of it. We need to keep an eye on that young woman; I don't want her getting mixed up in something dangerous or criminal.'

******

As Churchill's party left the NBC building he congratulated himself that the broadcast had been a success. He imagined how it would have sounded to those of his fellow countrymen and women who would have huddled around their radio sets on what he guessed was probably a cold and cheerless winter evening in Britain. The winter in Europe was already shaping up to be a hard one and forecasters were talking about an early snowfall. His talk would, he calculated, have warmed his listeners and stoked up their hope for an end to the distasteful humiliation of what had become recognized as nothing more than a thinly disguised occupation.

Martins drove the party across town and out to Floyd Bennett Field where a flight had been arranged that would take them to Washington. Although the new La Guardia Airport, which had opened the year before, was closer it was also more public. Both Thompson and Loughlin were insistent that they flew from Floyd Bennett and had negotiated a private charter with TWA. The afternoon had turned blustery and lumps of white cloud were scudding across the sky, driven by a strong, low wind. The flight would be uncomfortable.

Martins got the Packard right up to the front door of the small brick and concrete passenger building. Loughlin, who had been riding up front next to Martins, now jumped out and ran round to the curbside. After looking anxiously around, he opened the back door. Walter Thompson emerged first. He immediately went to the big glass and chrome door that led into the passenger terminal and stood guard surveying the surroundings, looking for anything unusual or potentially dangerous. Next Mary Shearburn got out and made her way to join Thompson, who pushed her through into the terminal. Finally Churchill emerged. As he did so, the door to the terminal opened and a man in the uniform of a TWA first officer and a stewardess came out of the building and walked over to greet him. After a short salutation and a handshake the party moved inside and Martins left for Croton.

There was no formality and the party were led straightaway out through the departure gate and walked the short distance to where a shiny silver DC3 sat perched on the runway. As they climbed the steps they could feel the plane being rocked by the strengthening wind.

'I'm afraid it's going to be a bumpy ride, sir,' the captain confided to Churchill.

'Never mind,' he replied with a schoolboy grin on his face, 'I'm used to bumpy rides. I once ended up getting myself chucked off the back of a camel in the Sudan – now that was a bumpy ride. It would be good if you could give us a softer landing than that.'

It was a very rough ride. Mary Shearburn was sick into a brown paper bag, but Winston seemed to enjoy it and kept them entertained with anecdotes from his days in pursuit of the Mahdi with Kitchener at Omdurman and how General Sir Redvers-Buller had made a complete botch of the Second Boer War.

'It was a bloody mess, you know. We marched our poor fellows in, dressed in bright red tunics like toy soldiers, and they got picked off by Kruger's irregulars all dressed like farmers and hidden in Nullahs half a mile away. It was slaughter. It was dreadful. It took a massacre before those arses in the War Office issued our chaps with khaki and kicked old Redvers upstairs.'

They touched down in Washington where they were met by a Navy driver and taken across town to the Shack. Waiting for them was a posse of press but Churchill waved them aside saying it was too soon to comment on how things were going in London. Inside they were taken to the Joint Chiefs' office where a group of military men headed by George Marshall were waiting. Some of them Churchill knew: Joe King and Hap Arnold he'd met before at the first briefing. Now Marshall introduced three more generals: Joe Stilwell and George Patton for the Army and Ira Eaker for the newly reorganized Army Air Corps.

Patton he knew by reputation but had never met. The man was physically big; his presence was such it marked him out even among a crowd of big men. He was well over six feet and even in middle age he was athletic. He was rumbustious and outspoken; sometimes the language was coarse and he often offended his fellow officers. But that was Patton and people around him accepted it because in the end he was a good soldier and he got things done. Enlisted and drafted men alike looked up to him and trusted his leadership and while some generals thought differently, he was popular with the President.

Patton greeted him warmly; there was none of the suspicion of Stilwell or the hostility of King about him. Churchill felt confident he had an ally. Better still, an ally who was known for his outspoken stance against German militarism and Churchill liked him for this part of his reputation alone. Now, face to face, he found the man every bit as large as his reputation: flamboyant, open handed and up for a fight. He liked what he saw. Here was a man he thought he could do business with. They shook hands and Churchill talked enthusiastically about re-arming Britain as soon as they had got the Germans under control. 'We need tanks,' he said, knowing Patton was a tank man himself and likely to support him.

George Marshall called everyone to attention and asked them to sit down around the large oval table that had been set up with pens and notepads opposite each chair. Marshall and his team were grouped along one side of the oval; opposite Churchill sat with Mary Shearburn, who would take notes. Loughlin had set up his Morse operation and waited for news from London. Next to him sat Thompson, though he was largely redundant there being little likelihood of potential assassins in the depths of the Shack.

'Gentlemen,' Marshall said addressing the group, 'we've got our Embassy in London monitoring the situation and the Intelligence Signals team upstairs are listening in to what they have to say. As soon as they have any news we'll get it. In the meantime, I'm asking Prime Minister Churchill to tell us how we can best help. I don't have to tell you that it is in our nation's best interest to have the British government properly in control of its own destiny – and particularly its own Navy.' He sat back and extended a hand. 'Mr Churchill, the floor is yours, sir.'

'I have to thank you once again for your kind reception. A short while ago I arrived on your shores clandestinely and disguised – some at that time rather unkindly referred to me as a refugee. Well, here I am again but this time in a different guise. Now those same uncharitable people might this time call me a beggar,' he smiled wryly and paused. 'I am, however, merely disguised as such and underneath I am wearing the trousers of the leader of a nation – though perhaps the belt needs to be tightened a little so as to prevent them falling down.'

A ripple of laughter went through the room. 'Good,' he thought, 'I'm getting them on board.'

'I'm not here as a supplicant. I don't have a begging bowl. I am here to seek a pact with an old friend, an old friend with a common interest.
'A terrible threat still stalks Europe and that threat, I believe, will shortly stretch out across the Atlantic to touch these shores. Indeed the Nazi jackboot has already set its imprint on this continent, north of here, in Canada. Unlike many, I do not believe the Germans when they say it is to defend against the ravages of communism that they are there. The guns that are presently pointing towards Russia could very easily be turned to point this way. The distance from Hudson Bay to the Great Lakes is not so far that it could not be covered quite quickly by mechanized forces – as we witnessed in France.

'If Hitler is to be stopped in his quest for world domination – if his insatiable appetite for other people's land and his unquenchable lust for spilling the blood of a generation is to be opposed and not appeased – then our two countries must stand united. I cannot stress too strongly the need at this critical hour for the United States of America to back us in our struggle to break out of the straightjacket into which some of my fellow countrymen have put us. Even as I speak, brave men are taking back the reins of the country and they have called upon me to lead them. I have taken up this challenge willingly but it is not a task that I take lightly. I have asked the President to help re-arm Great Britain and he has asked that I put my case before you, gentlemen, his advisers. Thank you.'

There was a lull as the assembled military men considered what had been put to them. King was the first to speak. 'Is the British Navy currently capable of keeping the Germans from crossing the English Channel – with an invasion fleet?'

'I believe it is. What is happening today in Britain is not a declaration of hostilities with Germany, although the Germans may take it as such. This is my country asserting its right to reject a treaty which Hitler sought to impose.'

'But Britain accepted the treaty in exchange for a cease of hostilities because you knew you could not withstand an attempt to invade.'

'Indeed, but things have changed and, as has so often been the case with Herr Hitler, we too have changed our mind.'

General Stilwell raised a finger. 'You have no air force – is that right? I mean it was disbanded by agreement under the Treaty. Isn't that so?'

'It is, but we have a plan which will reactivate our airplanes.'

'But you couldn't stop a German invasion with the Navy alone.'

'It would be very difficult.'

'And it will take time to get your planes back in the sky – in any meaningful number, that is'

'Our pilots are brave; they'll manage with what they have.'

'So you don't have a goddam plan; more of a gamble – and you want to drag us right along in there with you?'

Churchill had expected a rough ride but this was amounting to downright hostility. Marshall was getting irritated. 'Get to the point, Joe. Don't beat about the bush.'

'George, as I see it these guys don't have a prayer. They dumped themselves in it and now they want us to join them. Right now we couldn't afford to get into a fist fight with the Germans, and he's right,' he pointed directly at Churchill, 'there're a lot of Krauts up in the top of Canada. But they are facing the other way. However, if we throw in our lot with this desperate scheme and it goes wrong – well, hell, we could find ourselves in a shooting war on our own soil quicker than you can say Uncle Sam.'

Churchill was about to respond but he was cut short when a colonel from the Intelligence Signals was let into the room. 'Let's hear it,' Marshall said abruptly.

The colonel read from a sheet. 'This is the latest report from our London Embassy. Halifax and Chamberlain have resigned and the Parliament has voted down the Paris Treaty, as was expected. They report soldiers on the street everywhere and there's a public transport stoppage. There's no German reaction at the moment but there's a lot of radio traffic between Berlin and the Legation as well as between the Legation and the Kreigsmarine HQ at Ryde.'

Marshall looked up from his seat. 'Do we know what they're saying?'

'No General. It's in a code we haven't seen before but we're working on it. Generally the British plan seems to be working but we can't say for sure – it's too early.'

Marshall looked satisfied; the mood in the room was cheerful. 'Okay,' he said, addressing Patton in particular, 'let's get down to business. The British need armor. How many tanks can we spare and how long will it take us to get them to where they need to be?'

'Aren't we forgetting something here?' King butted in. 'Any assets we ship to the Limeys will have to go across the pond and we don't have control of those waters. We could end up in conflict with the Germans and the whole damn lot could end up on the ocean floor. I'm with Joe Stilwell on this one. We don't have a fight with the Germans, so why pick one? Let the British find their own way out of this. If they do, then fine. I don't have a problem with selling them a few guns – why, I'd even be in favor of them taking a few of Patton's tanks if he can spare them, but let's not jump into a ruckus we have no stake in.'

Churchill was on the back foot. His mood darkened and he felt some of the old blackness creeping into his mind. He knew Hitler would eventually attempt an invasion; without American support there was very little hope of holding him back. Roosevelt had promised to help where he could but he would be bound to go in whatever direction his Chiefs steered him. It was clear the Navy was not going to give its support and both Stilwell and King had a strong argument. Only Patton had seemed to be on his side, but now even he wavered.

'I don't think a handful of tanks are going to solve this problem – even if we could get them there in time – and time is something we don't have. I'm not a politician, thank God, but isn't there something called the Neutrality Acts that are supposed to stop us providing arms to belligerents? How're we gonna get around that little baby without Congress yelling foul? I think Joe is right – I think both Joes are right – we risk running ourselves into a war when we don't have to.'

King's face was masked with a false smile as he looked at the discomfited Churchill. He had not wanted this meeting and had tried to persuade the

President that they should have nothing to do with the British plea for help. Now he sensed the majority was going with him.

But Patton was not done. 'If there was some way to get the stuff to them it'd get my vote because it's my view those blockheads sitting up there in Canada represent a threat and we shouldn't damn well lose sight of it. In that respect I'm with Mr Churchill here. So why in the name of Holy Jesus Christ are we coming up with all this shit about pussy-footing around these bastards when everyone sat here knows we're gonna end up in a shooting war with those lousy Krauts sooner or later anyway?'

He turned towards Hap Arnold, who had listened but said nothing in the meeting. 'Hap, how does the Air Force stand in all this?'

Arnold took his time. 'It seems to me that the British need air support more than ground-based assets. It would, if the Germans tried to mount an invasion, be easier to keep them off the beach than to fight them on it. Air support and the British Navy could probably achieve that. I could lend my voice to that view – we certainly have the aircraft with the operational range. We could get them over there although we might run into some opposition on the way, but that's a risk we could countenance. But George here has put his finger on the sticking point – the real issue is how you get around the Neutrality Acts, and that's a job for the Executive, not for us in the military. My advice would be to go in strong on the diplomacy front. Get the German Ambassador in and make it plain the US could not tolerate interference or aggression. That, I believe, is the best we could do.'

Marshall nodded agreement. 'Yup, that's how I read it.' Stilwell and King just sat straight-faced and said nothing.

'One more thing I ought to say,' Marshall continued, throwing a glance first at Churchill before directing his remark to Patton. 'I don't share your view about a threat from the German presence in the north of Canada. I think their reason for being there is genuine enough. I don't see them as a threat to the US.'

There was another interruption as the Colonel of Intelligence Signals came back into the room. He passed a note to Marshall, then sat down. 'Alright gentlemen, listen up. This signal just came in from London hot off the wire. According to this the day appears to have gone well – though there is one report from one of our undercover people of activity around Downing Street and some kind of delegation has gone in. We don't know what that is about but if the Germans are talking instead of shooting then that's good news. It's getting late; I've ordered some refreshments to be served in the canteen. If anything else comes in we'll be the first to hear it.'

In the corner Loughlin sent out his call sign. 'I'll hang on. There's something coming in,' he said. 'I'll join you as soon as I've decoded it.'

CHAPTER 24

Southern England

Along a small road in Kent, just beyond Sevenoaks and not far from the RAF field at Biggin Hill, a convoy of articulated transporters turned off the road and disappeared up a lane towards a farm. The track was barely wide enough to take them but they were on the good solid chalk of the Kentish Weald. Chalk and flint; sound enough to carry the load of truck, trailer and cargo.

The day before, Linz had lost his tanks on the Great North Road. He had walked the quarter mile or so to where he had left them securely loaded on the transporters only to find they were without their crews – abandoned. There was no telephone in the area and he had marched in the teeth of a freshening wind another mile to Roxton where he was sure he would find one. Roxton was small and at first sight there was no evidence of a phone box. However, in the High Street he found a pub – the Royal Oak. Inside, the low ceiling beams almost touched the top of his head and he found himself instinctively ducking. The place was empty except for a man polishing glasses behind the bar.

'Do you have a phone I can use, please?' he asked the man behind the bar.

'Are you drinking?'

Linz was not expecting the question and looked puzzled for a second; then, as the translation worked its way through, he brushed it aside.

'No, no, just the telephone please.'

'It's for customers only,' the barman said curtly and went on polishing.

'Is there another one in the village?'

'No.'

Linz looked frustrated. 'I can pay you.'

The barman shook his head.

'This is ridiculous,' Linz snapped. 'What must I do?'

The barman put down the glass he was polishing and leaned intimately across the counter. 'Best if you buy a drink – then you'll be a customer. Customers can use the phone – simple really. What'll it be?'

Linz ordered a beer and paid, but didn't drink it. Instead he phoned the Legation to report that he needed a recovery vehicle and some drivers. By the terms of the Treaty they should be British but in this instance it was an

301

emergency so he would use Germans and argue the Treaty contravention later. As he left, the barman called after him. 'You haven't drunk your beer.'

'You drink it,' Linz called back, and headed off in the direction of the abandoned trucks.

When he got back the trucks had gone. At first he thought he hadn't walked far enough but when he carried on and reached the point where the lead transporter had broken down that had gone too. Only the tell-tale puddle of diesel remained to establish that this was where the vehicle had been – that, and the deep tracks cut into the field where its trailer had rested. He could barely contain his anger as he hurried back to Roxton. Someone would pay dearly for this, but who? He had an idea it was the lead driver and he now questioned if it was part of a bigger plot?

It was late afternoon by the time a driver from the Legation found him sitting on a bench outside the pub. A small black Mercedes 170 squeaked to a halt in front of the pub. Linz got in – it had not been a good day. He said nothing all the way back to the Legation.

Half a day's drive away from where he had lost it, Linz's convoy was now comfortably sheltered under the cover of an ancient pine wood far from the sight of even the most casual rambler. On the margin of the woodland it gave way to a field. Where, three months before, it had been covered with long-stemmed wheat, golden ripe and rippling under the early autumn winds, now it was replaced with dirty charred ground; still black from burning off the stubble. Alongside, a chalk track threaded its way over the ground, dodging round hedges and fording ditches for a couple of hundred yards until it crested a ridge. They made a strange sight strung out in a line: a long file of darkly clad men, silhouetted against the fading light, each one carrying a canvas holdall, in the middle of nowhere – seemingly going nowhere. As they crossed the ridge a large black timber-boarded barn came into view.

Reaching it, Alpha Six lifted an iron locking bar and let it swing down with a clank. He pulled open the door on creaking hinges and stepped inside. The floor was paved with large, irregularly shaped stone sets that had been polished smooth over the years since they were put their in the reign of Elizabeth the First. In the middle of the barn was a cast iron, potbellied stove with a very long roughhewn table stood next to it. There were benches with the table and some old spindle-backed chairs. On the other side of the stove and laid out randomly there were single bunks with straw-filled paillasses. The building was cold but it felt dry; the roof was in good shape and the loft was full of hay. Alpha Six lit a hurricane lamp. 'Welcome to our new HQ, lads', he said. 'Somebody get the stove going – it's bloody freezing in here.'

He lit a second lamp and handed it to another driver. 'There're more lamps in that cupboard over there. Get a few and hand them out; there's paraffin in the black drum outside. Careful not to spill it; we haven't got a lot and anyway I don't want this place going up in smoke. Right, two volunteers to go up into the loft. There's a crate up there with a few essentials. Let's get it down and get a brew going, then make some food. After that we wait – for further orders. Anyone got a pack of cards? I don't think much is going to happen till after the weekend.'

Alpha Six's group settled down for the evening. The stove was throwing out its heat and soon the air was thick with the smell of hot bully beef and cigarettes. The men laughed and joked about the last two days' work and the convoy they had liberated after the drivers had all conveniently disappeared – done a bunk. This wasn't the kind of work they had signed up for: they were paratroopers from the 44th, redundant after the regiment had been disbanded and, since there were now no planes to jump out of, they were making themselves useful elsewhere. They had been hand-picked by Charlie Armitage and seconded to MI5 – to deal with some of the dirtier work he knew would be coming over the horizon.

'Latrines are in the small copse out back,' Alpha Six said as an afterthought. 'They're fresh dug so the sides may not be stable; let's not fall in.'

******

At Northolt, Lovett's commandos had walked in through the front gate without a problem. Park had been in Kingston for three days and had already managed to get a handful of newly assembled Hurricanes over to Brooklands. On the streets around Lancaster Gate an astute observer would have detected a number of five-ton trucks, canvas-backed, with their rear curtains pulled together. Inside, soldiers from the Chelsea Barracks sat patiently waiting for Churchill's speech as the signal to erect barriers on all the roads leading to and from the Legation building. No one would be allowed to come or go.

In Hull the only difference to the daily routine at the German-occupied docks was that the transport drivers had not turned up for work. Instead a representative of the Transport and General Workers Union had presented himself at the Kommandant's office and served notice on him that there was a nationwide strike of all transport drivers. The Kommandant demanded to know how long the strike would last but the Union rep only shrugged and said he didn't know – he was only the messenger not the decision maker. The docks would be notified in due course. Ten minutes after he walked out through the dock gates a van drew up outside. Four men emerged from the back of the van and set up a picket. They took a brazier, a bundle of wood and a sack of coke out of the van and proceeded to light up a fire. When a German guard on the other side of the gates asked what was happening, the driver of the van laughed out loud. 'It's a picket, Fritz,' and he wagged a finger at him. 'Nichts drivers go in – nichts drivers come out. Alles kaput Fritz!'

In Downing Street, Armitage and James sat in Halifax's office and waited for Bevin and Dalton to return with Anthony Eden. There was no doubt about Eden's loyalty; he was a member of the Churchill family and had been Foreign Secretary for Chamberlain until he'd resigned over the Munich appeasement – but for security reasons they had kept him in the dark. They knew he would fall in with the plans so there was no reason to tell him; the fewer who knew, the smaller the risk the plot would be uncovered and the Germans tipped off.

By three o'clock the word was out that Parliament had voted almost unanimously to reject the Paris Treaty in its current form and renegotiate the terms. But there were no journalists in the press gallery; they had all scurried back to their offices as soon as the statement of the resignations had hit the floor of the House. In Fleet Street reporters and editors were frantically trying to get out a special edition.

Two hours later it would hit the streets in time for the home-going commute: 'BIG SHAKE UP AT NUMBER 10' the *Evening Standard* bannered. 'HALIFAX RESIGNATION – BEVIN, EDEN AND DALTON TAKEOVER' the *Daily Mail* shouted. Beaverbrook was silent on the matter – he sat on the fence to see which side Humpty Dumpty would fall.

The Times was more measured as it prepared its Saturday edition. It soberly reported the new government front bench line-up: Bevin as PM in a caretaker capacity until Churchill returned, Eden for Foreign Secretary and Dalton to be Home Secretary.

The phone rang in the office of Halifax's private secretary. He knocked and stuck his head round the door. 'Sorry, Prime Minister, but I have the German Ambassador on the line. He is requesting to speak to you direct.'

Halifax raised his eyebrows and looked over the top of his glasses. 'That is most irregular. Please ask him to contact the FCO.'

'He is most insistent.'

'Well,' he said to James, 'this is your show. I am no longer the PM and Neville is no longer Foreign Secretary, so it's rather over to you.'

'I'll deal with it,' Armitage said to the secretary. 'Put him through to the PM's line.'

'Good afternoon, Ambassador, I'm Sir Charles Armitage. I am standing in for the Prime Minister at this very busy time. How may I assist you?'

He put his hand over the mouthpiece but kept the phone to his ear. 'They know things are going on,' he whispered to James. 'They're demanding an explanation – he says they will strongly resist any attempt to alter the Treaty – now he's warning there could be the most severe consequences – they're

304

waiting on instructions from Berlin. Oops, here we go – they've got wind of a plot – and – they think we are behind the disappearance of eight Panzer tanks.'

He took his hand away from the mouthpiece. 'Ambassador, I can assure you this is not an attempt by His Majesty's Government to deceive your government in any way whatsoever, but I am sure you will understand that we are a sovereign nation and we reserve the right to make changes to our government as we see fit. It has always been the case that the Treaty had to be ratified by the British Parliament and in that nothing has changed. I shall ask the new Foreign Secretary to contact you as a matter of urgency, but I would be most grateful if in the meantime your government would refrain from any action that could precipitate any damage to relations between our two countries.'

There was the briefest of pauses. 'Of course – you too. Good afternoon.' Armitage put the phone down in its cradle.

'What was that last bit?' James asked.

'He's relying on us to act honourably.'

'That's rich coming from those thugs.'

'Yes,' Armitage observed quietly, 'better hold on to your seat. I think the firework show starts shortly.'

Bevin, Eden and Dalton arrived at Downing Street as Big Ben struck the hour: five o'clock – an hour to Winston's address to the nation. So far, the day had gone well. At half five they were joined by Alan Brooke, who reported that Lovett's commandos now had control of Northolt and Croydon. Tomorrow they would get aircrew mustered, then wait to see the German reaction. In Germany Hitler was on a train heading for Bavaria but his security was so tight and his movements so secret for fear of assassination attempts that he could not be contacted, even by his most trusted aids. It would be late Saturday, perhaps even Sunday before he could be told of events and by then the coup would be a reality. They had perhaps twenty four hours to get control of the skies over Britain; after that Park had calculated the air would be buzzing. Hull was the hornet's nest, he'd said, 'and we've just given it a good poke. Expect a swarm to come out of it.'

On the stroke of six Winston began his broadcast.

'Good evening, this is the BBC Home Service. There now follows a speech by the Right Honourable Winston Churchill, the Prime Minister. This is in place of the six o'clock news, which will follow immediately after Mr Churchill's address.'

'To all the peoples of this great nation of ours I wish you a warm and sincere greeting. I consider myself most fortunate to be able to talk to you this evening from the great city of Washington, where I have been engaged in talks with our friend and ally President Roosevelt for the creation of a transatlantic cooperation pact. This pact, I believe, will bring peace and prosperity not only to our country but to all the peace loving peoples of Europe …

[…]

'In conclusion, let me say that it is the intention of your government to make peace with Germany. We do not wish to go to war with them – or any of our neighbours – but let me make it plain to all who play the game of diplomacy that we shall not be bullied into some cheap contract that bargains away our sovereign independence for tuppence. Let it be clear, if we have to fight then we shall fight and we shall exact a terrible price from those who come against us. They should not deceive themselves that it will be another Dunkirk – it will not. This island of ours has been a free nation for almost a thousand years and the British people will never give up that legacy. So be of good cheer – let us brace ourselves for the fight, if there is to be a fight, but yet hope for peace and that bright future which is the right of all men, women and children everywhere.'

'Good speech,' James said, and everyone agreed.

Bevin, Dalton and Eden set about the task of putting together a negotiating team to face the Germans as soon as the storm broke. Eden proposed that they call the German Ambassador into the Foreign and Colonial Office first thing in the morning. A note was typed and sent round to the Embassy. They still had no idea which way they would jump, but planned for a head-on collision.

Late in the evening news came in from Park that Northolt was already thirty percent operational, and he proposed to send half that contingent up to Caistor, just south of the Humber up on the North Sea coast and within easy reach of Hull. There they could be ready for anything coming out of the docks and ambush it.

Caistor had one big advantage for Park. It had grass runways and had been primarily used as a training field. Remote from any habitation, in the middle of the flat fenlands and marshes it was isolated. As a result it had largely escaped the Treaty; there were no inspectors and pretty much everything had been left intact. The operational staff had simply switched off the lights, turned the key and walked away. The Germans would not be expecting fighters to be operating from there. But there was one even bigger bonus: Caistor had also been an ammo dump and a quick recce had shown that it was fully stocked. Earlier that day an elderly Dragon Rapide had flown north to get the place operational. When it touched down the crew found the field deserted, as expected. On board were ten men – as many as could be squeezed into the stripped out airplane – six mechanics who would keep everything flying, two armourers and two flight controllers; not much but it would do and Caistor would be a nasty surprise if the Germans tried to strong-arm their way down from Hull. That night 32 fighters took off from Northolt and flew to Caistor under cover of dark. Everyone got down safely except one Spitfire, which overshot the runway and damaged its undercarriage. At the same time the two Mosquitos were sent north. When word came back that they too were on station and fully armed Park was delighted; so far so good – he couldn't believe his luck. Now he had to get more crew operational, but that would be easier now the cat was out of the bag, security had become less of a risk. Once the politicians were in place the coup had more or less succeeded. All they had to do was keep them safe and in office so that negotiations could start. The worst they faced from here on in was that the negotiations would fail and they would have to pick up where they left off and re-engage the Germans in battle. True, they had been outgunned and outmanoeuvred in France but this was different. Here they were on home soil and they had learned a lot from Dunkirk. This time, if it came to a scrap Park was sure it would be different; there were a lot of good men he could call on and he was beginning to build up his inventory of planes.

******

In Portsmouth the day had started normally but at 3.00 pm that changed. As the statement was read out in Westminster the Provost Marshall and a commodore, David Briggs, from James' staff led a party of eight Navy Police to the Semaphore Building close to Number 1 dock. They entered the office of the King's Harbour Master (KHM) where they arrested the German observers who had effectively been controlling all naval movements in the Solent since Paris. Down at the main gate the guard had been doubled and the base quarantined. Only authorized Royal Navy personnel were allowed to pass. James had objected strongly when he was first shown the draft of the Treaty, which was to allow German joint control of shipping movements in and out of Portsmouth and throughout the waters of the Solent. He anticipated friction but the War Office and the Admiralty were implacable; it must be made to work. But as the months passed, German control began to creep ever further towards a total takeover of the entire command area. Kreigsmarine movements were taking priority; they were restricting the movement of his own ships. Two months in from Dunkirk he realized they were being gradually neutralized. That was when he had made his decision: the government had to be stopped; there would have to be an intervention, and it would have to be military.

In May MI5 had uncovered a German plot to abduct or kill Churchill. It could be either, they weren't sure. Alan Brooke and Charlie Armitage had come to James with a plan to get Churchill out of the country. With the help of Walter Thompson they would lift him out of London and make it look as if he had been killed. That would take the heat off; they needed somewhere to hide him and there was no safer place than on a ship in the security of the Dockyard.

After that, it was a short step to the final decision for a coup; Brooke and Armitage were in.

Commodore Briggs handed a list to the Harbourmaster. 'New order of movements,' he said.

The KHM ran his eye over the sheets. 'Jerry won't like this, Commodore.' He leafed through the schedule. 'This will bottle them up in the narrowest part. It doesn't give them much room to manoeuvre.'

'That's what we want, Harbourmaster. Jerry's had as much leeway as we're giving him. The order's direct from London. The government's voted to reject the Paris Treaty. He's about to get his sailing orders – back to where he came from.'

'Will they resist?'

'Don't know. Our ships have orders to confine them. Shoot if necessary; the rest is wait and see what develops. Keep an eye on them. I've put the whole base on alert; I'm putting armed sentries in every building.'

The Harbourmaster looked pleased. 'It'll be good to have that lot out from under my feet.'

When the Kommandant at the Kreigsmarine base in Newport on the Isle of Wight got the new orders to hold station and cancel all previous planned movements he immediately got in touch with his chain of command in Kiel. Something was not right. He was unable to make contact with the inspectors in Portsmouth. He needed orders on how to proceed.

The German response was not long in coming. It started with E-boat activity out of Ryde harbour. Five boats, each with 20 armed Kreigsmarine, came out line astern travelling at around 45 knots. Their wake ploughed a long white furrow of spume as they headed for Portsmouth.

The phonc rang on Briggs' desk. 'We've got five E-boats incoming. They're making a course directly for the harbour.'

'Let them in – then close the gate behind them. I'm on my way over.'

When they entered the harbour mouth two destroyers followed them in, taking up positions to blockade the entrance. Inside the E-boat captains ignored their enclosure and made straight for the Semaphore Tower.

They had come in on the bottom of the tide and now the head of the pier stood 18 feet above them. They had to fasten their lines to the iron rings set in the heavy wooden piles that formed the structure of the pier. Screwed deep into several of the piles were vertical iron ladders, slippery and seaweed encrusted. Each sailor had to climb one in order to reach the top. It took time to get all the men ashore, but there was no sign of any resistance. In fact, there was no sign of anyone; the area around the dock was deserted. The landing party crouched low and moved rapidly under cover of some small storage sheds that bordered the dock until they could see the entrance to the Semaphore building. There was now only a parade area left to cross and they would be in.

As the first of the landing party sprinted across, a figure appeared in the entrance to the Semaphore building, came down the steps and stood there watching them. In the same moment that he had appeared there was a deafening blast from a ship's siren: three short whoops in quick succession. A Corvette had rafted alongside the E-boats, totally enveloping them in its shadow. Its bridge was clearly visible above the sheds as it looked down on the men in the square. At the same moment a contingent of heavily armed sailors appeared on both sides of the square and took up defensive positions. Then two army halftrack machine gun carriers and an armoured scout car drove into the square positioning themselves directly in front of the landing party. They had been swamped. They were totally outnumbered – anything but surrender would be suicide. Briggs moved across the parade ground towards the captain who had led the shore party. It had been a risky strategy and he knew it would only have taken one wrong move and the whole thing could have ended up with a lot of killing. He extended his hand to the captain, who stood there still wondering what had happened.

'Wilkommen,' he said, using one of the few German words he knew. Instead of shaking his hand, the German snapped to attention and saluted. Briggs returned the salute. '*Sprechen ze Inglish, bitte?*', Briggs said, dredging into the bottom of his German language resource and hoping the answer would be 'yes' and not a string of incomprehensible Teutonic.

'Don't worry, Commodore,' the German said in perfect English, 'I was at Harrow before this war. I studied languages there; though there isn't much call for Latin in the Kreigsmarine.'

'Same with us really, old boy. Now to what do I owe the pleasure of your presence here? Why don't we go inside and talk about it.'

In a ground floor office Briggs sat the captain down and explained that it had been decided to freeze the position and go back to the status before the Treaty, but that this would be temporary while the leaders and diplomats tried to find a new solution to their mutual relationship. It was not the British wish to start hostilities, but they could not have the Kreigsmarine running around doing as it pleased without it being governed by a bilaterally agreed protocol. He put it as reasonably as he could and asked them to take that message back to his Kommandant at Newport. He threw in that he would be happy to meet with the Kommandant if it would help but thought it best left to the professionals. He didn't think for one moment the offer would be accepted.

The Germans left under the escort of the frigate and made their way back to Ryde. They had been allowed to keep their weapons. 'Might as well let them keep their dignity for the time being,' Briggs observed. 'I think we've bought some time but I don't know how much. Let's hope the politicians can work something out.'

Saturday dawned and everyone held their breath. Nobody expected it to pass without a major incident. Eden had readied himself for a flurry of protests from the Legation but things had gone quiet. He suspected they were waiting for the reaction from Hitler but he was still on his train. The meeting with the German Ambassador was formal, polite and uneventful. Eden used the tactic that Parliament had not voted to reject the Paris Treaty but to renegotiate some of the finer points. Both men knew this was untrue, but it suited neither at that moment to admit it. Instead they had a cordial conversation laced with the hopes that there could be a mutually acceptable agreement, sweetened with an apology from Eden that there had to be a suspension of the existing terms for the short interim period.

Northolt was now fully operational and there were five more Hurricanes over at Brooklands, making seven in all. Hawker finally had his production line operating at pre-Paris levels and although there were men on the Bofors guns in Kingston and the Chessington battery was now armed and ready, there had been no sign of the inspectors or any interference. That day, in the morning before first light, two Dakota aircraft transported men and materials to Caistor, bringing it up to squadron strength; most importantly, they had now brought in four cooks and rations. 'If they have to fight they can't do it hungry,' Park had said.

Halifax was still in Number 10 on Saturday morning and Chamberlain had passed the night in Number 11; he was no longer Chancellor of the Exchequer but it would take time to organize the move. He was, he told his wife that night, too tired to fight any longer and they would return to their family home at Heckfield on Sunday; he was at his end and he knew it.

******

James had spent the night at the Admiralty where he had his own living quarters. He was woken at six. After his bath he phoned his wife to let her know that he was fine. Next he phoned Armitage.

'How is it, Charlie? I've slept through it.'

'It's eerily quiet – business as usual – nothing to report overnight.'

'Good, I'll see you at Number 10. I'll be there for eight.'

In the Cabinet room Dalton and the others were already briefing the civil servants on the emerging situation. Everything connected with the Treaty was to be put on hold. Dalton had spent the first hour of his day at the Home Office setting out the strategy for the police. Every Chief Constable had been sent notification and specific instructions on how to manage confrontation with

German officials and, more importantly, Mosley's followers, who had formerly been known as the Blackshirts but who had now adopted the title of the British Black Shirts or simply the BBS.

James arrived at the same moment as Armitage. In the street outside the presence of soldiers was more evident and the barriers blocking the entrance and exit had been reinforced; two armoured scout cars now replaced the trucks.

The BBS had risen rapidly on the back of an opportunity that came out of the Treaty. Before the Treaty it had been a paramilitary riff-raff created by Sir Oswald Mosley. Mosley had been an admirer of Mussolini and later Hitler; his followers modelled their organization on Hitler's SS but they had never managed the popular following those dictators commanded. Mosley strutted, postured and gave noisy speeches, but had not been able to rouse an audience of more than a few hundred or raise a following of more than a few thousand.

That changed when he ingratiated himself with Mussolini. He had worked hard on Bastianini to get him an introduction and then persuaded Il Duce that a paramilitary force that was British but owed some allegiance to the Axis would be a valuable interface. Mosley had ambitions. Secretly he saw himself in the same role as the other two – even, in a grand delusion, as an equal partner at the head of a reorganized Britain. Franco had managed it in Spain – he could do it here. The difference was that Franco's starting point was that of an established General at the head of the Spanish Moroccan Army; Mosley stood at the head of a rag-tag, ill-armed, poorly disciplined and disaffected mob: Mosley's Blackshirts.

Nobody at the Paris negotiations had paid much heed to the clause in the Treaty that created a new agency in British law enforcement. There had seemed no reason at the time to see them as anything more than a jointly controlled instrument that would be brought in to deal with the arrest, where it arose, of German officials and military working in Britain. They were to remain under the control of the Home Office but in the service of the Legation at the same moment. The clause that allowed for the training and arming of the BBS to be carried out at their own cost and under the guidance of the Treaty had slipped through, barely noticed. It would after all absolve the British exchequer from an unwanted cost – it would save money if they were trained and armed by someone else.

The expansion of the BBS had been alarming. In May Mosley took a group of 100 men, handpicked, from the best of his recruits; men with political conviction – educated men and those with natural aptitude for command. They were flown to Munich by the Legation and taken from there to the Waffen SS training school at Bad Tolz. Six weeks later they returned to London and took over a building on the South Bank of the Thames near to the Rotherhithe docks in Bermondsey Street. The building was a disused factory with offices and had a complex of warehouses attached.

Local traders and residents were surprised to see the building transformed in a very short space of time from a rundown rat-infested derelict to a newly painted facade with the striking BBS badge adorning the front. High up on top the building was draped with crossed Union Jack and German Swastika flags.

The government was dismayed; now the cheap option had come home to bite them.

The docks and east London were ripe recruiting grounds. The unemployed, the poorly paid and those who felt exploited by the banks, the moneylenders and foreign immigrants formed queues to join up. In return they got a uniform, regular pay and they were armed; but more than this many felt they had gained their lost self-respect.

'The problem,' Dalton said to the others, 'is how we contain them. You realize they are better armed than the police – they're better armed than most of our own troops. The Germans have seen to that – Luger automatic side arms, Mauser machine pistols, Spandau machine guns – the list is terrifying.'

'Do you think they will try to resist?'

Dalton shrugged. 'Difficult to say. But if the Treaty goes they'll go, so what would you do in their shoes?'

Armitage looked blankly around the table. 'We've got people on the inside. One of them went to Bavaria in the first wave of trainees but they haven't reported anything yet. Have we got a plan?'

James agreed he had not. He had initially ignored them in planning for the coup. He had considered them still a small group and thought it should be possible to contain them if they swamped the area around Bermondsey and quarantined their building.

'Wouldn't it be better if we at least disarmed them?' Bevin suggested. 'Brooke should be able to find enough men to go in there and demand they hand over their weapons.'

James looked sceptical. 'I'm not sure they'd give up easily; don't forget they were SS trained. I could see a fire-fight developing. So long as we can keep them penned I think they're likely to stay put and see what develops.'

Dalton didn't like the idea: there could be shooting – people would get killed.

'I agree, I think we should leave them alone for the moment,' he said. 'We don't want to poke another hornet's nest. I've asked Mosley to come here on Monday; Anthony is going to raise the issue with the Legation on Monday. Let's hope common sense prevails. Monday will have given Berlin time to digest the Washington note. I imagine that will give them pause for thought.'

'I'm not so sure,' Eden replied. 'If Hitler goes through the roof he won't give a fig for upsetting the Americans.'

******

That evening Hitler's train arrived in Berchtesgaden where he was greeted by Admiral Canaris, head of German military intelligence, the Abwher. Signals had been coming in from London in a continuous stream since Friday. Now he had to break the news to Hitler. The fact was that the Abwher had not picked up any intelligence prior to Friday that there was a coup being plotted. Much of their focus had been on Churchill and where he was hiding. Their own plan to abduct him had failed. They had sent in two top operatives with orders to grab him and fly him to Berlin or kill him if they were cornered. Instead, they had been killed and Churchill had vanished. Hitler had exploded into a rage when he was given the news and now Canaris braced himself; it could well be the finish of him.

Out on the terrace a group of officers stood around watching the final sun's rays light up the mountains of the Obersalzburg. Hitler listened calmly to what Canaris had to say, nodding and looking thoughtful. Any moment Canaris thought to himself, he will blow up in my face. He finished his report and waited. Hitler, who had all the time had his hands plunged deep into his coat pockets took them out, blew on them and rubbed them together. He noted the concern spread across Canaris' face.

'Don't look so glum,' he said, 'this is excellent news.'

Canaris was used to Hitler's unpredictable responses but this caught him off balance. 'I don't understand, my Führer.'

'Let's go inside to the warm,' he shouted to the rest of the assembly on the terrace. 'We should celebrate some good news with gluwein.'

'The reason the news is so good, Wilhelm my friend, is this is what I had expected – it has just come sooner than I had calculated but that is not important. We have the perfect excuse to complete our takeover. Admiral Raeder will be delighted. We shall phone Berlin and give him the good news. And we also now know where Churchill is; that is a little extra good news.'

'It won't be easy to get him out of America, my Führer'.

'Then don't. Just kill him. Do you have a strategy to deal with the English plotters?'

'We're working on it.'

'Excellent, discuss it with me when you are ready.'

A frauline dressed in the traditional local fashion offered them the gluwein. Hitler smiled at her approvingly. 'I like to see these pretty girls in our national costume,' he said, 'they will make fine wives and mothers for the Reich.'

CHAPTER 25

Buchanan, NY, November 1940

He woke with a burning throat and a pile driver pounding in his head. The shaft of light coming through the narrow window told him it was day again but the light was less brilliant than before. It must, he thought, be cloudy out there. He reached out for the jug but it was empty. Lying there in the gloom, he struggled with his thoughts. They must have abandoned him – but why? Maybe that was the plan – maybe they wanted him dead. What if this was just some vengeful whim of Newman, and Parkes wasn't a real FBI man at all? But that couldn't be right; it had to be legitimate otherwise why check him in at the police station and tell the desk sergeant they were taking him to the house? His mind was spinning again with meaningless theories and random guesses. He had to get back to sanity. Then thoughts of Carey came crowding in on him; she would be desperate. It made him feel claustrophobic, smothered, suffocated. The sense of helplessness was overwhelming and profoundly depressing. It made him sad to think about her and he wanted to be there to comfort her. There was nothing for it, he would have to try to break out; but with what?

He hauled himself upright and looked around in the dim light. He got up off the bed and switched on the light. In the corner was the old cycle; that, he thought, might have something about it he could use – perhaps something heavy enough to attack the lock. He went over to where it lay, flat on its side, balanced on one pedal; the front wheel stuck up in the air like the head of some dying beast raised in a last forlorn attempt to lift itself to its feet. It looked as if it had just that minute been dropped there. He bent over it to have a closer look, but when he picked up the frame he could feel by its weight there was nothing really substantial to it. There was nothing much to it at all: it had a torch on the front but the battery had long ago corroded away, there was a mirror attached to the handlebars and a small leather bag hanging off the back of the saddle.

That raised his hopes – it was a tool bag. The straps were mouldy and the buckle rusted; it sagged limply to one side under the weight of its contents. He fumbled with his fingers at the buckle but the mold and rust had seized it solid. Inside he could hear the tantalizing clank of bits of metal. In the end he resorted to tugging at the bag until with a cracking, ripping sound the stitching gave out and the whole thing parted from the saddle fixings and rested in his hands.

314

Eventually he managed to get his fingers into a gap where the stitching had rotted and tore it open. He up-ended the bag and the contents clattered onto the ground. Carefully he picked through the small heap on the floor, looking for something that might be useful. The biggest items were two tire irons but he knew they wouldn't make a dent on the door or the lock. There was an insubstantial cycle wrench – nothing more than a thin piece of punched out metal. There was a tin box with some puncture patches and adhesive, and a very small screwdriver – nothing that would get close to forcing the door.

He sat on the floor for a while looking at the forlorn heap and trying to get his mind round the problem he faced but it was becoming hard to concentrate. Once more he found himself thinking about death. Was this really it; was this the end of the road? Leaning over the bike he looked at his image in the small mirror. Two gaunt eyes looked back at him. A blood vessel had burst in one eye and it was wildly shot through with a raw crimson blush. It must have happened when he fell and hit his head on the table, he thought. His face was covered in the stubble of three days and his forehead had streaks of grey where he had rubbed the grime and dust of the basement into it. At first he felt saddened by what he saw; he thought of Holly and Martha and how they must be taking his disappearance. He had no idea how it might be affecting Carey. He desperately hoped Mike had picked up the car keys and made the connection. Then the sadness began turning to anger. How dare they do this to him with no explanation, no charges, not even the threatened interrogation. The anger gave him energy. He got up from where he sat among the debris of the cycle tools and walked across to the door – there had to be a way out. He wasn't prepared to accept this lying down. At first he'd been compliant with their demands because he was an ordinary law abiding person and he was conditioned to the idea that you cooperated when challenged by properly appointed officers – but he'd traded that first for fear, now for a frustrated rage. 'I am not prepared to die here!' he shouted out, angrily kicking at the door. 'I will not die here – do you hear me, you bastards?.

There was no reply.

He stood in front of the door until the rage subsided – there had to be a way to break it. He went back to the cycle and looked at the tools. Standing by the small window he noticed it had started to rain. He rubbed the dirt from the glass with the sleeve of his jacket. The spots had turned to splashes as the rain picked up and the beating of the water on the glass pulled his mind back to how thirsty he was. The rainwater taunted him. It took a moment or two to sink in but it eventually hit him that all he had to do was break the window and he could get some of that water just by putting his cupped hands out through the gap. Picking up one of the small tire irons, he smashed it against the glass. The glass was thick and the tool simply bounced off. He looked around for something heavier, but there was nothing.

Staring out through the small opening, riven with frustration as the rain lashed at the pane he could not break, his anger again rushed up to fill his head. It was beginning to drive him crazy as he struck again and again on the glass and each time the tire iron simply bounced off; he had to find something bigger, heavier, stronger. He went over to the wooden table and examined it. It was solid but even if he managed to rip off a leg, he figured the wood was too soft to create the shock needed to break the glass. Then his eye fell on the metal-framed bed. The legs were squared tubes but they had solid iron feet attached – if he could get one off he knew that would have the mass he needed to go through the glass.

He dragged the bed away from the wall and tipped it over onto its side. Then he pulled on one of the feet. It refused to move, it was stuck fast to the leg; a thin veneer of rust had bonded the two inseparable. He tried the next one but it was the same; so were the others as he tried them in turn. Another solution occurred to him. If he could drag the bed to the window, raise it on one edge and slam one of the feet against the pane, that could do it. He had propped the bed on its side against the wall to get at the feet; now he pulled the bed towards him and let it fall with a crash to the upright position. It was heavy as hell and he was now quite feeble. No food, no water, no sleep; they all bore down on him. Only desperation and anger drove him on. His arm muscles were quivering from fatigue. He pulled at the bed but he couldn't shift it, the friction of all four feet on the floor was too great for him to overcome. He stood and looked at it, angry with frustration. Then he worked out that if he lifted one end of the bed, he might be able to rock it on the other two legs and walk it slowly to the window. The most difficult bit would be to get the bed end up to chest level. It would need one supreme heave to hoist it up to that height but once he had got it there he could transfer all the weight on to the other two legs and it would counterbalance itself. From there he would simply dance it one step at a time over to where he needed to get it. He got into a crouched position; like a weight lifter he braced himself. He knew he had to get it up with one pull; it would sap all his energy and he knew he wouldn't have the strength left to give it a second shot. He took a deep breath and closed his eyes. With one great heave he pulled himself upright and pushed the frame away from him. He felt it wobble slightly and then go light – it was pivoted on the opposite two legs – he'd managed it. Just achieving that lifted his mood and he let out a little whoop of elation. Carefully he pivoted the bed around one of the legs. Then something unscheduled happened – one of the feet that had been so firmly fixed wobbled and fell off; it hit the floor with a thud, narrowly missing his foot. The seal of corrosion around it had been broken; probably when the bed had been allowed to crash to the floor as he'd rolled it over earlier.

For a moment he stood, staring in disbelief at the object on the floor below him. Staring back up at him was a solid chunk of cast iron with a short length of tube embedded in it, the image of a stone mason's hammer. Tom stepped back and let the bed crash to the floor. He picked up the block of iron and felt its weight – this he knew would do the job. The glass instantly gave way and flew into shards on the ground outside. A blast of cool air hit his face and he felt the splashes of water where the rain bounced off the window ledge and arced across the sill into the room. He carefully knocked out the remaining jagged pieces that still lodged in the frame and then, reaching out through the gap, let the water splash onto his arms and into his cupped hands. At first he was tempted just to gulp some water as it filled his hands but his sense of survival, ingrained from his days of hunting, stopped him. Rubbing his palms together he would use the first two handfuls to clean them. When he finally allowed himself a mouthful it was sweet and soothing; the more so because of the effort that had gone into getting it. It took a while to gather enough to quench his thirst and more than once he choked and coughed as it went down the wrong way.

Now he turned his mind to how he could get out of the place. He had a solid tool with which to attack the door. Leaving the tin mug on the outer ledge of the window to collect water, he picked up his hammer and went over to assault the door. His first instinct was to hit it around the area of the lock as hard as he could. It only took two blows to show him that was not going to work; the door was extremely dense and simply absorbed the shock without moving.

He examined the whole thing more carefully. On closer inspection he noticed that the cement around the place where the lock mortice had been set into the frame had a small crack running horizontally away from it – a weak spot. It would take time but if he could chip away at the edges he might eventually be able to dig out the striker plate and then he would be out. He started work with the thin edge of the cycle wrench; driving it into the crack by hitting it with the bed foot hammer. The cheap metal wrench survived a dozen hits then bent under the pressure of the blows. It fell with a dull clatter at his feet, but it had left a fissure big enough to get one of the tire irons into it. He started the same process again. His forearms were struggling to swing the hammer and he kept hitting his hand as he missed the end of the iron, but he ignored the pain. Little by little, a chip at a time, small fragments began to crumble. This might be easier than he had dared hope. Putting an iron in the gap between the door and the striker plate he could now manage to rock it on the hinges. The wall around the hinges was now also beginning to show signs of small fractures. The more he rocked the door, the more pieces fell out. Again he tried hitting the lock but with little result – it was still too solid – it would just have to be the long, slow method, but he was making progress.

It was while he was inspecting the cracks around the hinges that he heard footsteps on the staircase; someone was coming down. Absorbed by the task, he had forgotten that there might be people in the house and anyway he hadn't heard anything for more than a day. Now a sense of panic grabbed him. The footsteps had reached the bottom and he could hear voices. He threw the tools clattering across the room, flipped the light switch to off and staggered back to the bed where he lay down and pretended to be asleep. There was a lull and then he heard the key go into the lock. The door opened and a shaft of yellow light from the stairwell split the room. A figure in the doorway flipped the light on and he saw through half-closed eyes a small elderly man with grey hair carrying a black bag; behind him stood Newman. The second man moved towards the bed and, as he did, Tom moved and groaned as if waking and then sat up. He looked suspiciously at the newcomer.

'Is this our man?'

'It is,' Newman replied.

'Good, good.' He looked at Tom benignly. 'Well, sir, I have come to give you a medical examination. Is that alright with you?'

Newman pushed his way round the older man. 'This is Dr Miller. He's here to see if you're well enough to be questioned. He wants to make sure you're fit and well.'

Tom swung his legs slowly over the edge of the bed and sat looking at them, not knowing what to make of it. He thought on it for a moment but he knew there was no point in resisting. 'Alright,' he said quietly.

'Lie back down on the bed please.'

The doctor took out a stethoscope, checked his pulse and pressed gently round the stomach area. 'Any pain here?' He looked up waiting for a response. Tom shook his head. Lifting his eyelids, the doctor shone a torch into each eye in turn. When the torch was turned off Tom could see nothing for a moment but two bright blue dots in front of him.

'Open your mouth please, as wide as you can'. He stuck a wooden spill into his mouth and pressed down on the back of his tongue. 'Hmm,' he said, 'seriously dehydrated.'

'I need some water.'

'You certainly do,' he said gently. 'We must see to that straightaway. Sergeant Newman, this man needs water and he needs it now. Would you kindly see to it please?'

Newman shouted up the stairs for Cardy to bring water. The doctor turned again to where Tom lay on the bed, his shirt pulled up to his chest. 'Thank you, I've finished. There is nothing basically wrong with you but you are dehydrated. Drink more water.'

As he left he took Newman to one side. 'We cannot do anything until he is recovered. He needs to be fed and he needs proper access to water – and stop beating him – it shows, and it's not helpful. Do I make myself clear?' Newman grunted something incomprehensible.

They left and Tom heard the key turn in the lock. He breathed an inner sigh of relief; they hadn't spotted his efforts to break out. They hadn't even noticed the broken window. After a while Cardy came back with a large brown paper sack; he'd been to a grocery store. He dumped it down on the table and looked at the forlorn figure sitting huddled on the edge of the bed. He shook his head and in a voice that had a tinge of pity in it said, 'There's salt beef on rye, salami and a jar of dill in there – it's the best I could find for the moment. I'll get you something to drink. After I'll see if I can take you upstairs and you can wash up; get a shave. That'll make you feel better.'

Tom glared back at Cardy, the anger welling up inside him. 'I'd feel better if somebody would tell me why I'm being kept here and what the holy fuck is going on?' He threw the words out with as much force as he could muster through the rawness of his still sore throat.

Cardy simply looked at him, then added soberly, 'You're in out of your depth, son. You should have kept your nose out of things – bad mistake.' As he left, the tenor of his voice turned to something more facile. 'Eat hearty,' he said, almost singing the words, 'I'll be back.' Cardy banged the door shut, then locked it. A few fragments and some cement dust dropped out of the wall and fell with a faint sound like a shower of gravel dropping on the floor.

Food had never tasted so good to him – not ever in his life before. The simple rye sandwich in that moment tasted better even than Martha's finest pies. He ate slowly, avoiding the temptation to bolt it and choke. The soreness in his throat was going and he felt his energy coming back. An older, less fit man might have needed rest after the ordeal he had endured over the last three days, but he was young and strong. His mind turned back to the task in hand – how to get out of there. They were in the house again so whatever he did he knew it had to be quiet.

The first thing to do was hide the tools. They lay scattered where he had thrown them across the floor. Picking them up, he stuffed them back into the saddle bag and tucked them under the back wheel were he figured they wouldn't be noticed. When he went back to the door he saw the cracks around the hinges had widened when Cardy slammed it shut.

The rain had stopped and sunlight had again come through the window. As it faded into late afternoon Cardy came back; now he was armed with handcuffs. 'Okay kid,' he said cheerfully, 'the doc says we gotta clean you up. Stick out yer paw, you're gonna take a wash.' He snapped the cuff around Tom's wrist and put the other end round his. As they got to the door at the top of the

319

staircase he was relieved so see that it was only a light wood-panelled construction; it would be easy to force with one of the tire irons – if he could get that far.

He stripped off and washed his body all over, standing in front of a large ornate china hand-basin with plated taps. He shaved with a safety razor that was sitting in the soap tray – it felt good to get the stubble off his face and wash out the grime of the basement with a piece of perfumed soap. He could see the extent of the garden out of the window. It was probably no more than 50 yards to the back boundary, which was hedged in by some overgrown woodland. Through the trees he could just see glimpses of water – the Hudson. The window, he noted, had internal bars – from outside it would look normal but from inside the bathroom it looked like a prison. It had been the same on the landing, he noted, as they came up the stairs to the first floor.

All the time Cardy stood back by the door and watched in case Tom decided to make a break for it. As they had come up the stairs that thought had been uppermost in Tom's mind; he'd looked for a chance – any chance – to run, but none had appeared.

On the way back down as they passed through the hallway Tom spotted a newspaper on a table. He motioned to it. 'Alright if I take this? it's pretty dull sitting down there.' Cardy just nodded and Tom grabbed it as they passed.

Back in the basement once more he sat on one of the chairs at the wooden table and leafed through the paper. He was feeling more human again as he waited to see what happened next, but he was confused. Why was he simply being held prisoner? Why had nobody questioned him? At least if they did that he would have some idea of what this was all about. It crossed his mind that perhaps this was some kind of interrogation technique; he'd heard rumors that the FBI used weird methods to get information out of tough criminals; was this part of what was happening to him now?

There was the sound of the key grating in the lock again. The door opened and Cardy came in with another food sack. 'You got a burger and fries and a coke – and some salad to keep you healthy.' He laughed at his own humor.

Tom looked at him sourly. 'Why am I being kept here?' he said pointedly. 'I'm entitled to know – I'm entitled to a lawyer – this is all irregular – what's this thing about?'

Cardy didn't look unsympathetic and for a moment Tom thought he might get some sort of explanation, but Cardy just shook his head. 'Don't ask me kid – I'm just the jailer. It was my job to arrest you.' He thought for a moment then said, 'Interesting that one ain't it – the Army couldn't arrest you on account of they don't have powers of arrest, and that Fed would have to get an order from a judge. So I had to step in because I have the powers of arrest vested in me. Kinda cool, huh.' He broke off for a moment then almost as an afterthought said, 'You don't somehow look like a spy to me – still what do I know'. Then, trotting out his mantra about eating hearty, he slammed the door and locked it. As the key turned in the lock it stuck for a moment and Tom saw the handle move slightly as the Deputy tugged on the other side to ease it. The key finished the turn and the lock clicked into place; as it did so another small piece of cement fell from just beneath one of the hinges and clattered on the floor.

He pulled a chair out from the table and sat down to eat, planning all the while to make more progress on the door. If he was going to get out he reasoned it would have to be in the early hours of the morning when they would be at their least alert. The trouble was he had no idea of time; the only indicator was the light coming through the window. He waited till what he thought must be around midnight and started work on the door again. There was still a lot to shift and the work was painfully slow. Once he thought he heard movements but nothing came of it. In the end he figured out that it would probably take another night, perhaps two, before he could get enough done to break open the lock.

He woke early the next morning feeling cold. There was a chill draught coming from the broken window. He got off the bed and turned on the light, picked up the newspaper and started to read it, wondering all the time what would happen next. The next thing was entirely unexpected – he could smell coffee, rich and tantalizing; then the usual key in the door followed by Al Cardy carrying a jug and a mug.

'I figured you could use a little coffee and there's a bagel in the bag. Nothing with it but it's good for dunking.' He set everything down on the table. 'I think the doc is coming back to see you to day. Could be they'll get round to asking you some questions – maybe clear up a few things. Who knows?'

'What did you mean yesterday when you said I didn't look like a spy? Is that what they think?'

Cardy was silent; he looked uncomfortable and just stood there with his arms folded. After a bit he said, 'I dunno kid. I shouldn't really be telling you this but I kinda like you. You've put up well with this shit.' He looked around the basement as he said it, grimacing at the squalor. 'Sergeant Newman has been on some kind of army business, some secret stuff up around Champlain, and then you and your pals turn up and follow him around – well, he got kinda suspicious.'

Upstairs someone opened the top door. 'Are you down there?' It was Newman.

Cardy shot Tom a glance. 'Must be the doc arriving. Good luck, kid – and I mean that.'

Locked back inside, Tom sat and waited. Cardy's words had set his mind running again. Now he was beginning to make sense of what had been happening. He could explain it if they would just give him the chance, just put the questions to him. He was sure he could sort this out. A feeling of confidence welled up inside him. He felt relieved; he could see an end to it all.

The key turned in the lock again; this time it was Newman and Dr Miller. Tom found himself smiling, almost pleased to see them standing there.

'Well now, you're looking a lot better son,' Miller beamed at him in a friendly manner. 'Sit down, sit down, and let me take a look at you.' Tom sat on the edge of the bed.

'Right, now take off your jacket and roll up your shirt sleeve, please. We just want to take your blood pressure – make sure it's not too high.' Miller opened his bag, set up the equipment and wrapped a band tightly around Tom's arm. 'Now I just want you to look up to the ceiling if you would,' he said politely.

Tom looked up and as he did he was conscious of a small, stinging sensation in the bound up arm. The sharp pain made him look down. For a split second he saw the hypodermic syringe and then the room turned upside down and he passed out.

As he came out of the drug he tried to move but his body felt as if he was buried in mud and he couldn't move his arms. Miller's face came into focus but it was surrounded by mist spangled with tiny glittering gold pinpoints of light. He thought he would pass out again but then things settled down. As the fog lifted he tried to get up. The suffocating weight had been lifted from his body as the last effects of the drug wore off but something wasn't quite right. Regaining full consciousness, he now found himself tied down to the bed. His arms and legs were restrained; he was shackled to the frame. Leather restraining straps held him down; wrists and ankles.

'Good to see you are back with us,' Miller smiled. 'How are you feeling?' Tom said nothing as he wrestled against the restraints.

'There, there, calm yourself son,' Miller said soothingly. 'Everything's going to be just OK. I would advise you not to struggle because you will only hurt yourself – the straps will cut your wrists, you know.'

As Tom looked around he saw that the wooden table had been pulled alongside the bed. On the table was a rectangular metal box with a small winding handle attached to one end and two wires screwed to terminals at the other. 'Do you know what this is?' Miller smiled at him, and tapped the top of the box with a carefully manicured index finger. Tom's heart rate was now through the roof. He was pretty sure he knew what it was and he didn't like it at all.

'Well?'

'It's a magneto.'

'Yes,' Miller spoke as if he were talking to a child. 'And if I turn this handle,' he gave the handle a couple of turns, 'it generates some electricity. Now this little slide here,' he went on, 'controls the voltage of that electricity – this way high, this way lower.'

Newman walked into the room. He had an ugly grin on his face as he looked at Tom strapped down.

Miller picked up the two leads and in that instance Tom recognized them as the ones he had seen sitting in the corner when he first arrived in the basement. 'I think we're nearly ready for a little test.'

He opened the crocodile jaws on the end of one lead and let it close on Tom's wrist. The teeth bit into the skin and he winced. 'There, there,' Miller said in a low soothing voice, 'just keep still and the pain will go.' The other clip bit into his big toe and again he winced.

'Now,' said Miller, this time in a sprightly enthusiastic fashion like a mother offering her child a treat. 'We're going to give it a little test.' Sitting at the bedside with his face close to Tom he smiled a wide, malevolent smile and started turning the handle slowly. The current flowed through Tom's body convulsing his muscles. He gritted his teeth, but then Miller increased the voltage and he screamed.

Miller stopped and let Tom rest for a second or two. Then he turned the handle again, this time whisking it round. At the same moment he twitched the slide giving a short jolt of high voltage. Tom's body jerked violently up, his back arching off the bed. He screamed again but this time it degenerated into a low, moaning sound as exhaustion set in. Miller waited for him to recover, then turned the handle again but this time very slowly. He watched with satisfaction as the muscles in Tom's arms and legs began to snake and twist. Miller stopped and waited for a moment. He moved his face very close to his victim. Tom was sobbing. 'Shush, shush,' Miller whispered, 'it's alright, it's all over.'

He reached over, unclipped the leads then released the straps. 'See,' he said airily as if nothing much had happened. 'It's alright and you'll be feeling fine in a few minutes.'

Tom looked back at him and then at Newman who had all the time been standing in the background watching. His face still bore the image of the pain he had just suffered. 'Why, Why!' he shouted. 'What do you want?' Newman stood there impassive and said nothing.

'Want,' replied Miller quizzically, 'we want answers – or at least Sergeant Newman here would like answers.'

'Answers to what?'

'To questions, of course.'

'Then for fucks sake why don't you ask me?'

Miller smiled. 'We shall, we shall,' then his voice tailed off into a more threatening tone. 'First you had to have a lesson so that you would know what you will get if you don't answer the questions truthfully – straightforwardly.'

Tom glowered; his face had gone red with anger. 'Then ask – I have nothing to hide.'

Miller stood up, 'We shall see, we shall see.' He put the magneto in its box and made ready to leave. 'Tomorrow,' he said abruptly to Newman. 'Tomorrow he will be ready for questioning. He needs twenty-four hours to think about the consequences, then he will answer correctly.'

Newman went over to where Tom sat on the bed and prodded him roughly in the shoulder. 'You'd better, or we'll fry your ass and serve it on toast.'

Miller looked exasperated. 'I've told you no violence. Is that clear!' Newman looked sullen but said nothing – he just grunted and nodded.

The door was slammed again but this time nothing fell out. The night's efforts had produced no progress as he came up against heavy reinforcing aggregate in the wall. The top stuff had come away easily but it was just the finishing screed. It was going to take a lot more effort to remove the layer underneath. He was back to a feeling of hopelessness. He lay down exhausted and thought about the pain from the electricity. It was a special kind of pain and it made him feel sick to think about it. He would tell them all they wanted to know; everything *he* knew – but what if they didn't believe him? What if that wasn't enough? What if they wanted more and he hadn't got any more?

The night passed slowly, interrupted by fitful waking moments and punctuated with bad dreams. When he did finally drop into a deep sleep it was nearly dawn. Cardy woke him with coffee and a doughnut. 'It's your big day kid. Tell it straight and you'll be OK.'

Tom found himself thanking him and for a single moment thought how strange to be thanking one of his tormentors. Actually, he reasoned, Cardy wasn't so bad; he had after all shown him some kindness unlike Parkes who'd been a cold son of a bitch doing things by the book. Newman he genuinely feared – it was obvious he was a psychopath. He was sure that left to him he'd almost certainly be dead by now.

Not long after he'd finished eating the door opened and Newman was there, leering and gloating. Cardy was standing behind him. Newman had a short leather-bound stick in one hand and he motioned towards one of the chairs with it. 'Sit,' he said dryly. 'It's your turn – you're on.'

He smacked the stick down hard on the table with a loud thwack. 'Okay mister, you've had the night to sleep on it – what have you got to tell me? It'd better be something good.' Newman sat down in a chair opposite him. Tom looked at the stick warily. Newman was idly swinging it from side to side, like a conductor with a baton.

'I have no idea what it is you want to know.'

Newman brought it down across Tom's thighs with a stinging blow. 'Maybe this'll jog your memory.'

'Hey Sergeant, no violence. You heard what the doc said.'

Newman snarled angrily at Cardy. 'I'm calling the shots here – if you don't like it don't stay.' Cardy looked uncomfortable. 'Get outa here, anyway,' Newman snapped. 'You're fouling my air.'

Cardy left. Tom braced himself for the inevitable assault. On the staircase there was the sound of footsteps descending. Newman started prodding Tom in the chest with the stick but hearing someone enter the room behind him half turned. 'What is it now?' he growled, expecting to see Cardy standing there, but it wasn't. Instead he found himself staring up at Parkes. 'You're just in time to hear the pig squeal,' he said casually.

Parkes ignored the remark and moved round behind Tom. He looked down on him and put a hand on his shoulder. 'It turns out you have friends in high places, son. Come on, you're free to go – I'm taking you out of here.'

Tom looked bewildered. 'Come on,' Parkes said, 'let's go.'

Newman jumped to his feet and put out a hand against Tom's chest and shoved him back down on the chair. 'Hold up, mister,' he said threateningly. 'He aint going anywhere until I say so.'

'Leave it, sergeant, I have direct instructions – right from the top of the tree. He's out of here. So stand aside.'

The anger welled up in Newman. 'He goes nowhere mister. He's mine and he stays here and you can get the hell out. You're forgetting this is my operation; this is a military intelligence matter!'

'You're overridden, sergeant. My orders come down from Hoover himself.'

'I don't care if they've come down from the King of Jerusalem. He's not leaving – but you are!' Newman's face was grim with anger, the veins on his temples standing out like fat worms, pulsing with every heartbeat.

Parkes calmly put a hand on Tom's shoulder. 'Come on, son, let's go. Collect your stuff from the station. Sorry you had to go through this.'

Shoving the agent to one side Newman got between them. 'You're not listening to me!' he yelled, at the same moment pulling a gun from inside his jacket. He waved it at Parkes. 'You're not listening to me,' he said again, this time more calmly but with menace in his voice. 'Go on, get out.' He motioned to the door with the nose of the automatic. Tom sat frozen to the chair – he didn't dare move for fear Newman would shoot him on the spot.

Parkes looked calmly at Newman. 'Don't be stupid, sergeant. Put the gun away.'

'Stupid! Stupid!' Newman shouted, the anger now seething in his face. 'How's this for stupid'. Newman fired twice and Parkes dropped as his legs folded under him. Both shots had gone through his heart and he was dead before he hit the floor. 'Who's stupid now, huh?' Newman went over and kicked the body hard, then turned to see Cardy standing in the doorway.

Cardy had met Parkes as he'd come into the house. When he was told about the order for Tom to be released he'd looked pleased. 'I'm glad,' he said, 'I kinda got to like him.' A few minutes later he heard the ruckus and had come to investigate. He'd reached the bottom of the stairs just at the moment Newman had fired the fatal shots. Now he stood ashen-faced in disbelief at what he had just witnessed.

'What the hell have you done!' The words were hardly out of his mouth when Newman put a shot into him and he went down to join Parkes.

Newman pointed the weapon at Tom. 'Right. Listen up and make yourself useful or you'll join them with a one-way ticket to the afterlife. Get that deputy and drag him inside.'

Tom did as he was told, all the time expecting at any moment to feel the shot that would fell him. If it hit him square he knew he wouldn't hear it or feel it – everything would just go black in an instant, without warning. He braced himself for it as he pulled Cardy's body out of the doorway and dropped it by Parkes. Newman stood over the bodies and in turn went through their clothing removing a gun, his badge and his pocket book from Parkes; with Cardy he just took his sidearm. Then he crossed to the door. 'Don't go away now,' he said laughing, slammed the door and locked it.

Tom sat down on a chair and stared at the corpses, stunned by what had happened. There was a high-pitched whistle in his ears still; the shockwave from the gunshots had temporarily deafened him. He knew now that his life was worth very little once Newman had got whatever information he was looking for and there would be no letting him go. He was in a closed end situation and the only way to resolve it was to kill Newman or somehow incapacitate him. He looked around for a weapon and then remembered the bed foot hammer; it was still there where he had thrown it. He picked it up and went over to the door looking for the best position to stand if he was going to ambush the killer.

The first thing he discovered was that Cardy's body was in the way. He got hold of the corpse by both arms and dragged it a few feet away. Pulling on the arms to shift the body he spotted a wrist watch. That would be useful; for the first time in days he would know what time it was. He took it off and put it in his pocket; the action made him feel strangely guilty, it was like robbing the dead. He pulled the body a bit further, then let the arms drop. As they fell he thought he heard Cardy groan. He bent down close and tried to listen but he could still hear the faint whistling from the shots. He put his cheek close to the partly open mouth and then he felt it; the faint draught of breath – Cardy was still alive. He heaved him upright then propped him against the wall. He grabbed the pillow from the bed and stuffed it behind his neck; maybe, just maybe he could save him. Undoing Cardy's shirt, he could see where the bullet had gone in. It had entered the body somewhere between the lung and the stomach – he had been lucky. The wound was still bleeding profusely and had to be stopped somehow.

Tom looked around; he needed something to bind it with but it had to be clean otherwise he could die from blood poisoning. The blanket on the bed was filthy. He went over to where Parkes lay and checked to make sure he was dead – he was well and truly gone. He had a handkerchief in one pocket but it didn't look clean; however, the necktie might be useful to hold some wadding in place – if only he could find something to plug the wound. The he remembered the cycle tire repair kit; that had patches and they were sealed up in little packets so they would be clean. He found the largest one in the tin. The mug with rainwater in it caught his eye – that would be useful to clean round the wound. Wetting an edge of Parkes handkerchief in rainwater, he managed to clean away the congealed blood. He patted it dry, then applied a generous smear of glue on the patch and stuck it over the hole. As he applied the glue he could smell it was spirit based and that was good because it might help sterilize the wound. He wrapped the tie round Cardy; there was a bulge of middle-age fat and it barely went round with enough to tie it off, but he managed it. Cardy opened an eye and looked at Tom. He opened his mouth but no more than a hissing of air came out.

'Don't try to talk. You've been shot; just lay quiet.' Cardy opened the other eye, then barely perceptibly he nodded. Tom glanced down at the patch; it had stuck fast – it would hold for the time being.

Back at the door he spotted one of the jump lead cables he'd noticed the first time he'd entered the basement. For a moment he thought of using it as a garrote; then another, better thought came into his mind. He went back to the cycle and found the screwdriver. Next he kicked at the spokes in the back wheel until one of them broke off. By bending and unbending the thin wire spoke, metal fatigue set in and he soon broke of the short piece he needed. Now he came to the delicate part. It was the memory of seeing the spark shorting in the light switch days before that now gave him the idea. He'd worried he might get a shock from it – now he planned to deliver Newman a shock that could knock him out, or at least disable him. It was a long shot but it was all he had – he knew enough about household electricity to know it could be powerful and dangerous. Now Newman could have a shock for a change; it would be poetic justice.

He unscrewed the cover and removed it to reveal the terminals. Making sure the switch was in the 'off' position, he carefully removed the live feed to the light and replaced it with the spoke, poking one end into the hole and screwing it in tight. Using the crocodile clips, he clamped one end to the door handle and the other he let bite on the stub of spoke projecting from the live terminal. All that was left to do was wait; then when he saw the handle turn – flip the switch.

He knew it would end up blowing a main fuse somewhere but he was banking on a big enough charge getting through before that happened. The spoke was thick enough to carry the whole load and, if it worked, Newman would get the full 110 volts – enough to kill a man.

He looked at Cardy's watch; 2.10 in the afternoon – Newman had been gone more than two hours. He pulled a chair over to the door and sat there ready to go the minute he heard the key in the lock. It was while he was thinking about and visualizing that moment that it occurred to him Cardy might have his own key to that door.

Tom knelt down beside him. 'How are you feeling?'

Cardy smiled back weakly. 'I'm okay,' he barely whispered. 'Thanks kid, I owe you if I ever make it out of here.'

'You'll make it. Listen, have you got any keys to the door over there.'

Cardy looked down to the pocket on the left side of his pants and inclined his head a little towards it.

Putting his hand out, Tom pressed on the pocket. His heart flipped as he felt the outline of a bunch of keys. He had to shift Cardy a bit and the man winced with the pain but when he saw Tom had got them he smiled through his gritted teeth and nodded approval. He stood in front of the door; looking at the bunch he selected what he thought was the most likely key. He had barely got the key in the lock when he heard the upstairs door close and the footsteps of someone coming down. Newman was back.

'Damn', he cursed under his breath, 'what lousy luck.' Half an hour earlier and he would have been out and clear away from the place. Now everything was hanging on the light switch working.

He pulled the key out of the lock, picked up the improvised hammer and waited. A key went into the lock and he heard the click. Then the handle started to turn and as the door started to open he flipped the switch. There was a blinding flash and a noisy bang like a firecracker as the fuse gave out, but the voltage got through. Newman screamed and was hurled backwards against the wall like a rag doll. Tom yanked the cable off the handle and the door swung open. Newman was alive but there was smoke coming off his left hand which was blackened and burned raw. He lay there in the stairwell groaning, his body blocking the way. Tom thought about finishing him off with the hammer but couldn't bring himself to do it; why bother – Newman was going nowhere. It was an error that nearly cost him his life. He was on the bottom step when Newman grabbed him by the ankle and pulled him towards him. Tom struggled and hung onto the stair rail. Newman was beginning to haul himself up but Tom got his foot loose and kicked him in the face. It opened up a split just under his eye. Newman grabbed the shoe again but this time it came off and he fell back. When he reached the top of the stairs Tom found the door there was locked too.

He looked down to where Newman was trying to pull himself upright. Tom tried to shoulder the door but it was useless – he was in the wrong position to get any force. Then he remembered Cardy's keys; he must have one. There were five keys on the ring and he knew which one fitted the basement door. He looked down to see Newman now on his feet, weaving around like a drunk. He fumbled with the keys then put one in the lock – it didn't fit; as he pulled it out he dropped the bunch and it fell to the third step. Newman had his hand on the stair rail and was glaring up at Tom; he had hatred tattooed all over his face. Tom stepped down and grabbed the keys and saw Newman put a foot on the first tread. He wobbled and stepped back, grabbing at the door to steady himself. As his hand reached out there was another sound like a firecracker and a flash of blue fire arced from the door handle into his fingertips. A residual charge had been loaded into the door frame after the first blast and now it found its way to earth through Newman. It wasn't as strong as the first one but it knocked him down nonetheless. Tom carried on frantically trying to find the right key; finally on the third attempt he found it. Opening the door, he looked down to see Newman once more on his feet. Locking the door behind him, he made his way to the front door. That too was locked. He looked into the front living room but that had bars on the windows; then he remembered everything was barred, as he'd seen on his visit to the bathroom.

There was one mortice key left on the bunch that he hadn't tried. As he put it into the lock and turned it there was a deafening explosion behind him as Newman shot his way through the stairway door; it flew apart like matchwood, splinters flying everywhere. Tom snatched a quick glance over his shoulder in time to see Newman level his gun at him, but he was through the door as the shot thudded into the frame. Tom tried to run but his legs were jelly. Like running away in a dream they just didn't seem to work. As he stepped off the sidewalk, he fell; now he was struggling to get up. Almost a week of near starvation, little sleep and beatings had caught up with him. Newman came through the front door and started down the short drive but, as he did so, the sound of a police siren made him hesitate. Tom lifted his head to see red and blue lights coming towards him. Newman cursed loudly, lifted the automatic to shoulder height and let two rounds go. Tom was half way to his feet but his body spun round violently and he fell to the ground. As the first police car screeched to a halt, Newman fired two more shots this time into its windshield, then finding a reserve of energy he ran at a surprising pace down the side of the house and disappeared into the woods.

A second police car arrived. Tom sat up and looked at the officers. 'I'm all right,' he said relieved, 'one of the shots just nicked me. There's a badly wounded officer down in the basement but I'm afraid the FBI man with him is dead.'

'Best you don't move sir,' the officer said, putting a reassuring hand on his shoulder. 'There's an ambulance on the way,'

'How did you know to come here?'

'Residents reported hearing gunshots and an explosion.' He laughed a little then said, 'you can't have a gunfight in a comfortable middle class neighborhood like this and expect nobody's gonna notice.'

The officer who had given chase appeared from round the side of the house. 'No sign of him – he got clean away.'

CHAPTER 26

Liberation and Betrayal

In Washington Churchill was formally recognized by Congress as Britain's Prime Minister, but it was a cautious statement; nobody knew how secure the coup was. Sunday passed without incident or much news. Loughlin remained in touch with Armitage and MI5 using Morse transmissions, monitoring regularly the progress of the takeover but after the first thrust everything seemed to be going to plan. The real test would be Monday when the first formal contact would be made with the Germans at a diplomatic level. So far, no shots had been fired at anyone; nobody had been killed. Lockouts, blockades and suspension of observers' access to most sites had at that point been the hallmark of the coup. Apart from Halifax and Chamberlain there had been no political casualties either. There was a heavy presence of troops on the streets but otherwise life continued as normal. Now everyone waited for Hitler's response.

In London Eden had met with the German Ambassador, but nothing concrete had come out of it. Later he saw Bevin and told him they had agreed to talks but they were still waiting for Hitler to decide on a time and a place. The Legation had no instructions at present.

'I think they're going to take it on the chin, Ernest,' he said confidently. 'I think they're too worried about deteriorating relations with Russia. The Molotov–Ribbentrop Pact is coming unraveled. I think their eye is on the east. If we let them keep Hudson Bay I think we can probably ditch the rest of this treaty business with minimum difficulty.'

'We should get Winston back,' Bevin suggested. 'We'll need him for the negotiations and it'll give the country a boost.'

'Yes, why not – it will show the Germans we mean business. We should get Armitage onto it. He's got a chap out there with Winston, I believe.'

Mosley met with Dalton at the Home Office. He arrived on foot in his BBS uniform but had come unarmed. 'He was actually quite civilised,' Dalton told the others afterwards in the Cabinet Office. 'I found him quite patriotic actually – not at all what I expected. He has given his assurance that the BBS will do nothing to interfere with the government. He even offered to assist in any way he could; said his force was at our disposal.'

Bevin looked unconvinced. 'Will he surrender his arms voluntarily?' he asked. 'That's the most important one.'

'That was difficult.' Dalton chose his words carefully, like a man who knows he may watch them come flying back home to wound him later. 'He says he will maintain his status until he sees where they are with any new treaty arrangement – but he undertakes to keep his men in barracks until negotiations are settled.'

On Tuesday there was still no word from Hitler; the coup was consolidating.

When Loughlin announced that they wanted Churchill back in London Churchill was delighted. 'Back in harness again,' he chortled. 'That'll be good.'

'It will take time to arrange, sir', Loughlin said cautiously, trying to damp down the expectation of instant action, 'and we can't let our guard down. We know they've got people out there looking to get at you. Getting killed at this point is going to help nobody and Washington is not the easiest place to guard you.'

'Then we should get back to Brunessemer,' Churchill announced. 'There's not much else to be done here anyway; I think were done with the jawing.'

******

Tom was in Peekskill Hospital; he had a gunshot wound to the right thigh. The bullet had missed the bone but it was going to take time to heal. At first he was registered and admitted as a minor hunting accident, but then they had put him into a private room and sat a guard outside his door. Two days after he had survived the basement he had his first visitors: Holly and Martha. She was beside herself with happiness. She sat there with tears rolling down her cheeks, stroking his hand and slowly shaking her head from side to side. 'My God we thought we had lost you,' she kept saying.

Holly put one arm round her shoulder and beamed at his boy. 'I wanted to bring Wheels with me but they said they wouldn't let him in.' Waving a finger and with a big grin spread over his face, he leaned closer. 'Now didn't I tell you,' he said jokingly, 'no good would come of messing with guns.' They all laughed together and it was the best kind of laughter – a soothing mix of joy and relief.

'Has anyone else been to visit?' Martha asked.

Tom shook his head. 'No,' he said, squeezing her hand. 'Not yet – just you. I expect the others will come soon but right now I just wanted to see you and Dad.'

'Police came and told us you'd been found.' Concern spread across Holly's face; it darkened, 'said maybe it had some connection to that young man from the garage being shot. They wanted to know if you had enemies. I told them I was damned if I knew anyone who'd want you dead. Is there anyone?'

'You can tell us if you're in some kind of trouble, son', Martha sighed. 'We'd understand, you know.'

'I'm as much in the dark as you are, Ma. I really don't know what's going on; but with that shooting – the guy from the garage – well – I think that was meant for me.'

'Why?' Martha whimpered through her sobs.

'I don't know – it's the God's honest truth – I don't know.'

A nurse let herself in and said they would have to go now because he needed his rest and she had to give him his medication. Outside Martha saw the policeman who was guarding the room. She approached him and in a soft apologetic voice said she was sorry to disturb him but did he know anything about what had happened to Tom. The officer said he was just a cop who had been told to check all visitors and turn away anyone unless they had a pass from the reception. He didn't know more than that though he thought the FBI were involved.

The next morning the nurse announced there were two visitors to see him if he felt OK. His first thought was Carey, but when the door opened he saw Dan Johnson from the office and behind him a soldier. The soldier was Fred; he didn't recognize him at first – the office junior had turned into a man.

They sat down awkwardly searching for something to say; Tom broke the silence. 'How's the Army Fred?'

'Oh, it's cool,' he said with an enthusiasm Tom had not expected. 'It really is Mr Jordan, sir – I didn't think I was going to like it at all but it turned out great.'

'Are you sure?'

'You bet. When my draft term is finished I'm gonna enlist and take the junior officers exam – I want to make it my career. I'm so glad I got drafted when I did.'

Tom laughed, 'It sure changed you.' They talked more of Fred and his new career, then they talked about the office and how the events in Britain had changed the risks in the market once again. Eventually Dan looked at his watch and said that everyone in the office had sent their best to him but they had to go. There was one thing though, he had forgotten to say. An FBI agent called round to the office the day after Tom was found.

'He asked if we knew where you might be. We didn't, of course. We didn't know you'd been found at the time. What's this all about, Tom – are you in trouble?'

'It's complicated, Dan. I'll tell you some time when I know myself.' He shuffled himself around to get more comfortable. 'Did the agent say who he was? Did he identify himself?'

'Sure, it's the first thing you ask – to see their badge. His name is Parkes.'

Tom froze. 'Are you certain?'

'Of course, he gave me a number to call if you came back to the office.'

'Do you have it?'

'Sure, I wrote it down. It's right here.' He pulled out his pocket book and handed Tom a slip of paper.

'Can I keep this?'

'Sure, why not – do you want me to call him?'

'No, Dan, whatever you do don't do that, and if you see him again don't tell him where I am. Instead you make an excuse. Get to a phone and call the cops.'

'Are you sure? Why would I need to do that?'

'Because he's not Agent Parkes. He shot Parkes and took his badge. I was there, I saw it happen. He shot me in the leg; that's how I got this. He's not an FBI man; he's a murderer. Now do me a favor. Tell no one at the office – or anywhere else for that matter. When you go out ask the cop who's sitting outside to come in.'

Carey didn't come to visit. As the afternoon turned to dusk and lights were switched on in the hospital he had other visitors. Just before the evening meal trolley came to his door two men in dark suits were let in by the police guard.

'We got your message,' one of them said in a deep southern accent. 'I'm Jones and this is Agent Polanski. We got your message. We were gonna come and see you anyway but we thought we'd give you a day or two to rest up.'

'You know who this man is?' Tom asked anxiously.

'Sergeant Henry Newman, US army recruiter – 'cept he's not.'

'I'm not getting it.'

His real name is Heinrich Neumann, born in the US to a German immigrant family, joined the army as a shooting instructor, volunteered to work undercover for military intelligence to gather information on disaffected expatriate Germans. He went over to the other side – he's a Nazi sympathizer, son, and he's on their payroll.'

'A double agent?'

'Now you're getting it. He's been on our watch list for a while now, then you and your buddies blundered in at Crows Crossing and caused a little flurry, you might like to say. You're lucky to be alive son.'

'Where does Cardy fit in?'

'Nice question. Deputy Sheriff Alan Broderick Cardy, regular officer, got drawn in to assist Neumann, thinking he was a bona fide government agent doing something for the military around Crows Crossing. When you boys turned up Neumann convinced him that his presence had to be kept secret and he needed to know if anyone had spotted him.'

'So he put out the story of the missing ranger so we'd report any suspicious activity we saw – and we did.'

'Right on the button, son.'

'So if we reported we'd seen Neumann and his men, he could alert them. Except we didn't tell Cardy.'

'That's right, you didn't. Instead you did the dumbest thing you could have done – you charged around in that old jalopy and chased after him. We figure that's why your old man's car got shot up.'

'Hell, I've been stupid.'

'I aint gonna argue with that.'

'The fellah who gave you the shock treatment is another one best avoided if you can. The good Dr Miller – real name Josef Mueller, also known as Doctor Death – Austrian national, professional killer and persuader, specialist in torture and extracting information, a real nasty bag of worms. Age around seventy. Hell, who would suspect a nice old guy like that?'

Polanski went over to the window and peered out into the dark. 'You've been keeping bad company, son. You're damn lucky to be alive.'

Jones grinned like he was enjoying the telling. 'Now we gotta keep you that way. You're one of the few people who've seen this garbage up close and lived to tell it. We're gonna catch them and when we do, why we need you to testify. Will you do it?'

'Try to stop me. Just one thing, though – what was Neumann doing up on Champlain anyway?'

'Shit son, we have no idea.'

'Couldn't Cardy tell you anything about it?'

'Maybe, but he's in no shape to talk right now. He's in a pretty bad way. I hear he owes you – you patched him up – that was pretty neat going son. I hope he pulls through.'

They made ready to go but stood there for a moment. Polanski, who had said little all through the visit, hesitated. 'Just one other detail. We would normally put you into witness protection but we don't have Neumann and right now we don't know where he is. We can't go chasing around looking for him – he could be anywhere. Our best shot at nailing him is you.' He seemed embarrassed to say it so Tom said it for him.

'You're going to phone that number and tell him where I am. I'm the bait in the trap. That's it, isn't it?' He looked at them angrily. 'Are you fucking serious!?'

Polanski twitched his head. 'Fraid so.'

Tom didn't like the idea at all. What if Neumann got through, crawled in under their radar, got to him? He would be defenceless in the hospital bed –

what then? Neumann was resourceful, desperate and determined. 'I don't like it – what if he gets by you?'

Jones tried to assure him. 'Hell, don't worry, son. We've got this place trussed up tighter than a turkey at a Thanksgiving dinner.'

'I still don't like it. Give me your gun.'

'I can't do that.'

'I need something to protect me.'

'That's us,' Polanski said firmly. 'We've got a dozen disguised officers here. They're everywhere; inside and out. They're janitors, gardeners, delivery men, interns – you're being well looked after.'

He ate the evening meal, then Holly and Martha turned up again – but there was no sign of Carey. He fell asleep with a creeping uncertainty that something had gone wrong.

Morning came and for the first time since he'd been shot there was no pain in the wound. When the nurse came to change the dressing she pronounced that it was healing nicely; much faster than she'd expected. 'That's being young for you – you mend real quick; you've done better than most I've seen.'

'Can I get up and walk around a bit?'

'I don't see why not. You might need a cane though – I'll find one for you if you like.'

It was good to be out of bed and on his feet again. At first he wobbled; the muscles in his legs had gone lazy from lying around in bed for days, but the strength slowly came back. He thought he might get dressed and go out into the hospital gardens. Just being outside would make him feel a whole lot better. When he told the nurse she said it was a good idea – so long as he was careful not to knock the wound and split it open. 'We can get those sutures out in a day or two. You're doing just fine.'

It was while he was sitting on a chair in the garden that he saw her. The day was bright and fine and the sharp morning chill had given way to something milder and not too cold. The nurse was walking towards him, waving and calling. Following close behind was the unmistakable figure of Carey. His heart jumped as he saw her; she had come at last.

Tom stood up and let her walk into his open arms, then he hugged her tightly. But when he went to kiss her she felt reticent and what he had waited for didn't happen. What should have been a long and warm sensation quickly terminated into something perfunctory – no more than if he had kissed his mother.

He let her out of his embrace. 'What's wrong?' he said – his heart now down in his boots, his initial happiness snatched away and replaced with that familiar cold, clammy blanket of anxiety. She was such a rollercoaster. She stepped back and looked at him.

'I hate hospitals,' she said, giving a little shudder. She pulled at her coat and wrapped it tight around her as if she were cold. 'They're full of sick people and people who are dying; it depresses me.'

He went to take hold of her again; this was the old Carey full of fears and phobias but he knew it would pass. She would melt into his arms, sob a little and then be the same lively, confused little girl he loved so much.

As he stretched out his arms and touched her, she pulled away. There was no sobbing or melting, just a slight look of guilt with a hint of remorse. 'I can't Tommy – I'm sorry – I can't. Things have changed; things are different now.' Her voice was cold and empty.

He stood there helplessly, unable to find any words, choking on the emotion that had welled up inside him. He had lost her – she didn't have to say it – he knew it. 'Why?' he asked in a flat, grey tone; all the colour had gone from his voice.

She rubbed her face with her hands and pulled at her cheeks not wanting to talk further, just wanting to run away. 'It happens,' she said as if she was in a trance. 'It just happens.'

'Why did it happen?' he persisted, struggling to find a way to hold her there. He knew she was drifting away and he couldn't stop her. Everything they'd had was now dissolving, slipping through his fingers like a handful of sand until eventually it would be gone and there would be nothing but memories.

'Why?' she said softly. She looked across his shoulder into the distance, not wanting to look him in the eye. 'I didn't know where you were; I thought you were dead – I cried to start with, then I met someone else. People do that, Tommy – people change. I'm sorry – I have to go now.'

He made one last attempt to salvage something to hold onto, something to hold near in the moment when the sad memory would come back to haunt him; something that would ease the pain. 'A goodbye kiss,' he said gently, 'something to remember you by?'

She shook her head. 'Sorry Tommy, I can't.' In that moment he felt the dull ache of resignation and he gave up the struggle.

As she left he caught the unmistakable fragrance of her perfume, the one he had first caught that day on the train. He watched her walk away, a tiny figure in the bleak November landscape; then it was over – it was finished. He wouldn't cry, he told himself; it isn't for a man to cry – he would keep it in – he would deal with it.

Tom sat back on the chair; his body didn't want to work and his mind didn't want to grapple with it. It was too painful. He was overwhelmed by it. This, he thought, is how it must be when someone you love dies.

He was still sitting there in the late afternoon light when the nurse came looking for him. His face was gently stained from some quiet tears that he could no longer keep back and he'd let fall as he came to terms with what had happened. 'We need to get you inside. What a beautiful girl,' she said cheerily. Then she noticed the sadness on his face. 'Are you all right?' she asked. Tom didn't answer; he just gave a little nod. She must have guessed what had happened and didn't mention it further.

At midnight he was still sitting awake in his room. Sleep wouldn't come and every time he closed his eyes he saw her. At first he thought he might ask the nurse for something to make him sleep, then he shrugged it off. Grow up, he told himself, live with it – but the pain was there, right in the middle of his chest – and it was strangely real. He'd never thought that something as abstract as an emotion could present such physical sensations.

This was no good, he told himself. He had to do something to take his mind off her. In the end he decided to go for a walk. He pulled on his outdoor shoes, opened the door and looked down the corridor. The cop on guard was dozing in the chair. That's not very encouraging, he thought, as he tiptoed past him. He ambled along until he reached the point where it joined another corridor. He looked right and left – it was empty in both directions. Which way, he said to himself, then turned right on a whim. He passed a general ward and, looking through the glass doors, noticed the neat line of beds. He could see the night duty nurse deep inside walking along checking on the patients.

It occurred to him that she was the only person he'd seen other than the sleeping cop since he'd left his room. So where were all the undercover people Jones and Polanski had talked about? The corridor came to a dead end at a laundry chute. He turned round and walked past the general ward again. The nurse had finished her round and was sitting down with her back to him. Anybody could be walking through here, he thought, and nobody would be the wiser. He came to where he had taken the right turn and this time carried straight on. The corridor was studded with doors carrying plates stating their function: X Ray, Fracture Clinic, Radio Therapy. This too was deserted; there was a spooky quality to the silence that surrounded him and it made him want to shout just to break it. He resisted and carried on walking until he got to where it seemed to finish. As he came to the end it took a right turn and, after another hundred feet, ended up in the main entrance to the hospital.

The reception was close to the main entrance where a nurse was sitting at a desk reading a magazine. He walked right past her before she saw him, then she looked up with a jerk. 'Oh,' she said, 'I didn't see you there. Can I help you?'

'Not really, I'm a patient here. I couldn't sleep so I thought I'd go for a stroll around, maybe go outside and take the air.'

The nurse looked surprised. 'You can't go walking around out there, it's bitter outside, Mr – sorry – what did you say your name was?'

'I didn't, but for the record it's Jordan – Tom Jordan.'

'Oh,' she said, 'there was someone in here asking for you earlier; a specialist consultant, I think. Did you see him? It was only about ten minutes ago.'

Warning bells started to ring. 'Are you sure?'

'Oh yes, Mr Jordan.'

'What did he look like – this consultant?'

'Well', she started to answer and then broke off. 'There,' she said, pointing down the corridor, 'here he is now, that's him there.'

Tom didn't stop to answer. He ran towards the front doors, ignoring the pain in his thigh as he felt the wound pop. The pain made him gasp and his legs seemed to be dragged down, making escape seemingly impossible. As he got out into the fresh air he yelled as loud as he could. 'Neumann! It's Neumann, for Christ's sake! Someone help!'

Neumann appeared at the entrance. Through the glass Tom could see the girl at the desk pointing to the outside. He kept on running now, dragging his leg as he went. It was more like hopping than running. Things started to play out in slow motion as he pulled himself along frantically, all the time cursing the dumb FBI for letting him in for it. He looked back and saw Neumann standing out front of the main entrance looking round in all directions. The lights in the drive held down Neumann's vision as he looked at an impenetrable wall of black. He moved in Tom's direction until he had breached the wall of darkness. Now he stood peering towards Tom waiting for his eyes to accustom to the dark. Tom tried to move on but, looking back over his shoulder, he lost his balance and fell into a shrubbery border. The noise alerted Neumann who started to move rapidly towards him. Then, somewhere out there in the night a voice shouted out, 'Hold it, mister, you're under arrest. Don't move!'

Neumann turned in the direction of the voice. There were three loud bangs in succession as he fired into the night and then ran. There was another bang, then another as the undercover team started taking shots at the fugitive. 'After him,' someone yelled, 'he's getting away.' There was a fusillade of shots, then a car door slammed. An engine roared into life and to the screech of tires and flying gravel Neumann made his escape.

Tom got to his feet and as he did so a figure stepped out of the shadows. 'Put your hands up high where I can see them. A wrong move and I blow your friggin head off.' Tom stood there, wondering what the hell was going on. 'I've got one of them,' the figure shouted.

Jones appeared. 'Oh, my lord, put the gun away, you dickweed. That's the boy we're supposed to be protecting. Sorry about that, son. He got clear out'a here.'

Tom shook his head in disbelief. 'How could you miss him? Who teaches you lot to shoot, for Christ's sake.'

When he got back to his room there were two officers guarding it. Neumann had killed the other cop; just broke his neck while he slept.

The next day Tom had the leg sewn up again. It wasn't serious so they let an intern loose on him. 'It's ripped a bit,' he said, 'and I'm going to give you a little jab to hold down the pain but it looks fine to me. You ought to stay here a day or two longer, but it's okay by me if you want a discharge later today. I can see how you might not want to stay.'

Mike stuck his head round the door, a mop of red hair plastered down with pomade and a big smile splitting his face. 'It's really good to see you, cara,' he said, using the Irish term of affection. 'How's the old leg there?'

'It's not too bad – yeah, not too bad.'

'I heard about the shenanigans last night. You really know how to have a good time,' he said, trying to make light of it.

'It was rough – that bastard Neumann – he's still out there. I don't know how he keeps managing to get away. He killed a cop last night, you know – right outside my door. I had a chance to kill him when I got out of that basement. I was going to cave his skull in with a hammer, but I couldn't do it. It's not easy to kill someone. I should've done it.'

'I heard.'

'Where's Tony? I expected to see him by now.'

'I don't know,' said Mike. 'I think he's busy right now doing something for his uncle. You know how Tony is.'

'Yeah, yeah,' Tom laughed, 'he'll be up to something cute, I'll bet. I often wonder what he gets up to when he goes off like that.'

'It'll soon be my wedding – less than a month till I lose my freedom.'

'You'll still hunt?'

'When I can, but married men have commitments, you know.'

'Yeah.'

'You'll come to the wedding, won't you?'

'Of course. I wouldn't miss it.'

Mike looked around the room. 'This all looks well enough,' he said. 'You've even got pictures on the old wall.'

'I won't miss it – I need to get out of here. I think they'll let me go tomorrow. Maybe you could drop by and pick me up? Dad still hasn't got the Chrysler back.'

'Consider it done.'

The conversation was running dry. 'Isn't it the oddest thing – you can gab away all day with your buddies but when you visit in a hospital you can't think of a single thing to say.'

'She left me, Mike,' Tom said drably. 'My girl dumped me'.

'I know, I heard.'

'She just walked away – I still can't believe it.'

'I'm sorry. It must be a hell of a hit after what you've been through. Does it hurt?'

'Yeah, it hurts – not so much now as it did. Some things hurt so much you wanna cry. Other times it hurts too much to cry and you just go numb – you don't feel the pain. This is one of those.'

'It happens. You'll come through it.'

'I know.'

There was a long, drawn out silence as the two men struggled to find something to say. Finally Mike broke it. 'She worked hard to find you and get you out, you know.'

Tom nodded without enthusiasm. 'Uh huh.'

'She and Tony – they really worked at it together.'

There was another pause. Tom pulled himself upright – somewhere in his head a light was switched on. He looked at Mike hard and he saw in his eyes what he had just guessed. There was no doubting what was there.

'It's Tony, isn't it? That's who's taken her. You knew didn't you?' Anger was written across his face; this was betrayal.

Mike sat, looking at him blankly, embarrassed by what he knew and how Tom had guessed it. He never was any good at hiding things; his face always gave it away. 'I'm sorry.'

Tom screwed up his face and winced at the thought of it – Tony and Carey.

'You knew didn't you? You've known all along – why didn't you tell me before? You could have let me know before she came here – it would have helped. I would have had time to prepare for it. It would have made it easier.'

'I'm sorry. How do you tell a friend something like that? I didn't want to dump it on you straightaway after you got out of that hell hole you were in. I thought it might be better coming from her.'

'It's been a shit couple of days. First my girlfriend dumps me, then some homicidal maniac tries to kill me, and now I've lost a friend. Anything else you can think of to go arse end up.'

He drew in a deep breath then slowly and noisily let it out. 'Pick me up tomorrow, will you; around ten if you can. No point sitting here feeling sorry for myself – need to get on and sort out my life.'

With that he closed the conversation. The visit was over – pretty much everything that had been was over with it.

******

'Hello girls. What's this coming onto the parking lot?' Jennifer was looking out of the window at a large black limousine that had just drawn to a halt. 'Swankeee,' she said.

'Bet it's some old rich guy.' Dolores was looking over her shoulder.

'Wrong – young and handsome – and clearly very rich; that's a chauffeur in the front. Dottie come and take a look at this, and he's coming our way.' Dolores fluffed up her hair, giving it some bounce and smoothed her apron straight.

Loughlin looked at the diner as he approached it. There were several cars parked out front and any one of them could be his. Inside he found a table and sat down. 'He's mine,' Dolores said as she started to make a move to the table.

'Nah nah, honey,' Jennifer said, wagging a finger, 'that's for Dottie. You're spoken for – remember hubbie; naughty girl.'

Dottie approached the table. 'What'll it be, sir?'

'I think I'd like a coffee please – but no milk, thank you.'

Back at the counter the other two girls gathered round her. Dolores shot a glance at him over her shoulder. 'He's English,' she said under her breath, 'don't you just love that accent? My God, I could pass out right here. Maybe I should do it; maybe he'd catch me and I'd wake up in his arms. Like Rudolph Valentino – and take me away in his fancy limo – and ravish me.'

'Maybe you'd just fall on your fanny and get a fat bruise,' Jennifer jibed.

'I wonder, did somebody leave a message and some car keys for me?' he asked Dottie politely when she came back with the coffee.

In that moment she felt a sense of déjà vu and instinctively looked towards the door, half expecting to see an FBI man standing there. 'I'll ask,' she said.

When she came back she was holding on to an envelope. 'Here sir, this was left. Are you Fred from Ealing?' He agreed he was and she handed it over. 'That's what it says on the packet; excuse me for saying it, but isn't that a kind of odd name?'

'I come from an odd country,' he said.

'Are you from England?'

'I am.'

'I hear things are in bad shape over there at the moment.'

'It's a bit shaky right now but it'll pull through.'

Another customer came and sat himself down at the counter. He idly turned to Loughlin. 'Were you in here a week or so back when that guy got lifted by the Feds?'

Loughlin looked blank. 'Sorry?' he said questioningly.

'The kid,' the customer persisted. 'He got arrested and carted off by the Feds except it now turns out they was nothing of the damn kind. Look – see here, there's the whole story. It was a kidnapping. They took him off up Buchanan way and tortured him; kept him locked in a goddamned basement for chrissakes. Look, it tells the whole story here. He escaped – he's a goddamned hero. I was here; I saw the whole thing, I'm telling you.'

'Can I see that,' Dottie asked, holding out her hand for the paper.

'Of course, miss. You was here too. Aint that so?'

'Yes. I'll let you have it back.' She retreated into a corner and read the piece. Somebody in the *Washington Post* had been tipped off and got the story from an insider. It had been syndicated and was probably in every paper round the country. It was graphic – it didn't pull any punches. There staring out at her were the faces of Parkes and Cardy. Now Parkes was dead and Cardy was lying in a hospital somewhere fighting for his life. She went cold at the thought of what had happened and how close she had been to it. As she gave back the paper she remembered the third man and realized that is who she had seen – the little old gentleman with the walking cane. The paper had called him a cold blooded killer who specialized in torturing people.

'Thanks,' she said, handing it back. 'It's unsettling when you think they were here, so close, especially the old one – the one who they say did the torturing.'

'Did you think he looked like a killer?' the customer demanded. 'I didn't see him, did you?'

'Yes, I did,' Dottie said in a low voice.

'What was he like, what was he like?' he said excitedly as he leaned over towards Loughlin. 'I'm telling you, mister, this was one hell of a creepy character. Like something out of a horror flick – Dracula or one of those creeps. What would you say, miss?'

'Actually,' she said slowly, 'no, not at all. He looked like a normal little old man – very neatly dressed and with a walking cane. He was standing over there by the men's room.'

A memory went snap in Loughlin's head; a connection fired a spark – and in a split second two images collided, then morphed into one. The old gentleman coming out of the dining room in the Washington Hotel and the elderly man in the men's toilets at the horticultural gardens in Wisley when he was warning Peters. They were the same; the two images coalesced. Wisley – that's where he had seen him before. Damn!

He stood up and went over to the counter to pay. 'Did you know the man in the newspaper by any chance, the one who was abducted?'

'He used to come in here from time to time – him and his friends. They go hunting up in the hills together. They'd meet here for breakfast then go off to shoot.'

'Would you know where to contact him? Do you have an address – perhaps a phone number?'

Dottie shook her head. 'No, not really. Why are you a reporter or something?'

'No, but I'd really like to meet him. If I give you a number could you ask him if he would call – if he comes in again, that is.'

She laughed. 'This place is becoming a regular messenger service for him.'

343

'Why do you say that?'

'You're the second person who left a message to call. The other one was a park ranger, Dave Hanson – comes in here regularly as well. I think they knew each other. He called him just before he got taken away.'

The car Amber Rose had left him was a black Ford; you couldn't get more anonymous than that, he thought, as he climbed in and pressed his foot on the starter button. On the drive back down to Dobbs Ferry he tried to put things together in his mind. The old man was Mueller and he'd probably killed Peters and his wife. There was an accomplice, Neumann, who was a double agent, and then there was this man, Tom Jordan, who must have seen something; he'd probably blundered into it and didn't know its significance. But why torture him? Did he know something? Did they need to be sure before they killed him that he hadn't passed something on?

If Mueller was sent to torture Peters then it was about finding Churchill – that was a given. The fact he was snooping around the Washington meant he was still looking for Churchill – and he was getting close. How could he know Churchill would be there – the story hadn't broken by then. There was a leak; there had to be a leak. The only one who knew they were there other than the White House was Amber Rose – was he the leak? But it still didn't tie in with Tom Jordan – what was the connection there? As he approached Brunessemer he was pulled over by a Highway Patrol car. At least the security around Churchill was working. Satisfied with who he was, they let him go on into the property.

Irena was preparing for the Thanksgiving weekend and organizing her guest list. It would be small: the Churchill party; her two daughters; Wendell, her son, if he could be bothered to make the journey; and Tommy. Like all the others she had read the story in the *Westchester Post*. He was a celebrity. Poor boy, she thought; everyone will want to meet him and she was determined to organize a dinner party in his honor once the inconvenient Mr Churchill and his entourage had left for England. Then they would be free from the constraints of all these security men snooping around the grounds, peering suspiciously at anyone who came to see her. She would invite all her friends and launch him into her social circle. After all, she reasoned, he and Carey were bound to get married so he will soon be part of the family.

Wouldn't it be nice, she mused, if I could announce an engagement at the dinner party – now that would be fun. Irena loved a plot and this one was forming up nicely in her mind. Never mind Thanksgiving; Mrs Martins could organize that. It was, after all, the same old thing year in year out; too much to eat and the same old family gossip brought out once a year and given the same tedious dusting down before bcing packed away for another year. A dinner party was always much more fun – so much fresh tittle-tattle, delicious scandals, and then there would be Tommy's story, which she knew would take them by storm. Finally there would be the crowning glory to top it all off – the announcement of an engagement. She rehearsed it in her mind, playing out the scene, savoring the triumph, imagining the moment.

Carey had not been home since the weekend and it was Wednesday already. How inconsiderate her daughter could be; Irena was bursting to give her the news of her big idea and she wasn't there . She phoned to say she was staying over in New York with a friend and wouldn't be back for Thanksgiving, but that was it. When Irena had tried to open up the conversation Carey said she would call again later, when she had more time; then she'd hung up. Since then nothing – no communication, nothing, complete silence. She went off in search of Vera the housekeeper. 'I think we need to order more drinks for the weekend,' she said. 'If Wendell condescends to grace us with his presence he'll probably drink the place dry.'

When Loughlin arrived and Irena heard the sound of a car coming along the drive at first she though it was Carey back at last. The door chimes rang and her next thought was the silly girl had forgotten her key. Patience opened the door and announced his arrival. Irena appeared in the hallway with a look of vexed disappointment on her face. 'Oh,' she said, 'it's you.' Never mind, she thought, and went off to find Clementine. She could enjoy sharing her big surprise with her; it was always much more fun if one had a co-conspirator.

Loughlin went in search of Churchill. He found him in the library dictating to Mary Shearburn; Walter sat in the corner reading a newspaper, watching over his charge. 'I'm writing something to Bevin,' Churchill said, looking up over his glasses. 'You'll need to put it into code and get it over to London on that tappety tapping machine of yours.' He laughed at his own humor.

Up in his room Loughlin set up the Morse and contacted London. When he had sent Churchill's instructions to Bevin he added an extra line. 'I think we have a leak – can you run me a check on Amber Rose?'

He waited. The Morse started to beep and the reply came back. 'Confirm, will run check; listen out.'

Back in the library Churchill had been furnished with a large whisky and had lit up a cigar. 'What news on the Rialto?' he quipped, paraphrasing Shakespeare.

'All quiet on the Western Front,' Loughlin joked back.

'In that case I suggest you pour yourself a drink. Then tell me how the arrangements are coming on to get me back to dear old Blighty.'

'That Army Air Corps commander – what's his name, General Eaker – he's going to fly us back in one of their new long-range bombers.'

'Couldn't we just sail back in *Tenacious*? That would be easier wouldn't it?'

'What, and risk running into another German U-boat? I don't think so. We can get you down at Northolt in a fraction of the time and at nothing like the risk. Anyway we can't get anything sorted out till after the holiday weekend.'
'Probably just as well. I wouldn't dare upset our redoubtable hostess,' he joked. 'I understand we are to be included in the dinner, together with all the trimmings.' He laughed again at his own joke then took another mouthful of his whisky. Patience announced dinner would be in half an hour and they all went their ways to dress.

******

Tom stepped out of the hospital and onto the street outside. The summer was long gone; the fall was passing and the prospect of winter was out there on the horizon – he could feel it in the chill of the early morning air. It was almost a month since his abduction by Parkes and Cardy. Then his world had been certain and his future had been full of promise. Now things had changed; nothing was like it was. All he wanted to do was go hunting, just to try to feel the comfort of his old life again; but he would go hunting alone. Mike would shortly get married and no longer had the time; Tony had betrayed him and was no longer counted a friend. It would be a solitary hunt but the smoke-scented air of the coming winter had excited him and he wanted to go, to be out there in the wild where he could feel free of everything and spend some time thinking.

He had tried to gather his thoughts in the hospital but, in spite of the care and the visits, he never managed to free himself from the images of the basement. At night he dreamed he was still there and woke in the early hours, choking and thirsty, stretching out a hand in the dark, feeling for that battered enamel jug. Sometimes he felt the electricity running through his body and he would wake with a jolt, his heart accelerating till it made his head spin. In the woods, up in the Adirondacks, with his rifle he would feel safe – and that would make things better; that would heal him.

Mike came to meet him and drove him home. 'It's good to be out of that place and smell the fresh air again,' he said to Mike as they arrived in Union Avenue and pulled up in front of the house.

'I can understand it, but you won't have the police guard will you?'

'It's OK. Wheels will wake the dead if anyone gets near the house – I'll sleep with the Remington in my room. I'll be fine. Besides it's Thanksgiving tomorrow – need to be home.'

'I'll leave you here,' Mike said as he saw Martha coming down the steps towards them. 'They'll want to have you to themselves for a while. Look out for yourself.'

'Rely on it; catch up with you after the holiday.'

CHAPTER 27

Thanksgiving

Thanksgiving dinner was the sweetest he could remember. As a child it was that enchanted time just before Christmas when he looked forward to the tastes and the smells that had been saved up all through the year and were now suddenly to be let loose to invade his senses. But over the years that had slowly melted away; special treats taken for ordinary as the country grew in prosperity and the scarce became commonplace. On this Thanksgiving Day things had changed; it was as if he had been thrown back to the time of his childhood. Things he had taken for granted in other times now took on a new dimension. Nothing had tasted so good for a very long time; the simple turkey stuffing had become the most exotic flavor that had ever been put into his mouth. The roasted pumpkin was sublime. He now knew that when you have everything taken from you and all that remains is your life, and a desperate struggle for survival, it sharpens the senses. Deprivation brings awareness, a sense of what you have lost. A little suffering, he had read somewhere, is good for the soul – it brings a taste of sweetness and makes you value what you have in your life.

But too much hardship, endured for too long, makes you bitter and you may never find your way back. He began to understand how the battle for the Forest at Argonne had driven Holly to the edge of the abyss, to a place from which he might never have returned. He could see how the dog had brought him back.

The Friday following Thanksgiving is a public holiday; everyone down to a kid in first grade knows that; Tom had forgotten. The alarm clock at the side of his bed clanged out the reveille and he woke with a jerk, looked at the dial, started to get up and then realized what he was doing. He sat on the edge of his bed and looked at the scar on his thigh – the wound had closed well but the scar was now bigger and quite ugly where it had been torn open when he had run from Neumann in the hospital grounds.

He got up and put on a heavy woollen dressing gown. The house was cold and the fires had to be lit. In the kitchen Wheels was curled up tight in his new basket. At the sound of Tom opening the cast iron door to the kitchen stove he opened one eye and then he sat up. He gave a wide, open yawn, stood up, stretched and trotted over to where Tom was scraping out the previous day's cinders.

'You can keep your nose out of that,' he said, grabbing him by the muzzle and giving it a squeeze. Wheels jumped back and let out a little bark, then scratched at the floor. 'Okay, ya mutt,' Tom said in a hushed voice and, going through to the back of the house, opened the door to let Wheels out into the yard.

Standing on the back step in the crisp morning, with the air he breathed out condensing to vapour like a dragon's breath, it felt good to be alive. Carey still hurt but he knew he had to move on; the pain would go. Back in the house he made coffee. Upstairs he heard Martha stir and then her footsteps on the stairs.

'I've lit the stove and the water's heating,' he said, as she came into the kitchen. 'I'm going to get washed. I think I'll go to the auto lot and see if I can't find something. Do we have any news on the old Chrysler?'

'Yes,' Martha said, coming over to him and giving him a small hug. She stood back and admired him and thought very briefly about how she had so nearly lost him. Just to see him standing there made her so happy she thought she would break into pieces. 'We can collect it any time. Maybe you could walk down there and get it this morning?'

'Okay,' he said, picking up his coffee mug and heading for the upstairs bathroom. 'I'll do that.'

On the stairs he met Holly coming down, his grey hair all spiked and knotted and his face bristled with morning stubble. 'Morning, son,' he said cheerfully. 'Did you sleep good?'

'Like a dead man, Dad. Like a dead man.' Only after he got to the top of the stairs did it come to him what he had said and it made him think. How different things could have been if events had shifted just slightly, if just one little insignificant event had happened a second later or a minute sooner. If Neumann hadn't come down those basement steps when he did, or did so sooner or later. What if Parkes hadn't come back to free him? What if Carey's father had not intervened to persuade whoever it was he persuaded to intervene? The list could go on forever, he decided, so he put it all aside. It was enough to be alive, back home and surrounded by people he loved. For the moment that would do.

It took him twenty minutes to make the walk to the police pound. The Chrysler looked the same except now, like him, it bore the scars of its encounter. They had that in common – they'd both been shot at and survived. Inside it had the comforting familiar smell of wood and leather. At first when he hit the starter the engine barely turned; it groaned lazily under the strain – it had stood for a month and now the oil in it was thick and cold. He let the battery rest for a minute or two then tried again. Just when he was about to give up it jumped into life with a lurch that shook the whole vehicle; then it was running.

It was such a fine day he would take a drive out. Anywhere would do, he just wanted to feel the motion of the road and sense the speed – to see the panorama of the countryside slipping by in a kaleidoscope of images. First, though, he would go home and let them know what he was doing. Right now Martha needed to know everything. The spectre of the unknown haunted her; it lay in ambush for her every time Tom left the house. The need to kiss him good luck was even more important – she was sure she had missed it on the day he was taken.

It was lunch time when he got back. They sat at the kitchen table eating Martha's home cooked meatloaf and talking about the neighbors. Tom said he thought he ought to cut down the old apple trees and plant something new – perhaps one apple and one pear in their place. They could be cut into lumber and left to season over the winter; they'd burn well in the living room fireplace next spring. The conversation went to Mike's wedding and Martha wanted to know everything. 'I don't know that much about it, Ma,' he protested. So what he didn't know she guessed at, punctuating her conjecture with remarks like, 'Well, what do you think?' or, 'You would have thought, wouldn't you.'

'What about that girl of yours?' Martha said quite innocently as she started to clear away the dishes. 'Have you seen her since all this happened? Poor thing, she must have been beside herself.'

Tom brushed it away; there was no point in talking about it. 'Oh, that never really went anywhere,' he said, trying to sound casual about it. 'We split up a while back.'

After lunch he discreetly went to his room, collected the Remington and a box of shells and smuggled them out of the house and into the Chrysler. He didn't want Holly or Martha to see; she, in particular, would only worry. He had told neither of them about the encounter with Neumann at the hospital but he was sure he would be out there; he wasn't going to be caught unarmed and defenceless again.

Out on the road he felt a little draught coming through the holes in the door where it had been shot up. Force of habit found him heading south towards Croton and, although he had driven that route so many times before, this time it somehow seemed different – fresher – he was seeing things he hadn't noticed before and enjoying them more.

Around Montrose he passed the truck stop where he'd held over from the storm before they went to Champlain – before they got caught up with Neumann. He thought about going in but it brought back memories of Carey and the hopes he'd had, so he ignored it and drove on by. When he came to Croton it struck him that if he kept going he would end up at Dobbs Ferry and he had no appetite for that, so in a random moment he decided to go to Jennifer's Diner instead.

The girls waiting on the tables all looked at him as if he was an alien. He could almost hear what was running through their minds. It was Dolores who came over to see him. 'What'll it be?' she asked curtly.

'Coffee, please.'

'Dottie isn't here. She's off for the holiday weekend,' she said, as if it had some importance.

What the hell has that got to do with me, Tom thought. He didn't say anything and let it ride. Dolores came back with the coffee and put it on the table in front of him. 'She left you a message,' she added.

Tom looked puzzled. 'Why?'

'I don't know why, buster.' She dumped a sugar shaker onto the table. 'I don't know what she sees in you at all quite frankly.'

'I think you must have the wrong guy. I hardly know her.'

'Well, read yer message. She said to be sure to give it to you if you came in – so why not just read it, huh?' She turned and walked away.

He unfolded the paper and spread it out on the table top.

Dear Tom,

An Englishman came by here on Tuesday asking for you. It seems he read about you in the Westchester Post and said he would like to meet you. He didn't say why but if you want to talk about it before you do anything I will be away for the Thanksgiving holiday but back on the next Monday. Anyway he left the number below if you wanted to call him. He seemed like a nice enough person.

Dottie

Call 077312

PS. I hope you are recovered from your ordeal – I read about it in the newspaper; it must have been awful.

He sat looking at the note for a while then downed his coffee. He left a dime on the table and got up to go.

'Hey, you wanna leave any reply?' Dolores called after him.

'Yeah, just say thanks when you see her.'

'Can you get that,' she said to the other girls after he'd left. 'You know she's eating her heart out for him and the heel just ignores her – like he doesn't know it. How can he do that?'

Back in the Chrysler he sat behind the wheel and read the note again. There on the wall of the diner was the phone booth he'd used to call Dave Hanson. Last time he'd used it the world had fallen in on him. What if he called the number and it turned out to be a trap set up by Neumann. He thought on it for a while. He put his hand out and touched the Remington – if it was Neumann and he turned up the odds would be different this time. No one would blame Tom if he shot him and killed him; he would claim self defence and no reasonable person would disbelieve him. But the note said it was an Englishman so it couldn't be Neumann, unless he had a sidekick who was English.

In the end he figured it was best to know who it was and deal with it afterwards. He would do it – he would call the number. As he dialed it up the numbers looked familiar. He was about to put in the last digit when he realized it was the house phone at Brunessemer. 'Carey,' he found himself saying out loud. His heart jumped a beat as an adrenalin rush went through his brain, numbing it for a second. Then he regained control. It couldn't be her – the note said it was an Englishman. He dialed the last digit. The phone was answered by Vera the housekeeper.

'The Taylor residence. Who's calling please?'

'My name is Tom Jordan, I think you know me.'

'Yes, of course,' she replied enthusiastically, 'who doesn't. I'm afraid Miss Caroline isn't here at the moment. She's gone to the country club.'

'It's not miss Caroline I was after, but thank you. Do you have an Englishman staying at the house at the moment?'

'We have three and two English ladies. Who did you want to speak with?'

'I don't know. Somebody left me a message to call.'

'Hold on. I'll go and ask.'

He waited as the sound of receding footsteps echoed off the marble paved hallway, then the sound of distant muffled voices. More footsteps, louder this time and more than one person.

'I'll hand you over,' she said.

'Hello, is that Tom Jordan?'

'Who are you?'

'My name is Fred Loughlin. Look, I'm sorry to jump on you out of the blue like this. When I left the message at the diner I had no idea you were a friend of our hosts here.'

'Okay, but what do you want?'

'I would very much like to talk to you about Dr Josef Mueller.' Tom didn't much like the idea of going back to Dobbs Ferry and he said so, but Loughlin thought it was important for both of them that they meet.

It was late afternoon when he arrived and the sun was just setting. A mist was already rising in the countryside around them; at Brunessemer it was turning into a fog. A security guard stopped him as he came in but said he was expected and to park the car away from the front door because they needed a clear view of anyone who came or went.

Inside Irena threw herself on him like her own son. 'You ought to know Carey and I are through,' he said quietly. 'She dumped me.'

'I know,' Irena said airily, 'but never mind, you're my friend too, you know. You're welcome here any time.'

She thrust her arm through his and led him into the drawing room where Aly and a fresh-faced youngish man in his late twenties, perhaps early thirties, were sitting together on a sofa. At first sight he concluded this was her boyfriend because they were cuddled up so close to each other, their arms linked. The man stood up and languidly offered his hand to Tom. It was an effeminate handshake and Tom took it that the man was most likely gay, so probably not the boyfriend after all.

'Wendell Taylor,' he announced.

'My wayward son,' Irena butted in, proffering an open silver cigarette case to Tom. 'Have one of these, darling. I'm sure you need one after that tedious drive. You'll have to stay the night – there's going to be a ghastly pea souper.'

Wendell pulled a sarcastic face at his mother and let the remark pass. 'Charmed to meet you,' he said, eloquently adding, 'Mother dear, you are so irascible. She's best ignored at moments like this,' then went on, 'I've heard all about you – well who hasn't – but what a ghastly business, you poor boy.'

'Put a sock in it, Wendell,' Aly said, jumping up from the sofa and shoving him aside. 'Tom, dear Tom, so good to see you safe'. She stood on her tiptoes and put her arms round his neck, kissing him hard on the cheek with a smack that was audible. 'We thought you were done for,' she said, then whispered in his ear, 'sorry about Carey. I tried to warn you she was a bitch.'

'Right,' Irena snapped, 'that's enough of you two. Come along, Tommy boy, there're some grownups want to meet you. They're in the library.'

In the library Churchill, Loughlin and the others were sitting talking. Everybody stood up as Irena ushered Tom into their presence. Loughlin stepped forward. 'Hello, I'm Fred Loughlin. Let me introduce everyone.'

There was the usual round of handshaking, then Churchill suggested that perhaps it would be more entertaining for the ladies if they joined Irena while the men did a little talking. Clementine took the cue – she was used to men getting into some kind of *Boy's Own* huddle with Winston and plotting one intrigue or another. 'Come along, Mary,' she said brightly. 'Irena, you lead the way.'

'Good of you to come on a dirty night like this,' Churchill said.

'I'm glad I did – I've heard a lot about you, sir. You seem to have gone through a pretty rough ride from what I see in the newspapers.'

Churchill laughed, 'Then that would seem to make two of us, wouldn't you say.'

Outside the fog had come down and it was hard to see much more than a dozen paces ahead. Under the outside lamps it sparkled white and gold as the ice crystals suspended in it danced like tiny stars. Walter Thompson stood, looking out of the window, peering into the impenetrable night. 'I don't much like this. Anyone could be moving around out there and we'd never know it.'

The guards in the grounds decided they had the same problem. 'Has anyone secured the main gate?' one of them asked his colleague as they met in the driveway.

'Not sure,' said the other man, 'I'll take a look,' and disappeared into the white swirl of the fog.

Not long afterwards the first guard thought he heard someone call, or shout, he wasn't sure – it could have been a screech owl, but more muted. He called out to his colleague and waited. There was only silence – then he thought he heard footsteps in the gravel. He called again but there was nothing. He took a flashlight out of his pocket with his left hand, unholstered his gun with the other then called again, but there was still no response. The flashlight was next to useless as it bounced off the water vapour revealing nothing but a blank wall of white in front of him. His range of visibility was no more than ten yards.

Slowly he made his way to the front gate, keeping to the middle of the drive. Either side the trunks of the great trees that lined it loomed menacingly out of the dark. He thought he heard a movement; the sound of a twig cracked under foot. He stopped and listened; there it was again, this time more audible. He turned abruptly in the direction of the sound. He stood rigid, hardly breathing, listening for it again. 'Come out and show yourself!' he shouted. 'I'm armed.' There was still no answer. He moved cautiously to within a foot or two of the edge of the drive. There was someone there, he could feel it. Then he heard it, a low moaning sound. 'Come on!' he shouted, 'I know you're in there – come out with your hands high or I start shooting.'

Without warning, something came out of the fog almost face to face and lunged towards him. He stepped back and let out a shocked yelp of terror. In front of him the body of the other guard fell heavily to the ground, a large steel needle protruding from his throat just below the jaw; the other end was embedded deep within his brain.

He stood rigid with horror for a moment then fired his gun three times in the air. 'Man down at the main gate!' he shouted, and kept repeating it until he thought his lungs would burst.

In the house they heard the shots and the muffled sound of shouts. Walter Thompson and Loughlin immediately reached for their own guns. 'Walter, you stay here and guard Mr Churchill. I'll find the ladies and bring them in here, then I need to find out what's going on outside. I don't suppose you have a gun do you?' he said, looking at Tom.

'I do. It's in my car round the back of the house; I'll get it.'

'Keep your eyes open. We don't know what's happening out there.'

In the hall he almost ran into Aly and Wendell coming out of the drawing room. Loughlin was right behind him, brandishing his .32 automatic. 'Tom, what's happening?' Aly asked, sounding panicky. 'I heard shooting.'

'Stay inside,' Loughlin ordered. 'There's someone out there.'

Wendell shrugged vampishly. 'I wouldn't dream of it, that fog would ruin my hair. Besides I'm sure you big boys will deal with it.'

353

Tom made for the front door. 'Not that way,' Loughlin shouted, 'if there is anyone out there you'll be a sitting duck in that doorway. Go through the kitchen.'

'Which way is that?'

'Come on,' Aly offered. 'I'll show you. It's quite exciting, isn't it?'

'Not if I get killed, it isn't', Wendell taunted her, camply clutching his hands across his heart. 'The excitement is all too much for a frail person like me.'

Irena appeared in the hall to find out what was going on. 'I'd better get the staff together,' she said. 'They'll be safer if they stay with Vera till this panic is over – whatever it is.'

The kitchen let onto a utility room and then an outside tradesman's alley with a gate shutting off the end. Tom opened the gate and peered out into the night. He could just make out the shape of the Chrysler, squat and square. 'Stay here,' he told Aly. 'Once I've got to the car go back into the kitchen, but don't bolt this gate. Lock the kitchen door, then open the window, tuck the key in under the ledge, then shut it again and get back to the others. Is that clear?'

'Yes, but what about you?'

'I want to take a look around.'

'Be careful,' she said and squeezed his arm.

'I always am.'

'I know, but be especially careful. You may run into somebody out there.'

'I know and I hope it's Mueller, because if it is I'm gonna shoot the bastard.'

He made it the short distance to the Chrysler, took the Remington off the passenger seat and stuffed his pocket with a handful of shells. Armed, he moved slowly into the fog, stood still and listened. He felt calm out in amongst the trees and the silence – it was like hunting. It was his environment – he felt at home. Gently he stalked the sounds of the night. The first trail led him to where the dead guard lay flat on the ground on his back with his mouth open in a grotesque last gasp; his eyes stared blankly into the fog. Three of his colleagues stood around him, one crouched down was examining the long needle stuck in his throat. 'Poor bastard,' he was saying to the other two, 'that's one hell of a nasty way to go.'

They all jumped up defensively as they became aware of Tom standing quietly beside them. He held up his hands to show he was friendly. 'I've come down from the house. We heard the gunshots.'

'He's OK,' one of them said. 'I let him in earlier.'

'What happened?'

'Somebody's got in. They killed Eddie here; we're going to comb the grounds but we're sticking in sight of each other. We don't want to end up like that – Jesus, what a way to go. That's a useful looking piece you've got there,' he said, motioning towards the Remington, 'd'ya wanna join us?'

Tom shook his head. 'No, but I think I'll take a look around on my own. You go on ahead and if I see anything I'll holler. I know how jumpy everyone is but try not to shoot me if our paths cross.' He stood and watched them until they disappeared, enveloped by the fog.

Alone, he listened to the silence, trying to pick up the tell-tale traces of movement. When it came, it wasn't the crack of a twig or an involuntary cough but the sound of glass breaking. Not a smashing and tinkling sound, but a discrete crack, muffled by a glued sheet of brown paper stuck onto a window. As stealthily as he would have tracked a buck he made his way back to the house, sticking to the soft ground and avoiding the gravel. Reaching the house he stayed back in the shadows, avoiding the shafts of light that spilled out between the gaps in the drapes. Carefully he started to make a circuit of the building until he found the broken window. It let onto the housekeeper's pantry and someone had climbed in. It was too high for Mueller to climb through, he concluded, so if he was the assailant then he had someone with him – maybe more than one, in which case Neumann was probably there as well. At least one of them must be in the house.

He needed to find the open door and that would tell him where they were. Brunessemer had doors right round it so he set out again to look. A few yards on from the broken window he found it; the door led into the office where Vera did all the household accounts. There was one small diamond pane set into the door and there was a light on inside. He stood stock still and listened; everything was still and silent. If this was how they got in, would this be the way they were planning to get out? Neumann and Mueller were professionals; they wouldn't have left their backs unguarded – they must have posted a man to watch the escape route. He grabbed a look through the diamond pane into the office.

There was a figure standing on the far side of the small room close by the door. To his right, sitting huddled together on the floor, he could see the housekeeper and the maids, Patience and Constance. He thought about rushing the man but if the women screamed or he got off a shot it would give everything away. He moved on round the side of the house till he came once more to the tradesman's alley, lifted the latch and slipped inside, drawing the bolt behind him. He found the key Aly had left on the ledge and gently put it into the lock. Slowly he turned it, wincing as it finally clicked and withdrew the bolt. Inside he locked the door again and made his way to where the corridor linked through to the front hall. He could hear the sound of voices coming from the library. He moved softly across the hall and stood by the library door, his back pressed against the wall.

The door wasn't fully closed and he could hear the distinct sound of at least one of the intruders; there was no mistaking it belonged to Mueller. He stood there not sure of his next move. He couldn't work out how many there were but he judged at least two, maybe three, and they were all talking in what he thought was German. Occasionally Mueller broke into English and when he did it was very clear they were going to take Churchill with them. He edged closer to the gap in the door; through it he could see Churchill; they had him on an ambulance stretcher and he seemed to be out cold. Mueller started to issue instructions but it was all in German and he had no idea what was being said. Then he broke into English, addressing the others in the room. 'Right, we shall go with your Mr Churchill, so say your goodbyes. Just be happy I have let you live.'

'Christ', he said under his breath, 'they're coming out.' He moved back towards the kitchen corridor. He knew he had to act but he needed space. If he could get out into the grounds he could easily ambush them; pick them off if he had to.

He stood outside the housekeeper's office then, taking a deep breath, he tapped on the door. The door opened and a man stuck his head out. Tom hit him as hard as he could with the butt of the Remington; he dropped like a sack. Constance let out a short scream but the others kept their calm as Tom with a finger over his lips gave a little shush. He pushed the body of the unconscious man into the office and shut the door. 'Help me,' he said to the three women, his voice charged with urgency, 'we have to get him out of here – now!' Outside they carried the body as far as they dared and dumped it in the bushes.

'Right. Now you ladies need to get out of here because when they come through that door I don't want you in the firing line. Go round to the kitchen, you'll find my car out back. It's not locked – just get in, keep your heads down and stay there until I come for you. Now go.'

He stood for a moment until they had been swallowed by the fog then stepped back far enough so that he could just see the light coming through the little window of the office door. He would wait there on the margin of the fog until they had all emerged and he could see how many they were.

Mueller was first through the door. He stood there waving a large flash light around him. A man came over the threshold at the front end of the stretcher then the other was clear; then a fourth person emerged. None of them was Neumann.

He waited for the last man to clear the door, brought the Remington up to his shoulder and stepped forward a pace so that he could be seen. 'Okay,' he shouted, 'that's as far as you go tonight gentlemen.'

Mueller turned the flashlight in his direction.

'Drop it – or you're a dead man.'

The party stood frozen like statues in a park.

'Put the stretcher down guys and do it slowly.'

He took another pace forward. Seeing who it was Mueller laughed. 'Herr Jordan,' he said mockingly, 'I'm surprised to see you still alive – but not for long I think. What have you done with Andreas?'

'Is that his name? I think he's going to need to see a dentist when this is over. Where's Neumann?'

Mueller said nothing. An ugly little smile crept across his face. 'Ah yes, the impetuous Heinrich. No, he isn't here I'm afraid – he had business elsewhere.'

From behind him Tom sensed a movement. He half turned his head and the bloody face of Andreas leered at him, a look of hatred and revenge coming through his shattered teeth. He had a rock in his hand. He brought it down hard, swinging it at Tom's head but he missed and instead caught him a glancing blow on the shoulder. Tom rammed the butt of the rifle into the other man's groin and there was a loud bang as the Remington loosed a shot in the struggle. Andreas fell with a groan. The two men carrying the stretcher dropped it and ran into the grounds. Meuller stood for a moment and pulled a Luger from his pocket but it snagged on his coat and he dropped it. He made it into the obscurity of the fog as Tom let rip with four shots into the dark. The fourth man in the party now bolted back into the house.

For a moment Tom hesitated, not knowing whether to chase after Mueller or go back and help the others. In that split second he thought of Aly and the others and decided they needed him more. He hopped over the stretcher with the drugged Churchill still on it and ran into the house. Tom caught up with the fourth man in the hallway. As the fugitive turned with a pistol in his hand and leveled it at him, Tom put a round straight through his kneecap. The force knocked him over and the gun clattered to the floor. Scooping it up he left the man writhing in agony, smearing bright red blood across the marble tiles.

Inside he found Clementine and the women tied together with electrical wire. Loughlin and Thompson were gagged and chained to the radiators. Loughlin had a nasty looking gash up in the hairline and was struggling to keep conscious.

'Quickly,' Thompson said, 'they've got Churchill.'

'It's all right,' Tom replied, 'he's out back – I think he's OK. Mueller got away but we've got two of them.'

A shout came from the corridor leading to Vera's office. One of the guards appeared, gun in hand and looking nervous; he recognized Tom and relaxed. 'We got two out back', he said, looking around at the chaos.

'Is he OK?' He pointed at the man with the shot out knee who had now propped himself up against the wall and sat holding the wound with cupped hands groaning with the pain.

'Shouldn't think so,' Tom replied casually as he cut the wire binding the women and set them free. 'Go back to the man on the stretcher and guard him.

357

I'll be out in a minute – and watch out for the one lying in the shrubbery; he's hurt but he sure isn't out of the game.'

Thompson and Loughlin presented a more difficult problem. They were cuffed and chained round the cast iron radiator and there was no sign of the key. The man in the hall looked sullen and grunted truculently in German. Tom looked down, making signs with his hands that he was looking for the key. The German said nothing. Tom tapped him lightly on the leg with the barrel of his rifle and the man howled in pain. Then he shouted what Tom guessed was a mouthful of abuse at him. 'He says the one you downed outside has got it,' Loughlin shouted from the library.

As he turned to go Aly appeared at the top of the stairs. She looked right and left then started to descend. 'Is it alright to come down?' she called to Tom. 'Wendell and I hid in my bedroom. Wendell's still in the wardrobe – he says he's not coming out till people stop shooting.' She reached the bottom of the stairs. 'What happened?' she gasped as she saw the wounded German and the blood smears all over the hall floor.

'It's OK,' he said, 'your mother needs some help with the others in there.'

A quick search of Andreas found the keys to the cuffs. Churchill was still out of it but his breathing was steady. The other two guards turned up. 'We think they've gone,' one of them said. Tom thought he looked relieved. 'We heard a car leaving and it sounded like it was in kind of a hurry. What d'ya wan 'us to do now?'

Tom looked up at the sky. The fog was clearing and he could see the stars. 'I don't think they'll come back. One of you stay here and keep an eye on this hoodlum.'

They dragged the half conscious Andreas into Vera's office, then carted Churchill back inside. 'Take him upstairs,' Irena instructed, 'and get him into bed. I've called Dr Matthews and he's on his way.'

In the library Aly was trying to clean up the wound on Loughlin's head. Thompson sat patiently and waited to be released; the keys fitted. 'You'd better go and sit with Mr Churchill,' Tom said. 'It'd be embarrassing if they came back and took him while we were all messing about down here.'

Thompson stood there looking around. 'I don't have my revolver – they took it. I don't know what they did with it.'

'Here, take this. I got it from the thug out there in the hall,' Tom said, handing him a Luger pistol. 'I'm going to get the maids and Vera. They're hiding in my car.'

Outside an ambulance drew up and a man with a doctor's bag got out and made his way up the steps to where one of the guards had now been posted. 'I'm a doctor,' he said politely. 'I believe there is an injured man inside'. The guard rang the doorbell.

When they heard the doorbell everyone froze. Aly looked up anxiously from where she was still tending to Loughlin. Only Irena was unfazed by the sudden interruption. She left Clementine where they had been trying to comfort Mary Shearburn. 'It'll be the doctor,' Irena said, getting to her feet. The German in the hall was rocking slowly from side to side, letting out a low moaning sound, trying to ease his pain.

The guard stood back and as he did so felt a stabbing pain in the throat. He looked down and in that last second of consciousness saw the steel needle being pushed upwards as it went through his soft palate and on up piercing the base of his brain; it thrust deep into the skull. He was dead. Another man emerged from the car and ran up the steps.

Irena opened the door – it wasn't Dr Matthews. For a moment she stood inert; it wasn't what she had so confidently expected to see. Mueller stepped across the threshold, roughly grabbing Irena and pulling her round to cover him. She caught a glimpse of her security guard lying prostrate on the steps and let out a short involuntary scream.

Aly ran out of the library but stopped dead and froze when she saw Mueller. He now had a gun pushed into Irena's neck. In the same instant the guard who had been holding Andreas walked out of the kitchen corridor into the hall. Mueller lifted the gun from Irena's neck and felled him with a single shot.

Walter Thompson came out onto the landing. The other man with Mueller had already started to climb the stairs as Thompson appeared and now had a gun trained on him. There was a stalemate but it didn't last.

'Put the gun down,' Mueller called out calmly, 'or this lady will not see the daylight again.'

Loughlin came to the library door, still having difficulty standing. 'You'd best do it, Walter.'

'Very good,' Mueller said, his voice laced with an evil laconic satisfaction, drawing out the last syllable of the words. 'Now we are hearing the talk of sensible men. Hans, take his gun and find Andreas. We have to get Herr Churchill back on his stretcher again. We can't keep his ambulance waiting. Now, everybody else back into the room. We have to lock you all up again; but this time there will be no release.'

Hans returned with Andreas. He was limping from the hit in the groin and his mouth was encrusted with dry blood; several teeth were missing and he was in a mood for revenge. He looked at the others in the library but couldn't see what he wanted. 'Where is the other one,' he shouted angrily at Loughlin, 'the one with the rifle?'

Loughlin shook his head. 'Too late. He left when the fog cleared.'

Andreas shoved his face up against Loughlin's and spat hard. 'You liar!' he screamed, then slapped his face so hard Loughlin collapsed.

'You lousy pig!' Aly shouted, and moved to stand between the German and Loughlin. Andreas responded by shoving her in the chest, sending her staggering backwards till she tripped and fell.

Mueller looked quizzically at Loughlin, who was struggling to regain his feet. 'He has a very good point you know,' he said quite calmly, 'where is the resourceful Herr Jordan?'

'I told you,' Loughlin repeated, 'he left, he's gone home. He's probably half way there by now – tipping off the FBI.'

Meuller smiled benignly. 'Perhaps it is so,' he almost sang the words, all the time mocking his victims, 'but I am sure we shall eventually find him and then Andreas can have his revenge.' For a moment he relaxed his grip on Irena.

Feeling the bond loosen, she made a move and jerked herself free. Mueller seemed unconcerned and she turned and slapped his face. Mueller took a step back and fired a shot into the floor between her feet. The bullet chipped the marble and whined as it ricocheted across the hall. Irena stood very still. Andreas looked at her white drawn face and laughed with pleasure at her fear.

'The next time, dear lady, I shall lift the sights a little higher and you will experience something far more unpleasant than the fear you now feel. Please stand close to me and do not do that again. Is that clear?' Irena made little nodding movements. Her top lip was quivering and for the first time in a long time she no longer felt in control – it terrified her.

They got Churchill downstairs. He was conscious but too feeble to walk. Hans and Walter carried him down on the stretcher and put him in the waiting ambulance. Everyone was corralled in the library; once again they were bound and shackled. Hans brought in a small suitcase, which he opened to display some wires and an alarm clock. Loughlin knew immediately it was a bomb.

'So mein fruende,' Meuller said coldly, 'it is time for us to say farewell. I shall keep this dear lady with me', he said, pointing to Irena, 'just in case Herr Jordan is out there. A little insurance you could say. You, of course, will know nothing about it since you will all now go to meet your god – or oblivion, whichever suits you. *Gute Nacht*. He grabbed hold of Irena by the wrist and pulled her in the direction of the front door. 'Hans, take her and keep your gun on her head so, if he is out there, Herr Jordan can see what will happen. Our intention should be clear.'

In the corner the man with the smashed knee tried to get up but fell back with a cry of pain. He put out a hand for help. 'So sorry, Gerhardt,' Mueller said, 'but it's not practical to take you with us. Besides what kind of life would you have as a cripple – and if you are caught here you will give us away.'

The German shook his head and put out his arm again for help. 'So sorry,' Mueller said and, putting his gun to Gerhardt's head, fired a single shot.

In the garden at the back of the house Tom was getting the women out of the Chrysler when he heard a crack; it was the sound of a small calibre pistol. He held up a hand for silence and stood stock still. He waited for a few minutes, all the time looking at the three women now cowering behind him. In the stillness of the night air he heard the unmistakable sound of someone walking very slowly in his direction.

'Back in the car,' he whispered to Vera. 'Take them with you and for God's sake keep them quiet.'

The path he was on led to the kitchen and, whoever it was, they were coming from that direction. A second shot cracked and this time it clearly came from inside the house. Something was not right. He moved off the path and stood close to the camouflage of a big maple tree. The night sky was now clear and his eyes had become accustomed to the low level of light. Then he saw the moon shadow of the approaching figure. In a single move Tom stepped out into the path and raised his rifle; there was a metallic click, clack, as he cocked the weapon ready to fire.

'Don't shoot me,' a voice said urgently in a hushed whisper, 'it's me – Wendell.'

Tom lowered the rifle. 'Jesus man, I damn near shot you. What's going on?'

'They're back. They've got Mother – and the Englishman – Mr Churchill. I came down the servants' stairs at the back. I saw that sadistic old man shoot one of his gang. He is one creepy pathological bastard.'

'Shush.' They stood and waited, all the while listening. Nothing. 'I need to get upstairs,' Tom said urgently. 'Can we do it from here or are we shut out?'

Wendell jerked his head in the direction of the kitchen. 'Come on.'

'Where to?' Wendell asked under his breath once they were inside.

'I need a clear shot from an upstairs window. I need to be looking down on them.'

'That'll be Carey's room.' For a single irrational instant he baulked at the idea of going back into her room, but it was no more than a silly thought and he let it go,

'I'm going to ask you do something for me,' Tom said, looking at Wendell hard and wondering if what he was about to ask was a step too far.

'Go on.'

'It'll be incredibly risky,'

'I'm listening.'

They stood by the window and looked down onto the drive to where the ambulance waited.

'In a moment they'll come out and down the front steps to that ambulance. There's three of them and I have to take them all out before any of them can shoot your mother. That's three rounds rapid and every one has to be a clean shot. I need a diversion – I'm afraid that has to be you.'

Wendell said nothing for a second or two, then he just shrugged. 'I suppose one has to sacrifice for one's mother,' he said flippantly. 'What do I do?'

'Simple really. You get back down there as quick as you can. Go round the house and wait by the corner nearest to where my car is sitting. You'll be able to see them from there. When they're halfway from the steps to the ambulance I need you to walk right out into plain site and shout at them.'

Wendell pulled a silly face. 'Shit, darling,' he said. 'That isn't risky, that's positively suicidal.'

'Can you do it?'

'I'll try.'

'Okay, let's go.'

With Wendell gone he opened the window. The long drape curtain was going to be an obstacle. He tried to tie it back but in the end he had to get rid of it. He grabbed a handful of the material and with a sharp jerk ripped it off the rail. He would need room to move around if he was to get all three. There was a pool of light flooding the front drive; at least he would have a clear view. He waited, trying to still his heart beat to give him the best chance of hitting his targets. As he slowly breathed in and out to lower his pulse he caught the distinct smell of her perfume; it was almost as if she was in the room with him. Then it came to him that he had chosen the very window he had stood at naked, that morning after they had first made love. What a long time ago it all seemed now as he stood poised at the same window about to kill three men.

Out in the night air a frost was beginning to settle and the steps were becoming slippery. Carefully Mueller and the others made their way down them and then cautiously moved towards the ambulance. There was no sign of anyone.

As Tom looked down from above, he could see that they all had weapons drawn. He would have to get Hans with his first shot to save Irena. After that he thought Meuller was more dangerous; Andreas was hurt and probably wouldn't react as quickly. He quietly prayed none of them would put a shot into Wendell.

The moment had arrived but there was no Wendell. They were perfectly aligned. There was nothing for it – he had to take the shots. As he pulled the Remington up to his shoulder there was a shout. 'You bastards! Put my mother down!' A rock came hurtling through the air, landing with a thump on Mueller's shoulder.

There were three loud bangs. Hans fell back with a jerk, loosing Irena and falling down behind her. The shot had hit him square in the forehead. Mueller flinched as the rock hit him and the shot creased his cheek; he ran. Tom was right about Andreas. He was the slowest, and in that the German was lucky because the shot was off target and although it hit him it only smashed his shoulder, spinning him round and throwing him down onto his face in the gravel.

For a moment there was the purest silence. Then, in the distance, he heard the sound of a police siren. Irena was standing in between the two bodies, shaking and crying uncontrollably. It was then he looked over to where Wendell had been and saw him lying lifeless on the ground.

He came downstairs once more and crossed the hall where the unfortunate Gerhardt lay dead. As he came out onto the top step he saw Irena. She was still crying, but he was surprised to see she was being comforted by Wendell.

He went over and prodded the corpse. There was no doubt about Hans; it had gone straight through his head; he wasn't going to be doing any more breathing. There was a Luger pistol lying next to Andreas; Tom kicked it far away into the shrubbery. Mueller was nowhere to be seen; he had disappeared into the night.

'I thought they'd got you for a moment,' Tom said, patting Wendell on the shoulder and sounding relieved.

'God, no darling. I just did my bit and took a dive. It was all up to you after that.'

No fewer than three cars arrived, with sirens blaring and lights flashing. Shortly behind them an unmarked black Hudson rolled in. Jones and Polanski got out, together with a third man, and went over to where Tom still stood looking at the bodies, wondering how it had all happened.

'My God!' Jones exclaimed in his languid southern accent. 'What *has* been going on here? You look like you've been having yourselves a war.'

'There's two more up here,' Polanski called from the top of the stairs.

A police officer came out of the house, stood on the top step and shouted in the direction of Tom. 'Captain, we got a whole bunch of people trussed up in here – and a bomb. We need to do something real quick.'

The third man left them and headed for the house. 'Okay,' he said, looking around at the nervous faces, all transfixed by the open suitcase. 'Let's see what we can do about this.'

Jones looked around him at the carnage. 'You nailed them good, son. That saves us a job. Of course, you'll have to explain how come we got so many dead bodies around here but, hell, I'm sure there's a good explanation.'

Tom shook his head slowly in sad disbelief. 'Are you planning to arrest me?'

'Well, strictly speaking, we should be taking you into the local station for some questions – but – given we already know most of the answers, I think we could leave it there. You will have to come and talk to the coroner some time though, but that can wait a day or two.'

'Where's Neumann?'

'No one knows. He disappeared up into the North. We think he's in Canada.'

363

'So I can't relax.'

Jones smiled. 'You can't relax. He's madder than a snake in a jar – but we'll be looking out for you.'

'That's what worries me.'

'What the hell is that noise?' Jones said, looking around him. There was a banging coming from the back of the ambulance.

'Christ,' Tom said under his breath, 'Mr Churchill.'

They opened the tailgate of the ambulance. Churchill stepped out and glanced around at the bodies. Flashbulbs were popping as the police now started to photograph the dead. 'I see I missed some excitement,' Churchill observed dryly.

Clementine came down the steps, followed by Aly and Thompson. She came over to Tom to thank him. 'Winston,' she said in a soft voice, 'I think we owe Mr Jordan a debt of gratitude.'

'We do indeed,' Churchill replied. 'You are a most exceptional young man, sir, and I both thank you and congratulate you.' Tom looked slightly embarrassed and mumbled his thanks.

'I need a favor,' he told Jones as they made their way into the house.

'Go on.'

'I need someone to go round to my parents and let them know I'm OK. They were expecting me home this afternoon and after the way things have been for a week or so back they'll be worrying. They don't have a phone.'

'It's done,' Jones said, laughing. 'Lord, I thought for a moment there you were going to ask for something tough – you know – like a beer or Neumann's head on a platter.'

'Whose is the black Ford sedan?' Jones asked, as things started to get back to normal.

'Mine,' Loughlin admitted. 'Why?'

'Where did you purchase it, sir?'

'Oh, over in Croton,' he lied. 'A contact supplied it'.

'Well, it's got phoney plates on it; probably stolen. I guess you'll be walking for a while.'

******

It took three hours and several vehicles to get the bodies away. During the clean-up they found a pair of Canadian plates in the cab of the ambulance. An officer handed them to Jones. 'Looks like they were planning to cross the border,' Jones observed casually. 'Seems like everything points north.'

The house was finally back to normal, but it was far from quiet. As soon as the police left Irena went straight to the cocktail cabinet. 'Come on,' she announced generally, 'we need a stiff drink. Vera, get Constance to mop the hall floor will you – it's beginning to smell – and why's the kitchen sink full of water with that thing in it?'

'That's the bomb,' Vera replied in a matter-of-fact tone. 'They say it's safe and they'll take it away shortly.'

'Well, I wish they would make it soon. It's most inconvenient to have a bomb in the kitchen.'

She insisted that they should get back to a normal routine as soon as possible because it wasn't good to dwell on excitement for too long. 'It is too late for dinner,' she announced, 'but Mrs Martins will put together some cold cuts and we can sit at the table like civilized people.'

When, a little later, the doorbell rang, everyone in the house froze but it was only Dr Matthews who had been on a house call earlier and finally got Irena's message. He cleaned up Loughlin's wound and said it didn't need sutures. He also administered a sedative to Mary Shearburn who he then ordered to bed.

'What actually happened here?' he asked as Tom escorted him to the door.

'Oh, nothing really. There was an intrusion and Mr Loughlin got hit on the head, but the police came and sorted it out.'

'Ah,' he said, 'that explains the patrol car at the end of the drive. They stopped me on the way in and wanted to know my business. Good to know they're doing their job.'

After supper Tom sat outside on the top step in the chill night air and looked at the stars. It had been one hell of a day. He had killed a man but he didn't feel anything – neither good nor bad. As he thought on it he supposed that must be how it was in a war: you killed the enemy not because you hated them but because if you didn't then they would kill you. The action was driven by fear and the instinct for self-preservation. If he felt anything at all it was the nagging thought that Mueller was still out there, still part of the equation; and Neumann, he was still out there too and that worried him.

Aly and Wendell came out and sat down next to him, one each side on the cold stone step. Aly put an arm around his shoulders. They sat there, looking up at the stars, their breath condensing like puffs of cigarette smoke, the crooked shapes of the trees silhouetted against the moonlight, giant and ghostly. Nobody spoke. They just sat there in the great still void of their individual contemplation.

Eventually Wendell broke the spell. 'You know, you're now the great hero of the hour, don't you? Imagine what my friends will say in Philly when I tell them I was there – that I know you.'

Tom didn't say anything in reply – just a small dismissive, 'Huh.'

After another spell of silence he nudged Wendell with his elbow. 'Actually, you were the goddamned hero,' he said, smiling and nodding approval. 'You stuck your neck out – that took nerve. All I did was shoot at a couple people. There are hoods out there who do that every day.'

'Yes, but I think that's pretty difficult for ordinary people like us,' Aly told him. 'Can you cope with it, do you think?'

'I think – probably better than I will with Carey. It was a really bad sensation standing in her room, smelling her presence and knowing I was about to kill someone – maybe more than one.'

'You shouldn't fret on her account,' Wendell told him. 'My dear sister isn't worth it. Carey is for Carey – she always has been, always will be.'

'Wendell's right,' Aly said, taking her arm from around his shoulder and turning to look at him head on. 'She's too hardnosed to get cut up over.'

'I just think she had it rough as a child; she told me about her childhood.'

Wendell looked knowingly at Aly. 'Well, I wouldn't get carried off too far on that one.' Aly said nothing but looked skywards, an expression of near exasperation on her face. She took in a deep breath, followed by a long and slowly exhaled contemptuous sigh.

'I think I'd better get going,' Tom eventually said.

'You could stay the night,' Aly said softly. 'I know Mother would feel more secure with you in the house.'

Tom let go a little sardonic laugh. 'I'm like jam to wasps right now. She'll be safer without me here than with. Besides, Fred and Walter are there and I hear there's a cop car just down the road. I'll come by tomorrow and maybe we could talk some more about Carey. It might help me deal with it a little better.'

It was past one in the morning by the time he got back to Peekskill. The subdued lights lining Union Avenue washed everything in a plaintive yellow. In the house there was a light showing in the front room; Martha had been sitting up waiting for him. When she heard the Chrysler hit the driveway a weight lifted from her heart, and when she heard the key in the latch her mood turned instantly from anxiousness to a comforting serenity.

'Sorry it's so late, Ma,' he said, folding his arms round her.

'That's all right; I told your father to go on to bed and I'd sit up for you.' Wheels trotted in from the kitchen and licked his hand.

He went to his room and dropped on the bed. It had been a nerve-wrenching day and he was all done in. A few minutes later he dragged himself to the bathroom where he fought to stay awake. While he washed he looked in the mirror; the face that stared back at him was drawn with shadows under the eyes – it looked older than it should. When his head finally hit the pillow he was gone in an instant, falling down into the dark velvet abyss of a deep sleep.

CHAPTER 28

Moments of Truth

Loughlin was back on the Morse to London; Churchill had to be moved. After the near kidnapping the day before he couldn't take any further chances. Tapping out his call sign, he waited. He'd had no contact with London since the attack; now he needed to let them know and get instructions. His mind was blazing with the events of the night. How had Mueller found them so easily, and what the hell was Amber Rose up to dumping a stolen car on him? Things were wrong; there was a leak somewhere. He had to find out where and plug it. Tom Jordan had left before he'd had a chance to talk about Mueller. He sat and waited for the Morse to start bleeping. The lump on his head was throbbing. Aly came into the room to take a look at the wound. She had arbitrarily taken charge of his care, a self-elected nurse – she ran to his every need. Now she was insisting on him getting rest as if she had some kind of stake in his wellbeing. Loughlin was flattered by the attention, but he had no time for this. He needed answers, not nursing.

'Don't get too involved,' Irena warned her daughter after she noticed the signs of infatuation. 'He'll be gone in a few days and I don't want you pining around the house like some love-struck schoolgirl. Besides, his life is not a good recipe for a husband. He's up to his ears in risk and heaven knows what danger.'

'Mother', Aly protested, 'don't move so fast – you'll trip over yourself.'

'My dear girl, I've seen that look before and I know where it leads. Finish your education first and then find a nice, steady, young man with prospects. Preferably a college graduate with a career in law – or something like that.'

Aly threw up her arms in exasperation. What was it with mothers that they forgot their own passions of youth so easily? Irena ignored the gesture. 'I'm going to take Clementine to Bloomingdales to do a little shopping. I need to do something to relieve the tension. Do you want to come with us? We can get some lunch somewhere nice.'

'No,' Aly shook her head. 'Tom's coming over some time. He wants to talk about Carey – poor fish. Where is Carey anyway?'

Irena waved it away. She had put up with Carey's whims since she had been a teenager and the latest adventure had gone too far. 'She's with that Italian from New York. Moved in with him for all I know. Your father won't be happy.'

'Shouldn't think he'll care.'

******

The invitation arrived for Mike's wedding. The postman handed it to him as he prepared to leave that morning for Dobbs Ferry. At first he thought he wouldn't go. He was sure Tony would be there and he really didn't want to meet him. It would be embarrassing because he knew they no longer had anything to say to each other; it had all been said and there was no way back. When a man steals from a friend it is a sad and desperate business; when the friend is down and defenceless it is irredeemable. There could be no redemption. But, as he drove down the highway, he began to change his mind. What did it matter anyway? Not after the events of yesterday. He'd killed a man. He'd taken a life and it appalled him that he felt no remorse. Yes, they would have killed him if they could, and they had planned to kill everyone at Brunessemer, blowing them to pieces with a bomb. Yes, they would have shot Irena and dumped her body somewhere, and yes they got what they had coming – only Mueller had escaped. But he, the executioner, should feel something, but he didn't and that preoccupied him – it nagged away at his brain.

When he escaped from the basement he could have killed Neumann. Just one blow with that improvised hammer would have done it, but he hadn't. Then he couldn't do it, his instincts somehow stopped him, wouldn't let him. Now, looking back, he wondered why. What had changed in him? Against that, the idea of meeting Tony at a wedding became meaningless. Tony had become inconsequential. He had shrunk, no longer larger than life, just another ordinary man; a frail human who had been hiding behind a myth. There is no Superman – everyone is vulnerable. It didn't matter anymore; nothing seemed to matter that much any longer. Was that, he wondered, what had happened to Holly, years back, at the Argonne Forest. He thought of Carey – that at least was normal. It still hurt, though not quite so much.

******

Martins drove Irena and Clementine out through the main gates. As they turned onto the road outside they came close to colliding with another car coming in. 'I know that car,' Irena observed. 'It's Carey and her Italian. I'm glad we got away before they arrived. I'm sure I would have been perfectly uncivil to him. I despair of that girl.'

'Children can be so difficult, even when they grow up. Of course, with the boys it doesn't matter. Winston has never grown up, but that's the male of the

368

species and they don't do much damage – other than starting wars. Girls are different – they can get into such emotional tangles.'

'Have you been to Bloomingdales before?' Irena asked, changing the subject.

'No, but I've heard about it.'

'Oh, you're in for a treat then.'

'I told Winston I was worried about leaving him this morning, after all that fuss last night, but he said he'd got his two bodyguards and would be fine. He then said he was more worried about how much money I would spend shopping. Can you believe that?'

'Men,' Irena said, laughing.

Aly saw the Cord from Loughlin's room where she had been sitting with him watching him operate the Morse. Oh God, she thought to herself, here comes trouble. 'It's my sister,' she told him. 'Have you met her? I can't remember.' She got up and went out to go down to the hall.

'No,' he called after her, 'and I'd prefer not – if you don't mind.'

'Suits me.'

They came in hand in hand, laughing together and looking the perfect image of lovers. Wendell had seen them arrive and he now appeared at the top of the stairs. 'Don't go into the Library,' Aly called to them as she trotted down the stairs. 'We've got guests in there. Use the drawing room. We weren't expecting you. Tom is coming over – it would be good if you weren't here when he arrives.'

'Well, little sister, you needn't worry. I'm only here to collect a few things then we're off. Hello Wendell,' she said dismissively, seeing her brother leaning over the landing bannister rail. 'You still here? I thought you would have scampered back to your precious chums by now.'

'Ooh, so bitter,' Wendell retorted.

She tugged on Tony's arm. 'Come on, darling, you can give me a hand. I won't need much – just a few rags. Isn't he just divine?' she grinned at Aly.

'So, what about Tommy?'

'Oh, you can have Tommy if you like. He's more your type than mine.' She pulled on Tony's arm, leading him up the stairs and along to her room. Aly was still standing in the hall when she heard Carey scream. The next thing she saw was Carey standing on the landing shouting down at her. 'What the hell's been going on in my room? The curtain's been ripped down, the window's wide open and it's in a mess.'

'I'll explain when you come down,' Aly said patiently.

They sat in the drawing room where Aly and Wendell recounted what had gone on. At the end, all Carey said was, 'Get me out of this place, Tony. I can't stay here any longer.' She bundled three cases and an armful of dresses into the trunk of the Cord and got in.

'What about the rest of your stuff?'

'You have it,' she told Aly coldly, 'if you can get into it.'

Driving along the approach to Brunessemer, Tom saw the Cord coming the other way and slowed down. Tony slowed as well.

'Keep going,' Carey said. 'I don't want to talk to him,' she shuddered. 'He's killed a man – and he did it standing in my bedroom; I don't think I ever want to see him again.'

Tom carried on to the house. When he had parked the car and gone inside he found Wendell and Aly waiting for him. 'I'm glad you didn't arrive earlier,' Aly said, kissing him on each cheek.

'Yes, I saw them on the road outside. Hi Wendell,' he put out a hand. 'You won't mind if I don't kiss you,' Tom laughed. 'I know it's the custom in Europe but this is America – thank God.'

Wendell smiled at his sister. 'I like him – he has a sense of humor.'

'And he saved our lives.'

'That too. We should find him a suitable reward. What would you like.'

'Nothing really. I came to see Fred. Is he around?'

'Upstairs,' Aly said, 'come on, I'll take you.'

'It's OK. I know my way.'

Loughlin was listening to London when Tom came into the room. He held up a hand indicating he needed quiet. As it came in he scribbled the message down on a pad ready to decode after the transmission.

'I didn't get a chance to thank you yesterday.' Tom waved it away. Loughlin began the decode; gradually a look of concern spread across his face. 'That's depressing,' he said under his breath.

'Bad news?'

'Could hardly be worse. I have to get Churchill out of here.'

He started packing up his equipment at the same time talking to Tom. 'Tell me about Neumann. What's he like, physically I mean?'

'Mid-forties, tall, probably six two, maybe a touch more, a hard-looking man, lean and mean. I figure he probably weighs in at around 200 pounds and not an ounce of fat'.

'I met a man like that in Washington. He had a wound around one eye.'

'When was that?'

'About three weeks ago'.

'Yes, that would be about right. He got that during my escape. Was it fresh?'

'No more than a day or two old.'

'That was Neumann then.'

Loughlin finished packing the Morse away. 'Thank you. I know where my leak is now.'

'Was it serious? The leak I mean.'

'Pretty much. They killed one of our agents and took on her identity. I didn't know it was a woman. Nobody bothered to tell me, otherwise I would have known.'

'Of course.'

'It seems they tortured her pretty badly before they killed her. It had all the hallmarks of Mueller about it. He killed a British policeman and his wife, you know?'

'No, I didn't.'

'Yes, the same nasty signature there as well. I must get Mr Churchill briefed and packed. We're going back to Washington to arrange his return to London.' He opened the door and ushered Tom out. 'Will you be around for a bit or are you going?'

'No, I really only came down to see you.'

'That was good of you. It's helped fill in some of the blanks.'

'Glad to be of help.'

Loughlin stood looking at him for a minute. They shook hands. 'In case we don't meet again, good luck.' He paused and then added, 'and thank you for flushing out Mueller. He's a swine – you did us a great service.'

Tom put his head round the corner of the drawing room door. 'I'm going now,' he called out.

'No, stay a bit,' Aly said. 'We want to talk to you. Come and sit down.'

He sat on the sofa. Aly came and sat down beside him. Wendell dropped himself into one of the large arm chairs opposite. There was an air of conspiracy about the pair of them and he wondered what was coming next.

'You know you're a bloody hero, don't you?' Wendell announced, grinning. 'Twice over. You escaped from captivity, then you rode to our rescue. Like a knight in shining armor. That deserves a reward.'

'It does,' Aly nodded enthusiastically.

Tom looked sheepish. 'I'm not sure about any of this.'

'Try not to look so sad,' she said gently. 'It must be awful but someone had to do it and you were the only one who could, so it had to be you. Try not to feel bad about it. No one else is; not Fred, or Mr Churchill or the other two – not even Mother – they're all relieved – she's gone shopping, for grief's sake. So we just wanted to tell you we understand and that you shouldn't let it hang heavy on your conscience, because you're a good man.'

He didn't know what to say. How do you respond to people who heap you with the victor's laurels when all you want to do is forget it? He wondered how Mike and his family might take it. It was bound to leak out. How would they feel about having a killer at the wedding feast – and he would have to face Martha, and especially Holly.

'Our father ought to give you a reward,' Wendell was saying. 'He's one of America's wealthiest men, you know. You saved his wife from being shot – and his precious house from being blown up.'

'I'm not sure he will necessarily thank you for saving Mother,' Aly said, trying to make a joke out of it. 'But the house – now that's another thing.'

'Since our father is not here present,' Wendell went on, seemingly enjoying the moment, 'we have decided to reward you on his behalf,' and he put some keys on the coffee table that sat between them.

Tom looked vacantly at them. 'What's this?' he said, pointing at the table.

'It's my car – that painted trollop of a French thing sitting out there in the garage. It's the car Father gave to me. He hoped it would somehow make me into the man he wanted me to be – fat chance. I'm giving it to you. It's no use to me. What the hell, I can't drive! What's more, I don't want to, why would I? I hate cars.' He stopped and looked at Tom; there was real sincerity in his eyes.

'You have it. I know you love it. Carey told Aly. So – here,' he pushed the keys towards Tom. 'It's yours – a gift from a grateful family.'

Tom said nothing. What could he say? He sat, shaking his head slowly, trying to take it in. 'I couldn't,' he finally said. 'I can't, it wouldn't be right.' He took a deep breath 'That's really kind of you but I just couldn't, and what would your father think? It was a gift to you.'

Wendell threw up his arms in horror. 'Beware of Greeks bearing gifts!' he shouted. 'It was a Trojan horse, for Christ's sake. He wanted to get inside my world and change it. That was the bribe money. It's an unwanted gift – please take it. It is only right someone should derive pleasure from it. Think of it as relieving us of our burden of guilt at having such a divine object cooped up in a stable where no one can see it.'

'Do acccpt it, Tom,' Aly pleaded. 'It would make us happy.'

'I can't,' he said flatly. 'It would always remind me of Carey.'

'Tom,' Aly looked at him seriously, 'you can't spend the rest of your life carrying a torch for our sister; she is just not worth it. She's manipulative, self-centered and devious. She does what she wants and to hell with how that hurts those around her.'

'I know,' Tom said, 'but she had a tough childhood. She told me about your father.'

'What was that?' Aly asked, raising her eyebrows.

Tom shuffled himself round to look at her. He wasn't comfortable with this conversation but went on anyway. 'The thing about taking advantage of her when she was just a child. That would mark you wouldn't it – explain some of the outbursts?'

Aly let out a little yelp of disbelief. 'What?' she snapped incredulously. 'She told you that story?' For a few seconds she hovered on the edge of saying something, then leaned over to Wendell. 'Will you tell him or shall I?'

Wendell looked heavenwards. 'You want the unexpurgated version?'

Tom didn't reply. He looked from one to the other of them and waited.

'Okay, listen up. Here it is in a nutshell. One fine morning our dear sister came down to breakfast in a really sullen mood. She hated the morning, she hated the world and especially she hated our father. Now it's important you understand something here. Carey had always been the center of attention, the golden child, the beautiful princess bathed in the adoring gaze of her admirers. When she was eleven years old she entered the Westchester County Little Miss America Beauty Pageant. Everyone told her she would walk it on account of she was so pretty. Everyone that is except our father who, rather meanly in my opinion, didn't bother to attend and when she said she wanted a tiara with real gemstones he said 'no'! Well, she didn't win – she came second to some blond-haired little angel from Tarrytown or some place around there. She never forgave him. So, come forward to that morning at breakfast. She's 15, not a good age for a girl, and she's a moody teenager. She's particularly pissed off with our father because he's grounded her and cut her allowance for reasons we won't go into here. Anyway, we're all playing the happy family at breakfast when Father says she should try to be more positive and happy with life.'

He stopped for a moment and looked over at Aly for consent to go on. Aly gave a quick nod of her head, signaling approval to continue.

'Well, Carey didn't take that too well. She banged her fork down on the table and shouted at him "I would if you'd just stop coming to my room at night and fucking me!" Then she got up and stormed off to her room. Well, you could have heard a dog bark in New York – the silence was that deafening. Our mother banished him from the house. He protested but she refused to hear it; she said if he came back she'd go public with it and ruin him. The rest is history.'

'So there's the answer, isn't it?' Tom said, still wincing at the story.

'Well, it would be,' Aly said, 'but there's a catch. It wasn't true.'

Wendell gave a little sigh of resignation. 'It was a lie, you see. Our father had not been screwing his little girl at all. Far from it, he had been ignoring her – she thought. Worse, she felt he spent too much of his attention on Aly. She hated him for it and this was her revenge.'

For Tom the revelation had just caused cerebral overload. He'd heard things he didn't want to hear; he felt the indignation rising in his chest. At first he didn't want to believe it. 'Did she tell you this?' was all he could think to say.

Aly nodded. 'It came out two years back when she was going through a particularly bad break-up with David, her man of the moment. She just blurted it out one evening when we were having cocktails before dinner. She just came straight out with it. I remember Mother dropped her glass and spilled her drink all down the front of her dress. I will never forget the look on her face. She'd spent years believing a lie. She still hasn't been able to bring herself to own up to our father. He ought to be told, but she'll have to do it.'

'Sorry,' Wendell said apologetically, 'it's better you know. Carey is for Carey. She always has been. She just can't bear not to be the center of attention; she needs to be adored – all the time. I don't know why she is how she is but I hope it helps you to understand things a little better.'

'I think I'll go for a walk,' Tom excused himself and stood up. He needed to be alone to get used to what he'd just heard. He was gone all that afternoon. At first he walked around the grounds, then he sat in the Chrysler for a while. Finally he drove into Dobbs Ferry and, finding the hotel, sat at the bar and ordered a beer. By chance the barman remembered him from the wild night with Tony when they had searched for the most beautiful girl in town.

'Say, did you ever find the most beautiful girl in Dobbs?' he asked, grinning at the recollection.

'No,' he said sadly. 'She was a myth, I found another girl though – but she turned out to be real ugly.'

'Friend, that's how life is. What you get into bed with at night aint necessarily what you wake up with in the morning.' He laughed out loud. 'You want another beer?'

'Why not.'

When he got back the place was deserted except for Aly. 'The Churchill party have all gone,' she said. 'Mother went with them to the station.'

'I've been a sucker, haven't I?' he said to Aly, 'a prize sucker.'

'You weren't to know.'

'I think Irena tried to warn me but I wasn't listening.'

'Come on,' she said, 'I know what you need – I've got just the thing for you,' and she led him off by the hand. On the landing they passed Constance. 'See to it we're not disturbed will you Constance – and if my mother returns just tap on the door for me.'

'Yes Miss Alicia,' Constance said and wandered down the corridor, giggling as she went.

'Should we be doing this?' Tom asked without any real conviction.

'Yes, it's the best medicine there is for your complaint. It'll help you forget – then you'll sleep nights much better.'

She took off everything without the least sign of being self-conscious. When she had stood there long enough for him to take it all in she pulled back the eiderdown and the blankets and carefully slipped under the silk sheets. 'Come on,' she said patting the bed beside her, 'pants off and get in here.'

For a moment he did nothing, 'I'm not sure I should. Your mother wouldn't like it.'

'Mother's not getting it – I am and besides she won't know. Do I have to tear those pants off you!'

He looked at her body draped in the silk of the sheets, like some sculpture of an ample Greek goddess. Her skin was soft and pale and her hair tousled where she had fluffed it up with her hands. What the hell, he thought, and taking off everything fell into the bed. 'Grief,' he said afterwards. 'You don't do things in half measures. That wasn't what I was expecting. Where'd you learn that from?'

'School,' she said lightly. 'We compare notes – all of the girls, well some of them anyway. We have a suggestion box; secret, of course. It's all in the school motto – it's chiseled in stone over the entrance.'

'What is?'

'The motto, silly: "Do it with thy might", that's what it says.' She sat up and her well-formed breasts looked so perfect, he wanted to kiss them. 'Go on,' she said guessing and, taking them into her cupped hands, offered them up to his face. There was a gentle knock on the door; it was Wendell. 'Mother's just got back,' he whispered. 'Playtime is over, children. Time to get up and get dressed. I'll keep her talking downstairs.'

Aly rolled over onto him, wriggled her body a little and gave him a last long kiss, pushing her tongue deep into his mouth. 'Now, you will feel a lot better.'

He took his leave of Irena, who looked at him as if she knew exactly what had gone on but said nothing. 'Thanks,' he said to Aly. 'You were right, it helped a lot'. At the front door he met Wendell and they shook hands warmly. 'I'd love to take the car but I don't think it would be quite right. Maybe one day, but not now. Thanks anyway.'

He took one last look at Brunessemer and decided he wouldn't be coming back again. On the drive home he thought about what he would say to the folks. In the end he decided to say nothing for the time being – with a little bit of luck, the story would be shut down. Irena had hinted that Warren wouldn't like it. A shootout at his family home would not be good for his image. He was well-connected and preferred a low profile.

When Tom had escaped from the basement and then gone into the hospital he had received a message from his section manager at Imperial Life telling him to take off as much time as he needed until he was recovered. His job would be safe. Now he felt he had taken all the time he should; he wanted to get back to normality. Just the simple act of going to work on the train again, walking from Grand Central to the office and signing in under the unforgiving gaze of Marilyn on reception would be like getting his old life back. He needed normality – he craved it.

He arrived at the office a little later than he should but, to his surprise, Marilyn, who always had a disapproving look for those who were not punctual, simply smiled. As he walked through the ranks of desks to the small glass enclosure of his office he sensed a strained atmosphere. Normally several of the incumbents scribbling notes and turning the handles on their calculators would look up momentarily and mutter a greeting. On this morning every head stayed assiduously down, every gaze glued to the work in front of it.

Dan looked up from the file he was studying. Fred's empty desk gave testament to his departure to the army and nobody had been found to fill it.

'Good to see you back, buddy,' he said in a slightly edgy voice. 'How are things? More settled I hope.'

Mavis came by with a bundle of files which she dumped on Dan's desk. 'Here you are, Mr Johnson.' She threw a timid glance at Tom but said nothing and quickly went back to her own desk. Adelle ignored him completely but he didn't pay much heed to it because she was never very communicative at the best of times. It was when Dan Johnson sidled uncomfortably up to him and said in a low voice, 'We need to have a little talk,' that he knew for sure something wasn't quite right.

They sat together almost in a huddle at Dan's desk. He pulled out a memo that had been sent round. 'I thought you should see this,' he said in a hushed voice, looking around him to see if anyone was in earshot. Tom read the memo. It was headed in bold with the words,

LET'S NOT MAKE A FUSS

Some of you will know Tom Jordan and some of you will have read about him in the press. He is returning to work tomorrow. This is a request from the President of Imperial Life, T.G. Garland, that we should all treat Mr Jordan with respect and not pry into the recent events of his life in the clear endeavor to make his return to work as comfortable as possible.

F. Brown, Senior Manager

Tom shrugged. 'Is this going to make things difficult working with me?'

'No, no, Dan Johnson insisted,' but he'd hardly got the words out when Marilyn from reception stuck her head round the door, then walked in and came over to his desk.

'Mr Brown would like to see you in his office,' she said flatly and without emotion. Tom often wondered if she had a sense of humor because she almost never smiled. She was married, he knew, because she had a wedding ring. It crossed his mind more than once that she might be trapped in a bad relationship. She hovered by the desk and Tom looked up enquiringly. 'Now,' she said, indicating he should follow her.

Frank Brown was the head of his department and generally you didn't go higher than that on a face-to-face basis. He was a very proper and urbane man with a slightly facile expression permanently fixed on his face. His voice was a little high-pitched for a male, not quite soprano but not far off it; it had a sing-song quality that was curious to listen to. He always dressed in a charcoal grey suit with a white shirt and a blue and white polka-dot tie. His nails were immaculately manicured.

Marilyn tapped on the door, then opened it to let Tom through. 'Come in, Mr Jordan,' he smiled. 'Please take a seat.'

Tom sat on the other side of the large, green leather-topped desk with its pens, inkwell and blotter all immaculately laid out. Nothing seemed disturbed or out of place and, as he looked at it, he wondered if any real work ever crossed that leather top. He had no idea why he was sitting there but imagined it had to do with the memo.

'How long have you been with us?' Brown asked.

'Nearly three years, sir.'

'Hmm, and do you like working here?'

'Very much so,' Tom started to feel slightly apprehensive – Brown seemed to be beating around the bush.

'Have you ever thought of some other career? Other than the world of insurance I mean, of course.'

'No, not really. I think I like it here. I like the work and I get by well with the people in my department.'

'Good – and, tell me, do you know who the President of the company is?'

'Yes, of course, Mr Garland.'

'Have you ever met him?'

'No, but I once saw him at a presentation here for the company's anniversary year.'

Brown stiffened himself in his seat, sitting more upright. 'I'll get to the point,' he said. Tom braced himself. 'You've made quite a stir in the papers recently. Did you know that T.G. Garland is related to the industrialist, Warren Taylor?'

'I didn't.'

'No, of course not.'

'He is actually the brother of Mrs Warren Taylor. I believe you know her.'

Tom got an uncomfortable feeling in his lower abdomen. This didn't sound good; he got the uneasy sensation he was witnessing his job going out the window. 'Yes, we have met.'

'Hmm, yes.'

'The family of Warren Taylor are very grateful to you for your help in recent events at the family home, which events are not at the moment in the public domain and they would wish it to be kept that way.'

377

So this was it. They were going to gag him, but they didn't need to because he was equally anxious to keep it out of the news. 'I wouldn't want this to come out in the papers either,' Tom replied, almost mumbling the words. 'It would distress my parents too much.'

'Of course, I understand, and that will be good news for our president and the Taylors. So we come to the second point. If it should come out you would, of course, be acclaimed a public hero – as indeed you already are in some quarters because of your unfortunate experience in captivity. Regrettably this might not be good for the image of Imperial Life. People are sensitive; they think of their insurance company like a solid rock, no dramas, no crises, their salvation in the face of a disaster. You see how that might not be good for the company's public image?' Tom just looked straight ahead. The axe was about to fall and he was looking at the executioner.

'The family would like to reward you but they can't do it publicly, so it has been decided to give you an early retirement pension on health grounds. Do you understand what that means?

'I think so.'

'You are being offered a substantial sum on leaving – which I am going to suggest is at the finish of this meeting – and a continuing pension of a sum equal to your present salary with annual increments as would be the case if you continued to work here.' He stopped to let Tom take it all in.

'How much?'

'The severance pay – fifty thousand dollars; tax free.'

'How do you make it tax free? I don't understand that.'

Mr Taylor has arranged it with the Treasury. You'll get a certificate.'

There was nothing for it but to accept; there was no other option on the table. If he didn't he knew they would find some way to be rid of him and at least this way he had some compensation. He signed an acceptance document. They gave him a copy and he left with a brown envelope containing a cashier's cheque. He didn't bother going back to say goodbye to Dan Johnson; it didn't seem appropriate.

On the train back to Peekskill he had time to think. This was the last time he would have to make this journey and he felt a strange nostalgia. Memories flooded his mind – the book on the seat, Carey standing on the station at Dobbs Ferry, Tarwids and the bear, hunting with Mike and Tony, lunches in New York, beers at Jennifer's Diner – all gone, all finished and washed away; and now his career – that was gone too. He didn't notice the journey passing until the conductor shouted out "Dobbs Ferry". He looked out through the window. Brunessemer was out there, back behind the town and the trees – Irena, Aly, Martins and the maids. He felt a pang as it sank in he would probably never see any of them again. It really was the end. He had to set his life on a new direction, he decided; he knew he couldn't live in the past. He opened the brown envelope and took out the cheque – $50,000 was a lot of money, too much to take in for the moment.

As the train pulled into Peekskill he had already made up his mind on where he was going next.

CHAPTER 29

A Change of Direction, 1 November 1940

He didn't tell his parents; he said nothing of the catastrophic events at Brunessemer, he said nothing of his lost job. Instead he put on a bright lie. The following morning he went to the bank to deposit his cheque. When it caused a fuss he told the manager he'd come into an inheritance. He then called the phone company and asked them to fix a line at the house in Union Avenue. Of course, he knew Holly would ask difficult questions; that was Holly, but he would tell him he needed it to keep in touch with the office and anyway he'd gotten a raise in salary and nearly every house in the street had one except them, and it was time they did.

In the afternoon he phoned Mike to say he planned to go hunting and would he care to string along. He couldn't, Mike told him; he had to go for a final fitting of his wedding suit, and it was an Irish tailor in Boston who specialized in traditional stuff and he'd be away for a couple of days – anyway, how come Tom was going hunting mid-week, he wanted to know; wasn't he back working yet?

Tom went hunting alone. He took the old Chrysler and the Remington and drove up state to where he knew there was a hunter's lodge. It was a shared accommodation but when he got there he found he was alone except for a ranger who had charge of it. It was what he needed – it would give him some thinking time. Out in the forest his mind felt freer. To start with he thought about Carey a lot but, as the days passed, it came to him there was something missing – the pain had pretty much gone. Now he thought of her less and settled in to the hunting.

It happened towards the end of the week when he had spent the morning tracking a big white-tailed buck. He finally came on it in a lightly wooded clearing. It stood on a mound unaware of Tom's presence downwind of it. It was the perfect shot as it stood with its profile sharp and clean against the skyline. It was the last day of the season; unlucky for this one, he thought, bringing the rifle up to his shoulder. Tomorrow and it would have survived for another season. He got the beast in his sights, his finger squeezed lightly around the trigger and, as he did so, the image of that night at Brunessemer flashed up in his mind – standing in Carey's bedroom, smelling her presence, lining up the shot on Hans. The deep bang from the shot split the air and echoed through the woods. The animal bolted in panic. Tom just stood there looking at the place where a moment ago the buck had been. He had missed the unmissable shot – the simplest, cleanest target you could get.

'There you go,' he said under his breath. 'There you go – that's my gift to you.'

Walking back to the lodge he mused on what he had just done. He knew it was a turning point; he'd lost the taste for something and he didn't think he would ever get it back.

'Good hunting?' the ranger asked him when he got to the lodge.

'I had a big white tail in my sights but I missed it.'

'Tough luck. Today was your last chance – season ends tomorrow.'

'I know. I think I'll be out of here tomorrow anyway. Got things to do.'

******

The flight from New York to Washington was uneventful. Churchill's party arrived without incident and went to a secure house in the Arlington district. It was quiet and anonymous but the accommodation was cramped.

'I shall miss Irena,' Clementine said as she unpacked her cases, trying to find enough drawer space. 'I rather liked that house. It had space, it was bright and airy.'

'Reminded me of a bunker,' her husband replied grumpily. 'Sort of place Hitler would feel at home in. I miss Chartwell, tradition, reliability, mellow bricks and mortar. You know where you are with that sort of thing.'

The phone rang. Mary Shearburn answered it and went straight to find Churchill. 'They want you at a meeting,' she told him, 'over at the Shack. They're sending a car here right now.'

'Ah,' Churchill said exuberantly. 'Let's hope they've organized my passage home.' He rubbed his hands together like a gleeful schoolboy.

Churchill took Walter with him for protection and Mary to take notes. During the short journey he dictated a new speech he intended to deliver to Parliament on his return. He was very confident, he told them both, that this was all going to turn out well.

At the Shack he met with the key chiefs: Marshall, Arnold, and King. Marshall was full of praise for Churchill, having survived the kidnap attempt and still looking so vigorous for a man of his age who'd been drugged, trussed up like a capon and generally had the hell bounced out of him. It was 'remarkable' he announced to the gathering.

'Let me just run through a few things first. Then we can get down to how we get you home.' They all sat round the table once more, the one from which Churchill only a short while ago had convinced them they should support him.

'OK,' Marshall said, 'the little things. All that gold on board the *Tenacious* has been put in safe store for you in Fort Knox. We can arrange transshipment back to London whenever you say. Two, I've arranged to supply your man Loughlin with a car – not stolen this time I'm pleased to tell you. Three, the cash from the *Tenacious* strong room has been put into an account with Chase Manhattan under your name – so Mrs Churchill can now go shopping.' At this everyone except King laughed.

'Now for the more important items. The State Department just issued a note to the German Embassy and a general announcement through the press that it recognizes you and your government to be sovereign – so hands off, Fritz. The President wishes you to know that he will support you in the difficult negotiations you have ahead of you with the Germans to dismantle the Paris Treaty. Now, about getting you home. Hap, how do we propose to do it?'

'We think it's too risky to just put you on board a TWA flight to London. The Germans would shoot it down if they knew you were aboard, that's certain.'

King looked sour. 'I don't see any point in jeopardizing American lives in repatriating Mr Churchill and his party back to where they came from. Why we can't just pack these people back into their own can and let them take their chances defeats me. That's how they got here. That's the way they should go back.'

Marshall pursed his lips and looked unhappy. 'Okay, but do you want to provide an escort to see them home safe?'

'The hell I do.'

'It's not necessary,' Arnold intervened. 'I've asked General Eaker to ready one of our newest Flying Fortresses. Mr Churchill and his bodyguard can travel back in that. It's armed to the teeth – nothing the Luftwaffe have would get near it. The rest of the party can go by passenger liner later. That's my suggestion, gentlemen.'

King didn't like it and said so. 'I still maintain we should not be risking American lives, airmen or seamen, in an adventure that is none of our business. Besides that, it will upset the Germans and we know we can ill afford to pick a fight with them at this time.' He sat back and folded his arms.

******

Alpha Six had left Kent early that morning and was now driving up Whitehall, crawling along behind a bus. As he came level with Downing Street the bus halted at a passenger stop; the traffic coming the other way was too thick to let

382

him overtake so he pulled up behind it. He sat tapping his fingers impatiently on the steering wheel, waiting for the passengers to get on and off the bus and cursing London traffic, when he happened to look towards Downing Street where his eye rested on four BBS men with what looked like Ernest Bevin and another man under their arrest. It was only a fleeting glimpse and he could have been mistaken, he told himself, but it looked odd. Alpha Six had been trained to trust nothing at face value and question anything even slightly odd.

The bus moved again, groaning and whining slowly along the street until it stopped once again and this time he could get past it. As he went round Trafalgar Square he noticed there were a lot of Blackshirts out, many more than usual; something was going on. He left the square and drove down the Mall a little way before turning into Spring Gardens, where he parked the car and left it. The day was grey and damp and he wrapped his navy blue British warm woollen coat tightly round him as he headed off to the Home Office, where in another persona he worked. As he walked up the steps of the building he noticed there was a BBS man there in place of the usual bobby. This wasn't right. The BBS man challenged him. 'You can't go in there,' he said brusquely. 'It's been closed down temporarily. New government orders.'

'What orders?'

'Can't say. It's closed, that's all.'

Alpha Six turned and walked quickly down the steps. Once out of sight of the Blackshirt he broke into a run until he got to the car. It took another ten minutes to get to the Chelsea Embankment where Charlie Armitage had his office. He walked in unchallenged; at least there were no BBS present but then again they shouldn't have been at the Home Office. Alarm bells were starting to ring. He walked up to the first floor where a woman sat in a booth behind a glass screen. He pulled a card out of his coat pocket. 'Richard Grainger,' he said, 'Home Office. I'm here to see Sir Charles Armitage.'

'He's not here. I'm sorry you've missed him.'

More alarm bells rang. They'd had a rendezvous set up. It was too important for Charlie to miss.

'Do you know when he'll be back?'

The woman looked around her surveying up and down the corridor, then leaned forward and quietly whispered, 'I think he was arrested. Half a dozen armed men from the BBS came in and dragged him away. They had a Home Office warrant.'

'Who else is here?'

'Well,' she said, still whispering, 'I don't think anyone is any more. They've been leaving all morning – I'm sure I'm the only one left.' She looked at him blankly like a lost child who isn't sure of herself. 'Do you think I should stay?'

'No,' he said, without giving it much thought. 'I'd go home if I were you. Do you know where they were taking him?'

'Bermondsey, I think I heard one of them say.'

'Thanks,' he shouted, running down the stairs. Things had gone wrong, that was clear. If Charlie had been nabbed then things could have gone dramatically wrong. He had eight stolen tanks sitting in Kent and only Charlie knew what he wanted doing with them. He had to lie low somewhere till he found out what was happening.

******

Bevin did not particularly like Number 10 as a residence, even though he would only be there until Churchill could get back. It was too big and too empty for his taste and he would rather be with his wife in their London flat. Hugh Dalton arrived, together with Eden, to start the process of the negotiations with the Germans. James had gone back to Portsmouth, where he had anticipated there might be trouble. Keith Park was at Northolt and Alan Brooke had gone north to organize army units to throw a cordon around Hull in case the Germans decided to break out. Hitler's response had caught them off guard. They had expected an angry reaction through the Legation with hostile posturing at best and outright assault at worst. In the event nothing had happened other than the Germans had asked for draft proposals for alterations to the Paris Treaty. There was no sign of aggression and no threats or intimidation. It was welcome but not expected. Now they had the task of putting together an agenda.

At the Whitehall end of Downing Street a car pulled up and five men got out. At their head Lord Halifax led the way. The Bren gun crew guarding the street came smartly to attention and let the party pass. At the front door the police officer saluted and called to the sentry inside to open it.

Eden was explaining the protocol of the proposed negotiations when the door to the Cabinet room opened and Halifax walked in, followed immediately by Mosley. He was flanked by three Blackshirts armed with machine pistols. Eden, Bevin and Dalton all stood up in a state of shocked disbelief.

'I'm sorry Anthony' Halifax said, 'I'm afraid there is no other way. We have to put a stop to this folly.'

Mosley stepped forward and his men fanned out around the room to cover any resistance, though there was little they could have done. 'You are under arrest for treason,' Mosley said with an air of arrogant authority, and drew a Luger pistol from the holster on his belt.

Bevin's response was to get angry. 'Put your toy pop-gun away and explain yourself, man. This is outrageous. We are His Majesty's duly elected government. Explain your business here.'

Halifax looked pained, but it was Mosley who said it. 'Not any more you're not. We are taking over. You are now prisoners of the Reich.' He raised his right arm in a Nazi salute. 'Heil Hitler.'

'Sorry,' Halifax said again, 'but it is for the best.'

******

The events in London had taken place in the morning and were concluded before midday. News reached Washington in the early afternoon by which time it was all over. In the Shack they were still debating the best solution for Churchill's return. Churchill had just reminded King that he was a recognized head of state and not some refugee seeking asylum when a note arrived from Signals Intelligence on the next floor up. The note was handed to Marshall who scanned it, then read it more slowly a second time.

'I think,' he said very deliberately, 'the decision has just been taken away from us. Something's gone wrong over there. The boys upstairs have just picked up a broadcast from the BBC. The government has backtracked and denounced the takeover. There have been some arrests – we don't know who or why but Halifax is back as Prime Minister.'

King looked over at Churchill. 'Looks like you're a refugee after all,' he sneered. His face wore a look of satisfaction. 'George,' he said, leaning towards Marshall, 'I think we should call this meeting closed for the time being until we find out what those devious Limeys are up to.'

******

In Arlington Loughlin had been on the Morse. He knew everything they knew – and some more.

'I've been contacted by someone using the call sign Alpha Six. I'm not sure but I think he's one of Sir Charles Armitage's men. There's been a counter-coup led by Mosley. Bevin and Dalton are in jail. I'm afraid they've got Anthony as well, sir. Sorry – but at least he's only under house arrest.'

Churchill sat in an easy chair, elbows on his knees, head bent and his cupped hands clasped across his forehead. A deep, black mood had descended upon him. It was a dreadful reverse.

******

Fighting had broken out around the Legation when a group of heavily armed Gestapo had tried to leave the building. They were now firing indiscriminately from the windows and the top of the building at anything that moved, soldiers and civilians alike. The tank regiment in Queen's Gate had sent two armoured cars with light cannon which for the time being were holding the position.

The two halftrack Bren carriers blocking both ends of Downing Street had retreated after a short gun battle with Blackshirt forces. The BBS had crossed Tower Bridge unopposed; a convoy of five-ton trucks made their way to the Whitehall end of the street where they set up two heavy calibre machine guns. The section guarding that entry point was quickly overrun with hardly a shot being fired. Seeing he was seriously outgunned, the corporal driving the carrier at the other end hastily retreated. For a while there was a stand-off as the colonel commanding the area looked for a superior to obtain orders. In the end it was Halifax who put a stop to everything. He came out of Number 10 and walked the short distance to the British troops. The colonel and a brigadier came through the defensive line, which had now been reinforced, and after a short parley were persuaded to withdraw back to the Horse Guards barracks while the politicians sorted things out.

Alpha Six drove east along the Embankment, crossing the Thames at London Bridge. Turning left he made his way along Tooley Street, patching his way towards Bermondsey through the narrow side streets of the South Bank. He came into Bermondsey Street and ahead of him saw the shiny black edifice that was the BBS headquarters. He had expected to see a heavy presence of men out at the front of the building but he had not anticipated a road block. Barriers had been erected 50 yards either side of the building, cutting the road on the east and the west. As he got closer he saw that he was being sucked into a funnel where vehicles were being stopped and checked. He thought about pulling over to the kerb and stopping to give him time to think or turn around, but he knew that would look suspicious. He noticed there were two motorcycles deployed at each barrier with armed Blackshirt riders. They were clearly pursuit vehicles that would chase down anything that tried to divert at the last moment. There was nothing for it but to go ahead and bluff his way through it.

He joined the queue of cars waiting to go through the barrier. As he inched closer his pulse quickened; he was being drawn into a potential trap. He had to keep calm, he told himself, because they would be looking for signs like sweating or nervousness. He arrived at the barrier and wound down the window, trying to look casual. The Blackshirt ducked down to look in through the window and in that moment Alpha Six decided to become Richard Grainger from the Home Office. It was a risky move, but it was his best chance. He held up his ID card. The Blackshirt looked at it and saluted.

'I think we've been expecting you, sir. Are you from Major Linz?'

He had no idea what was coming next but he was in with both feet. Instinct took over from rational thought. 'Yes, that's right.'

'If you pull over there, sir,' he said, pointing to the kerb right in front of the main entrance, 'I'll get someone to come down to you.'

Grainger moved the car and parked it. The Blackshirt called for another to take his place and came over to the car. 'Won't keep you a moment,' he said cheerfully and made off up into the building. Grainger sat there. His heart was beating furiously and he displayed all the signs that should have alerted them, but they now had some other idea in their heads as to who he was. Linz had legitimized him; he had some kind of mandate. Nobody noticed because he was what they were expecting. He thought about making a run for it but he knew he would not get very far before somebody got suspicious. He looked around for the most promising avenue of escape. He knew he was most vulnerable if he stayed inside the car because it offered no easy exit; he was in a cage. He made a decision.

He opened the door and got out, standing casually next to it leaning on the roof. He opened the back door and got a trilby hat off the back seat, pulling it down low over the front of his face. Next he took out a pack of cigarettes, went over to a man standing guard on the main entrance and asked him for a light. Moving around and being seen making small talk, he figured, would give him an air of being normal, of being one of them. A plan was forming in his mind: rather than running he could probably just casually walk away down one of the side streets. After that he would have to steal a car but that wouldn't be difficult. The most risky part of the plan was how to get round the cordon at the barriers. The eastern one looked the least heavily manned. He started to move towards it. He had an idea.

At the barrier he approached one of the men. 'I'm from Major Linz's office, waiting for someone.' The Blackshirt acknowledged him. 'I need a piss – okay if I just pop round the corner over there; just splash it up against the wall?'

'There's no need to do that, sir. We've got very modern facilities over there,' and he pointed to the HQ. 'Billy, show this gent the urinals will you – he's busting for a slash. You go over and see Bill. He'll show you. Up the steps and on your right, just through the doors.' Damn, he thought, what rotten luck.

He thanked the man and made his way towards the building. He had started to climb the steps to the front doors when one of them opened and a man with a clipboard came out and stopped him. 'Is that your car, sir?'

Grainger's throat went dry. 'Yes,' he croaked, and then coughed hard. 'Sore throat,' he said, thinking quickly.

'Can I see your ID, please?' This could be trouble. He pulled it out of his wallet and held it up for the man to read.

'OK, that's good. I need a signature – just here.' He unscrewed the top off a fountain pen and handed it to Grainger, who signed and handed it back. 'If you return to the car, sir, we'll bring him down and you can be on your way.'

He walked back down the steps and, as casually as he could, got back into the car. He sat and waited. He had no idea what was going on. He knew they thought he was from Linz and it was now clear he was collecting somebody. The fact that he had been asked to sign for the person pointed to it being someone in custody. How he would deal with that he had no idea, but it would give him a chance to get round the barrier and away. After that he hadn't a clue except that if it was a prisoner he was unlikely to object when Grainger let him go and made good his own departure for Kent and the tanks.

Two men came down the steps; one was in handcuffs. The passenger door was opened and the cuffed man was pushed into the seat. Grainger stiffened – it was Charlie Armitage. How lucky could he be?

But the luck quickly had the edge knocked off it. The BBS man with him got into the back seat. He was armed. 'I'll sit back here,' he announced, 'just in case he gets any funny ideas. It would give me great pleasure to shoot him in the back.'

'I don't think Major Linz would like that, do you?' Grainger said, trying to sound censorious.

'Sorry, sir.' There was contrition in the voice.

'Good,' he thought, 'he'll do as he's told.' The barrier was lifted and they drove east along the south side of the river. When they got to Woolwich a voice from the back seat said apologetically, 'Excuse me, sir, but shouldn't we be going the other way for the Legation?'

'We're not going to the Legation. Major Linz has another more suitable place for this kind of interrogation.' He turned his head slightly towards Armitage and lifted the brim of his hat. For the first time on the journey there was a look of recognition.

Now the problem was how to deal with the armed guard. Grainger had no weapon and although he'd had commando training he knew he had little chance with bare hands against a man with a semi-automatic pistol. He looked around the car for something he could use as a weapon, but there was nothing.

At Blackheath they emerged into open countryside. The needle on the fuel gauge was flickering over the empty mark and they would have to get petrol. 'We're nearly on empty. There's a garage up ahead; I'm going in there to fill up,' he shouted over his shoulder.

'Good. I could do with stretching my legs. There's not much room in the back here.'

As Grainger got out his foot struck something on the floor – a heavy steel starting crank had been slipped in alongside and partially under the driver's seat. An idea came to him. The guard was standing on the far side of the car and had lit up a cigarette. A pump attendant came over in a greasy, white overall coat.

'I'm not pumping petrol while you've got a fag on,' he complained to the guard. 'Move away over there if you want any fuel.' His luck had come back again.

'I'll check the oil while you're filling,' Grainger said loudly so that his Blackshirt would hear. He lifted up the engine side-cover, reached in and disconnected the main lead to the electrical coil. Then he dropped it down and fastened the side catches. 'Right,' he said, 'that's going nowhere.' He paid the attendant. 'Come on,' he shouted, 'we're under way again.'

He put in the key and pulled on the starter. Predictably the engine didn't fire. He did it two or three times more as the Blackshirt got to him. 'What's wrong?'

'Don't know – do you know anything about cars?'

The Blackshirt shook his head and looked doubtful. 'It's all magic to me.'

'Right, well give me a hand. I've probably got to use this.' He picked up the starting handle and brandished it. Then he unhooked the side catches and lifted the engine cover. 'Okay, we need to see if we've got a spark on the plugs to start with. I'll need you to get your head down and watch for a spark when I turn the engine over with this.'

'Down here?' The Blackshirt stuck his head into the engine bay. Grainger brought the heavy shaft of the starting handle hard down on his neck. His forehead banged against the engine block and he slowly rolled backwards onto the concrete forecourt. Grainger rolled him over and took away the pistol. He was out but he was breathing. Urgently he went through his pockets, looking for the keys to the cuffs but he couldn't find them. Damn, he thought, they must have been planning to un-cuff him at the other end. The Blackshirt was starting to groan but he hadn't regained proper consciousness. The pump attendant came over and stood looking. Grainger wondered what he might do. Maybe, he thought, he might not have seen the blow, but the attendant soon disabused him of that.

'Fascist bastard,' he said. 'You can't leave him here, you know.'

'Have you got anything I can tie him up with, some cable or rope?'

'I've got a roll of insulating tape. Wrap that round him a few times and he won't be going nowhere.'

'What are we going to do with him, Charlie?'

'We can't take him with us. Kill him, I suppose. Dump him out in the woods somewhere.'

'I'm not sure I like that. It's murder, you know.'

'Well, we can't take him with us.' Armitage looked at the unconscious bundle slumped on the back seat. Pity he only had that poxy little pistol with him. One of those Schmeizer sub-machine guns would have been handy.

'I've got a better idea. We find a cottage hospital in the next town and dump him on the doorstep.'

Armitage laughed. 'Dear boy, your charity will be your undoing one of these days.'

'Never mind the platitudes – and, while we're on it, what are we going to do with those bloody tanks I've swiped?' Grainger reconnected the coil and started the engine.

'You realise,' Armitage joked, 'this is the second time you've stolen the property of the good Major Linz. First you steal his tanks and now you've lifted me. You won't be popular if he finds out. Have you got a short-wave set at this hideout of yours? We need to get in touch with James and Brooke. God only knows what's going on.'

'No, but I've got a Morse transmitter.

They reached Sevenoaks as the light was fading. By the time they got to the barn and hid the car it was dark.

'I've got some heavy duty bolt cutters,' Grainger said, examining the handcuffs that were still holding Armitage's wrists captive. 'They'll make short work of these things.'

CHAPTER 30

New Beginnings

The salesman in the auto showroom was enthusiastic. He said it was the finest station wagon a man could buy. Ford, he said, had put their latest engine design into the model with a powerful V8 that would carry any load you could fit into its truly generous back end. It was the deluxe model, he assured Tom, pointing out the leather seats and the new column gear shift. There were brightwork trims around the lights and the beechwood side frames were crafted from the very best timber.

'And it's all yours for less than $900 dollars – on the road, with a free tank of gas. What d'ya think?'

'I'll take it,' Tom said.

After the Chrysler it was like riding on air and the man was right about the V8 – it really pulled when he hit the gas.

That evening, as he arrived home he found the man from the telephone company was there just finishing off rigging the phone line. Holly and Martha were standing outside looking up at it in wonder. There was an air of excitement as he came down off the ladder. 'That's it folks, you're all fixed up and ready to go.' Inside the living room Martha picked the receiver out of its cradle and polished the cream Bakelite with a soft cloth. Then she set it down and admired it.

Over dinner Tom broke the news to them that he had given up his job with Imperial Life and had enlisted in the Army as an officer cadet. There was a moment of uncomfortable silence as they got over their disbelief, then Holly said he was not altogether surprised. Martha smiled nervously and tried to put on a brave face and see the positive side of it but inwardly she felt overwhelmingly sad. She always knew that one day he would leave home but she had so hoped it would be to marry and set up house somewhere not too far away, and that there would be grandchildren and visits and birthdays and all those other things that make living so good. Eventually she could not help asking the question. 'Why? I thought you liked your job.'

It was going to be hard to find an answer to that without weaving a terrible web of benign deception. So, in the end he had to tell them the truth: what Frank Brown had said and why they didn't want him in the company anymore, but they had paid him handsomely to compensate him and he was content with that. He left out the bit about the events at Brunessemer and just kept it to the story of Parkes, Neumann and the basement. That was enough for the company to want him gone, he said, and he could see their point of view. And while it explained the mystery of why it was as it was, it did nothing to relieve the sadness cradled in Martha's heart, and that night, in the dark of their bedroom when Holly was sleeping, she worried quietly about it until she too fell asleep.

There was now only one other thing Tom felt he needed to do. He got up early and drove down to the hospital at Buchanan where Al Cardy was still recovering from his gunshot wound. It had been touch and go for a month but now, finally, he was on the mend. When he arrived for the visit the doctor caring for Cardy greeted him warmly. 'That was the most original piece of first aid I've ever come across, young man.'

Tom smiled. 'Yeah, I've got to admit, it was quite a novel way to stop a wound.'

On the ward he found Cardy sitting in a wheelchair. He looked tired but when he saw Tom his face cracked into a smile. 'You saved my life,' Cardy said, looking embarrassed. 'If it helps any I feel downright ashamed for my part in what happened. I was really stupid to get taken in by Newman like that.'

'It happens,' Tom replied, and held out a small packet to him. 'Here, this belongs to you.'

'What is it?'

'Your watch. I took it off you when I dragged you across the basement. Been meaning to return it – just never got round to it.'

'Thanks. You OK? Man, what a stinking mess this thing has been.'

'What were they doing up there with that boat, running around at night? And what was that equipment they had? What was that about?'

Cardy looked blank. 'I have no idea. Some kind of surveying for the military is what we were told. He turned up there one day with a letter from the Army requesting our cooperation and the sheriff assigned it to me. They wanted to make sure no one snooped on them, so when any newcomers were about I put out the story of the missing ranger. That way folk would report it if they saw Newman and we'd know they'd been seen. It was all about keeping their work secret and if anyone saw them they needed to know. It all seemed reasonable at the time. Then, of course, you come along and put the cat among the pigeons. Why did you follow us that day? That really spooked Newman. He was sure you were spying on him.'

'Just curiosity, I suppose,' Tom said, avoiding a longer explanation of the ruckus at the World's Fair.

'Well, that's one curiosity that nearly did do for the damn cat.'

They laughed and talked a little more, then Tom wished him good luck and left. He was none the wiser about Neumann and, as he drove north again, he kept looking in the rear view mirror, half expecting to see a black Plymouth tailing him. Neumann was out there and he was certain he would try something again. Then there was Churchill. He just couldn't see how that could be connected. Of course, it crossed his mind, Churchill had been at Brunessemer and so had he. Maybe it was coincidence but what if Neumann didn't know that? It would look like there was some deeper connection; and there wasn't.

******

The news from London was not good. NBC gave regular updates on their six o'clock bulletin.

Churchill and the others gathered around the radio to hear the latest. Britain now had a new provisional government, it announced. According to the BBC there was calm in the capital with only small pockets of armed resistance in the northern suburbs. As an emergency measure Parliament had been suspended and a governing council had been set up jointly under the control of Lord Halifax and Sir Oswald Mosley.

'That traitorous charlatan!' Churchill shouted at the radio in rage.

In an interview Beaverbrook had said he supported the efforts to bring peace and stability to the nation. The German Ambassador had made a statement that the Reich and its people applauded the events in Britain and would continue to cooperate in bringing about a peaceful and harmonious resolution to their differences.

'Diplomatic humbug,' Churchill grumped. 'Hogwash. The Nazi scum have gone in through the back door with the help of that Judas Mosley – and Halifax, the poor sap, is taken in by it all.'

Loughlin was all the while on the Morse, picking up news from Alpha Six on the real position. 'I'm afraid none of it is very encouraging,' he reported to Churchill. 'They've started to round up all your known supporters and associates; it's a witch hunt. The BBS are out in force and there may be evidence that they're being supported by SS units in Blackshirt uniforms. There is one bright spot, though. Some of the RAF boys are still flying and there seems to be a resistance force forming in the south-east. It's very sketchy but it sounds like they're fighting under your banner, sir.'

Churchill brightened at this news. 'Good, then we should support them. I think we need to work on that one. Let us try to encourage the resistance by giving it a central cause to focus upon. We shouldn't be sitting here passively, listening to events. We should be trying to do something positive to drive them. Tomorrow I shall speak with Marshall. We've got some money; we need to set up our own HQ – here in Washington. Mary, you've got some serious organizing to do. We shall need to recruit some help; there must be a few loyal expats who can be found in this city.'

'It'll soon be Christmas, Fred,' Walter Thompson said without enthusiasm. 'It'll be the first time I've ever missed one in England. I wonder if there's going to be a King's Speech this year.'

'Interesting one. I haven't heard anything on the grapevine about what they intend for the Monarchy.'

'Winston,' Clementine called from the hall. She came into the living room. 'Have you seen Winston, either of you?'

'In the garden I think, Mrs Churchill,' Loughlin replied.

'Well, there's a car here waiting take him to the Shack. Can you see if you can find him?'

******

'I'll get straight to the point,' Marshall said. 'The British have issued a warrant for your arrest and they're trying to arrange a hearing date in court this morning. They'll try to get an extradition order. They delivered a note to the State Department earlier requesting that you be detained, together with your team. They haven't included Mrs Churchill in the requests, though.'

'That's outrageous,' Churchill protested.

'There's more. They're demanding we hand over the *Tenacious* and her crew immediately and that we impound the bullion sitting in Fort Knox.' Churchill rubbed his forehead muttering expletives under his breath. 'It's not finished,' Marshall went on. 'The Germans have demanded we hand over your man Loughlin on a charge of murder and piracy.'

Churchill had gone to the Shack in high spirits with plans to set up a British government in exile. The news was a blow of staggering ferocity. 'Well,' he said in a measured voice after some careful thought. 'I hope the President and the Congress will oppose this cynical ploy to perpetuate mischief.'

Marshall looked doubtful. 'I can't speak for the court. That will be up to the judiciary but the President has already offered you the resources of the White House Counsel. He suggests you meet with them this afternoon.'

'I'm grateful to the President.'

'With *Tenacious*, the crew and the bullion, I think we can hold that off. We haven't recognized this provisional government as legitimate and I doubt we shall for a while to come. The Germans are going to be a bit more difficult. They're a legitimate state recognised by our government so they can't just politely be told to butt out.'

'I'll fight this,' Churchill said resolutely.

'I'm here to help,' Marshall assured him, 'but the President needs us to keep it low profile or the Germans will call foul. I don't think anyone is too worried about the rest. You'll understand that we shall have to appear to keep our distance.'

'I appreciate what you have already done. Perhaps I can ask for a little more assistance.'

'Go on.'

'I shall need to set up a fighting HQ – I need a suitable work space – somewhere I can operate from. The house in Arlington is really too small.'

Marshall looked relieved. 'I think we can go with that for you. There's not much space in this building here but I'm sure we can find you a corner in it somewhere.'

******

The marriage vows were taken by Mike and Eileen at midday in the Holy Name of Mary Church in the center of Croton. It was the first Saturday of December and the family had conferred long over the most auspicious day and decided this should be it. Tom deliberately arrived at the church just as the last of the guests filed in and chose to sit right at the back of the congregation.

A month before the wedding day he had enlisted as an officer cadet and reported to a training camp in Georgia. Now he sat discreetly at the back of the church where nobody knew him or noticed him. He was wearing the uniform of a trainee second lieutenant in the 1st Cavalry Division and his hair had been cut very, very short. They'd allowed him a 24-hour furlough for the wedding. He sat there in isolation and once again found himself thinking how different it might have been if the events of the past few months had not transpired. He and Tony would have been up front there with the close family; they would have been at the heart of it. Now it seemed inappropriate. He looked around for Tony but he wasn't there. Tom guessed he'd decided not to come for the same reasons that he had wavered.

When Mike and his best man strode to the altar they looked straight ahead so that neither of them saw Tom as he sat tucked away at the far end of a pew. The organ struck up the wedding march. The bride, accompanied by her father, was led down the aisle, with Shelagh and Rosheen carrying the long chiffon train and behind them Ruby with a bouquet of white carnations.

After the ceremony the couple led the way in an open-top Landaulette to Cutlers Hall amid a cacophony of horns blowing, trumpets being tooted and loud music emitted from the latest automobile craze – the car radio.

The main reception was held in the Hall's own ballroom. Built in an era when ballrooms were an essential part of any grand house, the one at Cutlers was large; it could comfortably hold a hundred dancing couples. At one end there was a raised dais for musicians. Tables had been set out, laden with delicately decorated platters of extravagant food. A New York caterer had been installed in the kitchens and waitresses had been hired to make sure the guests wanted for nothing.

When Tom arrived he could hear the strains of a traditional Irish folk group: a fiddle, tin whistle, drum and squeezebox. At first he recognized nobody as he idly wandered through the house. He had been looking forward to the wedding all year but now, as he mingled anonymously, he felt flat. The whole of the ground floor had been taken over by the guests. Everywhere there were couples dressed up for a celebration with the women clearly trying to outshine each other. Many of the men were dressed in kilts, which he supposed must be clan Mescal. Most of the people he had never seen before. A waitress with a tray came sailing by and as she passed offered him a drink. He took it and carried on wandering. He stepped into the ballroom which was full of younger people dancing. Everywhere there were children running about in little knots, shouting, laughing, bumping into adults and then breaking out onto the dance floor doing improvised jigs.

Shortly after he first arrived he had joined the queue leading into the dining room where the wedding guests were greeted in the traditional manner by the parents of the bride and groom. As he shook hands with them he realized they had not recognized him in his uniform with his nearly shaved head. The first to recognize him was Ruby. She was about to pass him when she stopped in her tracks and stared at him. Then her eyes widened in recognition and she virtually threw herself at him. 'Tom,' she squeaked with delight. 'Tom, you came, you came, I knew you would. Mikey said you wouldn't because he hadn't seen you but I was sure you would. Come on you must show him you're here.' She grabbed him by the hand and started to pull him along, but then she stopped and stared at him. 'Why are you wearing that uniform,' have you joined the army?'

'Uh huh,' he said, squeezing her hand.

'Gee, that's a bad haircut they've given you. Come on.' He trailed along behind her into the main living room where Mike and his bride were standing talking with his father and another man. They stopped their conversation as Ruby demanded their attention, shouting, 'Look, it's Tom. I told you he would come. I told you so!'

'My God,' Mike said, 'you've been drafted!'

'No, I've enlisted. I've decided to make a career in the Army. I'll be Second Lieutenant Jordan in another two months – if I pass out OK.'

'This is my wife', Mike said, introducing Eileen. 'I don't think you've met before.'

They hadn't met and Tom thought what a pleasant woman and told Mike he should be very happy to be so lucky.

'This is Dr Brent,' Mike senior said, introducing the other man in the group. 'He's a family friend as well as our doctor. We've known you a good few years now haven't we, James?'

'That's right, ever since I came to practice in Croton. I think you were one of my first patients.'

Mike senior spotted another man and called him over. 'Come here, Danny. I want you to meet the famous Tom Jordan – local hero, got shot in the leg by some really bad characters. Isn't that right?' He turned to Brent, 'You once treated Teddy Roosevelt for a gunshot – didn't he get shot in the leg in a hunting accident? Back when you were just an intern? Go on tell them the story.'

Brent chuckled. 'Yes, but it wasn't strictly in the leg. He was out shooting partridge or some game bird, if I remember right. He tripped, dropped a scatter gun and it went off; he shot himself in the backside. We spent hours picking out the little pieces of lead. Of course, we were sworn to secrecy and we kept silent because it could have ruined our careers. Poor old Teddy, I don't think he ever got over the indignity of it.'

There was a peel of laughter. Tom was holding an empty glass when he saw a waitress passing and asked her to fetch him another drink. As he did so he recognized her as Dottie, the waitress from the diner, and nodded in recognition. 'Hi,' he said in a low voice. 'What are you doing here?'

'Same as you – I got invited. Hang on there and I'll get you your drink.' She disappeared out through the door, giving a little wave in his direction.

James Brent looked askance at what he had just witnessed. 'Young man,' he said in mock severity, 'did I just hear you ask that young lady to get you a drink? It's usually the other way round in my experience of etiquette. Wouldn't you say, Mike?'

Mike senior nodded agreement. 'That would be my experience too.'

'I think you'll find she's one of the waitresses, sir,' Tom said respectfully.

'No,' Brent said. 'I think you will find she's my daughter. That's right, isn't it Mike?'

'I believe it is – yes, I believe that's right.'

When she came back in and handed Tom a glass he blushed right up to his scalp and he had no hair to hide it. As she walked away again Tom excused himself and followed after her. 'I'm sorry,' he said when he caught up with her. 'I didn't know. So your father's the local doctor then?'

'He is.'

'Hmm. There's one thing I don't understand.'

'Why I work at Jennifer's?'

'Yes.'

'I'm paying my way through college – I want to go into medicine. My parents hate it, of course, but I want to make my own way. I don't want to get something just because my parents hand it to me on a plate. Does that explain?'

'I guess.'

'Not such a dumb blond after all then.'

Oh hell, he thought, why, do I always put my foot in it? 'You could have told me.'

'You could have asked.'

They had reached the front door when he finally said he thought he would take a turn outside and wondered if she would care to walk round the gardens with him. It was cold but he felt the need to get out into the fresh air. She said she would, and inside she started to feel a warm sensation welling up from the anticipation that at last something had moved him. He didn't know it yet but she was already planning their first date. Now she had to get him to ask her.

They walked along, not saying much, and when he told her that he was only on a 24-hour furlough and had to get back to camp in Georgia she began to panic. This chance would never come her way again. He would disappear into the army and she had no way of knowing if he would ever visit the diner again. Salvation came in the form of three girls walking towards them along the path that led to a rose garden. They were all wrapped up in coats and at first he didn't recognize them. When they were almost on top of them he made out Mike's two sisters, Shelagh and Rosheen. Then, to his surprise, he realized the third girl was Aly. For a moment there was pandemonium as Aly shouted, 'Tommy,' and threw her arms around him. She gave him resounding kiss and then stood back to look at him.

'My God, they've run the lawnmower over you.' Shelagh and Rosheen also jumped on him and kissed him amidst shrieks of surprise.

'How do you know this man?' Aly said to Dottie almost accusatorily.

'He knows my father,' she replied, not bothering with a more elaborate explanation. There wasn't time for long dialogs, she told herself.

'We're Mike's sisters.'

'I know.'

'We're at Masters School in Croton. This is our friend, Alison Taylor – she attends there too.'

'That I didn't know.'

'Tommy used to go out with my sister,' Aly said cheerfully, 'until the dumb idiot dumped him. That's how I know him. Are you his new date?'

Dottie saw the opportunity and grabbed it. 'Would you say that?' she said hesitantly, looking up at Tom.

He looked down at her for a second and then said, 'I think I would.' He put his hand into hers and held it very gently until she squeezed his little finger and he knew they were going to spend time together.

They sat and talked till late in the evening and then he drove through the night to get back to camp on time, the memory of their goodbye kiss lingering with him all through the journey and even after, when he had parked the car and reported back.

She thought about him long after he'd gone and imagined where he might be on his journey. When she went to bed she said a small prayer for his safe return then, curling her knees up almost to her chin, she put her arms around one of the pillows and imagined it was him she was holding. When she got up the next morning she was walking on air.

'What did you think of him, Dad?' she asked over breakfast.

'Who?' he replied.

'Why Tom Jordan, of course, who else.'

Her father put down the newspaper he had been reading. It was as he had suspected since the time she asked for his help when the boy was in trouble. 'Quite a remarkable young man, actually,' he said after a little consideration. 'Are you sure you would want to be his wife? A junior officer's life means a lot of moving about, you realize.'

******

'They've arrested 11 more MPs. Together with Eden, Bevin and Dalton, that makes 14. They've moved them to Maidstone prison. There's talk of a trial; they say they'll hang Bevin. We need to do something about it.'

'What had you in mind?'

'Well, Maidstone's not far from here. It's not a very secure prison – I visited a couple of years back when we did a Home Office review. I think we could probably organise a jail break.'

Armitage rubbed an index finger slowly up and down the side of his cheek bone. 'It's risky,' he eventually said.

'I know,' Grainger said, 'but it's even riskier to do nothing. Can you imagine the impact on public morale if they start a witch hunt with wholesale executions? Jerry will have won.'

'How would you do it?'

'Cut the telephone lines, blow the front gate, then walk in and stick 'em up. The warders aren't armed. Bit blunt and old fashioned, I know, but it should work.'

'What about Eden? He's still at his house in Sloane Square.'

'No, he became ill and they've moved him. He's in Westminster Hospital. It shouldn't be too difficult to get him out. Now what are we going to do with these bloody tanks you got me to steal?'

'Well, the idea was to stop them getting to Portsmouth. We've done that; now we need to be more inventive. We need to find out how Brooke is doing – he could probably use them – and we need to know how things are in Portsmouth since the balloon went up.'

******

Churchill moved into his office at the Shack. He was pleased to have somewhere to operate. It was small, just three little rooms down the corridor from Signals Intelligence. They were laid out in a line: a front reception accessed the corridor and the other two sat as wings left and right of it. Mary Shearburn took up residence in the reception where she had a desk and a typewriter, and she could act as the front line for whoever came in. Churchill took over the biggest of the rooms, got in a large planning table and scrounged a good scale map of Britain. He had a desk with four chairs around it and a picture of King George and Queen Elizabeth hung on the wall behind it.

In the third room Loughlin set up the Morse with a permanent aerial and a shortwave radio receiver; that gave him limited access to monitor some of the BBC broadcasts. It wasn't perfect but he was happy they now had a secure base to work from and a regular flow of intelligence from the boys up the corridor who had been instructed to cooperate – but at their discretion. Information was now coming to them on an hourly basis. Loughlin listened to the BBC reports and noticed a shift in tone and content after Mosley had taken over. The Germans were using it for propaganda and the reports were not to be relied on. The only real source of information was through Alpha Six.

Every morning Loughlin compiled a report, which he passed to Mary for typing and she then presented it to Churchill who had started sticking coloured pins with little paper flags into the map. A picture was beginning to build. Loughlin then joined Churchill and together they analysed the position, making assumptions, though they were still not actually able to influence anything.

The day after settling in Churchill announced they needed a group identity, something for the British people to rally around. 'The British Independence Movement, that's what we shall be.' The name stuck but the Americans turned it around and shortened it, calling them 'The Independent Brits'.

He had, he announced, also decided to send out a daily shortwave broadcast to the British people, but they had no solution to the logistical problem of how to let people know their signal wavelength. It could only be discovered by chance or passed on by word of mouth. They had been operating for a week when

400

Loughlin received a tip-off through the Morse that there was a group calling itself Radio Free London broadcasting every day at six in the morning and again at six in the evening. It was not a government station and the story it revealed was very different from that of the BBC.

Following Mosley's takeover the BBC had reported cooperation from the Army, which had agreed to withdraw to barracks and support the new government. The conspirators had all been rounded up, it said. At the same time the newsreader had changed; it was now a man called Edwin Harvard. There was an air of contempt in Harvard's voice whenever he announced an item of what he called 'subversive activities' – there were also references to anti-government propaganda.

'I've finally got some hard news,' Loughlin reported excitedly to Churchill shortly after they had moved in. He looked at the pins in the map that were supposed to show the position of individuals and groups known to be loyal to him and opposing Halifax.

'You're going to have to change a lot of these,' he said.

******

In Hull Alan Brooke had at first kept the Germans penned in behind the dock gates largely through negotiation. It was agreed that until there was a diplomatic solution they would stay within what was potentially German sovereign territory and not attempt any incursion into the wider Hull area. But Brooke was cautious and he had installed concrete and steel anti-tank obstacles on the access road just beyond the sight of the gates. Behind these he'd sandbagged and brought up two 105mm field pieces and set up heavy and medium machine gun positions that would be able to concentrate fire on the dock gates and anything trying to come through them. He had divided two full regiments of infantry into a series of companies and deployed them along the flanks of the dock walls.

Now they waited to see what the politicians would do. All he had to hold the north was around a hundred thousand men with small arms and light machine guns – about one third of what had been rescued from the beaches at Dunkirk barely seven months before. There was little in the way of heavy weapons – most had gone out to France with the BEF and been abandoned in the retreat. The position was fragile and would not be able to withstand a full-on breakout by the Germans.

It had been six days since Bevin, Dalton and Eden had taken the reins of government and things were still calm. But the BBS were everywhere and there was a brittle feel to the atmosphere. Brooke knew it would be touch and go if the Germans decided to make a move. His observers reported a regular flow of aircraft and ships coming and going on the seaward side of the port. When news came of Mosley's takeover he strengthened his positions. By two in the afternoon the BBC had put out a news bulletin: Bevin arrested, a new government had announced a state of emergency and martial law. It ordered all military personnel back to barracks and declared a curfew starting at four o'clock. People were to stay indoors until a further announcement. Only BBS were allowed on the streets and curfew breakers would be shot on sight.

Brooke had set up his command center in the City Hall and there he waited for developments. Expect it any minute, he had told his small planning staff as he got the information. He sent news over to Park by dispatch rider, which took over an hour. By the time the rider arrived and had handed in the message Brooke's men were already engaged.

In a simultaneous thrust a heavy concentration of BBS attacked his rear. The dock gates opened; a tank rolled through the gap and immediately it was hit by both the 105s. It stopped as smoke poured out of the main turret but nobody opened the top hatch. There was a deep thud as the shell magazine exploded and blew the top off the hull. The turret was sent spiralling into the air – the lower torso of a soldier hanging out of the bottom, the legs flailing grotesquely. It then crashed back onto the ground where it bounced once and came to rest. Under cover of the blast, troops came pouring round both sides of the burning tank, diving for cover wherever they could find it. It was clear the men the Germans deployed were battle-hardened troops. They quickly established themselves behind the tank barricades that Brooke's men had set up and now they were settling in to consolidate. The mines were tripped but they had little effect; the blast went upwards and with the enemy lying flat on the ground in their firing positions the shrapnel barely touched them.

Less than an hour into the fighting Brooke had to order a withdrawal or they would be overwhelmed. Respite came when a group from Park's base came to his aid covering the withdrawal. A flight of Hurricanes beat up the ground, strafing the German positions with machine gun fire and holding them back while the British got away. 'We only got out,' he said later, 'because Parky's boys put up such a bloody terrific show.'

At Caistor, Park's squadrons had been flying all day but now he was beginning to run low on ordinance. They would fly maybe two or three more sorties and then that would be it. He sent word to Brooke that he was pulling out and sending his boys down to Northolt. As the light faded, the last DC3 transport took off and headed south. Park considered he'd been lucky. There had been nothing but Stukas coming out of the docks and they were sitting ducks for the Hurricanes. He had expected fighters but there weren't any. What he didn't know was that much of the Luftwaffe's resources had been diverted – shipped to Prince Edward Island in Canada.

402

Churchill got the first news of the fighting in the early afternoon, Washington time. Radio Free London put it out and then Alpha Six started to transmit.

Loughlin's late afternoon report made mixed reading. Churchill was disappointed when he heard the news that Brooke and Park were pulling back to the south. There would be nothing to stop supporters of Mosley and Hitler from taking over the whole country. It looked like the game was up before it was started. 'We should have re-armed when I told them in the thirties,' he said in disappointment.

Then news came in that James and the southern-based fleet had kicked the Germans out of the Solent. That improved his mood considerably. 'Good old Navy,' he shouted.

The Isle of Wight had been cut off and the German vessels there had surrendered after a short engagement in which two light cruisers and an undisclosed number of E-boats had been destroyed. The rest of the German fleet had fled north with James's ships in pursuit. They were harried all the way along North Foreland by ships coming out of Dover until they had passed through the Straits. There they came under fire from a shore battery which had been idle since the Treaty but which had not been decommissioned because no one could agree whether it was part of the Army or part of the Navy – if it was the latter then it could not be decommissioned. The ironic thing about the Treaty was that although Hitler viewed it as a mere subterfuge – a convenience that could be torn up when he thought it expedient – nobody had told the Legation or the Kreigsmarine, or the SS for that matter; they stuck to the letter of the document because it was the orderly thing to do. So it was that on this moot point the guns had been left operational and were now being used to bombard the fleeing Kreigsmarine.

In the north, Brooke's action had been defensive and took place only because the Germans and the BBS initiated it; James had pre-empted the position in Portsmouth because he had the luxury of men and equipment. He knew the Navy had the edge on the Kreigsmarine both in ships and seamanship. As soon as he heard the news from London he had no doubt that if he sat back and did nothing he would be removed and the fleet would be lost. It was an easy decision and he immediately signalled all ships to battle stations. Unlike Brooke and Park he had the advantage of an advanced battle plan; all senior ranks knew their roles. The Kreigsmarine commander at Newport was taken off-guard, still waiting for orders from Berlin. When those orders came he was already surrendering personally to Admiral James.

Churchill drew a line across his map from the Bristol Channel in the west to Ramsgate in the east; the line ran just south of London. He then drew a circle around Essex. 'This is what we could hold,' he said to Loughlin with some optimism. 'The West Country and the Home Counties, and that bit of Essex from the Thames Estuary up to the Suffolk border. It's the home of most of our naval forces – we should consolidate there; Surrey, Hampshire and Kent – all hills and dense woodland. If the Germans do invade they'll find it hard country to fight in – not good for armour.'

In Berlin, Hitler was irritated by the turn of events at Portsmouth but refused to take it seriously. It was not part of his bigger plan, he told himself. As he pored over his strategic map with his top generals he had already convinced himself that the British were a side show. They could probably hold on for a few months but in the end he could starve them out. So, he gave orders to blockade the south but not to attack or destroy the fleet. 'I can leave Mosley and the BBS to take care of the country from within,' he told his generals. He had plans for a great Atlantic fleet, and tonnage that went to the bottom would be useless for those plans.

The day after Brooke pulled back from Hull his men started to slowly shift south. Joining the rear-guard action there were camp followers: refugees were slipping down the country like grains of sand through a sieve. Whole families started to form columns, staying close to the army for protection. The numbers became too great for the BBS who were overwhelmed by the volume of those trying to get south and, after a few nasty incidents where Blackshirts had shot into the columns killing and wounding a number of refugees including children, Mosley was persuaded by Halifax to let the population choose its own place in the country. In the end it didn't matter, he argued, if they were in the north or the south because in the final analysis things would settle down, the Treaty would be ratified and there would be peace. So it was agreed they would concentrate on getting control of the armed forces. For that Mosley insisted he would take his lead from Berlin and would await orders. Halifax was disturbed by the idea of taking orders from Berlin and once again, as he had at the meeting with Hitler in Paris, he began to have his doubts about the wisdom of what he had done. He was uncomfortable with it and when he reached home that night he told his wife over dinner that he now had to search his conscience.

******

Mosley paced up and down the Cabinet room at Number 10. He looked at the portraits of past prime ministers hanging on the walls and saw himself there. I'll get one painted, he thought, why not – I am now de facto the leader of the country. Parliament had after all been suspended; MPs of every leaning had been disenfranchised and Mosley was now barely less than a dictator. There had been nothing like it since the Middle Ages.

He shifted his thoughts to the Legation. Linz was head of military matters but he had more rank than just an attaché – he took his orders directly from

Himmler for the political direction of Mosley's developing regime. Linz had instructed him that there had to be a Jewish policy, but it worried Mosley that this was not the right time. It irked him that his attempt to gain total control had not yet succeeded. Elements of the Army needed to be neutralised – he needed more time to recruit men to the BBS, which was only able to control pockets of the country. Linz was adamant that the programme be started without delay; Mosley complied. When, on the following day, his propaganda department issued Jewish Regulatory Order No. 1, it pushed matters between him and Halifax to a head. The order required the registration of all people of Jewish blood from four generations back.

Mosley waited for the visit he knew he would get from Halifax. He stood in the Cabinet room and rehearsed his response. I have to finish the interference once and for all, he concluded. Halifax would have to be eliminated from the equation. When the two men met there was already an unbridgeable gulf between them; now it would yawn even wider.

'Things have gone too far,' Halifax protested, 'Parliament needs to be recalled before implementing an order with such fundamental and profound implications. It must be voted upon – democratically.'

'Democracy is redundant. It's dead,' Mosely said flatly. 'Besides, the Legation would never allow a return to the old institutions.'

Halifax looked gravely at the other man; it confirmed his deepest fears. 'It is not given to the Legation to dictate such a thing,' he said – but without enthusiasm.

'On the contrary, Halifax,' Mosely said, and he took a few paces towards the door through which the other man had entered just minutes before. 'The Legation has both the power and the right. When Britain broke the Treaty and abandoned its obligations, it gave up it rights to self-determination. This is the natural consequence.' He stood stiffly, pushing out his chest with his shoulders held well back to emphasise his power. 'I am the Leader of this country and that position is both recognised and reinforced by the Legation. I have no intention of opposing them and triggering a full scale occupation.'

He waited for a moment to allow Halifax to give a response, but there was none. 'You had an opportunity to help shape this country as a part of a great National Socialist empire and you have failed to grasp that.'

Halifax moved towards the door. 'Is that what you believe?' he said somberly. 'It's a delusion – you are no more than a captive yourself. You are tied hand and foot with strings – you are simply a puppet. I shall have no more to do with this business. I resign.'

That evening at eight o'clock, as he sat at the table for dinner with his wife, two men arrived at the house and Halifax was arrested. He was driven directly to the Tower of London and locked in a cell to await trial on a charge of treason.

Satisfied that he now had total control of the politics, Mosley set about planning his campaign to remodel the country in the image of Germany. He would, he convinced himself with satisfaction, now build a great Aryan state – he would be its architect and stand at its head. That night, as he fell into that world of half reality which occupies those moments between wakefulness and sleep, he mused on his future and conjured a myth of his greatness out of the mists of approaching dreams. He would be another Hitler – even greater.

CHAPTER 31

Christmas 1940

It had snowed hard all day in New York, bringing traffic sliding to a halt and paralyzing the overground rail tracks. Nearly nothing came in or went out of Grand Central. In Croton eleven inches fell overnight and Highway 9 going north to Buchanan and Peekskill was blocked. Higher up in the Catskills there was four feet of snow already on the ground and the forecast was for more. Right up to the Canadian border the countryside was a white wilderness; small towns and communities were socked in until the ploughs could get to work. The message was to stay home and wait.

'Come for Christmas,' Irena had pleaded with Carey two weeks before. 'I've invited the Churchills, Nigel and some of the others. It will be so much fun. You can bring your new friend if you wish,' she had added as an extra incentive. Carey had said she would think about it but deep down she didn't want to go – she was happy where she was in Tony's apartment, just the two of them. In Miami Tony's father had similar ideas. 'Come home for the holidays, your momma misses you.' It was more of an instruction than a request. 'Giorgi and Gina are coming with the family. You need to be here. Bring the new girl if you want – what's her name?'

'Carey'.

'Good, then it's settled.'

Now the snow put a stop to everything – they were absolved.

The same snow that put a stop to movement up and down New York State extended in a line right up the New England coast and inland to Lake Champlain and the Canadian border; but there it stopped. That winter a phenomenon in the form of an extended duration of the El Nino effect had driven warm air up from the central Pacific into Alaska and across the Rockies to the east coast of Canada. As a result, the seasonal snow that normally fell, covering the whole of Canada and paralysing the north, this year fell as rain; the thermometer refused to fall below freezing. Hudson Bay was experiencing a freak mild mid-winter with very little snow – it was virtually ice free. While Washington was faring no better than New York where life was shutting down, life in Canada was still moving; people were getting about as usual.

Carey stood at the window and looked out across Manhattan. From behind the glass where she stood on a deep-pile carpet, warmed by the central heating, the scene was a magical wonderland: white, silent and glittering with a billion diamond crystals of ice shattering the light, splitting the colours – blues from reds, greens from purples, and throwing up miniature rainbows wherever she looked. The sun was going down and soon the street lights would come on and create another, different, enchanted scene.

Tony came over to her and put an arm round her shoulder, resting his head against hers. 'I could stand here forever,' she said in a whisper. So they stood and watched together as the last rays dwindled and the blue velvet of a night sky wrapped itself over the city. The street lights came on like rows of brightly illuminated beads and in apartment windows across the city Christmas trees could be glimpsed, draped with tinsel and coloured lights.

'I have to go out,' Tony said. 'I have a small errand to run for Uncle Giorgi.'

'Must you darling,' she said plaintively. 'Can't it wait? It's so cold out there'

'I won't be long, promise. I owe him a favor and I'd like to get it out of the way before Christmas – especially since we won't be going down to Miami.'

'It'll be nice to be here, just us together. I'm going to try cooking our own feast.'

He laughed and hugged her. 'Honey, you can't cook – you told me.'

'I know, but I've bought a cook book and I've been reading up on how to do it. You'll see.'

She followed him to the door of the apartment, kissed him and waited, listening to the hum of the lift as it descended. She went back in and ran over to the window in time to see him emerge from the building and start off down the street. She watched until he disappeared from her sight. She looked at the clock in the kitchen – it was 5.10. She found her cook book and, sitting in a comfortable chair, opened its pages and started to look at the chapter headed 'Your Xmas Feast From Scratch – Give Your Santa His Own Surprise'.

She would surprise him, she told herself. How hard could it be to follow some written directions? There were illustrations giving step-by-step procedures with oven temperatures and other useful information. She remembered as a child she had watched her mother cook, but as Warren Taylor became richer Irena had given up on household chores and employed others to do them. The art of the kitchen had become fogged by mystery. Things happened behind closed doors and from her adolescence onwards food simply appeared on the table without explanation and without questions. Inside her she felt a tinge of excitement. She had never before thought of herself as a homemaker but things had changed. She had found this thing which had all this time been missing from her life but which she never knew had been missing – someone to care for who was not just Carey.

At seven she got up to make a cup of coffee. Tony was not back; he'd been gone for two hours but she hadn't noticed the time passing. Now when she saw the clock it occurred to her that he should have been back by now and she started to worry. She knew she wasn't any good at dealing with anxiety so she went back to the cook book and tried to put it out of her mind. She started to make lists of things she would need. She would make a scratch cake and she would make her own stuffing for the turkey. That would require all manner of things she didn't have; she would have to do some last-minute shopping.

Twenty minutes later she shut the book with a snap and stood up abruptly – she was trembling. She went to the cocktail cabinet and made herself a drink to take her mind off things. He'd been gone two and a half hours – what sort of errand was that? She paced up and down for ten minutes, switching out the living room light so she could see down into the lit street below. Every time someone walked past she pressed her face to the glass hoping that they would turn and disappear into the front entrance of the apartments. She fixed a second drink and watched the clock hands as they passed eight. By eight thirty he still hadn't returned and now she had a sinking feeling in her stomach; a touch of nausea was creeping up towards her throat. Nine o'clock came and went. She was starting to panic; something bad must have happened, she was convinced of it.

She decided she would phone the police to find out if any accidents had been reported. As she dialed for the operator her hands were shaking so badly she had to put her drink down on the table. The operator answered. She was about to speak when she heard the sound of a key in the apartment door and his voice as he called out, 'Hi Hon – I'm back.'

She dropped the phone and immediately the trembling stopped; a wave of relief flowed over her. She ran to the hallway and went to throw her arms around him, but he stepped back holding up a hand that was cut and bleeding. There was blood on his coat. He looked pale and his face was tense.

'What happened?' Carey said, catching her breath. He said nothing for a moment, searching for the words to tell her what had happened – words he knew were going to cause her panic and anxiety.

'There was a fight,' he finally said. 'I've killed a man – some two-bit pimp.' He looked at the horror on her face and waited for her so say something but she didn't, she just stood staring at him. 'He pulled a knife. We struggled and he got stabbed. I walked home; I couldn't risk the subway – not with all this blood.'

The words hung in the air for a few seconds then fell on her, smothering her with a cold fear. She watched silently as he carefully pulled his arm out of the sleeve of the coat holding his hand up to stop the blood dripping on the carpet.

'Get me a sheet off the bed – I have to get rid of this,' he said, bundling the coat up into a ball. Carey got the sheet and held it out to him her arms stiff and lifeless like a zombie. He took it and spread it out on the dining table. He laid the coat open on the sheet then picked up two heavy candlesticks and dumped them in the middle. All the while Carey just stood there rigidly, frozen, unable to speak.

'That should weight it down,' he said under his breath. He wrapped the coat around them and tied the bundle in the sheet.

'If anyone asks, I slipped in the snow and fell – I've gashed my hand. Find me something to bind this honey, can you?' They patched up his hand and she poured him a drink. Topping up her own, they sat down on the sofa together and he told her about it. He was surprisingly unmoved by what had happened and his calmness helped to sooth her anxiety.

'What do we do now?' she asked naively.

'I need to dump this in the river. We can drop it off a bridge – it'll go straight to the bottom with all that weight in it. Come on,' he said, putting his arm round her and giving her a hug. 'It'll be OK – you'll see.'

She nodded nervously. 'What about the police. Were you seen there by anyone?'

'I don't think the cops will spend too much time on it – he was a small time crook. He tried to clip Uncle Giorgi for a bundle and I went to collect. It just went wrong, that's all. It's done – there's nothing I can do to undo it.' He had put on a brave face for her. Inside he wasn't so sure – what shit luck, the weasel had pulled a knife, it had been an accident but who would believe that? He would just have to wait it out and see what happened.

'We should go out to a restaurant. I can't cook with my hand like this. We can walk to the Italian; it's only a block away. There're no cabs still; nothing's going anywhere out there except the subway.'

******

Hitler returned to Berlin briefly during the second week of December. He had made some strategic decisions. They had come to him in a dream and he woke with a clear view of how his next move should be shaped; it had been an omen and he was a strong believer in the occult.

The weather in the east had turned bitter. The warm air that was keeping most of Canada snow-free had come up against a Siberian cold front and been pushed away to the south west, warming the tip of England and the west coast of Ireland as it went before veering into the Atlantic and sliding down the western edge of Africa. Back in the autumn it had come to Hitler that the time was ripe for a campaign against Russia. Inspired by the Wehrmacht's overwhelming victories in France and the Low Countries, he had plans to attack Russia and to take over that half of Poland still in Soviet hands. It was not a new inspiration –

he had always viewed his expansion as being eastward. Earlier he had signed a non-aggression pact with Stalin, but he viewed the arrangement as a redundant charade which had served its purpose and was now time expired. With the rest of Poland annexed, his armies would be free to move on to Moscow. But the weather had not obliged and the Soviet Union, like the east coast of America, was frozen solid, as now were his plans to march east; they would have to wait on the summer.

Earlier, on 18 December, Hitler had summoned his top generals from the Oberkommando der Wehrmacht to a briefing at the Reichstag building in Berlin. Included among them were Generals Friedrich von Paulus and Heinz Guderian. Here he had ordered the group to commence work on a plan to invade the Soviet Union. It was a plan which left most of those at the meeting uneasy. Russia and its soviets was a vast territory with a massive population that could be pressed into service under arms; his generals were apprehensive. Hitler had dismissed their concerns, insisting it was a corrupt and rotten society and would collapse easily in the face of superior German fighting skills. It will cave in, he had predicted – 'All we have to do is kick in the front door.'

Despite Hitler's enthusiasm and confidence the idea was still not universally well received by the military men gathered in the room. Admiral Raeder had urged him to finish off the British position first, but Raeder had more personal motives. He was in a hurry to grab the Royal Navy and subsume its considerable strength into the Kreigsmarine. Hitler had refused, saying that the British were finished and that it could be left to Mosley to sort out the last remnants of opposition in the south of the country. The struggle that was taking place in England was, he had insisted, a sideshow. It should not deflect them from his greater plan of expanding eastwards.

Everyone except Hitler and Goering left the meeting with misgivings. Heinz Guderian, in particular, was worried. As the Wehrmacht's most senior and experienced tank general, he criticised the plan as flawed. It ran the risk of being a long and protracted campaign which would not be suited to his tactics. Guderian had been born in Poland of German parents; his father was a colonel in the Prussian Army and the son had inherited the same sense of loyalty and military discipline – but he could be abrasive. Behind a rather jolly, round and avuncular face was a tough, iron hard soldier who often fell out with his fellow officers. He was not afraid to argue, even with Hitler. He was a soldier with his own ideas of how war should be prosecuted – most of all he liked to get things done quickly and done right. Among the others he was known as 'Schneller Heinz' (Speedy Heinz). As early as 1934 he had started to develop the strategy of armoured divisions acting in concert with air power as a fast mobile force which could produce a high-speed thrust – it had become known as *blitzkrieg* (lightning war).

Guderian stayed behind after most of the others had left the meeting with the purpose in mind of confronting Hitler. He saw dangers in the Russian campaign – technical difficulties they were not ready to overcome. Russia presented problems for waging armoured warfare. A winter campaign was out of the question, he advised Hitler; the vehicles would struggle to operate in the savagely low temperatures out on the Steppes. The spring is wet and the land turns to deep mud, he insisted. It could prove fatal for heavy armour. Any advance would be slow – worse, it could become totally bogged down – vehicles could not operate in such conditions. The autumn would be just as bad; only the summer could provide a viable window and that was short everywhere except in the south, which was only a small area. For the rest of the Soviets they had three months, maybe four, but no more than that.

There had been a fierce argument, but Hitler would not listen. If Goering could deliver with the Luftwaffe in these conditions, Hitler had shouted at him, then he was expected to do the same. When Guderian countered that there was no mud in the sky, Hitler went into a rage. Hadn't the army, under his inspired guidance, delivered the west in three short months, he railed. What was so different with the Soviets? It was a matter of distance, Guderian told him calmly. To cover and support that distance will require many more tanks and trucks, much more fuel, ammunition and food than can be delivered at the present time. Guderian was slightly taller than the Führer but Hitler looked him in the eye menacingly and told him that he, Hitler, was the Commander-in-Chief of German forces and, playing on Guderian's Prussian sense of his oath of loyalty, persuaded him to step down from his opposition. Hitler had trumped the argument and won the day.

Two days after the confrontation, however, Hitler summoned Guderian and Von Paulus to a private meeting, again at the Reichstag. He had, he said, reconsidered the campaign against Russia and had decided it should be shelved for later. Instead, he now ordered the two men to bring forward Operation Gottlieb. It was an operation so secret that only four other generals knew of it. It needs your planning skills, he told von Paulus, and it needs Heinz's tank strategy. When the two men left the meeting Guderian turned to Von Paulus. 'Well Friedrich, this is more to my taste than the Russian adventure.'

They parted and, as Von Paulus got into his car, he shouted over to his friend, 'I'll see you in 1941 – enjoy your Christmas'.

******

Tom got leave for the holiday and went home to Peekskill. The journey was long, cold and difficult. The train out of Georgia to New York was delayed but it ran. When he arrived at Grand Central the concourse was crowded and for a while nothing was operating. People sat on the benches and on the stairs – all waiting for news that their particular track was cleared of snow and their train could go. Steam rose from the barrows of the hot food vendors where queues of cold people formed to get something to warm them. But despite the cold they seemed happy enough – it was a holiday, the station was strung with lights and decorations; there was a big tree covered in baubles and brightly wrapped packages, and a band was playing carols. It was Christmas and Tom could feel it.

He finally made it home to the warmest of warm welcomes. Martha kissed and hugged him until he thought she would never let go. Holly was smiling broadly and slapping him on the back – and then there was Wheels, jumping up and barking excitedly. There were fires in all the rooms and the comforting smell of cookies and coffee spilled out from the kitchen. After dinner they talked long and late into the night; there was so much to say, so much to tell and for once in their lives it all seemed to be good. When he told them about Dottie, Martha almost passed out with delight and immediately wanted to know when he would bring her home to meet them.

'Well, if they can get the roads ploughed, I plan to go down to Croton and fetch her the day after Christmas.'

He had written to her twice while he'd been in camp and each time he got a letter back by return. Now he was impatient to see her again. As the memory of Carey faded, it occurred to him just how dumb he had been about Dottie, in not seeing her for the girl she was all those times he'd sat in the diner. Now, away from her, he realized how much he wanted her and how he would make up for it. The more he thought on it the more he concluded she was Miss Perfect for him. Mike had been right all along – now they were walking out together he could find the right moment and ask her to marry him. Each time he'd had a half-day pass he went straight to town and looked in the jewellery stores. He would buy her a ring, something nice, not too flashy, something with class. At night he looked at the picture she had sent him, pinned to the inside of his locker door. She had the most perfectly pretty face, framed by curling blond hair, with large blue eyes and a smile he would happily die for. He could barely wait to see her again.

The day after Christmas he took his time and drove down to Croton. At the front door he hesitated for a moment before ringing the bell, savoring the anticipation of that moment when he would see her again. She smiled and said, 'Hi Tom, come on in,' and led him by the hand through to the living room where her father and mother were waiting. James Brent was a friendly, comfortable man – easy to talk to.

'So, young man,' he said, 'you've come to take my daughter away for the day, have you.' It was more a statement than a question. Tom agreed he had but that he would bring her back not too late in the day.

'My folks would very much like to meet Dottie,' he said respectfully.

'Well, then, they've got a very pleasant surprise coming.'

'I think so.'

His wife let out a little laugh. 'Really James, you'll embarrass the poor boy – take no notice Tom. Go on the both of you and have a really nice day.'

They left and, as they got to the car, Tom took his chance and stole a kiss. She smiled and looked at him, then reached up and brushed his hair with her hand. 'It looks better now that it's grown a bit,' she said. All the way they talked non-stop – there was so much to say, so much to tell. She would graduate next semester and then go on to medical school. She had a placement lined up that was attached to Grasslands teaching hospital in Valhalla and she could barely wait to go.

'The house isn't as grand as your folks' place,' Tom warned her as they came into Union Avenue.

'Doesn't matter,' she smiled. 'I came to see your parents, not the house. I guess we'll get by.'

Martha could hardly contain herself. 'Isn't she just the picture,' she told Holly after they had gone. 'I'm so happy – what a lovely girl.'

Over tea they made a lot of small talk and Wheels came by to see what the fuss was about. He behaved himself and as a reward Dottie patted his head and gave him a biscuit. As he drove her home Tom asked her if she would be his regular date and she said she would very much like that. Two days later he was back at camp and missing her more than he thought he would. There wouldn't be another leave until passing out at the end of February – it seemed an eternity away and the days would go slowly. He wrote twice a week and twice a week she wrote back. Over at the diner there were squeaks of delight when the girls heard the news. Even the boys in the kitchen celebrated by banging pans and drumming on the table tops with their long-bladed palate knives. Walking home after work, she thought of him all the time and deep inside she smiled. Everything was going all right – she had her career and she had her man; what else could a girl want, she told herself.

******

In Washington things were quiet. News came in regularly but it was uneventful; things in Britain had reached a stalemate. Alan Brooke had pulled back to a line just south of London, leaving the Germans in Hull free to break out, but nothing had happened. Orders from Berlin were to let Mosley and the BBS deal with it.

414

They controlled everything north of the line Churchill had drawn on his map. Now they were preparing to move against Brooke's forces, but it would be slow. The BBS was short of men and recruiting had proved more difficult than Mosley had supposed. He needed officers, men who could lead and direct, but there was a reluctance amongst the educated middle class in the towns to become a part of what most people now saw as a quasi-Nazi organization. In the villages there was resentment at their strutting, bullying attitudes; the rural population had grown used to nothing more authoritarian than the village bobby and an undercurrent of discontent bubbled just beneath the surface.

Park was taking stock of what he had left in fuel, ammunition and spares to keep his planes flying. He had been obliged to abandon Northolt almost immediately after he had bailed out of Caistor. He knew he had to control the airspace along the south coast if he was to protect the Navy; he therefore spread his squadrons around the Kent and Hampshire airfields but that was as far west as he would go. His resources were already spread thinly and he knew he couldn't cope with long lines of communication and hope to hold them against a concerted attack. There was at least one bright spot for him, though: at Kingston the BBS had tried to cut off and close the Hawker factory but they had underestimated the determination of the garrison that Brooke had established there and had come with only light armoured cars. Fearing there would be close hand-to-hand fighting, the approaching BBS column avoided the narrow road that led along the edge of Richmond Park and instead used the Kingston Bypass. It was wide and open with three traffic lanes and gave the vehicles room to manoeuvre, offering a much better field of fire. To get to the Hawker factory they would have to go as far south as the suburban town of Tolworth, then turn east towards their objective. But by doing this they brought themselves in range of the gun battery at Chessington, which their intelligence had failed to spot. One of Brooke's observers in the attic of a large three-storey house in Tolworth watched their arrival, radioed the coordinates to Chessington and ranged the guns. By the third salvo the armoured cars were in trouble.

Another BBS group in a short column of troop trucks, which had decided to take a narrow route further east of the Bypass, was ambushed in the park itself and pinned down by machine gun fire; they abandoned their vehicles and retreated on foot through the cover of the parkland trees. What was emerging was that the fighting quality of the average BBS man was poor. Brooke's men, on the other hand, had survived Dunkirk and had been seasoned in battle. As the BBS fled back towards London, they left behind a valuable haul of arms, ammunition and vehicles. Brooke had ordered that wherever possible his men should avoid destroying vehicles – he needed everything he could get to replace his own losses.

Following that incident Armitage suggested to Grainger he should deliver two of the Panzer IVs to Kingston to beef up the defence of the Hawker factory.

******

Clementine contemplated the snow-covered garden and thought what a nuisance it was they hadn't been able to go to Brunessemer for the holiday. She missed the companionship of Irena to whom she had grown quite close. Instead she had arranged Christmas dinner at a restaurant for the whole group and told Winston he could not spend the day closeted in his little office playing war games. They went to church in the morning and then returned to the house in Arlington where she had organized mince pies and sherry to be served. As was their tradition they would not sit down to the feast until four o'clock.

'I've had to promise not to go out today,' he confided in Loughlin. 'The boss has grounded me – but that's not to say *you* can't,' and he nudged him and winked. 'Slip out and see what's happening. I can't put up with not knowing what's going on.'

When Loughlin got back he looked excited. 'They've got Anthony out,' he whispered to Churchill, as Clementine called them to say the taxis had arrived to take them to the restaurant.

'How?'

'No idea. I picked it up on Radio Free London; they put out a special bulletin. They say it's probably the same chap who lifted Armitage from the BBS in Bermondsey. They're calling him the new Scarlet Pimpernel.'

'That'll make the Christmas pud go down well,' Churchill grinned. 'Good show, eh?'

As they sat to eat, Churchill proposed the loyal toast, then announced the news. 'Anthony's free,' he said cheerfully. 'He's with Brookie and his men – safe for the moment. I give you Anthony and his family.' They all raised their glasses for the second time.

'Thank God,' Clementine said in a hushed voice. 'What a relief.'

******

The winter in the barn near Biggin Hill was uncomfortable. There were cracks in the timber-clad structure through which the wind blew and even the stove couldn't keep the occupants warm. The men sheltering there were hardened veterans but they found it tough; it was the hardest winter for years. The consolation was that it had practically halted any BBS activity. Grainger had persuaded Armitage to scoop up the best men of the 44th parachute regiment and shelter them in MI5. Over the past couple of months he had turned them into a sabotage squad, which he now intended to turn loose on the BBS and the Germans.

In the gloom of the hurricane lamps that dimly lit the barn Grainger's men huddled around the iron stove and turned on the radio to listen. 'This is the BBC Home Service; here is the six o'clock news. Good evening, this is Edwin Harvard.'

'A tribunal of three judges has this morning unanimously passed the death sentence on former Members of Parliament, Ernest Bevin and Hugh Dalton, for treason, conspiracy to overthrow the government and insurrection. In his summing up the Lord Chief Justice, Sir Piers Bannister, said the men had admitted to their crimes and had pleaded for leniency. They will be transferred later this week from Maidstone Prison to Wandsworth Prison, where they will be hanged.'

Armitage looked over to Grainger. 'We don't have much time if we're going to do something about it.'

'I've got a plan. Maidstone's in our patch now, isn't it?'

'Well, yes and no.'

'What's that supposed to mean?'

'It means yes it's our side of the line, but no we don't control it yet. Brooke's men are spread thin so he's just put a circle round the less important places and cooped them up.'

Grainger thought for a moment. 'How will they get them out and up to Wandsworth for the hangings then? They'll have to pass through Brooke's lines, won't they?'

'They'll fly them out,' one of Grainger's men offered. 'There're plenty of places to put a light plane down inside the town.'

Grainger scratched his head with both hands, ruffling his hair. 'In that case we'd better get on with it. If we can bust in and neutralise the BBS, has Brooke got enough men to fill in the gaps? Occupy it – bring it under our control?'

'I don't know,' Armitage shrugged. 'We'd better ask him.'

******

Four of Grainger's six remaining tanks clanked out of their woodland cover and headed for the main road to Maidstone. As they passed through the army cordon that formed their own defensive line they were joined by two companies of Brooke's infantry. Together with ten of Grainger's Special Forces it swelled their number to about two hundred and fifty. With the barrier lifted, they passed into no man's land and set off along the A229.

On the outskirts of the town they encountered the first BBS road block. It was manned by a company of Blackshirts and four German officers from an SS regiment. There was a pole barring the way and to one side a pit had been sandbagged and a machine gun mounted in it. The group manning the post had been standing around smoking and chatting. A wooden shed with a stove inside had been erected near to the barrier to give them shelter when the weather was bad. The day, however, was clear and although the air was still sharp from a morning frost, the whole contingent was outside. The first indication that something was happening was when they heard the low rumble of the tanks' engines. Then they heard the clanking, squealing sound of the metal tracks as the iron monsters ground their way across the stone-embedded tarmac surface of the road.

At first, they just stood there looking at the approaching tank, which was still in Wehrmacht camouflage and carried the black-cross markings of the German army. Then somebody on the barricade cheered and shouted, 'We've been relieved.'

The hatch was lifted on the Panzer. Grainger emerged and trained the tank's machine gun on the BBS men. Through the crisp morning air he heard the sound of a breach being cocked over in the machine gun pit. He fired a burst across the heads of the men manning it.

'Drop your weapons and put your hands on your head,' Grainger shouted. From behind the tank a dozen men appeared, all in irregular uniform and carrying an odd assortment of sub-machine guns. Even the more disciplined Germans could see there was no chance of resisting and threw their arms up over their heads.

The rest of the way to Maidstone was uneventful and they managed to get to the center of the town without any resistance. There were Blackshirts about, but surprisingly few, and they took the presence of the tanks as some kind of German reinforcement. Slowly and painstakingly they made their way to the prison. Grainger had brought four tanks with him; he placed one of them in front of the large heavy wooden gates to the prison. Another he parked in front of the police station, and the other two were deployed a short distance away to face the BBS barracks.

The first indication the Governor of the prison had was when a warder knocked on his door and breathlessly announced that there was a German tank at the front gate, but it had a British crew and they were demanding to see him.

'Open up', Grainger demanded in his perfect Oxford accent. 'I want the politicians you are holding – all fourteen and I want them now.' He leaned down from the turret to get closer to the Governor, 'Or I reduce this place to a pile of fucking rubble and dump it on top of you for a tombstone. Is that clear? Jolly good.'

The BBS barracks surrendered after only two shots had been fired. The high-explosive shells went straight into the main entrance and knocked out the retaining pillars. The whole of the façade of the four-storey building peeled away and fell into the street, throwing a cloud of dust over everything. Under the cover of the dust the BBS opened up with an assortment of small arms fire which pinged, zipped and ricocheted around the street; it made no impression on the armour. In the end a blast from the Panzer's flamethrower was enough to finish the business and the defenders suddenly changed their minds. As they filed out through the rubble of the collapsed building, covered in dust, some bleeding from their injuries, uniforms torn from their bodies by the blast, they became exposed for what they were – a group of well-armed but poorly led, badly shaken men. For most it had been their first and only experience of combat, and it was apparent from their faces they had not liked it. One by one they threw their weapons in a pile under the watchful menace of the tank, the nozzle of the flamethrower poking out threateningly towards them. They stumbled away, a ragged column of beaten men, the taste of dust and defeat mixed in their mouths like cement – nobody talked. Only the groans from the wounded punctuated the sound of shuffling feet as they began to feel the disabling pains of their injuries. Inside the building they found those who couldn't walk for their wounds and those who couldn't walk because they were dead. Raking through the rubble, they recovered the bodies of five men killed by falling masonry. Sitting on a toilet they found a sixth, a victim of the blast, he sat with his trousers round his ankles in serene repose. There was not a mark on him – the blast had pulled all the air out of his lungs and he had suffocated.

When Bevin and Dalton were handed over they were at first speechless. Then Bevin laughed out loud. 'Thanks, lads,' he shouted, 'you've just captured the new capital of England.'

They marched the straggling column of BBS men over to the prison where the governor now enthusiastically found enough cells to lock them in; then they waited for Brooke's men to arrive. Maidstone was now theirs. Slowly people began to gather at the scene of the destroyed building, asking what had happened; some cheering when they heard.

Bevin and the other politicians immediately moved into the Town Hall, declared it the only legitimate Parliament of Britain and set about putting together the instruments of government. It was, they knew, going to be a difficult task but now they had somewhere to operate from, and, even better, they were alive – not hanging off the end of a rope. It took two days to round up the remnants of the BBS; not all of them had been in the building that day. On news of the events, men had thrown away their uniforms. Some were found hiding at home – there was no shortage of vengeful informers to point a finger at them – some tried to escape across the Medway river, which now formed the new border with the rest of occupied Britain in that area.

Brooke and Park found a small building near to the Town Hall and set up their Command HQ. The next day they were joined by Armitage. Back at the barn Grainger and his men packed their kit, loaded the remaining tanks on their transporters and drove the convoy to the town. People at the roadside cheered them as they arrived and then gathered round to gaze at the monsters and touch them. Standing in Town Square, waiting for instructions on where they would be billeted, the men and their machines formed a strange and awesome spectacle like floats in a bizarre carnival. Children who came to gawp were lifted up by the soldiers and set down on the great iron beasts where they shouted to passers-by. Small, smooth hands patted the solid armour plate, in places four inches thick, and laughter rang out everywhere in the square.

'These tanks are bloody useful things,' Grainger told Armitage when he got back to the HQ. 'It was a good move of yours to pinch them.'

******

The phone on Mosley's desk rang. It was Linz; he'd heard about the rout at Maidstone. 'You must attend at my office immediately. I have to report this to Berlin.'

As he was driven the three miles to the Legation building, Mosley began to consider his position. He had lost control of Maidstone. Yes – but it was taken with German armour, armour that Linz had allowed to fall into enemy hands. Then there was another disaster – two loaded freight trains had disappeared; trains with food, ammunition, weapons and much more, all destined for his garrison in Maidstone. For weeks now the countryside had been relatively quiet, so it had been possible to keep the town supplied down the main line rail corridor. Trains had come and gone unmolested, although they had added the precaution of dedicated gun platforms front and back. The enemy stuck mostly to the towns they held and left the countryside to get on with its own life. The supply trains only had to cross a narrow strip along the Medway to enter the safety of the town – except that when they had arrived this time the town was no longer 'safe.' It had changed hands; Brooke was delighted with the gifts from London.

Linz was young for his rank – just 30, but it was war and the young were needed. He was Austrian but referred to himself as Bavarian; blond-haired and blue-eyed, he considered himself a true Aryan in the Nazi tradition – he didn't tolerate failure and could barely contain his anger at the ease with which Maidstone had been given away.

'It is clear your command is not competent to deal with the problems,' he said curtly to Mosley. 'I have requested a battalion of Waffen SS and we shall see if they can do the job for you.' The castigation stung Mosley. He left the meeting

420

determined to sort out his own problems before Linz could bring in others – others who might decide he wasn't needed.

In Washington, George Marshall got word of the fall of Maidstone from Loughlin, who'd had it in a report from Alpha Six. 'I just don't understand why they haven't gone ahead and swamped the British', Marshall told Roosevelt. 'It doesn't make sense – it flies in the face of military logic.'

CHAPTER 32

Georgia, 4 February 1941

It was graduation day. He would finally get his commission. There was an air of celebration about it; more of a party than a military day parade with families, wives, mothers, fathers and girlfriends, they were all there – witnesses on this most important occasion for the young men about to get their shoulder bars. The night before the event Martha, Holly and Dottie had driven down together and stopped the night in the town. Tom's brigade marched out to the strains of a band and were drawn up in ranks before the commanding officer. It was cold but the day was bright. Beyond the camp gates out on the streets the sidewalks were still piled with snow that had been shoveled and blown into banks, pushed in heaps up against buildings and fences where it would wait, frozen and grey, mired and flecked with black detritus from the street, until the thaw.

Martha was puffed up to bursting with pride. 'He looks so handsome in his uniform,' she said to Dottie as they stood to watch the ceremony. A colonel mounted the steps to the stage from which the cadets were to be reviewed and addressed. The graduation speech was short and emphasized the role they would play in shaping the new army that was now being developed. There was talk of newer and better weapons, the need to learn about them and to use their skills not only to develop their own careers but also to pass them on to the men they would be commanding. They would have a duty and a responsibility to the men under their command for their care and training whether in camp or on the battlefield. Finally they were reminded of the oath they would take later to loyally serve their country and the flag. The colonel finished; a cheer went up and the cadets threw their hats into the air – they were now junior officers.

'We've lined up something special,' Martha announced.

Every new officer got a pass – they could go out of the camp and celebrate their graduation till eight o'clock. After that they had to be back in their barracks where the following morning they would get their posting orders. Tom had no idea where it was he might be sent, but hoped it was somewhere north where he could be close to Dottie.

'I'd like to see you alone,' he told her when they reached the hotel where she and his parents were staying. 'There's something I'd like to ask you.' Dottie nodded, giving him a shy look.

They hung about in the lobby, waiting for Holly and Martha to go to their room, but Holly sat down in one of the easy chairs and picked up a newspaper. He settled in comfortably and showed no signs of wanting to move. Tom was frustrated. I have to fix this, he thought, and moved across to his mother who was talking to the concierge, getting directions to the restaurant.

'I'd like some time alone with Dottie,' he whispered.

'Of course,' she said, with a knowing look. She walked over to where her husband seemed like he was settled in for the duration. 'Come on, Holly,' she said, 'let's go to the room and freshen up before we go out.'

'You go on up,' Holly replied, with his head still in the newspaper. 'I don't need to freshen up – I'll just stay here and keep these young folk company.'

It was not what Tom wanted to hear and he shot a perplexed glance at Dottie, who had already guessed what was coming and didn't want his father getting in the way. She was about to say something but then Martha stepped in.

'Hollister Jordan,' she said imperiously, like a monarch dishing out a royal command. 'These two don't want you hanging around messing in their private moments. Come upstairs and change your tie or something.' She gave his arm a tug and the penny dropped. He looked at them sheepishly. Martha jerked her head towards the staircase; Holly got the message. 'Oh yeah, sorry. I think I'll change my shoes too while I'm about it. These new ones are nice but they're pinching a bit.'

Alone, they stood looking at each other. Tom fumbled in his pocket. 'I don't really know how to do this,' he said apologetically. 'I'm not very good at these things.'

Dottie waited patiently, her lips slightly parted as if about to say something. She held her breath as he finally managed to get a small box out from his tunic pocket. He opened the lid and there it was – a flawless diamond set around with rubies resting on a gold band. It was her moment and when he faltered trying to find the right words she beat him to it. 'Yes,' she said, her eyes wide open and looking deep into his. 'Take your time, but the answer is yes.'

A woman passing looked at the ring and then at Tom. 'Lucky girl,' she said chuckling. 'Hold on to it – hold on to both of them.'

Dottie smiled back at the stranger. 'I intend to.' Then she put her arms around his neck and they kissed a long, slow kiss, warm and moist and full of desire. 'I'm so happy,' she said, cuddling up to him and putting her arms round his waist. Tom looked down at her and in a hushed voice asked her to marry him. 'I thought you'd never ask,' she replied, and they both broke into laughter.

The clerk on the reception desk, who had all the time been watching, shook his head wistfully as if remembering something like that in his own life. Then he came out from behind his counter, his face positively beaming and enthusiastically congratulated them. When Holly and Martha came down, the first thing she did was show them the ring, then she kissed them both in turn. 'I think we should get some champagne,' Tom said.

The next day Tom got his orders; he was to report to Fort Bliss in El Paso, Texas – about as far away from Croton as you could get. He'd been assigned to the 1st Armored Division. What lousy luck, he cursed when he got his papers. 'Don't worry,' his drill sergeant had said when he told him. 'Wait six months and put in for a transfer; you're bound to get it.'

At Fort Bliss, when he told his platoon sergeant the advice, he laughed and saluting said, 'Pardon me, Lieutenant sir, but that's just army bullshit. No one goes nowhere with this here Division except to fight and I don't hear no gunfire coming out of New York State just now. You best marry the little lady and apply for quarters here.'

The first weeks passed more quickly than Tom had imagined they would. He wrote regularly to Dottie and she always wrote back. She was now at Valhalla and starting on her medical internship. Her letters were filled with the detail of her daily routine.

Grasslands Medical School
Valhalla
New York

February 6, 1941

Darling Tom
It is so exciting to be part of this medical school. We have a wonderful teacher, Doctor Cole – he's so patient with all the new students. I realize now I am not half as clever as I thought I was; there's just so much to learn. I do miss you so very much – when do you get your first leave ? I'm simply bursting to see you again.
We went to Grasslands Hospital today – it's my first time doing ward rounds. There were four of us students with a doctor and an intern. It was truly fascinating and I think I have made the right decision to do medicine. The intern said we'd better learn to do without sleep because once you're an intern you're up all the hours day and night. I really miss you so much.
All my love, my darling.
Yours forever.
Dottie

At first when he came to Fort Bliss everything seemed strange; it was not like training camp. He had been allocated to a platoon as second in command to a

Lieutenant Robert Duncan. Duncan was a tall, languid individual who looked more like a Hollywood star than a soldier. He was pale and slim with dark wavy hair, a polished Vermont accent and a Harvard education. He insisted on being called Bob when not in front of the platoon, which Tom found awkward since he had no empathy with the man. He was older than Tom by a year and a bit. As the junior officer in the platoon, Tom took instruction from Duncan but as the days passed he found himself taking on more and more of the duties and operating on his own initiative. Lieutenant Duncan was not a diligent officer; Tom thought him lazy and inclined to pass everything over to him. 1st Platoon was one of four that made up B Company, which was under the command of a Captain White. It comprised 38 men: a sergeant, two corporals and 35 privates, most of them were enlisted though he noticed there were increasingly draft men coming into the camp as Roosevelt's program to expand the size of the armed forces shifted up a gear. Every day he had a desk of paper to move: requisitions, requests from the men to be heard, medical inspections, kit inspections, parade drills; there wasn't time to think of much else. Only in the evenings did he find the time to miss her and then he would write her a letter and look at her picture.

On the second Monday after his arrival Duncan informed him it was weapons practice that morning and he'd ordered the platoon sergeant to make the men ready, then march them down to the range.

'You can take them for this one,' Duncan said, leaning back in his chair. 'It's dreadfully tedious standing out there in that goddamned desert watching them. You like shooting, don't you?'

'I don't mind.'

'Good, then it's yours.'

The insignia on the front gate announced that it was an armored Division but the reality was they didn't have a lot of armor. Their entire complement was only 37 M2 tanks – biscuit tins on tracks, Captain White had called them dismissively. White was a cavalryman; he preferred horses and didn't believe motor vehicles could ever replace the horse for encircling manoeuvres. He was too young to have been in the Great War – to see the mules and horses sliced through with shell-burst shrapnel, ripped to ribbons by machine guns, eyes wide in terror and screaming like demons from hell. He still held a romantic notion of the charge; bearing down on the terrified enemy, sabre drawn, yelling for blood – this was the ultimate glorious illusion he held dear to his heart with a pride that defied logic. One only had to watch a 50-calibre machine gun in action to know it was the ultimate dreamy folly.

The division also had 14 M2 scout cars, a handful of M3 halftracks and some anti-aircraft guns mounted on flatbed trucks. Not a lot really when he considered that just the columns the Germans had employed for the invasion of Poland had over two thousand tanks and although they were receiving new allocations on a daily basis, nevertheless, most of the regiments in the division were infantry. They knew nothing about these new instruments of war; they were foot sloggers, men who fought with rifles, machine guns and bayonets. It was therefore all the more surprising to Tom when he saw how bad the standard of marksmanship was.

Out at the range the platoon sergeant had the men in their firing positions and ordered them to commence free firing. After observing their dismal performance for a few minutes, Tom called the platoon sergeant over to him. 'These men don't know how to shoot sergeant – their standard is dumb. Who's been training them?'

'They don't get no training sir, not here. They just come down every Monday and fire off a few rounds. What you see is how they come to us.'

He barely believed what he was hearing. 'Well, we're going to have to change all that.'

'How's that sir?'

'We're gonna show them how it's done. It's called instruction, sergeant. Call them to attention please – we need a little chat with these guys.'

The men stacked their arms and gathered round in a semi-circle, standing at ease and wondering what it was about. It had to be important because officers didn't do much talking direct to the men, one private commented to another next to him.

'Corporal,' he said, handing the man a rifle. 'Let's see you shoot from the standing position; a full clip please – rapid fire.' The corporal shot off eight rounds then came to attention, returned to the circle and handed the rifle to the sergeant.

'Two out of eight hit the target corporal – twenty-five percent. If you ever get into a shooting war I don't much rate your chances of seeing out the tour.'

'Sergeant, give me a rifle.' He turned to face the men. 'Now watch and learn.'

Tom stepped up to the plate and shot his eight rounds. There was astonished silence as they looked at the grouping on the target. 'Okay,' he said, stacking the rifle and addressing the platoon. 'We're going to teach you men a few basics you seem to be lacking. Rule one – some of you men are pulling on the trigger. Squeeze, don't pull. If you pull the trigger you'll pull the gun off the target and you won't hit anything – and if the target you're shooting at is the enemy and he's squeezing while you're pulling – well, he's gonna get you. That'll be your war over and a sad telegram to your mother.

'Rule two – concentrate. Look at the target and bring the sight up to meet your eye, not the other way round.

'Rule three – if you really want to make the shot count and you have the time, regulate your breathing. In combat there probably isn't going to be the opportunity for that luxury, but here on the range you have the time – so practice it.

'Rule four – I notice some of you men blink when you fire. No blinking; you can't hit a target with your eyes closed.

'Sergeant, thank you. Let's see if they can put some of that into practice.'

Fort Bliss
El Paso, Texas
February 10, 1941
Dearest Dottie
Sweet heart, I had a salutary experience today. Some of the men we have here are so awful in their marksmanship I have had to institute a basic training procedure. This is especially true of the new drafted men who everyone around here calls the dog faces. I find it hard to believe that we still don't properly train our infantrymen in firearms proficiency. Tomorrow I'm going to put in a request to our company commander to set up a shooting competition with a three-hour gate pass for the prize; there's nothing like a gate pass to get the men keen. I miss you so terribly, honey – I try not to let it get to me during the day but as I lie here in my bunk I think of you constantly.
The rest of the time here is pretty dull with just a lot of routine paperwork to get through. I didn't realize until I came here just how many forms there were in the Army; you could chop down half a forest and still not have enough pulp to make the paper consumed.
The weather is good here but I miss the trees – there's nothing but sage brush and cactus for as far as the eye can see. I'm not sure when I get my next leave but I'll write you as soon as I hear.
All my love, Tom

15 February 1941
Dearest Dottie
Great news, my darling – I've been recommended for promotion, albeit a temporary rank but I am being made up to captain. The marksman training program I worked up went down real well, so well in fact I am now charged with rolling it out to every company on the base. It is an exceptional position though I shall stay on my existing pay grade, but I am more than content with it. I have written this hurriedly and won't say more at the moment because I am to go before a board this afternoon to plan the detail of the new task.
Still missing you desperately, all my love honey,
Your Tom

Grasslands
Valhalla
February 17, 1941
My Darling Tom
How wonderful! Is there any chance of you getting leave with the new post –
even a day pass would be lovely. I could get the train down and we could have a
day together. Everything here is as usual and I'm studying hard; I just hope I
can keep it up for the next three years. I've given up working at Jennifer's; it
was just too much to cope with. Of course mother and father are delighted but
they are right – I need all my time and energy for studying. I miss the company
of the girls though; they were fun but I'm finding the student group very
friendly, so that's alright.
I ran into Mike Mescal the other day. They are expecting their first baby and
he's over the moon; that was quick work. Anyway, he sends his best to you and
asks you to look him up when you're back and have the time.
Now for some rather shocking news, I'm afraid. Tony Gagliardi, who you used
to hunt with, has been arrested on suspicion of murder. It's sketchy; Mike didn't
know a lot about it but it seems he got into a knife fight and killed a man. I know
they betrayed you but I feel rather sorry for Caroline Taylor – in the end she
was quite besotted with him.
That's all the news my darling – I think of you always. Do let me know if you
can get a pass. Maybe you could enter one of your competitions for one of those
pass prizes; you'd be bound to win.
All my love as ever,
Dottie

Bob Duncan came into the office they shared and leaned on the door. When
Tom looked up Duncan jerked smartly to attention and saluted him, but it was
more of a joking gesture than anything. 'Permission to speak sir,' he said
mockingly.

'Cut it out, Bob.'

Duncan sat down at his desk. 'That's nice work, though. Wish I'd thought that
one up.'

'How's your shooting?'

'Frankly – fucking terrible.'

'Then you probably need to join the course.'

'I'm not sure that's a good move. There's an armored vehicle training exercise
this afternoon, though – we get to drive one of those halftracks that came in the
other day. Here,' he passed over the orders of the day typed on a single sheet of
paper, 'our attendance is required.'

The armored convoy made its way out into the desert led by a group of officers in four Jeeps. In their wake six halftracks and then four light tanks kicked up a plume of dust. A team of specialist mechanics in a truck hung back to keep out of the way of the grit spurting off the column, cursing the unremitting suspension and the heat of the day, damning the stupidity of the officers and swearing about everything in general. They were truck mechanics who knew their trade, but armored vehicles were something new. At the end of the Great War they barely existed and America had left it to the British and the French to develop these machines. Now truck manufacturers, White and Autocar, had started building stuff; big plates of thick steel welded together with Cadillac and Ford engines shoehorned into them. They were difficult to work on and they kept breaking down – nobody liked them.

Tom found his thoughts drawn back to an exhibit at the World's Fair – an exposition all about tank development. He'd picked up a magazine with pictures of a German armored column thrusting into Poland. He thought at the time how mean they looked, low and squat with powerful 75mm guns and very thick armor; crouching and prowling, looking ready to spring on their prey, metal-clad equivalents of the animals they were named after – Tiger and Panther.

As they stood round the halftrack Tom's first impression was how flimsy it looked when he compared it with what he had seen in that magazine. They took it in turns to handle the machine, driving it around the rough desert ground, across gullies, up and down dried out river beds. It handled well enough and went across areas of soft sand where you wouldn't have gone with a Jeep. But his recollection of the Germans was their armor was four inches thick. The halftrack and the tanks he stood looking at were made of plate only just over one inch thick and their armament was only 35mm, all right to fight infantry but other tanks – he had his doubts. He knew they were developing bigger, heavier equipment. He just hoped they would come up with something more substantial because if they got into Europe again he didn't like the look of the odds. He shared his thoughts with the senior instructor.

'Don't worry Captain,' the instructor said with an air of confidence. 'I've seen what's on the blue prints and it's world class.'

Fort Bliss
El Paso, Texas
February 18, 1941

Dearest Dottie
I can't believe my luck. I'm to be transferred temporarily to Pine Camp in New Jersey to set up a training program there so I'll be just up the road from you.

My transport is arranged for Saturday 22nd. The army is flying me to New York. I'll be taking the train up to Syracuse and I should be at Grand Central around midday, but my connection isn't till three that afternoon so we could meet on the concourse and maybe go somewhere for coffee – can you get away for that?

I shan't be sorry to leave El Paso, I don't really like the dryness of the desert and I miss the Adirondacks. There's nearly nothing to hunt out here, the land is flat, barren scrub, hardly capable of sustaining anything more than tumbleweed and cactus – I can't imagine why anyone would want live here. We took one of the M3s out on a border patrol yesterday – they get terribly hot in the midday sun and we mostly drive with all the hatches open. I'm not sure that would be so good in combat conditions. I had my first staff officer meeting with our Colonel and three other captains today. The idea was to hand over the training program and brief them in its roll-out across the division. I can't say I thought they were terribly enthusiastic – like White they are all horsemen at heart, though I can't see how wielding sabres is going to win us a war if we're unlucky enough to get dragged into Europe. I have to say nobody down here seems even remotely concerned that we shall get involved; I wish I was able to share their conviction.

Anyway, I must fly if I'm to get this into this evening's mail – let me know if you can do Grand Central. Miss you lots, all my love,
Tom

Croton on Hudson
February 20, 1941
Dear Tom
Something has happened which we need to talk over. I won't put it in a letter as it would be unfair and we need to do this face to face. I will be at Grand Central at 3.00 pm day after tomorrow and we can speak then.
Dottie

The letter kept him awake all night and he felt ragged in the morning. What the hell could it mean? Why was it so cold and formal? What could there be that was so serious she couldn't put it in a letter? He tried to phone her; the line was busy – he kept trying. Eventually he got through – it was her mother.

'It's me, Mrs Brent, Tom. I urgently need to speak with Dottie. Is she there please?'

'Oh, Tom,' an uncertain voice said at the other end of the line. 'Er, no, she's in Valhalla.'

'Do you know if she'll be back home for the weekend?'

There was another uncertain silence. 'Well, I'm not sure.'

'If she does come home could you ask her to phone me at the camp – I urgently need to talk to her.'

'Yes, of course.' The voice was stilted – not at all friendly.

After she had put the phone down she went into the living room. 'He's got a damn front phoning here after what he's done,' she said angrily to her husband. 'Do you really want to meet him tomorrow, darling?'

Dottie nodded. Her eyes were puffy and her nose was red from crying. 'I have to – I can't just leave it unsaid. I'll be all right.'

******

It was an eternity till they met. All through the flight Tom brooded on what could have gone wrong, what could have happened? There were no answers, nothing came to him. It gnawed at his gut and made him feel fragile with anticipation. His enthusiasm for everything else ebbed away: his career, his rapid promotion, the program – all shrank back into the shadows; nothing mattered except her. It seemed to have become the story of his life; just when things were going right lousy luck bushwhacked him and stole everything from him, leaving him with nothing but his determination to hold on to.

She was standing there in a dark red coat with matching gloves under the clock at Grand Central. As he got closer he could see from the way she looked at him that things were not good. 'Honey,' he said and went to hold her, but she held up a hand defensively.

'No, Tom – not now – not yet; we have to talk.' The station concourse was cold and her face looked tired and pinched. The sparkle in her eyes was gone and she looked at him with a strange seriousness.

He backed off a little to give her space, an expression of bewilderment on his face. 'Shall we go and sit down,' he said nervously, pointing at one of the concourse benches, 'or would you like to go somewhere more private – a café maybe?'

She shook her head. 'Here will do,' she said, going over to a bench and sitting down.

'What is it?' he said in quiet resignation, not certain what the answer would be and if he would want to hear it. He had ransacked his conscience for the last 24 hours and he couldn't come up with an answer. All around them people were coming and going but he noticed none of them – it was as if they were isolated in a wilderness, somewhere dark and cold, entirely alone.

She didn't reply but instead opened her handbag and, taking out a folded piece of a newspaper, handed it to him. He unfolded it; it was part of a gossip column from *The New York Times*. 'My father came across it,' she said in a dull voice.

The headline jumped up at him: 'Another of the Taylor Girls Hits Trouble'. He looked stunned but before he could say anything she stopped him. 'You'd better read it first.'

'Multi-millionaire industrialist Warren Taylor isn't having much luck these days with his two wayward daughters. As Caroline, his eldest, watches her Mafia boyfriend carted off to jail on a murder rap we hear daughter number two, Alicia, is pregnant. Eighteen-year-old Alicia, who is still at college, has been linked to Tommy Jordan, the young man who just a few months back made the headlines when he was abducted by foreign agents and held captive for nearly a month. Jordan, every inch the American hero, is tipped to be the father after he broke up with her older sister, Caroline. A top source has leaked that Jordan had a short fling with daughter number two just before he joined the Army. Jordan, who is now a rookie second lieutenant, has made no comment and Caroline is saying nothing ...'

Tom put it down and looked at her. The bench was cold but he felt colder. It had happened but he could hardly remember it. He'd killed a man and the sheer gravity of what he had done had swamped his senses; when she took him to her bedroom he went like a child, hardly thinking about what he was doing. It had seemed trivial at the time; he could recall the abandon with which they had made love but he didn't remember it as an act of loving. She had given herself up freely with no greater emotion than wanting to soothe the pain of someone she was genuinely fond of. He had succumbed to his lust, submerging himself in the warmth of her body to cover his wounds, dissolve his guilt. Dear Aly, he thought – now they would both have to pay.

'Well, is it true?

'It meant nothing,' he said slowly as the full impact of what he'd read sank in. 'It wasn't the way you think it was. I was in a bad way at the time.'

'Don't try to defend it, Tom. Just tell me.' She looked down at her knees and pulled the red coat over them. She had taken off her gloves and as she smoothed out the creases with her pale hands, he noticed the ring had gone – she was no longer wearing it. He read the message clearly and as she looked up, waiting for the answer, he caught a look of sadness in those lovely blue eyes and all he wanted to do was take her in his arms and make her world whole again.

'It happened before we met. My past isn't perfect.'

'I believe that, but this is different. What I want to know is are you the father?'

'I don't know. I could be. I don't know.'

'You know my family is catholic. My parents were horrified when they read it. You'll have to marry her.'

'I can't do that – I don't love her. I love you.'

'Then what in God's name were you doing climbing into bed with her?'

'It was before I met you.'

'No, you knew me long before that happened.'

'Not in this way – not how were are – were – now.' He couldn't find the words, it was useless he realized. He had lost her – it was in her face, it was in her words, it was in the way she had pulled away when he first tried to hold her. The numbness he'd first felt when he read her letter and then later when he'd read the news clipping had all gone and was now replaced with a sense of resignation.

'Couldn't we forget it and make up?' It was a forlorn plea. The words sounded feeble and as he said it he regretted it; it was like Carey all over again.

'No Tom,' she said, biting her lip. 'Thanks, but I don't want the Taylor girls' third-hand cast offs.' She looked like she would cry and he wished she would, but she didn't.

'No, it's too late for that. You have a child and you have to shape up to the responsibility you now have.' The sadness in her had turned to pathos. She was drained – she'd said all she had to say and she felt hollow. Two days before she had everything – then this. She was crushed, everything was broken, she just wanted to get away to some place where she could howl her heart out.

'I must go,' she said. She stood up and put out a hand in his direction. At first he thought it was a gesture of some kind of reconciliation – but it wasn't. 'Here,' she said, and handed him the engagement ring. 'You'd better give this to Alicia Taylor.'

Without turning to look back, she disappeared into the crowd on the concourse and he was alone with his thoughts. He sat on the bench with his head in his hands and tried to think. He had two hours before his train – there was plenty of time to think.

It felt like a bomb had exploded and ripped apart his whole life. In one devastating blow it shattered his dreams and his plans – they fell like a thousand shards of broken glass and he knew there was nothing he could do to put them back together. For a second time he was going to have to start all over again. This time, he vowed, there would be no women; from here on it would be his army career – he figured it was something he could rely on.

******

Marshall was sitting in his office when he got the news. Major Gregson from Signals Intelligence called him on the phone. 'You'd better come right down,' Marshall said.

Gregson rolled out a map. 'I think we've cracked Gottlieb.'

'Sonovabitch. I need to get on to the President right away. How soon can you get me a briefing report?'

'It's underway right now but we'll have a better picture if you can give me an hour.'

'You've got it. Oh, and stick your head round the door and give the Brits the nod on this one.'

Marshall had four phones on his desk, three black and one red – his hotline to the White House. 'Franklin, it's George – the Nazis have just taken out the government in Ottawa; they've put in a stooge, declared martial law and, get this, they've declared Quebec a Vichy French colony.' There was a moment's hiatus. 'I'll be right over – I need an hour to round up the others and get a status report from Signals. I don't like the look of it'.

He picked up another line. 'Hap, it's George. Have you heard about Canada? The Germans have taken over – they're all over the country with tanks, infantry, air, the whole bundle; they're sitting right on the US/Canada border. There's a meeting with FDR in an hour. Bring whoever you think will be useful. Signals are pulling together the latest for a briefing.'

When Churchill heard, all he said was, 'They'll be here next. You mark my words. Fred, run along and see George Marshall – he's bound to be going over to the White House and I'd like to be there. It is after all part of the British Empire that these criminals have just presumed to steal.'

Marshall did not want Churchill at the meeting. He would be divisive, he would fight with King and Stilwell, he would want to push the British interest and have a stake in it; he would want to interfere. Marshall confirmed to Loughlin that the Chiefs were indeed meeting with the President in just under an hour. They would let them have a briefing note on the outcome but it would be inappropriate to have a foreign head of state, even one as special as Mr Churchill, at a presidential meeting of that sensitivity even though, he conceded, the British had an exceptional interest in what had just happened.

They assembled in the Cabinet room just off the Oval Office. There were the four chiefs of staff, six army generals, four admirals, two air force generals, Henry Stimson, Major Gregson from Signals Intelligence, and the Secretary of State Cordell Hull.

They sat round the long rectangular table with Roosevelt at its head, Cordell Hull on one side and Henry Stimson on the other.

Roosevelt took a long look around the room. 'Gentlemen,' he began. 'I believe the hour is fast coming upon us when we will be looking across our northern border right into the eyes of hostile forces. Major, can you brief us on what we know – then we can go through what we think.'

Major Gregson got up and walked to an easel with a map of Canada which had been set up at the opposite end of the table to Roosevelt.

'For the last four consecutive days we have been getting reports from our agents in Canada of exceptional troop movements coming down from the

Hudson Bay area and feeding into all the main cities. Tanks have been moved by rail freight to Toronto and Ottawa in the east and we think Vancouver on the Pacific Northwest. Unlike the US the weather in Canada has been mild and favorable to these movements. This morning we got news that the parliament building in Ottawa and government buildings in Toronto and Montreal had been taken over by an armed militia calling itself the Free Canadian State Army. That was followed by radio broadcasts proclaiming the German-backed occupation of the country and the establishment of a new provisional government. It follows the same pattern we saw in London.

'For months we have been picking up random references to Gottlieb – which in translation means God's Love. Mostly these have been in Japanese signals where they use code Purple, which we compromised some months back. We think what we are seeing now is Gottlieb.

'We also think that for some time now Hitler has been planning an attack on Russia and as recently as mid-December was poised to go. Then for some reason it has been postponed in favor of Gottlieb. Our assessment is that he has decided to consolidate his hold in the North Atlantic before embarking on an eastward thrust. Our main concern is that he may have his eyes on the Alaskan oil fields and we should be taking steps to secure them.'

'The Limey's think they might be readying themselves for a strike at us,' Joe King butted in. 'What's your assessment of that?' King didn't believe in Churchill's theory but he wanted it out in the open to head off any support it might raise with the others. He was convinced the real threat lay in the Pacific with Japanese expansion. This, in his view, was where America had its real interests – Hawaii, the Philippines, all the small islands that dotted the ocean and formed America's patch. Britain was a dying colonial power, a nineteenth-century relic, whose primary interest was hanging on to its empire. So what, if it lost Canada that would only hasten its decline, which to his mind was a good thing.

'We've had discussions with the British group,' Gregson clarified, 'and Mr Churchill, and it's fair to say they make a strong case, but we don't see why the Germans would want to take on the US when we know they are about to mount a campaign against the Russians – fighting on two major fronts would be militarily untenable.'

'What if they abandoned the Russian campaign and decided to open a single front against the US?' King pressed him, knowing the intelligence community did not go along with the idea. He asked it nevertheless, trying to put the last nails in the coffin for Churchill.

'We have no evidence they are planning that – we haven't picked up any signals that would lead us to follow that line. All the intelligence we are getting says it's Russia. I suppose you might want to put the Army on a higher alert along the 45ᵗʰ parallel, but we do not see this as a real threat.'

Of all those present only Patton showed concern about the position. He didn't much like King. 'He's a sour-faced bastard,' he told his colleagues openly, 'always in a bad fucking humor.' Well he wasn't going to sit there and listen to this shit without putting in his two cents worth.

'All of this is true,' he said forcefully, 'but we're missing a goddamned trick or two here. It's my opinion there's not only a danger that the Krauts could decide to attack us. What if they take a beating from the Ruskies and it spills over onto us? Do we want the Soviets and their commi ideas in our back yard? I'd say "No sir," and I believe the American people would be with me on that one.'

Patton had split the consensus; of the army two generals were with him, the other three said they needed to go with what Intelligence said. The question, however, Roosevelt pointed out, was not so much what had happened but what if anything they should, or could, now do about it. Cordell Hull then threw in another complication.

The Monroe Doctrine had been an accepted part of US foreign policy for more than a century, he counseled. It not only precluded the US from 'meddling in the domestic affairs' of its neighbors on the American continent but also made it plain that it would not tolerate the invasion or control of any American continental state by European powers. The focus of the policy had been the South American states as they freed themselves from the colonial yoke of the Spanish and the Portuguese. Canada had been accepted as part of the British Empire since 1814, so it had de facto sat outside the doctrine and this had never been confronted as there had never been a problem to confront. Hull thought it had become a legal minefield. You could, he argued, take the view that this is a European power taking Canada by force, in which case the US had a right to intervene since it would affect its security. Conversely, he pointed out, it could be construed as simply the existing sovereign power rearranging its domestic administration – albeit in an unorthodox manner – in which case any action by the Americans could be construed as 'meddling'.

Then there was another dilemma. Patton was all for issuing a warning to the Germans to pull out of Canada or they would go in there and kick them out. This worried Roosevelt as it would push the Americans into a war with Germany for which they were still not ready. Hitler, he reminded everyone, had five million trained and battle-proven men at his disposal just in his land forces; America had less than half a million across the combined services.

Patton was for action. 'Go in and kick ass now – the longer we leave it the stronger they're gonna get. They're still pouring stuff into Hudson Bay but they could as easily steam right up the St Lawrence and then what sort of shit are we dealing with?'

King pulled his customary sour face of disapproval; he didn't like it. His ships would have to confront the Kreigsmarine. The last time they had discussed this he'd expressed doubts about the prospects of a victory at sea; but this wasn't 1940 – things had moved on, ships had been built, men recruited and his fleet was now moving towards superiority. But he voiced the same objection he had always deployed; he didn't want an Atlantic confrontation because he would have to call on the Pacific fleet and he was convinced Japan would try to capitalize on that.

At this point Hap Arnold came into the discussion. He was a long-time believer that there would have to be a confrontation with the Germans; he couldn't see how it could be avoided. Hitler, he warned them, showed no limit to his appetite for empire building.

'I'm with George in this. Our air force is certainly up to holding its own against what we know they have over the border, and if Joe can blockade and cut off the flow of new men and materiel coming into the eastern seaboard, well, then it should be a foregone conclusion.'

Roosevelt sat back in his chair. His face was solemn as he turned it over in his mind. 'Going to war is a serious undertaking for anyone holding this office; make the wrong call and you pay a high price to posterity.'

He looked right and left of him at his two political advisors. 'Henry, Cordell,' he said with an air of deliberation, 'we need to see if we can't find a political solution to this. I think we have to get the German Ambassador in and let him know how uncomfortable we're feeling right now. Let him know that they have to move back from the 45th and keep everything up north in Hudson Bay. I think we also need an agreement that they put a lid on any further supply coming in. Let us do that and see how they respond.'

He looked around the table for any further comment but there was none.

'Gentlemen, thank you.' With that he concluded the meeting.

******

Tom settled into Pine Camp and tried to put Dottie out of his mind. His emotional life had once more become a mess and it needed sorting out. Working on the program now had two mission objectives: train the men to shoot straight and at the same time salvage his emotional wreckage. The program developed well but the collateral damage from the breakup with Dottie clung stubbornly to the outer edges of his mind and would not let go. He missed writing the letters. Instead he wrote to Martha, but it wasn't the same and his heart was elsewhere.

Two weeks in and he got a weekend pass. He would go home, he decided, and maybe go over to see Mike. He hadn't spoken to him since the wedding and it would be good to touch base with what was left of his old life.

Martha was saddened when he told her they had parted but didn't pry into the reasons why, and he for his part didn't feel he had the heart for an explanation. So it was left unspoken between them and she never mentioned it again, though she could see the pain in his eyes. Although he talked enthusiastically about the army, his promotion and the program, the fire was no longer burning and those times when she came on him unawares she could feel the loneliness surrounding him.

When he'd married, Mike bought a house in Croton to be near his family; it would be company for Eileen and support once she had the baby. It was a newly built house with all the modern things they'd seen at the World's Fair. It wasn't large but Mike announced it would be big enough for his family because they were limiting themselves to three kids. It was good to see him again, Tom told him, because he needed someone to talk to and right now he was the only one who knew Tom well enough to listen and understand all those things that lay there in the past but which he couldn't explain to a stranger. They went into the kitchen where Eileen showed him all her new gadgets and gizmos. Everything had been designed to go together, the colours were bright and everything fitted together neatly – it was what they were calling the 'built-in kitchen'.

'You're looking very well,' Tom told her. 'Married life looks like it agrees with you.'

She smiled and smoothed her hands over the lump where her pregnancy was just beginning to show. 'I like it, you should try it.' The words were hardly out of her mouth when she realized what she had said. 'Sorry – I didn't mean …'

'Don't worry these things happen.'

'Come and have a beer in the sitting room,' Mike quickly offered, trying to rescue his wife from her embarrassment and putting a happier note on things.

The room was large and airy with big windows leading to a veranda on the back where it looked onto a garden. The garden was still a bit of a construction site, Mike admitted, but he had plans for it and Eileen wanted him to make beds and plant roses.

They sat in large, stuffed armchairs with brightly colored printed covers of linen, drank their beers, and talked about previous times – 'my better days,' as Tom put it.

'You've made a nice job of it,' Tom said, waving his hand across the vista of the room. 'It's a real home you have here.'

'I like it – we're happy.'

They hedged about with small talk for a bit, then Mike came straight out and asked what had happened. Tom explained the press clipping, the meeting on

Grand Central and the desperately brief interlude with Aly, but he left out the events that led to it, especially he avoided the killing of Hans. What was the point? It would only sound like he was trying to justify jumping into bed with her. Mike listened but said nothing for a bit, just slowly nodding his head and making a humming noise.

'What are you going to do – about Alicia I mean?'

'I don't know. I didn't know she was pregnant, I swear it. She hasn't tried to contact me – I guess I ought to ask her. What a mess.'

'Well it could be worse,' Mike joked, trying to lighten the conversation, 'and, after all, you survived that business with Newman.'

Eileen came into the room and the conversation stopped abruptly. Sensing she had interrupted something, she asked if they would like more beers. 'I'll go and get them then.' She came back, set them down on the coffee table and tactfully retreated to the kitchen.

Tom picked up his beer. 'Here's to us – what's left of us; God, how things have changed in a few months. It seems impossible. This time last year we were just three carefree guys who went hunting and hung out together. Now look at it. I lost a friend, a job and a girl, and joined the army; you got married and Tony's in jail; then I lose another girl, the only one I think I will ever love. What happened, Mike? What the hell ever happened?' He banged the flat of his hand down hard on the chair arm.

Mike shook his head. 'We moved on, I guess – that's life, things happen and people change – we all move on. It was a shame about Tony.'

'I often wondered about his life – he was always kind of private; I had no idea he was caught up in that Mafia stuff. You know what,' he said, changing the subject, 'you were right, Mike – that night in the Coco Club when you said falling in love is a slow business. I should have taken your advice and asked her out. Maybe none of this would have happened.'

He looked at his watch and stood up. 'I should go,' he said. 'I have to be back in camp by eight.'

Mike put a hand on his shoulder and they embraced as only two old friends can. Tom looked around him at everything. 'You're a lucky son of a bitch,' he said warmly. 'Look after all of this; it's worth holding on to.'

'It is,' Mike smiled, 'It is.'

Tom stuck his head round the kitchen door. Eileen kissed him lightly on the cheek. 'Come and have lunch next time you get a furlough.'

'I will,' he said, then took his leave of Mike at the front door.

'That's so sad,' Mike said, shaking his head. 'She was the right girl for him – I knew it the first time I saw how she looked at him. He didn't know it at the time but I could see it – and she was.'

'Doesn't your dad know her father – Dr Brent, isn't it?'

'That's right.'

'Couldn't you ask him?'

Mike looked horrified. 'Don't even think about it. Stay out of other people's lives; it never works.

'

******

It was Hans Thomsen, the German Chargé d'Affaire, who met with Cordell Hull on the day following the Roosevelt meeting. He was a genial man of medium height with dark hair neatly parted down the center. Hull had met him on several occasions prior to this meeting and had always worked well with him. However, this time there was something different about his air; he was dressed in a pale grey suit with a matching silk tie, a neatly folded silk handkerchief just showing in his pocket. The stiffness of the suit was matched by his demeanour.

Hull stood up as Thomsen was shown in to his office. Thomsen shook hands but there was no warmth in it. Then he did something unprecedented: before he sat he gave the Nazi salute. Hull looked at his secretary, who was sitting close by to take notes, shot her a glance that said, 'What is this about,' then quickly looked back to Thomsen.

'We have had the news from Canada,' Hull said cautiously, 'and I am bound to tell you it disturbs my government more than a little.' Thomsen was unmoved by the remark; his only response was to raise his eyebrows slightly and to adopt a quizzical look.

'We are concerned that the properly elected government has been forcibly replaced in a manner, which is, putting it mildly, at best undemocratic.'

Thomsen shrugged – another very undiplomatic gesture, Hull thought. Thomsen continued to sit in stony-faced silence. He waited and when nothing more was added by Hull he finally opened a dialog. 'Mr Secretary,' he said emphatically, 'I do not understand the point you are making – or even why you are making it to me. These are matters for the Canadian and British governments. Surely your questions should more properly be addressed to them?'

Hull knew well the game now being played by Thomsen and he found himself forced by protocol to join in. 'Let us just say that we are aware of the influence Germany has in these matters and that the orchestra does not play without a conductor. We would wish to hear a slightly different tune.'

'And how would you suggest we go about this change in what you call the music?

'You need to move the band a bit further away from our front door – in fact, a lot further away. The noise is making us nervous. For the sake of our continuing good relationship you need to pull back. We require a little more space around us – the freedom to breathe more easily.'

Thomsen stared intensely at Hull. He chose his words carefully. 'We do not wish to make anyone uncomfortable but I hope you will understand that we are now in an alliance with the British government as well as the Canadians; we have commitments to fulfil, treaty obligations. Germany has a legal right to be in Canada under the Paris Treaty but we are also mindful of the fact that there are neighboring territories who will feel affected – concerned. I have been instructed to inform you that the government of the Third Reich is anxious to maintain a good relationship with the United States of America and that we shall do all we can to secure that for the future.'

'Good,' Hull said, trying to sound conciliated, 'in which case you will be happy to know this can simply be facilitated by moving your troops and your tanks back to the north of Canada where they will not be perceived as a threat by the US.'

Thomsen seemed to consider the matter for a while. When he did speak there was a perceptible change in his approach; there was even just a hint of a smile. 'I can see,' he said thoughtfully, 'how you might feel under the current circumstances. I am sure my government will be happy to help in the matter. Now that I understand how you view the position I will communicate this to Berlin and ask them to make a suitable response.'

'Thank you,' Hull said, standing up and indicating that the meeting was over. Thomsen remained seated, however.

'There is another matter,' he said, politely following diplomatic protocol.

Hull sat down again. 'Go on.'

'Herr Churchill and Herr Loughlin. If we are to have a cooperation in the matter of the withdrawal it would help greatly if there was some reciprocation. I am sure you will understand the immense importance of a gesture like that.'

Hull stood up again. 'I will give it my full attention but you must understand that I cannot override a decision of our courts – not even the President is above the law – but I will see what can be done.' This seemed to please Thomsen and when they shook hands for the final time he was effusive and warm.

Later Hull told Marshall, 'I could cheerfully have slugged the Nazi bastard there and then – but it would have been a breach of diplomacy.'

'Did you believe him?' Marshall asked.

'About pulling back if we handed over Churchill and the other one?'

'Uh huh,'

'Yes, I think so. I got the impression they aren't too interested in us – more they want to consolidate their position all around the Soviets. They're cozying up to Japan right now because that gives them a handhold east of the Urals;

Canada does something similar in the west – so, yeah, I could go with that. Of course, I still don't trust them further than I could throw them.'

******

The snow slowly melted and the eastern seaboard got back to normal movement again. Irena called Clementine to say that she was coming to Washington the following day and would very much enjoy the opportunity to have lunch and maybe do a little sightseeing. They could also do some shopping, though she insisted Washington was not a patch on New York and that led her to suggest that she should bring Winston back up to Brunessemer for a week some time soon and they could do a Broadway show and dine at the Stork or the El Morocco. 'It always gives so much pleasure to spend some of my husband's money,' she said. 'It would be such fun and Martins could drive us there and take us home later.'

They met at the Willard, which Irena said she thought was an extremely dull hotel from the outside because it reminded her a lot of Brunessemer, but the interiors were so elegant, so Belle Epoch, she could forgive the exterior and just close her eyes until she got in through the front door.

'We must go to the bar,' she positively insisted. 'We can sit on those high stools and lean our elbows on the counter top and drink cocktails like a couple of *high society gals*,' and she laughed hilariously at the idea.

'You know what I like about America?' Clementine said after the second cocktail.

'No, what is it you like about America?'

'You can sit in a bar and have a couple of drinks without some old fuddy-duddy looking all sour-faced at you and disapproving; it's so refreshing.

By the time they sat down to lunch it was nearly two, which Clementine thought a bit late but Irena assured her it was the perfect hour because the crowd had eaten and left so you always got better service. Over lunch she told Clementine the latest gossip then, looking surreptitiously around her, let slip that Aly was expecting. 'Can you imagine it?' she said quietly almost under her breath. 'My otherwise intelligent daughter let's herself get pregnant – stupid girl. Now she's insisting on keeping it – she doesn't have to but she insists. I told her Dr Matthews could arrange a clinic but she won't hear of it. I just don't understand her.'

'Who's the father?' Clementine asked conspiratorially.

'She won't say at the moment – which is even sillier, but we have our suspicions.'

'Who?'

'Well it could be that young man who my eldest daughter was walking out with – mind you, I think they did more lying down together than walking out together.'

At this, both women let out a howl of laughter which caused some other diners to look in their direction. An elderly man with what Clementine took to be his wife pulled a long face and a waiter hovering nearby was clearly unimpressed by the behavior.,'Oh dear,' Clementine almost smirked. 'That waiter looked most disapproving.'

'Such a handsome boy,' Clementine remarked after they had settled down again, 'and so gallant. It's a shame really that they broke up. But what makes you think it's him? Has he come clean?'

'Well, it was that gossip columnist in the *New York Times* who suggested it.'

'But what does Alicia say?'

'Oh she's saying nothing. She's covering for the boy – whoever he is.'

When lunch was finished they went over to Georgetown where the best of the shopping was to be had but Irena was right, there was nothing to compare with New York. The city was altogether more conservative; it had no edge to it. So instead they went off to look at the Lincoln Memorial and Capitol Hill. Lincoln, carved in cold stone, looked severely at them and reminded Clementine of a number of politicians she had met – serious men with an over-inflated sense of their own importance and a poorly developed sense of humor.

'Winston is not at all like that,' she confided, looking up at the unsmiling Lincoln. 'He can be rather mischievous, you know – quite like a naughty schoolboy sometimes but he has an enthusiasm for ideas and likes to get on with things. He's not at all like the others – that's what I think attracted me to him. This is all a great adventure for him. He misses Chartwell, though'.

The two women stood and looked at the statue, both caught up in their individual thoughts: Irena with the two girls, Clementine with Winston. Why did Winston always want to find a struggle to engage? He'd done it all their married life and there were times when she could find it most irritating. It was exciting when they had first met and married all those years back but they were getting older and he showed no signs of wanting to give up. It really was time he sat back and let others do these things, she thought.

'How are things going in England?' Irena said as if she had read Clementine's thoughts.

'It's quiet at the moment. Winston thinks the Germans will help that ghastly little man Mosley take over the southeast. We have so many friends there – I just wonder what they will do. I fear for some of them. They're shooting people, you know; there are executions every day. It makes me sad to think of it.'

'I'm sorry; but at least you will be safe here.'

'Winston is not so sure, you know. He worries Germany will attack America and you'll get pulled into the war.'

'Warren holds that notion, too, but I find it hard to believe. I'm more concerned about my two foolish daughters – and as for Wendell,' she threw up her arms in a gesture of despair. 'Let's not depress ourselves with these things, it's half four – I think we should find somewhere to have tea.'

******

Churchill was outraged when he heard what Thomsen had suggested. 'They act like criminals!' he shouted. 'They are not to be trusted.'

The case for the extradition of Churchill and Loughlin was due to be heard later that week in the District Court. Neither man was certain of the outcome. Churchill had been advised not to worry unduly since the German argument was clearly political and the court would not act on that basis. Loughlin was a different matter; he had boarded the German U-boat and taken prisoners without any proper legal standing. There had not been a state of war between Britain and Germany at the time. On the contrary, the Paris Treaty was still being upheld by the Halifax government. Then there was the matter of the Kreigsmarine men; Loughlin had killed one and severely wounded another. Loughlin claimed self-defence but the Germans were calling it murder and it was aggravated because he had scuttled the sub, opening up the seacocks and sending her to the bottom. The crew had been taken hostage, unlawfully imprisoned while they themselves were lawfully arresting the crew of *Tenacious* at the request of the British government. It looked messy and no one was sure which way it would go.

The day before the hearing was due Churchill took him to one side after dinner. 'I think you ought to be making preparations to go underground, Fred. If things go the wrong way you'll have a better chance on the dodge. If the Germans get their way you're a dead man – you know that don't you?'

'I do – I've made some preparations – I've got someone who will hide me; I won't say because what you don't know can't hurt you. They're bound to ask you and I know how you dislike lying.'

'Thank you, that's most considerate but when it comes to this pack of rats my conscience would be clear.'

At five o'clock, as Irena and Clementine were finishing their tea, NBC interrupted its afternoon broadcast with news that fighting had broken out along a broad front in England. At the office of the British Independence Movement Churchill was preparing his broadcast for Radio Free London. Fred and Walter Thompson had settled down in the room next door to monitor the BBC News that NBC were at the same time reporting on.

444

'Sir, you need to come in and listen to this,' Loughlin shouted through the open doorway. Mary left her desk to join them, standing around the shortwave radio. The half-mocking tone of Edwin Harvard poured out through the receiver like a slick of oil.

'In Kent and Hampshire there has been fierce fighting as government forces backed by elements of the German Wehrmacht started on their operation to bring the southeast of the country back under the control of the authorities. The German Legation announced this morning that it has pledged to support the legitimate government of Sir Oswald Mosley. Units of heavy armour and two brigades of Waffen SS, originally bound for their base in Hudson Bay, are to be sent to the naval base at Hull. Elsewhere it has been reported that elements of the defected British fleet have entered the Thames Estuary and bombarded government installations at Gravesend. One cruiser is reported to have been hit and damaged – there were no reported losses of government forces. In a separate incident Jewish dissidents paraded along Whitechapel Road in London's East End demanding the withdrawal of the Jewish Compulsory Registration Directive. The demonstration was broken up by the BBS; 27 protesters are reported to have been killed or injured in clashes with government forces. A captain of the BBS sustained head injuries and two police constables are known to have been hospitalised in the riot that ensued. In a statement to the Governing Council the National Leader, Sir Oswald Mosley, said that the rebels should lay down their arms and immediately sue for clemency. He said that the current position of a state within a state would not be tolerated and he pledged to crush the dissidents without mercy and impose the severest penalties on the ringleaders.'

'It's started,' Churchill said solemnly under his breath.

******

The following day they got the news of the court verdicts. Churchill was in the clear; the judge had thrown out the application on the grounds that it was purely political. He had made particular reference to the questionable legitimacy of the Mosley regime; he ruled they had failed to establish their bona fides as a sovereign state in every interpretation of the word.

The news for Loughlin was not good. 'You need to pack your bags, dear boy,' Churchill said, commiserating.

'It's done.' he replied, 'Everything's arranged. I'll leave this afternoon if that's all right?'

The extradition application had succeeded and the judge had ruled out an appeal on the grounds that Loughlin could not dispute the charges in fact. The events had been well documented; his response had been self-defense and that,

445

the judge decided, should be tried in the jurisdiction of the alleged crimes. In this case they had occurred on board vessels on the high seas. This, the judge ruled, was the sovereign territory of Germany in the case of the U-boat and they had a right in law to try the case in Germany. With the charge of murder, this had taken place on British territory but since the victim was German this too should be tried in Germany subject to the agreement of the British government. There was a counter-argument: in Churchill's case the British government had not been accepted by the court as legitimate and therefore it should be applied equally to Loughlin. The judge conceded it could be interpreted so, but in any event this was more properly argued in the German courts. Accordingly, at the end of the proceedings an order was made for the arrest and extradition to Germany of Mr Frederick Anthony Loughlin.

Hull sat stiffly in his chair and looked unsmilingly at Thomsen. 'Hans, you've got half of what you wanted – that's the best that can be done. Now I'd like you to keep your end of the bargain.'

'We would have preferred Churchill.'

'Not possible.'

'I don't know how it will be received in Berlin.'

'You could make a fresh application – you probably have a case. It wasn't you who were thrown out, it was the Brits.'

'We shall see.'

'No, we had a deal.'

'I'll see what can be done,' Thomsen said as he got up to leave the meeting. After he had gone Cordell Hull picked up the phone.

'Get me Hoover will you.' He sat back in his chair and waited, the instrument pressed to his ear.

'John – it's Cordell. This extradition – I want you to slow your boys down a bit on that. Let's see which way the Krauts jump before we go doing anything we might regret.'

Two hours after Loughlin had left the house in Arlington an officer of the court and a police officer stood at the front door with a warrant for his detention pending extradition. When they were told he was no longer there they politely shrugged and left. Their quarry was already in a car heading north to another place.

CHAPTER 33

Manhattan, 1 March 1941

'I do hope we're in good time to see the whole show.'

'I wanted to see this last year,' Dottie said.

They had taken the train from Croton to Grand Central and then a cab to Broadway; the crawl through the evening traffic had set Eleanor Brent fretting but eventually the cab drew alongside the curb in front of the new Odeon cinema with time to spare. Bannered in lights across the front of the theater a poster announced the show: *Gone With The Wind – Now In Its Second Record Breaking Year.*

'There ya go, folks,' the cab driver said heartily, obviously hoping for a tip. 'They say it'll be the biggest hit of the movies this year. I can't see it myself – me, I like a good horse opera, yes sir, gimme a western any day – that's more to my liking. I hear this new movie with John Wayne is real good – *Stagecoach.*'

Dr Brent thanked the cabby. 'Maybe we'll do that,' he handed over the fare saying, 'Keep the change.' The driver looked at the bill in his hand and then at the meter. He grunted a grudging 'thanks' that said he'd expected more.

Inside, settled into the plush comfort of the red velour-covered seats, they waited for the lights to go down. As the glow from the bulbs dimmed Dottie found herself thinking about Tom. It had been more than a few weeks since that awful meeting on the concourse of Grand Central but she couldn't get him out of her mind. There were moments when she wished she had just pushed it under the carpet and carried on with their lives as if nothing had happened, but then her strict catholic upbringing would leave its mark in guilt on the rest of her life; she couldn't bring herself to do it. The truth had to be faced – Tom had a child on the way; he had to do the right thing and carry the burden of his actions. Still, she could not get him completely out of her mind and at night she often dreamed about him, that he was holding her in his arms or they were walking in the woods together – waking to a deep nostalgic sadness. There were times it would stay with her all day, a lingering emptiness that refused to be satisfied.

'America Marches On,' a stentorian voice announced as the silver screen flickered then filled with light and images. It was the NBC Newsreel; there was to be no B movie, the main feature ran an unprecedented four hours. The newsreel rolled and the soundtrack started to play stirring patriotic music. Then images of soldiers, young Americans, mere boys with guns. 'Say hello to the heroes of tomorrow,' the hidden voice proudly announced. 'Our boys train hard in America's heartland here at Fort Knox while some of the latest in good old American know-how is being rolled out and the 3rd Armored Corps puts its very latest hardware on display. America's enemies had better watch out – this man's army is no pushover.'

'Canada!' Images of more military; convoys on the move, trucks filled with soldiers, smiling, waving for the cameraman; then a flight of the latest fighter aircraft roar overhead. 'Hot on the heels of the change of government in Ottawa,' the disembodied voice intones with a sonorous gravity intended to impart the seriousness of the situation, 'German troops have begun appearing just north of the 45th parallel; movements are being monitored and our border forces are being strengthened. President Roosevelt says this is only a precaution but has sent a note to the German Government of Herr Hitler telling him to back off. Uncle Sam won't put up with this kind of shenanigan in his own backyard and Fritz had better believe it.'

The images made her think of Tom again and she wondered how he was coping. She thought he might be sent north; Mike had said so. She had been to the library and looked at a map of the border in an atlas. It made her feel better just seeing it on the paper page; she couldn't picture where he might be but she could imagine him out there somewhere. Afterwards, as she'd walked home, she told herself it was no good going on like this. She had to put it down – she had to let him go – there was no future in it.

Lost in the comfort of the enveloping dark she felt her mother's hand on her arm; she'd guessed what must be going through her daughter's mind and wanted to let her know she had her support – just silently, no need for words. Dottie patted the hand to say thanks mom, thanks for understanding. The two women looked at each other, a fleeting glance; there was the merest hint of a tear, tiny, bright like a jewel, reflecting back the silver light from the screen.

The newsreel went on with images of the struggle taking place in southern Britain where the independent fighters of General Brooke were holding out against the continued onslaught of Blackshirt and SS assaults. They were boxed into just three counties in England, their shrinking air force still holding out against the Luftwaffe, 'but for how long can they hold on?' the voice asked. 'Only the strength of the Royal Navy is keeping this gallant little group of resistance fighters out of the clutches of the Nazi monster. Admiral James, commanding the Royal Navy fleet is now firmly in control of the southern seas around Britain and has driven the Germans north to seek sanctuary in the City of Hull where they have been successfully corralled by the British. Take that Adolf – and you know where you can put it.'

The news was coming to an end; time for the lightweight story, the feel-good story, the one to finish on a high note. The marshal music ended abruptly and the soldiers faded, giving way to a picture of a young couple coming out of City Hall.

'New York society is all of a flutter today when it missed what might have been the wedding of the year,' the voice said, this time cheerily. 'Standing on the steps of City Hall in New York, Alicia Taylor, the youngest daughter of Industrialist Warren Taylor has just tied the knot with English fiancé, Fred Loughlin. Mr Loughlin, an aide to the exiled British Prime Minister, Winston Churchill, has recently been the subject of judicial proceedings for extradition by Germany on charges of sinking a Nazi U-boat and capturing the crew whilst at sea in a British destroyer; but now he's married to an American girl these charges will have to fall away because we don't allow our own people to be extradited – especially by despots and dictators. Of course, there are some who say Mr Loughlin is hiding behind his new wife's skirts, but we don't believe it. You get the last word on this Fred. Whadya say?'

The cameraman pulled in close; the faces of the happy couple filled the screen, giant images with mouths twenty feet wide. Dottie instantly recognized Aly. Her heart jumped so fast it made her head feel fuzzy – she put her hand over her mouth to stifle an involuntary gasp; the other one was the man who had come to the diner looking for Tom. When he spoke the accent brought back a vivid flash of that day.

'This is a love match,' he replied to camera in his clipped British accent, all the time smiling politely at the insinuation, 'it has nothing to do with avoiding Nazi extradition. I fell in love with Alicia when we first met – it was love at first sight. As for the charges, I took on the Germans man to man in fair combat and they came off worst – they're just sore losers, that's all. Alicia and I are extremely happy.'

'Looking at them we believe it,' the voice boomed gleefully, 'so, tough luck, Adolf – give this man a medal we say.'

The music rose to a crescendo, THE END emerged through the image – then it was gone. The audience waited in silence, a faint crackle from the sound speakers as the main feature reeled its way through the projector. Dottie turned her head towards her mother. James Brent was silent – his face bore the expression of a man lost for something to say. They sat there, the three of them, with more questions than answers but nobody gave voice to them. The film rolled and the music droned. Dottie drifted in and out of the story as it unwound, taking in no more than a sense of it, not following the plot. Her mind refused to stay in one place; it ran off into her own confusion, wildly throwing new thoughts into her mind. By the end of the movie she was exhausted but had little notion of what had played out on the screen in front of her.

They sat in the back of the cab in silence; nobody spoke until they got to Grand Central.

'Well,' Mrs Brent said, trying to make some kind of conversation as they got out of the cab – anything would do, she thought, just to break the horrible spell that was now gripping them. 'What did you think of that? You could see why she went for Clark Gable – what girl wouldn't – and Ashley Wilkes was such a limp drip. What did you think of Scarlet O'Hara? Wasn't she flighty?'

'She was horrible,' Dottie replied flatly without enthusiasm. 'Selfish and self-centered. The dresses were lovely – I hated the character.'

Deep inside she sensed something had gone badly wrong with her life – the shades of a terrible mistake had stirred; now it began to haunt her like some ghastly phantom. To begin with she had felt empty, sorry even for Tom who had clearly been dumped by Aly – this was like the movie she had just watched. Next her mood changed to anger as the realization of what she had sacrificed out of a noble sense of duty hit home. The train journey back to Croton passed with difficult conversations about the movie – conversations nobody really cared for – conversations for the sake of breaking the silence. Occasionally James Brent threw a meaningful glance at his wife but they didn't dare broach the subject they knew was running its course through their daughter's emotions.

Back at home and before she went to her room she kissed them both, then pausing for a moment said very simply, 'I think I might have made an awful mistake, and now I have to do something about it.'

James Brent looked at his wife; he said nothing. She looked back cautiously, shrugging her shoulders as if to say I think we should stay out of this for the time being.

She couldn't sleep, it wouldn't come. Her head was full of questions, questions, questions, and there were no answers – just speculations and what ifs. She turned over but it didn't help; she lay on her back and stared at the ceiling, she lay on her right side, she lay on her left side, she tried tucking her knees up under her chin – nothing worked. In the end she sat up and, propped against the pillows, turned on her bedside lamp to read a book. That finally worked; feeling the drowsiness in her eyes she slipped down under the blankets and drifted into sleep.

In her dream she was chasing Aly Taylor with a hockey stick but no matter how hard she tried to hit her the result was feeble, it had no impact, the stick felt like it was made of straw – and all the time Aly was laughing.

******

The telephone rang; it was sitting on the table in the cavernous front hall of Brunessemer. Patience answered it, 'It's for you, Miss Alicia,' she shouted in the general direction of the drawing room.

'I do wish she wouldn't shout like that,' Aly said to her mother.

'I have to see you,' said the voice at the other end of the phone. It was a woman's voice and it sounded edgy – unsettled. 'I have to see you – today.'

'Who are you? Do I know you?'

'I'm Dorothy Brent, Dr Brent's daughter. We met – just briefly – at Mike Mescal's wedding.'

'Oh yes, I remember you. How can I help?'

'I have to see you – there's something I need to know.'

'Well, couldn't we talk about it now – while you're on the line?'

The voice hesitated. 'It's about you and Tom Jordan. I have to see you – it has to be like that.'

Aly thought for a moment, running through her memories trying to figure out what it could be. 'Okay,' she finally said, 'but not here.'

'Where then?'

'There's a café nearby the railroad station – I'll meet you there.'

The two women looked at each other across the table.

'Okay, so what is this about – let me have it.'

'I have to know,' Dottie said, looking stiff-faced. 'I have to know why you've married this Englishman and not the father of your child.'

Aly looked over the top of her coffee cup at the girl sitting opposite and wondered exactly what she was talking about. 'The last time I saw you, you were with Tommy Jordan. Are you two still together?'

Dottie shook her head but said nothing. Aly waited, but this girl – who she hardly knew – she just sat there staring at her. 'Okay, tell me again – I don't think I'm getting the message too clearly.'

'I know you slept with Tom – you're pregnant – you're expecting his child and now you've married someone else – why?'

As she said the words Dottie felt the indignation welling up inside her. Sitting looking at this over-privileged woman – not even a woman really, just a spoilt college girl too rich to care what she did to anyone else. She wanted to slap her face, push her off the chair she was so smugly perched on.

Aly was shaking her head slowly, a look of disbelief on her face. 'I think you've got yourself a little mixed up here. Where did you get this crazy notion?'

'It was that woman in the *New York Times*. You can't deny it – it was there, in the paper – I read it myself.' She dug into her handbag and pulled out a scrap of newsprint. She smacked it down on the table, turning it towards her opponent.

Aly carried on shaking her head in disbelief. 'Who the hell believes what they read in a gossip column, for Christ's sake?'

451

'But it's true – you *are* pregnant and you *did* sleep with Tom – and you *have* just married that Englishman.'

'All correct,' Aly replied at last, beginning to see where the conversation was heading. 'But you're playing with the wrong piece of the puzzle and it doesn't fit.' She stared sadly at the wretched-looking girl in front of her.

'The child I'm carrying is Fred's, not Tommy's.'

'But you slept with him?'

'True, but I also slept with Fred and it's his baby – not Tom's.'

Dotty clammed up. She hadn't expected this – in fact, she hadn't known what to expect. She had just blundered in and now she wasn't sure what came next. She felt angry – she'd been caught off balance. This was supposed to be the moment of truth but the truth was turning out to be something different.

'How do you know?' she snapped angrily.

'Simple – I was pregnant before the incident with Tom. Dr Matthews confirmed it nearly a week before.'

'And you still slept with Tom – how could you?'

'Listen,' Aly said, a touch of sympathy in her voice. 'There are some things you ought to know – because it wasn't the way you think.'

'So how was it?' Dottie replied testily. She wasn't going to be fobbed off with some flabby excuse about spur of the moment passion; it'd better be good.

Aly drained her coffee cup, put it down slowly and looked hard at her. She knew she would have to tell her the story of that night, who Tom had killed and why, how she'd led him off to bed; he'd been in a state of shock, he was still trying to get over Carey leaving him for his friend, he'd been a mess, he was pretty much sleep-walking, how did she explain all that? Worse, they had all been sworn to silence over the affair; the FBI, the police, Warren Taylor had seen to that, he'd had it gagged right the way to the top. Now she had to break the oath and let someone else into the circle and she wasn't sure if the angry woman sitting in front of her would keep the silence. But the truth had to be told; she decided she had no option.

'I'm going to tell you something,' she said slowly and deliberately. She paused briefly, trying to judge if she could trust her, then went on, 'and then afterwards you're going to forget all about it because it can't be mentioned to anyone – talking about it won't change what happened. I want your word on that. Do I have it?'

Dottie said nothing, just nodded her head numbly wondering at that moment what was coming that could possibly be so dreadful a secret.

Aly searched around trying to find the words. It was going to be difficult to start the story but she got it under way; when she had finished she reached into her handbag and took out a pack of cigarettes. She offered it to Dottie, who was now in a state of absence; drifting in a vacuum.

'I don't,' she said feebly. She sat there, a dejected heap of regrets and anger as it sank in that she had given up the man she loved because she'd swallowed the made-up slander of some cheap journalist looking to sell a story. But it was all too late for regrets – she had sent him away, dumped him and burned her bridges.

'I threw him over for this, you know,' she said vacantly. 'We were engaged and I gave him back the ring and told him to go away – to go away and do the decent thing – live up to his responsibility to his child – and now it turns out there is no child, at least not his.'

Aly sat there saying nothing, letting Dottie ramble on till in the end the self-recrimination dried up. She felt sympathy for her, but she was now being self-indulgent and when she finally finished off with the words, 'I didn't know any of this – but it makes no difference, he's gone and he'll never come back', the sympathy went out the window, taking the patience with it.

'God, give me strength!' Aly hurled the words out in a tone charged with exasperation. 'I don't know who out of the two of you is the most stupid – you or that crazy sister of mine. She dumps him for some low-life Italian Mafiosi and you tell him to take a hike without even finding out if the story is true! What the hell is wrong with you!'

Aly was now pretty much shouting. A woman at the next table gave her a pained looked and raised an index finger to her lips, indicating that the noise was unwelcome. Aly shot her a patronizing smile that said 'butt out', but she dropped her voice to not much more than a whisper. 'Tommy Jordan is most likely the best man you'll ever meet – do you not understand that? There aren't a lot around to match him. There are probably only two good men in the whole of America: I just married one of them and you told the other to shove off. Are you crazy!?'

Dottie was not feeling good. She felt physically sick with anguish over what now seemed she had carelessly thrown away. 'I don't know what to do.'

'There's only one thing *to* do – go after him, tell him you love him. He'd jump at the chance of having you back.'

'Do you think so?'

'Of course. You're an attractive and otherwise intelligent woman – other than this lapse into temporary insanity. What sensible guy would not want to marry you?'

'You've been so kind.'

'Yup, and you've been so dumb. Now go and do something to make it right.'

******

453

'Have you seen this,' a major called after Tom, holding out a sheet of paper in his hand.

'I don't know, sir, what is it?'

'Orders; just down from Division – increased readiness. There's one sitting on your desk. You'll need to get your men briefed.'

'Is it serious?'

The major looked disinterested, 'Shouldn't think so, by the look of it I'd guess just some routine politicking.'

The order had come down through the chain of command from the office of the Joint Chiefs. The border with Canada was to be reinforced against what was thought to be the unlikely prospect of an incursion by German units now sitting on the other side of the 45th parallel. It was not a high alert, just a precaution. It listed crossing points to be manned, new checkpoints to be set up and, most bizarrely, a need for all this to be highly visible; the strategy was to let the Germans know the border had been strengthened with the aim it would act as a deterrent.

Later that morning Tom got a summons from the Camp's commanding officer, Brigadier Moses Rubin. 'I've orders to send you north to join your regiment. 1st Armored has been sent up to the Canadian border; you're to link up with your company at Plattsburg – it's already there. Transport's been arranged. You go within the hour.'

It was a disappointment; things had been going well with the program and now he was being moved on. The prospect of rejoining Bob Duncan, Andrew White and the others left him without enthusiasm. He guessed they would be delighted to be up there in the Adirondacks, it was good riding country and he was sure they'd bring horses with them. It was inevitable they would want to patrol the border on horseback, it was natural. They were cavalry and the countryside was rugged and wooded; too thick for motorised infantry or tanks and, of course, they would insist on him riding too and he wasn't that happy on a horse. The program would be handed over to others and he would miss that. He guessed he would also lose his temporary rank and be back to second lieutenant. Once more, he found himself questioning what it was in his life that no sooner had he gained something he valued he lost it again?

He wrote to Martha and Holly to let them know what had happened. For a brief moment he played with the idea of writing to Dottie, but the thought passed – it would be pointless.

It was a long ride in a Jeep, near on five hours. They bumped across poorly paved roads, passing newly sown fields with here and there new green shoots of wheat showing, then passing through small towns and hamlets. The private assigned to drive him was a blabbermouth; he talked non-stop. Not only that but it seemed there was nothing in the whole damned universe he liked. He was from North Dakota and said he thought New York State was a very crowded place. He was used to wide open spaces and here he complained you were no sooner out of one township than you were into another. There were too many trees, there was too much traffic, the chow wasn't good, the beer was thin, the beef in the burgers was fatty, people ate salad with their steaks – what the hell was that about? – And they had no idea how to run a rodeo. Tom pulled his greatcoat up around his chin and decided to feign sleep. 'Private,' he said, 'you'll excuse me if I sleep a little. I was up most of last night.'

'Sure thing, Captain,' the private replied, but carried right on talking. Somewhere about the halfway mark he finally ran dry, leaving Tom with his thoughts at last.

They found the divisional HQ a mile or two out of Plattsburg at Cumberland Head on the edge of Lake Champlain. Curious, he thought to himself, who would have guessed last year I would be back here – and under such different circumstances. His mind drifted to Tony and Neumann and Al Cardy; how everything had changed for each of them. He wondered how Tony would handle the jail; he wondered how Carey was taking it – badly he guessed, she wasn't ever any good with a crisis. Cardy should be back in Crows Crossing – he might go and look him up. Then there was Neumann – he was still out there somewhere. He didn't think of him that often these days but there were those odd moments when he found himself wondering where that would all end. Maybe he would just give up; who knows, he could be dead, killed in an auto accident or some such thing. Maybe he'd gone back to Germany where his family had come from originally. He couldn't find an answer so he was content for most of the time to let it settle in the background. Just occasionally he found himself looking over his shoulder or into the rear mirror of the car – but there was never anyone there. It was the kind of thing you might carry with you for the rest of your life and never find the answer – and it would eventually die with you and be lost to history like most of everything that happens to most people.

Divisional HQ was a bivouac; a tent city with everything under canvas except the C.O. and his staff. The Army had rented a farmhouse from a local family who no longer worked the land and instead had moved to Plattsburg where they owned a general store. The C.O. would be comfortable in the farmhouse, sheltered from the cold spring weather, though the men would find it hard after the hot dry desert air of El Paso.

Tom reported and traded in his captain's silver bars. There was one consolation which made him think that not everything goes wrong, though; his second lieutenant's gold shoulder bar was exchanged for a silver one as Colonel Hamilton, now his senior officer, announced a promotion board's decision to make him up to first lieutenant.

455

'You'll get the full pay grade that goes with it,' Colonel Hamilton grinned, shaking his hand then saluting. Tom didn't really care about the pay; he was already rich beyond his needs, but he knew he shouldn't say anything. He would gladly have exchanged the pay for one letter from Dottie.

Life at Cumberland Head was less than comfortable. The weather had been wet, the fresh spring rains leaving well-trodden pathways ankle deep in mud. Men sloshed and squelched from ablution tents to the Quartermaster stores to the PX and to the vehicle parks. The mud got everywhere; once it was on his boots it proceeded to climb up the legs of his uniform till it got to his knees. It didn't matter how carefully a man picked his path through it – the mud would get him. The engineers threw down metal grids for the vehicles to cross and wooden duckboards for the men, but as often as not they then sank into the slurry of mud and so more had to be thrown on top. After a miserable three days of briefings and strategy meetings, Tom was grateful to finally get his onward orders. He was being sent to join his platoon with 'B' company; they were billeted at Rouses Point, about forty minutes' drive to Champlain then five miles east. When he got there and discovered they were housed in solidly built wooden huts he felt relieved; the mud at Cumberland Head had found him wishing he was back in the desert around El Paso. 'I'd rather breathe hot dust than chew on mud all day,' he told Bob Duncan as he settled in to their shared quarters.

He was right about the horses; the moment he stepped out of the Jeep he could smell them – a mixture of sweat, manure and piss. 'We've brought a string with us,' Bob Duncan announced cheerfully. 'They'll be useful to patrol in this terrain. There're enough to go around. I've cut one out for you – it's a mare – she's not too lively,' and he laughed. They think I'm some kind of blue collar man, he told himself, not quite their kind.

'Come on,' Duncan said, after he'd unpacked his kit, 'I could do with a drink.' They walked over to the mess; as they went Tom noticed the ground was hard and stony – that was good he told himself – no mud here. At the bar Andy White and another cavalryman, a second lieutenant Simon Newhart, were already drinking. Newhart, like the other two, had what Tom called the mark of aristocracy on him. White was quite short but had that slightly arrogant bearing that comes from the confidence of a privileged upbringing. The other two were tall and well groomed – their accents so refined as to be almost English; he felt out of place. The bar talk was all horses and where the best riding was to be had. As he looked at them he wondered if they would be any good in a tight corner.

Just before dark he strolled round to the tactical vehicles park to get a look at what asset strength they had. It was pretty slim pickings. There were only four tanks: two M2s and two of the latest Stuarts. There was also a halftrack. It sat there in one corner, its forward sloping snout-like engine cover and the two narrow windshield slits like eyes giving it the appearance of a dog's face – like some mournful hound tired of waiting for its owner. He sniffed at the cold night air; the odor of horses had gone, replaced with a strong mix of fresh oil and gasoline – it was more to his liking. Standing there, the irony struck him – they had more horses than armor.

The following morning bloomed bright and clear with small wisps of cloud pushed along by a brisk breeze. Tom was obliged to join the other three; they would take a section of the platoon and ride up to the border for a reconnoiter. There were only four properly trained horse troopers in the platoon: Corporal Ransom and Privates Delgado, Rogers and Halliday. The section mounted. With the four officers out front and the troopers bringing up the rear they went off at a trot, then settled into a steady gallop for a while. The road ran straight for about three miles, running through arable fields backed by woodland, after which it started to bend right and left for the last mile and a bit until it reached the border with Canada. At the point where the road intersected the frontier there was a log cabin; smoke curled out of the chimney and the smell of a wood fire, bacon and fresh coffee said somebody was home. Straddling the road there was a red and white painted pole hinged at one end with a heavy metal counterweight balancing it. The other end rested in a cupped stirrup mounted on a post where it was fastened with a short chain and a padlock.

Inside the cabin three border policemen were setting about fixing breakfast. The cabin was built on a platform with a decked veranda out front and three steps down to the road. The stars and stripes hung from an inclined staff over the front door and another fluttered from a masthead, where it was raised every morning and lowered at dusk. It was just one of the many back doors into America that pierced a border stretching nearly three thousand miles from the shores of the Atlantic clear across to the Pacific.

Captain White dismounted and tethered his horse to the rail edge of the veranda. The others stayed in the saddle, their horses occasionally snorting. Steam came off their twitching flanks driving off the heat generated by the ride.

As he put his foot on the lower step the door to the cabin opened and one of the policemen stepped out onto the deck. He looked at the military horsemen. 'Morning to you, gentlemen,' he called out. 'You're just in time for breakfast, if you'd care to join us, feel free.'

The section dismounted and tethered their horses. 'Delgado, stay with the horses,' Simon Newhart ordered as he got down from his mount. 'We'll fetch you out some coffee.'

Over bacon and eggs the talk was all about the German activity on the other side. The road had risen up a steady gradient starting around two miles back from the frontier; it had gone through a dozen or more switchbacks with the woodland hugging close to its margins. The trees had been cleared on the approaches both sides of the barrier and there was a wide open stretch running a good five hundred yards to where a roadside board announced 'Welcome to Canada'. Beyond the board the road turned and the woodland once again asserted itself on the edges. It was impossible to see anything beyond that point, but everything had been quiet anyway.

The officer running the post held the rank of captain and they were normally a six-man contingent: three on three off, turn and turnabout. It was not a busy crossing point and had only been built during the prohibition years to deter bootleggers. Now it was still maintained more by default because nobody had got around to standing it down. But things were due to change and they would be joined by the Army. It was however, more about showing the American flag than opposing any serious threat, White explained to the policemen.

'Well, it's pretty dead around here most of the time – especially these last few weeks; nothing came up from the Stateside,' the Captain observed, 'but then everything south from here was locked down with the snow.'

'We did have one guy through about two weeks ago, though,' one of the other officers remarked. 'According to him there was a lot of military traffic further north up Ottawa way, but he claimed it was almost deserted when he came through the Canadian post up the road.'

'That's pretty much what we expected,' White replied, stuffing a strip of bacon into his mouth. 'We could do with some water for the horses, then I think we'll take a ride along through the trees for a mile or so in each direction, just see how easily someone might get round your post.'

'There's a water pump out back – it's a good fresh spring, help yourself. The border is fenced on both sides for two hundred yards in each direction. After that it's pretty rough country, it makes its own barrier.'

Later, when they came back from their reconnaissance White announced that they would be stationing one of the tanks and the halftrack at the post together with a platoon. That, he thought, should be enough to convince any watching Germans that they meant business; uninvited visitors were not welcome.

As they left, Corporal Ransom reported having spotted a light flashing right up on the edge of the road where it turned out of sight. He thought most probably it was the sun reflecting off field glasses. 'Fritz is watching us,' Newhart remarked. 'That's good, that's what we're here for.'

Returning to Rouses Point, Andy White wrote his report and sent it down to Cumberland Head. It was taken by a motorcycle dispatch rider who would wait on Colonel Hamilton's appraisal and an order for White to consign elements of armor and a platoon up to the police post. It came back, 'Operation approved,' just before 17.00 hours; White would choose the platoon and brief the men next morning.

With the order came an instruction to reassign the lower commands: Bob Duncan was to remain the officer in charge of 1st Platoon, Tom was moved to 2nd Platoon, Simon Newhart was to get 3rd Platoon and a new man would be appointed to 4th Platoon, but in the meantime Andy White would have to take care of it. This made up B Company, a total complement of 152 men and four officers.

Officially they were B Company, 13th Cavalry Regiment, 1st Armored Division. In reality they were lacking any meaningful identity and 1st Armored had come out of a hastily devised plan hatched sometime in the late thirties when – paying heed to the experience of the Great War and taking a lesson from the armored thrust into Poland by the Germans, and given the latter's formidable success – Army Chiefs concluded there should be a motorized arm to their forces; one that was armored and mobile. So there was created a curious beast they named the Mechanized Cavalry; it was an uncomfortable creature.

Its problem came in trying to mix the horse with the machine and create a manual that applied equally to both. Some officers despised the machine and lived for their horse; some of the men, especially the draftees, could not ride a horse. In a pure cavalry regiment grooms had been important players with the role of keeping the mounts in prime battle condition. These had to give way to the mechanics and engineers required to keep the armor moving and battle worthy. This mix of personalities, tasks and loyalties proved difficult to manage and often produced tensions and a lack of cohesion. It also produced tactical issues: when Captain White had taken a section up to the border it was an unorthodox composition having as many officers as men because he decided to go on horseback, eschewing the more normal Jeep; also he didn't have enough men who could ride.

The real problem, however, lay in the largely officer-led conviction that the horse was both tactically and ethically superior to the machine. Horses, it was argued, did not break down or run out of gas, they could move through tight terrain, jump over obstacles and get places inaccessible to tanks and armored cars. An uncooperative snobbery had grown up around this creed and would eventually have to be tested.

White made the decision to deploy half his force on the border and keep the other half in reserve at Rouses Point. Early the next day he led a short column out of the base and headed for the police post. It presented a bizarre spectacle: White, Duncan and Simon Newhart on horseback leading 1st and 3rd Platoons loaded into troop trucks together with their kit and canvas tents. This was followed up by the halftrack and one of the Stuarts with an M2 bringing up the rear. It bore more resemblance to a showground parade proclaiming the start of a rodeo than it did to a military expedition. White was so confident in the routine nature of the exercise on which he was embarked he had not included a medic or any engineers to back up his two platoons; he calculated he was so close to camp that if he needed the extra support it could be called up on the radio. Besides, he was just one of many small encampments that were now being set up all along the Canadian border to let the Germans know that it would be folly to encroach on US territory; they would cross the border at their peril.

The column arrived in stately procession. White, having led a spirited gallop after the second mile of the journey, now let them amble the last bit at a lazy pace. In the distance across the border both Duncan and Newhart saw the same flashes of sun glinting on glass that Corporal Ransom had reported on their first visit. All three took out their field glasses and trained them on the wooded margin away in the distance.

'Can't see anything out there,' Bob Duncan commented, and got down off his horse.

'They're out there watching,' White confirmed, getting off his own mount. 'Good – that's why we're here – to be seen.'

The section set up its bivouac around the back of the post close to the water pump. The men were carrying combat rations but with no kitchen so they had to rely on camp fires. The three officers were more comfortable, bunked down in the post and eating with the policemen. Although they would not be there for more than a week at a time it was decided that for more than 70 men they needed a mobile kitchen – and a latrine unit to supplement what the men had dug in the woods. Having assessed the position, White ordered a pit to be dug and its perimeter sandbagged to make a nest for the .50 calibre Browning machine gun. The men spent the first two days digging further defensive ditches; observation posts were prepared and the front of the cabin was heavily sandbagged.

At the end of day two, White declared himself satisfied with the preparations and they settled in to a routine; horse patrols made forays up and down the wired area of the border and then on deeper into the dense hilly woodland. Squads on foot made routine patrols in the nearer vicinity of the post, but nobody expected to see anything. It was the end of the first week and the section was preparing to be relieved the following day. Nothing had happened and the men were beginning to get bored. White wrote his first report to HQ at Cumberland head.

The next morning he instructed the radio operator in the halftrack to call for a dispatch rider. At just after 07.00 hours a young soldier, riding an Indian motorcycle appeared at the camp just in time to see Simon Newhart, Corporal Ransom with troopers Delgado and Rogers depart for the morning patrol. The motorcyclist took off his heavy gauntlets, unstrapped his helmet, unslung his dispatch bag and sat down to wait while White sealed up the report. The section sergeant, a huge barrel-chested man with a service flash from the Great War, offered him some coffee. Sergeant Roberts had been a private when he had fought in France – just a teenager who'd enlisted because it had seemed like a good idea at the time and, anyway, there was not a lot going on in his small town in Kansas. He was 41 years old and had known nothing but the army. He had once met a girl and thought to get married but somehow it never happened because he said she had wanted him to leave the army and get a civilian job. He had put it off and in the end she wouldn't wait and they parted. 'I like the army,' he told the dispatch rider, 'I like to be out in the open and using my hands, it gives me a sense of freedom.'

'What do you think about this lot?' the rider asked, waving his hand towards Canada.

'Hard to say,' Roberts replied, 'but don't underestimate the Krauts. They're hard men and know how to fight; I saw that in France – I was at Belleau Wood and Amiens with Pershing. That was a goddamned hard fight; they were determined alright – and totally ruthless.' He pulled out a pack of cigarettes and offered them; the dispatch rider pulled one out and lit up.

'You don't look hardly old enough to be riding that motorcycle – how old are you son?'

'Twenty one; I got drafted. I'm finished my time in 11 days – hope I won't be called back. Mind you, I'll miss that', he said, indicating the bike propped up on its stand. 'They make good machines that Indian Motorcycle Company – I might buy myself one when I get some money.'

******

At 07.00 hours that morning, Tom strolled over to the officer's mess and got himself some breakfast. The weather for the day looked fair and there wasn't much activity in the camp with half the company gone to the border. He had some papers to move off his desk; a report to HQ which would be short on account of the quietness of the situation. He figured he should go up to the border and talk through the changeover with White; he could get a feel for the way things were panning out and plan any changes to their disposition. He had a problem though. He couldn't leave the camp without an officer and with the other three up at the border he was all they had left. There was a new lieutenant posting due that day to take over 4th Platoon but he had no precise arrival time so he would just have to wait. Then at 07.50 a Jeep turned into the camp with the new man on board.

Second Lieutenant Lawrence Brennan – Lee Brennan to his friends – was a young man of medium height, slim build and a fair complexion that looked like it wouldn't stand too much sun. He had transferred to 1st Armored from the

461

newly formed Armored Force School at Fort Knox and, having got his commission, found himself on a transport heading north. He had arrived at Cumberland Head on the previous day; there he'd been given a very short situation briefing and, after a day enduring the mud, was moved out to Rouses Point. Tom was pleased to see him – 4th Platoon needed its own leader – someone they could bond with. Brennan was the younger man, 22 against Tom who was nearly 28 but his experience with armored vehicles gave him an edge, especially over the older cavalry men. Tom liked that and warmed to the new man – here was somebody living in the present, somebody who understood the new technology and how to use it. He finished his breakfast and they went together to review what was left in the vehicle park. After a short walk round the vehicles they had there Tom briefed him on what was up at the border. Brennan pulled a long face. It was not impressive, Tom admitted, but he lived in the hope that they would get some of the newer, heavier stuff that he'd been told was now coming out of the factories.

'There's a lot of better stuff than this,' Brennan told him. 'These bean cans are already out of style.' He walked round the M2 then climbed up onto the Stuart. 'Last year we thought this thing was awesome. Don't get me wrong, it's still a pretty damn good infantry support vehicle but I wouldn't want to go up against anything heavy in it.' He climbed up onto the hull and lifted the command hatch – then he let it drop with a clang. 'Still too thin.' He jumped down to the ground again. He put on a grim look and shook his head, an expression that said, 'I've seen garbage cans that looked tougher than this.' Walking back he became more cheerful; the new stuff's okay – it's got thicker plate – and they've replaced that peashooter with a 75mm cannon; guaranteed to stop anything dead. Hope we get some of it soon.'

They toured the camp. Tom showed Brennan who was who, what was what, and where everything was kept; it was a small camp and it didn't take long to do the round. In the end he got 4th Platoon fell in and presented its new officer. After the men fell out they wandered back to the office where Tom formally handed over control of the camp to Brennan.

'I'm going up to the border,' he announced. 'You okay to keep a handle on things down here for an hour or so till I get back?'

'Sure – you go on ahead,' Brennan said confidently.

'I wanna see how things are laid out up there; need to meet with Captain White and the others.'

The driver from HQ, who'd been getting himself some coffee in the men's mess, now waited for further orders. He sat propped up against one of the fenders, his legs stretched out, a tin mug in one hand, a cigarette in the other. Seeing an officer approach he ditched the cigarette, threw the coffee onto the ground, put the mug down on the hood and jumped quickly to attention.

'Is there anything else I can do here sir?' he said, throwing up a salute.

Tom thought about getting up to White's bivouac; the Jeep was handy. Why not? 'You can drive me up the road a bit, private. There's a section up there I need to visit.'

They had not gone far when Tom asked the driver to pull over. He got out of the Jeep and looked around at the open countryside, bright in the morning sunlight. It was only about three miles to White, the day was clear and crisp, the walk would be good. 'You can stand down,' he told his driver, 'I think I'll walk it from here.'

The driver turned around and headed back towards the camp and the road to Cumberland Head; slowly the sound of the Jeep faded till he stood there alone in the midst of the near still landscape. Only a ragged black crow perched on a distant oak cracked the silence; its plaintive call drifting on the barely perceptible breeze. He started to walk at an unhurried pace, soaking up the morning air; it was fresh and sweet and still sharp from the touch of an earlier morning frost. It was good to be alone sometimes, just to let his thoughts meander over nothing in particular. He was thinking idly about Wheels when the thought was interrupted by a distant popping noise. He stopped and listened – nothing. He started to walk then there it was again, very faint but it was there. He stopped again; there was a deeper sound like muffled thunder muted by the distance. Out there deep into the horizon he saw something moving, at first just a black dot against the blue of the sky. It was definitely moving and it was heading his way. There was the sound of an engine slowly getting louder. It unsettled the crow; the bird gave one last rasping 'caw' and launched itself from the branch, flapping away over the treetops till it disappeared.

******

White came out of the post, stood on the veranda for a moment and looked into the distance. He thought he saw a movement on the Canadian side out where the road turned and the trees started. He decided to go back inside to fetch his field glasses when he spotted the dispatch rider sitting with Sergeant Roberts. Calling him over, he handed the report to the rider with instructions to take it straight to Cumberland Head, then he headed back to the post. As he did there was the sound of a rifle shot. It came from the direction of Newhart's patrol. There were more shots, then the short burping sound of a burst from a submachine gun; the next minute the horsemen came crashing out of the woods.

'Germans!' Newhart shouted, 'twenty or thirty, they've come round the far side of the wire.'

'Sergeant,' White yelled, 'get the men fell in and get that dispatch rider out of here. Corporal, get that Browning over here.' They formed up into a defensive line, fanned out at the back of the post and waited. There was silence.

'I think Corporal Ransom may have downed one of them,' Newhart said, 'but we need to get in there and flush them out. We're sitting ducks at the moment.'

The words were hardly out when Bob Duncan came running round the back of the post, head down and weaving. 'There's something coming down the road, looks like tanks. You'd better take a look.'

There was no doubt it was an armored column; the grumble of the engines and the clanking of tracks was now audible.

White ran across the open ground to the halftrack and, as he did so, there was the sound of small arms fire coming from the back of the post. He reached the halftrack. 'Radio Operator, get HQ on the line, tell them we're under attack – and then warn Lieutenant Jordan at base. I'm expecting incoming fire from that lot any moment.'

He ran the short distance to where the Stuart had already fired up its engine and was making to move into cover of the trees. 'See if you can put a round into that lead tank.'

The gunner raised the elevation of the Stuart's main gun and fired. The shot found its mark, hitting the front of the tank squarely. But as the secondary charge fired the shell simply bounced off, leaving the German still advancing. The armor was too thick for the puny 37mm shell. There was a gasp of horror from White as he witnessed the feeble result of the event. The Stuart was carrying the heaviest arm they had and it had proved inadequate against the oncoming German tank. As the gunner lined up his sights for a second shot a battery of incoming fire was suddenly unleashed. Somewhere in the barrage was a shell that took out the halftrack. It was a direct hit; the armored snout reared up like a monster poised to pounce and then, with a second explosion, flipped over onto its back, black smoke and flame gushing from a gaping ragged hole in its cab. There was no sound of distress from within; the blast had killed the entire crew instantly.

'Shit,' White shouted, 'there goes the radio. Dispatch rider – get the hell out of here. Get to Rouses Point – we need help and fast!'

The Stuart took a second shot but it missed. The German column was now beginning to fan out; shells were landing all round them.

At the back of the post men were hunkered down behind the sandbags, flattening themselves into shallow trenches dug on the first two days; hollows they never dreamed they would use when they dug them. Then the shapes of German helmets began to appear on the edge of the woodland; shadowy forms in grey coats, their square tin hats easily recognized. The men of 1st Platoon saw Newhart go down. He had stood up with some insane idea in his head that if he got to his horse he could get in behind the enemy and attack their rear. It was an absurd and reckless notion ingrained in his cavalry officer's training – an instinctive response that went hopelessly wrong. The corporal and his two-man team got the Browning into position and began spraying the woods in front of them. The .50 calibre rounds ripped chunks out of the trees, sending splinters in all directions. It was no more than fifty yards across the clearing to the fringe of the wood, but the Germans stayed back just inside where they were difficult to see. Only the muzzle flashes gave them away; but they were clever, seasoned soldiers – they fired then moved, then fired from another position. From the cries in the woods 1st Platoon knew they were having some success but it was chaos and as many as they thought they had killed more seemed to pour in and replace them.

The M2 came trundling round the side of the post, firing into the wood with its main cannon and two machine guns. Men had formed up behind it led by Bob Duncan. 'Sergeant,' he yelled frantically. 'Get your men on their feet we have to get into them. If you sit there you're a dead man – get in behind the armor.' As the M2 got closer the men in their shallow foxholes started to make a break for it. Roberts took his chance; he knew he couldn't stay where he was. Armed with a Thompson submachine gun he stood up and made a run for the M2, firing as he went. He got no more than three or four desperate paces before he went down in a hail of fire as several Germans in the wood saw their target. He fell where he stood still firing the Thompson, hit so many times bits flew off his body. The effect on the other men pressed hard into the ground was demoralizing and no one else tried to move. The M2 got as far as the fringe when it shuddered to a halt, hit by an anti-tank rocket. A second rocket pierced the wafer thin armor and exploded inside, killing all the crew except the commander, 2nd Platoon's Sergeant O'Hagan. Scrambling desperately through the hatch he made it to the ground where he died like Roberts, shot to pieces. Duncan threw three grenades into the wood then took a bullet in the head.

Behind the M2 the rag end of 1st Platoon started to run out of ammo. Now the Browning jammed, the breach recoil mechanism overheated; they had lost their last heavy weapon. Nervously they watched for targets to emerge from behind the trees. Someone in one of the foxholes shouted, 'Remember your training, squeeze don't pull – eyeball your target – control your breathing – don't shut your eyes – make every shot count.'

Morale was ebbing low. The only possible salvation was reinforcement from the base and the hope that the dispatch rider had got through to HQ. Cumberland Head was a long way off and men began to hold fire, preserving the last few precious rounds. Things were going badly but they were about to get worse.

There was a deafening explosion behind the men dug in. They felt the heat as the blast rushed across them. Lying flat they were saved from the flying fragments as the post took a direct hit from a howitzer shell; it shredded the timber building into matchwood, killing the three policemen inside. The ruin of the building instantly blazed, throwing a screen of choking smoke across the clearing. It gave the Germans in the wood the opportunity they needed and, under cover of the pall thrown across them by the fire, they came out of the trees and began to kill at close range. There was another loud explosion as the Stuart was hit. It instantly brewed up and burned the crew alive; a hideous screaming pierced the air as the men trapped inside were cremated by the fierce flames from burning gasoline, their cries punctuated by the thud of ammunition as the fire exploded the shells inside the vehicle.

This was war as Andy White had never imagined it. The horses were all dead, their soft bodies cut down by shrapnel and rifle fire. There was no glorious charge with flashing sabres, just this ghastly carnage and the noise of people screaming amidst the crack of rifle fire, the sputter of machine guns and the deafening explosions of shells. It was worse than his wildest nightmare. It was chaos, it was confusion, it was mayhem and all against the backdrop of a scene from the Apocalypse. He was losing his ability to command; all his assets were being destroyed in front of him – it was futile and in the end he gave up.

He surrendered to a tank commander wearing the uniform of the Waffen SS; a ferret-faced man with darting eyes and very blond hair. Obersturmbannführer Joachim Metz looked around him at the devastation with an air of satisfaction. He leaned down from the turret of his tank to Captain White. 'Did you think your foolish display would stop us from coming? All you did was convince us that America is feeble. You are a nation of decadence. You people are corrupted by the dregs of the sub-humanity you have let take over your society. We have come to cleanse you.'

From behind the burning remains of the post more German soldiers were emerging from the woods. Slowly the Americans stood up raising their hands as they got to their feet. Out of more than 70 men only 19 had survived the fire fight. They were herded over to where Metz was still lecturing Captain White. He broke off to survey the battered men and smiled. He was surprised by how easy it had been, how primitive their equipment was and how unprepared their strategy. Metz had taken part in the thrust through the Low Countries with Guderian when they had rolled up the French and the British like a Persian rug. This was going to be the same and with America and its industrial capacity, together with plenty of oil and steel, it would be easy to crush the Russians. Germany was the master race – we are the inheritors of the earth, he proudly told himself.

'So,' he said airily to White, 'what shall we do with you now?' He shook his head in an admonishing gesture at the captured Americans. They stood with heads bowed, battered and defeated. Two men had been wounded but the rest were physically unharmed. They had just run out of willpower along with their ammunition.

'We are your prisoners,' White said rationally in a dejected tone. He had never before considered what followed on defeat because he had never expected to find himself in such a position. He had, in fact, never thought he would face battle – at least not this kind of unforgiving hell. He had nothing to draw on and could only wait for whatever it was to come.

'Quite so,' Metz agreed. 'Normally I would send you back behind my lines to Ottawa or somewhere, but I can't spare the men – and I am in a hurry. I shall have to put you somewhere where you will not be a nuisance.'

'So what do you propose to do?'

'What can I do,' he said, more as a statement than a question. 'Oh, I know.' Metz smiled down benignly at White then shouted something to one of his men. There was a momentary lull and in that time it dawned on White what was about happen. The blood drained from his face and with a look of abject supplication he implored Metz to consider the men and their families.

Metz shrugged it off. 'They should have considered this might be their fate when they became soldiers – this is the risk we all take.'

'What about the Geneva Convention?' White was saying, as he heard the weapons cocked.

Metz seemed to waiver and for a moment White's hope rekindled. Metz nodded to his firing squad; they shot the prisoners in a cacophony of gunfire. The men died almost without a groan, scythed down like ripe corn. Then there was silence – broken only by the tinkle of the last spent round as the empty jacket bounced along the paving. There was a terrible silence. White reeled under the shock of what he had just witnessed. He was about to shout at this animal, to tell him what a low, callous bastard he was when everything went black and he too was out of it. He fell to the floor, shot through the head. All along the road that stretched out behind the pathetic little pile on the ground that was White's lifeless body, the road he had been guarding, the road leading back into Canada, a long column was forming; tanks, mechanized guns, infantry, ordinance trucks, fuel tankers and every kind of support needed for an invading army. Meanwhile the same scene was being played out at more than a dozen crossing points along the border as Operation Gottlieb got on the road.

Hidden just round the first bend inside what was still in that moment US territory the dispatch rider, sitting astride his Indian, had seen it all. Too stunned to move, he finally pulled himself together, kicked the engine into life, crunched into first gear and accelerated away. A Stormtrooper who had detached himself from the main group and gone into the woods to relieve his bowels now saw the rider and took a shot at him. In the time it took for the German to operate the bolt on his Mauser rifle the Indian was disappearing round the next bend in the road. The rifle barked; it was a grabbed shot, fired blind as bike and rider disappeared.

The boy on the Indian was unlucky; the bullet flicked through the early spring leaves, snatching and clipping them as it went until finally it found its mark. It hit the satchel slung over the rider's back but that wasn't enough to stop it. It tore through the leather, split a thick wad of paper and went into his lung. It didn't kill him but he felt the pain like someone had punched him between the shoulder blades real hard. After a few minutes the pain became sharper, more localized, more defined; he began to find difficulty in breathing – he was operating on one lung. On the road ahead he saw a single figure walking towards him. He was beginning to feel faint, his grip on the throttle was failing – the machine was beginning to slow and with that slowing started to lose its gyroscope effect; it began to weave. He was closer to the figure now but it had become much harder to control the machine. At around 50 yards he lost it; bike and rider both went down together, sliding along the paved roadway until finally, with all the momentum exhausted, it came to a halt, the front wheel hanging into the roadside drainage ditch. He was dimly aware of a face staring down at him.

Tom pulled the rider clear of the bike; he looked at the blood on his hands. 'We need to get you to a medic,' he told him calmly. He looked at the motorcycle then back to the rider; his face was white as marble and he was now coughing little flecks of blood. He had to do something and quickly. Hauling on the handlebars he got the bike upright and put it on its stand. Gently he pulled the rider to a sitting position and propped him against the machine. He was no more than a kid, Tom thought – and now he was probably going to die.

'They're coming,' he said feebly, 'they killed everyone, just shot them down where they stood. We have to warn Headquarters – they'll be here soon.'

'Save the talking,' Tom said calmly, 'it'll only make things worse. If I ride this thing do you think you can stay on the back, hang on to me – it's less than a couple of miles to camp?'

'I'll try,' the boy wheezed. 'Can you ride a motorcycle?'

'Well, I can ride a bicycle,' Tom said, trying to make light of the situation, 'and I can drive a car – so I guess it shouldn't be too difficult if I put the two together. Do you think you can stand if I haul on your arm?'

It was painful and it was difficult but they got themselves on the bike. As they wobbled erratically down the road towards the camp he knew that if the boy fell off he couldn't stop to pick him up again. If what the boy had said was correct the Germans were right behind them. They made it to the camp; Tom skidded the machine to a halt. The boy fell sideways off the back and thumped onto the ground.

'Medic, medic!' Tom yelled. 'Over here on the double – we need a medic!' Men came out of the huts at the sound of the shouting. Three medics arrived all at the same time.

'Right,' Tom shouted, 'just listen up – don't ask questions – we've got a goddamned emergency. Private, find Lieutenant Brennan and get him here on the double. You,' he said pointing to one of the medics, 'get an ambulance and get this man in it. Then get the hell out of here and over to Cumberland Head.'

'He may die if we move him, sir.'

'He'll die if you don't – just do it!'

As the words came out of his mouth there was a roar overhead and a plane with a Swastika tail marking flew low across the camp, raking it with machine gun fire as it passed.

'What the hell was that?' a private said, looking skyward open mouthed.

'We're being attacked, soldier. Get your rifle and find some cover.' He looked around as men now started to run in his direction.

'Sergeant Costello,' he yelled at the top of his voice, 'get your ass over here.'

Brennan and Costello arrived together and Tom rapidly laid out the position. He'd barely finished when they heard the sound of the plane returning. 'Take cover,' he shouted as loudly as he could, then threw himself to the ground and crawled under the steps of one of the huts. The plane came in low again firing its machine guns; then, as it passed overhead, a dark, sinister lump detached itself and fell from the underside. As it landed there was a flash and a bang; the ground shook. A fountain of earth spurted into the air then rattled back down on the hut roofs. They were lucky – the bomb hit the parade ground and did no more than leave a small crater. All round the camp men had taken up makeshift firing positions and were shooting rifles at the attacker – but without result. From its pit near to the front gate a Browning machine gun stuttered, but it too seemed ineffective. The corporal on the Browning couldn't work out why he hadn't hit the damn thing; it was right in his sights, for God's sake.

Tom scrambled to his feet. 'It'll be back,' he said urgently. 'Sergeant, get some drivers. I want every vehicle in the parks out of here and on the road. Go straight to Cumberland Head – we can't defend this position, it's too damned exposed; and sergeant don't let them bunch up, they make a better target. Split 'em up and spread 'em out – send some of them on the Champlain road and some down the lake shore to Coopersville. Don't hang about and do it now on the double. Lieutenant Brennan, find Corporal McAndrew. I want him and a squad of our best marksmen over at the machine gun dugout as quick as you can. Then get everyone else onto vehicles and move them out. Leave me two Jeeps or a truck – whatever you can spare. Let's do it.'

As vehicles and men streamed out of the camp, the squad got down into the dugout. It was a cramped circular pit about eight feet in diameter with a small canvas cover on a frame that could be pulled across for weather protection or moved if it obscured the field of fire. The last vehicle passed by the dugout and droned off down the road, the whine from its rear axle differential getting fainter and fainter – and then it was quiet; an eerie stillness settled over the camp. There was no sign of the raider, no sound of an engine. Maybe it wasn't coming back. Tom didn't believe it – where there was one there would be more, he was certain. There wouldn't be much time to brief the squad so he would keep it to the minimum. The men huddled there, squatting down behind the sandbagged wall, hugging their rifles and listening for the sound of an aircraft.

'OK,' Tom said, looking at the apprehension on their faces, 'listen carefully. I don't have time to go into the reasons so you'll have to take what I say on face value and trust that I know what I'm talking about.'

'Yes sir,' they chorused in unison as if they were on the parade ground. Every one of them was happy to have someone who seemed to know what he was doing. In their minds they were feeling like children and Tom was their father figure.

'When that plane comes back I don't want you to fire at it – I want you to fire in front of it. Is that clear – in front of it?' The men murmured and nodded, indicating they understood.

'If he comes in straight and level take your aim about ten or twelve feet in front of the prop. Corporal, you wait until he's around fifty yards away and then you open up vertically on the Browning. I want a stream of lead straight up into the sky.' He paused very briefly and looked around.

'OK, here's why. That plane's an FW 190. Flying straight and level he'll be travelling around 400 miles an hour; if he comes in on a shallow dive he could be going 450. He'll be around one to two hundred feet when he gets to us. I won't bore you with the statistics but at the muzzle velocity of our weapons a bullet will take around a twentieth of a second to reach its target. This target is about thirty feet long and in the time it takes your round to reach its mark it'll have moved on by around fifty feet. So if you shoot at it you're gonna miss it. Is that clear?'

'Yes sir,' they chorused again, this time more positively. It was good to have a leader who was smarter than they were – and certainly smarter than the enemy. They felt they would survive. They waited and listened but nothing happened. The minutes passed and still nothing – slowly they relaxed a bit; perhaps he wasn't coming back after all. Eventually a low droning coming from the north signaled it was back. Men got into their firing positions; the droning got louder, then they saw it – a squadron of black specks against the afternoon sky; they were heading for Cumberland Head. After a few minutes one appeared to have changed direction and was looking like it would pass to the west of them. 'Damn,' Tom said under his breath, 'he's going for the trucks heading for Champlain.'

At five hundred feet the pilot of the 190 had a perfect view of the countryside around him. Down among the patchwork of fields he could clearly see the trucks and the armor dotted along the roads moving like children's toys; little models in a table-top game. Away to the west he could see the camp now seemingly deserted – he wouldn't waste his time on that. He'd dropped the single bomb he'd been carrying so there was no point in beating up the Stuart that was clanking steadily along the main road; even his heavier wing-mounted cannon would not get through its armor, and besides the tank was fitted with a pair of anti-aircraft machine guns, so why take the risk? Better to shoot up a soft target that couldn't bite back. He picked on a line of well-spaced troop carriers. As he lined up to make the pass he could see the faces of the men peering out of the canvas back; he got right down under a hundred feet, eased his airspeed back to a slow 250 mph and, at a hundred yards, pushed his thumb into the firing ring on the control stick; the guns raked the back of the truck. The rounds ripped through the bodies of the men inside; they smashed through the back of the cab hitting the driver. The truck went out of control and veered across the road into a field where it rolled slowly to a halt. Men clawed their way out of the back, falling onto the ploughed earth; some so traumatized they could make no noise even though they were clutching at the holes in their bodies, blood streaming through their fingers, struggling with smashed bones. A field ambulance that was ahead turned and raced back to where the stricken men were spread across the ground. While they patched up those they could it was too late for most of them; men died as they bled to death, some drowned in their own blood as their lungs filled and they suffocated, others just died from trauma. The medics did what they could, crowding the survivors into the ambulance, leaving the dead where they lay. There was no time for niceties, barely time for a prayer, they had to move on.

The 190 pulled up and banked away to the right, then turned back on itself; the pilot looked down in triumph at the kill. On the ground there was nothing the fleeing vehicles could do; just keep moving. Each man hoped he would not be the next target. Their luck turned for the better when the pilot decided to call it a day – his fuel gauge was showing less than a quarter. He turned his plane east; he would overfly the camp to make sure there was nothing left there of strategic importance. If there was he had enough cannon and machine gun ammunition in the belts to deal with any stragglers; if not it didn't matter, it would be routine reconnaissance and he would still be able to report a good day's hunting.

In the dugout they heard the drone of the 190's radial engine. Tom held up a hand for silence. It was getting closer, less than five hundred yards. They heard the pilot throttle back and they watched as the plane dropped down to around a hundred feet; it was heading straight towards them.

'On my command,' Tom said calmly, 'you know what to target.'

At what Tom judged to be around fifty yards he yelled out the order. There was a deafening crescendo of gunfire and the air filled with metal rain as the 190 hurtled across the top of them at less than fifty feet. They could feel the roar of the engine vibrating in their chest bones as it skimmed them so close it felt like any man could have reached up and grabbed it by the tail. It was all over in a fraction of a second. The men stood up and watched; there was a murmur of disappointment as the 190 started to bank and climb, turning towards them.

'I could swear we hit it,' a private said. 'I saw bits drop off.' He jumped out of the pit and ran a short distance to where he picked up a small fragment of metal. He waved it triumphantly in the air. 'Yup, we hit it okay.'

'Action stations again,' Tom shouted, 'and keep your heads down because he knows you're here and he'll come in shooting.' The plane completed its turn and everyone got down as low as they could.

'Look, that's smoke, isn't it?' someone shouted. Everyone stood up; there was a discernible puff of smoke; then it turned to a plume, a thin line of billowing black smoke.

'Son of a bitch,' someone else shouted, 'we got it – we hit the bastard.'

There was silence as the 190 started to lose height; flames appeared from around the engine cowl. Seconds later there was a bang and a cloud of grey smoke, this time from the engine. The plane stopped flying; it stalled and fell out of the sky. The volatile fumes in the near empty gas tank blew out a fireball and that was an end to it. A spontaneous cheer went up from the pit. Men jumped up and down; they laughed and hugged each other, patted each other on the back. Tom let them have their moment of celebration; it was good for morale, he told himself, but the German column couldn't be far off and they'd probably seen the fate of the downed 190. He needed to get them out of there while there was still time.

'Corporal,' he shouted, 'let's get this show on the road. We need to get out of here. Every man with his own rifle – and we'll take the Browning.' They bundled into the two vehicles Brennan had left behind; a Jeep and a one-ton truck. Tom stared hard into the fading light; there was no sign of anything in the air. Thank God, he said to himself.

At Cumberland Head radio traffic was flying around like scared starlings. They had survived the first attack from the squadron of FW 190s. Telephones rang non-stop as reports came in of incursions all along the border. E-boats were reported moving down Lake Champlain in force. Further west on Superior, Ontario and Huron the same pattern was emerging.

******

Up in Pembina, which was nothing more than a hamlet out in the deserted grasslands of North Dakota, a solitary farmer ploughing with a tractor saw a long line of what he took to be trucks way out on the horizon, and wondered what they were doing there. This was remote country; more than one truck in a day was an event. He looked for a while, shading his eyes against the low, early morning sun; then he dismissed it and went back to his ploughing.

A short while before the farmer had seen the line of what he took to be trucks, a battalion of fast-moving German armor had arrived at the single red-and-white striped pole that defined the Canadian border and there came to a halt. A soldier climbed down from the turret of his armored scout car, looked around briefly, and seeing no one leaned on the weighted end of the pole and watched it rise to the perpendicular position. The way ahead was clear. The column got on the move again and forged its way south. Not a single shot had been fired; the post was unmanned. Turning east, it moved down Route 75 and headed for the first small community at Hallock; again it was unopposed – the route and the flat, ploughed countryside around it was empty of life, deserted. As it arrived at Hallock and passed along Main Street people came out of their houses to look, driven by curiosity. Women with children stood on the sidewalks and stared; some waved, thinking it was their own army on exercise. One man announced confidently that it was in his opinion a barn storming carney – some kind of travelling show – and he said how he hoped it would set up somewhere near so they could get a lick of the entertainment.

But the travelling show kept on going, skirting around Grand Forks and moving on to Fargo. Here it changed direction and headed in a straight line across the farmland of flat fields into Minnesota; it was perfect tank country – flat, firm and devoid of trees. As the column pushed on, odd reports started to come in about strange sightings out on the highway. The first police patrol to make contact came face to face with a forward scout car in a remote area on Highway 2. The officers inside the car were not sure what to do. They came to a halt twenty yards from the column and for a moment just sat there dumbstruck, looking down the road at a sight they were finding difficult to comprehend.

'Hell, I think they're Germans,' one of them said, seeing the swastika pennants flying from the wireless antennae of the lead vehicles. 'What in tarnation are they doing here?'

He didn't have to wait long for an answer, but neither of the men would have the time to consider its import. They both died instantly; a 35mm shell ripped through the windshield and exploded the gas tank in a ball of searing orange flame – and they were out of the game.

******

In Washington that morning nobody seemed to know what was happening but a steady stream of reports was now coming into the Shack with every passing minute. At first they were sporadic and incomprehensible. The German incursions had happened too fast and occurred in places that were far and remote. There were few eye witnesses to their progress and where there were they were overtaken before anyone could find anyone else to tell it to.   The previous night most of America had slept without even guessing something might be wrong. Not till the following morning did the majority of the country understand the gravity of the situation as they sat down to eat their cornflakes, their waffles and maple syrup, their ham and their eggs, sunny side up or easy over – they heard it on the radio. Unsurprisingly a good number of listeners thought it was a new radio drama. The story of Orson Wells and the panic of *The War of the Worlds* was still fresh in the collective American memory. A lot of people, it turned out later, thought it was just another hoax – but they were wrong. This time the aliens were real and the killing was real, and it was going to take more than a nasty head cold to defeat them. they were witnessing not the War of the Worlds but the Second World War. It had arrived on their doorsteps – along with the morning paper.

******

'Fred, good to have you have you back. Sit down and take a look at this – the balloon went up early this morning.'

Loughlin pulled up a chair. There was a section of a map showing the Canadian border – black jagged arrows slashed across the line of the 45th parallel.

'I told them, did I not,' Churchill said, prodding a finger here and there at the arrows. It wasn't a question; it was a statement of fact. He had raised the probability of a German invasion from across the Canadian border more than once but they hadn't listened. Only Patton had taken him seriously and it now turned out that only Patton was prepared.

There was a knock and Mary stuck her head round the door. 'General Marshall has asked if you could go to see him urgently.'

'Come on, Fred, I think we're on at last. Now maybe they'll listen,' he grinned as they walked the short distance along the corridor to the Chiefs' Office. Inside a group of anxious faces were poring over a map. There were faces he recognized: Hap Arnold, Ira Eaker, George Marshall, others he hadn't seen before – and then there was King, pulling his usual sour face. He's going to find this hard to swallow, Churchill thought. Major Gregson, the Intelligence Officer from SI was running a hand over the plan of the unfolding attack. Everybody looked up as they entered. 'Winston,' Marshall called out with an air of warmth that immediately put Churchill on guard. He surreptitiously nudged Fred. 'They want something,' he said out of the corner of his mouth.

They moved over to the group and waited to see what came next. King did something unprecedented: he held out his hand to Churchill and forced out what was probably meant to look like a smile but turned out more of a grim grin. It caught Churchill off guard for an instant, but he took the hand that was offered and shook it anyway. It was a hard bony hand, cold and leathery like the man himself; it was like shaking hands with a thinly gloved skeleton. 'It seems you were right all along,' was all King said, and even that sounded like it came grudgingly. Marshall made room for them at the table.

'They broke in here,' he said, tapping a section of the map indicating the top end of the Hudson Valley, 'here on Champlain, here at Rouses Point, then right across to North Dakota. We don't think they'll go for anything further west – they're fenced in by the Rockies. We think two armored Divisions crossed the border into North Dakota at around 07.00 this morning; heavy and light tanks, halftracks, anti-tank guns and infantry in support. That was this morning, but more came in behind it and it's rapidly becoming a full army group; and they have air support – though thankfully not a lot.

'There's a major waterborne thrust on all the lakes from Champlain to Superior,' he swept his hand across the map, generally indicating the extent of the area the Germans were trying to cover. 'And they've spread themselves on a wide battle front; that makes it difficult to confront because we simply don't have men in the right places. Worse, where we have managed engagement we've been comprehensively knocked out; we're being hit all over park. As of right now we're losing this ball game – that has to change.'

He looked across at Arnold. 'Hap, it's your turn to show and tell.'

'We've got every serviceable airplane heading in that direction and we're establishing forward bases along a line around fifty miles south of where they are right now. We daren't get any closer just yet; the enemy are moving fast and there's a danger we'd be overrun. I don't want to lose stuff on the ground. We're putting fighters and ground attack aircraft into the front line to start pounding their armor.'

He waved a hand at Eaker, indicating it was his turn on the stump. 'Ira'.

'We've requisitioned all the civilian airfields across the northeast and we're getting the heavy bombers in place to strike. We've got reconnaissance out there looking for targets but it's going to take time. As of this moment we're getting what we can airborne. We're going after the Canadian airfields, railway yards and bridges to start with, then the ammo dumps, fuel supplies and vehicle parks – but it's not going to be easy. They have pretty much everything on the move, and in the end there's a limit to what can be done from the air. It won't replace ground forces – men in tough boots with rifles.'

Marshall looked around the faces again. 'It's clear from what we have that the Germans are trying to create a pocket. They're making a wide circling movement through Minnesota, clear across to Vermont where they look like joining hands with the east coast thrust – probably somewhere east of the Hudson River. Inside that pocket, if they succeed, they'll have Detroit, Chicago, Cleveland and Pittsburgh – a lot of the industrial heart of America – and they'll be knocking on the door of New York. Tucked up under the lakes, they'll be able to supply themselves on a front so broad we will be facing real problems. Yes, General Eaker is right we have to have men, and tanks, on the ground face to face with the enemy fighting for every inch of the ground – but ...'

He stopped abruptly and this time looked at Churchill.

'... the problem is we barely have enough men to do that. We can probably hold them along that line but this is ultimately about numbers. We have to stop their resupply – men and materials. We have to cut their line of communication. If we don't the build-up will prove fatal – we'll be overwhelmed. The only way out of this a blockade; we have to stop the flow coming into Hudson Bay – and the whole of the Canadian east coast. To do that we need more ships in the Atlantic. We can't take them away from the Pacific – the Japs would be all over the west coast the minute we deplete the Pacific fleet. We can't build our way out of this – there isn't time. The only other resource open to us is the Royal Navy.'

He stopped again, drew breath. 'Winston,' he said casually, 'I think this is your call.'

Churchill didn't respond immediately; heads turned in anticipation. 'I think we can probably manage that,' he said.

King looked approvingly at him. 'Good, we can talk about the nuts and bolts after this meeting.'

'It was,' he said to Fred when they got back to their own office, 'the only time he could remember seeing the old sourpuss look even remotely like a happy man.'

'That's settled,' Marshall said. 'We'll need a meeting with Admiral James. I suggest the Azores.'

'There is one other thing, though.' Churchill stood there with his thumbs thrust into his waistcoat pockets; he sensed an opportunity for a bit of horse trading.

'That is,' Marshall raised his eyebrows – he was not expecting strings.

'Recognition. I can't be fully effective without it – I need authority. I will need the US to officially recognize my authority as the elected leader of Britain and withdraw any recognition of Mosley and his henchmen. The legitimate government is the one in Maidstone.'

'You've got it,' Marshall said looking relieved. 'Now let's get down to the nitty gritty.'

CHAPTER 34

South East England, 2 March 1941

Something had changed; something was different. The first indication came when the pressure on Brooke's front line eased; dispatches filed after engagements noted the numbers of Wehrmacht in the field had reduced. Field commanders were reporting fewer contacts with the enemy along the length of their defences and when they did come they were less aggressive; there was an absence of SS. Intelligence reports coming to Armitage were bringing in the same message: where engagements took place they were now almost exclusively with BBS forces, who lacked the resolve and ferocity of their German collaborators. This was disquietingly strange for Brooke; the more so because towards the end of the previous year, sometime before Christmas, the Luftwaffe had established a forward base operating out of Croydon; fighters and ground attack Stuka dive bombers. For three months they had been putting pressure on Park's flyers.

At the end of February Grainger had taken six of his men on a hit-and-run raid into the suburbs of London. Their target was the airfield at Croydon.

Armitage had called him the day before. 'Brooke and Park want someone to go in and sabotage the field,' Armitage told him. 'I've volunteered you. Go in and wreck as many aircraft as you can and, if the opportunity presents itself, why don't you see if you can blow the munitions dump as well?'

The week before the operation two of Armitage's agents in London had left a cache of plastic explosives, detonators and some Sten guns at a safe location. They were stored with a garage owner, a trusted partisan, in his workshop close to the airfield. All Grainger's team had to do was get in and get out.

The day before the raid they made their way from Biggin Hill, where Park now had his main fighter base, and set off for the Medway, which still formed the frontier with Mosley-controlled England. Crossing the lightly wooded open countryside under cover of dark, they got across the river and broke in behind the BBS lines. In the early hours of the morning just before first light, they emerged from the protection of the woods at the outskirts of the small Surrey town of Banstead. Dressed as factory workers and with forged papers, they walked into the railway station and purchased tickets for Croydon. It was not long after they came out of Croydon station and they'd started to make their way to the rendezvous at the garage that they first noticed the absence of Wehrmacht soldiers on the streets. The garage owner said he'd noticed the same but didn't know why. There had been a lot of activity over the past months, particularly around the airfield, but recently he hadn't seen any at all.

'There's been a change,' he told them. 'I don't know what happened but looks like Jerry's pulling out.'

That night they collected the arms and explosives then set out for the airfield, travelling the short distance in a delivery van with a night pass; they made their destination without incident. This Grainger found unsettling; he had expected to be challenged at least once on the route but they saw no one, just a solitary bobby who ignored them as they passed by. The plan they had was not complicated; as always Grainger liked to keep things simple – complicated plans he knew from experience had too many things that could go wrong – and if they could go wrong then sooner or later they would go wrong. So the plan was straightforward.

They would drive the van up to the gates and, relying on the strength of their fake papers, gain access. The first objective was the control tower; they needed to neutralise the radio operators. After that they would split into three groups: Grainger's target was the ammo store; the other two groups were to lay charges under as many planes as they could get to. The detonators were timed to blow at 90-second intervals starting with a big bang from the ammo dump. They would get out the same way that they got in – drive out through the main gates. They would have less than two minutes to get out after the first charge was timed to blow. If anything went wrong before that, if they were discovered or challenged, they would have to shoot their way out.

'Each man looks to himself,' he had told them at the end of their briefing.

The plan was audacious and risky but Grainger was relying on that very audacity to keep the Germans off guard – nobody would be expecting an attack so far inside occupied territory. He was banking on them being half asleep.

He had relied on taking the Germans by surprise, but in the event the surprise was sprung not on the guards at the gate or the operators in the control tower – it fell on them. When they got there the main gate was unguarded. A few yards inside there was a gatehouse but it was in darkness. They sat there with the engine running and waited, expecting to see a light come on and a guard to emerge – nothing happened. At first Grainger suspected a trap and he ordered his men to get out of the back of the van and find cover. Nothing happened. He got out from behind the wheel and cautiously walked up to the gate, trying all the while to look casual – it wasn't locked. As he stood there in the eerie silence he half expected at any moment to hear the shout of a challenge, but there was nothing. Something's not right, he kept telling himself as the uncertainty of his position played out. He had to do something, he couldn't just stand there. He pushed on the gate – it opened with a metallic squeak and a groan. Quickly he moved over to the gatehouse; the door had been left open, there was no one inside. This, he thought, is bloody careless of them and went back to the van. 'Let's be bold,' he told the others, 'We'll just drive in and help ourselves – if they're this sloppy it'll be a piece of cake.'

But what he found was neither what he had expected, nor was it a piece of cake. It was just simply deserted; it had been abandoned. The hangers were empty; there was nothing in the ammo dump; everything had been taken – the place was empty.

******

In Berlin Hitler gathered his High Kommand. He was planning another master stroke; he wanted his crack troops for a greater scheme. There was little place in this new grand plan for Britain or the British; they were a maritime nation and what he had in mind was not a war at sea. Admiral Raeder had for some time argued for an all-out assault to finish the British business once and for all, and to subsume the British fleet into a greater Kreigsmarine, but his constant requests only served to irritate Hitler, who angrily pushed them aside. Now Raeder was absent from the gathering, excluded because he would try to deviate from the plan, try to nudge it off course. Hitler knew his game – he was a good mariner but he didn't understand strategy the way Hitler did.

'Can he not see,' he ranted to the small coterie of generals gathered in his office, 'Germany is a continental nation, part of a great contiguous land mass. This is the real living space I must have if I am to create the greatest Empire the world has ever seen.' He thumped the table with both fists.

'It stretches from Franco's Spain in the west to the Pacific coast of China in the east; my interest and my plans lie here, not in some insignificant offshore island that does not even consider itself to be a part of Europe.' He brushed his hand across the map in front of him, the back of his hand symbolically sweeping away the island and the English in one dismissive stroke. It was a distraction, a small concern to be bypassed, left in the wings while the greater game was played out on the main stage. Later, when the big victories had been gained he would attend to it.

'I shall isolate them,' he declared and stabbed the air with a forefinger. 'They will come running to us begging forgiveness, crying to be let in – like a child pleading with its father – you will see. Then we shall make them wait.' He pounded the table again and laughed loudly; the sycophants gathered around him laughed in unison.

There were moments when he believed that the bond with the English, in particular, was strong enough to bring them round by their own choice, when they would clamour to become part of the great German family of the Third Reich. Gottlieb was succeeding. It was bringing him victories, rapid victories just as it had in the Low Countries and France. He read the reports from Guderian and Von Paulus with growing enthusiasm. He was elated; they were loaded with a heady, intoxicating sense that his armies were unstoppable. The industrial north was secured, overrun in days. Hadn't they extended the frontier of Canada down below the line of the Great Lakes almost without a proper battle? The Americans, he had predicted, would not know how to fight – they would have no stomach for a fight. It was another great victory and it was perfectly timed for his address to the Reichstag.

******

'Colonel Hamilton wants to see you sir.' Corporal McAndrew stood to attention and saluted. The air in the tent was damp and cold. The ground under the canvas was soft; one leg of the table he was using as a desk had burrowed into the floor, tilting it to an uncomfortable angle. The last time he'd been there the camp was a sea of mud – now it was an ocean. Everywhere men were on the move, splashing around, skidding on the duck boards, pulling down tents, packing up bivouacs. Cumberland Head was being evacuated; departing vehicles churned up the saturated ground and headed towards Plattsburgh, the nearest defendable point. They heard reinforcements were coming up from the south, but the news was sketchy and the rumor was that the Germans had already outflanked them. Coming down Lake Champlain with a fleet of fast assault craft, they had easily taken Burlington on the east bank. On the western edge of the lake they had overrun Port Henry and Crown Point.

When Tom heard that he briefly gave a thought to Al Cardy at Crows Crossing; it would be occupied by now. It occurred to him that was what Neumann had been doing there – he'd been surveying for the invasion, checking out the lay of the land. Obvious with hindsight, but who would have guessed it then? There was a time when the discovery of that simple truth would have excited him; now it passed as unremarkable. Neumann no longer mattered – wherever he was; only the here and now mattered – the task in hand. He made his way through the mud to the farmhouse where Hamilton had his HQ. Inside it was warm and dry.

'Lieutenant Jordan'.

'Sir', Tom replied.

'I have a job for you.'

'Sir.'

'Gather up what's left of your platoon and Second Lieutenant Brennan's; hand pick two more platoons and make up a replacement for Captain White's – poor devils. You'll reinforce 'A' company, they're dug in on Highway 9. You're the rear guard; you'll fight a holding action while we get the rest of this stuff over to Plattsburgh. We can't defend the position here; I don't know for how long you can pin them down – we're promised some air cover but it's any man's guess. When you get my signal pull out.'

'Sir'.

'I'm putting you back up to Captain – it goes with the job.' He pushed a pair of silver bars across the desk towards Tom. 'And get someone to paint another bar on that tin hat of yours. Good luck – it's a lousy job, I know, but you're the only man I have with any battle experience – so it has to be you. Find the best men you can.'

Away from the farmhouse Tom went looking for Brennan. He found him in what was left of the officer's mess. 'It's a bit early for that,' Tom nodded in the direction of a large tumbler half full of Kentucky whisky.

Brennan shrugged and when Tom told him the mission they'd been handed, he picked up the glass and downed it in one noisy gulp. 'I don't want to die sober,' was all he said.

'Get your men together; we'll assemble over at the armored vehicle compound – what's left of it.'

Tom went off to find McAndrew, cursing his rotten luck again. He came across him sharing a smoke with a sergeant close by one of the mustering points where men were being loaded into trucks. That was convenient – he needed a replacement for Roberts.

'What's your name, sergeant?'

The man dropped his cigarette and snapped to attention. 'Rossi, sir.'

'What's your company?'

'C Company, Arizona Rifles, sir.'

'How many men have you got?'

'Still here, sir?'

'Still here, sergeant.'

'Two platoons, sir – and a medic.'

'Good. That's exactly what I need – where's your captain?'

'Gone to Plattsburgh with Charlie and Dog Companies, sir'.

'Any officers left?'

'Just the two Lieutenants, sir.'

'Okay, Sergeant Rossi, you're with me now, orders from the Colonel. Round up your men and find your officers, then get them over to my tent; McAndrew will show you where that is. Corporal, get the rest of our men over there too – and while you're at it find me some scoped rifles. Do it on the double – we don't have too much time.'

They came upon 'A' company dug in on either side of Highway 9; the ground was flat and clear, there was no cover at all and Tom wondered why they had picked that point – it was a lousy position to defend. Four M3 antitank guns had been wheeled out in a fan and covered with camouflage nets, but they'd be easy to spot and just as easy to knock out. He found the officer commanding 'A' company standing in the open, looking up the road through his field glasses. They exchanged formalities: Captain Daniel Brown had been at Fort Bliss when Tom was there but they had never met. He wasn't surprised; it was a big place and Brown was running a catering unit. What the hell was Hamilton doing putting a cook out to command a rear guard?

'I volunteered,' Brown told him. 'I only have basic training but I hate kitchens.'

'Who's your top sergeant? We need to get ourselves in a better position than this?' He looked around him at the flat, open countryside. They were ducks sitting there waiting to be shot; he had to move them. Further up, the tree cover thickened; that would be a better spot.

Tom called the sergeants together to brief them. There were only two of them, Rossi and Cleaver, but he was relieved to find they were both regulars – enlisted men with a lot of training behind them but they had never seen action; only his old platoons had come under fire. The first blooding, he knew, could be terrifying and it was anyone's guess how the new men would react. Some would let their training take over and just do what they had to – but some would hesitate, they'd think too much, they would be unpredictable; they were the ones who were most likely to be killed.

Up in the new positions he felt more comfortable. The ground rose steeply to a ridge on one side and was covered with good mature trees that were already thick with late spring foliage. He would put three marksmen up in the trees where they would have a clear view of the approaching enemy; there was nothing like snipers to slow down advancing infantry. Not knowing where the next shot might come from naturally made men cautious, reluctant to move – it kept their heads down.

Getting the guns into position had been difficult. The tow vehicles would not penetrate the heavy undergrowth. They manhandled them as far up the sloping ground as they could and cut away some small trees to give a field of fire that covered the road for more than a thousand yards. The one advantage they now had was the rising ground to one side of the road and the thick woodland on the other; advancing vehicles would be hemmed in, unable to get off the road – they would be in a box. Behind them from the top of the ridge the ground dropped away steeply, falling down into a good sized pond – almost big enough to call a lake; beyond that was more woodland and then the shores of Lake Champlain. In his mind Tom had already worked out his line of retreat. That would be their escape route when it came time to pull out, him and the snipers; the others would go first, falling back down the road to where their transport had been left. He talked it through with Brown and when they were agreed they instructed Rossi and Cleaver. The men then settled down to wait.

McAndrew had scrounged four 30.06 Springfield rifles back at the armory in Cumberland Head; they were all scoped for sniping. With these he could do a lot of damage to the enemy morale. He set about choosing his three best marksmen: McAndrew would be one; he picked the other two from what remained of his old platoons – Privates Pratt and Zuckerman. They were men he had trained and knew he could rely on to make a shot count. He placed them in the trees high up on the ridge where they would get the longest view to the horizon.

'Take out officers wherever you can,' he told them. 'It'll disrupt the chain of command.'

Then, having chosen his own spot, he went down to the edge of the road, crossing over to where Brennan had settled in a section with a bazooka. They would stay covered and out of sight, held in reserve for anything that got past the first assault. He would use the M3 field guns to knock out what they could of the lead vehicles. It had to be after they'd entered the box. If he could do that, it would block the road and they should be able to hold the enemy in a bottle neck. He had a mortar squad zero their sights to drop onto the road just behind where he thought they would hit the lead vehicle. He knew the Germans would push their infantry through the woods. It would be the job of the snipers to slow them down and then it would be up to the rest of the men in close combat – the rifles and the machine guns to hold the ground until they got their orders from Hamilton to pull out, or ran out of ammo – then the main body would retreat back to the vehicles and make a break for Plattsburgh. The snipers would be the last men out – the last point of resistance, covering the withdrawal of the others. They would each take their chances, melting away into the woods and trying to regroup at the pond; after that he wasn't sure. That was the plan and if it worked they should be able to buy Hamilton the time he needed to get away to Plattsburgh. He didn't really believe they would get the air cover, but if it came that would be a bonus. He would rely on what he had in place and make the best of it.

Just after three in the afternoon there was a shout from one of the men posted forward as a lookout. 'Something coming down the track.'

Tom raised the scope to his eye and trained it on the object. He held it there for a moment, getting it focused. He shouted for Sergeant Rossi. Rossi came forward, keeping in the cover of the trees. 'It's someone on a bicycle,' he said quietly. 'Tell the men to hold their fire; I don't want to give away our position. Just let him come on in and when he's close enough snatch him.'

As it got closer he could see the cyclist was a soldier, but the battledress was khaki not the field grey of a German. The soldier was dressed like an American, but was he a dogface or some kind of decoy put up by the Germans to spy out the land? 'He's pedaling hell for leather,' Brown noted as he took a look through the scope. 'Who do you suppose he is?'

'No idea.'

When the cyclist was nearly on them they took up positions in the undergrowth. Then, as he entered the trap, two men jumped out and grabbed him, lifting him bodily off the bike and hauling him back into the bushes. The cyclist let out a howl of profanity as he was bundled roughly over to where Tom and Brown were waiting. Tom instantly recognized the man – it was Corporal Ransom

'What happened?' Tom blurted out incredulously. 'We thought you were dead.'

'I was,' Ransom replied, brushing himself down and looking angrily at those who had manhandled him, 'or at least those Kraut assholes thought I was. They rounded us up and we thought they were going to take us off into Canada – prisoners, but then they opened up on us. I hit the deck the second they started firing. Delgado was in front of me – he got it good and fell on top of me. There was so much blood I must have looked like I was dead too.'

He stopped as one of the men offered him a cigarette and lit up. 'Anyway,' he went on, blowing a long stream of blue-grey smoke through his nostrils, 'the Krauts just left us there. So I waited till dark and slid out as quietly as I could and made it back to Rouses, but you'd all gone. I found a bike and made it here.'

'What's it like up there?'

'Thousands of them – tanks like you never saw before; howitzers, field guns – mobile ones, bigger than I've ever seen – mounted on tracks – got their own engines.'

'Did anyone else get out?'

'I don't think so. They shot Captain White, straight through the head – murdered him like he was nothing. The Kraut that did it – he was a mean looking sonofabitch.'

Tom knew he ought to send him to Hamilton to debrief, to make a report, but he knew if he did they'd send him on to Plattsburgh and he needed him here. Ransom had battle experience, he'd been under fire and that had value. Besides, he told himself, Hamilton already had the story from the dispatch rider. He had his moment of guilt knowing he was probably condemning Ransom to death – he had no illusions about the risks – they were not all getting out of there. The moment passed and he gave it no more thought. There was a job to do and it was their bad luck it had fallen to them to do it – but they were there, there was no one else – they would have to do it.

It was not long after Ransom arrived that they saw the head of the column. It was led by a scout car running fifty yards out front. Behind the car the first of the tanks became visible – grey smudges on the horizon. He got as close as he could to the edge of the road without breaking cover and called across to Brennan. 'There's a scout coming. Keep down and let it through. Don't do anything until you hear the M3s open up. Let it go down the road if you have to – we can take it out later.'

Scrambling back up the slope, he stopped at the first of the guns where Brown was squatting down, scanning the horizon through field glasses. Earlier they had picked out a large crooked maple at around six hundred yards and about half way into the box – this was to be the marker for the M3 guns.

'Wait till the first tank reaches the marker. We want enough of them inside the box – I wanna see a real New York style traffic jam.'

As it reached the edge of the box the scout car slowed, then stopped. 'Damn, he doesn't like it', Tom cursed under his breath. 'He's not sure about that,' he said to Brown, as the column began to catch up.

The first of the tanks reached the car and it too came to a halt. The hatches on both vehicles opened; heads appeared, they were scanning the woods and the road ahead, field glasses glinted in the afternoon sunlight. Tom knew the sun was with him; it was on his back and hung low in the horizon. It was making things difficult for the Germans looking into it; it was making them cautious. Then he heard the engine on the scout car; it was on the move towards them. 'Let it go through,' he said to himself, then called out to Rossi. 'Everybody to hold their fire. The guns go first – pass the word.'

The growl from the approaching car grew louder. It was in the box, then it was there in the road below them – it felt close enough to touch. Slowly it moved through their line, the smell of its hot exhaust penetrating up through the trees. The noise reached a crescendo, then started to abate, decreasing as it got further away until finally it was inaudible. Everything was quiet; somewhere in the treetops a bird began to sing, then another joined it. There was no sign of the scout car returning, but still the column stayed put – nothing was moving. He thought about his options and concluded there weren't any other than to stay put. Brown nudged him and handed over the glasses.

'I think we've got a visitor,' he said, pointing skywards. A small black mark in the sky was droning towards them.

'Spotter plane!' Tom shouted. 'Keep covered.'

The plane that was heading towards them then veered off in the direction of Plattsburgh. At the same time they heard the deep-throated rumble of a tank engine; the column was on the move.

'They're going for it,' Tom called out again.

It seemed to take forever for the lead tank to reach the marker. Twice it halted and each time he thought they were on to them. Finally its tracks crossed the imaginary line by the maple. The M3s thumped out their first rounds. Three shells hit the lead tank; the hull ruptured and it lurched to a halt; smoke poured out of the top hatch and through the gaping holes in its body. The tank commander scrambled out of the turret and onto the burning hull but, before he could jump clear, there was the crack of a single shot and he went down – taken out by one of the snipers; Zuckerman claimed the kill. Then all hell broke out as the mortar team began lobbing bombs into the vehicles further back. It was no more than minutes before incoming rounds started to rake the woods and they took their first casualty – a drafted man. Six months earlier he'd have been just any other John Doe working in some office or depot somewhere, with family and friends; maybe he owned a car, maybe he had a wife, kids – who knows – but it didn't matter. None of it mattered to him anymore. He was out of it – he was dead; just another letter by an anonymous hand that would fall through someone's door and most probably wreck a life.

Wehrmacht men in grey coats with blockhead tin helmets and black leather boots streamed from the far side of the burning column, making for the cover of the trees, filtering their way towards Tom's positions. The guns kept pounding away at the stalled column, raising their sights, trying to get to the vehicles further back. For the first twenty minutes it had all gone Tom's way but now the tide was beginning to turn. Somebody shouted, 'We've got visitors – they're into the woods.' It was followed by the rapid cracking of a Browning automatic rifle firing in short bursts. Shells started to explode around them as the Germans got their own mobile guns to bear. For a while they were falling randomly as they raked the hills, but as the battle progressed they started to find their mark. An hour in and they were fighting at close quarters; another hour and the casualties began to pile up: Cleaver was dying, ripped open by shrapnel from a German shell; both the lieutenants from Rossi's Arizona Rifles lay dead, together with two privates from 1st Platoon. He had no idea how many were wounded and, when the antitank guns were down to their last rounds, he passed out the orders for the men to withdraw, keeping the machine guns till last. When they had gone it would be down to the snipers alone; they would be the last to get out. The light was beginning to fade and it would soon be dark; there had been no signal from Hamilton and no air cover. Tom passed the word to McAndrew and the other two snipers: pull out – each man for himself – rendezvous at the edge of the pond if you can make it

.

******

General Guderian set up his HQ in Detroit. The two divisions which had penetrated North Dakota and run through Minnesota like quicksilver now joined up with the eastern arm of the pincer under the command of Von Paulus. The maneuver was complete – they had established a strong line carving out the industrial heartland of the north east. Now they were preparing to move on New York. The first phase had been a text book exercise in fast armored warfare and even its most ardent practitioner, Heinz Guderian, had been surprised by the time in which it had been accomplished. In Berlin they drank a toast in champagne to 'Schneller Heinz'; Hitler called him his greatest general.

The Swastika flew briskly over the Stock Exchange building in Chicago, driven by a strong onshore wind. It flapped vigorously, cracking like a stock whip. It was the motif of control by a new regime; the Stars and Stripes were flying too but, by order of the military government, they had to be smaller – a symbol of their subjugation. The city was proving difficult to police. Unlike Europe the local population were not cooperating. There were collaborators, of course; they could be seen walking the streets after the six o'clock curfew, identified by their red and black swastika armbands. They formed the committees that now kept watch over the factories, seeking out saboteurs, malcontents, potential resistance to law and order. They were succeeding in holding down opposition, but the air had a feel of grumbling discontent that rippled just beneath the surface. Orders went out to make examples of communities that were suspected of disaffection to the Nazi cause.

Einsatzgruppen – SS death squads – began to appear on the streets. At the same time rewards and privileges were being handed out to all levels of officials in the civil administration; bribes to change sides. It was important to keep these large cities functioning, to keep their industries working and producing; they were to be key elements in Hitler's next great adventure.

******

Irena knew it would not be long before they arrived. She had no appetite for what she thought might come and was not hanging around to greet them. Martins loaded cases into the Packard; they would all travel together.

'Do come along,' she called irritably to Aly. 'You don't need your whole wardrobe – you can buy new in Washington,' then added derisively, 'I'm sure some Nazi frau will fit into them.'

Aly came struggling down the steps with a box in her arms. She took each step awkwardly, the pregnancy now beginning to show. Seeing her paused half way down, Fred dropped the case he was carrying and ran over to help her. 'You must take it easy darling,' he gently chided her, 'think about the baby.'

She smiled back and handed over the box, pressing both of her hands into the small of her back to ease the ache of carrying the extra weight in her belly.

'What's in that?' Irena called out to her.

'Hats.'

Irena threw up her hands and screwed up her face in exasperation. 'You don't need that many hats. You can buy hats in Washington. Leave them, I need the rest of the space for more important things.'

Aly dumped the box down on the steps and went over to Fred. She stood there leaning on his shoulder, trying not to get emotional. She knew Irena was right but she was finding it hard to think rationally. At first when she found she was pregnant she had felt defiant and assertive – they would have to treat her like an adult, deal with her in adult terms. She had reveled in telling friends at Masters because it made her feel special, daring, even superior to her peers; she was the center of attention – somebody important. But as her term progressed the changing hormones in her body brought on new feelings: anxiety about the coming birth was heightened by the uncertain future, the unknown outcome of the war, the sense that an advancing evil was not far away – just up the road – hiding in the shadows – grotesque and dark. She knew she didn't need the hats but the hats were more than just hats to her. They were her touchstone with the past – a past she now feared she could never recapture; they were something to cling onto – like a child's old bear, a little worn out toy. They were her security blanket.

Constance and Patience stood at the top of the steps, suitcases by their feet, waiting for Mrs Martins. They would all go to the station together and take the train to New York where they would board the Greyhound to Washington.

'What's the new house like?' Aly asked idly, as she sat balanced on a suitcase trying to get a grip on her emotions. 'I hope it's not pokey.'

'I don't know,' Irena replied without enthusiasm. 'You're father has organized it. No doubt it will be some huge, ugly, modern cave – a reflection of your father's impeccably bad taste.'

She went back up to the house again and stood in the hallway. Constance and Vera had spent the morning covering the furniture with dust sheets; it looked ghostly – ready to be haunted. She walked through the rooms one at a time pulling at a sheet here and there, adjusting the drapes, looking to see what else she had forgotten – things that ought to be taken. She'd heard that German soldiers were looters and spoilers; they would wreck the place if they moved into it. She'd never much liked the house but the idea of strangers sitting on her furniture, eating in the dining room and, worse, sleeping in the beds had left her angry and repulsed. She went into the kitchen where Vera had lined up all the wine bottles from the cellar and all the spirits from the cocktail cabinet. Irena started opening the bottles and pouring the contents into the large Belfast sink.

Such a waste, she thought: good chateau bottled Bordeaux, fine Burgundy and a lot of very good quality Rhenish wine; Hocks, Gewürztraminers, Rieslings, all German – she wasn't going to leave that for them.

'What are you doing, Mother?' Aly demanded, raising her voice in a pejorative tone, not really expecting an answer.

'Well, if I can't drink it I'm determined they won't,' Irena replied truculently. 'If they come here they'll only wreck the place and I'm damned if they're going to do it all fired up on my booze.'

'And if they don't come here?'

'Well, we can always buy some more.'

She stopped and stood quietly looking around the kitchen. 'It's ironic, don't you think?' she said, going back to the task of depriving the Germans of a good Chateau Latour, 'Tommy was right when he told us there would be a war. We all laughed about it then – funny really, it all seems such a long time ago – and now here we are, almost in the front line. I wonder what happened to him – he enlisted after Carey threw him over, didn't he?'

'I met the girl he was dating. She knows the Mescals. She said he was posted up near the Canadian border just before this happened so I suppose he must have been in the thick of it. Did I tell you she dumped him too?'

'No, you didn't.'

'Well, she did – all over that stupid gossip column. Poor old Tommy, he always seems to get the rough end of things.'

'Silly goose,' Irena said, upending the last bottle. 'There that's done – that makes me feel a whole lot better.'

******

The house in Washington was no surprise. Tracy Place on 23rd Street North West had been built in 1927 and was a reflection of everything Irena knew to be dear to her husband's heart.

'He could have designed it himself,' she said disparagingly. It was a single rectangular block in white concrete, steel-framed windows and an overbearing entrance hall. Even the steps leading up to the elevated front door spoke of Brunessemer. There were eight bedrooms in two wings leading off a central landing. Each had its own full bathroom and the master suite had a large dressing room. The staircase was hung on slender chromed steel poles that rose to the ceiling, giving a sense that the whole structure was somehow floating. The concrete treads were finished with polished grey and white marble tiles. It was topped with a sinuous bannister rail, again in chromed steel, which snaked its way softly upwards following the profile of the treads. At the base, the midpoint and the top there were large lamps in pairs; their shades, designed to represent flaming torches, had been cast in pink frosted glass.

Irena and Aly stood in the hallway, looking at the staircase not sure of what to say. In the end Irena broke the silence and expressed their mutual view. 'Hollywood,' was all she said, but the air of contempt was undisguised.

'It's a refuge, Mother,' Aly said consolingly. Although Irena did not like Brunessemer, across the years she had grown comfortable in it; she knew where everything was and everything was where it should be. Now she was faced with the tiresome task of doing it all over again – finding the new places, and even buying new things.

'The furniture is ghastly. It has to go – I couldn't possibly live with it. I shall call Clementine and ask her advice. She has such good taste.'

Fred helped Martins bring in the cases; things piled up in the hall. Mrs Martins, who had arrived that afternoon with Constance and Patience, was busy sorting out the kitchen. Only Vera the housekeeper had stayed on at Brunessemer. 'I'm not afraid of these Germans,' she had said bluffly when Irena asked if she wanted to go with them to Washington.

Clementine came to the rescue in a taxi. It was, she said, the least she could do for her good friend who had been so hospitable to Winston in his hour of need. Together they went to the Willard; six o'clock was not too early for cocktails, Irena assured her. She wanted advice, she confided in Clementine, advice on furniture, advice on colors for the walls, advice on the drapes, advice on the crockery and the cutlery. They had left everything behind at Brunessemer, she told her friend. The invaders were already nearly at Peekskill and nothing seemed to be stopping them – Roosevelt's administration seemed to be as paralysed as the man himself. It would not be long before they were knocking on the door of Manhattan.

'It's funny,' she said thoughtfully when the conversation turned to Brunessemer, 'but I can't stand the idea of those vile creatures living in the place. I would rather they bombed it, burned it to the ground. I shall never be able to live there again.'

Clementine put a hand on hers and patted it gently. 'Let's hope they don't get that far down the Hudson.'

'What does Winston say?'

'Not much to me but I hear more than he thinks I do. He's convinced the tide will turn shortly now the Generals have at last got themselves organized.'

'Well, I hope so because I'm not shifting out of Washington even if they get down here. One house move is enough.'

'Quite so, and anyway you should not be worrying about that – leave it to the men. You'll have a christening to plan shortly – that's far more important. Do they have a name for the baby?

491

'Charles Frederick James for a boy, Charlotte Louise if it's a girl.'
'I like them. I approve.'

******

At the end of May Hitler issued new orders: Von Paulus was to take New York. Neither Guderian nor Von Paulus wanted to move the front further south; their lines of communication were stretched and they needed time to consolidate. Their supply routes too were in danger of disruption. At the beginning of the campaign they had lost only a handful of tanks to American resistance but that was now changing. Raids by ground attack aircraft had started to take their toll. Eaker's bombers were getting through and there were more fighter escorts.

Guderian complained to Reichsmarschall Goering that they lacked enough fighter cover and his tanks were now sustaining losses to the increased strength of the enemy air attacks. It was compounded because in the North Atlantic Admiral James had joined hands with Joe King and had begun a blockade of the Canadian ports. Materiel was still getting through but it was reduced; unless greater resources were put into the campaign, Guderian warned Hitler, Gottlieb could stall.

On the morning of 30 May Guderian issued orders to the 3rd Tank Division. A brigade under Joachim Metz, now promoted to *Oberstleutnant* following his successful campaign in the Champlain salient, was to lead an armored thrust down the eastern bank of the Hudson. An SS tank brigade prepared to press east from its base in the suburbs of Detroit, through Utica and join Metz at Albany. There they would push south on both sides of the Hudson, piercing the city at Yonkers.

Von Paulus was unhappy. Managing the civil administration in so many large urban centers was soaking up manpower – men he would need to put into the front line if they were to meet Hitler's ambitious objectives. The position was further complicated by the level of criminal organization that existed, especially in the cities. Police chiefs were willing to carry out their duties in accordance with their oath of office, though most did so grudgingly, sparingly, and with a strict adherence to their rules of procedure. But the willingness evaporated as it came down the chain. At street level hoodlums and officers alike now found themselves on the same side; strange compatriots – men with a common cause and a shared discontent, unhappy men, men with guns; there were a lot of guns. Chicago and Detroit were under control but it was uneasy, on a knife edge.

'I am expected to hold a city where perhaps half the male population are armed,' he again complained in a letter to his wife. 'It is quite the most impossible task.'

Trying to hold the balance were more than half a million Wehrmacht men on the streets of the cities and towns inside the German lines. But even with this number they were stretched; New York threatened to tip the balance. Von Paulus sent a message to Berlin: he needed more men. Hitler refused; he had a different agenda. There would be no further reinforcement of Gottlieb.

There is a group – a small group, an intelligence report had stated. This group has killed four Wehrmacht officers and one member of the Gestapo. It is a criminal group and must be hunted down and made an example of German justice to the people who are sheltering them. The assassinations all took place in the North Shore district of Chicago.

Guderian threw the dossier down on his desk. 'Criminals,' he spat the words out like a mouthful of bad food. 'Criminals,' he repeated to his adjutant who had brought him the report. 'This is the work of professional hit men.'

The officers were strolling along the waterside beach when they had been gunned down. A car had crawled slowly along the curbside. A man with a Thompson machine gun leaned out of the passenger-side window. The Thompson rattled, spraying the Germans with a ribbon of fire, killing them where they stood. A Gestapo man, dressed in plain clothes – but who might just as well have had a swastika flying from his Homberg because they all look the same in their black leather coats and their badly cut suits, the killers joked afterwards – was also shot as he pulled a pistol from his coat pocket and tried to intervene. No one had come forward to identify the killers. This was the seventh attack of its kind since the occupation – two in Detroit, one in Duluth, four in Chicago – all officers, all off duty, all in broad daylight, all drive-by shootings, and nobody had been arrested.

Guderian stood silent while he thought about it. Resistance was to be expected after an occupation; they had experienced this in Poland, in the Low Countries and in France. The answer was simple: find some scapegoats. It didn't matter if they were the real culprits; just round up a handful of likely men and execute them – publicly. Invite the press, why not, the Americans like a spectacle and they should have one. It should be sent out to the radio stations. Shoot a newsreel and get it across the front line. Give it to the networks – let everyone see that you could not mess with the Third Reich and then not pay. Yes, he would let the SS do the job. They did this kind of thing well; this was their business.

******

It was barely three weeks since the invasion. The Americans had been unable to hold a line anywhere. After Cumberland Head they made a stand at Plattsburg. It was a short, bloody affair. Hamilton was hopelessly outnumbered. The

493

promised reinforcement never appeared; it had stalled and been cut off further south by the pincer movement coming in from the Dakotas. When the word came to pull out, what was left of Hamilton's force made a ragged retreat down to Albany, harassed all the way on their eastern flank as the small shoreline towns of Lake Champlain fell like dominoes. Albany, too, soon fell. German armor completed its encirclement and although the news that Patton was advancing, coming up the Hudson with a large tank force, gave the defenders hope, it was not in time to save the city. The retreat was a rout.

The remnants of Tom's men had straggled in behind the line at Plattsburg before it gave way. Brown and Brennan made it back safe; they brought what was left of the two companies with them. Just before the German attack hit their lines Corporal Ransom came in with three walking wounded, carrying a fourth over his shoulder like a sack of potatoes. There was no sign of Tom or the snipers. After they fell back to Albany, Colonel Hamilton wrote letters to the families: Zuckerman, Pratt, McAndrew and Tom were now all posted as missing in action – either captured or, more probably, dead.

When the German advance finally halted it was not because of resistance put up by the Americans but only because Guderian and Von Paulus had outrun their own supply lines. They had captured not just a large swathe of territory but a densely populated one. They needed time to consolidate. This was not France with its small towns and scattered rural hamlets that could be rolled over in a few days. The population inside the German encirclement was estimated at more than fifteen million; these cities were huge and dense. The buildings were concrete and steel, not the brick and timber farmhouses of Holland or the medieval stone villages of France – they towered many stories high; they weren't pushed over easily. And now they had these cities they had to be controlled. The shock of invasion would soon wear off and the inhabitants would start plotting, forming resistance groups, committing acts of sabotage. Guderian knew if he let things rest as they were he would have trouble on an industrial scale.

What he needed was a terror campaign – something that would send out a strong message. There was an expert, a man to do the job, and he was already to hand, less than a day away by road, stamping his mark on the rebellious population of Ottawa.

The road from Ottawa was long, straight, flat and tedious; it was also rutted and potholed. Recent tank movements had disrupted the paved surface; they had chewed through the macadam and broken its back, turning it into a ploughed field. Gangs of local laborers worked day and night trying to repair it; and then there was the filling in of bomb craters left by Eaker's B17s.

Convoys of trucks, obstructed and slowed by lumbering horse-drawn carts, ground their way down towards the new front line, compounding the damage;

trucks laden with essential war loads to keep Guderian and Von Paulus supplied. Bumping and dodging its way through the relentlessly unending column of plodding traffic, a faster moving staff car headed south. In the rear seat the occupants held onto the leather straps that hung from the door pillars. The powerful Mercedes 770K klasse bucked at every pothole, jumped and jarred on each encounter with the deep ruts, scattering a shower of bitumen fragments and stones from its wheels and trailing a plume of fine muddy mist in its wake.

The passengers, a senior SS officer, an *Obersturmbannführer* (the equivalent rank to a major in the Wehrmacht) and his staff assistant, a high-ranked SS NCO *Hauptscharfuhrer*, rolled from side to side as the car slalomed its way through the endless column of field grey vehicles strung out along the highway. They watched out of the windows with satisfaction at the tide of men and materials moving south and recounted with satisfaction the good work their Einsatzgruppen had accomplished in destroying the heart of the resistance in Ottawa. Their death kommandos had targeted one group in particular to which they owed their success in a terror campaign that had scoured out the resistance – eliminated its leaders, purged all opposition. In what had been commended by Himmler himself as an inspired tactic, they had targeted the women. The victims they sought were the mothers, those with babies and very small children.

The inspiration had come to him in Poland when the Obersturmbannführer witnessed the killing of a woman. In her arms she clasped her baby, enfolding it close to her breast, shrouded round with a ragged shawl – a tiny pathetic bundle, its mewling cries piercing the silence of the cold air. As she stood there in the bitter cold grey light of the morning of her execution she had, at the final moment, turned her back on her executioner in a hopeless attempt to shield the child. It availed her nothing and as she fell so the child fell with her. An awful moan of despair rose from the mouths of the witnesses and he noted that the death of this one woman and her baby had caused more anguish than the public killing of half a dozen partisans machine gunned in a public place, tied up to stakes.

At that moment, as the woman and her child lay on the frost-hardened ground and he listened to the desperate wailing of the others, he realized he had stumbled upon a particularly potent tool. Providence had devised an effective demonstration; by shooting a mother through the back with a high-powered rifle so that the shot penetrated not only her body but went on through to destroy the child she held in her arms, he could instill a fear and an obedience into his terror campaign that no other method had hitherto afforded him. This public demonstration of ruthlessness had satisfying results because the spectacle concentrated the fear of their men and dissuaded most from joining the resistance. Young men had handed themselves in and turned informer for dread of seeing a mother or a lover in the death queues that were formed up for public execution.

'The death of the innocents, my dear Vogel,' the senior man observed, 'is far more effective than the execution of heroes.'

******

A BBS staff car drew up to the kerb outside the German Legation building in Lancaster Gate. The driver jumped out and ran round to the other side of the car and opened the door. Mosley emerged; the driver stood to attention and saluted with a raised arm. Mosley stood for a moment then pulled his military peaked cap tight onto his head and marched resolutely up the front steps.

'I do not understand why you are withdrawing. It makes no sense – we are close to a decisive victory. Why now?'

Linz sat at his desk in his room at the Legation. It was a large room, a room of very elegant Georgian proportions. It had high ceilings and two large cut-crystal chandeliers; the parquet flooring in polished cherry wood was dressed with an expansive pure wool Wilton carpet of a most ornate floral design. There were velvet drapes in dark blue with extravagant gold silk ties holding them back in swags to reveal floor to ceiling windows giving excellent views across to the park in the distance. He sat straight-backed, arms folded and disinterested. He looked dispassionately at Mosley who, dressed in his black crew necked sweat shirt and military cut jacket, appeared out of place and at odds with the room. Linz thought him a trivial man, not militarily competent, just another strutting politician with ideas beyond his abilities.

Mosley walked back and forth in front of the desk; he was agitated. His German support was being run down; the SS had gone and now the Wehrmacht was pulling out. 'You will have to settle these things on your own,' Linz said in a matter of fact voice. 'We have trained your men. We have supplied you most generously with weapons. The task should not be too difficult. Huh?'

'I need to retain at least one division. I'm sure with one more hard push we could take Maidstone – then it would all be over.'

Linz clucked his tongue against the roof of his mouth, making a tutting noise. 'It is too late for that. You should have made the push while you had the resources. The Führer needs these men elsewhere – those are my orders. Besides, you will still have our military advisers – we are leaving them in place.'

'I need tanks, not advice,' Mosley said belligerently.

'That is another thing. Why have you still failed to get back those stolen Panzers? I am most unhappy about that.'

Linz waited for a response but Mosley just stood there looking sullen. Linz ignored him and started to look through the papers that had arrived in the morning's despatch from Berlin; the audience was over. Mosley prepared to leave; he clicked his heels, an action designed more to break the difficult silence than anything else, then he raised a hand in salute. 'Heil Hitler.'

Linz nodded. 'Heil Hitler,' he replied in a flat tone, then added, 'You can keep one regiment of Wehrmacht infantry for one month. I suggest you make good use of it while you have it.'

As Mosley briskly descended the marble stairs his mind was frantically pulling together a plan. He would make an all-out push across the Medway and thrust deep into the flanks of Maidstone; there were still planes in Hull he could use for air support, so long as the Germans were prepared to commit them. He would need the cooperation of Linz's advisers if he was going to get his air cover. In the past he had largely ignored them. This was his country and deep in his psyche he denied he was just another Hitler vassal; he was an independent leader – he believed that to be true. He had, after all, always set the agenda for the conduct of operations; he devised his own strategies; he formulated the policies that ran the country; he considered himself his own man; but now he would have to go to them to get what he needed. He would have to stand back and let these Germans direct his operation. That rankled.

Outside the Legation his staff car waited but his driver was nowhere to be seen. There was a man waiting at a nearby bus stop. 'Have you seen the driver of this car?' Mosley shouted. The man at the bus stop walked halfway towards him, then hesitated as he saw his bus approaching.

'I think he went to the taxi drivers' tea stall,' he shouted back to Mosley, 'over there,' and he pointed to where a dark green wooden kiosk stood on the pavement providing refreshments to the taxi men.

Mosley hovered on the pavement for a moment then decided to go in search of the delinquent driver, but as he did so the missing man appeared from behind the kiosk and, seeing Mosley, walked smartly back to the car. He opened the door, aware of the hostile gaze of his boss. Mosley got in, settling himself into the comfort of the back seat. He needed to think – he had to get this plan into operation without delay.

'Bermondsey,' he ordered imperiously. The car moved smoothly down Park Lane heading for the BBS headquarters. Once there he could call his chiefs together and brief them on his great plan. By the time he reached Victoria he had already formulated the broad outline for the thrust and was working through in his mind the stance he would take with Linz's advisers.

Going round the Broadway the traffic was messy, crisscrossing, trying to change lanes and get into the right position for the next turning. A bus got in the way as it tried to cross in front of them to pick up passengers from a stop. The driver braked suddenly, causing Mosley to be thrown forward out of his seat. In the same moment that Mosley lost his seat a small tumbler device which had been stuck to the underside of the car flipped. It should have flipped when the car left the kerb in Lancaster Gate but it was faulty and it had failed to respond to the motion of the vehicle or the uneven road. But now the violent jolt from the sudden braking set it free to do its job.

With a click that was inaudible to the occupants of the car it sent a tiny electrical charge to a detonator embedded in a packet of plastic explosive. There was a flash and a thump, which kicked the car into the air. Inside, the shock broke the driver's spine; he sat there paralysed, unable to move or speak. The floor pan under Mosley's seat was two-inch armour plate; it buckled but it didn't burst – he had survived. Two quick witted passing pedestrians pulled the driver clear of the wreck but when they tried to get to Mosley they found they could not open the rear door.

Dazed and confused, Mosley tried to get out of the car but the chassis had distorted and the heavily armoured doors that had been designed to protect him now held him prisoner. He could smell the petrol from a rupture in the fuel tank as it poured out underneath the car. When the volatile liquid reached the area where the bomb had been placed it encountered a fragment of glowing metal. There was another explosion – this time a muffled 'whoompf'. The tank exploded. Mosley was roasted alive in his own personal oven, choking on the smoke; there was no air in his lungs to utter a scream, it was all over in less than a minute. When finally the fire brigade got the car open he was long dead, burnt to a crisp – unrecognisable. There would be no masterly thrust into the flanks of Maidstone. The game had changed.

'Mosley's dead,' Armitage told Grainger.

'Is he, by Jove   how did that happen then?'

'Somebody put a bomb under his car. Any idea who might have done it?'

Grainger shrugged. 'Fraid not – good someone's done it though.'

Armitage changed the subject. 'I have another little job you might like to consider, Dicky.'

'Consider? Does that mean I have a choice?' Grainger smiled, knowing full well he did not.

'Not really, but I like to sound reasonable.'

'Never let it be said you were that, Charlie. What have we in mind?'

'It will involve a little excursion – a bit of travel outside the comfort of this nice town we inhabit. Let's go for a stroll – it's a nice day and I could do with the fresh air. I'll tell you as we walk.'

******

The death of Mosley passed almost unnoticed in Berlin. To Hitler, now absorbed with his newest inspiration, Barbarossa, it was of little consequence; it was delegated to an official in the *Reichskommissariate*. The *Reichskommissariate* had a simple function: its job was to find and create those intermediate officials who ran the machinery of state. The first response was to create the office of *Reichskommisar*, which was a position almost equal to that of a colonial governor but when Linz was offered the post he opposed the idea. Britain was, he insisted, an ally not an occupied territory, and he did not want to create more opposition than already existed in the rebellious southeast of the country. He proposed an alternative – he would accept the position of *Gauleiter*, a sort of Mayor; a position whose powers were hidden by a veil of diplomacy and political backroom dealing. He could twist arms in private, behind the scenes, away from the public view; he would be a puppet master.

The weather was bright and sunny but not yet hot – it was still only May. Linz crossed Bayswater Road; a long brisk walk would be good – he could go through Hyde Park and admire the office girls strolling during their lunch hour. He filled his lungs with the fresh air of the late spring. Here and there the remains of the daffodils still clung on to their blooms, dotting the banks of the Serpentine with little blobs of yellow. At Piccadilly he marched across to Green Park, picking his way through the near stationary traffic which had jammed right on the Circus where three conflicting traffic lanes merged. A cacophony of shouting and hooting, overlaid with the sounds of overheating engines, rose from the street as the traffic struggled to inch forward through the chaos. He crossed Green Park, leaving the din behind.

Walking along the edge of the park, shadowing Constitution Hill, he encountered a group of Household Cavalry exercising their horses and stopped to admire their mounts as they ambled by, snorting and flicking their tails. He smiled and one of the officers offered him a laconic salute. The smell of the animals drifted into his nostrils and reminded him of home – he liked to ride in the forest but it was a long time since he had been there; he was not really happy in the city – he had been brought up a country gentleman and he missed it. When things were more settled he would go home and retire to his parents' country estate with his wife, Renata, and their two daughters, Friedle and Gerda. He was missing them. It was more than six months since he'd had any leave; it was overdue but this business with Mosley had made it difficult to get away.

At the end of Constitution Hill he crossed the Mall and went into St James's Park. People were out feeding the ducks on the lake and up towards the Whitehall end a military band in ceremonial red jackets was playing martial music from a bandstand. An audience of men and women, some tourists, some office workers, sat on rows of chairs eating sandwiches. At the end of each piece the bandmaster turned and bowed to the crowd, who clapped politely and for just the appropriate amount of time. Then he turned back to the musicians and, tapping on his music stand with his conductor's baton, sent them again into the strains of some well-known and well-loved marching tune.

Linz left the park and made the last stretch to Scotland Yard. He stood for a moment recalling the last time he had visited. How things had changed. Inside he was formally received by the new commissioner, Bertram Bines, who had also temporarily stepped into Mosley's shoes; Bines was a short, square man with a crooked smile and bad teeth. His thinning brown hair had been cut in the Hitler style, now fashionable amongst the BBS, and glued to his forehead with Brylcream. His upper lip sported a close-clipped shaving brush moustache; another homage to the Führer, though in truth Linz thought it made the man look slightly ridiculous, more like the Hollywood comedian Oliver Hardy than Hitler. Bines was one of the new breed brought in by Mosley. Often they were men of small intellect and poor education, men who were at home on the street or in a pub brawl. Not a lot of grey matter behind that forehead, Linz found himself thinking.

Bines was clearly impressed by the visitor, demonstrating it with an oily smile and inviting him to sit. It crossed Linz's mind that the last time he had been there it was to see Peters, a much better man in his opinion. Then he had been investigating death and here he was again on a similar mission. How strangely the world turned – Mosley had been there with him and now he was gone, dead, burned to a cinder. He wouldn't miss the posturing, all that strutting about striking ridiculous poses. He wouldn't miss him at all, but he had left behind a power vacuum and that had to be filled. He looked at Bines. If this was the calibre of the men left he didn't hold out much hope. Maybe he should accept the post of Reichskommisar after all. Bines offered him coffee, but he declined.

'Are there any witnesses?'

'There are,' Bines said without enthusiasm, 'the driver of the bus, one passenger on the top deck and any number of pedestrians – but they're not much use. Just a flash and a bang is all they're saying.'

'The driver survived. Have you interrogated him?'

'I have. Says he thinks he was lured away from the car while it was standing outside your office. He went to get a cup of tea and he thinks the bomb was planted then.'

'Is there anything left of the device?'

Bines shook his head glumly. 'Not much, they found the remains of a tumbler – that probably set it off.' His expression changed to one of perplexity. 'Can't understand why it didn't go off sooner – must have been faulty.'

He handed the heat seared piece of metal to Linz who turned it slowly in his hand. To place a bomb like that in broad daylight in front of his office –

someone had taken a big risk to do this thing; he would have to be a bold man indeed, a man who dared take extravagant chances.

'Do you have nothing on the case at all – no leads, no what it is you call hunches? Is there anything to work on?'

Bines looked vacantly back at him; his fat, pudding face and watery eyes offered nothing; his mouth stuffed full of excuses, mumbling about how difficult it was. There was one thing, he said, a line that one of his detectives had been pursuing on another case – the one where a prisoner had been hijacked from the Bermondsey HQ.

'Go on,' Linz said slowly.

Bines lifted the phone on his desk – the same phone Peters had used on that visit. The man who came in with the file was the old sergeant. Still here, Linz thought, some people have a sense of survival. Bines opened the file and picked up a photo. He passed it to Linz.

'We got this from the Home Office files. We think it's the same man who did the lift, though we can't be certain. Of course, he's long flown. Bound to be on the other side of the Medway, if you ask me.'

Linz studied the photo. The face was familiar. His mind switched back to the events of that day when he and Peters had confronted each other over the German corpses and there had nearly been a shoot-out. Then that young man from the Home Office had breezed in and, with almost clinical expedience, had settled matters. It was the same man. It was also the same face that had been with him in the tank transporter, the driver of the lead truck, the one that broke down, the man who stole the Panzers. The same man was now staring at him out of the photo.

Grainger's cover was blown – Linz now knew the man he was looking for. Curiously it made him feel better about the theft just by being able to put a face to his thief. This, he concluded, must be the same man who had so audaciously walked out of Mosley's Bermondsey stronghold, who had lifted his prisoner, Sir Charles Armitage; the same man who had spirited Eden out of the hospital in London; led the attack on the BBS barracks in Maidstone. He must have planted the bomb under Mosley's car; he was convinced – this was his assassin.

He came back from Whitehall with a sense of satisfaction. He knew his quarry – now he must find a way to catch him. Bines thought he was on the other side of the line, in which case he was almost certainly in Maidstone. The question was how to hook this fish. A plan started to develop in Linz's Teutonic brain. He would lure him across and he knew just the bait he could use.

******

The trains were no longer running beyond Croton. The Germans were in Albany and might soon reach Peekskill, but it was still possible to get there by bus. Dottie stood in the queue and waited to buy a ticket.

Her bus stood in its bay under a grey steel canopy that gave some pretense of protection from the elements for its passengers as they boarded. It was a big ugly Mack diesel smelling of carbon, exhaust fumes and hot rubber tires. The polished corrugated aluminum of its bodywork was streaked with dirty rain and spattered with mud thrown up by wheels. The driver's uniform was crumpled and looked as tired as the man wearing it; it had been sitting behind the wheel too long, the seat of the pants had become shiny from the friction of the man who was wearing it, sliding his backside on and off the rough leather driver's chair. The patent leather peak of his cap was cracked and the strap round its brim was now held in place with a bobby pin. It was not promoted as a premium way to travel and these images were not misleading.

As a rule she didn't travel by bus; they were always crowded and the working men who used them to get to their place of work and back home again leered at her. Blue collar workers – mostly they had jobs in the lumber sheds and paper mills; they smelled of their trades; they smelled of glue, they smelled of ammonia, they smelled of fuel oil and they smelled of sweat – and some smelled of booze. One time, when there was a rail car conductors strike and she had been obliged to take the bus, a man sitting next to her had become uncomfortably familiar, deliberately pressing himself against her thigh.

She boarded and took a seat close to the driver where she felt safest; she was not long seated before a large overweight woman dumped herself down next to her, gasping asthmatically from the exertion of climbing aboard. She smelled like she could do with a bath – but at least it wasn't a man.

The ponderous diesel engine clattered into life. The vehicle started to reverse, sliding slowly out from under the canopy until fully emerged like a giant bug crawling out of its chrysalis – it waited. There was a high-pitched whining, grinding sound of metal resisting metal as the driver searched around for first gear, finally locating it with a crunch. There was a further moment of inaction then it lurched forward and they were off. The ride was rigidly uncomfortable, the poorly upholstered seats barely disguising the shock of each pothole it sought out and fell into.

At Montrose the bus stopped to allow passengers off. Dottie silently prayed the woman next to her would be one of those to get down; her prayers were answered – the good Lord was listening. They stopped again at Buchanan and she looked out to where she could see the police station. They had taken Tom there. She had never seen it before, why would she? There had never been anything to bring her to this very ordinary small town, but now she found herself with an urge to investigate it, to see the house where they had held him.

Maybe, if they ever got back together they could come here. 'What are you thinking of?' she scolded herself. 'Why would he want to come back to relive that memory?' The bus lurched into life again and headed up the Albany Road. She watched the fresh, early summer foliage waving, brushed by the air from the bus's slipstream.

As the tree lined road started to give way to the outskirts of Peekskill she turned her mind to what she would say. She hadn't let anyone know she was coming. At first she thought she would; then the fear struck her that Tom might answer the call and tell her to go to hell and she couldn't run that risk. If he was going to say it, he had to tell it to her face. Then at least she could plead with him. It was, she knew, much easier to put the phone down on someone than it was to turn them away on the front porch, to slam the door in their face.

She stepped off the bus and onto the sidewalk. The old anxiety was back; uncertainty invaded her mind. She was trembling again; a nervous frisson tingled on her shoulders and around her stomach. Her teeth wanted to chatter together and she gave a little shudder as she tried to pull her body together – get control of the nerve endings, stop them sizzling. She could see the house as she turned into Union Avenue; the front had been newly painted white and there was the single strand of a telephone wire draped across the street in a gentle arc, wired into the insulator and attached just under the gutter, connecting the telephone that Tom had given as a gift to Martha and Holly.

The nervous jitters revisited as she mounted the steps. Was this such a good idea? Well, it was too late anyway because before she could make any decision the front door opened and there was Martha.

For the briefest of moments the two women stood there; bound in a kind of limbo they looked at each other, neither seeming to know what was to come next. It fell to Martha to break the spell. Smiling a little sad smile, she held out both arms and in an invitation to embrace, took hold of Dottie and hugged her. 'I always knew you would come back,' she said in a hushed voice.

'Is he here?' Dottie asked nervously, looking around the hallway, half expecting to see him appear from the living room.

Martha shook her head slowly. 'We got a letter,' was all she said, then she led her into the house and out onto the back porch where Holly was dozing in the midday sun, Wheels stretched out beside him. Seeing someone new, the dog got up and trotted over to acquaint himself with the stranger. He sniffed at the hem of her dress and then, recognizing the smell of a friend, sat back on his rump and looked up waiting for some kind of reward. Dottie let her hand drop and ruffled the fur on his head. The small docked tail wagged; he put his muzzle up and licked her hand.

'Holly,' Martha called softly. 'Wake up honey, we've got a visitor. Look who's come to see us.'

Holly opened both eyes; seeing Dottie he smiled. He paused for a second or two in which he assimilated the moment then he hauled himself out of the chair and hugged her warmly. She felt she was at home among friends; all trace of the nervous anxiety that had gripped her when she had approached the house had gone. Only the absence of Tom spoiled the moment – made it incomplete.

Holly went off to the living room. When he returned it was with the letter in his hand – the one he had received from Colonel Hamilton.

'We got this a while back,' he said in a dull flat tone, trying to mask his emotion. 'I'm going to write to the Secretary for War – see if we can find out more, see if they have any news about him.'

'We live each day with hope,' Martha added quickly, but Dottie could see from the sadness in her eyes that there probably wasn't much hope to be had. 'It's a terrible thing this war – who would have believed it. When Holly came back from the last one we really thought that would be an end to it – and now – well here we are again.'

They talked for a bit before Martha announced to Dottie that she would fix them some lunch and the two of them went off to the kitchen where they could have some women's talk.

'What will you do now?' Martha asked as she cut slices of meat loaf and placed them onto a flat oval dish then covered them with a rich brown gravy.

'I don't know – I thought I might enlist in the medical corps. They're crying out for nurses and I ought to put my skills to good use. It somehow seems trivial just to sit at home while the boys go out and get themselves killed.'

On the bus journey home she made up her mind to enlist. Men were dying and she felt the need to do something. Tom was out there somewhere still fighting, she was sure. She had to believe that, she refused to give up on him – to admit that he might even now be lying in a field somewhere – dead.

When she got home she told her parents what she would do. She had thought they might try to dissuade her but they didn't. She was glad – her mind had been made up and she didn't want to change it.

******

The night was quiet and although there was a moon, in the woods it was dark. Overhead the thick canopy of the trees blocked out the sky except where here and there bright stars sparked pinpoints of white light through the gaps in the leaf cover. There was a muffled crack of twigs being crushed under the feet of something moving. Tom crouched down, waiting to see what was coming his way. A few yards off to his right he could see the edge of the water – the large pond at which they had agreed to rendezvous. It shone, silver lit under a strong clear moon. There it was again, the sound of movement; it was getting closer. A minute or two later a shadowy image emerged from the shelter of the woods and stood on the shoreline; it was a man. Backlit by the moonlight bouncing off the lake, it presented a perfect silhouette but the body of the figure was obscured and dark, blotted black by the bright light behind it. He was expecting the others but old habits told him to wait, to be cautious, just in case it was not what he thought it was.

There was another sound; the figure on the shore turned to look in its direction and at the same time bringing a rifle to the ready. It was McAndrew – or was it? He couldn't be sure the Germans had not already started to comb the woods for them. He waited till another shadow emerged and presented its silhouette alongside the first. A few minutes more and the two were joined by a third. It was what he had been waiting for. He called quietly and the three shadows turned abruptly, revealing who they were. 'Corporal,' he called in a low voice, 'over here.'

'The Germans are everywhere,' McAndrew whispered. 'The woods are crawling with them; Zuckerman here nearly tripped over one of them coming up the slope from the road.' Zuckerman nodded vigorously. He was a small man of Levantine origin; slight but wiry with dark furtive eyes and a sharpness about him that gave him the air of a fox. McAndrew knew him to be a top marksman and for this reason had picked him for the squad. Pratt, by comparison, was the antithesis to Zuckerman – a tall, laconic Texan with a laid back manner and a lazy drawl. But there was one thing he shared with the other man – his exceptional ability to shoot, especially over distance. Pratt could hit a target unerringly time after time at a distance of a mile.

Tom motioned the men back into the cover of the wood. Crouched in a huddle, the three of them waited for Tom to set out the situation. 'I don't think we can get to Plattsburgh along the highway; it's too exposed. So we have to make it across country. That should be OK so long as we do it under cover of dark.'

He looked at his watch. 'It's 00.47; it doesn't get light till 04.00. That gives us a bit over three hours to cover five miles of rough country – shouldn't be too tough. We need to keep inside the cover of the woods until we get away from the edge of this pond. After that we head into more open country which should make the going easier. We should strike the lake shore just west of the town and we can work our way in along the beach. Any questions?'

Pratt rubbed his chin. 'Yeah, what in the name of anything is that girlie ring you wear tied onto your dog tags, sir? I saw it when you got your shirt off and I thought that's the darndest thing.'

Tom pressed his hand onto his chest and felt the engagement ring Dottie had handed back to him on Grand Central. 'This, Private Pratt,' he said slowly, fingering the ring, 'is the epilogue to my dreams.'

505

'What the hell's an epilogue – sir?'

'An epilogue, Pratt, is the final word.' Pratt looked confused.

'Forget it,' Tom said. 'Are there any proper questions?'

There were no questions. They set out along the line of the pond; the undergrowth made the going slow and after half an hour Tom judged they would have to take the risk and get out into the open countryside if they were going to make Plattsburgh while it was still dark. As they moved away from the edge of the woods the undergrowth thinned and they waded through waist-high brush and small bushes.

Another hour passed, then the ground changed again and gave way to worked arable land. They halted at the edge of the first field. 'Wheat,' said McAndrew and grabbed a handful, snapping off the ears of unripe grain and smelling them.

The crop was full grown but not yet ripe. It stood four feet tall – enough to hide them if they crouched down, but who would see them anyway? They marched through the young plants, leaving a trail of crushed, slender green stalks in their wake. They emerged from the field and passed through a hedgerow into another planted out with cabbages. There they stood for a moment assessing their position. It felt eerily exposed.

'I don't think we're much more than a quarter mile from the highway,' Tom said quietly.

Then Zuckerman pointed to a dull glow on the horizon. 'That must be the light from Plattsburg.'

Pratt bent down and sliced the top off one of the cabbages with his bayonet. 'That's a weapon, not an eating iron,' McAndrew observed admonishingly as Pratt stood back up straight and examined his prize.

'Try it,' Pratt said, offering a piece of the green heart of the cabbage to McAndrew, 'it's good for you.'

McAndrew pushed it away. 'I thought you Texans only ate beef,' he said distastefully. 'I hope you aint going all maggoty on us. I heard tell you country boys had funny ways.'

Pratt said nothing but stuffed a large piece of the cabbage core in his mouth and crunched on it. He was about to respond when Tom held up a hand.

'Stow it.' The air was still, they stood and listened. Away to the east there was a dull rumble.

'Tanks.'

Pratt dropped the cabbage and grabbed up his rifle from where he had set it on the ground. Tom signaled to duck down and follow him. They crossed the open field at a trot, not stopping till they reached the next dividing hedgerow on the far side. Over the hedge there was a large expanse of fallow land – it stretched clear across to where on the eastern side it lay up against the highway. Filing into it, coming off the highway, were tanks.

'At least twenty, maybe more.' Tom squinted through his field glasses as he tried to count the shadowy lumps of steel that were less than five hundred yards away. 'Damn!' He pushed the glasses back into his pocket. 'They're getting into position to move on the town – we need to get out of here. There's no way we'll get into Plattsburg now.' His mind ran franticly over his options.

'Change of direction,' he told the others. 'We make for the shore east of us – look for a boat, there're plenty of folk fishing in these parts. We need to get round Plattsburg and down the lake.'

He had hardly finished when the sound of incoming fire broke the silence. A round roared over their heads with the noise of an express train ripping apart the sky above them. In Plattsburg the defenders were ranging their guns. They were in the firing line.

'Let's move out of here before one of those hits us,' Tom said calmly and they set off on the double following the line of the hedge. Behind them the noise of the battle for Plattsburg now split the air and the sky was lit with the brilliance of bursting munitions. As they put distance between them and the fight, Tom looked back. The horizon was now shimmering with flashes. The white phosphorous dots of tracers wriggling in ragged arcs across the sky reminded him of fireworks. Fourth of July briefly crossed his mind, but these were not fireworks. The tracers were looking for targets – there must be planes up there. They needed to get clear before daylight; they had about an hour before sunrise.

CHAPTER 35

The Hudson Valley, June 1941

Patton had finally got his new tanks; but it wasn't just the hardware, he had more men as well – grunts, dogfaces, foot sloggers – the boys who would double up behind the armor and do the hard business of fighting. At last he was ready to make his move. With his new army he was working his way north up the corridor of Highway 9 – the road to Croton.

A division of mechanized infantry ground its way along the edge of the Hudson. Painfully, slowly, it closed the gap with its objective. The summer dust kicked up by tracks and tires was visible for miles, floating like smoke on the still air. This was Patton's spearhead. In the tip of the spear was his new weapon, the latest version of the Mk3 medium tank – a creation of brutish ugliness that looked ungainly and dated against the crouching low lines of the German Panzers. Its clumsy-looking high profile meant it stuck out in silhouette on the horizon, which was never a good thing if you were being shot at. Nevertheless it had virtues: very thick armor and a hard hitting 75mm cannon that would punch holes in most of what Guderian could put up against it. Tank for tank it outmatched the Panzer; and so it was that it not only gave cover but comfort to the dogfaces who tramped along behind it. They felt the playing field was leveling out – they were getting more confident.

Jennifer's Diner stood empty, the windows boarded, the doors barred, the car park weirdly silent – empty. A hand-painted sign on the outside said simply:

TEMPORARY CLOSURE
GONE TO FIGHT THE WAR
! FUCK OFF FRITZ !

Down the road at Dobbs Ferry the talk in the hotel bar was all about the new stuff coming up the valley with Patton; stuff that would 'whip those Nazi asses good and hard' the barman told anyone who was listening. William Knudsen, the quiet Dane who had been brought in by Roosevelt to organize the 'Arsenal of Democracy' program, was doing his job. Industry was working; Warren Taylor was producing steel; American Car and Foundry was turning it into tanks and giving them to Patton. Further south at Rock Island arsenal in the mid-stream of the Mississippi, way beyond the reach of German bombers, the foundry was cranking out shells and mortar rounds, small arms ammo, grenades and field pieces.

In the west – which had been spared the *blitzkrieg* because, like Switzerland, it was protected by mountains – the North American Aircraft Company now moved to Seattle was rolling out a new fighter they were calling the P51, the Mustang. Hap Arnold and Ira Eaker were turning the road from Ottawa to Chicago into a ploughed field; making life difficult for Von Paulus and his supply line.

After three months of defeats things were beginning to look a little better, but still one problem remained: they needed even more men, the General Intake had not caught up with the early losses; men had been killed, men had been captured. Patton was getting his hardware but again he was running short on manpower, the men who would have to slug it out with the enemy; an enemy that was tough, battle-hardened and determined. When the first attacks came the American GIs had been no match for their German opponents. They had folded in confusion – lack of experience had betrayed them and the Wehrmacht scythed through their ranks and piled the dead high and bloody on each battle encounter. Slowly things were changing as the men who survived hardened their resolve. Field promotions were welding new platoons and companies together; they had leaders but they still needed more men; without more men they could lose the war.

Patton sent a blunt message to Marshall and Stimson. 'I've got the tin ware but it's no fucking good without a man to squeeze the trigger.'

These were the resources America had at its disposal.

North of the occupied line Von Paulus and Guderian did not have their own Knudsen; instead they now had to rely on a different tactic to make the factories and the workers produce what they needed for their war. Its name was terror.

Two days after it had set out, the Mercedes, which had bumped down the road from Ottawa carrying two SS men, arrived at Von Paulus' operational headquarters in Chicago. Von Paulus had installed himself in City Hall, removing most of the mayoral encumbrances, who he squeezed into cramped accommodation in a nearby building. Only the Mayor and a small staff were allowed to stay for the sake of essential liaison and good order in the running of the city. Not that that worked. There are criminals everywhere, Von Paulus complained, and they are armed. If this was how they ran their cities he felt no surprise that the Americans were losing as badly as they were.

The City Hall building sat on an entire block, a street flanking each side. It contained over four hundred separate rooms on ten floors spread across nearly an acre of land. Von Paulus and his key staff occupied the top floor where he enjoyed an uninterrupted view across the rooftops to Lake Michigan and out onto the horizon. In off-duty moments he liked to stand by one of the big windows and look out at the ships maneuvering onto the Navy Pier. He wrote to Constance, his wife, saying how much he liked the view and how it was a beautiful city but lamented the bad parts, describing how it was marred by disorder and some very poor housing districts – districts where it was dangerous even for his soldiers to go, where curfew patrols went only in vehicles and never on foot. 'Everyone,' he wrote, 'seems to carry a gun and this is proving a very severe problem. Unless we can disarm this population I don't see how we shall ever hold our position.'

Of the two SS men now entering the building only the officer went up in the elevator; the lower-ranked Vogel was left to loiter in the large marble-faced lobby where he stood watching the coming and going of clerks and minor officials. Stepping out of the elevator, the officer emerged into a long, well-lit corridor with a good quality carpet laid down its length. At the far end he observed a sentry posted outside a large door and deduced it would be the General's office. He was ushered in by a secretary who sat in the outer office where there was no view, only a frosted glass panel in a door that let onto the corridor where the sentry stood. Entering the inner room he came to attention, his cap tucked under his arm; he gave the obligatory Hitler salute.

'SS Obersturmbannführer Heinrich Neumann reporting for special duty,' he announced. Von Paulus returned the salute but did not get up. Instead he indicated that the officer should sit. Neumann pulled up the chair and waited.

'You have an excellent record of results in your work, Neumann,' he said. 'We have a very big problem here, one which particularly plagues the larger cities. It will require some extraordinary measures if we are to combat it.'

Neumann looked smugly confident. He had dealt with bigger problems and, besides, he knew America and American ways – he had, after all, been born there. He knew their sensitive spots and how to touch them, how to make them raw with the most exquisite pain until they would do anything he asked of them – just to make him stop.

'We have our little ways, General.'

'Good, then I shall arrange for your briefing. Your quarters have been allocated; I think you will find them satisfactory. I would like you to start work right away. That is all; you may go – and good hunting.' Neumann got to his feet.

'I need results, Obersturmbannführer. Too many of my men are tied up trying to keep order and that is unsatisfactory. I need them in the field; they are soldiers not policemen. Results – do I make myself clear?'

Neumann snapped to attention and saluted, 'Yes, Herr General.' As he descended in the elevator he smiled at the prospect of the coming operations.

'Come, Vogel,' he said when he rejoined him in the lobby. 'We have some interesting work to do. You will enjoy it; I know you will.'

510

On the following day a notice appeared on the wall of a building close to the North Shore. Another was pasted to an A-board at the entrance to a gas station. Then one appeared stuck to the window of a bakery. Groups of men wearing collaboration armbands walked the streets of every district, sticking and nailing the notices to lampposts, telegraph poles, doors and windows. They shouldered satchels stuffed with them. They pushed them under the windshield wipers of parked cars; they even nailed them to the doors of churches.

The groups roamed the city in bunches of four to six men, armed with iron bars and clubs. Anyone who complained about the posting was beaten up on the spot. Mostly it was some small-time shop owner who made the mistake of confrontation; the punishment meted out was swift, vicious and indiscriminate. Nobody was spared, not old men, women or children – not even dogs. Opposition was unacceptable – it was not tolerated.

On a street in the Southside district a group of four men walked into the bar of the Crystal Peacock nightclub and there stuck a notice to an ornate gilt-framed mirror. It was Friday and they were getting ready for a busy night, so when the manager, Franco Delarosa, saw what had been done he blew up angrily. He strode over to the mirror and tore down the notice, not bothering to read it. Delarosa was not a man to be messed with. He ran this club; it was his territory – he wasn't putting up with any bullshit from a bunch of Nazi sympathizers. He screwed up the paper into a ball and hurled it in the face of one of the men. The others stopped and turned to look at Delarosa. They glared menacingly at him, a look of affront in their eyes. Delarosa shaped up to them.

'Get out'a my club, you worthless bums,' he snarled, grabbing one of them roughly by the jacket and shoving him towards the door. 'Go on. Get out'a here.'

At this a second man moved brusquely towards Delarosa; his stance was threatening. He prodded him with the blunt end of a thick metal bar, jabbing him in the ribs and taunting him. 'Back off, fatso, unless you want some of this.'

A scuffle broke out. Delarosa punched the man with the iron bar. 'Chew on this, punk,' he shouted and made to hit him again, but before he could get in the second blow the others turned on him. He took several hits before he fell to the floor. A barman stepped in, trying to protect Delarosa's body as he lay on the floor being kicked, but he too was knocked down. The noise of the fray brought two club bouncers to the scene. They were followed by some kitchen staff. The poster men ran, shouting threats and abuse as they fled.

Delarosa was lifted to an upstairs room and laid on a sofa; he didn't look so good. Somebody called for an ambulance but it was too late – he was found to be dead. One of the blows rained down on him had cracked his skull; his brain had hemorrhaged.

Later, after things had died down, a kitchen porter clearing away the debris of the brawl, righting fallen tables and removing a broken chair, picked up the ball of crushed paper that had started the ruckus. As he unraveled the notice he saw it was spattered with Delarosa's blood. He smoothed it out on the top of the bar and read the text.

PUBLIC EXECUTION NOTICE
08.00 Saturday June 10th 1941

**Reprisal for the shooting of
four German officers and
a member of the Gestapo
on the North Shore.
Twelve female residents
of the City of Chicago
will be summarily executed
by firing squad
in front of the City Hall
By order of General Friedrich Von Paulus**

The KP, who was merely a teenage boy, carefully folded the notice and tucked it into his pocket. He'd never seen an execution before. He'd once read about one in a book at school but that didn't seem real – this could be interesting. When he got home he told his brother about it and showed off the blood-stained notice like a trophy. They decided they should go and watch it; it might be more entertaining than a ball game – which is exactly what Neumann and Vogel wanted.

Neumann was quartered in the luxurious Drake Hotel where he had been allocated a suite. From there he was a short walk to City Hall. Vogel had a room in a boarding house on East Monroe.

The death of Franco Delarosa had not passed unnoticed. That night the club had a visitor, a special guest, a member of the Southside Outfit and *capofamiglia* of one of the most prominent crime families in Chicago – Tony 'the Beast' Bardetti. He had come to pay his respects to Franco, whose death he now volubly lamented. They had been like brothers; they grew up as kids in the same neighborhood – they lived less than a block away from each other. More importantly, not only was the Crystal Peacock a joint on his patch, Tony Bardetti owned half the place. Accompanying him that night, also paying respects, was the other shareholder, a member of a New York family – Giorgio Gagliardi. Together they sat in Bardetti's office on the first floor. A waiter came in with coffee and set it down on a table.

'How is it down there now?' Bardetti asked him. 'Are we ready for tonight?' There was a party due in at ten; important people, men with interests in the City and across Illinois. It would be champagne, gambling and girls through till dawn.

'I've cleaned up the damage in the bar, Mr Bardetti. We're in pretty good shape now.'

'The city has gone to rubbish, Giorgi,' Bardetti said as soon as the waiter had closed the door on them. 'Ever since these Germans arrived. Nobody goes out any more except they get a special pass.'

'Let's hope they never get to New York – ha! We'd go broke.'

'I have to speak with the Mayor – he owes me.'

'Does he have influence – with these Tedeschi?' He used the Italian word for a German like it was a pejorative.

Bardetti sneered and shook his head. 'Who does? They have no interest in business. Only they want to go around destroying things – telling people what to do – sticking their noses in where they don't belong.'

'You heard about the executions tomorrow?'

'I did. Who killed their people? Do we know anything?'

'Partisans, I hear – Polacks – some guys from the North Side, Avondale I think. They're a bit pissed off about what happened when the Tedeschi took over their country.'

Gagliardi shrugged. 'Can you blame them?'

Bardetti was about to suggest they added a shot of brandy to the coffee. He liked a café corretto in the afternoon. It was civilized, he would say, and anyway it reminded him of the old country. But before he could get the words out the door burst open and there was the waiter again – this time breathless and panicky.

'The poster men,' he rasped. 'They're back and they're wrecking the place.'

As he spoke there was a commotion, the sound of furniture being thrown around, shattering glass and a lot of yelling. Bardetti got up and moved across the room to where a vitrine stood fixed against the wall, filled with crystal champagne flutes and brandy goblets. He reached up to one of the glass doors and, putting his hand on the ornate carving that surrounded it, pressed a small concealed button. There was a click then a whirring sound as the whole vitrine slid sideways revealing an alcove. Inside, neatly racked, were a number of guns. He grabbed a Thompson machine gun and threw it to Gagliardi, then picked out a sawn-off shotgun and stuffed his pockets with shells. Gagliardi cocked the Thompson and both men walked briskly out onto the landing from where they could see the wreckers at work.

Gagliardi reached the top of the stairs where he was confronted by a man with an axe coming up towards him. He raised the axe above his head with one arm and bounded up the stairs, two at a time. It was pointless; there was the short rapid sound of the Thompson – bap, bap, bap – the man fell backwards and, still gripping the axe, slid and bumped back down to the bottom where he lay in a motionless heap. In the same moment, leaning across the landing balustrade, Bardetti loosed a round from the shotgun. The poster men stopped wrecking and stood frozen, looking from one to the other, not sure of what came next. Bardetti and Gagliardi came down into the bar, their guns trained on the three remaining wreckers.

'Up against the wall, punks,' Bardetti shouted angrily. The men dropped their axes, moving sullenly and slowly to one side of the room. Bardetti crunched his way across the debris of broken glasses and mirror fragments that covered the floor. Walking close to one of the men, he hit him in the belly with the butt of the shotgun – then as the man doubled in pain he smacked him across the side of the head with the barrel. The man dropped to his knees grunting from the pain, finding it hard to draw a breath. Bardetti brought a knee up sharply under the man's chin, hitting him hard and knocking him backwards. 'Lousy informer – lackey – testa di cazzo.' He went into a rant of Italian expletives, each time kicking the lifeless body of the man on the floor.

'What are we going to do with this filth?' he called out over his shoulder.

Gagliardi stood back and watched, slowly shaking his head but saying nothing. He approved of the beating; it was justice for what these two-bit turncoats had done. Not just for breaking up the joint, after all hadn't they done that to the competition themselves? During the days of the Prohibition competition for territory had been fierce. A lot of guys got themselves killed, that was natural; but this, ratting on your own people – to a foreign invader. That was treachery – that demanded proper punishment. He inclined his head downwards and lit a cigarette.

As he raised it again he noticed a movement at the other end of the room where a door led into the kitchen. There was a man standing there who had not been there before. At first he thought it must be a commis chef because he was wearing a black and grey uniform. But it wasn't and, as he watched and wondered who it was, he noticed the man was holding a submachine gun. Next, the lobby door at the opposite end was flung open. Four soldiers in the uniform of the Waffen SS moved quickly into defensive positions, rifles trained on Gagliardi and Bardetti. The man from the kitchen now moved casually through the wreckage towards them. He wore the insignia of an officer on his uniform though Gagliardi did not know what rank it was. He smiled a very malignant smile, an evil patronizing smile that said something nasty might be going to happen. Gagliardi knew they were in trouble.

At first Bardetti thought they were cops come to see what the ruckus was about. It had probably been reported by some right minded citizen, he concluded, and he turned to put out a handshake. It was a bad move; he was shot by one of the SS men who mistook the sudden movement as a threat.

514

Bardetti fell and as he did Gagliardi let the Thompson drop from his grasp – he knew he had no chance.

The officer walked up to him and in perfect American ordered Gagliardi to face the wall. As he did so the officer shot him twice in the back of the head, then walked to the center of the room. He looked around for a moment or two and then spotting some of the bar staff cowering behind the counter asked them politely to 'stand up please.' One of them started to shake and began to cry; he realized he was about to die and as the fear spread through his body with a cold and numbing sensation it paralyzed his brain. He felt the warm trickle of urine run down the inside of his leg as his bladder gave out and he pissed himself. He was barely twenty years old and now it was all going to end.

The officer surveyed the pathetic fear-ridden group who presented themselves in front of him and laughed. They waited for death – but it didn't come.

'Don't look so worried,' he said, still smiling the same satanic smile. 'You're not going to die,' and here he chuckled, 'at least not today. You are my witnesses. Go home and tell your families, tell your friends – this is what happens when we don't get cooperation. It is my lesson to you – tell someone you know what happens to the enemies of the Reich.'

He stared at the stunned audience for a moment or two longer then, as abruptly as he came he went, taking his men with him. The two surviving poster men followed them, making a hurried getaway, stripping off their swastika armbands as they went and tossing them in the gutter – fearing they could become targets for revenge.

When news reached the ears of his family that Tony the Beast was dead they called a meeting. Other outfits were invited. They were cut off from the Commission that in more normal times would have met to decide on who was responsible and who would exact the revenge. The Mafia Commission was in New York but, no matter, they were still talking down the wires. There would be a reckoning.

At the Drake Hotel Neumann called room service for some champagne. When it arrived he poured two glasses and drank a toast to the Führer. 'You should have been there,' he told Vogel. 'It's a pity you missed it – you would have enjoyed it.' He raised his glass for a second toast.

'Here's to our work.' He smirked with satisfaction then, looking at his watch, added, 'Hmm, ten o'clock. You know, Vogel, the guests at the Crystal Peacock should be arriving about now – won't they have a surprise.'

******

James Brent sat at the breakfast table and confronted a plate of eggs and hash browns. On the table next to it, folded neatly, was the morning edition of *The*

515

New York Times. He picked it up, shook out the folds and looked at it. The picture he saw that morning was spread across the front page of every major newspaper in the country, and it shocked the nation to its core. It showed the bodies of the reprisal victims executed in Chicago: women and children, at the very instant they fell – crumpled, leaning forwards, staggering back, limbs sprawled about them as if dancing out some grotesque ritual. Perfectly timed, the photo caught the moment of their deaths in a grainy black-and-grey limbo and froze it for eternity. The executioners and the executed, facing each other across a few yards; the tiny puffs of smoke visible from the barrels of the rifles as they spat out their awful sentence of annihilation. The face of the officer giving the command to this death squad caught, mouth open, shouting the last words the fallen would ever hear; he carried the look of evil and bore the resemblance of Cain.

Further down the column he came across a quote from Churchill, who had been asked for his comment. 'Long after this war is over and forgotten,' Churchill had said bitterly, 'this image will remain – a startling testament to the vicious nastiness of which men of ill will in their dark nature are capable.'

James Brent found it struck a chord. Now his daughter was about to join the conflict. The thought chilled him but he knew she had to go and there was nothing he could do or say to change her mind. Right across the nation the sons and daughters of America were making the same decisions.

Neumann had arranged that the execution should be filmed in motion. He wanted the maximum impact; the viewers of this grim spectacle should see the faces, hear the cries and feel the terror. He arranged for two canisters to be sent across the front line then mailed to the offices of NBC and Pathe News. But the exercise failed. The content of the film was considered too obscene in the nature of its images to be passed for public exhibition. In making the message so terrible, so terrifying and inhuman he failed to get it across – and in that way he defeated himself.

The mood in Washington swung between outrage at the event and angry frustration that they were powerless to stop it from happening again. Everywhere there was gossip; rumor was rife and there was speculation that the Germans would soon be knocking on the door of New York. They were already in Albany and were moving steadily south down the Hudson.

******

Aly saw the same paper that James Brent had read and, although they were more than two hundred miles apart, it pulled on shared emotional strings. Their positions were the same: they both had people they cared for who were in danger of getting in harm's way, they both shared the same anxieties and forebodings. The only difference between them was breakfast – hers was just a piece of toast with a cup of tea. She couldn't eat; she was nearly at the end of her term but she still felt sick with the pregnancy. Added to this she was depressed, although Irena brushed it aside saying that was natural at her stage. The photo in the paper did nothing to help and she burst into tears. For Fred – who had always seen her as self-assured, assertive, even bullish – this was a new Aly and it worried him. Now he found himself torn between his duty to Churchill and his duty to a new wife.

Congress was clamoring for retribution. Pressure was being piled onto Roosevelt to do something. The people of America, the Speaker in the House said, wanted to hear some good news and this Democratic administration had made one God-awful mess – though he omitted to add that he was one of those who had tried to limit the expansion of the armed forces in the preceding years. There were a lot like him around and Henry Stimson wasn't slow to remind them.

When Loughlin got to the office that morning he was met by two men. He recognized them instantly: Jones and Polanski, the FBI agents who had been at Brunessemer the night Tom Jordan had stopped Mueller and the others. 'These men would like to talk with us, Fred,' Churchill said. Loughlin's first response was to be on his guard, but Churchill seemed relaxed so maybe he shouldn't worry.

At Churchill's invitation they all sat around the map table. Jones pulled a photograph out of a leather portfolio case he was carrying and dropped it on the table. It was a blow-up of the photo on the front pages of America's news sheets that morning. Jones flipped the picture round so that Loughlin could see it the right way up. He tapped a fingertip on the image of the SS officer with the open mouth giving the order to fire.

'Do you know this man? Have you ever seen him before?'

Loughlin looked hard at the image. 'No, I don't think so.'

Jones looked surprised. 'Are you sure?'

Loughlin shook his head slowly from side to side. 'It's not a face I'd forget – but, no, I've never seen him before.'

'You met a German agent when you first came here,' Polanski said.

'The one passing himself off as Amber Rose?'

'Yes. Could this be him?' Polanski pointed to the SS man again.

'No, I'm sure of that. You're thinking of Heinrich Neumann.' Loughlin looked from one to the other, then added, 'That man is not Neumann – Neumann is altogether taller, much more athletic. No, that's not Neumann.'

'Certain?'

'Positive.'

Jones and Polanski looked disappointed, then Jones asked, 'Do you think you would recognize Neumann ...' and he waved his arm generally in little circles, indicating there was maybe some uncertainty, '... if you saw him again – that is?'

Loughlin shrugged. 'Yes, I think so – why?'

'Oh, just thought we might need you to ID him sometime,' Polanski said, seemingly unconcerned.

They thanked Loughlin, said how nice it was to meet him again, then after the pleasantries they left. 'What was that about?' Loughlin asked Churchill after they had gone.

'I'm not really sure – but since you ask me I'd say someone is hatching a plot. It has that feel about it.'

He changed the subject; there was little to be had from trying to second guess what the FBI was up to. His mind was across the Atlantic. He wanted to get back there but for the moment Roosevelt was set against the idea. If anything went wrong he was handing the Germans another victory and that was a risk he didn't need to take. From England there was more news: Halifax was to be tried for treason and if found guilty he would be executed.

'They've moved him out of the Tower,' Churchill said casually. 'His health is deteriorating, they say. Not surprised really – it's a damp, cold old place. They've stuck him in Westminster Hospital.'

'Why bother, if they're going to kill him anyway?'

'Public consumption, dear boy. It needs to be made to look fair, you know. Besides, a trial makes for good propaganda and they need a show after Mosley's killing. Shan't miss Mosley, I must say.'

Walter Thompson, who now stood in regularly for Loughlin on the radio and the Morse, stuck his head round the door.

'Just in from Radio Free London,' he said. 'Jerry's secretly planning to put in their own man to replace Mosley – and they've put a reward of a thousand quid on the head of that Scarlet Pimpernel bloke who lifted Mr Eden from under their noses. They've named him. He's an ex-civil servant from the Home Office – a chap called Richard Grainger.'

In the outer office Mary Shearburn took a call. Roosevelt had ordered a meeting of the Chiefs but this time Churchill was invited.

There was news. At the end of May, General Bradley, one of Marshalls rising stars, was now two divisions strong and together with the newly formed 82nd airborne had started pushing up under the Dakotas, testing the German lines. Vinegar Joe Stilwell was on the northern margin of the Appalachian Mountains where his forces were sealing the routes south.

'The Germans are boxed in by the terrain,' Marshall announced, 'forests and mountains – ridges too steep to move vehicles, valleys with fast-flowing rivers.

It's not good terrain to carry out an invasion. It's guerrilla country; it favors the defenders – it isn't a battlefield Von Paulus will want to take on.'

He stood up and went over to a wall map. 'Any expansion of the theater has to be towards the eastern seaboard and down the Hudson valley. This is his only practical option and right now he looks like he's taking it.' He tapped on the map with a pointer. 'They are already in Albany.'

The advance down to Albany had been another textbook exercise in lightning warfare. The Americans were still learning lessons, still under strength, fighting local actions with local resources, still being massacred and still retreating. They had yet to get a big enough build-up of men and equipment concentrated in one place to make a stand and win a battle. Outgunned and outnumbered, they could do no more than slow the advance.

As one commander put it after falling back from his position, 'It was like trying to stop a cart rolling downhill when you're standing on ice – you can slow it down but you were always gonna be slipping backwards.'

Marshall stopped to draw breath, then smiled. 'Now for the good news. Yup, there is finally some good news. I just got a report that Patton has engaged the enemy and held them a few miles north of Croton on Hudson.'

It was a cause for celebration. Finally something seemed to be going right.

******

The bell on the front door did not ring; instead it buzzed. It was a hideous sound, Irena declared when they first arrived, but there again she thought it a hideous house throughout. She liked it no better than she did the house in Dobbs Ferry – less, if anything, because at least there she had the comfort of familiarity. She repeatedly told Aly she had no doubt her father chose the house just to annoy her with that ghastly modernist buzzer. She would have it changed if only she could find a man to do it, but there were hardly any tradesmen to be found. The city had been scoured of its men to feed this wretched war, she complained.

'It's Miss Caroline,' Constance announced, opening the door to the sitting room where Irena and Aly were drinking tea and discussing the prospect of the birth.

Carey stepped in through the open doorway; she stood looking at the other two. It was more than six months since they had last seen her – not since the shooting at Brunessemer. Aly was shocked to see how pale and gaunt her sister looked. Her make-up looked carelessly applied and she had an air of hopelessness about her. There were dark shadows under her eyes; her shoulders slouched around her body; she looked tired. Irena got up and embraced her but it was a gesture without passion. Carey allowed herself be hugged but that too was perfunctory.

'You don't look well,' Irena said awkwardly, leading her eldest daughter to a chair. Carey sat down, not bothering to take off her coat. Instead Irena peeled it off her and draped it over the back of the chair. She sat there like a zombie. Aly got up with difficulty, hauling herself off the stuffed sofa that enveloped her. She went over to Carey and kissed her.

'It's been a long time, Sissy,' she said, reverting to a name she used to call her when they were kids. 'What have you been doing with yourself?'

'Not too much lately,' Carey said, looking down at her hands and twisting her fingers nervously together.

'I'm sorry about Tony,' Aly said, trying to sound sympathetic even though she had not liked what little she had seen of the man and even less about what she had heard. 'It must be hard.'

Carey went to say something, but the words stuck in her throat and instead she started to whimper – then she began to sob. She pulled a handkerchief out of her bag and sniffled into it, trying to get control of her emotions but it was all to no effect and she broke into a full-throated blubber.

'I can't handle it,' she sobbed as soon as she got control of the crying fit. 'It's so awful just to see him there – in chains – behind glass.' She stopped just long enough to draw a deep breath then said pathetically in a low, resigned voice charged with the emotion of despair, 'They won't even let me touch him.'

Aly tried to comfort her with an arm around one shoulder as her sister sat there crying, the handkerchief held over her snuffling nose, rocking back and forth on the chair trying to ease her pain. Irena had got up and left the room – and came back with a large glass of bourbon.

'Here,' she said, 'try this. I find it's good when the world's looking black. Go on – take a good slug,' and she pressed the glass into Carey's limp fingers and forcibly clamped them around it. 'Right,' she said firmly, sitting back down again. 'We've done the poor me bit. Now what do you want me to do? You do want me to do something – that is why you're here isn't it?' Nothing was said.

'Good, we've got that out of the way. Do you want me to speak with your father?' Carey shook her head and started to sob again. Irena began to lose patience. Carey had always been self-indulgent and the sympathy was wearing itself out.

'No? Then what? If you have some idea, tell me.'

Carey broke off from the sobbing. 'Father won't help me but your friend Clementine could – she's married to a man who's close to the President. If you could just talk to her.'

Irena looked at the wretched woman in front of her and wondered how her daughter had come to this. 'Sweetheart,' she said quietly, 'it would be no use.

Your friend killed a man, he's been convicted of murder, he has to pay for what he did. We all have to be responsible for our actions, darling.'

Carey burst back into tears again, pleading with Irena to do something. 'It was an accident,' she said through waterlogged eyes, 'a terrible, bloody accident – and these bastards, these judges, they took revenge because they hate him and his family.' Her tears were giving way to a rant. She clenched her fists till her tiny knuckles turned white; she banged them on her knees.

'None of you like him,' she said, now with more than a touch of venom in her voice. 'I hope the bloody Germans win this war; at least he'd have a chance, which is more than this fucking lot will give him. I hope they come in and smash everything. I hope you'll all pay the price you're making him pay. How many men did Tommy kill and they called him a bloody hero.' The rage turned back to helplessness again as it burned itself out and once more the tears flowed and the pathetic little sobs returned.

Irena had seen her daughter like this before, long ago and in another life. This was Carey's resort whenever she felt she had been dealt a bad hand. In the past Irena had just let it flow until it blew itself out, knowing that Carey would move on. But this was different; everything was different – life had changed beyond all imagination and it would be a long time, if ever, before things came right. Worn down by the vision of despair in front of her, Irena gave in.

'I'll see what I can do,' she said cautiously, knowing what was being asked would be near impossible. 'I'll try,' was all she would commit to.

On his way home that evening Loughlin pondered his day. He had news of his own to tell Aly and he wasn't sure how she would take it; he wasn't sure how he should break it. But before he could begin to explain she greeted him with the news that Carey was staying for a few days and she was in a very fragile condition. He took off his jacket and fell into a soft chair while Aly poured him a drink. They sat together, his hand on her belly feeling their child as it kicked and turned inside her, and Aly told him all of what had happened. He could see she was upset by what was happening to Carey – it would not be a good time to tell her about his day. He decided it would keep till tomorrow when maybe things had settled down a little.

The following morning over breakfast he broke it to her. 'I have to go away for a while – I've been put on an assignment,' was all he said.

Aly didn't like the sound of that one little bit. 'Can you tell me anything?' she asked cautiously.

'I'm sorry sweetheart – it's very hush hush.'

'Will you be gone long?'

'I don't know. Can you be brave? I really need you to be brave.'

Aly looked at him longingly. How much she loved her Englishman, she thought to herself, with his funny accent and his very precise manner. 'Uh, huh,' she said as she moved her head perceptibly in a little nod of consent to the question. 'When do you go?'

'Tomorrow.'

She wanted to say something but she didn't. Instead she thought of Carey and understood more clearly how she was feeling. It's hard to suddenly have someone close wrenched away from you, she told herself.

CHAPTER 36

The Champlain Canal

The night air was warm; all along the canal banks frogs were calling; croaking and yapping, trying to get a mate – it was the season.

Through the blackness a small wooden row boat was drifting on the current, which was picking up pace approaching the last lock before the slow, oily green water would finally be let free and flow into the Hudson. Lock seven marked the end of the Champlain Canal at Fort Edward. They only had to get around this and the way was open, clear through to where they calculated the American forces would be.

It was McAndrew who had found the boat pulled up on the lake shore not far from Plattsburg. They had rowed it to the bottom of the lake to the point where the Champlain Canal started. There they had carried it a short distance overland to circumvent the first lock, which was already in German hands, and then under the cover of darkness started their journey down to where it would join the Hudson River. During the daylight hours they took the dinghy out of the water, concealing it and themselves in the woods that flanked the Canal, and there they slept. Finally they had nearly reached the end of the journey.

About a quarter mile upstream from lock seven they hauled the boat out of the Canal and onto the bank. Quickly and expertly they went through the now familiar routine. Laying the two oars across the gunwales, they lashed them tight to the oarlocks. Then, with a man on the end of each oar, they lifted the craft and walked steadily down the towpath. They had bypassed six locks this way since they entered the Canal at Whitehall on the southern tip of Champlain. They traveled at night, keeping to the edge of the waterway, trying to choose the most deserted bank.

By the time they reached lock seven they had exhausted their K rations. They would have to go into the next small town to find something. Tom was gambling that the Germans would now be thin on the ground. He knew from what intelligence there had been when they bailed out of Cumberland Head that enemy forces had taken all of the towns on the east bank of Lake Champlain and they had spotted sentries and gun emplacements when they came through the lock at Whitehall. It was clear the Germans were moving their forces south –

that had to mean New York was the next big target. Once there, it was no more than a hop, skip and a jump to DC.

Lock seven was active, the banks on both sides of the canal bathed in strong yellow light from flood lamps mounted high above it. A gun battery had been installed on one of the quays; they counted no fewer than five E-boats moored on the downstream side of the lock. This was not only the gateway to the Hudson coming south all the way from the St Lawrence Seaway in Canada, but it joined the Erie Canal further downstream at Albany, opening up the route through to the industrial area of Detroit. It was a natural conduit for invasion.

Nearly all the traffic they had encountered on the water was military. Each night for three consecutive nights they dodged the large, armed barges that now plied the waterway; steel leviathans, black and rusty with anti-aircraft machine guns mounted fore and aft. It was apparent the Germans were using them to carry supplies and men down to the Hudson.

On nights when there was no moon the only way of knowing one of them was close was from the throb of its engine. The German crews ran them blacked out for fear of air attack and more than once they had been surprised by one of these monsters and found themselves under the bows about to be run down.

If they could get onto the Hudson Tom felt sure the going would be easier; the river was wider and the water flowed faster – there were no more locks to circumvent. There was another thing: the banks of the river were mostly roughhewn, cut by the passage of water and time, not made by the orderly minds of men, unlike the neatly finished edges to the canal which offered no refuge in which to hide. On the river the margins were irregular, thick with waterside shrubs and overhanging trees, punctuated by inlets and intersected by small streams. There were discreet places where a small craft could lay up and not be seen by the other river traffic. The barges, laden and sitting low in the water, would stay well away from the shallows around the banks, out in the centre stream, avoiding the risk of running aground.

But if one problem had gone it was quickly replaced by another. They were beginning to feel the toll of hunger and it was making them weak; they would have to go ashore to find food and take their chances of running into a German patrol. They couldn't do it in broad daylight – the only clothes they had were their field combat uniforms. 'We need to find somewhere quiet,' he told the others, 'somewhere small, somewhere the Germans are unlikely to be.'

So as the day broke in a rose-colored blush they had guided the boat into a creek where the water was fresh and where they had been able to wash and drink. They had lain hidden there throughout the day, sleeping in the undergrowth and taking turns to watch. As the light faded they left the boat drawn up onto the shallow sandy bank of the creek and struck out in the direction of some lights they could see glimmering on a hill. Tom judged them to be around one or maybe two miles away.

The lights were closer than Tom had anticipated. Not long after they left the boat they emerged onto a narrow country road which made the going easy, and so they came on them less than twenty minutes march from the creek. He stopped and listened, holding his hand up to signal the others to halt. He sniffed at the evening air; his nose picked up the scent of kerosene. They were not the electric lights of a modern house; they were storm lanterns, the sort used by farmers and homesteaders in the less populated areas. Good, this was somewhere remote; there were unlikely to be Germans. He moved his men cautiously up the road and closer to where the lanterns were burning.

The dark outline of a barn began to form, its wooden shingles picked out by the dull yellow light. Then he got the warm smell of livestock – cattle. They were in luck – it was a farm. A short distance on from the barn was the house, its windows illuminated and welcoming. There was a raised wooden porch running across the front punctuated by heavy planking steps leading up to the front door.

'Okay,' Tom whispered, 'listen up. Corporal, take Pratt and go round the far side of the barn – make a wide sweep. Zuckerman, you come with me – we'll go the other way. We meet up on the far side.'

'You think maybe there're Krauts here?' McAndrew asked in a barely audible whisper.

'I don't think so – but if there are let's find them before they find us.'

McAndrew and Pratt quietly faded into the dark. Tom gave them till a count of ten – they were taking the long route round. He and Zuckerman only had to cover one side. 'Stick close to the barn wall,' he told Zuckerman. 'That way we'll be less conspicuous.'

They reached the corner. It was all clear; the only sound came from the animals inside as they shifted about in the forage. The open ground between the barn and the house was deserted except for an old Ford stake-back truck parked close to the front steps. After a few minutes McAndrew arrived. 'All clear,' he reported.

'Good, OK, but let's just be a little careful. You men spread yourselves along the wall of the barn. Cover me, keep the house in your sights. I'm going to pay them a little visit.'

Crossing the ground quickly he made his way to the house; from inside a dog began to bark. He heard the sound of the latch being sprung; someone was opening the front door. Tom reached the cover of the truck seconds before a splash of light spilled its way across the porch and onto the ground where he had been standing. The figure of a man filled the frame of the door, then the form of a large dog. The man stepped out onto the porch and stood there. The dog followed him out and sat on his haunches beside him all the time, uttering a low growl. There was the sound of scratching and the rasp of a match being struck – it flared into life and briefly lit up the face of a rugged, middle-aged man. The match flickered then left a small trail of sparks as it was shaken lifeless by the hand holding it. In its place the red glow of a cigarette.

The man now slowly descended the wooden steps; the dog followed. The light from the doorway fell on the side of him; he had a shotgun tucked under one arm, his hand thrust deep into the pocket of a pair of battered denim pants. He reached the bottom of the steps and stopped. 'Who's there?' he called out in the direction of the truck.

Tom waited, not knowing how jittery or trigger-happy the farmer might be. The last thing he wanted was to get his head blown off after all he'd survived. 'Captain Jordan,' he called out calmly, 'US Army.'

He moved very carefully out from behind the truck and into the open; the dog saw him and started across the ground towards him, snarling and barking, but before he reached him the farmer yelled out for it to stop. Tom was thankful that it did – it was a large ugly crossbreed with a square head and powerful jaws; there was probably some mastiff in it somewhere.

The farmer stood still and said nothing, sizing up the man who had come out from behind the truck. 'You'd better come on in, Captain,' he said, jerking his head in the direction of the house. He whistled to the dog which, seeing his master acting friendly towards the intruder, dropped its aggressive stance and loped lazily back up the steps and into the house.

Inside a nervous looking woman in her middle age emerged from the kitchen. Her face was lined and weather-beaten from a life of work outdoors. She wore her hair tied up in a bun, which was still a fashion for country people. A few wayward strands of grey-streaked hair fell across her forehead which, on seeing a stranger, she smoothed back into place.

'Who's this, Calvin?' she asked furtively.

'This here's Captain Jordan,' he said reassuringly to her, then turned to Tom.

'Why don't we go through to the living room where we can talk?'

The question didn't call for an answer. Instead he led Tom into a large room with a heavy wooden table at one end and easy chairs circled around a large open hearth at the other. There were three young women settled in the chairs, all of them engaged in sewing.

'These are my daughters,' the farmer said, acknowledging them briefly. The three women got up and smiled shyly at Tom. They all seemed to be close in age: late teens and early twenties, Tom judged. The oldest came forward and put out her hand in a genteel greeting. Tom took the hand and gave it a perfunctory shake, bowing slightly at the same time. She was a strong looking woman with a fresh, open face and dark eyes. He noticed the hand was roughish and guessed she helped around the farm.

'It's very nice to meet you I'm sure,' she said. 'We don't get many visitors out here.' The other two looked on, smiling but saying nothing.

'Well, we're just passing through,' he replied. 'I'm Captain Jordan.'

The farmer looked at Tom, then at his daughters. 'Joanna, take your sisters and go help your momma,' he said, dismissing them. They looked disappointed but obediently gathered up the garments they had been sewing and went off to the kitchen.

The farmer reached up to the mantelpiece over the fire hearth and took down a tobacco pouch; he sat in one of the easy chairs and beckoned Tom to do the same. He offered Tom the pouch. After they had rolled two cigarettes and lit them the farmer leaned forward, fixing Tom with a confidential gaze.

'I'm Calvin Fletcher and I farm this land hereabouts,' he said like he was making a statement, 'milking cows mostly. My granddaddy built this house and that barn out there.' He leaned back in the chair with a look of satisfaction.

'I lived in this house when I was a boy and when I took a wife she came to live here too. My maw and paw passed on some years back; now it's my three daughters you just met – Joanna the eldest, Marianne the middle, and Susie the young pretty one. We had a son but he got took sick when he was just a month and he died. Didn't have no more after that. Pity because sons are useful on a farm, but the girls pitch in and together with their momma we get to make a living.'

He paused to draw on his cigarette then blew out a stream of acrid grey smoke into the air above him.

'That's me and where I fit in these parts. So what about you? What brings you here, Captain – you on the run from them Germans? And just now you said *we* to my daughter. Are there more of you outside – in the barn maybe?' Tom nodded but declined to comment on how many they were.

They sat for a while and talked, Tom recounting the events of Cumberland Head, the fall back to Plattsburg and their journey down the waterway from Champlain, finishing with, 'I don't even know exactly where we are.'

'Well, it seems like you and your boys have had a pretty rough time,' Calvin Fletcher said earnestly. 'I'd consider it an honor to have you sleep over.' He hesitated for a moment then added, 'I'm happy to have an officer under my roof but with three girls in the house I'd feel more at ease if your men was to sleep in the barn – I'm sure you know what I mean. Oh, and as to where you are – you're just north of Stillwater. That's the nearest town, but don't go there – it's full of Germans right now. I hear they're heading down Albany way.'

He went quiet and looked down at his hands. 'Looks like we're done for,' he said, as if he was almost too embarrassed to say the words. 'There's no stopping them.'

The house had been built in the Dutch style on three floors, timber clad with overhanging gables and strong wooden storm shutters. When they had finished talking Joanna brought him something to eat – cold ham, cheese, dill pickles and a coarse country rye bread, black and almost sticky. Afterwards she showed him to his room at the top of the house; it was sparsely furnished with a wooden cot, a pillow and a thick feather cover to sleep under. They must have been European settlers, he thought, looking round at the simple furnishings. There was a framed picture of a religious scene hung on the wall and a small square mirror. In one corner a hand basin was set on a small table and there was a single chair with a string seat. The only light came from a single candle in a holder with a glass cover to protect the flame from blowing out.

'I'll bring you some water,' Joanna said, and left him there to think about what he and the men should do next. If the Germans were still between them and Albany he had to find a way round them. The river was getting crowded; it was too exposed. They would have to go overland from here on in.

There was a tap on the door and Joanna came back in with a large jug filled with water and a small bar of soap. 'That's the best we can do, I'm afraid. I'm sure you must be used to better.'

'That's fine,' Tom assured her and she left, closing the door carefully.

A few minutes later there was another sound outside his room and when he opened the door it was the middle girl, Marianne.

'Hi,' she said almost in a whisper, 'would it be okay if I came to talk to you a bit?' She came in without waiting for an answer.

'We don't get many visitors,' she said coyly. 'It's nice to talk with someone new.' She sat on the edge of the cot and started to smooth out the creases in the thick down cover. 'Why don't you sit next to me for a spell', she said, giving him a broad smile. She pulled on the hem of her dress lifting it up then letting it settle back down just above her knees. The thin cotton clung to her, tracing seductive curves in the rise and fall of her thighs. She was making a play for him and he knew it was probably not a good idea; not the best way to repay a man's hospitality by screwing his daughter. What if he walked in on them, caught them in the middle of the act? He could be putting the safety of his men at risk.

He struggled with the dilemma but in the end the rising urge bound up in his hormones got the better of common sense. He gave in and sat down next to her. He put a hand on her knee and slid it up the smooth inner thigh; she parted her legs just enough to let his hand go all the way, then leaned across and kissed

528

him. She was wearing no underclothes – she had come with clear intent and now she got what she came for.

As she got off the cot and smoothed down her dress she let out a little giggle and, touching his lips with her finger, made a shushing noise. 'Let's not tell,' she said in a hushed voice.

Shortly after she had gone there was another tap on the door. He opened it; Joanne was standing there. 'I've got some food for your men downstairs. Paw thought it better if you come with me to get them bedded down.'

Downstairs Mrs Fletcher had lined a wicker basket with a cloth and put cut bread, still warm bacon, cheese and a covered pot with soft cooked eggs in it. 'I hope this'll be alright for your men,' she said timidly, almost apologetically.

'It'll be fine, ma'am. We're most grateful.' It went through his mind that she was a bit of a mouse, probably worn down by the hardship and isolation of her life. He got the notion that she might be disillusioned – there was definitely an air of resignation, almost indifference in the way she addressed life and those around her. It brought on a pang of guilt about what had happened with Marianne; he felt it was a betrayal.

Tom picked up the basket and waited for Joanne, who had brewed a large jug of coffee and was pouring it into a round canteen to carry it out and down the steps.

'I guess you had a visit from Marianne,' she said casually on the way to the barn.

Tom wasn't sure how to answer. 'How do you mean?' he replied lamely.

'I could smell her on you when I came to your room. She always uses the same cheap scent when she goes out man hunting; dime a bottle down at the general store.'

There was an embarrassed silence then Tom said, 'I don't feel too good about it.'

'You shouldn't feel bad – that's Marianne's way. She'll have the pants off any fellah she meets – she's like a bitch on heat. Don't worry, I won't tell.'

In the barn McAndrew and the others had already staked out their places. The smell of coffee and bacon filled the air. McAndrew had put together a makeshift table to set the food out and now they sat on upturned milk churns and got stuck in.

'It's darned good to feel clean again Captain.' Pratt said as he sat to the table and bit into a thick slice of hickory smoked bacon. 'That's the first real wash I've had in more than a week.'

Zuckerman nodded his agreement, his mouth too full to say anything. He stabbed at two eggs sitting on a slice of dense country bread and stirred them about with his fork. Zuckerman was a Jew but only middle of the road, he joked, when challenged over some of his eating preferences. He wasn't going to let that get between him and the bacon piled high on the board in front of him.

******

It was just getting light when Tom was woken by a presence in the room. It was Joanne. 'You have to get out of here. Now – and quickly.'

He sat up and rubbed at his eyes; they were bleary from sleep but his mind was functioning. 'What is it – what's wrong?'

'Get dressed, I'll explain. Paw has gone out. I think he's gone to alert the Germans over in Stillwater. They could be here any time. You need to get your men and go; get as far away as you can.'

'Why would he do that?'

'He likes them; he thinks they will do good for America. His mother, my grandmother, was Bavarian and his patriotism leans in that direction. He's always been a Republican. He hates Roosevelt and all the Democrats – he blames them for the depression years. You have to understand we're farmers – we suffered a lot in those times.'

She almost pushed him out of the room. As he reached the bottom of the stairs he came face to face with Mrs Fletcher; she was holding a bundle wrapped in a sheet. 'You'll need these,' she said in her small, nervous voice. 'It's clothes for you and your men. You can't go out in what you got on – you wouldn't get a mile. There's a lot round here think like him. Good luck, young man.'

She pushed the bundle into his hands. 'I don't know what to say.'

'Say nothing', Joanne said impatiently. 'Just get moving.'

'We can't go back to the boat,' he told McAndrew. 'He knows where it is. We'll have to go across country.'

Dressed in ill-fitting clothes – too small for Pratt's lanky frame and too long in the leg for Zuckerman – they struck out along the road leading to the main highway that would take them in the direction of Albany. They walked on the paved road; it was easier and faster than working their way through the woodland but they stayed close, ready to dive for cover at the first sound of any approaching vehicle.

At noon they reached the edge of the Hudson again; they were just upstream from the town of Mechanicville where the railroad crossed the river on an iron girder bridge. They hadn't had sight of a German all morning. Tom looked at the bridge and assessed their chances; they could walk it, but they would be exposed. McAndrew didn't much like the look of it and said so. There was nobody to be seen around and they would stick out – 'like a hooker at a church weddin', he said.

'We look like hobos,' Tom argued. 'What's more natural than a bunch of bums walking the tracks waiting to jump a boxcar?'

'True,' Pratt replied, 'but if we get pulled by a cop and he looks in our knapsacks – well it might take some explaining why we got four stripped down Springfields and a bundle of rounds.'

'Hunters?' Zuckerman suggested.

Pratt grinned. 'Make up your mind, Zuckerman, I thought we were bums.'

Zuckerman laughed. 'Now he calls me a bum. Did I say I was a bum? No, it was the Captain here who made that suggestion; I prefer to be a hunter.'

'I think that decides it. We stay this side of the river.' Tom pointed over to the far bank and upstream to the north where the road to Stillwater disappeared behind the trees and to where a truck hove into view – then another close on its tail, and another. He shoved a hand into his knapsack and fished out a rifle scope. 'Germans,' he said to McAndrew, passing it over to him. McAndrew put the scope to his eye.

'Yup, it's our Kraut friends again.'

'They're going to Mechanicville. It's supplies. I think that means the town's probably already in their hands.'

'So where's the front?' Pratt chipped in as he looked through his own scope at the convoy.

Tom turned towards the south and pointed generally to the horizon. 'Somewhere out there. Can't be close or we'd hear the guns, I guess.'

Zuckerman looked worried, holding his hands out like he was about to pray, staring up at the open sky then turning his gaze on Pratt. 'Maybe our guys are being rolled up so fast we won't catch up till they're in Georgia.'

Pratt shook his head in disbelief. 'Geeze, Zuckerman,' he said despondently. 'You're a pessimistic sonofabitch.'

'No, I'm a realist.'

Pratt laughed. 'I liked it better when you were a bum.'

'A hunter,' Zuckerman corrected him, 'a hunter – I was never a bum. I'll have you know I'm the son of a good Jewish tailor. I come from a nice family – and he calls me a bum.'

'Stow it you two,' McAndrew grunted. 'Which way, Captain?'

'South, I think, Corporal. We need to stay away from that town, though. We'll rest up when the light goes.'

Three miles later their plans changed. Ahead of them a house appeared close to the edge of the road. A little further on there were more; they were walking into the eastern edge of Mechanicville where it spilled across the river onto the western shore. A few houses down and they encountered their first people of the day. A small knot of men and women were gathered at the corner of a street where the road led to the only bridge across the river connecting them with the main town.

They stood there looking sullen, arms resolutely folded, their faces painted with the long brushstrokes of indignation. These were unhappy people. At the foot of the bridge the focus of their discontent stood to attention in front of a newly erected sentry box. Beside him another Wehrmacht soldier dressed in field grey shouldered a rifle with a bayonet fixed. The two guardians of the bridge stared back warily at the group.

'Howdy, folks,' Tom said, casually edging closer to get a better look. 'How long's this been going on?'

A man nearest to him turned and looked at him suspiciously. 'You new in town?'

'Yup, just got in today.'

'They came down from Stillwater more than a week ago. There wasn't a fight even, they just walked in and our boys just slunk away in the night. Cowards to a man, if you ask me.'

A woman in the group with tear stains on her cheeks, her eye make-up smudged, stared vacantly at the bridge. 'They've cut off the town. They won't let nobody in or out. My son's over there – he's only five and they won't let him cross. What kind of people are they, for Lord's sake.' She collapsed into a flood of tears and while the others were consoling her McAndrew sidled up to Tom. 'Captain, I may have a solution for you.'

They detached themselves discreetly from the group and walked a short distance to where they found Zuckerman and Pratt on the forecourt of a gas station. Zuckerman had his head under the hood of a Chevrolet sedan.

'There's no one here,' McAndrew told him. 'The place is deserted. I figure they're probably up the road staring at that bridge.'

The groaning of a starter motor came from the bowels of the Chevrolet then the engine kicked into life. Zuckerman came out from under the hood, his face wreathed in a lean grin. 'She's all yours, Captain,' he laughed loudly. 'Fueled and ready to go.'

Pratt looked impressed. 'Where did you learn to hot wire?'

'I worked as a mechanic when I left school.'

'Hang on, I thought you said you were a tailor,' Pratt jibed.

'My father was a tailor, you putz. I was a mechanical apprentice.'

Pratt smacked his forehead. 'First you're a bum, then a tailor and now I find you're actually an auto thief. I'm getting confused here – somebody help me out.'

'Not a bum,' Zuckerman said testily as he climbed into the back of the Chevrolet. 'I have never in my life been a bum.'

With Tom at the wheel they slipped quietly out of town. McAndrew produced a map. 'I picked this up back there. I left a nickel on the cash desk. I left a note too – I said this man's army had requisitioned the car and they should ask Uncle Sam to give it back when the war's over.' He looked a little uncertain and added, 'I hope that was OK.'

'I guess it depends on who wins this war,' Tom replied.

They found a road that headed south east. It would get them away from the river and they would try to skirt round Albany and find the front line – if it existed. Maybe Zuckerman was right; maybe they'd never catch up with the retreating Americans.

******

Not one more step back. That was the order from Patton's headquarters.

Albany was gone; it had been a week of bitter fighting and in the end the Americans had been forced out, but they were learning. It was, Guderian observed, getting tougher to flush them out. They were becoming battle-hardened, resistance was fiercer, the cost of capturing territory was rising; the price of real estate was going up.

After Albany, the road lay open – now it was the turn of Peekskill.

A ragged stream of retreating military and fleeing refugees choked Highway 9, all heading south. It was a strange rag-tag bunch of fighting units. The remnants of Colonel Hamilton's men had fought a slow and desperate retreat all the way from Plattsburgh. Every mile had been bloody and slow; very few of his original force now survived though the number of men under his command had swelled in spite of the terrible losses. At each stand he had been joined by National Guard units and local militias, though they still lacked the heavy equipment it would take to stop Guderian's advance.

Patton addressed his commanders standing on a wooden stage in the Assembly Hall of Croton College. In more normal times students might have stood there to give their valedictory and receive their degrees. But college was out for the duration. The good folk of Croton had gone and those who were staying on were mostly too old for learning.

'I want every man behind this line,' he said banging a wooden pointer against a large map on the wall. 'This is where we are going to give Hitler's gang a good hard kick in the balls – one that they won't forget. I intend to show these assholes who is boss around here.'

The pointer hit the map just north of Croton. 'Buchanan,' he emphasized each word by banging the pointer on the chosen spot. 'Not perfect, but the best there is to be had. Look at the terrain; the Hudson on one side and swamp, forest and big rocks all over the other. Anything that gets into that will be in trouble – it's not good ground.'

He paused to let his audience think on it. Below the rostrum a sea of faces waited on what came next.

'If they want to get to New York – which we well know is their objective – then they have to come down here.' He scraped the pointer up and down Highway 9. 'There is no other route and this is the best position to defend from. Now, when I say defend, don't run off with any ideas that we are only planning to stop their advance. I'm going to start pushing them back up the road they just came down and we won't stop until we kick their asses back into Canada – and then on some more until we push these ugly bastards back into the Hudson Bay where they crawled out of it.'

He went silent again and waited for the questions. A colonel close to the front raised an arm. Patton nodded. 'What about the men coming down from Albany – will they keep fighting the rear guard action?'

'No. I've issued orders to get them to retreat into our defensive line as quickly as possible. In the intervening moment the air force will bomb the hell out of anything that comes out of Peekskill. That should give everyone time to get home.'

Another hand went up. 'I heard the Germans have death squads carrying out reprisal killings all over the place. Can we do anything to stop it?'

'No – not at this time but our intelligence boys are pinpointing the perpetrators. We know who they are and when we get to them we're gonna beat the living shit out of them.'

'General, sir,' a voice called from the back of the hall. 'I just got up from Valhalla with a medical training unit but there doesn't seem to be a location designated to set up the clearing station.'

'The clearing station will be up at Montrose, behind the Buchanan front line. See General Ambrose's staff – they'll fix you up. Okay now, all officers on logistics report to my office by 0800 hours tomorrow and let's get this show on the road.'

******

'Is this the clearing station?' Dottie looked at the field full of tents set out in rows behind the railroad depot.

'That's it,' the officer said, 'everybody under canvas for the time being. If the general's right we'll be setting up at the Presbyterian Hospital in Peekskill before you know it.'

'Well,' she said in a voice that spoke of consolation, 'I guess this close to the railroad track means we get the wounded in and out quickly.'

534

June 21, 1941
Montrose, NY
Dear Dad

So it's started. I was woken by the guns opening fire at four yesterday morning and they've been pounding away ever since. I'm not allowed to say much about it but I thought you and Mom would like to hear that I am well. The station is very quiet and we are waiting for the first casualties – but nothing yet. I am finding the experience not a little frightening but I am not the only one and I am sure I will measure up when the test comes.

I received my officer commission insignia this morning when I arrived, a little silver bar, which means I am now a lieutenant. All the girls automatically get promotion to officer rank, which they tell us is good for the morale of the men who come in on the stretchers. Of course it also means they have to do as they are told, which will make our job easier.

There's not much more I can say just now so I send my love to you and Mom.
Your affectionate daughter,
Dottie

'Casualties arriving – on the double,' somebody shouted as they ran along the rows of tents. Suddenly nurses and general medics were everywhere.

The first train from the front arrived. Men were coming in on stretchers having been patched up in the field stations. Now the wounds were being unwrapped and there was blood pouring out everywhere. It was no worse than she had expected but it shocked her nonetheless to see so many casualties. Their wounds were terrible; she had seen bad accident cases in her short time at Valhalla – victims of auto crashes, people with broken limbs from a bad fall. She had even been there when they brought in a gunshot wound – but this was another whole dimension in human misery. These were bodies that had been ripped, mangled and shattered – and the flow was relentless. By the end of her shift she was exhausted, mentally and physically; she wandered back to her tent and fell into her bunk where she slept until she was roused to meet the next incoming train and the pandemonium started all over again.

'Too many of them die,' she said to the nurse who lay in the next bunk. 'I never realized how terrible a war could be.'

'One of them who came in said that Patton's advance had bogged down. He said they were being "scythed down like summer wheat". Kind of poetic language for a soldier. He was just a dogface. There wasn't much we could do for him; he just slipped away, poor boy – babbling about his mom. It's odd how many of them do that – they're just kids most of them.'

******

A column of tanks had stopped just north of Buchanan. The ground that Patton had thought would give the enemy problems was now being used to their advantage. Somewhere up ahead, concealed by the woods and the uneven terrain, a group of anti-tank guns had stalled the advance; pinned down by the fire the lead tanks were taking a pounding. Two of them sat burning after taking direct hits. The column had stopped and pulled back, leaving the two stricken M3s to burn.

'General coming,' an officer shouted. A Jeep pulled up abruptly beside the front tank and Patton jumped out. Always a soldier to lead from the front, he had come forward to see the problem for himself.

The tank commander leaned down from his turret and saluted. 'They're in the woods up ahead, General. Self-propelled artillery, I'd hazard a guess; big calibre by the way they're punching holes in us.'

'We'll call down some artillery fire,' Patton called over his shoulder as he climbed back into the Jeep. 'See if Ira's got anything in the area,' he said to his NCO, 'maybe we can bomb the motherfuckers out of there.'

They bucked off down the road, Patton hanging on to the grab handle on the dash. 'Jesus, these Jeeps are a damn fine vehicle,' he shouted at the driver, laughing loudly. 'Good old American knowhow.'

He was happy in spite of the holdup at Buchanan. The wind had changed – he knew they were winning. For the first time they had halted the Germans and now they were pushing them back. It would be bloody, he accepted that, but in the final analysis he would win. All the days when they were losing, when they were taking terrible beatings, when they were fighting suicidal holding actions, slowing down the enemy advance – all that time he had used to build up his fighting force. Backing him now, waiting in the wings was the biggest concentration of men and machines ever assembled on the American continent. He knew that Admiral James and Joe King had wrested control of the North Atlantic; they were throttling Von Paulus's supply lines. Eaker's new Flying Fortresses were pounding the roads leading south; and, best of all for the airmen, their new weapon – the Mustang fighter – had finally given them a match for the German's much feared FW190 and Messerschmitt 109e.

Soon Von Paulus and Guderian would be on a diminishing return. The Germans had banked on being able to harness the factories all across Michigan and Illinois; the war production of hundreds of small foundries and engineering workshops were to provide parts to keep their machine running and repaired – but it wasn't happening. There was sabotage, go slow, stoppages – men walked away and didn't come back. The death squads of Neumann and Vogel were kept busy coercing men to comply but they would never be able to match what lay at the disposal of Patton. They would lose.

******

Chicago was simmering in the June sun; the temperature was up in the eighties. It was also simmering with resentment over the reprisal killings.

Of all the people in the city that summer the families of Giorgio Gagliardi and Tony Bardetti were probably among the most resentful and unhappy. The two families had talked just a few days after the slayings. They agreed they should consult with the Commission in New York and now they wanted a meeting. The Commission had been set up in the thirties to control the rash of vendettas and killings that had marked the mobs of that period, causing chaos and uncertainty. The families had got together and agreed that they should have a professional body which could properly regulate reprisals for the whole Mafia – all the families across the nation, put a stop to the random killings, end the vendettas. They had formed the Commission and elected its members. It was a criminal organization but it was strangely democratic and the families consented to be bound by it.

It wasn't long after the occupation that some family members rediscovered holes in the German lines, backroads and forest tracks where they could cross freely and at will, clandestine routes they had used back in the days of Prohibition to avoid the Feds. These were the wormholes through which the Bardettis passed to join hands with the Gagliardis in New York and there they organized a meeting with the Commission before which they laid their petition for a just retribution. Everyone agreed the actions of the Einsatzgruppe could not go unattended – there was honor at stake.

Von Paulus was outraged. He slammed the dossier he had just read hard down on the table. He got up and walked to the window and stood for a while, looking at the waters of the river. The tranquility of the scene helped him regain his composure.

'More killings. Six this time, all officers of the Wehrmacht, all in different parts of the city and all murders carried out by organized criminals.' Neumann stood rigidly to attention and said nothing. He knew who was responsible and he would exterminate them like vermin.

'I tell you, Obersturmbannführer,' Von Paulus shouted in frustration, pointing at the document he had just read. 'There are more criminal gangs in this one city than in the whole of Germany.'

Von Paulus returned to the table and seated himself in his chair. He picked up the dossier again and waved it at Neumann. 'Valuable officers,' he said irritably, 'one of them a colonel. Another was one of Guderian's top tank commanders. It's bad enough to lose a good man in battle but a criminal killing, murder – that is wasteful. Experienced, well trained officers cannot easily be replaced.'

'Permission to speak, General,' Neumann said resolutely.

'Speak.'

'We know who did this, Herr General. Vogel, my aide, is already rounding them up as we speak. He has gone with an SS assault group. We will teach these people to respect the Reich. We will make examples of them.'

******

The Bardetti home sat back from the road in a quiet street on the North Shore at Highland Park. It was a peaceful neighborhood. The house was still in mourning for its eldest son, Tony, and everywhere there was black crêpe de chine, black veils, black suits – nothing wore color. It was a week since the funeral and they expected a visit.

'They're coming,' a voice shouted from upstairs. Roberto, the youngest son, the one they all called Bambino, flew down the staircase jumping two steps at a time. In his hand he clutched a cumbersome pair of ships binoculars. At the bottom he was met by Ercule, his grandfather – the head of the house. The Bardettis were an old family, conservative in their ways and living three generations under one roof. They had lived in the neighborhood since 1893 and they had grown prosperous from their business interests. But since the invasion things had not been so good. The six o'clock curfew was ruining the club business – people had to get passes; city hall officials and local police chiefs were growing fat – huge bribes were demanded and paid. Those who for years had run the protection rackets now found they had to pay protection money themselves.

'How many?' Ercule asked the boy, patting him on the head.

'One car and a truck full of men.'

'How many men, Commandante?'

'I think there are ten. Maybe a few more – but not much more.'

'Now,' the old man said, 'I want you to go down into the cellar and stay there. Don't come up until I call you. Will you do that for your grandpappa?'

'Of course,' Bambino replied respectfully.

Ercule went into the large French-style salon that served as the family room. Sitting round in a semicircle the remainder of the family waited: Ivana, the grieving widow; her daughter, Christina; and her brothers Marco, Giovanni, Maurizio and Bruno. 'Ivana, take Christina and go to the cellar, I have sent Bambino down already. Go, join him and stay there until this thing is settled.'

He looked at his four sons sitting around him; beautiful young men in their prime each with a future in front of them and a life of promise to live out. Marco, the eldest son, had a wife and two beautiful daughters. Giovanni, the second boy, would marry next month into one of the most powerful families in Chicago. Maurizio so talented and gentle, now studying to be a musician – and

538

Bruno, the youngest; tough, the hard man of the quartet – he would have followed his father.

'Okay now,' he said, addressing the line of expectant faces. 'We have two choices. We can throw down on them as soon as they reach the house and take our chances that we kill them all – in which case, we have to leave our home and make our way down to New York because they will never leave us alone. Or I try to talk to them and buy our way out. Which is it to be? But hurry because they will be here any moment.'

One by one they agreed. 'Talk is best, papa.'

Ercule waited on the front steps.

The car that led the truck full of men entered the gateway to the garden and circled round the drive; it came to a halt a little way off. It was followed by the truck out of which men jumped. They spread out and took up firing positons. Two of them had stayed in the back of the truck manning a heavy machine gun, which they trained on the front of the house. Ercule came down the steps and walked towards the car and the man he took to be in command. Hauptscharführer Vogel turned to look into the eyes of the older man advancing towards him. A man with a camera who had been sitting in the back of the car now got out and began taking photos.

'Good morning,' Ercule called as he came closer. 'How can I help you gentlemen?'

Vogel pulled a pistol and leveled it at the grandfather of Bambino. 'You can help by getting into the car – and, by the way, we are not gentlemen.' He pushed the elderly Ercule into the back of the car with an unceremonious shove.

The car moved off towards the gate, but instead of leaving it stopped by the truck which now stood between the car and the house, giving it shelter. Vogel wound down the window and, leaning out, shouted something in German. The air burst with the sound of firing. Ercule sat and watched in horror and anger as his sons were rapidly despatched in the hail of fire. The boys put up a short futile fight; their arms were no match for what they faced. Rounds from the heavy machine gun burst through the walls and the timber casements, smashing glass and bodies alike, ripping apart everything that got in the way with shocking, irresistible violence and a deafening crescendo of noise. Like a violent storm, the enfilade of metal lashed the building, shredding everything it washed across; pieces of stone and brick flew off the façade showering down on the roof of Vogel's car twenty yards away. Chunks the size of a man's fist gouged out the masonry where heavy calibre rounds tore them off the building and hurled them scuttling and bouncing onto the driveway.

Then it was over.

Vogel got out of the car dragging Ercule behind him. The old man was crying like a child.

The SS men now moved from their firing positions and ran up the steps. They jumped through the frame where the ornate door had once proudly hung; it had been blown off its hinges and lay smashed on the floor. One by one the broken bodies of his sons were brought out and dumped on the ground in front of him.

'You see,' Vogel said smiling, 'there is nothing you can do for me.' He kicked the head of Marco the eldest boy. 'Nothing,' he repeated.

Ercule fell to his knees among the corpses and let out an awful wail.

'Ah,' said Vogel, as much to himself as the old man blubbering at his feet, 'this is a pleasant surprise. What have we here?' Ercule looked up to see Ivana, Christina and Bambino being herded out of the wreckage of the house.

'No! No, please,' he pleaded, staggering to his feet, 'for God's mercy.' He lunged at Vogel who cuffed him with the back of his hand, sending the old man back down to his knees.

Vogel looked at his new prize. Ivana stood with her arms around her two children, holding them close. She spat at Vogel and cursed him, calling him a cowardly pig. Vogel shrugged. What did he care for her curses? How many times had he been cursed by such women – he had lost count. They were only words and she would soon be made to swallow them. Her time would soon come to beg.

'Let me have the boy,' he said to her. The anger in her eyes now turned to fear and she held Bambino even closer. One of the soldiers wrenched him free and for the moment he stood in front of his mother motionless not knowing what he should do.

'Come here, little boy,' Vogel said in a soft, inviting voice. 'Come along – I'm not going to hurt you.'

Timidly Bambino walked the few steps to reach Vogel who bent down towards the boy and stroked his head, but it was a malignant gesture. Christina began to cry. It drew her to Vogel's attention.

'Hmm,' he wrung his hands together intertwining the fingers then, turning them outwards, cracked his knuckles. 'Take the girl,' he said to the man nearest to her. 'Let the men have some fun with her. Then when they have finished, shoot her.'

He smiled malignantly at Ivana, who screamed and then pleaded. 'Let them take me. Do what you like with me but please not my daughter – she is innocent.'

'Precisely,' Vogel smirked, 'that is what is so attractive, whereas you – you are old and not at all innocent – or attractive for that matter.'

In the house Christina was screaming, 'Mother, help me!' It was unbearable. All through the process Vogel stood holding on to Bambino, occasionally smiling at Ivana until there was the sound of a pistol shot and the screaming came to an abrupt halt. Ivana hung her head and wept bitterly.

'There,' he said, 'it's all over.' Now Bambino started to cry. He pulled away from Vogel and ran to his mother.

'Now, who will be next?' he asked. 'I shall spare one of you. You shall be the witness; you shall tell all your friends – all those criminals who have been murdering good German officers. I shall let one of you live to spread the message. Which one should I chose?'

Ercule had struggled to his feet. 'Spare the boy, in God's name. You can't kill a child.'

'Oh, but I can,' Vogel assured him. 'I have done it often – and why not? Boys grow up and become men and men become soldiers and soon I will find myself fighting them. So why not save myself the trouble?'

He turned to face Ercule. He raised his pistol and was about to hit him with it when he changed his mind and, turning back, stepped across to Ivana where he wrenched the boy from her grasp, pulled him away and, looking down at him, said, 'So, little boy, you choose. Tell me which one shall I shoot and which one shall I let live. You say – is it your mamma here or your grandpappa there? What do you say, hmm?'

At nearly, but not quite, seven years old the boy was old enough to comprehend what was happening but too young to understand the reasons. He stood there bewildered; he looked at his mother then at his grandfather, wondering how he could make such a decision. There must be some answer to this puzzle. He felt like he was back at school where the teacher sometimes made him stand out front and answer a hard question. This was the same and, as at school, he didn't know the answer. He didn't understand why grown-ups did this kind of thing.

The demand to give an answer was lifted from him when another car arrived through the gates and an officer got out. He looked like an honest man and Ivana instinctively called out, 'Please help us.'

Neumann had been given a message that Vogel was at his work and now he joined him. The two men talked for a bit; Bambino took the opportunity to run back to his mother where he clung on to her.

Neumann came over to them. 'Well, young man', he said cheerfully. 'I hear you can't make your mind up.' Bambino looked down at his feet – this is how it always was at school.

'So,' Neumann said, 'I shall help you.' He took the boy by the hand and with the other unclipped the flap on his holster, removed the pistol and shot Bambino through the head.

Ivana howled from a depth of despair that only a mother losing a child can feel. Then, letting loose her reason, she gave full voice to the anguish. 'Oh God, no!' she screamed. 'No, no, no! Oh God no.'

'He was too young to live, Vogel,' Neumann said in a matter of fact voice. 'The child would not have made a good witness.' Then he turned to Ercule and shot him twice in the chest.

'And he was too old. Let us go,' he commanded. 'She can clean up the mess. It will make the message clearer for her – something she will never forget.'

As the three vehicles left the wretched Ivana, kneeling on the round rocking back and forth, the limp and lifeless body of her son clutched to her, a few curious faces began to appear at the gate. They had heard the shooting and the screaming – now they came to see what it was about. Behind her in the debris of her life a fire had broken out and the house began to burn. For fifty years it had been the family home; now there was no family and no home. The men were all dead; only the women remained – cousins, wives, daughters – the line had finished. It was the end of Bardetti.

The lesson handed down by the executions was as Neumann had calculated; it struck fear into the minds and hearts of those who read about it in the newspapers or heard it broadcast by the propaganda-controlled radio. But as word of the outrage spread across the frontline and into the living rooms of unoccupied America it also endowed the two SS men with an unexpected legacy. It had reached the White House and now Roosevelt demanded it be stopped. He put a price on their heads and then he sent a message to Patton.

'I want these bastards, dead or alive, but preferably alive so I can put them on trial. Go in and get them George.'

CHAPTER 37

What Price a Hero

'Listen.'

Tom stopped the car. Nobody spoke; they wound down the windows. In the distance there was a sound like muted thunder. 'Artillery – where are we?' he asked McAndrew.

The corporal unfolded the map and spread it out across the dashboard. They had driven all day, patching their way south, zig-zagging down country backroads, sometimes no more than tracks trying to stay east of the Hudson and away from the German columns moving south. They had seen almost nothing – just the occasional farm wagon and a few cars. Nobody had stopped them and they had stopped for nobody. When they did come across isolated hamlets they drove straight through, stopping only once at a remote gas station to get fuel.

'It's kinda hard to say exactly, this map aint so smart. My best guess is somewhere west of Yorktown Heights.' He stuck his finger on the spot.

They all sat motionless and listened, trying to determine the direction of the sound. 'I think it's north from here,' Tom eventually said. 'I think we've broken through their line – I think that's coming from Peekskill.'

There was a whoop from the back of the car as Pratt and Zuckerman cheered the news. He turned the car west towards the firing and, as it got louder, he suddenly recognized his surroundings. 'We're in Cortlandt Manor. I know this place, I used to hunt here.'

They bumped along another unmade track that passed a lumber mill; the mill was deserted. The workers must have got the hell out of there, Tom thought to himself, probably a bit too close to the guns for their liking. The track merged with a logging road and continued to run eastwards. He stopped again to listen; the guns had gone silent.

'We must be close to the Albany Post Road,' he was saying to McAndrew as they pored over the map. McAndrew was about to agree but his response was wiped out by an ear-splitting bang that shook the car, making it jump. At first Tom thought they had come under fire.

'Get out, get out!' he yelled at the others as he dived out through the door, hit the ground and rolled away from the vehicle. He hugged the ground in search of cover. There was another violent bang and then another. He looked around and, seeing a ditch, ran to it and threw himself in; the others followed. There was a short lull and then they heard the sound of heavy diesel engines. He signaled to the others to stay down.

Keeping low, he climbed out of the ditch and almost ran into a gigantic armored vehicle. It was fitted with the biggest cannon he had ever seen. He pressed himself tight behind a tree. The engine noise abated to an idle, then stopped; it was almost on top of him. There was the clang of hatches being opened and then the sound of voices. Carefully he crouched down; slowly he inched his way along the ground, putting some distance between him and the vehicle. Far enough into the cover of the trees he worked his way back to the track and found the others.

'Tank destroyers,' he told them in hushed tones. 'The biggest gun on tracks I've ever seen, there're three of them – they're monsters. I think they're pulled back from wherever their firing position was and they're just sitting there in a big dished hollow.'

'What do you want we should do?' McAndrew asked.

'We get the fuck out of here, that's what we should do, Captain sir,' Zuckerman chipped in.

'For once I think that's right. There's nothing we can do here. We should try to get to our own lines. We must be close.'

They got back into the Chevrolet and Tom let go the hand brake. They had been sitting on an incline and now it served them well. He didn't want to start the engine too soon for fear the Germans would hear it so instead he let the car roll down the incline. Slowly, silently, it began gathering momentum; he let the speed build up until, sure he was far enough away, he crunched the gear lever into second and let out the clutch. There was a jerk and a sharp sideways skid on the back wheels as they resisted the dirt surface, then the engine fired and they were away. Tom put his foot hard to the floor, disregarding everything except the road in front.

'We don't want to do that too often,' he shouted, all the time watching the road ahead for signs of more problems. The track seemed to go on forever and with every twist he half expected to encounter Germans. Each time he came to a dogleg he held his breath; they could be anywhere in the woods waiting with an armed roadblock. Then he saw it – about a hundred yards away there was a road junction. Again he held his breath.

'This could be something,' he shouted as, without warning, they hit Highway 9. One minute they were on a logging track and the next they popped out onto a fully paved highway. He recognized it – but which side of the line were they? Within minutes he found the answer as a military truck came towards him. It had a big red cross painted on it – it was an ambulance, an American ambulance. 'Yeh man,' Pratt shouted from the back. Minutes later they were confronted by a group of white-helmeted men – military police. They had two jeeps pulled across the road and a makeshift barrier of wooden poles wrapped with barbed wire. A sergeant stepped forward and held up his hand. Tom clutched inside his shirt and came out with the dog tag hanging round his neck on a chain. They had made it home.

A master sergeant with a Thompson slung over his shoulder took him in to Patton, who was poring over a map with two senior officers. He recognized one of them. Colonel Hamilton looked up and seeing Tom greeted him warmly.

'Glad you made it,' he said, shaking his hand. 'I've told the General here about the gallant stand you and your men made at Cumberland Head.'

Patton grinned at him. 'We need more boys like you, Captain. I hear you did a damn fine job – there's a citation in this for you.'

'Thank you, sir,' Tom replied, 'but it was more than just me. I had three very good men with me.'

'I hear you came on some Kraut tank killers back in the woods. *Jagdpanzers*, my intelligence guys tell me – armor five inches thick. Can you pinpoint them on this map?'

Tom leaned over the table and traced his finger back along the line of the logging road towards Cortlandt, then up northwards in the direction of Peekskill.

'They were around here,' he said, stabbing the spot with his finger, 'close to 9 but further north than where we joined it.'

Patton was frustrated. They were blocking his advance and he couldn't find a way to flush them out. He had lost another two tanks to them. 'They keep damn well shuffling around and the air force can't seem to hit them,' he complained.

'Sir,' Tom said, 'would you mind if I made a suggestion?'

'Go on'.

'The easiest way to neutralize them is not by hitting the vehicles, sir. Take out the personnel and the vehicles are useless. My suggestion is you go for the men not the machines.'

'How would you do it?'

'A small squad, say, six men – all marksmen – and a sergeant who's seen action, so I can split the force if I need to. If we go back up that logging road we could work our way round behind them. The ground's swampy back there so they're limited in the tracks they use. All we need to do is find some high ground.'

'Okay, you've got it. Hamilton, give him what he needs and let's see if we can't get this show moving again.'

Tom found the others preparing to go back down to Croton for a rest and broke the news to them. Zuckerman and Pratt groaned, but McAndrew was up for it. They had an hour to get ready, he told McAndrew, and waited in his tent for the rest of the men. When the sergeant Hamilton sent him turned up with the three extra men he found himself confronted by a familiar face.

'Ransom,' he said, jumping up from his chair, a look of pleasant surprise on his face. 'Good to see you made it.'

'Pleased to see you got through too, sir.' The two men shook hands warmly.

'They made you up to sergeant – that's good. Did Colonel Hamilton tell you what the job is?'

'He only said some kind of mission behind the lines.'

They spent the next hour planning the strategy and briefing the men. As the sun slipped below the trees and the shroud of night drew across the sky they set out to retrace their route up the logging road. They went bundled into a Cadillac limousine, which Tom had borrowed from a brigadier. It was a strange way to go to war but it had a distinguishing merit: the engine was quiet, densely soundproofed and, as they rolled silently up the track, they knew it gave them the best chance of getting through where the rough hum of a truck would probably have given them away long before they reached their target.

They got as far north as Tom dared go without hitting the outlying districts of Peekskill. There was a half-moon shedding just enough light and once their eyes had become accustomed to it the car settled down to a good pace, all the time driving without lights for fear they might be seen by the enemy. Finally they left the car and set out on foot, making a slow circle around to where Tom figured he had last seen their quarry. In the silence of the night woodland he felt at home – as if he were back in better times tracking a buck with the others, Mike and Tony.

For a short spell he found himself wondering how they were. Mike now had a son; Tony was sitting on death row; and here he was about to kill or be killed. How strangely it had all turned out. It was far from what they had imagined in those happier days sitting in the diner drinking coffee – and then there was Dottie; maybe he would never see her again.

He was jerked out of his nostalgia by the sound of voices – German voices. They had found the quarry. He signaled to the others to wait back then, beckoning to Ransom, he picked his way towards the sounds until they came upon them in the same hollow where Tom had last encountered them. The machines were parked loosely in the hollow where there was enough firm ground to support them; their crews were spread out around them, some sitting on top of their vehicles, others sitting on the ground their backs leaning against the massive iron tracked wheels. On two sides the ground rose steeply in a thickly wooded scarp. On the third side there was a pond backing away into swamp. It was a safe, defensible position for their vehicles. The Germans had chosen it well; the woodland trees provided cover from the air.

Only on the fourth side was there any firm ground. This was the way they had come in and this is the way they would move out. The corridor was only wide enough to take one vehicle at a time so they would have to go in single file before they could fan out and choose their firing positions to ambush Patton's tanks. The flanks along the valley in which Highway 9 sat were flat and firm with a loose covering of trees and light shrubby growth – ideal for the Germans to operate in once they were out of their protective hollow. Each machine held a crew of five so they had fifteen to contend with.

'Just over two to one and we have surprise,' Tom whispered to Ransom. 'I like the odds – I think they run with us.'

'How do you want to play it?' Ransom asked, keeping his voice low. Tom cast his eye across the clearing. 'I want you up there,' he said, pointing to the ridge that marked the end of the box. 'Take Pratt and Zuckerman; they're our best marksmen. Position them well apart. I'll go in with McAndrew and the others head on – we'll make it a plain old-fashioned stick up. The shock should be enough to make them come quietly. You take one tank apiece – decide which and cover it. If anyone makes a move take 'em out.'

'It'd be less risky just to sit up there and pick them off.'

Tom shook his head. 'The quieter we can do this the better. For all I know they may have friends close by. Let's not advertise ourselves if we don't have to.'

They waited until three o'clock in the morning, just before first light, to get into position. Then, with McAndrew and the three other men whom Ransom had brought, Tom walked into the open end of the box where he found a sentry dozing against the first machine. Finding himself with a gun at his head, the man dropped his weapon and threw his hands in the air. Pushing him roughly forward to cover himself, Tom moved to another man who was sleeping and nudged him with his boot. The man woke abruptly and, like the sentry, gave up without resistance. Men were beginning to wake as Tom finally found what he was looking for – their force commander.

'Tell your men to surrender,' Tom said curtly, hoping the German would understand. He did – for once Tom thought the luck was running with him.

'You're surrounded,' he said. The German looked about him; Tom could see he was weighing up his chances. Others of them were looking edgy. The officer looked at the Americans confronting him: three privates, a corporal and a captain. Three to one, but they had the drop on them.

'Sergeant Ransom,' Tom shouted in the direction of the ridge, 'give 'em a couple of warning rounds.'

From two sides of the box half a dozen shots rained down on the armor of the machines, clanging and ricocheting off the hard metal. It was enough.

McAndrew and the others began rounding up the crews, searching them for weapons, throwing them into the pond as they found them.

Ransom came down from the ridge with Pratt and Zuckerman, who were both smiling like cats who'd just found the cream. 'Pratt, you and Zuckerman get the brigadier's Caddy and deliver it back to him. And no joy riding on the way – I want it back without a scratch.'

'At last a rich man,' Zuckerman joked. 'I get my own Cadillac – and it's a limmo.'

Pratt shook his head in a mock sad gesture. 'I liked it better when you were a bum.'

'Not a bum,' Zuckerman was protesting as they left. 'Not a bum – I was never a bum.'

'What do we do with this lot?' Ransom asked, waving his gun in the direction of the prisoners who were now sitting on the ground, cross-legged with their hands clasped behind their necks.

'Commandant', Tom shouted. The German stood up. 'Who are the drivers?' The officer called out three names and the men stood up.

'Get them into the machines,' Tom told McAndrew. 'Put one of our men in to guard them. The rest can ride on top where we can see them. It's the quickest way out of here.'

Patton's sergeant came on the double, saluted and almost breathlessly said, 'General, sir, it's Captain Jordan. He's back and he's got them – all three – they're parked up the road a bit with fifteen prisoners.'

That lunchtime there was a celebration in the officer's mess, but the day that had started so well finished badly. Colonel Hamilton brought him the news.

'I'm sorry to tell you this. Pratt and Zuckerman have bought it. One of our patrols found thc brigadier's car up on the logging track. It was pretty badly shot up – their bodies were inside. From the damage it looks like they were taken out by a Kraut air attack.'

'Thanks for letting me know,' Tom said with a touch of sadness; but this was war and people died and it was best not to get too close to anyone, so he made it a rule not to. 'Do you want me to write to the next of kin?'

'No, I'll do that.'

'They were good soldiers. They ought to get a citation – even if it is posthumous.'

'I'll make sure they're mentioned.'

As the day ended Patton called him to his office.

'Captain,' he said, pulling hard on a big Havana and blowing the smoke away over Tom's shoulder, letting it drift into the corner of the room. 'I need more men like you, men who can work on their own initiative. You did a damn fine job today – now I want you to do another one for me.'

He stood up and hauled on his belt, pulling his pants up tight around his arse. 'I'm making you up to major. It's a field commission because I need you to take a command and you'll need the rank to do that and I can't trust those tinhorn politicians in Congress to get off their flabby asses and do it in time – but I'll see to it it's permanent.'

He sucked on the Havana fiercely, making the end glow incandescent and sending a shower of sparks into the air. He stabbed the air with it, emphasizing what he was about to say; then he launched into it. 'I know you know what's been going on with these death squads across the line. I've read your file; you had first-hand experience with one of them before this war started.'

'Heinrich Neumann.'

'That's the asshole,' he said, stubbing out the last quarter of his Havana and grinding the butt hard into an ashtray like it was Neumann's face.

'You've read about what his gangs have been doing. He acts like he's immune, but he's not. The FBI has had him on their wanted list for killing one of their men, right here in Buchanan – but of course you know all about that.' Tom agreed he did.

'The President wants this bastard stopped, but he wants more. He wants to put him on trial – the American people want to see him put on trial. He's put a price on his head, though; that's more for public morale than anything else. I don't think anyone is about to rush out tomorrow and try to claim it.'

Patton paused for a moment. When he resumed it was with a note of satisfaction in his voice and a grim smile on his mouth. 'But now, see here, he's picked a fight with the Mafia – and handled right that could be real helpful.'

Tom pondered on what Patton had said and waited for more, not sure of where he fitted in to this. He didn't have to wait long.

'Right now we believe he's in Chicago and we'll know for sure when he commits his next filthy act. The President wants him lifted out of there and I've promised him I've got just the man to do it.'

He stopped again and, tilting his head slightly to one side, looked Tom full in the face. He raised his eyebrows and waited for the response. Tom knew he would not be allowed to refuse and, anyway, the idea of getting his hands on Neumann held not a little vengeful appeal; there were scores to settle.

'I'd be happy to do it, General – but I need a little time to think about how.'

'Okay, good. Take some time. In the meanwhile I arranged for you to have your office here in my headquarters. Let me know when you have a plan to discuss.'

Patton stood up; the meeting was at an end. 'Thank you, Major,' was all he said.

Tom saluted and left. Now all he needed was a plan but he wasn't sure what. He was bivouacked in one of the hundreds of tents crowded together in a canvas city that stretched all the way from Buchanan down to Montrose. Coming out of the HQ building he found a Transport Corps private leaning on the hood of a Ford pickup, taking a leisure break and smoking a cigarette in the late afternoon sunlight. The image it struck was one of pleasant tranquility – a quiet, peaceful contradiction of the reality that surrounded them. His mind flicked to images of Zuckerman and Pratt, their shot-up bodies now lying cold in canvas bags somewhere, waiting for their final journey home. There was no mileage in dwelling on it. He co-opted the young GI and they drove to collect his kit then moved it into a house where he had been billeted, close to the HQ where he was now to be operating.

That evening he went for a walk and as the last rays of the sun gave up their light to the darkening blue of a clear evening sky he found himself in Hoover Street, looking at the house he had been held in by Neumann and Cardy. He knew then that he should have killed Neumann when he had the opportunity. How different the whole of history might have been had he committed that single act. But, then again, he thought how different his life might have been if he had never chased after Neumann and Cardy that day at Crows Crossing. He stared for a while longer at the house until, telling himself he could go on saying 'what if' until infinity ran out and it would still not make a jot of difference, he idly ambled back to where he was staying.

Later he went to the small mess that had been set up at the back of HQ for Patton's staff and got himself a drink. Sitting at a table looking at the men around him he realized he knew none of them. It had been a feature of his career that he had been moved on like some nomad wandering back and forth, following the fortunes of the seasons ever since he came out of cadet school. Everyone he had known in 1st Armor was dead – only Ransom and McAndrew remained from Cumberland Head and even they were shortly to be moved on. It was as if nothing stuck to him. He was the essence of the proverbial rolling stone; there was no moss to be had.

Eventually he saw a face he knew – Colonel Hamilton together with another officer with the rank of captain. Hamilton was a man in his forties, dark-haired and sophisticated. He had a reputation for caring about his men and there were those who said he had taken the slaughter at Rouses Point personally and now bore the burden. Touches of grey were showing at the temples and his eyes looked heavier than they should for a man of his age. He pulled up a chair. 'Mind if we join you?' he said, indicating that they would sit with him.

'Of course,' Tom replied, starting to get up but Hamilton put out a hand.

'That's OK, stayed seated.' Hamilton sat down and raised the glass he already had in his hand. 'Here's to a short war and a good one,' he said cheerfully.

'I'll drink to that,' Tom agreed.

'This is Captain Menzies,' he gestured towards the other officer. 'He's from Army Press Corps.' Hamilton took a sip from his glass. 'The President is anxious to have some good news to get into the papers. Menzies here is looking for a story. He thinks you might provide it.'

Menzies leant forward, adopting a conspiratorial stance. 'We'd like to run with the story of how you captured those Germans. We need a good picture. I've seen those tanks you brought in – I think if we could get a mock-up of you and your boys marching down Highway 9 leading those tanks you captured that would make a fine front page. Pathe wants a news clip; *Stars and Stripes* like the story, and I think we could make the front cover of *Time*. What do you say?'

Hamilton nodded at Tom, indicating he would expect acceptance. 'Good,' said Hamilton before Tom had a chance to respond. 'That's settled then.'

Menzies downed his drink and stood up. 'Thank you, Major. I'll send someone round to your office in the morning to fix up the arrangements.'

'We have to do our bit for morale,' Hamilton said, seeing that Tom was not altogether happy with the idea of being pushed into the public eye again. Every time he was, it seemed there was a price to pay and something unwanted quickly followed.

'We're putting on a dance over in the school building on Saturday,' Hamilton said, changing the subject. 'We're inviting personnel from the Medical Clearing Station at Montrose. There's going to be a lot of pretty nurses there. You're a single man, aren't you?'

Tom admitted he was. Hamilton was quiet for a moment; the shadow of something crossing his mind showed in his face. He hesitated a little, then asked, 'I wonder if I could ask a favor of you.'

'Ask on, sir.'

'My daughter would like to go to this shindig but her husband is away in New York. Do you think it would be OK if I asked you to escort her – as a special favor? I realize it would cramp your style with some of those pretty nurses, but I would be most grateful.'

'It would be my pleasure, sir.'

The billet he had been allocated was the most comfortable place he had stayed since he'd left home and it reminded him of his own room in Peekskill. For the first time in a while he found himself with time to think about Holly and Martha. Word had come down from the front that the Germans had moved forward from Albany to confront Patton's advance, which had reached the fringes of the outer suburbs of Peekskill. For days beforehand elements of the American defenders of Albany had poured down Highway 9 together with a stream of refugees who, seeing the retreat, had themselves decided to gather what they could and flee.

The stories of the death squads, and the prospect of the *Einsatzgruppen* being among them, had terrorized much of the population of Peekskill and the young women, in particular, had been sent packing by their menfolk. A vulnerable woman in an occupied town was a liability most of their men wanted shipped out of reach.

******

Holly had watched all morning as the townsfolk began leaving; many had been panicked by the sight of their own soldiers heading steadfastly south.

'I'm going down to the railroad station to see what's going on,' he called out to Martha. She hurried to the door where he was putting Wheels on a leash and gave him the obligatory kiss he had to have before she would allow his departure.

'Don't be long.' She looked anxiously up and down the street; she had been talking only that morning with her friend and neighbor, Irene, who had told her how everyone believed the Germans would be there by tomorrow.

Holly reached the station after a few minutes' walk. Wheels, who had trotted along so purposefully beside him on a slack leash, now settled obediently on his rump and watched the frantic activity as people with too much baggage pushed and shoved their way onto each departing train. Everywhere military police were herding the crowd, channeling them into files, trying to impose some order on the jittery mass.

An MP looking across the street, and seeing this solitary figure with his dog sitting obediently beside him, walked over to ask if he could help. 'Are you planning to go along, grandpa?' he said patronizingly. Holly looked at him blankly.

'Do you want me to see if I can get you a place on the train? Do you have anyone with you?'

'No,' Holly replied in a subdued tone. 'I don't think I'll join that pack of fools – but thanks for the kind offer anyway.'

'Are you sure now?' the MP persisted.

'Why would I run – and where would I run to anyway? I live here – this is my home. I fought this lot in the last war. We didn't beat 'em by running away.' The MP shook his head, a little bemused by the sight that presented itself: a stubborn old man and a small dog.

'Cowards,' a voice from somewhere on the other side of the railroad office called out. Holly walked away and as he rounded the building to go back home he saw the heckler. A man of about his age was berating a convoy of army trucks that was heading out of town onto the Old Post Road in the direction Croton.

When he got home he told Martha about what he had seen. They sat in the afternoon sun and wondered how it had all come to this. They still had no news of Tom, though they no longer talked about it if they could avoid it – the prospect might have been too painful to contemplate. Instead they silently kept their hopes alive with the thought that he might still be out there somewhere. They were not to know that around that time he had not been so far away – skirting round Albany, trying to get to Patton's line.

Two days after his walk to the railroad station the first Germans arrived. The town had become almost ghostlike. Many had left, locking and boarding their houses as if they were anticipating a storm and would return later after it had passed. Others stayed inside and waited, not knowing what to expect. It was Sunday; Holly and Martha had been to church for the morning service. Inside, with only a handful in the congregation, they had all sung the hymns loudly; be strong, the minister had encouraged them, carry on as normal, avoid antagonizing the enemy. God will shelter you in this time of need.

They had reached the house and Holly was unlocking the front door when the sound of a vehicle caught his ear. He turned to see an armored car traveling slowly along Union Avenue. A man stood in the vehicle with his head and the top half of his torso exposed through the roof hatch. Every few yards, he threw a handful of small paper leaflets out onto the sidewalk. Holly stood there, watching the vehicle as it progressed to the end of the street then, turning left, it disappeared. Martha said nothing; she waited quietly on the top step of the porch as Holly descended to the drive then went out onto the street where he picked up one of the papers. He read it, screwed it up into a ball and tossed it back onto the sidewalk.

'It says this is now German territory,' he told Martha as he opened the front door. His voice had become flat and taciturn, and it worried her because this is the way he was before.

'Says we should stay inside for the next twenty-four hours and anyway not go out on the street after six o'clock; says they may shoot us if we do.' They went inside and he slumped into his armchair. He said nothing; the old hopelessness began to enfold itself around him – he was slipping back to the way he was. Martha made tea but it didn't seem to help; Wheels sat on his haunches looking confused, letting out little whining noises, sensing something was wrong but not knowing what.

There was more depressing news to come. The Germans announced they were setting up a civil administration to govern the town. They were calling for able-bodied men to form district committees – committees that would patrol the streets, enforce the curfew and inform on dissidents. Three days after the appearance of the armored car in Union Avenue men with red and black swastika armbands appeared on the streets as they had done in Chicago and all the other places where the Nazis had dug themselves in.

Late in the afternoon of the day the armbands appeared Martha told Holly she had something distressing to tell him. Alan, their mild mannered neighbor, was wearing the swastika. He had been appointed head of the local district committee. Alan, the timid clerk who was retired and wore starched collars, now roared like a lion and strutted like a peacock. When Holly challenged him he simply said he wanted a secure life and he believed the Germans would bring order and stability.

Later he told Martha he had lost his temper and told Alan that a man who sold his freedom so cheaply would gain nothing in the end but the bitter taste of slavery. Alan, he said sadly, had threatened to denounce him as a dissident.

The next day he heard artillery fire coming from the south and it lifted his mood. He had never thought to be cheered by the sound of guns, but he knew what it meant – America was fighting back.

CHAPTER 38

Return to Brunessemer

Tom arrived at his new office for his first morning and found McAndrew there waiting for him. 'I've been put on attachment to your office, Captain,' McAndrew told him. 'Colonel Hamilton's orders, sir.' He saluted and stood stiffly to attention.

'Stand easy,' Tom replied. He shuffled the papers on his desk then walked over to the window that looked on to the gardens outside. The day was bright again and warming up to be another hot one. He watched a small flock of birds squabbling in a tree; everything was quiet and normal – it hardly seemed possible that there was a war being fought just a bit on up the highway.

'See if you can rustle me up some coffee, will you Corporal. By the way, what do they call you when there's no one around?'

'Mac, Captain. Mostly they just call me Mac.'

'That'll do – welcome aboard, Mac.'

He sat down at the desk and looked at the blank sheet of paper in front of him – he still did not have a plan for Patton. McAndrew came back with the coffee. 'There's someone here to see you, Captain.'

'That'll be from the press team – wheel 'em in, Mac.'

In Tom's view it was a day wasted. They lined up the captured Jagdpanzers and hauled a group of German prisoners from a compound where they were being held for interrogation and lined them up in front. It didn't seem to matter to the press team that these were not the same men Tom had captured – it was a story. They rounded up Ransom and his three men to mount a mock guard. Then, with Tom and McAndrew, sitting atop they rumbled the three monsters and its dejected column down the road like a circus parade while a Pathe cameraman and some Army photographers got their pictures. Only Pratt and Zuckerman were missing – everything else was pretty much as it was.

After the show was over Tom went back to his office. He confronted the clean sheet of paper that sat staring up at him from his desk. He still didn't have a plan for Patton.

******

'I don't believe it,' Aly called out incredulously, as her husband packed a case with the clothes he thought he would need for his mission. 'Fred, it's Tommy, Tommy Jordan, right here on the front page of *Time*. Come and look at it.'

Fred stopped what he was doing and came to see what it was about. He took the magazine and, finding the page with the story, read it out loud to his wife. Irena had found a similar story in her morning edition of the *Washington Post*.

'Well, my gosh, just look at that. Who'd have guessed it when we first met him? Do you remember how shy he was then?' She waved the paper at the other two saying, 'I must tell Clementine – she'll be tickled pink by it. They've promoted him to major. That silly sister of yours should have stuck with him. You realize when this war charade thing is over he'll be one of the most eligible young men in America. He's got money, you know. Your father gave him god knows how much when they conveniently shoe-horned him out of Imperial Life. I bet they're regretting that one now. What an asset to have a hero like that on the board.'

Aly looked dismissively at her mother. 'This war is not over yet by a long stretch. He'll probably get himself killed taking risks like that – then how eligible would he be?'

'Well, so long as he finds himself a girl and gets married beforehand so there's someone to mourn him. That's what matters – rich, single and dead is such a waste.'

Aly shrugged off the remark as facile and typically Irena. She had her own man to think about and a baby due sometime in July. Now he was going away for who knew how long and getting involved in who knew what; she had no time for Irena's gossip or empty-headed society philosophy. All she could think of was how long they would be apart and what risks he might be taking. He saw how it played on her fears but there was nothing he could do or say to help; he had been sworn to secrecy both by Churchill and by Armitage before him; and now the FBI.

******

'Do come over, Clementine,' Irena said down the phone. 'There is a new range you could just die for at that couturier just off Penn Avenue; the one we went to a while back. I really do need a new outfit for the christening next month when Aly's baby comes. Besides I want to talk to you about Fred and what Mr Churchill is up to. Yes, I know it is probably all terribly secret but it'll be safe between us girls.'

She laughed and hung up. 'I'm going out,' she told Patience who had opened the front door for her. 'Please let Miss Alicia know. Tell her I'm meeting Mrs Churchill – we're going shopping.' Irena still referred to her daughter as Miss when addressing the staff. She had somehow not managed to adjust to the idea that Aly was now Mrs Loughlin and no longer her teenage daughter.

They were in the cocktail bar at the Willard, drinking an early afternoon Vermouth, when Clementine announced that they might be going back to England quite soon. 'Can you do that,' Irena looked surprised, 'with this war going on? How are things in England? Nobody tells me anything – least of all my son in law.'

Clementine threw up her hands as if to say don't ask me. 'I think there are improvements; I can't be sure because Winston rarely tells me anything until either he's done it and it's gone wrong or he's just about to do it and won't be dissuaded from it.'

'How very irritating men can be.'

'I do know one thing though. Since that ghastly man Mosley was assassinated Winston thinks the Germans have lost interest in Britain. He let slip that there may be some other agenda and Hitler doesn't want to waste his forces over there.'

'What sort of other agenda?'

'No idea, my dear – not a clue.'

Irena looked at her watch, it was almost five. 'Shall we have another of those rather nice Vermouths?'

'Why not? I think there's time. Listen, I've had quite a good idea; why don't I come over to you for supper this evening? I'll bring Winston along and you can grill him; he'll probably tell you more than he does me. He's a great fan of your husband, you know.'

'Well, he's a lousy judge of character is all I can say on that count. But never mind that, I would love for you to come over. He drinks champagne, your Winston, doesn't he?'

'My dear, he drinks anything – and often too much of it – except of course beer. He has no taste for the socialist drink, as he calls it.' They both laughed then went into a discussion about the hat Irena had purchased. She pulled it out of one of the many bags she had accumulated during the afternoon's excursion and placed it daintily on her head, inclining it at various angles for Clementine's critical appraisal.

Over supper Churchill cheerfully drank the champagne that was offered and made light conversation about how beautiful Washington was and how pleasant the long days were. Irena artfully moved the talk around to the war and what he thought about the position in England. On this he became more guarded, but it was clear from his tone that he was optimistic. His friend Alan Brooke was on the offensive, he said confidently. Admiral James now had control of British waters and the Kreigsmarine had been pushed away from the Channel right into the arms of Admiral King.

'The Royal Air Force has been most courageous, madam,' he said with an air of intimacy; Winston can be so charming when he wants to be, Clementine had once told Irena, and now she saw it for herself as he generously answered her every question.

'And it has been hard for them,' he went on, 'but now America is supplying us with a regular airlift of all manner of things, including their latest fighter, I believe the balance to have been tipped.' At this point he raised a glass and proposed an impromptu toast.

'Parky's boys,' he said jubilantly. Then he added that he was indeed looking forward to returning to his beloved country and reconstituting a proper democratic parliament. He had missed the House of Commons most dreadfully, he admitted, but with the puppet Mosley gone and the country effectively leaderless, now he considered was the proper time for him to return.

'I do not think that the British people will put up with this German Gauleiter for long and I am most sorry that Halifax is in the Tower, but he failed to get the country behind him. Let's hope he survives the experience. I'll let him out on good behavior,' he joked, and then shouted, 'Hah, it'll be good to be back on the floor of the House.'

The conversation flowed and Churchill made much of Patton's advance up the Hudson, but when Irena pointedly asked him what his plans were for her son-in-law his mood changed; it was as if a tap had been turned off. There was an awkward silence and nothing more was forthcoming.

It was late before the evening broke up and Irena was preparing to retire for the night when the door buzzer sounded. 'It's Mister Wendell,' Patience shouted to anyone who was close enough to hear. She took his coat and he wandered off into the drawing room where he poured himself a drink and fell back into one of Irena's stuffed sofas.

'What do you want at this hour?' she asked him frostily.

'It's Carey, Mother. She needs help; she's drinking too much and I worry about her sanity. We have to do something.'

'Well, it's a bit late to be worrying about her sanity. That went off with the birds a long time ago.'

******

On the night of the officer's dance Tom put on his dress uniform and made his way to the Hamilton quarters. His mind was elsewhere and he was not enthusiastic; he was preoccupied and still struggling with Patton's plan. The front line had moved forward but the Germans were well dug in and resistance was stubborn. He was in no mood to dance, least of all with somebody else's wife. Mrs Hamilton presented her daughter, Lucille; she was a tall, slender young woman with a lot of glossy blond hair and a good figure. This was not what Tom had been expecting. When they entered the dance hall they looked for all the world as if they had just stepped out of the silver screen. If there had been a Hollywood scout in the house he would have snapped them up for sure, one junior officer at the bar was heard to say. As they stepped onto the floor another voice with a face unseen said, 'Now that's what I call a good-looking couple.'

As the evening progressed Lucille began to dance closer to him than was comfortable and when, after a slow waltz towards the later part of the evening, she clung round his neck and placed her head on his shoulder he decided it had all got too much. He could feel more of her body than was good for him; this was the daughter of his Commanding Officer and she was married, for god's sake. This could lead him to places he didn't want to go. He made his excuses and headed for the men's room.

On the margin of the crowded hall two nurses stood each with a drink in hand and a man in attendance. Dottie had decided she would go because she had seen his picture in the forces paper *Stars and Stripes*. It had made a big deal out of 'everyone's hero', Major Tom Jordan, and when her friend at the clearing station had shown her the story and Dottie said she knew him, there was nothing for it but she would have to go and introduce them.

She had agreed but omitted to tell her friend just how well she had known Tom. Now, on the edge of the dance floor, she was a witness to the intimacy between the Hero and his partner. Inside she felt a flood of anguish rise up and consume her. Of course, she told herself, he was bound to have found another girl – and why not? She'd given him the brush off, hadn't she.

'It was a mistake to come here – I have to leave,' she said, apologizing. As she fled back to the clearing station the anguish turned to anger and she physically slapped her own face hard – so hard it stung. A vision of the last parting at Grand Central when she had sent him packing loomed up in front of her. How could she have done such a thing? How in god's name could she? She kept saying over and over 'you stupid woman, how could you have sent him away like that', but in the end it did no good and, with reason finally conquering emotion, she rationalized that he had no notion of how she felt and it was inevitable he would find someone else.

At six the alarm went and she made her way to the mess where she got breakfast. The nurse who had been with her the previous night came and sat alongside her. Laverne was a brash New Yorker with hair as dark as Dottie was blond and an accent as strong as her will. She was from the Bronx and before arriving at the clearing station they had met only once briefly at Valhalla where she had been a nursing assistant in the local hospital. At Montrose they had

559

formed a close working relationship, though it had not become a close friendship.

'What the hell was that about last night?'

Dottie stared at her plate, pushing a morsel of waffle round and round, mopping up a small pool of syrup. 'It was a mistake, that's all – I should never have gone.'

The other girl raised a quizzical eyebrow. 'Go on.'

'Do we have time for this?' Dottie said, not sure she wanted to get deeper into the conversation?

'We've got twenty minutes – tell me, I'm fascinated to hear. After all it was my evening too.'

'We used to see each other. We were engaged; he bought me the most beautiful ring with a diamond the size of a dime and rubies all around it.'

'Rubies,' the other girl chipped in unenthusiastically. 'Not good – they say rubies bring sorrow.' Dottie brushed away the remark.

'So what happened? Let me guess – the heel walked leaving you with a broken heart and a rock that sounds like it's worth a pile.'

'No, it wasn't like that. I gave back the ring; I dumped him.'

Laverne laughed. 'You're kidding me. Nobody could be that stupid.'

'I could,' she said, sighing glumly and she set out the whole story of Grand Central and the clipping from the *New York Times* and then the discovery that nothing was as it seemed.

Laverne slurped noisily on her coffee, thought for a moment, then said, 'Listen honey, I'm no expert but I'd say he was probably caught on the rebound and the floozy he was wearing round his neck last night was nothing more than compensation. He's probably pining his heart out for you right now. Why don't you go talk to him?' Dottie was not convinced, but it made her feel better to have shared the full story with somebody else.

There was a call on the address system that announced another trainload was arriving from the front. The fighting had been bitter – they would have a busy, bloody, day in front of them. There was little time for her own feelings and she buried her thoughts. Half way through the day she lost the first of her patients, a young lieutenant. He died in the comfort of a morphine dream as the blood ebbed away from his wounds. There were too many bullet holes to staunch and in the end she just sat next to him, his hand gently holding onto hers as the tide of his life ebbed from him, and then he was still. He was the first of three that day and, although she had become inured to it, she somehow never quite managed to throw off the pang of sadness each death brought with it. She sutured, transfused and plugged wounds, set bones in casts and helped boys get up onto their crutches and into a transport for home. At the end of her shift she was exhausted; but although the patients got up and moved on, the scraps and fragments of their broken lives stayed on to dwell with her.

'You can't let it get to you,' a well-meaning captain told her as they struggled to save a boy of no more than 18. 'Remember, you're a professional and these guys rely on you to stay cool and focused.'

At this point she drew consolation from the fact that she was a respected member of a team who saved more lives than they lost and she tried not to let her private life get in the way. She knew she had to push her emotional demands into second place, but they were there all the same. Deep down and pushed well to the back of her mind there was always Tom and what might have been.

As she prepared for an early night she resigned herself to the reality that it was probably all over between them, but she would go to see him just for the sake of what had been – and to say how sorry she was for what had happened on Grand Central.

******

A Pontiac Silver Streak painted army brown with a crystal Indian-head hood mascot and white wall tires picked its way slowly through the tide of traffic that was coming south towards it – traffic that was trying to get into New York City. There were a lot of upstate plates; these were refugees fleeing the fighting around Peekskill, their belongings strapped to roofs and fenders. Desperate faces peered out through grimy windshields, many of them not knowing where they were going or where they might end up. They just wanted to get as far away from the enemy as they could. Driven by fear – stories of rape and rumors of mass shootings – more than logic, they honked their way through traffic jams, bottlenecks, flats and breakdowns, clogging the incoming routes and creating a traffic cop's nightmare. The army driver cursed every time a car strayed onto his side of the highway as faster, more able vehicles tried to hustle past the slower ones. The passenger was a man of about 30, wearing a trilby hat and a tweed jacket; he bore the hallmarks of an academic. As the Pontiac swerved and lurched against the oncoming flow it occurred to the passenger that he had witnessed this in Europe as the Germans had sped across the Low Countries; the sight made him uneasy.

After Yonkers the route heading north split. The Pontiac took the left fork onto Highway 9 and pointed its long snout in the direction of Hastings. It was a quieter drive, the traffic thinned and as the road hugged the banks of the Hudson, the houses and buildings gave way to tree-lined verges of grass and shrubs. The driver relaxed and his passenger admired the scenery.

561

It was the same road along which Tom and Carey had driven in another summer but neither the sergeant driving the car nor the passenger sitting languidly in the back seat had any notion of what had been.

As they left Hastings they were stopped by a highway patrol and the passenger was asked for his papers. They said they were on the lookout for fifth columnists and aliens, especially people of German extraction who might be trying to get across the line.

From Hastings they made good time up to the next small town on the route. As they entered the outskirts they passed a large sign – WELCOME TO DOBBS FERRY. They drove into the town and through the center. The passenger, looking out of the side window, saw a hotel; he made a mental note – it might be a good place to get a drink some time. Then they turned right, heading away from the river and as the town gave way to woodlands the driver announced they had arrived, turning sharply through a large set of iron gates onto a sweeping gravel drive. There, in front of a big white house, two more identical brown Pontiacs were parked.

The driver jumped out smartly and got round to the door but he was too late and his passenger was already standing on the bottom step, looking up at the grand modern house.   Brunessemer, he said to himself as he read the inscription over the doorway; he thought it an odd name.

A woman in her middle age anticipated their arrival and opened the door before he got to it. 'I'm the housekeeper,' she announced. 'My name is Vera. If you would please follow me and I'll show you to your room. Tell your driver to go to the kitchen; the other drivers are there – I'll get him something to eat.'

They walked across the black-and-white marble floor, past the place where Gerhardt had been shot through the head, then mounted the grand staircase. 'The rest of the party are in the library,' Vera said coldly as she let him into a bedroom. 'Mr Loughlin has asked you to join them there as soon as you are unpacked.'

Then she added as an afterthought, 'Please try not to break anything.'

******

Corporal McAndrew was sitting at his desk in the outer office reading *Stars and Stripes* and admiring the picture of him sitting on top of the German tank killer when a private from the gatehouse entered and said there was a visitor for the Major – a female.

'Wheel her in, Mac,' Tom said, wondering who it was that had come to see him. For a moment his mind sprung to the woman from the Army Press Corps wanting another interview, but when the door opened it revealed an unexpected surprise.

There was an awkward silence as she sat down. 'Carey,' Tom said in a voice that displayed total bewilderment. 'What are you doing here? How did you find me?'

Her face bore a tiny, agonized, apologetic little smile. 'You're famous,' she said in not much more than a whisper. 'You're all over the papers and on the newsreels – it wasn't hard.' She looked around his office for a moment. 'You've done well,' she said. 'I'm glad – you deserved it.'

'Thanks,' he said without conviction. He was beginning to feel distinctly uncomfortable and wondered what she was there for. There was another short silence.

'It's nice to see you again,' he said, but it was a meaningless platitude because it struck him that he was now quite indifferent to the frail, rather tired-looking figure who sat across the table from him. This was not Carey as he had remembered her. There was the slightly cloying smell of alcohol on her breath and he quickly realized she had already been drinking. It crossed his mind that she had probably needed a boost to her courage to make this meeting with him. She was not at ease; this was not the light and carefree Carey he had known. If he had any emotion for her now it was pity.

Then it came out – all in a rush, so fast that he couldn't at first take it in.

'Oh Tommy,' she said, her eyes wetting with the start of tears, 'please help me. I'm desperate. Nobody wants to help me. Mother won't ask her friend Clementine; the Churchills are close to President Roosevelt but she won't ask them. I don't know what to do any more. I need your help – please.'

He took her hand and clasped it with both of his, trying to calm her. 'What is it you want?' He had meant to say it sympathetically but there was a firmness in his voice which stopped her short so that she pulled away from him and, dabbing at her eyes with the back of her hand, regained her composure.

'Tony is on death row – you know that don't you?' It sounded awful when she said it so starkly like that and, for the first time since he had heard about it, he was struck by the full weight of what that meant.

'Yes I know,' he said in a subdued voice. 'Mike told me – but I don't see how I could help.'

'You could help. I know you could – you know General Patton, you're a hero, people will listen to you. Please, Tommy. The President could grant him an amnesty or whatever it is they call it. I know you hate us and you think I betrayed you, but it wasn't like you think – we couldn't help ourselves. Please, please help us. Oh god, it's so awful, I can't bare it any longer. Please help.' She stuttered to a halt and let the tears flood down her face. Her makeup-smudged red eyes now implored him to do something.

'Couldn't your father do something? He's well connected, knows a lot of the right people. After all, he managed to get me out of that darn difficult position. He went right to Hoover, as I understand it.'

The tears stopped. The way she looked at him changed. A mixture of disbelief and indignation spread across her face and she started to shake her head slowly from side to side. 'You don't know do you,' she said in a tone of disbelief. 'My god, you don't know.'

He looked at her bewildered. 'Know what?'

'That wasn't my father who got you out of there. That pious bastard wouldn't lift a finger to help anyone if there wasn't a profit in it. It was Tony, didn't anyone tell you that? It was his Uncle Giorgio who pulled the strings that saved you – not my father!'

He hadn't seen that one coming – for a moment it rendered him speechless. 'Couldn't you ask him to help?' He grasped at the straw it offered because he couldn't think of anything else and it was the first thought that entered his head. 'After all, if he can get to Hoover that must be good, mustn't it.'

Her face dropped again and in a voice that was beginning to crack she said wearily, 'He's dead. The Germans killed him a while back – he was with a friend in Chicago.'

Now his head was spinning. How in the name of hell was he going to be able to help was all that ran through his mind as he sat in front of this distraught, sad creature who he now hardly recognized. He had only one thought and that was to get her out of his office.

'Look,' he said, trying to find some palatable words, some placebo to keep her calm for the moment until he could gather his thoughts, 'I'll see what I can do. I'm not sure about Patton but there are others – I'll try.'

He took her hand again and patted it. 'I'll try.'

For a long time after she left her words nagged at his mind. He tried to imagine what it must be like for Tony sitting in a cell waiting for his fate as the hours passed; going to sleep, dreaming another world, then waking to reality. It took him back to the house on Hoover Street and he tried to equate it with his friend of the past, but that was different – Tony was an institutional prisoner and there would be no hope of escape. It took a while for it to sink in but when he eventually got there he no longer held any bitterness against the two of them, only sadness at their plight and the way in which things had ended. However shit he thought his life had been, however bad the luck dished out to him, it was nothing compared with the rotten hand they had been dealt. He would try. He had no idea how for the moment but he would try; he would give it his best shot.

'Colonel wants to see you, sir – his office as soon as you're free, he says.'

'Thanks, Mac.' It was the diversion he needed. He put Carey out of his mind and went back to thinking about Patton's plan; ideas were at last beginning to form.

'Come in, Tom,' Hamilton said, standing up to greet him. 'Have a seat. How are you?'

'Thank you sir, I'm good.'

'The reason I've called you in is General Patton has asked that you attend a briefing, Tom. It's away from HQ so you'll need a driver – you can see my sergeant on the way out. Now, I wondered if you'd come up with anything for the operation because I think he's expecting something today. I thought you should know in advance – that's all. Wouldn't like you to be caught on the hop, as they say.'

'That's appreciated, sir.'

'No, no. I like to look after my officers – it's good for morale.'

'Well I'm working on it.'

'Good to hear it. Oh, and thanks for looking after Lucille; she seems to have enjoyed herself.'

'It was my pleasure, sir.'

******

'Where are we going, private?' he asked the driver as they turned right and joined the highway heading south.

'Dobbs Ferry, sir. A big country house, a real rock pile of a place called Brunessemer.'

******

When Vera saw him standing there at the door she greeted him with a broad smile. 'You don't know how good it is to see you again, sir,' she said warmly. 'The house is overrun at the moment with these.' She waved her hand in the direction of the MPs who now seemed to be spread liberally around the grounds.

'Thanks Vera,' he said. Inside he paused in the hallway to look at the familiar surroundings. 'It feels kinda weird to be back here again.'

'They're in the drawing room, sir – you know the way.'

As he stepped inside the room five faces turned to look at him: Patton he was expecting; Dobson, a captain from Intelligence he'd met at HQ in Buchanan; Jones, the FBI agent, he knew as well. Then there was Fred Loughlin – that was a surprise, he had not expected to see him; and, finally, an unknown man who seemed, by their intimacy, to be with Loughlin.

'Good you're here, Major,' Patton said. 'Gentlemen, this is Major Tom Jordan. Some of you will have read about him. He's going to be sharing his ideas on how we get this thing done.' Loughlin moved forward and greeted him.

'Tom, my dear chap, it's good to see you again. Let me introduce you. This is a colleague from England.'

The unknown man shook Tom by the hand. 'Richard Grainger,' he said, 'British Intelligence – MI5.'

Patton led the way into the dining room where coffee and soft drinks had been laid out on the table.

'Let's get down to business,' he said brusquely. 'You are all aware that our Commander in Chief, the President, wants this man Newman or Neumann put on trial for multiple charges of murder. Our British friends here have their own reasons for getting in on the act.' He looked directly at Loughlin and Grainger.

'Neumann commissioned the murder of a senior British policeman and his wife,' Grainger said. 'We have good reason to believe the infamous Dr Mueller actually carried out the killings. We also want him on charges of the attempted kidnap of Mr Churchill while in Britain.'

'You will also be aware,' Loughlin added, addressing his remarks to Jones, 'that he murdered a British undercover agent in Washington.'

Jones, who had his arms folded on the table in front of him, now leaned forward. 'Let me summarize. The FBI has a warrant for Neumann's arrest for the murder of Agent Parkes. We also want his sidekick, Joseph Mueller, for multiple murders. We would like to have them both publicly tried and executed. We also want them on charges of spying. If we can get them, these guys are gonna fry.'

He looked around the table, then added, 'First we have to find them, of course, but I leave that to you, gentlemen,' and here he waved a hand in the direction of Tom and Loughlin.

'Second, the President has put a hundred thousand dollar reward on the head of Neumann, dead or alive. This was a mistake because we don't want his dead body; we can't publicly try a dead man.' He looked over at Tom again. 'You have to get to him before some trigger-happy bounty hunter brings us his head on a plate.'

He paused for a moment, then went on, 'and just to complicate things for us, Neumann has picked a fight with the Mafia. One of his squads wiped out a whole family in Chicago and they're gonna be looking for revenge. So we need to get him before the mob bumps him off.'

He paused again. 'Fortunately it's not all bad news. We know the Chicago families have routes through the lines; we know they have been meeting with the Commission in New York since the killings. We are presently trying to talk with them. We're gonna need their help in this business – especially we need to persuade them not to kill Neumann. We have an agent working on it.'

Somewhere in Tom's mind a dime dropped into a slot, rolled silently down an inclined groove where it knocked out a pin that released a spring that flipped a switch to complete a circuit – and a light went on. He had hit the jackpot. It is a rare occasion in life, and   especially it was so in Tom's life, that things work out so that everything drops into place – the perfect fit. For once it had – they had the dream team: Tom, the hunter who would find their quarry; Loughlin, the detective who knew the quarry, how they operated and spoke the language; Grainger, the expert in making things disappear. To this Tom could now add a fourth dimension.

'I think I have a plan,' he told Patton, 'but it requires some flexible thinking.'

CHAPTER 39

Redemption
The office they sat in was panelled in dark stained oak. It was large and dimly lit. The windows looked out onto a skyline of grim grey industrial-style buildings and the light coming through them appeared cold even though outside it was another warm bright June morning. A man in a grey check suit and matching waistcoat sat behind a solid oak desk. The worn brown leather set into its top had an air of humorless no nonsense; ink stains marked the passing of careless moments with a pen and there were several traces of rings left by hot cups that should have been set down on saucers. Tom found himself wondering how many death sentences had been signed on its tawdry scuffed surface.

The man behind the desk carefully read the paper he had in front of him, then satisfied that it was properly set out he turned it through 180 degrees and pushed it across the leather top to Tom.

'I'd be grateful if you would sign this, Major Jordan,' he said politely, offering a fountain pen at the same moment. Tom glanced at the paper, signed it and handed it back.

'Thank you,' the man said and got up, taking the paper with him. 'My officer here will take you to the front gate if you would be so good as to wait there.' He shook hands with Tom and nodded politely to Carey.

Tom looked at her and wondered how she would take it. Her face was tense and her fists clenched tightly into two little balls.

'I want you to promise me you won't lose control.' She said nothing but nodded her head vigorously – like a child who wasn't really paying attention.

The man in the grey checks appeared with his paper again. At first Tom thought something had gone wrong; Carey looked anxious. A prison officer came through the inner gate and there behind him was Tony. He was thinner; the clothes he had gone in with no longer quite fitted him and his face had a slightly gaunt appearance – but it was the same Tony. Seeing him there in his ill-fitting suit looking a bit like a scarecrow, Tom realized he had no appetite for a grudge.

'He's in your care now,' the man in the grey checks said, handing Tom the piece of paper which he had earlier signed. 'I hope the Army makes good use of you Gagliardi. Good luck anyway.'

'Thank you, Warden,' Tony replied, still a little fazed by the speed of the change in his life. The three of them walked out into the full glare of the summer sunlight.

When they reached the car Tom embraced his old friend, slapping him on the back as if nothing had happened. Then, standing aside, he held the rear door open like a guard of honor at a wedding feast and ushered them both in. As he drove away he knocked the rear view mirror out of line to give them what privacy he could.

'I've got you one night, then you report to my office for duty,' he called over his shoulder.

They left Ossining and drove south, leaving the grim fortress of Sing Sing prison to its remaining unfortunate inmates. Tony never looked back. Instead he buried Carey in his arms and thought how good it was to have a life again, to have a future. He would survive this war; he knew he would and then they would get married, raise a family and live a quiet life till they were old and had surrounded themselves with grandchildren.

They drove as far as Dobbs Ferry and stopped at the hotel. Carey didn't want to stay at Brunessemer so they took a room there. It must have crossed Tony's mind, Tom thought – the irony of it – the very hotel in which he and Tony had started their search for the most beautiful girl in town.

When they had gone upstairs the barman, seeing Tom standing there and recognizing him, said, 'Say, you're Major Tommy Jordan, aren't you? An honor to have you in my bar.' He grabbed Tom's hand and pumped it up and down vigorously. 'Are those folks friends of yours?'

'They are.'

'Should I know them? He looks familiar, and what about her?'

Tom resisted a smile. 'He is my oldest friend – and she's the most beautiful girl in Dobbs Ferry. I came looking for her once, a long time ago, but in the end it was my friend who found her.'

A smile of recognition spread across the barman's face. 'Of course,' he exclaimed, 'I remember. Well darn me, it's you.'

'That it is,' Tom replied, 'that it is,' and he then left for Brunessemer where he had plans to hatch with Grainger and Loughlin.

CHAPTER 40

The Road to Chicago, July 1941

The battle for the Peekskill suburbs had become a stalemate but Von Paulus was for the moment content they had brought the American advance to a halt. Nevertheless, he did not like the position in which Guderian now placed his forces. The front was too narrow, constrained by the Hudson on one side and the bad terrain on the other. While this kept the Germans locked up, it also stopped the Americans from breaking in. Frustrated, Patton decided he would throw out a pincer across to the eastern seaboard in an attempt to cut into the side of the German line on land that was flatter and favored his tanks. But in doing so he raised the prospect of weakening his forces at the Peekskill bottleneck; he was still short of men but the balance was slowly being redressed and the quality of his draftees was improving as training programs took hold.

If Patton was drawing the Germans over to the east, Tom argued, then they should go west and up through Indiana. It was wooded country, riddled with back roads and farm tracks – they were unlikely to run into any German patrols and once they had reached the lakes they could just stick on the main highway until they reached Chicago. They could hide in the traffic; they would just be another vehicle moving west.

They left early the following day in an old Model 18 Ford with fake Illinois license plates and a flat head V8 grumbling away under the hood. It put Tom in mind of the Chrysler – it was a jalopy but it was anonymous. More than that it was a good car to ride the country lanes and rough farm tracks they would need to use if they were to cross the line and penetrate the German-held zone without detection. A few miles from Dobbs Ferry and just before Tarrytown they turned onto the Tappen Zee Bridge where they crossed the Hudson. The Germans, they knew, were in Monroe just a few miles to the north, but they had been blocked from coming further south on that side of the valley, first by the mountainous country, but more now by the presence of Stilwell's forces who were waging their guerrilla-style war along the southern edge of the German-occupied zone. And so the front line was fluid and hard to define, with both sides probing the defences until they made contact, then skirmishing and withdrawing.

On the afternoon of their departure, not long after they had set out, there was another visitor at HQ.

'I'm sorry, miss,' McAndrew told her. 'I'm afraid the Major left on operations this morning.' She had wanted to know what kind of operations but, of course, he would not tell her. She knew it would be something dangerous and it entered her thoughts that she may never see him again. Back at the clearing station Dottie made up her mind not to think of him anymore; there was no point in it. She had a 48-hour furlough coming up and she would go home and spend it with her parents. When this war was over she would go back to Valhalla and finish her studies. If she met somebody that would be good, but she was not going to let it get in the way of her life. She would have a career in medicine and if that was all there was, that would be enough.

Seven hours out they reached Columbus, still south of the German line. It had taken them longer than they thought; the route had been crawling with US army patrols checking everything that moved. This was General Omar Bradley's First Army Corps getting beefed up. They concluded they should have stayed further south; it was longer but they would have saved time. They still had another four or five hours before they could cross so it would be touch and go getting into the Chicago safe house before the six o'clock curfew.

Somewhere west of Dayton they took a turn off the main highway. The road narrowed and in place of the flat arable plains woodland started to crowd in on them. The land was getting hilly, the road got narrower until it became a track with the leaves of the saplings that spread out from its edges slapping against the windows.

'There's a small town up ahead,' Tony said. 'There's a gas station. I'll call my cousin – he'll get us in.'

It wasn't so much a town, more a collection of buildings where two dirt roads crossed each other. There was a general store on one corner, a feed barn on another, and a gas station on a third. After that there were a handful of tarpaper and clapboard shacks with picket fences and wire keeping the hens and the livestock from roaming. Tom pulled the car to a halt outside the gas station and Tony got out; he disappeared inside. A mangy dog that had been lying in a dust bath taking the sun came over and sniffed at the wheels. It lifted a leg and pissed on a tire, then satisfied he had marked it as his property went and fell into the dust bath again.

A short while later Tony reappeared. 'About a quarter hour,' he said. At that Loughlin and Grainger both got out to stretch their legs.

'What was it you did back there in England?' Tony asked casually.

'He used to steal things,' Loughlin said wryly.

'What sort of things?'

Grainger took out a pack of cigarettes and offered them around. 'Just things,' he said, dismissing the question.

'Were you any good at it?' Tony persisted.

'I once liberated eight tanks from a rather careless German major.'

'Impressive.'

'He also steals people,' Loughlin said, butting into the conversation. 'That's his specialty.'

'Where I come from we call that kidnapping,' Tony said, with an air of mock disapproval.

Grainger laughed. 'That's why I'm here, dear boy.' The sound of an approaching vehicle brought the conversation to a halt.

'Help's arrived,' Tony said as a car appeared at the crossroads. A ratty-looking station wagon with rust-eaten doors and dented fenders stopped next to them. It was a typical farmer's car – uncared for and used for everything. The driver got out. He embraced Tony who spoke briefly with him, then they left.

They followed the station wagon for a short distance, then turning off the road both vehicles started along what was no more than a line of two ruts left by others who had passed that way. After half an hour of bumping and lurching along unmade tracks, through gullies and across farmer's fields, they arrived at a homestead. They were in the back of beyond. The countryside around was flat but thick with green corn that stood higher than a man and stretched for as far as the eye could see.

'This is as far as I go,' their guide said. A man came out of the house with a roughly drawn map – just a few lines on a scrap of paper with the names of some towns scratched on it. While he pointed Tony in the direction they had to go, a woman in an old-fashioned cotton dress with a Dutch sun bonnet appeared from the kitchen of the house and pressed a brown paper sack on Tom.

'Here,' she said in a low voice, 'something to see you along the road. Avoid stopping at the diners and the truck stops,' she advised earnestly. 'Germans are everywhere all over.' She handed them a quart jug. 'Cider, it's good – made it m'self. Good luck.'

The man with the map added a last warning. 'The first town you hit is McGuffey, just here,' he laid a finger on the spot. 'You might find Germans, there again you might not. Hereabouts is no man's land. Sometimes we see them, sometimes we see our own guys – just depends. From McGuffey just keep going north. Don't go further west. Keep away from Fort Wayne – Germans everywhere, they're thicker on the ground in those parts than the hairs on my old dog.'

He broke off and looked up at the sky, shading his eyes from the sun. 'You should make Toledo inside the hour but you might be pushed to get to Chicago before the curfew. You take care now.'

They took their leave and, driving through the cover of the corn, found their way out onto the road to McGuffey. The town was small and the road ran straight into Main Street, past a bank and a handful of stores then out the other side. There were not a lot of people in evidence and Tom felt comfortable that they were still probably in a peaceful area. They left the town and picked up yet another near deserted country road. They were on a relatively straight stretch when in the distance ahead they saw another vehicle join the road from a side turning.

'I don't like the look of that,' Tom muttered to Tony as they started to close on the vehicle in front.

'Slow down,' Tony suggested. 'Let it get some distance on us.'

Tom eased up until the vehicle was lost from sight around a bend. He slowed the Ford to a halt and stopped. He turned to Grainger and Loughlin in the back. 'Germans, I think. Looked like some kind of armored car but I couldn't be sure at that distance.'

'We need to get on,' was all Loughlin said. Grainger said nothing, but nodded in agreement.

As they rounded the bend the road ahead was clear. They began to climb through some small hills with the road switching through a series of tight bends.

'Shit, Germans,' Tom shouted, as they came out of particularly sharp switchback. There they were blocking the road in front of them. Looking back over his shoulder, Tom realized they must have been watching them from above as they made the long, slow climb. When they drew closer he saw it was the same armored car that had been in front of them.

A soldier with a steel helmet and a rifle got out and stood with one hand held up to stop them. He leveled his rifle as Tom stopped the car short of him. As he advanced another two emerged from behind the armored car.

'I don't like this,' Tom said under his breath, 'we could do without it. Fred, can you get to the guns?'

Loughlin and Grainger shuffled forward, trying to lift the back seat under which they had concealed their weapons. Loughlin pushed his hand down through the gap they had managed to open; he could feel the cold metal of a barrel but his fingers weren't able to get a good enough grip to pull it through. The first soldier was now level with the windshield. He motioned with the barrel of his rifle for them to get out. The other two were moving towards them, rifles at the ready. Tom opened his door and cautiously stepped out, raising his hands to show he had no weapons. An officer now got out of the armored car, the final member of the crew, Tom calculated. He had a pistol in his hand.

Grainger opened his door and slowly he got out, leaving Loughlin with just a little more space to pull one of the guns clear. In his mind Loughlin had a plan but it would be touch and go; he was pretty sure at least one of them would be killed in the shootout. At last he had the weapon cradled in his lap. The first soldier stood back a bit, distracted as Tony now opened his door and slowly got out. It was now or never Loughlin told himself.

He opened the door and got out. The bark of a rifle shot split the air and for a split second everything froze in time. Tom watched as the officer jerked backwards, his pistol falling from his grip. He saw the soldier nearest to him raise his weapon and looked for cover but there was none. There was another crack, followed by several more in quick succession. Grainger and Tony had ducked down behind the cover of the car as Loughlin finally got clear of his side and brought a Thompson up to his shoulder. He looked around, not quite understanding the scene. All four Germans were lying in the road but he hadn't got off a shot. He stood for a moment not believing what he saw. Tom, who a few seconds earlier had expected to die, now started to move towards the lifeless bodies. Grainger and Tony came out from behind the car. There was an eerie silence.

'What happened?' Grainger called out uncertainly into the now quiet air. They looked around for an explanation but there was nothing – the place was deserted.

The answer came from the roadside a few moments later, as a man armed with a machine gun appeared, pointing it menacingly at Tom. Another armed man stepped out from the scrub bushes that lined the road, then another and another; in all they were nine in number. They were not Germans.

'Stay where you are, boys,' the lead man shouted as he advanced towards Tom. 'Just want to see what we've got here.' He looked over at Loughlin who now had the Thompson at the ready.

'I think it would be good for your health if you just laid that to one side,' he said, motioning to Loughlin to put down the gun. Loughlin laid it carefully against the car and stood away from it.

'Who are you?' Tom asked as the man reached him and, as he did so, he noticed he had a band of calico cloth buttoned tightly around his right bicep. It had been cut from a small flag and bore remnants of the Stars and Stripes on it. Another of them had tied the same material around his head as a bandana. They were wearing the flag.

In the background he caught sight of some of the men now moving the bodies off into the scrub where they had begun to strip them of their uniforms.

'Who I am is not your business,' the man with the Stars and Stripes said belligerently. 'The point is who are you and what exactly are you doing on this here particular stretch of road, huh?'

Should he tell him? Tom had his doubts, but these were clearly not Germans. They were some kind of partisan group. Could he trust them? Should he risk it and blow away his cover? His options were limited.

'Major Thomas Jordan, United States Army,' he finally said. 'We're here on a special mission for General Patton.'

The other man's expression became less aggressive. 'Can you prove it?'

574

'Nope, you'll have to take my word for it.'

The other man thought for a moment, then smiled. 'Colonel Don Hall, Jefferson Irregulars – the only Americans fighting north of Bradley's phoney front line. Welcome to the real war.'

'What will you do with this lot?' Tom pointed to the armored car and the pile of guns and uniforms next to it.

'Booty,' Hall grinned. 'We'll dig a small hole and bury the bodies. I like to do things decently – not like them Germans. If things had gone the other way they'd have hung our bodies up at the side of the road and let the birds pick bits off us. We'll hide the car until we find a use for it – maybe paint the banner on it.'

'Can I have two of the uniforms – to fit us,' Grainger butted in pointing to himself and Loughlin and glancing sideways at Tom. 'They could be useful.'

'Sure, why not.'

After they had cleared away all signs of the events that had happened they sat for a while and talked. They drank the cider the woman with the Dutch bonnet had given them and Hall explained how there were now a growing number of clandestine militias being formed in enemy territory, fighting hit-and-run raids on isolated German patrols. He knew of one as far away as Duluth and another in Pittsburg. They were springing up all over, but there still weren't as many as there could be. 'We've got the guns,' Hall insisted, 'all we lack is the courage to use them. Why we could whip these blockheads easy with just the guns a man has in his house. Everybody's got one; the country's awash with guns. That's our strength,' and he laughed out loud at this. 'Hell, you can't occupy a country like this for long without getting your head blowed off by someone.'

They took their leave to a cheer and shouts of good luck from the militia.

'Why Jefferson's Irregulars?' Tom asked as his parting shot.

'He's the man we owe it to,' Hall said thoughtfully and he wrinkled his nose. 'A right to bear arms,' he added wistfully, 'that was him who gave it us.'

Before they reached Toledo they stopped in a quiet spot. Loughlin put on the uniform of the dead German officer. With his fluent grasp of the language he was confident he could pass himself off as a member of the Wehrmacht. Now they would be able to travel after curfew. Grainger put on the other uniform – a corporal; he would pass himself off as Loughlin's driver. His German was adequate but not more than that. The tunic was baggy but if nobody looked too closely it would do the job. Tom and Tony climbed in the back.

If they were stopped it was agreed Loughlin would do the talking. The story was he had recruited the two in the back as collaborators. As Tom put on one of the red swastika armbands worn by collaborators, which they had brought with them as their disguise, the thought crossed his mind that they might have had some hard talking to do if Hall and his men had searched the car and found them. They might even have joined the Germans in their shallow grave.

'You'd better keep schtum and just mumble if we're challenged,' Loughlin told Grainger. 'You speak German with an Oxford accent. Did you know that?'

'Not surprising', Grainger retorted. 'I did my degree there. Got a First in Classical Greek – not a lot of use really.'

The rest of the journey went without incident until they crossed the state line where they came on a road block. It was tucked away so it couldn't be seen until they were right on it. A soldier stepped out with a paddle that read STOP, but when he saw the officer sitting up front he stood back, saluted and waved them through.

By 7.30, with the evening light still strong and the air still warm, they parked the Ford in the secluded driveway of a solidly built mansion in a respectable quarter of Chicago and went inside to lay their plans.

CHAPTER 41

Retribution

Ivana Bardetti – in widow's weeds and still mourning her husband, her children, her brothers and her father – demanded retribution. The Commission had heard her and granted the right. Now she needed someone to deliver it for her.

The Gagliardi family were more than just associates of the Bardettis. Giorgio Gagliardi had been a close friend of Tony the Beast. There was a true quid pro quo in the contract that was now proposed. Tony Gagliardi had been the go-between and, although it was a most unnatural marriage with the strangest of bedfellows, it would work because it served all parties' interests equally.

Tony was now the true representative of the Gagliardi clan who wanted payment for the death of Giorgio. With the help of the Bardettis he had got Tom and the others into Chicago and it would be down to him and his family to get them back out again when the time came.

For their part Tom, Loughlin and Grainger would deliver Vogel into the hands of Ivana. There was only one sticking point: the Gagliardis wanted Neumann killed into the bargain. Tom proposed they strike a compromise: if they stepped away from that position and got him across the line with Neumann alive then, Tom promised, they would get the reward.

Hands were shaken and the contract was sealed.

******

Von Paulus stood shaking his head in disbelief. Guderian looked at him dumbfounded.

'I find this very hard to comprehend, my friend,' he said. 'Sit down, Heinz. Have some coffee; it's real and there's not a lot of it to be had any more.'

Both men sat and looked at the orders that had just been delivered by the Berlin courier. Hitler was about to launch Barbarossa, his invasion of Russia. Von Paulus had been recalled to command the sixth army. Guderian would take over.

'This is pure madness – to open another front when we are stretched in this campaign here. How does he expect us to keep delivering him victories when he keeps tying our hands together?' Von Paulus sipped at his coffee, his sharp features drawn with a look of exasperation. 'I need more men just to police the territory we have conquered and he asks me to expand the campaign and at the same time he steals my resources.'

'We could take men away from policing,' Guderian suggested, 'offer bigger bounties to our cooperative friends; increase civilian patrols – that might release up to a hundred thousand more front line men and officers.'

Von Paulus did not like the idea. Most of the collaborators would defect the minute they sensed any weakness, he told Guderian. It was already proving difficult to keep order in the cities with those collaborators they already had. They were unreliable and then there was the new threat: militias, irregular armed civilians. Paramilitary groups were forming; men in makeshift uniforms, living rough, roaming the woods and the hills. They appeared, struck and disappeared like phantoms.

'This isn't like France or Poland,' he observed with pessimism. 'This resistance is endemic; it's wholesale and it's well armed. That's the problem, it's too well armed. I've ordered the immediate execution of anyone captured.'

Von Paulus could not stop the resistance without a change in strategy. He thought they should increase the work of the *Einsatzgruppen* and he said so, but Guderian was not convinced. 'These retribution killings are causing resentment. They will just stoke the fires of our problems.'

Von Paulus changed the subject. 'Let's leave the SS to do their work and we'll get on with ours. How is the battle for Peekskill?'

At this Guderian looked more sanguine. 'It's been improved by Patton's encircling move to the east. He is like us Friedrich – stretched and short of men. He has robbed his position in Peekskill to attack our flank. I think the advantage is with us.'

'But for how long?' Von Paulus was becoming morose on the subject. 'He can resupply – we are having increasing difficulty. I've heard reports that Raeder is losing control of the Atlantic. That leaves us with only the domestic capacity. Local industries are not producing what they should. They are inefficient and plagued by criminal sabotage. But that is not the real problem. It's men we need – where are we going to get them from?

******

In Washington they couldn't believe their luck when the news came through. Marshall immediately reported to the White House.

'They're going to lose,' he told Roosevelt.

Churchill announced that he would pack his bags and go back to England as soon as a flight could be arranged. Everywhere the mood was lifted – except for

578

one household: Carey and Aly both had men out there somewhere. Neither knew if they would ever see them again.

******

The main lobby of the Drake Hotel was busy. Guests and visitors milled about looking for information at the concierge desk, ordering coffee, picking up newspapers and wandering off looking for friends or colleagues. In this crowd a captain wearing infantry insignia made his way to the main desk where he tapped on a silver domed bell and waited to be attended.

'I am looking for Obersturmbannführer Neumann,' he told the girl who had come to ask him what he wanted. 'I have an appointment,' he added. The girl thought his accent a little strange but he was a foreigner and they all sounded odd to her American ears. She rang up to the room of Herr Neumann, but after a minute without an answer she concluded he must be out.

'You can ask the concierge,' she said, pointing to a man in a black waistcoat with fine gold stripes on it.

'I'm afraid Herr Neumann is no longer with us,' the concierge said rather disdainfully. 'You could try enquiring at City Hall. I believe he has an office there.' The officer thanked him and left.

Ten minutes later the same officer presented his military warrant card to a civilian clerk in a reception kiosk on the main concourse of City Hall. The young man squinted at him through thick-lensed spectacles and asked politely after the reason for his visit.

'I need to see Obersturmbannführer Neumann urgently,' he said. 'I have some vital information for him.'

'Very well. Wait over there,' the young man said, pointing to a row of chairs against a wall. 'I shall see if he is available.'

The Captain waited and after a short while saw a man dressed in the uniform of a staff officer walking towards him. He stood up as the officer got to him and, raising an arm in salute, said, 'Heil Hitler,' but without any real conviction.

'The Obersturmbannführer is no longer in Chicago,' the staff officer said. 'He has gone to Albany where there are problems for him to deal with. However,' he added, 'his assistant, Hauptscharführer Vogel, is still in Chicago and you could try leaving a message if it is a matter of importance.'

The Captain looked agitated, saying that the matter was urgent; he knew of plot to abduct the Obersturmbannführer and he knew the whereabouts of the plotters. The staff officer on hearing this merely said that there were constant threats against the Obersturmbannführer but they usually came to nothing. However, he would contact Vogel by telephone and inform him.

'Wait here,' he said. 'Hauptscharführer Vogel may wish to speak with you.'

The Captain sat down again and waited.

Vogel was an ugly man, as ugly in his features as in his nature. His mouth was pinched with a cruel, leering expression when he spoke. He was not as tall as Neumann and slightly built. He wore his hair shaved tight to the scalp. His neck muscles were scrawny like a turkey and the skin sagged under his chin, partly obscuring the line of his jaw. His eyes appeared dark and beadlike and peered through steel-framed glasses. It was a callous, cruel look that had terrified many of his victims.

He brought this gaze onto the Captain and asked what this was about.

'I have uncovered a plot against Obersturmbannführer Neumann. I think they plan to abduct and kill him.'

Vogel looked bored. 'There are many such plots. I have reports of them every day. They mostly amount to nothing – loud-mouthed boasting in beer halls.'

'I think this is different.'

'Tell me, how did you uncover this plot?'

'One of the collaborators has infiltrated the gang. They are Mafia.'

At the mention of Mafia Vogel shifted his stance. 'Mafia,' he sounded interested. 'Where is this collaborator now?'

'On the North Shore. I asked him to wait there. He was frightened to come here – he thinks they may be watching him.'

Vogel put his hand over his mouth and squeezed at his cheeks with his bony fingers. 'All right,' he said, 'let's go to see this informer of yours. Wait here, I'll get a driver.'

The Captain looked happier – now at least perhaps something might get done. 'I'll wait in my car. My driver is parked out front. You can follow me.'

'You have a car,' Vogel said, brightening. 'Good, let's use that. It will save time.'

The Captain led the way to where the car was standing at the curb. There was a corporal sitting at the wheel ready to go. He opened the rear door and they both got into the back.

It took no more than a few minutes to reach the North Shore esplanade. There they saw a man with a swastika armband standing on the sidewalk. As the car came to a halt the man opened the door. He looked at the two sitting in the back then over his shoulder to see if he was being watched.

'Move over,' he said to Vogel, and got in beside him.

'So,' Vogel said. 'What is it you have to tell me?'

'You won't much like it.'

'Why don't you tell me and I'll let you know if it offends me,' Vogel sneered.

The collaborator pulled a machine pistol from under his coat and pushed it hard into Vogel's neck.

'We are going to kill you; how does that sound.'

Vogel went pale.

'I said you wouldn't like it.'

'Who are you?' Vogel snarled at him. 'You won't get away with this. Kill me and you'll be hunted like a dog. Neumann will come after you.'

'I'm rather banking on that,' the other man said, pushing the muzzle harder into Vogel's neck. 'And my name, since you have asked, is Tom Jordan – Major Tom Jordan of the United States Army – and you are my prisoner.'

'Hauptmann!' he snapped at the Captain next to him.

'Sorry, old chap,' came the reply. 'Wrong again, I'm afraid.' He pulled a pistol from his pocket and rested it in the crook of his arm pointing the muzzle at Vogel. 'Fred Loughlin – British Special Branch. Hard luck.'

As the car drove up to the house and Vogel saw the shattered and burned ruin of the old Bardetti mansion he knew this was the end of the game for him. Standing on the charred steps, Ivana Bardetti and her three sisters-in-law waited for their revenge. Tom got out, then turned and pulled Vogel out by one arm and forced him to kneel at the foot of the stairs.

Ivana Bardetti walked up to him. She held a short, thick piece of lead pipe in one hand and an automatic pistol in the other. She hit him hard in the face with the pipe, breaking his front teeth. He rocked under the ferocity of the blow but stayed upright.

'Putana!' she shouted at him in Italian. 'Pimp – this is for my son.' She fired a single round at his genitals. Vogel was stunned by the shock but as the pain flooded in he let out a howl and clutched at the wound.

Ivana contemplated what she might do next to this pig who had tormented her as he had killed her son and violated her daughter. She wanted him to suffer; she had prayed for this moment but now God had delivered him into her hands she hesitated.

'I can't do it,' she said, turning to the wives of her brothers. 'Let's put an end to it.' She raised the gun to his head and put a single shot into his brain – just as they had done to her boy, Bambino.

Vogel fell in a pathetic heap with the blood pumping out of the hole in his head. The other women came down the steps to the corpse and one by one they kicked it in ritual revenge.

'You'll need to do something with the body,' Tom said. 'Neumann isn't here. We have to go to Albany. We can't bring him all the way back here; it's too risky. I'll ask you to get a message to Patton for me, but we'll find another way to get back across the line.'

Ivana said nothing but indicated with a slow movement of her head, a barely perceptible nod, that she understood.

She took Tony's hand then embraced him. 'Our family will always be in your debt,' she said hoarsely through her tear-choked throat, then she kissed him.

One by one she thanked the others. Finally, with everything said that could be said and with no other gestures to be made, they got back into the car and left. It was a three-day drive to Albany and there was a risk of being stopped if they traveled after six. They would have to find out-of-the-way hotels to put up overnight, but there was nothing for it; if Neumann was in Albany that's where they had to go.

Nobody spoke as they drove back towards the east. Tom contemplated what he had witnessed and found it hard to come to terms with what had happened. Killing is an ugly thing. Not for the first time it was dawning on him; he was beginning to understand how Holly had come to feel the way he did about guns.

The journey to Albany was easier than they had imagined. They were stopped twice on the second day. The first occasion was a road block as they crossed a state line but the guard there was too bored to do more than give their documents a cursory glance. Later that day, as they passed through the small town of Bowling Green, they picked up the sound of a siren.

'Well, damn me if it isn't the sheriff's men,' Grainger said, looking in the rear view mirror. 'What do you suppose is exercising them?'

'I think,' Tom said laconically, 'you were probably speeding – and I noticed you jumped a stop sign around Main Street.'

'I'll try to be more careful, dear boy. Shall I pull over?'

'Probably better had.'

The police car drew up behind them and an officer got out, taking out his ticket book getting ready to issue. 'OK,' he said, as Grainger rolled down the window, 'what's your hurry, bub?' but then when he looked in and saw the German uniforms he changed his mind and simply bid them a good afternoon and a safe journey.

'I like this,' Grainger joked. 'Wish I could do that in Blighty.' The others were less amused; it was a risk they didn't want to take a second time. Grainger was told to watch his speed and stop for red lights.

As the journey progressed another problem insinuated itself into Tom's thoughts. Albany was smaller than Chicago but there they'd had contacts and they'd known where Vogel was to be found. In Albany they knew no one and Neumann could be anywhere. It was not as if they could just walk into City Hall and ask his whereabouts.

Inside the car the only noise for hours was the rumble of the V8; conversation had long since dried up – only occasional remarks on the passing scenery punctuated the silence. The tedium of endless stretches of monotonous tarmac and distant horizons left the passengers in a torpor; nobody had said anything for miles. Each man was tied up in his own world of speculation about the next phase of the mission. It was Tony who was first to open the conversation.

Coincidentally his mind had been wrestling with the same dilemma that was exercising Tom's mind.

'I don't know if any of you guys have been thinking what I've been thinking,' he said in a very deliberate voice, 'but how exactly do we find Neumann? I mean he could be damn near anywhere in this town. For all we know he may not even be here anymore; he may be someplace else by now.'

'Good point,' Tom agreed. 'I've been thinking about that myself.'

'I've been thinking too,' Loughlin joined in. 'We need to get rid of this car – and while we're about it these uniforms too.'

'How so?' Tom asked.

'Look at it this way. Vogel must have been missed by now; they'll be looking for him. If anyone working at the City Hall saw him leave with me then they'll be looking for the car too. The same goes for this kit. I'm carrying dead man's documents and someone will be out there looking for him; same goes for Grainger here. We need to find a new car – steal one if necessary.'

'No need,' Tom said. 'I've got a car not a hundred miles from here, just down the road at Peekskill. It's sat on my parents drive.'

'Okay,' Tony acknowledged, 'that solves that one. So what about Neumann? Where do we go with that?'

'Simple,' Grainger called across his shoulder. 'If we can't find Neumann then why not let Neumann find us? Same rat trap that caught Vogel. Lay out some bait and when he takes it – snap!'

'So what do we use as bait?'

'I'd have thought that was obvious – our gallant Major, Thomas Jordan. From what I've heard he would be irresistible to brother Heinrich.'

'You know what? I think he's right. The only way to deal with this is to announce my arrival.' Nobody said anything for a while as each one of them thought through what came next.

'In that case,' Grainger eventually said, picking up the previous conversation, 'don't dump the fancy dress. I think we'll need the uniforms for just a while longer.' Then, laughing, he added, 'I *must* find a tailor – this jacket fits me like a sack.'

******

Martha was standing at the kitchen sink, attending to her chores and thinking of nothing in particular, when the sound of footsteps coming onto the porch made her look up. At first she didn't believe what she saw.

'Oh, my Good Lord,' she said under her breath, and then with a scream of delight she ran to the front door, yelling as she went. 'Holly, Holly, come quick it's Tom! He's alive, oh my sainted aunts he's alive!'

583

She flung the front door open and there he was – the son she thought she had lost, her only child she thought she would never see again. She just grabbed him, threw her arms around him, then let all her emotions burst out of her with tears of joy punctuated with little whoops of laughter. She hugged him, then looked at him, then hugged him again until finally Holly and Wheels came into the hallway and he pulled one arm free to reach out and touch his father. Holly shed a silent, stoic tear but quickly wiped it away. They moved into the living room with Martha still clinging to one arm for fear he might dissolve, Holly with a hand on his shoulder, gently patting it, and Wheels carried away by the commotion and excitement, barking and jumping up at him for attention.

He sat on the sofa and for an hour or two he told them everything that had happened while Martha made endless tea and Wheels, having taken up a place of importance on Tom's lap, looked from one human to another, wondering what it was all about but sensing it was something good.

'I can't stay long,' Tom said, 'this is sort of unofficial leave. I have a job to do then I have to get back to Patton. Try not to worry too much. We are winning – this will be over soon.'

He took the car a couple of blocks away and left it at the side of the road, coming back for the station wagon. As he reversed onto Union Street he thought he saw the front room curtains move in the neighbor's house. Holly had warned him about Alan.

As he took Route 9 back up to Albany a plan was beginning to take shape in his mind. Tony's connections had found them a safe house on the southern edge of the suburbs – quiet and convenient. 'I have a plan,' Tom told the others, 'we can set our trap in Peekskill.

At eight the following morning they left the house to merge with the commuting traffic and worked their way south. As they got closer to Peekskill the nature of the traffic changed. Wehrmacht vehicles now dominated, running up and down the route like a busy column of ants – new stuff going south and old damaged stuff coming north. 'Lot of wreckage coming up,' Tom observed casually. 'The fighting must be stiff.'

As they reached the outer suburban fringe they could hear the rumble of heavy guns. Ahead of them the traffic had stopped moving.

'Someone better take a look,' Loughlin said. He got out and went forward to investigate. Still dressed in the stolen uniform, he walked uneasily to the head of the queue knowing that at any time he could be challenged. By now he knew they must be on the lookout for someone of his description and the documents would easily give him away.

'It's a road block,' he told them as he got back into the car. 'They're checking everyone's documents. I think it's time to abandon ship.'

'Right, everyone out,' Tom said. 'We have to fake a breakdown. I can't think of anything else.' They pushed the car to the side of the road, lifted the hood and propped it up on a stay. Tony pulled a canvas bag out of the back and they set out to walk a little way back up the highway till they came to a side street.

'It's a bit of a hike but this should get us into the center,' Tom said. Things improved with a rare piece of good luck. A man in a flat back pickup truck slowed down and asked if they wanted a lift. His left arm was bound with a red and black swastika band and seeing the German officer and his retinue thought he might score a few points by making himself useful.

'That's good of you, neighbor,' Tom said and got in with the driver. 'Just follow my directions, it aint far.' Loughlin and the others climbed into the back and sat on a pile of lumber. The pickup dropped them in Union Avenue on the corner with Bay Street, a short distance from Tom's home. As they got down from the truck the driver asked the officer to put in a good word for him. Loughlin thanked him and said he would be sure to make a note of who he was and pass it on.

They watched while the pickup reached the end of the street and was out of sight. 'You and Grainger take the avenue. They don't know you so they won't get suspicious. I'll circle round the back with Tony.'

Bay Street was no more than a track running behind the yards of the houses on Union Avenue – it was flanked by woods and open space. Midway along, Tom found the yard they were looking for; up against its close-boarded fence was a mature oak tree. The tree had been there as long as he could remember; he had climbed it often as a boy and way up in the branches was still the remnant of a tree house he had built there. The tree was now in full leaf so the timber platform that he had built from solid planks all those years ago could not be seen. But he knew it was there – every fall slowly revealed it and in the depth of winter he could see its hard black silhouette lodged in a hefty crook of the gnarled branches from his bedroom window. The full thick canopy would give good cover.

Tom cupped both hands for Tony to put a foot in. 'If we get out of this alive I'd like to think we could be friends again.'

Tony winked an eye at him. 'Depend on it,' he said.

Tom lifted him high enough so that he could grasp the first of the lower branches. He grabbed hold of the strong lateral limb; it bowed a little but easily took his weight and he hauled himself up to the first of the thicker branches, from there it would be easy to climb the rest of the way.

Bending down Tom opened the canvas bag and took out a rifle. He threw it up to Tony who caught it and hung it by the strap on a small branch next to him. Now Tom threw up a satchel filled with ammunition pouches.

'Good hunting,' he said in a hushed voice as Tony disappeared into the upper levels of the foliage. 'Stay safe.'

He moved a few yards further on then gingerly he pulled away three boards from the fence in front of him. They came away easily. Alan, his neighbor, had neglected the back of his garden; the heads of the nails fixing the boards had long ago rusted away and they gave up without a fight. Once in, he waited for a signal.

******

'There's someone at the door,' Holly called down from the bathroom where he was shaving.

'I'll get it,' Martha shouted up the stairs.

She opened the door to see a short, well-presented elderly man with a Homberg hat and a walking cane. He took off his hat politely and explained that he had come to see them about their son Tom. Martha showed him into the sitting room and called up to Holly that they had a visitor.

'I hope nothing is wrong,' Martha said, looking anxiously at the man. 'He was here just yesterday.'

'No, no,' he replied reassuringly in a calm urbane voice. There was, Martha thought, a slight hint of an accent – he must be foreign.

Wheels trotted in to inspect the new smell he had detected from his box in the kitchen. He looked up at the stranger, who was now sitting on the sofa. He sniffed at his shoes and then deciding he was not hostile sat on his rump and looked up to see if he would get any attention.

'What a nice little dog,' the visitor said, stroking Wheels on the top of his head.

Holly came into the room and the man stood up. 'How can I help you?' Holly asked politely.

'I am looking for your son. Are you expecting him back again?'

At this, Holly looked suspiciously at the little elderly man in front of him. 'And you are?'

'My grandson was with your boy at Cumberland Head – Lieutenant Brennan. I haven't heard from him or his unit since then and – well – I thought perhaps he might have news of him.'

'I'm real sorry to hear that,' Holly said sympathetically. He knew what it was like to wait, never knowing what had happened. 'I genuinely don't know when he will be coming back. I'll surely let him know you called.'

'That is most kind of you. why don't I leave you with my phone number and when he does come back I would be most obliged if you could ask him to call me.'

'You're most welcome,' Holly said, rubbing his newly shaved chin, 'but I don't know if he'll be back any time soon.'

Mr Brennan thanked them both for their courtesy and said he would take his leave but very much hoped they might meet again. 'Perhaps,' he added, 'when this difficult war is over and things are back to normal.'

'I don't know,' Holly said after Brennan had gone. 'What did you make of that?'

'He seemed a nice enough man,' Martha replied, 'very polite I thought.'

'Hear those guns,' Holly said, breaking off the previous conversation, 'they're getting closer.'

'Will you look at that,' Martha called to Holly from the kitchen. 'I've just seen two German soldiers go into Alan and Irene's. What do you suppose that means?'

'Not a clue and don't care,' Holly called back from the comfort of his chair. He picked up a newspaper. Wheels jumped up and made himself comfortable on his lap, resting his chin on Holly's knee. 'Maybe they've got themselves arrested – that'd be good.'

The two Germans Martha had watched walking up the front steps of Alan and Irene's house now stood under the cover of the front porch and paused for a moment, looking in through the windows. One of them rapped loudly on the glass pane of the door. When he opened the door Alan's initial reaction was one of surprise at finding an officer and a corporal standing in front of him. The corporal had a rifle slung over his shoulder.

'We need your help,' the officer said. 'Do you know the district headquarters?'

'Of course, sir,' Alan replied, 'it's not five minutes from here.'

'Good,' the officer said. 'We have put the house of your neighbor under surveillance. We are watching the house for a visitor. Have you seen anyone suspicious coming there?'

Alan nodded his head vigorously and told them he had seen Tom. He also described the elderly gentleman who had also been there a short while ago. He had no idea who he was or what his business was but he had never seen him before – he was sure of that.

'I want you to take a message to the district headquarters for me.'

'Of course,' Alan said eagerly. He was flattered that they should ask for his help – it made him feel important. When this was all over and the Germans had won he fancied he might obtain a post in the civil administration if he could only make his mark. Here was an opportunity perhaps.

'Irene, look after the officer while I'm gone,' he instructed his wife. 'I shan't be long.' He got his bicycle out of the garage and pedaled off furiously down the avenue.

'Those guns are getting louder,' Irene said to the Captain, then added, 'I'm sorry but I don't know your name.' He snapped his heels together in a gallant fashion and gave a little bow. 'Frederick Loughlin, madam,'

'You sound quite British,' she replied, looking a little surprised.

'Indeed, I am madam, but don't fret about it – you're in good hands.' He politely waved an arm inviting her to sit in an armchair, which she did. She said nothing; she could think of nothing to say.

Grainger went out back in his baggy tunic and signaled to Tom that the coast was clear. 'I have to get my parents out of the house,' Tom said with an air of urgency. 'They have no idea what's going on – I want them out of harm's way.'

'Oh, you're back. That's real nice,' Martha crooned with delight as Tom came back into the house.

'You had a visitor,' Holly said, then told him about Brennan. Tom looked at the number that had been left. It was not one he recognized. He dialled it anyway, curious to know what the news was about Lieutenant Brennan but when he got through and asked for the man by name a voice at the other end said it was a wrong number and hung up.

He looked at his parents: first at his mother, then at his father, and finally down at Wheels who was sitting next to Holly. How the hell was he going to explain this was all that kept running through his mind? There was so much history, so much water under the bridge, so many bizarre events, so many complicated twists and turns. He braced himself and then launched into it.

'I know this is going to sound strange but you have to leave the house and you have to do it now.'

Holly and Martha both looked at their son as if he had somehow lost his reason. Holly had started to say he didn't understand but Tom stopped him short – there was no time for rational argument. This was not the time for debate.

'Listen,' he said insistently, and with all the gravity he could muster. 'Some Germans will arrive here shortly. They will try to kill me or capture me. There will be shooting and stuff flying around and anyone here will be in the greatest possible danger – and I don't want you to get hurt. So you have to leave. Do you understand!'

Martha stood motionless, not knowing what to say or what was happening.

'If we go, then you should come with us,' Holly protested.

'Dad, I can't. There isn't time to explain.'

'Tell me as we go, can't you?'

'No – I can't.' He raised his voice and clenched his fists together in exasperation, like a man praying. 'I have to be here; I've lured them here; I've set a trap. I have to arrest one of them and take him back across the line, to General Patton. Don't you see? It's why I came back – it's my mission.'

He stopped and looked at them. They said nothing, but he could see they were now resigned to doing as he asked.

'Get what you need in case you have to stay out overnight. I've got a car just up the road – I'll get it. Please be ready when I get back. We have very little time.'

******

'Wait here,' a clerk in charge of the front desk said officiously and walked away with the note Alan had handed him. He waited for what seemed an inordinately long time. After a while he looked at his watch – he had been there nearly half an hour but still nobody came.   When he next looked at the time it had passed the fifty-minute mark. He went to the desk and enquired again. The clerk who had taken the note was not there and he called to a woman sitting at a typewriter. At first she ignored him but he kept rapping on the sliding glass glass window of the hatch. Eventually, after he had mustered the courage to slide it open, he stuck his head through the gap and called to her. She got up from her machine and walked testily over to him. She made it clear she didn't want to help but after a stiff conversation she eventually agreed she would go in search of the clerk who had taken the message.

Alan sat back down and waited. He started to worry – this could not be right. The woman came back and said someone would be out shortly, but he was to wait there. After another half hour, when he was wrestling with whether to leave and perhaps run the risk of upsetting someone or stay and perhaps get a reward, his struggle was interrupted by a man in an SS uniform. The face that stared down at him was particularly humorless.

'Follow me,' was all he said, and started off down a corridor. When they reached the end they turned a corner into another corridor. It was ill lit and smelled damp. Halfway along they stopped and a door was opened. Alan stepped inside; there were some chairs and a desk but nothing else. The walls were bare save for a picture of Hitler and a telephone hung on a bracket; the windows were caged on the exterior with barrel bars like a prison.

'You will wait here,' the SS man said without emotion then, stepping back into the corridor, he banged the door shut and locked it. Alan shivered. He didn't like this at all – something was very wrong. He had heard of collaborators suddenly disappearing, but why him? He had done nothing wrong – he had served the Germans loyally.

In the street outside a large black open-topped staff car arrived at the building and stopped. Neumann jumped out and ran up the steps of the headquarters building, taking them two at a time. Inside an aide snapped to attention and took his coat, hung it up and followed Neumann along the corridor.

'If they think we will fall for this a second time,' he shouted back to the aide, 'they are more naïve than I took them for.

The SS man who had locked Alan in now unlocked the door. At the sound of the key he stood up. 'Sit down,' Neumann ordered.

He took a pistol from his holster and banged it down on the table, then he pulled up a chair and sat opposite the now trembling Alan. He stared across the table at him, assessing the calibre of the man – not a plotter, he concluded.

'Tell me,' he said, leaning towards Alan, 'what sort of man is this Captain who has sent you on this mission to me?'

'Just an ordinary German officer,' he replied. He was now visibly shaking with fear and expected that at any moment something awful would happen. He had heard about the violence of the SS from others, but had not expected to face it himself. Now he wished he had never taken up his position as a district organizer.

Neumann pushed a grainy photo across to him. It was a man in civilian clothing but there was something familiar about the face and the way the subject stood. 'Is this the man do you think? Is this your Captain?'

Alan squinted at the picture in the poor light. 'I think it is. Yes, it looks very much like him.'

The phone hung on the wall by the door that he had noticed when he first came into the room now rang. The SS man took it off the hook and listened. 'Ja,' he said and held out the instrument in the direction of Neumann, who got up and took it.

'I've found them,' a tinny voice on the other end said. There was a short conversation. Neumann smiled. 'Most excellent, Mueller.' He hung up the phone.

'So, I think you are telling the truth.'

'Thank you – can I go now?' Alan asked pleadingly.

Neumann stood up and grinned. 'No, you will stay here until I have concluded this business – then you will be free to go.' He left and the SS man slammed the door. Alan heard the key turn in the lock. He sat there alone, wracked with insecurity and fretting about Irene; he was near to breaking down.

******

As he turned onto the driveway Tom saw the front door was half open; there was a suitcase on the porch ready to go. Thank god for that, he thought. There wasn't time for further resistance or explanations; he had to get them away. He left the keys in the ignition – Holly would have to drive; he had to stay. If Neumann had taken the bait he could be there any moment. Inside he heard

590

Martha calling for him. Her voice sounded strange, edgy and not like her usual self. He guessed she must be feeling the strain.

He went in through the front door and sensed a movement behind him. There was stinging pain in the back of his neck as something hard hit him; his legs gave way and he struggled to see as a green haze blurred his vision. He fought to hold on to his fading consciousness; slowly he won and, hanging onto the door, pulled himself to his feet. There he found himself face to face with the visitor in the Homberg hat. It was Mueller; he held a gun at his head. In the other hand was his walking cane; it had a heavy silver ball on the handle with which he had felled Tom.

'Ah, Mr Jordan,' he said, 'so nice to see you again, my friend.'

Mueller steered him into the kitchen. There was Martha; she had been bound to a chair. Tom flushed with anger but there was nothing he dared do. He knew Meuller would kill her without hesitation. His mind churned, searching for answers, but nothing came to his aid.

'Where is your father?'

'I don't know,' Tom lied. 'Gone out. He went out an hour ago.'

There was a sound behind him. Wheels wandered in idly and stood looking at Mueller. The dog sensed things weren't right and a growl started deep in its throat. Mueller waved his cane at it; the dog was irritating him. The growl turned to a bark and Wheels darted at Mueller and went to bite his ankle. Mueller kicked him away but when he came back for a second attack the German swung his cane and brought the heavy end down hard on the dog's skull, which split – killing the dog instantly.

'No, no,' Mueller said quickly, as he perceived Tom about to move in anger. 'I will shoot your mother if you do not do exactly as I tell you.'

'If you love her – and what son does not love his mother – you will sit calmly while we wait for Obersturmbannführer Neumann, or Sergeant Henry Newman as you know him. We all have a little unfinished business.' He rubbed a finger along a scar on the side of his face where Tom had so nearly put a round through his head.

'Herr Neumann is very upset that you killed his good friend and colleague. Poor Vogel – it was you I imagine who killed him, was it not?'

He was interrupted by the thump of another shell exploding, much closer this time. Mueller's face carried a tinge of concern and Tom spotted it. It must be Patton's front line on the move, he thought, and a vain, vague hope came to him that the cavalry might come riding over the hill to their rescue, but it wasn't to be.

Instead Holly, who had been upstairs, now appeared in the kitchen doorway, a look of shock and disbelief spread across his face.

'Come in,' Mueller said, waving the pistol in his direction. 'I will kill her and then your boy if you do anything stupid.' For a moment he wavered, not knowing what to do; then seeing Wheels laid out on the floor – lifeless, his head in a pool of blood – he let out a low, anguished moan.

'You've killed him,' he said pathetically, kneeling and picking up the lifeless corpse of his dog. 'You didn't have to kill him – he was just a little dog.'

'Stop moaning, old man,' Mueller sneered derisively. 'Go and sit in another place – your sentimentality sickens me.'

Holly looked at his son and his wife, and then at his dead pet. He felt useless, worthless, humiliated and utterly degraded – he was powerless, and he knew it.

'You killed my dog, you killed my dog.' He kept repeating the mantra as he turned his back on his family and trudged into the hall. There he sat on a chair with poor Wheels cradled on his lap and began to shed tears – slow remorseful tears for what his life had become. He was nothing and the truth of it crushed him.

******

The doorbell rang. Irene went to get up but Loughlin put out an arm and stopped her. 'I'll go,' he said, as if he were speaking to a child, 'just in case it's an unwanted visitor.'

He opened the door and found himself facing Neumann, who shot him point blank in the chest. Loughlin just stood there staring in disbelief, one hand clutching the wound. Shock took over – he felt nothing. As his knees began to give way, Neumann shoved him and he fell to the ground.

Hearing the shot, Grainger grabbed his rifle and dodged into the kitchen just in time to see Neumann step over his friend's body. There were others with him – maybe six or seven, Grainger reckoned, as he bolted for cover in the back garden.

'Get him!' Neumann ordered 'Kill him, we don't need him.' He looked into the living room where a terrified Irene had become hysterical. She flinched as the sound of rapid shots came from the rear of the house.

'Where is Tom Jordan?' he yelled at her. She shook her head, blubbering that he wasn't there. 'I don't know – I don't know,' she kept repeating.

Outside in the back yard the men of Neumann's *Einsatzgruppen* had run into Tony's sights. There were three shots in quick succession: the first three casualties fell, each man as he came out through the back door. They lay in a pile. Behind them the other attackers were pinned in position by crossfire from Grainger, who had hunkered down behind a pile of lumber stacked by the woodshed. He looked up to the foliage where he knew Tony was hidden.

'We have to get out of here!' he shouted. 'You first – I'll cover you – see if you can get round to the Avenue.'

******

Neumann stepped out of the house and made his way across the front garden, single-mindedly disregarding the firing all around him. He shouted to the rest of his men, who were sitting in a truck parked casually at the curbside, to get into the house and take the heavy machine gun with them.

'Blast them out of there,' he ordered.

Methodically he crossed the drive onto the Jordan property then made his way to the side of the house. His actions were calm but inside his head he was writhing with anger. Jordan had thwarted him too many times and now all he wanted was revenge. He would kill him slowly and painfully, and with Mueller there it would give him pleasure to watch.

As he reached the porch at the top of the steps he noticed a number of Wehrmacht infantry men running in the street below. 'What's happening?' he called to one of them.

'The Americans have broken through,' the soldier shouted back.

Ignoring them, he stepped across the threshold and into the hallway where he immediately felt the coolness of the house; outside the sun was bright and hot. It took a moment or two for his eyes to accustom to the subdued light. The first thing he saw was an old man sitting on a chair sobbing, a dog lying on his lap; they seemed oblivious to him and he ignored them.

'Mueller,' he called out.

'I am here,' a voice replied from the kitchen.

'Well now, we must be quick, Mueller, because I think we may not have much time.'

'Which one first?'

'Oh, I think the woman, don't you? Let the boy here suffer a little – he deserves to.' Neumann slapped Tom across the face, making his nose bleed. 'Who is the old man sitting in the hall sniveling?'

'He's nobody,' Mueller said casually. 'He's distraught because I killed his dog.'

'Bring him in. His sentimental grief will add to the pain for our friend here.'

Mueller went into the hall. Holly had gone – only the limp corpse of Wheels was still there, draped across the chair where he had been sitting. 'The old man has gone,' Mueller said. 'Shall I go and look for him?'

'Never mind him,' Neumann replied, 'we can deal with him later. It will be good to let him grieve a little.'

Meuller looked up and down the hall but it was empty. Maybe he was in the sitting room, he thought, and went to look there. As he came out and into the hall again he saw a shadow move. Holly was standing there at the foot of the stairs. 'Come here!' Mueller shouted harshly at him.

'You killed my dog,' Holly replied almost mechanically, 'you killed my dog.'

'It was only a dog, you stupid old man – just a dog. Come here.'

Holly raised his arm and then Mueller saw it. He was holding a rifle, Tom's Remington. He had gone upstairs to Tom's room where the gun had been propped against the wall just behind the door. He had found a box of shells where Tom kept them in a drawer and he had loaded the gun. He had not put his hand on a gun since he left the Army at the end of the Great War and he had sworn never to do so again. Now that oath seemed empty. Here he was, faced with evil men who would kill everything he had ever lived for and there was no other way. He put the stock of the rifle to his shoulder. The muzzle gaped at Mueller's face. He wasn't sure he could do it.

'It's useless, old man. You can't save them - we will kill them anyway. Put the gun down.'

Holly hesitated. 'Yes, I know you will.'

There was a deafening explosion and Mueller jerked backwards, his chest caved in under the impact of the high-calibre hunting round.

Neumann grabbed Tom and spun him round to shield himself, then inched towards the doorway. He pushed Tom's head out into the hall. He peered cautiously over Tom's shoulder and saw Holly.

'Put the gun down, old man, or your boy gets it and then your wife. Throw the gun down where I can see it.'

With his head in full view Tom could see Holly standing by the stairs. Mueller was well and truly dead, crumpled up against the wall – half sitting, half crouching where the force of the shot had thrown him.

'Don't do it, Dad, he'll kill us all if you do. Don't mind me, take him down – save Ma.'

Neumann forced him into the hall and made for the front door, firing at Holly as he went. He pushed Tom stumbling down the steps towards the truck where his men had been, but there was no sign of them. The street outside was in confusion. Men were running. There was a halftrack coming down the Avenue – a German halftrack with an SS pennant. He dragged Tom out into the street and waved the armored vehicle to a halt. There was a very senior tank officer behind the wheel; the men in the back of it looked to be dead.

'I need to get my prisoner away. There's another one in there I need to get. Come down and help me.'

'Get out of my way!' the officer yelled back at him. 'The Americans are here. There is no time for prisoners. Leave him and get in if you value your life.'

'Traitor,' Neumann said calmly, and levelling his pistol shot the tank officer dead. It was a just end to Kommandant Joachim Metz, who only months before had murdered the men from 1st Armor at Rouses Point and had callously killed Captain White. Justice had finally laid its hand on him.

'Climb in,' he ordered Tom, prodding him in the back with his gun.

Tom put a foot on the running board of the halftrack and climbed up. As he did so, Neumann jumped sideways and hopped a couple of paces, then fell on the sidewalk. The next thing there was Tony running towards him, weapon at the ready, pointed at Neumann. Coming down the steps of the house was Holly clutching the Remington and across the way Grainger appeared from around the back of Alan's house. Then he heard the rumble of machinery and, looking up, saw a column of Patton's favorite tanks coming down the Avenue, infantry fanned out behind them. He got down from the halftrack and walked to where Neumann lay on the ground, cursing and holding his leg.

'That leg aint never gonna work again,' Tony said, shaking his head.

Holly came over to him. 'Here,' he said, handing Tom the Remington. 'You may need this. I have to go look after your mother. She's alright but she's a bit shook up at the moment.'

Neumann kicked out wildly at Tom with his uninjured leg. 'Kill me,' he sneered. 'Why don't you shoot me? You don't have the guts, do you?'

Tom shook his head. 'I'd like to, but that'll be for others. Henry Newman, I'm arresting you on the orders of General Patton and the United States Government for the murder of FBI Agent Parkes, of Giorgio Gagliardi and Anthony Bardetti, as an accessory to the deaths of other members of the Bardetti family, and for espionage against the nation. You'll be tried publicly and then I guess you'll go to the chair.'

Neumann spat at him.

As the tanks and infantry rolled past, it fell to Grainger to shout for a medic. 'Fred took a bullet,' he told the others. 'He's in a bad way. I don't think he's going to make it.'

'Don't you think it's ironic?' Tony said after they had carted Neumann away. 'I killed a man by accident in a knife fight and they sentenced me to death. I've killed maybe a dozen today and they say I'll get a medal. How do you work that one out?'

CHAPTER 42

Epilogue to All the Dreams

Irena was back at Dobbs Ferry. She had never been able to quite get on with Washington; it was cliquey and gossipy and the shopping was poor. In the end, she had to admit it, she actually missed Brunessemer. Besides, her friend Clementine had gone back to England; gone with her husband to reclaim their country.

Patton had pushed the Germans into Canada and then on north all the way to Hudson Bay. Finally they had pulled out altogether. But it was not Patton in the east or even the combined thrusts of Bradley and Vinegar Joe further west; in the end it was the growing irregular militias and the random killings by armed civilians that made the German position ultimately untenable. It was argued by some that this was a true echo of the Founding Fathers' belief that an armed people could not be subjugated and that the right of the people to bear arms was the greatest defense against tyranny – though not all agreed with that.

As he retreated, Guderian repeated Von Paulus's complaint made some weeks before when he was recalled to Berlin for Barbarossa. 'It is impossible to hold the ground,' he reported to Hitler, 'where almost the entire male population is armed.'

At last they had the Germans on the run. Now Roosevelt and Churchill plotted to take back Europe. The tide was on the turn. In Croton and all the way down the Hudson things were getting back to normal.

It was the fall again. The summer of '41 was waning, the year was coming to an end. It had been a month since the capture of Neumann and there had been a great deal to do: reports to write, hearings to attend, ceremonies and inaugurations. Tom had become America's most popular soldier and it seemed everyone wanted him at their shindig.

Come September he felt he'd had enough and he put in for a weekend furlough. The message came down from Colonel Hamilton that he should take a month – he had been in the field continuously since Rouses Point and he should rest up.

First, he would go home for a few days. Martha could hardly let him go from the moment he walked into the house. Holly had got himself a new dog, which he was calling Wheels Junior, but in the end he dropped Wheels and just called it Junior. He said it brought back too many memories and just made him sad – there wouldn't be another Wheels.

They had never properly discussed what had happened that day but it had wrought the final change in Holly. They sat on the back porch together and watched the sunset. Tom looked across the fence to the pile of lumber that Grainger had hidden behind, and at the house that for as long as he could remember had been home to Alan and Irene.

They had found Alan, a sergeant and an infantry squad, cowering in the corner of the room he had been locked in at the Nazi District Headquarters. He had been there for two days and nights without food or water. They took him to a hospital, but when he got back home he became reclusive. Irene went to pieces: she never properly recovered from the trauma of the attack. Then one morning a car came for them and they simply disappeared. Holly had no idea why or where to.

'I haven't really had a chance to tell you, Dad, just how proud I am of what you did.'

Holly shrugged. 'It sometimes takes strange things to wake a man up. I'd been sleepwalking for years, but I'm OK now. How about you son? You saw some pretty mean things?'

'I think I've changed. I think I begin to understand how you were feeling all those years – about the guns and the killing. I don't know. I suppose I feel different – that's all.'

'Well,' Holly said, drawing out the word slowly, 'I guess it's not the guns so much – they're just bits of metal and mechanism. It's how we use them. I had to shoot that sonofabitch – I had no option. Sometimes we just don't have a choice.' He stopped and considered what he had said. He shook his head – it was as if he didn't quite approve of what he'd said. 'Yup, it's not about the gun. It's about who's holding it – that's all. It's about the people.'

They sat on the porch until Martha called them in for dinner, then afterwards went back out. All three of them talked about better times and sipped a little bourbon.

Early next morning the phone rang. 'It's Wendell,' the voice on the other end of the line said. 'I wondered if you had the time to come down to Brunessemer. There's something I need to tell you, but it has to be to you personally. Do you think you could make it?'

It was nine o'clock and they had just finished breakfast. 'Okay,' Tom said, looking at his watch. 'Is it important?'

'Yes, I think it is.' Wendell sounded hesitant, like he might be about to say what it was, but he didn't. So there was nothing for it, he would have to go down there.

The drive down to Dobbs Ferry was a swirling mess of memories and nostalgia as he passed things and places that had filled up his life with pain and happiness, good times and bad times. As he passed Jenifer's Diner he saw they were open for business again. It set him off thinking about Dottie. In all the chaos and killing he had temporarily forgotten her and now this one sight brought her back. She would be here in Croton, he thought, or else at Valhalla – or maybe she had stayed on and gone north into Canada with the troops. The Army still needed nurses.

He puzzled over the call for the whole of the journey. He had no idea what Wendell could possibly need to say to him face to face. Then the thought struck him that maybe Fred Loughlin had died. After the shootout in Union Avenue he had been shipped down to a hospital in New York. He'd been in pretty poor shape and nobody really thought he would make it through. Tom hadn't seen him since that time but, there again, he had seen nobody. It had been impossible to get away – he had a lot of catch-up to play.

Brunessemer had returned to what it had been the first time he had gone there; it was as if nothing had changed. Martins was in the driveway polishing the Packard to a peerless gleaming black, and when he rang the doorbell he was met by the broad smile of Patience who welcomed him in and directed him to the drawing room. The only difference was the sound of a baby crying somewhere upstairs. He went into the drawing room where he found Wendell and Aly.

'Wendell,' he said cheerfully, hoping that he was not about to hear bad news, but from the look of sadness on Aly's face and the sombre tone of Wendell's response he realized it was definitely going to be bad news.

'Carey has died,' Wendell said, beckoning Tom to take a seat. They sat and looked at each other across the elegant Mackintosh coffee table. It was the last thing that could have entered his thoughts. He had been so sure it was Fred who would be at the core of Wendell's message that he had left no room in his mind for any other thought. Aly looked at him, waiting for his response. She was not sure how he would take it; she didn't know how deep in his heart her sister might still be.

'How did it happen?' was all he said.

'Booze,' Wendell said, as if it didn't really matter what she died of. 'She drank herself to death. It started after Gagliardi went inside [the family never referred to Tony by any other than his family name; it was their way of saying he was not accepted, that they didn't approve]. It was downhill after that. Her body couldn't take it. Renal collapse and liver failure – that's what finally took her.'

Tom didn't know what to say; there are times when it is better to say nothing. He was sad, yes, but the news failed to strike deep into his emotions. He had passed on from Carey a while back; he knew that when she had come to see him in Buchanan. He had looked at her then and realized that the flame that had set him alight back in New York had gone out. It had been extinguished and replaced by a little flickering sadness, not of loss, but at seeing her so unhappy.

'Poor Carey,' Aly said, trying to hold back her emotions. She had been determined not to shed tears in front of Tom but it was difficult. She never really felt close to her sister until now – and now it was too late. 'She was so happy for a while and then she lost it all. How terrible.'

'When's the funeral?' Tom asked, because he could think of nothing else to say.

'Next Friday. Will you come?'

'Of course.'

'Let's talk of happier things,' Wendell said, as Irena came into the drawing room holding her grandson. 'Look who has come to join us.' He got up and took Aly's baby in his arms as if he were somehow more proprietorial than a mere uncle.

The sight of new life revitalized the air and tore away the veil of gloom that had hung like a funeral shroud over the room. Aly jumped up and took her boy away from her brother; cradling him in her arms, she took him over to show Tom.

'This,' she said, 'is Charles Frederick James. Charlie, say hello to your uncle Tommy.' She held out the bundle to Tom saying, 'Here hold him – but make sure you don't drop him.'

Tom felt the warmth of the child against his chest. 'Yes,' he thought, 'I could do this, I could be a father,' and it occurred to him that he would quite like that. Of course, he would first have to find the right girl. That was when it dawned on him that he no longer knew any eligible women and that, in fact, he now inhabited an all-male world – the army.

'What news of Fred?' he asked Aly as he handed back the baby.

'Yes – he's progressing. It'll be a while and we're not sure how complete the recovery will be, but I hope to have him home before Thanksgiving. Will you come to us for Thanksgiving?'

The invitation was, Tom knew, just a device to end a conversation that she didn't really want to have, but he said yes he would anyway. Then, having wished Fred a speedy recovery, he made his excuses and said he really had to get back to Peekskill. He ritually kissed the baby, hugged Aly and said how sorry he was about Carey.

Irena and Wendell took him, arm in arm on either side, to the door and lingered with him for a moment on the top step. Irena gave his arm a little squeeze. 'You know,' she said, 'I never thought I would hear myself say it – but it's nice to be back. Washington never felt like home. I'm so grateful you didn't let the Germans get here and ruin it all.'

Tom chuckled. 'It wasn't me. It's Patton you have to thank for that – and all the anonymous grunts that followed his tanks.'

'Yes, but they couldn't have done it without you,' she insisted.

At this they all laughed. Then, almost as an afterthought, as if he suddenly remembered he had forgotten, Wendell took something from his pocket. He jingled the keys to the Bugatti in front of Tom's nose. 'I want you to have this,' he said. 'You've earned it - and I won't accept a no.'

'Take it, Tommy,' Irena insisted. 'I know how much you loved that car. You've done so much for us – please take it.'

'Okay,' was all he said. He took the keys from Wendell and after hugging them both he made his way down the steps. 'I'll come back for it,' he called up to them, and then he went.

As he left he looked in the rear view mirror and, seeing the tall trees in the driveway, a memory flashed through his mind of the days he had spent with Carey. Deep down he had known it could never last and, watching as he drew away and as the image grew smaller, he knew he had long ago accepted it. Now she was gone and not even her ghost remained to haunt him.

The funeral was a miserable affair. Arriving at the cemetery he saw Tony standing alone and apart from the family, a long black coat draped across his shoulders even though the day was still warm. He had a dark black Fedora with the brim pulled down over his eyes, as much to protect him from the glare of the others present as the glare of the sun.

He hadn't seen Tony since they had said their farewells to each other at Peekskill. With Neumann came an end to his commitment. Roosevelt commuted his sentence to the equal number of days he had served and the Army recognized his contribution by awarding him the Purple Heart, though it had been controversial. Patton had recommended the Distinguished Service Medal but there was opposition from the Army Board because of his criminal record. Tony really didn't care, and Carey's funeral was the only time he would ever wear it. He had lost his favorite uncle and now Carey, the only things he ever really loved in his life and it was a bitter vacuum he inhabited. Tom stood by his side through the mournful proceedings and then, hugging his old friend after it was over, they said their goodbyes and parted.

Afterwards Tom went back to Brunessemer and did his best to make small conversation. He hardly knew anybody present at the wake though he recognized the two men from Kolinsky's Gallery, the two young men who had vampishly referred to her as 'the Vision of Loveliness' and laughed at her. It was clear they didn't remember him and there was nothing to be had from resurrecting the event, so he let it pass. He politely drank the drink that Patience served him and spoke briefly with Nigel, the artist, who did remember him. He saw Jerry and the other one from the tennis club whose name evaded him and their two socialite wives, Cynthia and Margaret, but apart from a polite nod they avoided each other.

Only Irena, Wendell and Aly really knew him. Irena wept a little, very privately, on his shoulder and said, 'Promise you will come for Thanksgiving.' He said he would and then after a warm handshake with Wendell and a kiss for Aly he faded out of the scene. He had come by train and Martins had met him at the station, just like the old times. He went round to the garage where Martins had opened one of the auto shed doors and now stood there smiling. Tom got behind the wheel of the Bugatti and, with the engine grumbling through its exhausts, he drove it slowly out. He shook hands with Martins, who looked at him as though he were his son and with a discreet smile on his face said, 'It is a very fine motor, sir, and I know it has been put into good hands.'

******

In London, as July turned to August and as Hitler became more embroiled in the mire of his Russian campaign, the last of the German Division that Mosley had pleaded for was withdrawn. It left Brooke free to make the break out from Kent and, with more of James' ships free from North Atlantic duty, a flotilla of three light cruisers and five destroyers sailed up the Thames and took up stations in the Pool of London. The light cruiser HMS *Arethusa* dropped anchor in mid-stream opposite the Houses of Parliament, though it was a symbolic gesture. Parliament had not sat and the building had been closed up since Mosley took over more than a year earlier.

On that day Bines – who had now temporarily taken on the role of leader of the BBS in place of Mosley but who had retained his post as Commissioner of the Metropolitan Police – was in an emergency meeting at Bermondsey. This dual position, which had at first seemed a stepping stone to becoming the most powerful man in Britain, now felt less promising as Brooke's advance gathered pace. Men who had been persuaded to follow Mosley and who believed in his ability to hold on to power were now less convinced by his replacement; slowly his support was being dissolved as surreptitiously men drifted away, leaving uniforms in lockers, burning identity cards, throwing into the river anything that might connect them with the organization that had become the most reviled institution in the country. Every day men disappeared, slipping back into the slums of the East End where they would be as hard to capture as a handful of smoke.

Bines was wavering; he was no longer sure what to do. His dilemma lay in the fact that there was nobody who wanted to step into his shoes and nobody he could wholly rely on. The top echelon of the organization had never been strong and Mosley had always made sure that he was the dominant force. He had avoided promoting anyone he thought might challenge him and so, with his parting, there formed a vacuum. It was the legacy of single-minded autocratic leadership – it left no room for succession. Supreme leaders commonly fail to consider their own mortality and refuse to acknowledge that there must someday be a reckoning with the dark spectre of death. So it had been with Mosley. Now the legacy clung to Bines like a leech it stuck to him like shit on a blanket and he could find no way to get it off: nobody wanted the job – it had a bad odour about it.

The meeting was stillborn, it was impotent. The wellspring of this impotence came from the fact that nobody present had anything to offer Bines. They looked at him blankly but said little. They had not been schooled in strategy; they had grown used to being under the control of the Wehrmacht and the SS. Those were the forces which had shaped the day-to-day command decisions and issued the tactical guidance. They had been the head of the serpent, but now there was no head. Furthermore, it hadn't even been chopped off; it had more fallen off – not even that, it had just taken itself off somewhere else to be another head – on another serpent. Bines was adrift. Linz had been right in his assessment.

At first light a contingent of Royal Marines had come ashore at Spice Wharf, where they had been cheered by the dock workers. They made their way along the wharf road until they reached the gates leading into Bermondsey Street, where they were confronted by a squad of lightly armed BBS. The Blackshirts were so surprised to see them, they dropped their weapons and surrendered without a single shot being fired.

The Marines went on the double along the edge of the wharf at Shad Thames, emerging into Tooley Street and headed for the Bermondsey headquarters. At the approach to the building they encountered the only resistance of the day when they came under fire from a scout car armed with a turret-mounted machine gun. The firing was erratic and poorly aimed; news had already started to filter through of the ships in the Pool and BBS morale was beginning to crumble. After receiving return fire and on seeing the Marines lining up for an assault, the crew of the scout car tied a white handkerchief on the end of a rifle and pushed it up through the hatch where they waved it nervously to a chorus of 'Don't shoot – we surrender.'

Two Marines then ran forward and laid a charge of plastic explosive against the grand front doors of the HQ, then blew them off their hinges sending them hurtling into the building. It was not that the doors had been secured but that the Captain leading the squad wanted to make a statement and to let those inside the building know what they were up against. Several smoke grenades were thrown in – and then they waited.

In an upper room the shock and the sound of the explosion brought the meeting to a premature conclusion. As the smoke filled the corridors, a stream of gasping men emerged with their hands in the air. There had been no appetite for a fight. The only shot came from one of the upper floors when a BBS sergeant leaned out of a window and fired at the Marines below. His shots were random and the aim was poor. As he fired for the third time a Marine got him in his sights; he fell with a dull thump into the street – dead. The sight was enough to convince the rest and in particular Bines, who emerged waving a white table napkin he had taken from the officers' canteen. The game was up and he concluded he'd best give in.

Chartwell
1ˢᵗ August 1941
My Dear Irena
Home at last and back in dear old Chartwell. Winston is so happy to be here again. He made his first speech on the floor of the House yesterday and they say you could hear the cheering all the way to Piccadilly Circus – though I think there may be some exaggeration in that.
I do so hope that you are now settled back in Dobbs Ferry again. It was a frightful upheaval and I know that you were never very fond of Brunessemer, though for my part I must say I found it bright and airy and rather an easy house to live in. We are so grateful to you and your husband, although I never met him, for the kindness and hospitality shown during our long stay in America. Should you come to England I would be so delighted to have you stay here with us at Chartwell – I suspect you would warm greatly to the historic charm of the house, though I have to say that keeping old houses clean and tidy is not an easy task and not one I would recommend without help to hand.
What an adventure it was. Looking back, I can hardly believe it happened and I must say I don't think I would welcome that much excitement again; normality can be a little plain but it is nice to have the certainty of order in our lives again. You will no doubt have read that the last of the Germans were evicted from Hull. Winston counselled that they should be allowed to retreat since he says we are still not fully ready to engage Hitler in all-out war. It is so good to be able to shop again in London without constantly seeing them strutting about the place.
I was so pleased to hear that Aly and little Charles are thriving and it is great news about Fred – let's hope he is out of that invalid chair soon. It is quite remarkable what doctors can do these days.
Do write and let me know how things are.
Your true friend,
Clementine

******

A keen-eyed constable on duty at Kings Cross spotted what he thought was a suspiciously furtive man boarding a train bound for Hull. The man was tall with fair hair and a military bearing. He was carrying a small attaché case. What alerted the constable to the man was that the case was chained to his wrist and this, he concluded, was not a common sight. He had seen this kind of arrangement only with couriers carrying important documents or items of high value that may be stolen by snatch thieves. As the constable approached him the man looked agitated, so he decided to turn away and let him board the train, reasoning that once on board he could more easily be detained, should that prove necessary, because there would be less facility to make a dash for it. The constable went to find the guard and warned him that the train should be held at the station while he went for help.

The constable returned with a sergeant and a plain clothes detective. On boarding the train they saw the man seated in a first class compartment. As they stood in the corridor looking through the glass partition of the compartment door, the detective began to have second thoughts – he needed to be cautious. If this man was travelling first class, he reasoned, he must be important and if he was important and was upset by this intrusion he might lodge a complaint. If he was important enough that complaint could blight his promotion. The detective made a career decision and left the compartment, taking the two uniformed officers with him.

'I have to be careful,' he told the two officers. 'If this man is a VIP and we upset him we could all be for the high jump.'

They stood for a while discussing their options. The guard came over to them; he had been waiting for the all clear to let the train go. 'I can't really hold it any longer,' he explained. 'The 11.24 from Sheffield is due in – I have to get her away.' The detective was in a quandary.

A man in a belted raincoat and a trilby hat then solved the problem. He had walked along the train, looking up at the windows. As he came to the compartment where the suspicious passenger was sitting, he tapped on the window. The man inside the first class compartment brought his face to the window to see who it was attracting his attention and, as he did so, the man in the raincoat pulled out a revolver and shot him – twice. The assassin dropped the revolver and ran, but a quick-thinking ticket man who was standing at the entrance to the platform slammed the metal trellis gate shut. The fugitive ran into it and fell back. Before he could make any further efforts to escape, the detective and his officers grasped him and snapped on some handcuffs. The train had to stay where it was and the 11.24 had to be rerouted to another platform.

The constable felt inside the pockets of the dead man and pulled out a passport with a swastika embossed on it. Inside was a picture of the dead man and underneath his name and title: Major Auguste Baron von Holstein zum Linz.

Linz had become just another victim of the Polish resistance. His killer was quietly spirited away by MI5.

******

A week after the funeral Tom got a call from Mike Mescal.

'Not good news, I'm afraid. Tony is dead. He took his own life.'

There was a long pause. 'I'll come down to see you.'

'Of course, but come to my parents place. I haven't told Eileen and I don't want to distress her – she's expecting our second. When will you come?'

'This afternoon if that's OK.'

'Of course. I'll see you later. It's terrible news.'

He drove down in the station wagon – it somehow didn't seem right to take the Bugatti. It was nothing he could put his finger on, but it seemed frivolous. Perhaps it was just the memories it stirred; he felt it was better to leave it behind.

It was only a short while since he had last seen Mike, but as he drove in and parked on the gravel in front of Cutlers Hall he got the sense the house had lost something familiar. It was as if he was a stranger – Mike and he had become strangers.

It was not the passing of time but the passing of events that now somehow managed to put distance between them. It was a time that had been packed with many things. A lot had happened; they had lost the shared experiences they'd had in those better times. Mike was now a family man; he had a child and another on the way – he was settled. Tom was a soldier. He had seen death and the ugly face of war, the destruction of lives. Things were different for him. He saw the gulf opening between them like a man standing on the stern of a ship as it pulls away from the dock, sees his friend on the shore slowly drawing away from him, receding into the horizon – the water between them was widening.

As he climbed out of the car he saw a familiar face. Ruby stood on the front step, looking coyly at him. It helped to add a touch of the old normality. 'You've grown again,' he said as she came out to meet him and linked her arm round his. 'How old now?'

'Thirteen,' she said and she tugged on his arm as she always had when he arrived at the house, pulling him towards the open front door. 'I'll soon be catching you up.'

'I don't think the numbers work quite like that.'

'Oh yes they do,' she said, wagging her head from side to side. 'Mom told me girls grow up faster than boys. So you see, one day I'll catch you up.'

'Well,' he laughed, 'who am I to contradict your mom.'

She put on a more serious expression and looked at him as if some deep thought had gone into what she was about to say. 'Would you wait for me – till I grow up?'

'Honey, I'll be an old man when you grow up,' he said, grinning and trying to make light of it, 'but you know what, I'm real flattered you asked. That makes a fellah feel good.'

She shrugged. 'I think it was real stupid of Doc Brent's daughter to throw you over like that.'

'Well,' he said, 'she had her reasons.'

'I still think she was stupid. I wouldn't have done that.'

'Tom,' Mike Mescal senior called to him as the pair came into the house still arm in arm. 'Come in, come in. Ruby tell your brother Tom is here.' They went into the study and sat in the large buttoned brown leather chairs to wait for Mike.

Mike senior slowly shook his head in a gesture of disapproval. 'It's a terrible thing suicide; I don't know where he'll be laid to rest. There'll be no churchyard that'll have him – that's for sure.'

Shortly after Mike joined them he got up and made his excuses, leaving the two friends to share the sad event. Mike went and found a decanter of Irish whiskey and two glasses; he poured two fingers in each and handed one to Tom.

Tom took a slug. 'How did he do it?' It was the first question that came to his mind, but as he spoke the words the tragedy of what had happened made him wish he had put it less bluntly.

'He shot himself,' Mike said without any sign of emotion. 'He couldn't go on – not without Carey. It broke him.'

'How do you feel about it?'

Mike rubbed his brow with the tip of finger. 'We weren't close, not after what happened with Carey – but you know, I can understand what drove him, what drove them both. Passion is a powerful thing. They were almost like classical lovers really – Romeo and Juliet, that kind of thing. Funny, but I think I feel closer to him now than I did when he was alive.'

'He was a hero in the end, you know. He saved my life in the showdown with Neumann.'

Mike ignored the remark. 'What ever happened with you and Dorothy Brent?' he said, changing the subject.

'It didn't work out.'

'Do you go hunting these days or do you not have the time?'

Tom ran his fingers through his hair and screwed up his face as if to say that's a difficult one. 'You know,' he said at last, 'I think I lost my appetite for it. I've shot too much in this war – too many people. It's not the same anymore. I know how my dad felt when he came home from the first European war.'

'How is he – your dad?'

'Well that's the most confusing thing of all. You see, after he shot Mueller I thought that would be the end – that he would fall back into the old despair,'

'And?'

'And nothing – he's as right as rain. If anything, he's better than I've ever seen him. You know Mueller killed his little dog Wheels? It was as if he had taken revenge for the dog. You know how at the end of a movie, when the bad guy who's been evil all the way through the second reel suddenly gets it; you know how that makes you feel good? Well, that's how I think it was for him. He got closure from it. He's got himself a new dog. He goes rabbit shooting with a scatter gun. Damned if I know.'

They made a little small talk, mostly about Eileen and his growing family, and Mike poured more whisky.

When they had talked themselves out Tom got up. He said goodbye to Ruby, who kissed him and then looked all shy and silly. 'Stay in touch,' Mike told him. 'Call by and see Eileen and the kids some time – don't drift off.' Tom said he wouldn't drift off but as he got behind the wheel and pulled away from the house he knew that the friendship was not the same anymore. In its place Mike had Eileen and the children, and the expectation that he would one day fill his father's shoes and carry on a dynasty.

As he drove out of Croton he passed Jennifer's Diner. A hundred yards further on he stopped and turned the car around. It was no good, he couldn't resist going back to take a look - just for old time's sake. He parked up where he had always parked up and, for a second or two, half expected to see the Cord draw in alongside him.

In the diner they were all new faces – new girls. He sat in his usual place and ordered coffee. When the girl came back with it he asked if any of the old staff were there, those who were there before the invasion. She said she didn't think so but she would ask. He was sitting looking out of the window when a voice said, 'Oh my god, it's you.' He turned and looked up to see Jennifer standing there.

'Tom Jordan,' she said, almost breathless. 'Well, you became a goddamned hero if ever there was one. How are you?' With that she slapped him heartily across the shoulders. 'What happened to that lovely little blond we had here, Dottie? Did you two hit it off?'

'No. We lost touch when the war started. I wondered if she might have come back here.'

Jennifer shook her head. 'No, honey. I think she joined the nursing corps. Last I heard she was up at Montrose. That's a downright shame. You two were just right for each other – you know that, don't you?'

Tom looked sheepish. 'I guess you're right.'

He sat for a while longer wondering about where she was and what had happened. If she had joined the Medical Corps he could probably find out where she was now. He could even just go and ask her parents – they lived in Croton.

******

There was a tap on his office door.

'Yes, Mac, come in. I've got a small task for you. I'd like you to get on to Army Records. I'm trying to track down a young woman who I think was a nurse in the Medical Corps. I'd like to try to find her if we can.'

'Sure thing, Major. Does she have a name?'

'Naturally – Dorothy Brent. Here,' he took a photo out of his pocket book.

Mac looked at it. 'I think I saw her. She came here the day you took off for Chicago with the two Limies. She came asking after you.'

He felt a little sense of excitement at the prospect that she might want to see him again but he wasn't going to fall into the trap of expectation. He'd been there before and it had ended in pain. He really didn't want his life disrupted, but nevertheless he felt lifted by the prospect of seeing her again.

'Let's go to it, Mac.'

It took Mac a week to come back with the answer that he didn't want to hear. 'She was listed as missing in action – somewhere up around Champlain. It looks like a forward field unit got hit by the Germans in a counter attack. Her file has been closed. Sorry, Major – real sorry.'

Tom took a deep breath and let it sink in. 'Thanks, Mac,' was all he said as he felt the disappointment wash over him. 'Same old Jordan luck,' he said to himself. 'Never good.'

He went outside into the late afternoon sun and wondered around to the motor pool where he kept the Bugatti. A corporal mechanic in the engineers had taken on the car's maintenance and as Tom arrived he found him standing a few paces away looking thoughtfully at it, listening to the motor purring with the hood up and the light reflecting off the brightly polished aluminum engine.

The mechanic looked round as Tom approached. 'Beautiful,' he said, 'like a pretty woman – but less temperamental. You won't get up one morning and find she's left you.'

'True', Tom said, 'not unless somebody else comes along and steals her.'

He hung around for a while just looking at the car, then decided to take it for a drive. He needed some time to think. In the car he was alone with his thoughts, which was what he wanted. It took a while but finally he concluded there was no mileage in raking over what might have been. It was the past; here and now is what he had and he needed to make the most out of it. Maybe someday he would meet someone and get settled like Mike or Fred, but for now he had the Bugatti and his army career. He was well-heeled and still young – there was bound to be someone out there just waiting for him.

'The War Department wants to start up a new marksman training program,' Hamilton had told him. 'I've recommended you to advise on the set up. You'll be based at Fort Hamilton, New York. The name's a coincidence – nothing to do with my family,' he laughed. 'I think this will be an opportunity for you to get away and have a change of surroundings. Corporal McAndrew let slip this place holds a few unhappy memories for you.'

Fort Hamilton was in Brooklyn, close by the Battery just across the bridge in Manhattan. On the first weekend after his arrival he decided he would go and explore the island again – it was a while since he had been there and he just wanted to make its acquaintance again. He got a driver from the motor pool to drive him across the bridge and drop him around Midtown; from there he began to walk. In the early evening he found himself on Lexington Avenue. It stirred a memory and after looking right and left up and down the street he made a decision and started to walk. The sun was dipping fast behind the high towering buildings and casting long shadows across the streetcar rails running down the middle of the thoroughfare. He walked along till he came to Number 645 and there he found what he had been looking for – Tarwids. The bear was still there, sitting in the window with his champagne cocktail, and when he went in it was like he had stepped back in time. He sat down at a table close to the bear and ordered a Manhattan. When the waiter had served his drink he raised his glass to the creature: 'Cheers,' he said quietly. 'It's just us now, pal.'

Four drinks in, a young woman, who at first he took to be a hooker, came and sat opposite him. 'Do you mind?' she asked politely.' He shrugged indifferently.

'So,' she said, 'what's a good-looking guy like you doing drinking all alone. That's not right.'

'I'm not alone,' he said. 'I'm with him,' and he pointed his cocktail at the bear.

'Do you make a habit of drinking with bears?'

'Not especially, but this is an occasion.'

'What sort of occasion?'

'I've come to say goodbye to an old friend,'

'The bear?'

'Sort of.' The Manhattans were starting to get the better of him and he knew he was rambling. 'I used to come here with a girl – we used to talk to the bear. He was a friend, but then – '

'She left you,' the woman completed the sentence for him.

'Something like that.' He looked at his watch. 'I have to go,' he said abruptly and stood up. He left without looking back. In another place at another time he might, he thought, have stayed and talked, but he had promised Carey he would never go there with anyone else and it would have seemed like he'd broken his promise if he stayed. He decided there and then he would never go back again. Outside he took a last look at the bear, saluted and went in search of a cab.

April 1, 1942 – All Fools Day

At last he was through – the job was done. It had taken until the following spring to finish setting up the program, but now it was done. The handover to his superior officers complete, he got a lift to Grand Central and went home to Peekskill. It was a good homecoming. He couldn't remember a time when Holly had been on better form – in higher spirits. Junior had grown and he could hardly tell him from his namesake, who Holly had laid to rest in the garden under a heavy rock to stop the foxes burrowing in. He had marked it with a simple wooden cross bearing the legend 'Here lies a hero' carefully carved on it. It's a hard cherry wood he told Tom – it'll outlast me.

'I thought I might go away for a few days,' Tom announced over breakfast one morning. 'Go up to the cabin at Crows Crossing, maybe do a little fishing.'

Martha didn't much like the idea. Deep down she thought it would awaken old memories, break open the old wounds. She knew he was physically capable, probably more than any man, but she had doubts that surrounded his emotional strength. After Carey and then Dottie he seemed unable to make a relationship. She didn't know why but she knew it to be so. He wasn't outwardly unhappy; it was just he no longer seemed to care – it was as if he couldn't be bothered.

'I don't see any grandchildren,' she would sometimes say to Holly. It was sad; she was slowly resigning herself to the idea, but she didn't like it.

The Neumann trial was due to start soon. Tom would have to take the stand and give evidence. He would have to relive the events of the past three years all over again. So perhaps it would be good for him, she argued to herself. Get away for a spell – just do something idle like going fishing. He left the next morning, packing a rod and the Remington, though he had no intention of doing any hunting. Anyway it was out of season. Martha insisted on the ritual parting kiss – she wasn't running any risks this time around –then he left

.

******

The ranger approached carefully, not quite sure of what to make of him. He had the Remington slung on his shoulder and a pair of field glasses in one hand, scanning the woods below him.

'Hello mister,' the ranger said. 'It's a good day to be out in the wild.'

'It is,' Tom agreed.

The ranger moved closer, keeping one eye on the rifle. 'You wouldn't be planning to shoot anything with that gun you have there, would you?'

'No.'

'That's good. You know it's outside the hunting season for everything at the moment?'

611

'I do.'

'So you're not hunting then?'

'That's correct. I'm tracking.' He let the glasses drop till they hung by their strap, swinging gently round his neck. 'I like to be out in the woods – just to be here. Tracking gives me a purpose.'

'Uh huh. You from around these parts?'

'No, I'm staying in the cabin down on the lake – Shelstone Farm. I'm doing a little fishing.'

A look of recognition lit the ranger's face. 'I think I heard about you. You're the guy who patched up Al Cardy from the Sheriff's Office over at Crows. Is that right?'

'How is he? I thought I might drop by and see him.'

'Oh, he's fine. He's no longer the Deputy, he's Sheriff now.' The ranger looked him up and down, then put out a hand to shake.

'Pleasure to meet you,' he said warmly. 'Okay, well you take care, mister. Shall I tell Al I seen ya?'

'You do that – and let him know I'll call by before I go back.'

The afternoon was coming on as he made his way back to the cabin. He worked his way down across the ridges. The smell of the spring air and the sound of the birds lifted his spirits – it was a good decision to come here, he told himself.

Approaching the cabin, he saw there was another car pulled up alongside the station wagon, a black Plymouth sedan. At first he was instinctively suspicious; it had shades of familiarity – it raised memories of Neumann in his mind. Then it sank in – it must be Cardy come over to see how he was doing, and he relaxed again. As he got to the car and was about to shout 'Hey Al,' the door opened and the driver got out, but it wasn't Sheriff Cardy.

'Dottie?' He stood there mouth open, not really sure of what to say.

'Hi,' she said, sheepishly. 'Martha told me I'd find you here.'

He said nothing. He just stood there looking at her. 'He doesn't want to see me,' was her first thought.

'How,' he eventually blurted out, 'I mean, I don't understand – Army Records – they told us you were missing.' She stared down at her toes for a moment.

'I was. The dressing station got overrun, but I hid. I was posted missing but it was a mistake – I guess they never put it right.'

There was another interlude of silence. He searched for something to say but nothing would come – his mind had gone blank. He had long ago written her off as lost to him. He had become used to a life without anyone.

'I saw you at that dance in Buchanan – the officer's dance – when they invited the nurses,' she said. 'I came along that night.'

'You were there?'

'I saw you dancing with that blond girl, so I left.'

'Ah, Lucille,' he said, slapping his forehead, 'my commanding officer's daughter. He asked me – he virtually ordered me – to escort her. Her husband couldn't take her; he was in New York.'

'She was married?'

'Yup, still is as far as I know.'

'I looked for you,' she said nervously, 'afterwards. I wanted to apologize for Grand Central but they said you had gone on a mission.'

'Chicago'.

'I read about it.'

'Tony is dead – did Mike tell you?'

'I haven't seen Mike since I got back. I heard about it though. How awful.'

The conversation dried again. Dottie tried to think of something to say but nothing came. She knew she had lots to say; she had planned what to say and rehearsed it all the way on the drive up from Croton. Now she couldn't get it out.

'Well, it was nice to see you again,' she said a little sadly. 'It would be nice if we could meet again.'

Tom said nothing for a moment. Instead he just shook his head. 'I don't think,' he said deliberately, 'that is such a great idea. It's not good meeting and parting again like this.'

That was it then. She couldn't get any words out and instead gave several little jerks of her head. She bit her bottom lip and tried desperately not to burst into tears. It had all been for nothing.

'Listen. We could compromise,' he said. 'How would it be if I asked you to marry me – that way we wouldn't have to go on meeting like this?'

'Oh yes,' she said, letting the tears fall, 'I thought I'd lost you. I thought you'd never ask me again.'

He pulled a handkerchief out of his pocket and handed to her. 'Come on,' he said, folding her in his arms. 'I know an Army chaplain who owes me a favor.'

ACKNOWLEDGEMENTS

It is routinely said that writing the manuscript is just the beginning and the real work that goes into the making of a book does not commence until the author puts down the pen. This, however, is only true in part. First comes the idea, the kernel of the nut that will make the story; then before the words spill onto the paper there must be research – the inquiry that gives the story its substance, its authority and its credibility. In creating this tale of 'what if' there was a lot of delving into the real history of the world on the brink of a war; on the people of the time, what they wore, how they spoke, how they lived their lives and what they thought; the mindset and the values of ordinary men and women as well as the famous and the powerful. In the process of this research I relied upon many sources to whom I am thankful.

But what of this '*real work*' that follows the writing? This, for many of us who write, is less work than it is a chance to be sociable and to discuss that thing we have created during our solitary task of getting the words onto the paper. This can be fun because you are surrounded by people who share your enthusiasm and your hope. To these people the author owes a great deal not just for their sterling efforts in getting the book to work but, more importantly, for the praise that keeps our spirits up in the moments of doubt, and equally for the criticism that keeps our feet firmly on the ground and guides the rewrites – there are always rewrites.

For all of this I acknowledge a special debt to my wife Liz, who encouraged me to work and took on the monumental task of copy-editing the work. To my American editor and good friend, Linda Amstutz, who made sure I used the right terminology: that I called the pavement a sidewalk, the windscreen a windshield and pointed out that Michigan was a state and not a city. To David Povilaitis, guru on presentation and promotion in the electronic world, and to Jami Jennings, his partner, for those memorable evenings on the balcony with glasses of rosé wine to hand, watching the sun go down over the Corbière hills.

I also offer my gratitude to my Beta Readers – especially Linn Hunter – those hardy, durable souls who volunteered to plough their way through the manuscript right to the end, then tell it how it is. These are true friends because they have the courage to tell you the truth even if it is unpalatable, putting aside flattery and an urge to spare your feelings. As a first taster of the fruits, their words are valuable beyond measure. Theirs is an unenviable task because they may have to tell you your child is ugly then share a drink at the bar without regret or embarrassment.

Printed in Poland
by Amazon Fulfillment
Poland Sp. z o.o., Wrocław

49591965R00371